I0584858

Stormbird

Books by Karen Turner:

All That & Everything

Broughton Hall series:

Torn
Inviolate
Stormbird
Counterpoint

Stormbird

Karen Turner

Published in 2023 by Karen Turner

www.karenturner.com.au

First published in 2018 by Fisher King Publishing, UK

STORMBIRD

Copyright © 2018 Karen Turner

The moral right of the author has been asserted.

All rights reserved. Without limiting the rights under copyright restricted above, no part of this publication may be distributed, reproduced, stored in a database, introduced into a retrieval system, or transmitted, in any form or by any means (electronic, mechanical, photocopying, recording or otherwise), without the prior written permission of both the copyright owner and the above publisher of this book.

This book is a work of fiction. Names, characters, businesses, places, events and incidents are either the products of the author's imagination or used in a fictitious manner. Any resemblance to actual persons, living or dead, or actual events is purely coincidental.

Designed and typeset by Look Up Media
Initial design and typeset by Fisher King Publishing, UK

Cover design by bluewrenbooks.com.au
Cover image by bigstock.com

ISBN: 978-0-6450002-5-2 (pbk)
       978-0-6450002-0-7 (ebk–ePub)

NATIONAL LIBRARY OF AUSTRALIA

A catalogue record for this book is available from the National Library of Australia

For those who didn't believe,
and those who did and never gave up.

Chapter 1

March 1941 – Broughton Hall, near Wolstone, Yorkshire

"U-boat."

"Have you told the children?" Olive asked.

"Mary already guessed." Jessica was tired. She heard it in her own voice. "It was on the wireless. She recognised the name of the ship."

"How'd they take it?"

"All right, I think. It'll take time."

A wet snorting came down the telephone line as Olive blew her nose. She drew a shuddering breath. "There must've been survivors. Are they certain?"

"They said there was no doubt." Jessica stared dismally at the War Office telegram in her lap and swallowed painfully. "Forty or so survivors... Jon wasn't among them." Jessica paused, her voice quavered and the tears finally spilled over. She added, "They never found his body."

Olive snuffled again. "But it's... "

"Empty," Jessica supplied. "The children and I, we won't have a grave or... anywhere to go to... rem-remember..." She choked and couldn't continue.

There was a momentary silence as Olive gathered herself. Then, "Now you're free," she stated flatly.

Jessica gasped. "What!"

"Well it's true, isn't it? You never loved Jon in the first place."

"Don't say that! How can you say that at a time like this?"

"Oh, for goodness sake, Jessica! I'm not trying to be unkind. It's the unadulterated truth."

Jessica realised her mother's grief was making her cruel – angry too. Anger would feel better than the agony of grief.

"You married him because he was already part of the family," Olive went on, sobbing now. "He was safe – you always... play it... so safe! *Oh, God*!"

Jessica mopped her eyes, listening to her mother's anguish on the other end of the line. "Now's not the time," she said softly, as Olive gradually quieted.

A drawn-out silence followed, during which Jessica heard various thumps and the creaking of floorboards overhead. Fumbling in the pocket of her pinny, she drew out a hanky and blew her nose. "Mum, I think Thomas is up. I'll have to go."

"Righto love." Olive seemed to have pulled herself together. "Will you be all right?"

Jessica dragged in a shaky breath. "Of course. I'll be fine – nothing ever happens out here. It's you and Dad in Leeds... every time I hear a plane go over... I wish you'd–"

"Don't. Your father's not closing that shop."

"I know, I know..."

"Look," Olive's voice was thick and wet, "if there's a bomb with my name on it, it'll find me wherever I am."

Jessica made a humourless, huffing sound. "You'll ring later?"

"Will do."

Jessica hung up quickly before she heard the dead click in her ear. She worried about her parents. *And I've got that much room here*, she thought. *Too much room for just me and the twins.*

The Gerries were regularly bombing Leeds, York and other parts of Yorkshire – her parents could be killed while sleeping in their beds.

Jessica took a fortifying breath and pushed herself off the telephone stool. Smoothing the apron over her skirt, she went into the kitchen.

The fire in the range had burned down. She wrenched open the firebox, threw in a log and slammed the door on the snapping orange sparks.

I'll have to cut more wood.

Sighing, she passed a hand over her throbbing eyes. She'd cried herself out eighteen months ago when Jon hiked his navy issue haversack onto his shoulder, kissed her and the children, then trotted down the Broughton Hall drive. Eager for adventure, he'd never looked back.

Useless to tell him that he belonged here because Jessica knew, in his heart, Jon wouldn't have agreed.

The lump was forming in her throat again. She swallowed hard and glared at the ceiling as she heard a loud thud from somewhere near Thomas's room. She made a tutting sound and muttered, "Don't wake your sister."

***

"I'd be 'appy to teach you anytime, Missus," her steward said, sliding into the driver's seat and slamming the car door.

"Now, why would I learn to drive when I have you as my chauffer, Sam?" Jessica responded playfully.

The man snorted, shifted the gears and the car lurched off.

"You're right, of course," Jessica conceded, soberly. "If there's an emergency or something, I should be able to drive."

"Exactly so," Sam agreed. "Troubling times, these." He navigated a series of pot-holes in the lane and the Daimler's springs squeaked and groaned.

Six months after Jon joined the war, Jessica advertised for an odd-jobs man in exchange for rent-free accommodation.

The old gardener's cottage at the end of her drive needed to be lived in – like everything on the estate, without human intervention, it quickly became run down.

Sam Clay had responded to her advertisement, bringing his wife, Marg, with him. The arrangement had worked perfectly and, Jessica reflected, she felt more secure having the couple nearby.

She watched the Yorkshire Dales roll past; fields of green broken by sporadic patches of snow, and bordered by low walls, constructed decades ago from local stone.

She drew a deep breath. "How long will you be in Wolstone?"

"Depends 'ow long you need."

Jessica considered. "Not long, I shouldn't think. I need to go to the haberdasher's and the grocer to get – oh!" She broke off to rifle through her handbag.

Her steward threw her a brief sideways glance, "Forgot summat?"

"Thought I'd forgotten the ration books... they're here." She pushed them safely towards the bottom of her bag.

Sam made the right-hand turn onto Bridge Street and crossed the River Wharfe into Wolstone. "Where do you want me to drop you?"

"Just up here... past Courthouse Street... perfect. Thank you."

Sam pulled up outside Walker's Haberdashery and Manchester. "I'll pick you up from 'ere in say, an hour?"

"Make it half an hour." Closing the car door, Jessica waved him off, and decided to visit the grocer first.

Wolstone's main street was busy and vibrant, even though it wasn't market day. Jessica dodged a young woman pushing a pram and an elderly gentleman getting along with a walking stick. The sound of the stick tapping on the flagstone footpath was drowned by the roar of a lorry bearing a cow and calf. It left a stinking pall of fumes in its wake and Jessica was grateful when she went into the grocery shop.

"Thass all there were to't," the customer was saying. A bell jangled above the door as Jessica closed it behind her.

"Ah'd be tellin' 'im t' bugger orf if 'e were sat 'round me 'ouse like tha' doin' nowt all day. Tell 'im t'get orf 'is bloody arse'n start workin' down in't mill. Betty's quite 'appy t'take ex-servicemen."

"Ah would, Lillian, but tellin' 'im and shiftin' 'im are two diff'rent things, aye?"

"By gum, don't ah know't!" The shopkeeper turned to Jessica. "Mornin' love, got yer book on yer?"

"Yes, and my children's too."

"All right, Lillian," the customer said. "Ah'll see yer down a t'pub Friday night." She avoided Jessica's eye and left the shop – the bell over the door jangled merrily as she closed it.

After three years in the region, Jessica was still an outsider. In the past, strangers to a village would have simply been eyed with suspicion. The advent of war, though, had drawn communities closer making it difficult for newcomers to fit in.

At least the children have assimilated at school – that's something, Jessica thought, as Lillian took Jessica's ration books and read their addresses. "Oh, thass right, yer live in't old 'all out near Jackson's 'eath."

Jessica nodded. "Broughton Hall. Do you know it?"

The woman began collecting items off her shelves and stacking them on the counter.

"We all know tha' place, love. Me old Dad used to go't school wi' Francis Broughton. Spent a few weekends up at 'ouse. Reckoned it were 'aunted, 'e did."

"Oh." It was all Jessica could think of to say. She watched the sturdy woman move with practised ease along the rows of shelving, reaching for packets and tins. She called out items and put them on the counter without waiting for Jessica's reply, "Tea, sugar... sweeties – o' course yer want sweeties, yer've got kiddies," she muttered, more or less to herself. "We all laughed at 'im, o' course," she went on. "Imagine 'im believin' in ghosts 'n' such rubbish! Butter?"

"Sorry?"

The shop assistant turned. "Butter? Says 'ere yer don't

normally take yer ration o' butter."

"No, thank you."

"Good-oh." She continued, "Meat, yes... no cheese. Yer don't take cheese neither?"

Jessica shook her head.

"Right ye'are." Lillian ticked the items off in the ration books and began boxing them. "Now... soap, lamp oil... ? Y'ain't got 'lectric up a t'all?"

"No."

"Fit this in yer 'andbag?" Lillian held a packet of Velvet soap. "Won't fit in't box."

"Yes, I'll carry it separately."

The bells jangled again and Jessica turned to see a man just closing the door.

"Oh, 'ello Nigel, love. With yer in a tick."

"No rush, Lillian," the man responded, pulling his ration book from a string bag. Jessica recognised Nigel Bright, one of the sons from A. J. Bright and Sons, the district's largest milk pasteurisers.

Even though Nigel had to be in his fifties, and his father long in his grave, he was still, one of the sons.

"Mornin' Mrs Barrow," he said with a cordial nod.

"Hello Mr Bright," she replied, politely.

"'Ow them cows o' yers doin'?"

"Very well."

He nodded. "Thass good then. Tell tha' man o' yers t' come talk to's. Gov'ment's keen t'buy as much milk as we can deliver. Wantin' t'powder't... send t'troops on't front."

"I'll tell him." *They're my cows*, Jessica added to herself, resentfully. *You could talk to me.*

Nigel and Jessica fell uncomfortably silent, each watching, with apparent great interest, as Lillian tallied Jessica's bill.

Jessica paid, collected her ration books and scooped the box into her arms. "Thank you," she said over her shoulder, pulling open the shop door. The bell jangled as she closed it behind her.

She'd only gone half a dozen yards when she remembered the soap she'd left behind.

"Lucifer's balls!" she muttered, returning to the shop.

Nigel was leaning on the counter. Lillian's face was contorted with displeasure. "Imagine! Livin' up tharr in't shabby old 'ouse... raisin' them poor kiddies on 'er own. She stood right where y'are now, not sayin' nowt more'n yes, no. Mousey thing... no personality. 'Ow she won tha' 'andsome fella she were married to I'll nivver know!"

Nigel snorted, "Apparently, 'e didn't even wait t'be called up – volunteered 'e did!"

Lillian grunted with satisfaction. "Why wouldn't 'e though, wi' tha' cold fish a t'ome –Gerries'd be more welcomin'!"

The two broke into laughter.

Dizzy with mortification, Jessica slowly backed out of the shop. The bell gave an incongruously cheerful jangle.

***

Jessica was waiting outside Walker's Haberdashery and Manchester when Sam pulled up in the Daimler. The box of groceries was at her feet and a parcel of fabric was tucked under her arm. Her eyes felt puffy and she was blowing her nose.

Sam got out and put the box on the back seat while Jessica climbed in the front passenger side, tucking her hanky up her sleeve.

Jessica stared absently out the window, brow furrowed. *Why don't I ever stick up for myself? I let everyone walk all over me... talk about me like that... I'm not cold... I just never know what to say... always feel so awkward.*

From time to time, as the Daimler bounced along the country lanes, she felt Sam stealing curious looks at her but she was disinclined to speak.

They were nearly home before Jessica said, "Saw Nigel Bright this morning."

"Oh aye?" He glanced at her as he drove.

"Wants to talk to you about supplying more milk."

"Righto," Sam said, after a brief pause. "I'll see 'im when I take the cans up tomorrow."

She nodded and they continued home in silence.

***

Jessica regarded the tangled mess at her feet. The ruins of a once beautiful terraced garden slumped before her: dilapidated walls; cracked and broken flagstones; and the dried-up stumps of formerly magnificent roses. Even the hardiest of plants would have given up the fight against the choking, rampant bindweed that had taken over.

She made her way around the back of the house to her straggly, untidy vegetable plot and hunkering beside it, inspected the matted weeds and the sprawling bindweed strangling everything.

Selecting a clawed tool, Jessica set to work dragging up a large spread of weeds to reveal the thin, sun-deprived spears of young growth beneath.

As she worked, she recalled her husband's comments after they'd first moved to Broughton Hall.

Jon had stood on the porch surveying the gardens, the terraces and paddocks, the remains of a small orchard, beyond which, in the middle distance, a cluster of thatched cottages comprised the village of Jackson's Heath.

"It's worse than I thought," he'd said, grimly. His voice had been deep and resonant; it never seemed to fit the slenderness of his frame. But he'd been tall – Jessica wore a pair of his old trousers for her gardening work and had to roll up the legs.

"Bloody mess," he'd observed, adding, "Well, Jess, you

wanted the place."

"We could only afford it because it's in such a state," she'd reminded him. "And it's not like we're on borrowed time. Neither of us is going anywhere."

He'd laughed then, squeezing her shoulder as one friend to another.

Barely six months later, war was declared and Jon had gone, the lure of adventure proving irresistible.

Jessica had regularly received Jon's naval salary, roughly £28 each month. Now of course, that would stop. Yet Jon had religiously contributed three pounds each month to an insurance policy – enough to pay out their mortgage.

"The place might fall down around your ears," he'd told her, handing over the policy document, "but nobody'll take it from you."

Jessica hadn't understood at first. Now she did; it's a hard admission – even in the privacy of your own heart – that your husband married you purely to thank your parents for taking him in when he had nowhere else to go.

She sat back on her heels, clapping her gloved hands to remove the dirt. "Oh Jon," she sighed. If war hadn't taken him away something else would have.

The garden hummed with bees industriously gathering from early daffodils and the crocuses that were growing wild among the weeds. Although it was technically spring, the sun was a silvery disk in a watery sky and the air cooled early in the afternoon.

A flash in the corner of her eye reminded her that she hadn't seen the children for a while. Turning, she expected to see one, or both, of them.

It was Sam, returning from the lower paddock near the orchard, deftly rolling a cigarette as he walked. Jessica observed him take a box of matches from his pocket and pause to light his cigarette. Exhaling a cloud of fragrant blue smoke, eyes heavy-lidded, savouring the flavour of his tobacco, he stood watching Jessica's small herd of cattle.

Sam spent most of his time with the cows and attending to various tasks around the property. It was too much for one man alone, but since Marg had appointed herself head housekeeper, Jessica could help.

Jessica returned to her work, charged with a new sense of purpose. *For the time being, I'll grow my vegetables. But one day... how I'd love to return the gardens to their former glory.*

And the gardens had been beautiful. She knew this because she'd seen them in her dreams – seen them so vividly they could not possibly be of her own imaginings.

Dreams aside, Jessica was growing accustomed to glimpsing fleeting, formless shapes. Sometimes a voluminous outline, other times the solid figure of a teenage girl, melting into the shadows. Lately, though, the figures had become more distinct, and, Jessica would not soon forget the feeling of a dog brushing past her in the dark one morning outside Thomas's bedroom door.

While the visitations were never threatening, they did make her wonder who the girl might be, and the dog, and why they appeared. Jessica blew a stray hair from her face and stripped off her gloves to retie her plait.

"Mummy?"

With a jerk, she looked around. "Mary! You scared me!"

"Sorry, Mummy."

Jessica climbed woodenly to her feet. "Blimey, I'm so stiff I feel like I've been here for days."

"Only hours," her daughter replied. "Mummy, could I do some work in the orchard?"

"The orchard?" Jessica was surprised. "What do you want to do down there?"

Mary picked up one of her mother's gardening tools and toyed absently with it. She was looking towards the outbuildings, beyond which were the remains of an apple and plum orchard. "I wanted to pull out the weeds, tidy it up. It could be nice. Daddy says..." The child's voice faltered and her eyes suddenly welled.

Blinking hard, Mary seemed to compose herself. She went on, "Daddy'd said we'd get more fruit if the trees weren't crowded with weeds."

Jessica felt her own eyes filling and grief tightened her throat. She touched Mary's shoulder gently, "Daddy was probably right."

Mary sniffed. "I wanted to... pull out the weeds," she murmured. The gardening tool dropped to the flags with a clatter and the girl burst into tears.

Swallowing the painful lump in her throat, Jessica went to her knees and pulled her daughter's shuddering little body against her own.

When finally, the child grew still, Jessica took a hanky from her pocket and mopped the girl's puffy face.

"We sometimes need to let our sadness out," she whispered. "Don't ever try to hold it in, promise?"

Mary nodded.

"You all right now?"

Mary nodded again.

"Good. I'll organise some tools for you so you can start tomorrow."

***

That night, Jessica lay in bed, a child lying stiffly and wide-eyed beneath each arm. Engines droned overhead, malevolent, deadly; destinations, Leeds, Huddersfield, York and Sheffield, and the intermittent, *blat... blat... blat...* sounded in the distance.

New words had entered the English vocabulary; Luftwaffe

was a name synonymous with evil. Its planes were Dornier, Junkers and Messerschmitt; harsh sounding and unpleasant on English tongues. *Blitz* was the German word for lightning; *Blitzen*, a lightning strike – every *blat* was a lightning strike.

Another *blat*; a building razed, a home destroyed, lives extinguished.

And a U-boat killed my husband.

Jessica wouldn't telephone her parents in the morning. Disconnected lines only added to her anxiety. They'll ring when they can.

She hugged her children close and squeezed her eyes tight to hold in the tears.

***

Sometime during the night, Mary returned to her own room, but as morning arrived, Jessica found herself clinging to the edge of the bed with the tasselled fringes of the bedspread dragged across her shoulders. Thomas, curled on his side, had positioned himself in the centre of the bed, sheets and blankets mounded around him.

Jessica smiled, envisioning Thomas's future wife and the battles she would wage.

Winter was almost gone but mornings were still very cold. Jessica's room had an old relic of a fireplace complete with an ancient iron poker. She doubted a fire had been lit there for at least fifty years; the chimney was probably filled with derelict birds' nests.

Yawning, shivering, she slipped out of bed and pulled on her dressing-gown. Thomas murmured something inaudible, sighed and slept on.

Downstairs, Jessica poked a twist of lit newspaper at the kindling in the firebox. It ignited enthusiastically. She filled the kettle and put it on to boil, then turning, was startled to find

Thomas behind her.

Sleepy-eyed, with his strawberry-blonde hair sticking up like a crest, he stood in the door, barefooted and wearing only his pyjamas.

"What's the matter, love?" she said, going to him. "Aren't you cold?"

"I... saw someone. In your room." His voice was thick with sleep.

Jessica crouched before her son and looked up into his face. "You saw someone? Good dream or bad dream?"

"Wasn't a dream." He rubbed his eyes. "But I wasn't scared. It was just... a dog and a girl."

Jessica's heart skipped a beat. His words recalled the caress of fur against her leg. Shaking off the notion, she took her son's cold hands and chafed them briskly between her own. "What were they doing?"

"Just sitting. On the floor, on the mat next to the bed."

Unbidden, a vision of a dark-haired girl and border collie flew into Jessica's mind.

Before she could think about it, Thomas went on, "She was older than me. Dressed in funny clothes."

The skin on Jessica's arms prickled. She asked carefully, "Did she say anything?"

The little boy shook his head. "I don't think she saw me."

"Well," Jessica said, smiling, "Sounds like a rather nice dream, don't you think?"

Thomas yawned.

"Tell you what, go upstairs and wake Mary. Get dressed nice and warm, then go out and collect some eggs for breakfast, hmm?"

"All right, Mummy."

"Good boy."

Vaguely unsettled, she watched him pad away. So it's not just me seeing things.

***

A short time later, the kitchen was warm and fragrant with the combined smells of toast and eggs frying in burnt butter.

"It was my favourite dream ever!" Thomas's voice rose over the spatter and snap from the frying pan. "Australia needed two to win. Tom Wills facing. One ball left –"

"Sounds like a stupid dream," Mary muttered.

"Mary," Jessica warned over her shoulder. "Ouch!" She rubbed a spot on her cheek where a spitting egg had caught her.

Thomas ignored his twin. "I was bowling. I kept thinking, What would Hollies do? Hollies doesn't like googlies but I thought he'd probably bowl a googly this time... Wills would never expect that!"

"You'd know, I suppose," Mary remarked, dryly.

"Mum, tell her to stop," Thomas cried.

"Mary, let your brother tell his story. Go on, Thomas." Jessica slid the eggs on to three plates and brought them to the table.

"But I already told you, that's when I saw the girl."

"Girls don't play cricket!"

"Mary!" Thomas glared at his sister, his face glowing hotly beneath a scatter of freckles. "I woke up... just before I did my run up – I'd decided to bowl the googly. She wasn't playing. She was sitting on the floor in Mummy's room... with a dog."

Mary made a rude noise. "Well, it obviously was a dream."

"Was not!" Thomas's bottom lip stuck out.

"Was so!"

"All right, you two," Jessica interrupted. "Eat your breakfast."

"Hasn't Granny rung yet, Mum?" Mary asked, dipping a toast soldier into her egg. "That why you're snappy?"

"I'm not snappy!"

Her children exchanged glances, their own dispute apparently forgotten.

Jessica tucked a strand of auburn hair behind her ear. "I don't think I'm snappy."

"You never *think* you are," Mary said with solemn eight-year-old wisdom. "But you're always snappy the morning after the planes go over and you're waiting for Granny to ring."

As if on cue, the hall telephone bell gave a shrill ring and Jessica jumped. Mary shot her a look that said, *I told you so*, then returned to her eggs.

Chapter 2

Jessica snatched up the receiver. "Mum?"

"Yes, it's me."

"Thank God." She exhaled in a rush and flopped on to the telephone stool. "Were they close? We heard them go over."

"I thought you might've. Look, we're getting used to them, you know? As soon as the sirens go off we drop what we're doing and go down into the cellar. We're quite comfy."

"How's Dad?"

"He's fine; he was playing cards with Reg. He's on a winning streak. Reg reckons –"

"I wish you wouldn't be so flippant."

Olive fell silent. When she spoke again, her voice was low, resigned, "What else can we do?"

There was silence again before Olive continued, "It's quite cosy. We've got that old cast-iron stove... we boil the kettle... make cuppas."

Jessica sighed. "As long as you're all right."

"We're all right. Our street is all right and none of our friends've been hurt. Apart from old Mrs Godfrey, but she forgot to turn the gas off... went to light a ciggy. Oh, but there's good news!"

"We could do with that. What is it?"

"They got two of them," Olive said brightly. "Shot down two planes last night."

"Two? Bloody hell!"

"Our boys did a marvellous job! Wonder you didn't hear it. That anti-aircraft regiment up top of the Chevin did it. Planes came down outside Wharferidge, not far from you – a Junkers and a Messerschmitt."

"Really? A Messerschmitt? Last I read, the Gerries weren't using them yet."

"That would explain all the excitement then." Olive chuckled delightedly. "Derek Watters, that man from the army barracks? Well, he came into the shop this morning. Told your father they think the Junkers was accompanying the Messerschmitt to see how it got on." Olive snorted. "I'd say it didn't do too well at all! Reckoned the Messerschmitt got a couple of bombs away before they brought 'im down though. You didn't hear the guns, then?"

Jessica realised she was holding a piece of toast. She bit into it. "Not a thing," she replied, chewing. "Pilots would've died of exposure. Freezing it was, last night."

"Searchlighters went out... found them all. Three of them, two pilots and the bomber. One had a broken leg – should've put him out of his misery, I say."

Jessica made a noise of agreement. She swallowed the toast. "Where are they now?"

"Derek said they took them to that camp down Redmires Road–" Olive broke off at a voice in the background. "Love, I must go. Your father's wantin' his morning tea – says 'ullo."

"Hullo back! All right Mum, I'll let you go."

"Love to the children."

***

Jessica had expected Mary to quickly lose interest in tidying the orchard and was surprised when several days later the girl continued to work. Mary had spent the weekend tearing out the weeds and plant litter from between the rows of trees, piling it all in the wheelbarrow and trudging up to the refuse heap behind the woodshed.

On her knees, weeding the kitchen garden, Jessica allowed her mind to drift. She recalled when she and Jon had decided to raise their family in the country. Neither could have foreseen the extent to which the world would change. They had barely settled into Broughton Hall when the war intruded, and Jon, along with many others, had not waited to receive the official call.

With her husband's departure, Jessica's vision of the home and gardens they'd create together became a fanciful dream.

"Mum!" Mary's shout cut through the early spring afternoon. Sam was carrying a pail of water into the stables. Jessica saw his head jerk up at Mary's cry.

Mary was standing at the corner of the wash-house. "Mum, Mr Clay, come and look!" She waited to be sure her mother was following before disappearing at a run towards the orchard.

Jessica and Sam found Mary squatting on the ground beside a tangled mess of blackberry canes. "There's something under here." Mary turned a white face towards her mother. "I thought I saw a hare run in and... Mr Clay," she said, slightly out of breath, "look!"

Sam gingerly pulled aside the brambles. Jessica, peering over his shoulder, could just make out what appeared to be a small headstone.

"Think it's a grave?" Mary asked. Her voice was a mixture of curiosity and wonder.

"Pass's the secateurs," Sam said. He cut away the spiny tentacles while, intrigued, Jessica waited beside her daughter.

As he worked, the canes fell away to reveal a small, weathered headstone. Despite having been shrouded in weeds and brambles for countless years, its carefully carved inscription was still reasonably legible:

DARLING JEMIMA
12 MARCH 1806 – 22 SEPTEMBER 1817
Loved forever and never forgotten

***

"Oh, Mummy..." Mary edged closer. Jessica felt the girl's

hand creep into her own.

Sam grunted as he hauled himself upright. "Well, Missus..."

Recovering faster than the adults, Mary leaned towards the stone. "A little girl... about eleven." She straightened. "That's sad."

Jessica frowned. "Who would put this here? Sam, is this even legal?"

Her steward passed a hand over his thinning scalp. "Dunno."

"Mum," Mary whispered, "nobody knows but us."

Jessica looked at Sam. He gestured uncertainly, "Girl's got a point. Besides, it's been 'ere over an 'undred years."

Jessica gave a little shiver as the sun dipped behind a bank of clouds. Dampness in the air suggested rain was imminent.

"I can pull all the weeds out, Mum. I can make it nice!"

"Well..." Jessica was still uncertain. "Sam?"

"It's been 'ere so long I don't s'pose it'd matter."

"Then I'll start straight away," Mary decided.

***

"Mummy?"

It was later that same day and Jessica was elbow-deep in soapy water, determinedly scrubbing Thomas's best pair of trousers. The boy had managed to get grass stains on the knees and was, consequently, not her favourite person.

"What is it?" She didn't pause in her work and it was several long moments before he spoke again.

"Mummy? I want to tell you something."

"Phft!" She blew at a stray hair but it was stuck to her steam-damp cheek and wouldn't budge. "What?"

"Mummy," he paused.

"I don't have all day, Thomas." She dried her wet hands and grasped the box of Rinso, holding her breath. The advertising claimed it was anti-sneeze but that didn't seem to apply to her.

As soon as she poured it into the water, the powdery residue rose and the familiar itching began.

Jessica wrinkled her nose irritably. "What is... is... ah – ah shoo!"

Extracting a hanky from her apron pocket, she blew her nose and turned to her son. Her ill-temper quickly evaporated when she saw his expression. "What is it, love?"

"Mummy, there was a man. Last night, outside my window."

Alarmed, Jessica dropped before him, her hands on his little waist. She stared hard into his face but he didn't seem afraid.

She, on the other hand, was quite afraid. Carefully modulating her voice, she asked, "Where, exactly, was he?"

"Out there." Thomas pointed through the wash-house door towards the stables.

"What were you doing out of bed? What time was this?"

"Late, I don't know what time."

"Perhaps –"

"I wasn't dreaming!" he cried. "Mary says I dream things, but I don't!"

"I didn't say you were."

"You thought it," he said, accusingly. "I couldn't sleep so I was looking out the window and that's when I saw him."

"What was he doing?"

Thomas shrugged. "Just looking around."

"Perhaps it was Mr Clay?" Jessica suggested hopefully.

Thomas shook his head firmly.

"How do you know?"

"It was dark, but I could see it wasn't Mr Clay. He was too tall."

"Well," Jessica rose and took his hand – her washing forgotten for the moment, "I'll ask Mr Clay if he knows anything, hmm?"

"Okay, Mummy." He brightened instantly, pleased to be taken seriously.

"Okay? What's that mean?"

"Jack Ramage said the Yanks staying at his house say it all the time. Means all right."

"The Ramages have Yanks billeted, have they?"

"Mm-hm. Jack says they came before Christmas... brought tanks with them for our soldiers. Jack reckons they don't do owt but hang around. They share things with him, chocolate and this stuff you can chew on for ages. Jack says it tastes like mint. Mummy, can we get some Yanks to stay with us?"

Jessica rested her hand on his slim shoulder as they strolled up the path towards the house. "I think we're too far from Leeds. They prefer to be closer. Where's Mary?"

"Still weeding in the orchard."

"All right, why don't you go help?"

He shook his head, disinterestedly.

"Well go practise your reading or something; I have to finish scrubbing the stains out of your trousers. Okay?"

He grinned. It made his nose crinkle and she thought he looked cute. "Okay!"

Jessica watched him go into the house. *I'd better talk to Sam.*

***

"We're going to be late!" The voice, young and insistent, was close to her ear. Jessica was jerked into wakefulness. The sun was streaming through the windows and Thomas was peering into her face.

"Mummy, we're going to be late!"

Jessica's limbs felt heavy and she longed to return to sleep but her son's face, inches from her own, bounced in front of her.

"C'mon Mummy."

"All right, Thomas" she said, at last. "Give me a moment."

She pushed to a sitting position and ran both hands over her face.

"I can't be late, Mummy. Michael's bringing his new puppy to school to show us."

Jessica glanced at the bedside clock as she shuffled into her slippers. "You won't be late."

"But what if I miss the bus and –"

"Thomas, you won't be late," Jessica insisted. "Go downstairs and pack your satchel. I'll be there shortly."

Jessica dressed automatically, still half-asleep and feeling mildly distracted, then went downstairs.

"Have you eaten?" she asked, entering the kitchen.

"I made us toast," Mary said.

"Good girl," Jessica responded absently. She was bewildered by vague, disconnected threads of a dream she'd had during the night. In it, two young men – one fair with brilliant green eyes, the other dark and impressively handsome – dressed in Regency costume, were sitting in her parlour.

Oblivious to her preoccupation, her children munched through breakfast and chattered to one another.

"Mummy, who's Patrick?" Thomas suddenly asked.

Jessica snapped back to the room. "Patrick? I don't know any Patricks."

"You must," Thomas said, swallowing his toast. "You said, Patrick while you were asleep. Anyway, what do you think about Michael? His puppy's called Angelo because it goes so well with Michael. That's clever, don't you think?"

"Yes," Jessica agreed. "Very clever."

"So, *I* thought," he continued, "if *I* got a puppy I'd call him Cromwell."

"Good thing you're not getting a puppy then," Mary said. His sister was seated across the table from him, her satchel at her feet. "Thomas Cromwell was killed by Henry the eighth. You look tired, Mum."

"I am tired but you shouldn't let me sleep so late."

"You're normally up early. You must've needed to sleep," Mary reasoned. Turning to her brother, "Go get your satchel, Tommy."

"Don't tell me what to do!"

Mary sighed and regarded her mother archly.

"Get your satchel, love," Jessica said, gently. The boy huffed a little but obediently left the room. Jessica addressed her daughter. "All right, what is it?"

Mary lifted her shoulders in a shrug. "You're worried about stuff... the war and all. You're tired because you can't sleep."

Jessica filled the kettle and put it on the hob. "Of course I'm worried. Everyone in England's worried." She yawned and raked her fingers through her hair. "But you shouldn't be."

Mary nodded, only eight years old but with an odd, sometimes confronting, wisdom. "I'm worried too Mummy – but I think it's going to be all right. We're safe here, so far from Leeds."

Jessica nodded. "I just wish your Granny and Grandad would come live with us."

Mary was about to respond when Thomas bounced into the room. "Come on," he urged his sister. "Before we really are late."

Mary threw her mother a farewell smile, grabbed her satchel and followed her brother out the door.

***

"'Ow's it going?" Sam came to stand beside her as Jessica inspected the bare earth of her kitchen garden.

"There's still more to be cleared over there," she pointed to a far corner, "but it's pretty much done. What sort of vegetables do you think I should plant?" She glanced at her steward, "What'll grow?"

"Anything, I reckon. Spinach, silver beet, turnips, carrots... all kinds o' stuff. Will the kiddies eat things like that?"

"Mary usually will, without complaint, and Thomas'll do

whatever Mary does, though he'd never admit it."

Sam smiled fondly and shredded tobacco into a cigarette paper, expertly rolling it into shape.

Jessica gazed towards the paddock; the cows were chewing their cud in the afternoon sunshine, their eyes heavy, almost mesmerised. "Even though they're twins," Jessica went on, "they're so different. Mary is serious, like me – seems older than she is. Thomas is adventurous and daring, like Jon was."

"Missing their father?" Sam sounded casually interested. He continued shaping the cigarette though Jessica knew she had his attention.

"They're doing all right. More resilient than I expected."

He nodded and put the cigarette between his lips. "And you?"

Jessica continued to watch the cows. *What about me?* she thought. *I'm a widow at twenty-eight. What's that* supposed *to feel like?*

"I'm not sure," she answered slowly. "I miss him, of course, but – you have to understand, Jon and I... we grew up together... like brother and sister. I loved him but it was... different," she finished, lamely. "I said my goodbyes the morning he left. The morning he left me," she whispered as though to herself.

She inhaled resolutely, and changing the subject, she said, "Did you talk to Nigel Bright?"

"Aye. They're wantin' to purchase as much fresh milk as they can from farmers round the district. They need us to keep delivering every morning and they'll take more if we can produce it."

Jessica looked impressed. "More than we sell them now?"

Sam nodded, cupping his hands round his mouth to light his cigarette.

"Will they pay?" she asked. "Are they good for it?"

He exhaled a plume of smoke, "Oh they're good for it. Government's their biggest customer. After it's pasteurised, it's powdered and shipped to the military. Bright and Sons pay by the ten gallon can, but only full ones. They weigh 'em," he added, pre-empting her next question. "I'm driving out there later to pick up a dozen more cans, so we can up our sales – as many as we can fill. They'll take a couple o' vats of cream too."

"As long as we keep some of that for butter," Jessica reminded him. "Marg exchanges it, along with eggs, for bacon and sausages in Wolstone."

"Now," Sam said, "we gotta grow the 'erd a bit. Fortunately, some of the lasses are in calf."

Jessica sighed. "Let's not separate them from their calves too early, Sam."

He smiled indulgently. "Soft 'earted, eh? Well, you're the boss and I gotta get back to work."

**

The spring afternoon was warm and the perspiration beaded on her forehead and dampened the back of her work shirt.

Jessica finished turning over another section and jammed her pitchfork into the soil. It swayed like a drunkard as she straightened, massaging the small of her back and admiring her work.

Pleasant as the sun was now, evening still descended early and it would quickly grow cool.

Jessica was thinking she should begin packing away her tools when on the edge of her hearing, came the relaxed clopping of a horse. Curiously, she strolled around the side of the house to check.

Shading her eyes against the low sun, she saw with surprise, a mahogany-coloured horse approaching her front porch. As the rider noticed her standing at the corner of the house, he directed the horse over.

"Whoa, girl," the stranger in the saddle reined-in on the grass before her. The mare snorted and whuffed at Jessica, while the rider lifted his hat in greeting.

"Afternoon," he said cheerfully. "Nice day for it." He nodded towards her gardening clothes.

"Yes," Jessica responded. "It is..." she paused uncertainly. *Where's Sam?* "Can I help you with something?"

Jessica rubbed the horse's velvety nose, waiting and scrutinising the man as he dismounted. His eyes were an unusual brown. Jessica thought they looked like chestnuts; they formed crescent shapes as he smiled at her. He wore a dashing little moustache, like Errol Flynn in *The Charge of the Light Brigade*. "I'm Robin Tyler... " he stuck out a hand. "You probably know my father, Albert?"

Jessica shook his hand, "Um... No. I'm Jessica Barrow."

"Pleased to meet you – *Mrs* Barrow? So," he looked around, "you alone...?"

The alarmed expression on her face evidently surprised him. He took a quick step backwards. "I'm sorry, that didn't sound right." He smiled apologetically and spoke quickly, "I'm recently discharged – shrapnel in the leg," he indicated his right thigh. "Dad's on his own. Has a small farm over Jackson's Heath way." He waved in the general direction.

"I see," Jessica murmured. She was distractedly wondering if this Robin Tyler was Thomas's mysterious prowler. If so, what was he doing lurking about private property in the dead of night?

Glancing round, she spotted Sam heading towards the stables. He was carrying a canvas bag. "Just a minute, if you please, Mr Tyler. Sam!" she called. The older man gave a visible start and turned abruptly. "Could you pop over, please?"

For a fleeting moment, indecision flashed across Sam's face before he seemed to gather himself, "Ah... o' course. Just a moment, then."

Jessica turned back to Mr Tyler, "My husband... U-boat. He

was lost at sea."

"I'm sorry to hear that." He smiled gently.

He's not quite as good looking as Errol Flynn, Jessica decided, as Sam joined them. He'd left the bag somewhere and now stood beside Jessica, hands on hips, openly looking the newcomer up and down.

Jessica introduced the two men – *it wouldn't hurt Mr Tyler to know there's a man on the property*. Sam said, "What's the purpose o' your visit, then? There summat we can 'elp you with?"

Mr Tyler's smile remained in place. "Got home a couple of weeks ago; meant to call in earlier. Riding past just now and thought I'd come over."

"Right," Sam responded and Jessica thought he looked cagey. Perhaps he's being protective.

"Dad's getting up in years," Mr Tyler was saying. "Can't manage the heavy work like he used to."

Jessica nodded towards the mare. "Your father has horses?"

"Mm-hm, a couple like Allegra here." Mr Tyler scratched the mare's neck affectionately. "Mainly it's sheep. Wool. He supplies a weaving business in Leeds."

"Should be doing a roaring trade then," Jessica observed. "The military wants wool for uniforms."

"I keep telling Dad that but he's happy with his small flock. You have cattle, I see. Dairy?"

Jessica nodded, wishing he'd get to the point of his visit. "Like your dad, I don't keep a big herd. Enough for a bit of income and fresh milk and butter for us."

While the conversation continued, Jessica was aware of Sam shuffling beside her. She wondered abstractedly what might need his attention so urgently.

"Do you ride, Mrs Barrow?" Mr Tyler's question called her back to the conversation.

"No, not me. My daughter does. Mary has a pony."

"I missed Allegra while I was away. It's good to be back in the saddle – we both enjoy the wind in our hair." He laughed and pushed his hand through his thick curls, tousling them into Errol Flynn rakishness.

Jessica laughed politely, while Sam huffed sullenly. He cleared his throat and said, "Well, if you'll excuse us – things to do before it gets dark."

"Of course," Mr Tyler said. "Dad'll be wondering where I am. Told him I was going into Wharferidge and wouldn't be too long. Nice meeting you, Mrs Barrow," he nodded towards Sam, "Mr Clay."

The pair watched as Mr Tyler remounted. He gathered the reins and kicked his horse into a trot down the drive, then took the lane towards Jackson's Heath.

"Hmm," Sam said, thoughtfully scratching the stubble on his chin. "What d'you make of 'im, then?"

"Seems friendly enough. You weren't though."

"Friendly?" Sam shrugged carelessly. "Can't be too sure of strangers these days."

"Not a stranger, is he? Not if his dad lives just over there." Jessica waved towards the village beyond her orchard.

"S'pose."

Sam made to turn away but Jessica stopped him. "Thomas saw a man standing by the stables in the dark the other night."

Sam frowned. "A man?" he repeated. "By the stables?"

"You haven't seen anyone loitering about have you? A vagabond or …?" she gestured uncertainly.

"Nope." Sam's response was dismissive. "Well, back to –"

"Probably dreamt it," Jessica said. "We'd know if someone was lurking about, wouldn't we?" She peered at her steward, seeking reassurance.

Sam seemed impatient. "S'pose. I'll be in the dairy if you need owt."

She chewed her cheek thoughtfully as he strolled off.

***

The following day, a balmy afternoon suggested that spring wasn't far off and the cows in the field lowed gently, anticipating the coming of evening. Jessica sat on the porch, shelling peas and enjoying the slanting sunlight, while awaiting the school bus that would bring Mary and Thomas home.

The porch steps descended to the dirt driveway that bisected the front of her property and led to where the Leeds Road passed her gate.

From the scars in the grass, it was evident that in years gone by, the driveway had cambered to the left in a graceful half-moon curve. Now it was a lumpy track with a bend in it. The Leeds Road, originally a lane, had been widened over the years, gradually swallowing Broughton land.

If I had the money... Jessica thought, *I'd restore that driveway to its former elegance.* It was a fanciful notion as there was so much more pressing work to be done.

And despite the progress she'd already made in the garden, she'd only just scratched the surface, for the house behind her was aged. Its stones were pock-marked and greenish-grey with lichen, after years of exposure to harsh Yorkshire weather. The great double front doors were desperately in need of painting and they creaked badly, although age had not detracted from their craftsmanship.

Each had been hewn from a single length of oak, and bore a lion-head knocker in the centre.

Jessica took a deep breath and tucked loose coppery strands of hair behind her ears. So much work to be done – so little money, and the whole country in the same boat.

If something needed doing, you either did it yourself with the few resources available or decided it didn't need doing after all.

The Wolstone townsfolk thought she was mad for living in this decaying house – and perhaps she was – but she had seen its potential, even if Jon had not.

Jessica's reverie was interrupted by the sound of a lilting childish voice singing a song. She cocked her head to better hear the tune: *Whistle While You Work* from Snow White and the Seven Dwarves, except that the words were different.

Thomas strolled through the gate, satchel slung over one shoulder, cap pushed off his forehead.

"Hullo, Mummy," he greeted her as he came up the drive. "What're you doing?" He paused at the foot of the porch steps looking up at her.

"Shelling peas for tea. What was that you were singing?"

"Oh, something some of the lads were singing today at school. Henry Davies said he heard it somewhere."

"Can you sing it for me?"

He grinned, shyly. "I could, but you'd laugh at me."

"Why would I laugh? Where's Mary? Didn't she come home with you?"

"No. She was walking home with Peggy Walsh," Thomas told her disapprovingly, adding, "They said they had secret stuff to talk about."

"So, come on. Sing your song for me."

He smirked, "Turn your back."

"How about I keep shelling peas?" She lowered her gaze to the bowl, smiling to herself as his thin voice began, hesitantly at first, then building.

"Whistle while you work, Hitler is a twerp, Goering's barmy, so's his army, whistle while you work."

She looked up. He was waiting uncertainly, his russet eyebrows raised expectantly.

"That was brilliant!" She held her arms out and he trotted up the steps and into them. "Very clever, and you sang it so well."

"Hullo Mummy!" Mary was coming up the drive. Jessica turned, her arm over Thomas's shoulder, but he wriggled away and ran to his twin.

"Have you heard the Hitler song?" he asked, brimming with new confidence. "All the lads are singing it. I can teach you if you like."

Jessica got up and pushed her chair back to the wall where it normally stood.

"Mummy, Peggy's grandad is making her a sledge for next winter," Mary told her.

Jessica contained a melancholy sigh. Grandfathers were taking on fathering roles these days; another reason her father should be here – if not for his own safety.

"Oh?" she said.

"She said I'd be able to play on it too. That would be all right, wouldn't it?"

"If Peggy's mum says it's all right."

"She did today."

"Did you go to Peggy's house?" Thomas sounded put out.

Jessica pushed open the front door and her two children ducked beneath her arm into the dim entry hall.

"You like her, don't you?"

Thomas was quick to deny the charge and was about to launch an attack of his own when Jessica interrupted. "Go upstairs and change out of your school clothes. Do you want some bread and butter before tea?"

"But Mum," Thomas cried, his argument with his sister immediately forgotten. "Can't I play outside for a bit?"

Though it was spring and the days were beginning to lengthen, evenings still closed in early. Even now the sky was turning lavender and the shadows of the trees were stretching across the lawn. "Not tonight, love. It's not summer yet and it's getting dark already." Ignoring his protests, she headed towards the kitchen with her basin of peas. "Go upstairs," she called over her shoulder.

Jessica moved about the kitchen. *I must take that letter from the army to Jon's insurance company. I can make a claim,* she thought, filling the kettle and putting it on the range. *Imagine paying off the mortgage!* "Wherever you are Jon, I'll be forever grateful for your foresight," she said aloud.

"Tommy, stop singing that stupid song!" Mary's bellow rang through the house.

Jessica smiled at the ceiling and took out a cup and two glasses, placed them on the kitchen table, then reached for the tea canister. The one-scoop-for-each-person-and-one-for-the-pot guide had been modified due to rationing. Jessica tried to get by with just a quarter scoop. Wasn't too bad if she let it stew for a while.

"Damn!" she cursed. The wood basket was empty and the firebox needed feeding. Moreover, they would need wood for the evening. Thomas must have forgotten to refill it – one of the chores he regularly forgot.

She knew Sam kept wood in the stables for the steam engine to avoid going down to the woodshed – the path could be treacherous in the dark, icy mornings when he fired up the milking machine.

Being sure to remove the kettle from the hob first, Jessica went outside through the garden door. She'd been right to keep Thomas in – it was already dusk and the shadows were deepening, shrouding the shapes of trees and outbuildings. Iron-grey clouds filling the sky didn't help.

Making her way to the stables, Jessica sniffed the air. Damp: they were certain to get rain tonight and quite soon too.

The path wound past the wash-house to the stables, which, to Jessica's surprise, were open, the large door gaping like a mysterious black hole.

Should've brought a lantern, she told herself as she stepped cautiously inside. She could see the silvered outlines of farm tools hanging from the rafters overhead. Some were stacked against the walls, visible through the darkness. Shapes she knew well, that were innocent in daylight, became sinister and unfamiliar in the dark.

Beyond here, was a penned area where warm, heaving bovine bodies milled about in the straw. A corridor ran the length of the building; Jessica knew the wood was stacked at the far end, past the cows, stalls and the space where Sam kept the milking machinery.

The shadows grew thicker as Jessica edged along. Her fingertips groped the rough-cut stone of the walls. Her feet inched over the uneven cobbles.

Foolish to be so nervous; the only ghosts here were the gentle spirits of horses and cows. Yet tonight the hairs at the back of Jessica's neck spiked and her hands felt clammy.

She hesitated. Her breathing was shallow.

Peering into the shadows, she just made out the woodpile hunkering like a miniature pyramid at the darkest point.

She forced herself to take another step; her feet felt leaden.

Something wasn't right.

Darkness has a way of feeling empty. This darkness did not feel empty and Jessica's senses shifted into high alert. The skin on her arms began to tingle.

Silly woman! she scolded herself. Eyes intent on the inky outline of the woodpile, she stepped over a bundle of rags on the floor.

Without warning the rags exploded into movement!

Jessica shrieked and fell backwards. A milking bucket clattered loudly as she tripped over it. She landed heavily on her backside, whacking her head on the stone wall.

Shocked and slightly dazed, Jessica huddled in fright as the pile lurched and grew before her.

Eyes widening in horror, she pressed further into the unyielding stone behind her as the apparition rose, a formless, terrifying shape looming over her.

Jessica gaped in disbelief. Her feet slipped and scrabbled on the cobbles, trying to push away, but she was trapped against the solid stonework.

Her heart was thumping so hard it hurt. As she strained to see through the dark, Jessica was unknowingly emitting high-pitched squeaking sounds.

Run! her addled brain shouted *Get up! Run!* But she was half-crazed, insensible with fear.

Her breath was coming in rapid, rasping gasps while her lungs screamed for oxygen. Hugging her knees to her chest, Jessica shrank into herself, balling tightly, transfixed by the ghastly spectre swaying drunkenly before her.

Whimpering in abject terror, she heard the gritty scrape of it moving across the cobbles; the sound becoming distant beneath the pounding of the blood in her ears.

The human brain can only accept so much before it snaps shut, denying what it sees. At this point, Jessica's senses began to reel. Her vision swam, blurring around the edges. A loud buzzing started in her head; she was on the brink of hysteria.

Oh, God! I'm going to pass out!

And just as the thought entered her tortured mind, the hulking shape staggered. With a tremendous shudder, it collapsed, like an empty sack, on the stone floor at her feet.

Chapter 3

When Jessica was five years old, she'd visited the Ilkley Farmer's Fair. Spellbound amid the jostling crowd, she had watched as The Phenomenal Walter disappeared right before her very eyes!

Walter must truly be Phenomenal, she thought, *because he wasn't just Phenomenal Walter, but* The *Phenomenal Walter*.

Enthralled, she'd waited as the sequined Zelda slowly raised the Enchanted Cloak over The Phenomenal Walter's head. With bated breath, the audience of farmers, tradesmen and children, waited, mouths hanging open and eyes on stalks. Then suddenly, with a great flourish, Zelda whisked away the Enchanted Cloak and The Phenomenal Walter's stylish black suit collapsed to form a pile of empty clothes on the scuffed floorboards of the stage.

***

In the sinister shadows of the stables, as Jessica's senses slowly returned, any number of thoughts could have flashed through her mind. But as the apparition collapsed into a heap of rags at her feet, she was absurdly reminded of The Phenomenal Walter.

Jessica wanted to believe she was living through a nightmare. But as the panicked buzzing in her ears subsided, she found herself huddled on the cobbles of the darkened stables, wedged painfully between a wheelbarrow and the wall.

It was no nightmare – it was real.

Slowly, a skeletal, white hand extended towards her, fingers clawing and desperate. The spectre groaned, long and low, a sound vaguely like, *"Hair-clai..."*

Jessica's heart gave a painful thud and her eyes darted frantically about... a weapon... anything! But it was dark and there was only the bucket, lying where she'd tripped over it.

"Hair-clai!"

Moving quickly, Jessica snatched up the bucket, and grasping it by the rim, poised for attack. If the creature came closer, if it made one move towards her, she would wield that bucket like a mallet.

But as she crouched there in the increasing darkness, the shape made a hoarse gasping sound and the bony hand dropped with a dead slap to the stone floor.

Jessica held her breath, listening intently for what seemed a very long time, while her blood pounded in time with her heart.

Oh, God! It's breathing, she thought as a shallow rasping filtered through the gloom.

Her eyes darted between the shape on the floor and the door, beyond which she could see the purple evening sky.

If she could get out of here... get to Sam. *What if the children come looking for me*!

That thought forced her into action. Still gripping the bucket, Jessica slowly pushed to her feet, knees trembling, back sliding up the wall.

She felt the ripples of the stone drag at her cardigan. Her entire body shook and her breath was coming in short, sharp gasps. The amorphous shape on the ground made no move but Jessica lifted the bucket – ready to wallop it, if it so much as twitched. Mustering her courage, she inched forwards, peering intently. It remained unmoving.

She edged a bit closer... another step.

It's... Christ! It's a man! And the smell; she detected the ripe smell of unwashed male underlying some other tang – metallic.

Blood!

With a strangled cry, Jessica fled with a pace to rival Jesse Owens. She fairly flew over the cobbles, lunging towards the door.

Blind to everything but her need to escape, Jessica plunged through the stable doors and slammed hard into a body. Its arms clamped around her, holding her firmly in bands of wiry muscle.

Gasping with terror, Jessica fought like a wild thing.

"Missus!" the man panted. He ducked the determined sweep of the metal bucket. "It's me... S'all right!"

Jessica was deaf with terror. She fought with an insane strength, but the man held her tightly.

Suddenly he gave her a violent shake, "Jessica!"

Jessica was startled into awareness. When the bands around her loosened, she slipped free and staggered drunkenly. Something in her mind clicked into place. Wheeling around, she cried, "Sam? Sam! There's a man... a man!"

Like a crazy woman she returned to throw herself at him. In relief, she grasped his jumper, eyes darting frantically between her steward and the stables behind him.

"A man!" she panted, still brandishing the bucket.

Sam ducked, then patted the air before him to calm her. "S'all right! Missus, it's all right."

But Jessica wasn't listening. She clutched his bony shoulders, "There's a man! A man... in there!"

"I know." Sam was unruffled. "I know. Calm down."

"I thought... I thought I was seeing... I don't know what... who is he?"

"Shhh, 'e won't 'urt you."

"How do we know? We must call –"

"Hush, we don't need to call anyone. 'Ee's a pilot – 'e's no threat!"

"A pilot!" Sudden, relief made her giddy. She slumped against him. "You know him? Oh thank God... I thought –"

"'Ere, you'll kill someone with that!" Sam took the bucket. Placing it on the ground, he quickly ushered her further into the rapidly lowering night.

Jessica was still trembling with the force of her shock. She ran a shaky hand through her hair, gradually regaining control.

"That man... a pilot? What's a pilot doing here?"

Sam drew in his breath. "Brace yourself." He took her by the shoulders and held her firmly. "'E's a Gerry."

Jessica blinked at him uncomprehendingly. "What?"

Sam drew in his breath and released it resignedly. "'E's a *German* pilot."

"*What*!" Jessica cried, aghast. Suddenly her heart rate shot up again. Grasping handfuls of his clothing, she hauled him towards her. "A *Gerry*! What the bloody hell!"

"Shh, Missus."

"A-a-" Jessica stammered. Her face was ghostly and the whites of her eyes shone wildly. She shot a look over Sam's shoulder, anticipating an attack at any moment.

Clutching her wrists, Sam gave her a gentle shake. "Missus... it's *all right*."

"No, it most certainly is not all –"

"Jessie, please, listen to me." Sam talked quickly, trying to get the details out, trying to make her understand. "'Is name's Anton. 'E was shot down t'other week. 'E were found unconscious an' bleeding... 'e's not well, Missus. 'E's badly wounded."

She watched his face and saw the plea there – and something else. Sympathy?

"Oh my God!" she gasped in disbelief. "You're looking after him! We need to call the authorities – the Home Guard – immediately!"

She took a step towards the house but he held her elbow. "That's why I didn't tell you."

Her heart was pounding out of time and her hands were shaking uncontrollably. "Christ Sam, we can't keep him!" she exclaimed incredulously. "He's not a pet, he's the bloody enemy!"

"Missus, please, 'ear me out."

But Jessica's fear was turning to anger. She pulled away and marched towards the house.

There was purpose in her step and Sam hurried to follow. "All's I could think was what if that were my boy?" he said, jogging to keep up with her brisk stride. "What if some Kraut lady were kind enough to take 'im in... feed 'im and nurse 'is wounds?"

"So what!" Jessica spat over her shoulder. "Let the authorities nurse his wounds." She quickened her step but he kept pace.

"Wait!" Sam grabbed her arm again.

Rounding on him, she shook off his hand. "His kind killed my husband!" she cried furiously.

"His kind... killed my boy..." Sam's voice broke.

Jessica thought it would have been better if Sam had been angry, but even through the evening shadows, she could see the dampness glistening on his cheeks.

They stood, a yard apart, breathing heavily.

Unexpectedly, the shock overcame her. Jessica's legs gave out and she dropped to her knees on the broken path, head in hands. She was aware of Sam hovering above her, watching uncertainly. Her chest hurt with every heaving sob. She stammered, "They... they killed... my husband..."

Irresolutely, her steward squatted before her and gently took her hands from her face. "I'm sorry, honestly I am," he whispered, tears trickling down his own face. "But 'e's little more'n a lad. We couldn't turn 'im in... we just couldn't."

Jessica remained kneeling, working to compose herself. Something Sam said struck a discordant note. She slowly raised her eyes.

"*We?*"

Sam looked sheepish.

"Marg's in on this?" Jessica demanded. "Well," she sighed, "she's your wife. Of course she's in on it."

Jessica forced herself to speak firmly. "This is my land, Sam

Clay. I have a right to know who's on it."

"We... we couldn't... we weren't to know 'ow you'd take it... and we've been that worried about 'im."

Jessica deflated. Sam seemed to have aged in the minutes of their struggle. All the fight drained from her. She said, "He's badly wounded?"

"Broken ribs, we think. Marg bound them but 'e's in a bit of bother. Now we think 'e's getting pneumonia."

"Pneumonia?"

Sam nodded. "If 'e's got that, it'll go badly for 'im."

He released her hands as she fished in her pocket. Pulling out a hanky she mopped her eyes and blew her nose, then with a final, resolute breath she climbed to her feet.

Sam rose with her, waiting, his face white and stricken.

"Well," was all she said. Shaking her head as though to clear it, Jessica took a deep breath. Her hands trembled as she tucked stray hair behind her ears. "What now?"

Her steward shrugged and suggested cautiously, "I could introduce you?"

Jessica sniffed wetly. "You're serious, aren't you? What if he's dangerous?"

Sam grunted. "Poor sod 'asn't the strength of a newly 'atched chick."

Seconds passed while Jessica considered. It was now full dark and a night bird called to its mate in the nearby forest.

"All right," she said finally. "If he's living in my stable, I'd best meet," *the bastard,* "him."

Sam led the way. The stable was completely lightless now but he went directly to the bundle on the floor. Crouching, he whispered, "Anton?"

The bundle twitched and dragged in a wheezing breath. "*Hair clai? Ist... Ihnen?*"

Ah-ha! Jessica almost said out loud. *Herr* Clay! She hunkered curiously beside her steward.

"Aye, lad," Sam responded gently. "'Ow you feeling?" Sam put a hand to the man's forehead, "Blimey, you're burning up! Let me get you summat."

Sam reached into a darkened corner, withdrawing a cloth in one hand, a flask in the other. He shook the flask experimentally. It sloshed. "You 'aven't been drinking owt. No wonder you're poorly. Gotta keep those fluids up."

He opened the flask and poured its contents onto the cloth. Water dripped on the floor. Folding the cloth into a rectangle, he instructed, "Relax now," and placed it on the man's forehead. "You'll be 'ungry, I reckon. *Hungrig?*"

Jessica watched in wonder. In how many homes, stables and sheds, across England, was this going on? How many honest English people were caring for the enemy? Quite a few, she decided, given that it was going on in her own stable, at this very moment.

While she watched, Sam delved into the sack she'd seen him carrying earlier. Another *ah-ha* moment. She edged forwards, "Sam, I –"

With a small, sharp cry, the man on the floor started violently. "*Was!*"

"Steady, Anton... s'all right." Sam threw an accusing glance over his shoulder. "Anton, this's Mrs Barrow... Frau Barrow... remember I told you about 'er? She owns this place."

"She... knows? About me?" Coming through the darkness, though the breathing was laboured with pain and congestion, the disembodied voice was heavily accented. *A Kraut!* She told herself. *The enemy! Husband killer!*

"She were in 'ere before. You scared 'er, 'alf to death," Sam said, lightly. "What the bleedin' 'ell you doing up 'ere anyway? You should be down the back!"

"*Entschuldigung...* I am sorry."

"S'all right, lad."

"Sam," Jessica tried again. "Now I know about him, you could use the lantern."

"Oh aye, of course." She heard him move. "Got used to working in the dark. Now, where'd I leave it?"

"Here." The lantern was by her side. It rattled, metal on glass, as she handed it to him. Sam struck a match and touched it to the wick, replaced the glass casing over it and sent shadows leaping and scurrying into corners.

Jessica and the young man on the floor regarded one another cautiously.

The first thing she noticed was that he was filthy. The second was how small he was – or seemed to be. As it was, he was curled on one side – he seemed to be protecting the other. His knees were drawn up and the cloth – it looked like one of Marg's face-cloths – was draped over his brow. In the light of the lantern, she could see he was wearing a uniform – but not any style of uniform she'd seen before. It was this, more than anything else about him, that screamed foreign.

It was a long, tunic-like shirt that, although stained, seemed to be flecked in white and some other darker colour – blue perhaps – and loose-fitting trousers with numerous pockets and zippers. His boots were black and caked with dried mud. They seemed to be made of heavy leather, and what could possibly be shearling, and were tightened with black leather straps around his legs.

Dirty, unshaven and dressed as he was, he looked fierce and very dangerous. Jessica took an involuntary step backwards. Immediately, a change shadowed his face. His expression, although shrouded in fatigue and pain, had initially been open, even hopeful. Now it turned wary. He shot a quick glance at Sam, before returning to her.

"I am... pleased to meet you, Frau Barrow." He spoke haltingly, his accent guttural. The hairs on Jessica's neck rose.

Turning to Sam, she said, "He speaks English! I didn't expect
_"

"You may address me directly, Frau Barrow." Breathing
carefully through his pain, the German tempered his words with
a small, cautious smile. But he'd got his point across and Jessica
felt her face warming.

"I'm sorry. That was rude of me. I'm... surprised, that's all."

"I lived... United States," he said with difficulty, his breath
wheezing in his chest. "I speak English."

"Never mind that now," Sam interrupted. "Anton, 'ere, eat
this."

Sam handed him a sandwich made with thick slices of bread
and what appeared to be meat filling.

Jessica watched as the German took a bite. He chewed slowly,
dutifully, seemingly without hunger, all the while regarding her
through hooded, pale eyes. Difficult to tell their colour in the
dimness of the stables, or the colour of his hair as it crested from
his skull in dirty hanks. Beneath the grime and sprouting beard,
his cheekbones were what her mother would describe as refined;
the hand holding the sandwich was square, with long pianist's
fingers.

Her eyes returned to his face.

***

As Jessica studied him, Anton was making a similar
assessment of her; auburn hair and pretty, freckled face. She
was all apricot and cinnamon with eyes that seemed to be gold-
speckled in the flickering lamplight.

Herr Clay took a bucket and turned it upside down. Drumming
on it, he said, "Sit, Missus. Better than standing there."

Anton took a second bite from the sandwich, watching the
woman tuck her skirt beneath her thighs and prop uncomfortably
on the bucket. She continued to stare at him but he thought she

didn't seem as afraid any more.

He swallowed with difficulty, his throat felt raw and he was burning up. He put the food aside. Herr Clay removed the cloth from his brow and he felt its lack immediately. But it was rinsed and replaced and Anton allowed his eyes to close with relief.

***

"*Mum!*"

All three gave a start. Jessica turned an anxious face to Sam. "Oh, God! The children!"

Sam opened his mouth to speak but Mary's voice rang out again, "*Mum... You outside?*"

Jessica went to the stable door. *How am I going to keep this from the children? What child could possibly keep a secret this big? What if he's dangerous? How do I protect them?*

"Mummy? Where are you?" Thomas echoed his sister. He sounded concerned.

"Coming... don't come out, it's too dark. I'm on my way." Turning to Sam, "I'll be back... tomorrow. I..." there were so many questions. She faltered. "We'll talk tomorrow," she ended and dashed into the night.

As she rounded the wash-house, the garden door stood open – a big rectangle of yellow light framing the black shapes of her children.

"Coming," she puffed.

"You were gone for ages, Mummy," Thomas whined.

"I was checking one of the cows. Everything's all right."

"Everything's *okay*," he corrected.

"Stop trying to talk like a Yank," his sister admonished.

Thomas made a face at her.

"Inside, you two. Now!" Jessica herded the pair into the kitchen. She turned the key in the lock, and for the first time in her memory, she dragged a great lump of wood from behind the meat safe and grunting, hefted it in her arms and slid it home through the iron bands secured to the door-frame.

Jessica saw her children exchange glances, before they turned away.

Chapter 4

March was the time of year when the garden came to life. Trees and flowers blossomed and bloomed, seemingly overnight, and Jessica's garden was a hive of industry as bees collected pollen and birds built their nests in anticipation of the young soon to come.

Although it wasn't a sunny morning, Jessica decided the breeze would be sufficient to dry her washing. She hung the last of it on the line, then hoisted the lever that swung the wire high into the wind and secured it in place.

Drawing herself up to her full five-feet-four-inches, she took a deep, spring-scented breath and looked around. The kitchen garden was nearby. It was slowly undergoing a transformation and soon, the earth would grow warmer and the seeds she'd planted would burst through the soil, spearing skyward in their quest for life-giving sunlight.

The clothes-line was situated near the wash-house and other outhouses. A broken, uneven path led towards the stables where her milking equipment and Mary's pony, Spencer, were housed – along with a German fugitive.

God, if the authorities find out... It didn't bear thinking about. So, she determinedly put the matter out of her mind – for now at least.

***

As the morning progressed into afternoon, Jessica paused in her work. She was clearing the last corner of the kitchen garden. Resting for a moment, she watched the birds roosting in the trees. The chill wind reminded her that it was still only March and winter was not so distant as to be completely forgotten.

Digging the hard earth had quickly warmed her, and every so often she straightened and wiped her sleeve across her brow.

It was Saturday, and Thomas and Mary were happily pursuing whatever business children pursued when not at school – they'd not yet come hungrily asking about tea.

"'Ow's it going?"

Sam stood looking down at her. She sat back on her heels and shielded her eyes to look up at him.

"Making good progress."

He continued to hover over her.

If he thinks I'm going to enquire as to his patient's welfare he's got another thing coming.

She expected him to say something else but he stood restlessly moving from foot to foot. Her sweat-dampened skin quickly cooled and she gave a brief, involuntary shiver.

He noticed and asked, "You'll be finishing up soon?"

"I suppose so …"

"Righto then. Call me when you're ready. I'll put the tools away for you."

"Oh," she responded, mildly surprised. *Saving me the trouble of another confrontation with his Kraut, I suppose*, she thought grumpily. "Thank you."

Sam lingered a moment longer and Jessica regarded him thoughtfully, before returning to her work. She felt gritty – digging, pulling weeds, planting – it was dirty work, and it was hard work, particularly when there were rocks, like this one, that wouldn't budge.

Bracing her weight on her knees, Jessica leaned forwards, trying to dislodge the rock with her gloved hands. She brushed away the dirt, tearing up the roots of some long-dead plant. Working doggedly, gradually she exposed lines that seemed curiously straight.

"What's that?" Sam asked, peering into the hole.

"I don't know." Jessica grunted with effort as she laboured to dislodge the lump. "I thought it was a rock. It's some kind of

…" She rapped on it with a knuckle. It gave a distinctly metallic sound. "Lucifer's balls!"

It's a box!

The ground seemed to heave beneath her knees and her stomach lurched sickeningly as misty images from a recent dream came floating back.

An old woman … late at night … digging a hole...

But that surely hadn't been real! She shook off a sudden uneasiness and resumed her work.

Sam hunkered beside her, watching as she pushed her fingers into the soil and gently extracted the box.

***

Jessica sat at the Clays' scarred, old kitchen table, Sam on one side and Marg on the other, each with a steaming mug of tea.

The box, caked with dirt and riddled with a cancer of rust, sat on a sheet of newspaper before her.

"What's it got on the lid?" Marg was peering over the rims of her spectacles at the initials embossed on the dented top.

Sam leaned in for a closer examination. "Looks like a U … p'raps a V? No wait, I reckon that's 'alf a W."

Gazing at the box, Jessica felt the room recede and the gossamer threads of her dream returned to whisper about her. The night breeze had been cool, the moon drifted behind ribbons of cloud. Like a slip between time and space, Jessica had distinctly heard an aged-cracked voice, say, *Margaret Maria Washburn. Were it your life, would you have lived it differently?*

"M. M. W." Jessica murmured.

"Blimey woman, will you open it?" Sam cried. "Suspense's killing me!"

"Sam!" Marg admonished. "Let 'er take 'er time."

Jessica gave herself a shake. "You're right. Let's get on with it."

She drew the tin closer and lightly wiped the lid with a damp cloth. The initials stamped there were legible now and clearly read, M. M. W.

About eight inches long, four wide and six deep, the box could hold any manner of items. Yet as the last traces of dream evaporated, Jessica knew that whatever it contained was something of significance.

"Pra'ps you're a millionaire now," Sam joked, but Jessica barely heard him over the excited pounding of her heart.

The latch on the box hung limply, and as she touched it with a gentle finger, its decayed moorings crumbled. It dropped to the newspaper amid a rusty lump of soil.

With a hand on either side, she eased open the lid.

Sam and Marg leaned forward, sucking in their breaths.

At first, Jessica thought it was simply a dirty old rag, but closer inspection revealed something wrapped in a filthy piece of canvas that smelled of earth and mildew. As though performing delicate surgery, Jessica tenderly lifted the package from the box and placed it on the table.

The cloth was cold from the ground but seemed to be in one piece.

With her heart beating faster by the second, Jessica carefully peeled away the folds of canvas to reveal what appeared to be a book. Although age-mottled, Jessica could see it had once been bound in beautiful red leather.

"*Whew* ..." Sam gave a low whistle.

Rotating the sheet of canvas, Jessica examined the book's spine. "It's holding together really well ... it's just dirty."

"Open it," Marg urged. "Must be summat important."

Jessica stared at the book and she heard the old woman's words again, "*Were it your life, would you have lived it differently?*"

"It's a memoir," she whispered, and ever so gently, opened it.

The leather gave a soft creak; a single sheet of paper, folded in half, lay beneath the cover. It was discoloured with age and spotted with mould. *Only the highest quality paper would have survived so well.* With great reverence, she slid out the page and opened it.

It felt brittle in her fingers but miraculously bore few traces of its habitation beneath the ground.

Placing it flat on the table before her, Jessica raised her eyes to the couple sitting eagerly forward in their chairs. "C'mon, lass," Sam urged. "What's it say?"

Jessica cleared her throat and took a deep breath. She began to read.

14 March 1871

You have found the diary, as I knew you would. Are you a relative? I know not. But I have spoken with you in my dreams and I have seen you sometimes in my waking hours. You walk these halls, your lovely auburn hair swinging with your step.

Here, Jessica paused. A fluttering had begun in her stomach, quickly becoming a sickly feeling. She knew it was foolish, but it was as if the letter addressed her personally.

She looked up at the Clays – they seemed more interested in what the letter said than in whom the auburn-haired person was.

Sam gestured impatiently, "Don't stop now!"

But Jessica's hands were trembling and her mouth had suddenly gone dry. She swallowed hard and continued.

You walk these halls, your lovely auburn hair swinging with your step.

I know not if you are aware of me, for somewhere deep inside I know that you do not exist in my time. And for this reason, I entrust this to you.

Allow me to introduce myself. I was born Margaret Maria

Washburn on 17 February 1809. This book was placed into my care and I was entrusted with a sacred duty – a duty I carry out this night.

This is a fascinating, sometimes painful, sometimes joyous story. But it's not my story.

The note documented the life and marriage of Alexandra Broughton, and as Jessica read aloud, occasionally squinting to decipher faded words, her stomach leapt at an incredible, intriguing knowledge; it was no coincidence that Jessica's house was called Broughton Hall.

Alexandra must have lived within those very walls!

As Jessica continued reading the note, a picture grew in her mind of a young girl with unruly brown curls, rambling about this lovely old house accompanied by a dog.

She went on to describe a request, many years later, from Alexandra to visit her in her marital home.

By then in her sixties, Margaret had made the journey.

The day before I was to return to Yorkshire, Alex spoke to me privately, both of us knowing we would likely never see one another again.

She showed me a scuffed, red-leather bound journal and explained that Patrick had given it to her for Christmas, the first Christmas he'd spent at Broughton Hall. She invited me to read it, explaining that she had documented her life ... she had neither secrets nor regrets.

Finally, her voice a thin thread, she leaned close to my ear, and I know I made no mistake in comprehension when she said,

"Meggie, please take this journal home to Broughton Hall." Pressing the well-loved book into my hands she added, "It's for the lady ... You know of whom I speak. Keep it safe for her. Let her find it... somewhere..."

As Jessica came to the end of the letter, all three sat in thoughtful silence. Jessica's hands had grown cold and clammy. Somehow, she knew, that she was *the lady*. It was to her this letter was addressed.

But that's crazy. I must be going crazy, Jessica thought, yet there it was: *you walk these halls, your lovely auburn hair swinging with your step.*

No, it's too impossible. How could it be addressed to me? Yet the words resonated in her chest like a baritone. And more profoundly: *Somewhere deep inside I know that you do not exist in my time. And for this reason, I entrust this to you.*

No! Jessica's mind snapped. *It's too crazy and I'm being ridiculous – just because I have auburn hair!*

But what about the dream she'd had in which that old lady buried the box... what if it had not been a dream? What if she had somehow, incredibly, witnessed it happening?

Lost in thought, Jessica gave a little start as Marg spoke. "What're you going to do now?"

"Read it, o' course," Sam said.

His wife shrugged, "Or keep it safe until after the war... until you can take it to some museum or summat."

The couple lapsed into speculative discussion but it barely registered with Jessica. Her brain was still trying to gather the strands of an impossible notion and weave them into sense.

Chapter 5

Jessica couldn't sleep. She lay in bed, very still, listening for the faintest sound, the slightest hint that the stranger in her stable was moving about outside.

But why would he? The man couldn't stand let alone walk. He'd been there for days, weeks, without making any effort to approach. He didn't appear dangerous. The opposite in fact, for he'd seemed genuinely afraid of her.

But Jessica's mind would not rest.

Suddenly, she remembered the man Thomas had seen from his window that night.

Of course! Who else could it have been?

Dear God! How long has that bastard been hiding in my stables? And how long has Sam known about him?

Suddenly other things started to come clear, like Sam's restlessness when Robin Tyler was visiting.

Now Jessica was wide awake; sleep was impossible. She struck a match and lit the lamp. Somewhere in the forest, an owl hooted. His mate answered, and Jessica glanced towards the window.

Her eyes lit on the tin box she'd dug up in the garden. Pushing herself to a sitting position, she reached for it and lifted the lid. The cloth-wrapped parcel nested within.

Jessica spread the oiled cloth across her lap and revealed the scuffed, red journal. Gently lifting the cover and moving aside the letter, she turned to the first page of writing.

Sections of it were blurred or faded with damp and age, but for the most part, it seemed extraordinarily well preserved.

The date at the top read, *June first, 1830.* The handwriting was neat with curling, old-fashioned flourishes.

I'll read you one day, she promised the journal as she folded its protective cloth covering over it and returned it to the tin box.

Suddenly a shout below her window startled her. Holding her breath in surprise and afraid to move, she listened intently.

"Missus! You 'wake?"

She relaxed with relief. *Sam. But at this hour?*

Jessica shimmied off the bed and ran to the window, unlatched it and leaned out. Her steward stood below, looking up, twisting his flat-cap in his hands.

"Sam! What on earth...? You'll wake the children."

"Missus, you must come! It's the young man – summat's wrong."

She tutted irritably. *Isn't it enough we could all go up for harbouring the enemy, but we have to fret about the bugger's health as well?* "All right," she said resignedly. "Give me a moment. I'll come down."

***

Should've worn something warmer, Jessica thought as she stepped into the night. Sam was waiting by the garden door with a lantern. The air was icy; dampness seeped into her dressing-gown as she followed him round the kitchen garden towards the stables.

Her breaths formed puffs of vapour before her face; the smells of damp earth and grass seemed stronger in the night. Neither spoke as Sam pushed back the door and lit the way into the hay-filled barn. Compared with the outside cold, the interior was humid from the mingled breath of slumbering cattle.

Jessica heard the wet gurgling of the German's breathing before she got to the stall. As she knelt over him, she felt the heat radiating off his damp skin; he was practically steaming with fever.

"I'm 'oping 'e's just taken some kind of chill," Sam said from behind her. "I'm 'oping it's not... you know?"

"Hmm." Jessica moved cautiously, as one would towards a

wounded animal, and gently, placed a hand over his forehead.

"My God," she murmured. "He's burning up."

As a child, Jessica had visited an elderly neighbour who had pneumonia. The last time she'd seen the woman alive, the old lady's complexion and breathing were very much like the German's were now.

"He should be indoors... in a proper bed," she told Sam. *I'm going to regret this*, she told herself. "He needs someone to watch over him... fluids, aspirin."

"Aye, e's got blankets but 'e keeps kicking them off."

"He will. We need to bring the fever down – it's way too cold and damp in here."

"And 'e won't eat nowt."

Jessica sighed heavily. "Sam, he needs a doctor. He should be in a hospital. We're going to have to –"

"*No!*"

She stared at him. The lantern light threw the lines of his face into craggy relief. His grey eyes looked black and hard – determined. "No," he repeated. "'anding 'im over to the authorities will kill 'im."

"What would you have me do?" she demanded in a hoarse whisper. "He's extremely ill, he has a raging temperature. He'll die if he doesn't get proper treatment."

"'E'll die if we turn 'im over! You think they'll care about 'im?"

The German chose that moment to moan, his legs kicked uselessly in the hay, hands clawing at the neck of his shirt.

"*Heiss... zu heiss...*" he muttered, head lolling from side to side.

"What's he saying?" Jessica wanted to know.

Sam shrugged. "Dunno, but I reckon 'e's 'ot. Look at the sweat pouring off 'im, poor sod."

Indeed, the man's hair was plastered to his temples and

forehead, and perspiration ran in glistening rivulets down his neck.

Jessica rose, the better to stand her ground. "Sam," she began hesitantly. *What was it Jon used to say? Stand tall – don't let them see you're vulnerable.* "Sam, I really don't –"

"I'd take 'im down to the cottage if we 'ad space but we 'aven't room to swing a cat."

"What?" she demanded. "You think *I* should take him in? That he should be moved into *my* house?" Jessica gaped at her steward in disbelief.

Sam removed his flat cap and scratched at his scalp. "Well... you do 'ave all that space."

"Out of the question! He could be dangerous."

"'E's 'armless! Well-educated! What do you think 'e 's gonna do?"

"I don't know what he's going to do. That's the problem!"

Sam wasn't backing down and Jessica sensed she was losing the argument. The words, *out of the question*, had always worked when her father said them. Why, when she said them, did they never command the same respect?

"But Mary and Thomas –"

"Mary and Thomas are –"

"He's *German*!" she cried, frustrated.

"He speaks *English*!"

"Not much with an accent like that!"

She sensed the argument swing in her favour, but suddenly the young man gasped, "*Gott! Hilf... mir!*"

She stared down at him, thrashing about in a feverish delirium at her feet, and felt the first pangs of guilt. *He was so young, so far from home and caught up in this bloody war just like she was. Were his people, at this moment, weeping over a letter saying he was missing in action? He would have parents, a sweetheart or a wife. Had they received the same kind of official letter she had?*

Automatically, she glanced at his left hand. The absence of a ring didn't mean anything; Jon never wore a wedding band. And just like Jon, this young man was guilty only of loyalty to his country.

Sam obviously saw her wavering and played his trump card. "Missus... 'e's just a lad."

"Blast you Sam Clay!" she muttered angrily.

***

Jessica wanted to wait until the children had left for school before they moved the German pilot. Despite the freezing temperature, Sam and Marg agreed to sit with him throughout the remaining hours of the night.

When Jessica went outside just before six the next morning, a crisp frost covered the garden and lawn in glittering white. Marg and Sam were shivering beneath a shared blanket, each hugging a lukewarm hot water-bottle, and grateful of the hot tea and toast she brought.

They'd spent the night applying cool compresses to the German's chest and forehead to stop his temperature rising further. While the patient seemed less distressed, the fever was no less severe.

Jessica leaned over him. In the pearlescent light of dawn, his complexion was a dirty grey colour. When his eyelids suddenly fluttered and popped open, Jessica was mildly startled. She had a glimpse of bright blue, but they were glassy, unseeing.

Relieved, she escaped to the house before the children got up.

Once she'd seen Mary and Thomas safely on the school bus, Jessica set about preparing the spare room at the end of the hall – as far from the children's rooms as possible.

The room she chose was ordinarily used for storage, and it took Jessica and Sam most of the morning to transfer the boxes and crates to another room and move in a spare bed.

***

It was almost midday when Jessica straightened and blew away a strand of hair loosened from her plait. Having made up the bed with fresh linen and blankets, it now occurred to her that the German was filthy – they couldn't possibly put him in that clean bed in such a state.

Sam'll have to bathe him – damned if I'm doing it! Besides the obvious fact that he was a man, she was certain she didn't want to be alone with him. *If Sam was so sure the German meant them no harm, he could bloody well look after him.*

The man would need to be brought into the house, stripped naked, scrubbed and dressed in …

Jessica made a sound of irritation and went down the hall to her own room. Most of Jon's clothes were still in the wardrobe, including his green-striped pyjamas. Taking them out of the drawer, she ignored Jon's distinctive smell still clinging to the flannelette.

She left the pyjamas in the bathroom.

By the time she returned to the stables, Sam and Marg were trying to rouse the man. They'd had some small success, though he seemed confused and weak.

Sam and Jessica supported him, all the while mindful of his broken ribs. Marg followed with his pack and leather pilot's jacket.

"I've drawn a bath," Jessica gasped, as they manoeuvred him through the garden door. She had guessed he wasn't too tall. Once they got him to his feet he was a little taller than he'd appeared, but not much. Jon had been six foot one. This man was shorter; five foot nine, best guess.

He was very thin, but a virtual dead weight, which left Sam and Jessica, neither of whom were big, half-dragging, half-carrying him from the kitchen, up four steps, right turn in a narrow corridor, up another four steps, right turn and along the hall to the main staircase.

Pausing at the bottom, Sam gripped the man's chin and gave his face a little shake. "Anton! You're gonna 'ave to 'elp us. We gotta get you up them stairs."

Obligingly, the German attempted to lift one foot after the other. The trio made a slow and ungainly ascent, stopping regularly for all three to rest.

By the time they reached the landing on the upper floor, they were puffing. The German was sweating profusely, his face above the thick, dirty beard was the colour of a suet pudding.

"Straight to the bathroom," Jessica directed.

Sam and Jessica half-dragged the German down the hall while Marg held the bathroom door open. It was warm; the furnace in the corner was stoked and roaring and steam hung in the air.

Sam turned to his wife, "I'll manage all right if you can 'elp me get 'is kit off and get 'im into the tub."

"Take that wrapping off his ribs too," Jessica ordered. "He's struggling to breathe as it is." She went to leave, "Oh, and throw his clothes into the hall. I'll boil them up in the copper. I've left a pair of Jon's pyjamas on the stool in there."

Sam nodded. "Right y'are."

Besides Jon's pyjamas, Jessica had left Jon's shaving brush, mug and razor.

She noticed Sam frowning dubiously at them. "I ain't never shaved another man before."

Marg grinned. "I 'ave."

"When?" Sam demanded. His wife's grin grew mysterious and he eyed her narrowly. "Well?"

Jessica smiled, enjoying the exchange between them.

"Silly apoth!" Marg admonished. "When I were nursin' in Flanders in seventeen, of course."

"Oh aye, of course."

By now they'd sat the German on the stool where he sagged

against the wall, breathing in wet, shallow gasps. As Jessica left them, Marg was unbuckling his boots and Sam was dragging his pilot's tunic over his head.

***

Later in the kitchen, Jessica was stirring a pot of soup when Sam came in. "'E's in bed … all clean and shaved."

"Is he all right? Does he need anything?"

"Marg's with 'im now. The bath did wonders for 'is fever – seems more settled now."

"Good," Jessica murmured. She almost meant it. As she stirred the soup, she noticed Sam sniffing the air appreciatively and realised it was after one o'clock and none of them had eaten since six that morning.

Just then Marg arrived in the kitchen. "Sleeping, poor love. Amazing what a scrub-up'll do. He's younger'n I thought – younger than our Charlie."

"You think?" Sam thought for a moment. "I'd say they're of ages."

Who cares! Jessica wanted to shout, leaning wearily over her sink. She was more concerned about keeping her children safe from the bloody Gerry in the house.

Marg's eyes settled on her with understanding. "It'll be all right," she said gently. "I'll sit with 'im at night until 'e's better."

Jessica threw her a grateful smile but Marg had already turned away, returning upstairs.

***

The fact that the house was silent meant Jessica could forget – sometimes for as long as ten minutes straight – that she was harbouring a German fighter pilot in her spare room.

Going about the day's chores, Jessica put a load of washing in the copper, although she omitted the German's putrid uniform;

she couldn't stomach the idea of washing his filthy clothes with her children's or her own.

She stuffed the Gerry's clothing in an old chaff bag and stashed it in a corner of the wash-house. *I'll worry about it another time.*

Later, she pulled her clean washing through the wringer, then took it out to the line.

Meanwhile, Sam had milked the cows and taken the full cans to Bright and Sons. The remaining half-can, Jessica poured into shallow dishes to allow the cream to rise.

From there, she went out to the garden to continue her weeding and planting.

***

Some time later, Jessica returned to the barn and found the cream had completed rising. She skimmed it and set it aside in an earthenware jar. As her dairy operation was relatively small, she tended to collect the cream over a few days before churning it into butter. It produced a richer flavour that way.

Spring was the perfect time for churning; the summer was too warm and made the butter too thin, while winter churning resulted in a product that was slow to set and difficult to work with.

After jarring the cream, Jessica was surprised by the time. It only wanted an hour or so before the school bus would rumble up the Leeds Road returning Thomas and Mary home – unless they'd decided to walk with friends.

Her work done, Jessica could no longer pretend the stranger did not exist. During her years at school, she'd learned that the protocols of the 1929 version of the Geneva Convention made provision for the treatment of wartime wounded. If the Gerry recovered after being so ill and feverish, he would be thirsty, hungry … *bloody hell, he'll want to go to the toilet*! If she refused to take care of his needs, she'd be in breach of some international treaty!

She smiled sardonically. *Who would have thought – meek little Jessica Barrow, torturing her very own prisoner of war*!

Not funny really; Sam and Marg were right. If some German woman found Jon, she would hope the woman dealt kindly with him.

Marg had left the Kraut sleeping relatively peacefully an hour ago. She'd promised to return after tea, but begged Jessica to unbend enough to check on him.

Jessica stood outside his door, listening for any sound from within. Nothing.

With a deep breath, she turned the handle and pushed. The door creaked open but the shape in the bed didn't stir as she stepped into the room.

He slept on his side facing the door. Marg had drawn the curtains and the room was dim. Jessica slowly approached the bed.

Washed and freshly shaved, the man before her was no longer the fearsome monster she'd imagined. He was much younger than she'd first thought; no more than 25 years old by the looks of him. His light brown hair had been closely cropped in accordance with most military standards, though was longer and tousled on top. His nose was straight, if slightly wide at the bridge, his cheekbones, as she'd previously noted, were high and well-formed and there was a slight cleft in his chin.

But it was his mouth that drew her gaze. Beautifully shaped, the lips slightly apart, it was the kind of mouth that might smile often and laugh easily.

He was attractive in a way that brought to mind those Norse raiders she'd seen in history books. Unbidden, the word Aryan entered her head – he was the perfect example of a word that, until recently, was a description with no greater importance than Oriental or Caucasian. Yet these days the word held a new, evil connotation.

The man before her, wearing her husband's pyjamas, eyes darting behind closed lids and breathing stertorously, was her enemy. If she were to take a gun, place it between his closed eyes and pull the trigger, who would condemn her? Could the laws of the Geneva Convention be used against her?

She doubted it – a woman protecting her children.

Shocked by her own thoughts, the colour rose in her cheeks, for as he lay there, he looked as he was; a young man, recruited by his government to fight for his country. He had no more control over his destiny than English lads had.

These men were torn from their homes, to face the worst horrors man can devise, by governments whose actuaries perform probability calculations to determine the number that will or will not return to their families. Jon was among the number that did not return, and while this young man might eventually contribute to the same statistics, Jessica knew she could not stand indifferently aside waiting for him to die.

Suddenly, she understood why Marg and Sam had wanted to care for him. She sucked in a long breath and drew herself up, unconsciously squaring her shoulders.

Very well. If it lies within my power, I will help return you to health.

Doesn't mean I have to like it, though.

Chapter 6

The day after the Gerry had been moved into the house, his condition rapidly went downhill.

Marg hovered about his bed, day and night, mopping the perspiration from his face and trickling small amounts of water into his mouth. She smeared petroleum jelly on his cracked lips and combed the hair from his damp brow.

At intervals, she jammed a thermometer beneath his tongue, clamped his mouth closed, and held her own breath, as the mercury rose up the slim glass tube.

Shaking her head vexedly, she murmured, "Poor bugger's on fire."

Jessica stood by the bed, watching helplessly. The children had gone to school and she wondered for how long she'd be able to keep the German's presence from them.

She tried to go about her normal business. Today, she had enough cream to make butter. Usually she found the rhythmic motion of the dasher therapeutic; a time to tune out and lose herself in the repeated up-and-down movement, as the butter gradually separated from the buttermilk inside the glass churn.

But the German was constantly on her mind, and by mid-afternoon, she couldn't put it off any longer. She went upstairs.

Marg's face, etched with lines of worry, told the story. "Not doing so well," she said to Jessica. "Pneumonia's got a good 'old on 'im. Breakin' me 'eart, it is."

Jessica contained a bitter sigh. *Lucifer's balls! What am I going to do with a dead Kraut?* Immediately berating herself for being so uncharitable, she closed the door quietly on her way out of the room.

***

The morning of the third day, Jessica saw the children on to the school bus then visited the patient.

Marg was asleep in a chair while the young German appeared to be resting more peacefully.

Not wishing to disturb them, she made to back out when Marg gave a start and was immediately wide awake. "Wha–what's 'appening?" Her eyes darted from the Gerry to Jessica and back.

"I came to check... didn't mean to disturb you. Can I get you anything?"

Marg stretched. "No, I'm just tired. We 'ad a bad night last night."

"Oh? I didn't hear anything."

"No, you wouldn't." Marg's tone held a hint of resentment. "I tried to keep the poor sod quiet."

Well, you wanted to keep him, Jessica thought churlishly, although the other woman's peevishness made her feel guilty.

Marg went on, "I reckon the fever might've broken, though. 'Opefully 'e's turned a corner."

Jessica nodded. *So, he lives. What will I do with him then?*

Marg laid a mothering hand on her patient's brow. "Not outta the woods yet, are you, love? Still got a long road to go."

Jessica's mouth was a grim line. She was looking towards the future whereas Marg's only concern was for his immediate welfare. Regardless of whether he lived or died, Jessica could see no way out of the situation without incurring the wrath of the authorities.

She was starting to feel out of her depth; a potentially dangerous man was beneath her roof and Marg was clucking and fussing over him, salving her grief over the loss of her son. Returning to the kitchen, Jessica slumped on to a seat and ran her hands through her hair.

Shit! What have we got ourselves into? She wondered as a cold serpent of fear roiled in her belly.

***

That afternoon, Jessica stood over the German's bed while Marg tucked the blankets around his shoulders and smoothed down the bedspread.

"He ate a bit of soup," she whispered, indicating the small bowl by the bed. Then she turned to Jessica, regarding her narrowly. "You sure you're all right to watch 'im?"

Jessica opened her hands. "Go to Ilkley, Marg. I promise I won't murder him in his sleep."

Marg snorted and Jessica added, "Go!" She made a shooing motion. "Go! You've been looking forward to seeing your friends all week... you said, he's out of danger and Sam's already brought the car round."

"What if 'e –"

"If you don't go now, the children will be home from school before you get back," Jessica said, marvelling. She took off her cardigan and draped it over the back of a chair. "It's a wonder they haven't found out about him already."

Marg stared at her in surprise. "What?"

Jessica frowned. "I said –"

"Jessie," Marg interrupted, taking a step towards her. "The children know. It were them what found 'im!"

Jessica's mouth fell open before she clamped it shut, gritting her teeth angrily.

"Thought you knew," Marg muttered. She quickly left the room.

Alone with the German, Jessica flopped on to a chair and stared vacantly into the fireplace.

Marg had built up the fire, let it reduce to coals and banked it so that it glowed red and gold. Occasionally it popped and sparks showered the tiled hearth.

The laboured breathing of the man in the bed was loud in the room.

I don't believe it! Jessica thought bitterly. *Sam and Marg, and even my own children! They all knew and kept it from me.*

She rested her elbows on her knees and propped her chin in her hands. *What on earth was I thinking, bringing him into my house?*

She sat for a long time, her slippered feet angled towards the fire. Finally, she took a deep breath and drew the mysterious memoir from the pocket of her apron. She'd planned to read it while sitting with the Kraut – had been looking forward to it – but had been too busy stewing over her children's betrayal.

Now she held the journal in her hands and examined it. It must have been very expensive; its red leather cover was aged, naturally, but the quality of its pages was clear in their texture and endurance.

Carefully, she opened it and turned to the first entry. The handwriting was easily legible. She began to read:

I was born Alexandra Rose Broughton on May 22nd 1795. I grew up one of three children of Lady Miriam Broughton and Sir Dudley Broughton. We were not an important family, but my mother brought money to her marriage.

Jessica read for the better part of an hour and became engrossed in the story of Alexandra Broughton's life in this very house during its heady Regency heyday.

Occasionally she glanced at the German and as he continued to sleep, she returned to the book.

Papa enjoyed his naval career, returning infrequently to England, visits that resulted in Simon, me and Anne – in that order.

One day in 1806, Papa's ship sailed and did not return, and Simon, at only fourteen, came into his inheritance.

The Gerry groaned and stirred in his sleep. Jessica rose quietly and went to his bedside. Laying a light hand on his forehead, she was satisfied that he was feeling cooler and not so clammy. As she watched, he stirred again and began to cough. It was a harsh, chesty bark.

It woke him, but he seemed dazed, somewhat detached from his surroundings. Jessica plumped pillows behind him and looked around for something to relieve the coughing. Marg had left a bottle of Irish Moss on a table. Jessica quickly poured a measure and, cupping the back of his head, held it to his lips.

The Gerry drank unquestioningly but it was still some time before the coughing subsided. At length, his shoulders relaxed. She helped him to snuggle down and he curled on his side, exhausted and perspiring from his exertions.

Jessica remained standing over him. His eyelids fluttered for the briefest moment, then he slept again.

She studied his unguarded face – certainly a young face, but not an inexperienced one. For even in repose, the youthful features had a veneer of maturity and the skin beside his eyes was slightly crinkled from squinting into the sun.

Perhaps he's a country boy, she thought.

The fire had burned down and the room was cooling. Jessica added a log and poked it to life before returning to her chair. Marg had left a blanket folded over its back. She shook it out and draped it over her knees, tucking it around her feet, then, taking up the journal, was about to continue reading when she paused and raised her head, listening intently.

There, the distinctive pitch that seemed to find an echoing tone somewhere in her solar plexus, building, growing steadily.

Planes.

Fighter jets.

A daytime raid, designed to target public locations, to terrorise, disorganise and disrupt civilian activities. Daytime raids caused more destruction, more casualties.

The skies had been quiet lately. There had been no planes since the night when...

She shot a glance at the Gerry, sleeping peacefully in the bed, and recalled her mother's tinny telephone voice, *Searchlighters went out ... found them all. Three of them, two pilots and the bomber...*

"Hmph!" Jessica scoffed, adding *sotto voce*. "Looks like they missed one."

The droning grew louder; a steady, ugly buzz that reverberated through her bones. A glass resting on the table made a bright, tinkling sound against the Irish Moss bottle. Jessica nudged them apart.

Turning back to the Gerry, she started in surprise.

He was watching her. His piercing blue-grey eyes were intense and unwavering. Jessica and the German pilot stared at each other as the sound swelled overhead, vibrating and filling the room, before gradually fading, the pitch adjusting with the distance. Only then did his gaze slide to the window through which the sky was a pale, spring blue.

Probably wishes he was up there, blasting us out of our homes, she thought, drawing a shaky breath.

His eyes swung back to her face and he regarded her steadily. "*Es ist ordnung.*" It was the first time he'd spoken in days. His voice was rough, very guttural.

She swallowed uncertainly. "Are you hungry?"

He paused so long that she wondered if he'd understood. She was about to repeat her question when he nodded slightly. "*Ja*. Little."

I suppose he could have some more soup, she thought

grudgingly. She'd hoped the soup would last a couple of days but it wouldn't if she had to feed the bloody German airforce!

Her thoughts must have shown on her face for he attempted a conciliatory smile. "I am... sorry that I cause trouble for you."

Yes, you are causing trouble!

"It's no trouble." She turned away.

***

It didn't take long to heat a small amount of soup. Jessica put it on a tray with a spoon and returned to the German's room. She found he'd shuffled up slightly but didn't appear comfortable. Putting the tray on a table, she took a spare pillow from the cupboard and plumped it behind him.

Close enough to touch him, she noted the dark shadows beneath his eyes and lines of fatigue and pain etched round his mouth. In a moment of sympathy, she automatically placed a hand on his forehead.

"Your fever is down," she said. He was looking up at her, his eyes steady on her face. *How old is he? He seems so young – Sam said he's a fighter pilot. Can't be that young.*

"*Ja*. I feel... better."

He was looking at her strangely. His eyes were more grey than blue now, and following her. To hide her discomfort, she collected the food tray and brought it back to the bed.

"Can you feed yourself, er ...?" She didn't know what to call him. Sam and Marg called him Anton, but she couldn't bring herself to do that. He was not her friend – he was her enemy.

If he noticed her stumble it didn't show on his face.

"*Ja, danke.*"

Jessica placed the tray carefully across his lap. "Don't spill it," she snapped, then turned towards the door.

He inhaled appreciatively. "It smells *gut*."

She didn't respond.

"*Warten!* Er wait... please. Will you stay?"

Jessica saw the appeal in his face, and against her better judgement, hesitated. For here was a young man, lost among strangers and far from home. He'd been shot out of the sky, wounded and dangerously ill. While she was afraid of him, he was no doubt afraid of her, and what she might do.

She might turn him over to the authorities.

She might call in the Home Guard or the army.

Jessica had decided to care for him, but he could not know that and the anxiety on his handsome young face gave her pause. Though he didn't seem afraid, she realised he simply didn't want to be alone.

Returning to his bedside, Jessica pulled over the chair. Marg's rug was lying over its back. She draped it over her knees.

He smiled. It reached his cheeks and seemed to lighten the shadows beneath his eyes. "*Danke schön.*"

Taking up the spoon, he began, very slowly, to eat. She felt uncomfortable watching him, so she opened the journal and resumed her reading.

When I was eleven, a collie bitch owned by one of our tenant farmers had whelped and one of the pups, the runt, was not expected to survive the night. My brother, Simon, showed me the pup the evening she was born saying that if she were still alive by morning she was mine.

Huddled overnight in the stables, with the pup bundled snugly under my cloak, I kept my vigil. At intervals, I put her to her mother's teat, pushing her stronger siblings aside and coaxing her to suckle. The next morning, she was still alive.

I continued in this fashion for an entire day and the following night, and the pup made rapid progress. On the third day, I named her, Jemima.

Jessica gasped. Jemima? Wasn't that the name engraved on the headstone down by the old orchard?

"*Was ist?*"

The German spoke and she looked sharply at him. "What did you say?"

"I..." He broke off in a fit of violent coughing.

Jessica leapt up to take the tray from him before soup spilled everywhere. She put it on a table, then braced a knee on the side of the bed, supporting him with an arm round the shoulders, until the coughing subsided.

Finally, he relaxed and she exhaled. The coughing worried her – it seemed so violent and painful.

"Are you all right?" she asked. The force of it had left him red-faced and gasping for breath. He swallowed and nodded.

She moved away, groping behind her for the chair, sat and continued to watch him. After a moment, he looked at her, slightly flustered. "*Es geht mir gut* ... all right ... I am all right."

"Can you eat? Would you like more?"

He nodded again. "*Ja* ... I would ... if you please."

She was gratified he was eating well for she'd been disturbed by the protruding bones beneath her hands as she'd held him; scapula and clavicle, sharp and hard, and sticking out more than they were three days ago when they'd carried him up here.

Although, he'd been wearing his uniform then, now he was only in pyjamas. She gave him the tray again and resumed her seat.

"What are you reading?" He asked, nodding towards the journal on the floor beside her feet.

His face was open, interested. It would be churlish of her to be unfriendly, yet taken off guard, she hesitated. "Um ..." she picked up the time-worn book and showed him. "It's a memoir – someone's life story. I found it in the garden."

"*Wirklich*? I mean ... this is true? You found it ... in the *garten?*"

She leaned forward. "Yes, it was buried. In a tin box. It's the story of a girl who lived here. In this house."

"How long...?"

"How long ago?"

He nodded.

"According to a letter in it, it was buried in eighteen seventy-one."

"Oh *ja*! A long time then."

He'd continued eating and now was nearly finished.

"You've done well with the soup," she remarked, smiling without realising it.

He noticed and smiled in reply. "Will you read it to me?"

Jessica was taken aback. *He's trying to be friendly. Either that or he's waiting for me to lower my guard.*

"I wouldn't want to disturb you," she began, doubtfully.

"It is all right," he said, still smiling. "I am not very busy."

He was infectious. She felt her mouth turn up. *What harm could it do to read to him?* she wondered. *And anyway, it might help him sleep.* She said, "I haven't got very far. I can go back to the start."

"I would like that."

So, she turned back to the introductory letter from the old woman, Margaret, and began to read:

You have found the diary...

Jessica read for a good half an hour, pausing now and then to take a sip of water. The Gerry listened, coughing occasionally but otherwise was silent.

When she got to the part about the dog, Jemima, she looked up and said, "We found the dog's grave in our garden."

"Oh *ja*? She loved this dog very much."

"Yes, I imagine she did." Jessica watched his face, she was growing curious about this man. Who was he and what sort of person dropped bombs on innocent strangers? "Do you like dogs?" She'd asked the question before she could stop herself.

"Oh *ja*! I have two dogs at my home."

"Two?"

"They are both pinschers. Do you know that one?"

"I have heard of it but we don't have them round here. Our dogs are usually working dogs, like farm dogs."

He nodded. "The pinscher was ... breeded for work too."

"Bred."

"Bred? They are *gut* for hunting *und* protecting the property."

"Do you live in the country?"

"Oh *ja*. My parents have a small farm. We have sheeps *und* chickens. The pinscher dogs are very *gut* for guarding the sheeps. That is their breed, but my dogs are too... er... *verwöhnt*."

"Wervont?" Jessica repeated, quizzically.

"*Verwöhnt*. What you say when something is lazy, or ... not made to do the work."

"Umm, spoilt, perhaps? Like a child can be spoilt?"

He thought for a moment, then, "*Ja*, I think it is this. Spoilt."

"So your dogs are spoilt?"

He grinned. It made his eyes glisten, bluer than grey now, and smoothed the harsh lines that fatigue and illness had scored into his face. "*Ja*. They are spoilt. They live in the *Haus und* sleep beside the ..." he pointed to the fire.

"Fireplace."

"Fireplace. We say *der Kamin*."

Jessica smiled. "Yes, that would be considered spoilt by our standards too."

"No matter. I think that there is much er... cruelty in the world. If my dogs are spoilt, that is all right."

Jessica sat back in her chair and regarded him narrowly. Her face grew hot from the sudden anger that surged through her.

The German stared at her in confusion. *"Was ist?"*

She was not usually one for confrontation, but with him lying there in *her* bed, eating *her* food, and telling *her* about cruelty – him a German! The nerve of the man; talking about the cruelty in the world when he and his kind were perpetrating cruelty on an unprecedented scale!

"What is wrong?" he persisted.

She opened her mouth to speak but the words didn't come. She closed it again, glaring at him.

"I have upset you?"

When finally she spoke, her voice was low and taut. "How *dare you* speak to me of cruelty? You... you barbarian!"

He looked confused and mildly hurt. *"Was...?"*

She rose and gathered her things, preparing to leave. "Please," he said, eyes widening in alarm. "I do not understand! *Was ist* this barbar-ian?"

"You!" She stabbed a finger at him. "You, you bloody Kraut!"

"I –"

"All you bloody Germans, and *you*, in particular, flying over our homes... murdering innocent people in their beds... terrifying children... old people!" The words came tumbling out of her as though a dam had burst.

She stood over him, snarling at him in a hoarse stage whisper, while all the grief and fear of the past two years of war poured from her in a torrent of uncontrollable outrage.

Her face flamed and her heart pounded yet she continued, undeterred, and insensitive to the distress on his face. "You talk about spoiling your dogs while you, and thousands like you, torture and persecute millions – you... I, I should have... bloody well killed you when I had the chance! Should have left you to die!"

Suddenly she clapped her hands over her mouth, eyes

glistening and face burning with mortification.

"Oh, God!" she gasped behind her hands.

He stared at her mutely.

Jessica dropped into the chair, head in her hands. She thought she should apologise – *knew* she should, but could not bring herself to do so. How could she apologise for something that was intrinsically within her?

***

Anton watched her. He felt her anger as she raved at him and saw her distress as she realised what she'd said.

She all but collapsed into a chair and sat for a long time with her head in her hands.

Herr Clay had told him Frau Barrow's husband had been killed by a German U-boat which no doubt explained her bitterness. But witnessing her confusion now, he realised she wasn't as heartless as she'd have him believe.

Anton let her sit for a while and compose herself. When at last he spoke, his tone was gentle. "I can understand that you feel this way."

Finally, she raised her head to meet his eyes. She looked as unhappy as he felt.

"It is not my family that does these things," he explained gently. "We do know what is happening. We are powerless, *ja*? *Und*, you know that our cities are being bombed too? Our homes *und* villages... I wish it were not so."

***

She had hurt him, Jessica saw, but she felt no satisfaction. She dropped her eyes, sucking in a deep breath to steady herself.

He went on, "I can see that my being here is... er, difficult for you. If you will allow it... allow me to go free... tomorrow I will leave. I will not trouble you any more."

Jessica felt in her pocket for a hanky. Finding none, she wiped her nose on her sleeve.

"You're not a *prisoner,*" she snapped, unable to keep the edge out of her voice. "But you're not well yet and anyway, you've nowhere to go." She sniffed and cleared her throat. "I, I don't think you need me to sit with you."

"*Nein, danke.* I shall sleep now."

She nodded, eyes downcast, and whispered, "You don't need to leave." Then, taking another deep breath, she hauled herself from the chair and left the room without looking back.

*****

The kitchen was warm with the smell of toast and butter when Mary and Thomas took their places at the table the following morning.

Thomas had been out to the henhouse early to collect the eggs for their Saturday breakfast. Eggs on toast was a treat many didn't enjoy these days, although eggs weren't yet among the items on the government's rationing list. Jessica expected that sooner or later they would be; every day new items were added.

Each household was encouraged to be self-sufficient. The Ministry of Food was running a vigorous *Dig for Victory* campaign that recommended growing vegetables and keeping rabbits and chickens for meat. It was considered unpatriotic, even obscene, to have a lawn. Every spare inch of ground grew, or fed, something edible.

Those with land were persuaded to share and trade what produce they grew. Marg traded Jessica's cream, butter and eggs for meat and other staples.

Jessica took the eggs Thomas had collected, fried them in butter and put two on each of four plates. She then placed a plate before each of her children, the third at her own place on the table and the fourth remained on the range to keep warm.

The children didn't notice. They were busily arguing the merits of the government sanctioned, National Loaf, which was the only bread available.

"Michael hates it!" Thomas declared of his school friend. "So do I. It's a dirty colour and you have to chew it and chew it for ages."

Mary seemed to consider Michael's opinion irrelevant. "It's not that bad. Besides it's good for you."

"It can't do you any good if it's so horrible you can't eat it," Thomas retorted logically.

"Just be thankful you have bread at all," Jessica said, taking her seat.

"But what about the extra stuff they put in it?" Mary wanted to know.

"Calsorum," Thomas informed them, knowledgeably.

"Calcium," Jessica corrected, "but you get plenty of that through our milk and butter. Not everyone has access to those."

"Oh." Thomas broke the yolk on his egg and spread it around his toast. "Mummy, what's that other plate for?" He pointed with his knife.

Jessica suppressed a smile. "Don't wave your knife around, love. It's for the visitor from the stables." She spoke casually cutting her toast, aware that a heavy silence had fallen over the table. "Oh, by the way," she glanced up and caught her children exchanging alarmed looks. "He's now in the spare room at the end of the hall."

Still, they were silent and Jessica continued eating as though nothing were amiss. Finally, she put down her cutlery. "When did you plan to tell me?"

Mary recovered faster than her brother. "We didn't want to worry you, Mummy."

"Besides," Thomas added, "we thought he'd gone."

"Yes, indeed he has gone – into our spare room." Jessica

leaned forward, the better to drill home her point. "I'm not going to ask you why you didn't tell me. But I want you to understand what this means. Do you have any idea how important it is that nobody finds out about him?" She levelled her gaze intently, first on Thomas, then his sister. "It must be a secret. I'm very, *very* serious. It can only be us and Mr and Mrs Clay who know."

God, what am I thinking? They're only eight!

"Can you do that?" she asked. "Can you keep such a big secret?"

Thomas nodded energetically, brimming with the excitement of intrigue, while Mary gazed at her solemnly. "Of course, Mummy. We kept it secret from you, didn't we?"

Jessica tutted irritably. "Yes, yes you did. But this is much more serious than keeping it from me. If anyone, and I mean *anyone* finds out about him, he'll be taken away and..." *Where is the line between stressing the need for secrecy and terrifying your children?*

"We'll never see him again," Mary finished for her.

Jessica sighed. "Exactly. We'll never see him again."

Thomas was staring at his breakfast. Looking up, he said, "Mummy, he's nice. I wouldn't like it if he went away."

"He made us laugh," Mary added. "He told us funny stories and said we could call him Mr Bird."

"Is that so? Mr Bird?" Jessica looked from one child to the next. *If he's making a joke about flying, I'll –*

"Tommy told him about cricket but I don't think he understood."

Thomas frowned at his sister. "He did so! He said it sounded like good fun."

"Liar!"

"Shh!" Jessica hissed. "When did you first know he was there?"

Thomas shot a glance at his sister and Mary shrugged. "You

might as well tell her everything, Tommy."

"Remember I told you I saw a man outside my window one night?" the little boy asked and his mother nodded. "Well, I thought *you* thought I was making it up. But I know what I saw, Mummy! I *knew* I'd seen a man. So, I told Mary and we went to look."

Jessica sucked in a quick, horrified breath. "You *what*!"

"We found him straight away," Mary said, quickly. "He was in the stall at the back – the one Mr Clay uses for storage. There were hay bales across, like a wall, and Mr Bird was behind them lying on the ground."

"I don't believe this!" Jessica cried, in frustration. "What would you've done if he was dangerous, hmm? Did you think about that? A strange man, Thomas? Hiding in our stables and you went *looking for him*?"

"I took my cricket bat."

Jessica gasped, appalled by the thought of two eight-year-olds on a manhunt, armed with a cricket bat.

"Don't you realise how dangerous that was?" She glared at her son and daughter in turn. "What if he'd attacked you? What if he *hurt* you?"

Reprimanded into silence, the twins stared sulkily at their plates.

Jessica grunted angrily and flicked a hand towards the table. "Finish your breakfast."

Thomas sniffed but Jessica refused to feel guilty for raising her voice. These were dangerous times – the children needed to understand.

Nevertheless, she softened her tone. "Come on, eat up. Then we'll take his tray upstairs together."

They obeyed, finishing their meals in chastened silence while Jessica rubbed her temples. She could feel a headache coming on.

"Mummy?"

She looked up, wearily. "Yes, Thomas."

"Um..." He paused uncertainly but Jessica wasn't feeling patient.

"What is it?" she demanded, annoyed.

"Mummy, the man I saw that night... it wasn't Mr Bird."

Chapter 7

Mary and Thomas scampered up the stairs and along the hallway. Jessica followed with a tray of toast, eggs and a mug of tea.

"Slow down," she warned as they neared the Gerry's door. "You don't barge into someone's room unannounced."

Thomas arrived at the door first, socks skidding on the floorboards. His knuckles hovered before the door, waiting for his sister to join him before he knocked.

As Jessica approached, she heard a response from within and nodded. "All right, go on."

"Hello, Mr Bird!" they shouted in unison as they bounded into the room.

"Good morning!" he greeted them cheerfully, although his eyes were on their mother.

"We're so happy you're here," Thomas cried. "Mummy knows now so it's okay to talk to you."

Mary said, "We thought you'd left without saying goodbye."

"I would never do that. Not to my two young friends."

"We didn't tell Mummy, Mr Bird," Thomas said. "She found out all on her own."

"We promised we wouldn't tell." Mary added, and Jessica caught the defensive glance her daughter shot at her. "Mummy said she'll keep the secret too."

Thomas's expression grew rebellious. "I don't know why, though. Jack Ramage tells everyone the Yanks are staying with him. He brags about it an' all!"

"Your mother is right," the German said. "I must leave if I am found here."

"But how come Jack tells everyone about the Yanks?"

Jessica was helping the German shuffle to a sitting position. He threw a beseeching look at her.

"Thomas, we've talked about this," she said, placing the tray over the convalescent's lap. "Things are not that simple."

Mary snorted derisively. "It's because the Yanks are the goodies and Mr Bird is one of the baddies."

Thomas made a cry of protest but Jessica quickly cut him off. "Enough now, Mr Bird is entitled to eat his breakfast without you two behaving like the Spanish Inquisition."

"*I* know, Mum, but Tommy takes a bit longer," said Mary, rolling her eyes. "He's younger than me, Mr Bird, so he's slower."

The German laughed but Jessica exclaimed, "Mary! Never talk about your brother like that!"

Unrepentant, Mary grinned at the man in the bed who had begun tucking into his breakfast. "It's true, I'm fourteen minutes older. Mummy likes to protect him, which proves my point."

Thomas didn't seem quite sure whether Mary was serious or not. He stood looking from his sister to his mother and back, a guileless smile on his face.

Jessica made a herding gesture, "Come on, out! Let Mr Bird eat his breakfast in peace."

She watched as her children moved to the door, waving to their friend. "Aren't you coming Mummy?" Mary stood on the threshold.

"In a moment. Mr Bird and I need to talk."

Mary nodded and followed her brother out of the room. "And close the door, please," Jessica called after them.

Once they were alone, Jessica turned to the German. "Well, *Mr Bird*," she said with significance. "What's with the name?"

He looked up at her, chewing slowly. The morning sun was streaming into the room. It fell across his hair shooting golden highlights through the light-brown strands.

Reaching for the mug of tea, he took a sip, swallowed and said, "I do not understand."

"Are you making a joke? Because you fly planes?" She suddenly realised how petty she sounded but it was too late now.

"It's not very funny if you are."

His brow creased slightly. "Forgive me but I do not know what you mean."

"Why did you call yourself Mr Bird?" she barked.

His brow relaxed and he smiled. "Because it is my name. I am –"

"You are German!" she snapped. "*Bird* is not a German name!"

"No, it is not," he agreed patiently. "But Vogel is my name *und* it means bird."

***

Anton watched the heat flood Frau Barrow's cheeks. "Oh, God!" she murmured. "I'm so sorry." She didn't seem to know where to look, so busied herself smoothing his bedspread. "I don't know what's got into me. I thought you were being spiteful or something. I'm not normally so... argumentative."

"Frau Barrow," he said gently. He paused, waiting for her to look at him. When finally, she met his eyes he smiled at her. Realising that in the revealing morning sun, the ravages of his recent illness would be stamped on his face, he assembled his expression into something open and friendly. "You are protecting your family."

Jessica grimaced apologetically. "Still, I'm being unforgivably rude to you, *again*."

Anton indicated the chair beside the bed. "Sit with me, please. Ask me anything, if it makes you feel more er … comfortable. I will answer honestly."

He picked up a slice of toast and bit into it, watching her appreciatively. There was something about her, despite his wariness of her, something he couldn't put a name to.

***

Jessica looked out of the window. From where she sat she could just see the swaying tops of the trees in the distant forest.

There was so much she wanted to know, but not the sorts of questions she could, in fairness, ask. Things like, *What kind of person drops bombs on a town knowing people are sleeping innocently below?* What answer did she expect him to give to a question like that?

But she was curious. And she was suspicious too. Was it purely by chance that he ended up here, on a property inhabited by women, children and one elderly man?

She raised her eyes and caught a strange look on his face. He didn't wait for her question. His voice was very low as he spoke, "Your gunners shot down two airplanes that night – a Junkers *und* a Messerschmitt."

Jessica breathed in slowly, then said, "I heard they found three men – two pilots and a bomber."

Her hands were growing clammy. She was reasonably safe for now, while he was prone in bed, but it wouldn't be long before... *Don't let them see you're vulnerable,* Jon's voice echoed in her head.

The German sipped his tea. "*Ja,* that is right."

But he's recovering. When he's fully recovered ... what will happen then? He's growing stronger every day. She steadied her voice. "They thought they found all the crewmen. How were you missed?"

He hesitated and Jessica sensed she was about to learn something the officials did not know – if he trusted her enough. But why should he trust her? *She* didn't trust *him.*

The German studied her face for a long time and it seemed the oxygen was being sucked from the room. Jessica had stopped breathing and tension shimmered between them. Finally, he said, "You are a very pretty lady."

The air burst from her in a nervous laugh. "You said you'd be honest. Don't flatter me to avoid answering."

He grinned charmingly. *He's accustomed to using his looks to get his own way.* She cocked a disapproving eyebrow.

"Well," he admitted, "it is true: you are pretty *und* I am trying to flatter you."

She flushed with embarrassment while a worm of suspicion whispered in her ear, *He's trying to distract me, or win my confidence. Either way, I mustn't let my guard down.*

"I did think," he continued, "that I should not tell you, but then, it is no secret now." He drew a breath, drained his tea and put the mug resolutely on the tray. "The Messerschmitt was a test airplane. When they... er, *prüfen* the airplane they will see."

"Proofen? What's —"

"*Prüfen* is... when they try to find out about something."

"To... investigate?"

"*Ja*, investigate, or..." He frowned thoughtfully. "I have not spoken English for two years. I forget words. I want to say, examine. When they examine the Messerschmitt they will see, so it is no secret."

"What isn't a secret?"

He grinned again and she wished he wouldn't; it made her forget the monster he was. "The truth is," he went on, "that the Junkers carried three men. The Messerschmitt, this one in particular is the *Sturmvogel* two-six-two. She carries a crew of one. When your men found the three airmen, they would have thought the two flyers were from the Junkers *und* the bomber was from the Messerschmitt."

"But he was from the Junkers too?" she guessed.

"*Ja.*"

"Then, they didn't realise that the Junkers carried three men – there should have been a fourth airman?"

He gave a short nod. "*Ja. Das ist richtig.*"

Jessica regarded him steadily. Summoning her confidence,

she said, "You're the bomber from the Messerschmitt."

It wasn't a question. He inclined his head in agreement.

"But the Messerschmitt wasn't designed as a bomber."

His eyes locked with hers. "You know a lot about them." When she made no comment, he gave a small shrug and went on, "But you are right; she is a fighter, *und ja*, I was conducting a bombing test. There is some discussion among my, er... superiors. The Messerschmitt was designed as a high-speed jet fighter, not a bomber. She is the fastest plane ever built but she only carries two bombs. They want her to carry more but the added weight will slow her. Until it is decided, the Messerschmitt will not be fully operational. I was conducting a test flight; if we are testing with live ammunition, we generally do so over enemy territory."

Jessica shuddered. "How thrifty of you," she muttered darkly. "If I know something about bombers," she added caustically, "it's because we English have a small interest in what will be blowing up our homes. Presumably you haven't been testing planes the entire war?"

"I am a fighter pilot." He eyed her cautiously. "The Messerschmitt will enter service *und* they will expect me to continue flying her."

"You fought in the sky and shot down our planes? And you dropped bombs on Leeds before you tested the Messerschmitt?"

It was a long time before he spoke, and when he did, his voice was without emotion. "I flew the Junkers. It was the job they gave me. They will expect me to continue when I return home."

He hadn't spoken with any arrogance or malice, simply stated facts. But in that moment Jessica felt as though the cogs in some vast machinery were slowly cranking into movement. She whispered, "*If* you get home."

She hadn't intended to speak out loud. But she had, and the words could not be unspoken. The attractive lines of his face grew hard and he eyed her with a wariness she had not seen since his recovery.

She was sorry for it, but what did he expect? *We're in the middle of a blasted war*!

His voice was even and without emotion when he said, "I will sleep now, if you do not mind, madam."

He hadn't finished his breakfast but she nodded, inexplicably saddened, collected his tray and left the room without another word.

***

"Mummy?"

"In the stables, Thomas," Jessica called. She was watching Sam as he examined one of the cows.

"Mummy, we've got a visitor."

Sam straightened and Jessica saw his eyes slide guiltily to the stall where the German had once slept. Thomas and Robin Tyler stepped through the door.

"Hullo," Tyler said, cheerfully. "What have we here? Mother-to-be?"

"Hullo, Mr Tyler," Jessica turned to where Sam stood, calloused hand resting casually on the cow's rump. "Yes, it's her first and Sam's keeping an eye on her. Seems bigger than she should be."

Sam narrowed his eyes at Robin, "Know owt about cows, Tyler?"

"Nothing, as it turns out."

Sam sniffed, disdainfully.

"Mr Tyler's father keeps sheep," Jessica told him. The tension between the two men was instant and thick.

"Aye, I recall." Sam looked the newcomer up and down, then, "What can we be doing for you?"

If Tyler noticed Sam's bluntness he didn't show it. He addressed Jessica, "I came to ask if you and the children would care to accompany me to Wolstone for the May Day fair? It's on a Thursday this year, but the games and market stalls continue all through the weekend. I thought we might go on Saturday for the parade."

Sam made a snorting noise and Tyler glanced sharply towards him. Jessica spoke quickly, "May Day's not for a couple of weeks yet. I hadn't given it a thought." *And would prefer not to think about it now.* She smiled sweetly. "It's a very kind offer, Mr Tyler, but –"

Thomas tugged her sleeve. "Oh, Mummy! Can we go? It'd be such fun."

"Looks like I've one taker," Tyler said, smiling at the boy. "What do you say, Mrs Barrow?"

"I bet Mary'd want to go," Thomas added.

"Well..." Jessica cast about for an excuse to decline and came up with nothing. "What exactly did you have in mind?"

"I thought we could drive over in my motor. Early in the morning... make a day of it, eh? What do you think?"

"A lot o' work to be done 'ere," Sam growled into his chest.

"Surely one day won't hurt," Tyler said. "Promise to have your boss home before evening milking."

Sam looked unimpressed. "C'mon, Norma." Slipping a rope around the cow's neck, he led her out through the door.

"I'm not really Sam's bo –"

"Norma?" Tyler asked, archly. "He named the cow?"

"Norma Shearer. He names them all after actresses."

"Simple folk..."

Jessica regarded Tyler thoughtfully. His comment had been tempered with a half-smile and she decided it wasn't meant unkindly.

"Mum, please say we can go to the fair," Thomas begged. "Wait! I'll go fetch Mary!"

He dashed off to find his twin and Jessica was left alone with

Robin Tyler.

"Your man doesn't like me very much, does he?"

"He's worried about the cows," Jessica said. "I rely on him an awful lot."

"Do you rely on him for *all* your decisions?"

The question stung but Jessica smiled gently. "No. Sam helps me a great deal. I couldn't do without him." *Why am I explaining myself?*

"And there's no one else around, no farm girls or..." he shrugged and eyed her curiously.

Jessica felt the skin prickle on the back of her neck. "No, it's just me and Sam," she knew she sounded defensive, "though Sam's wife helps around the house a bit."

Tyler opened his mouth to respond but was interrupted by Thomas's running return; his sister was strolling a distance behind him.

"Mr Tyler, this is Mary," Thomas said, breathlessly, sliding on the straw-littered cobbles.

"Hullo, Mary. You look very much like your brother."

"We're twins," she told him flatly.

"But we're not *identical* twins," Thomas clarified unnecessarily.

"I see. So," Tyler went on, turning to Mary, "your mummy and I have been talking about what time I'll take you to the fair."

No, we haven't, Jessica thought, indignantly.

"What time?" Thomas asked, hopping from foot to foot. "Are we really going in your motor?"

Tyler laughed and ruffled Thomas's hair. "What time suits you, Mrs Barrow?"

"Early, Mum! Straight after breakfast!" Thomas pleaded, clutching at her arm.

Jessica sighed. "Shh, Thomas! We'd be pleased to accept your invitation, Mr Tyler. Pick us up whenever it's convenient for you."

"Hurrah!" Thomas shouted.

"Mary," Tyler said, "I understand you like horses."

Jessica glanced towards Mary. The girl nodded mutely, apparently unimpressed by the man.

"Would you like to visit my stable some time? I have a few thoroughbreds including a magnificent Friesian – you'd love him. His name's *Krijger* – that's Dutch for Warrior."

Mary smiled coolly. "That'd be nice, Mr Tyler."

For a girl inclined to fuss over any sway-backed old hack that passed the gate, Mary seemed surprisingly reticent. Jessica felt prompted to respond in the manner Tyler probably expected.

"What a good idea," she said, with a heavy dose of enthusiasm. "Even *I* would enjoy seeing a Friesian. One day –"

"Well then, I'll take you to see him after our May Day outing, before bringing you home."

Damn! That didn't go the way I'd hoped. "Oh, lovely." Jessica smiled circumspectly.

"Excellent! Then that's settled." As Robin Tyler strode confidently down the driveway, Jessica watched from the side of the house.

"Can do without the likes of 'im nosing about," Sam grumbled coming up beside her.

Jessica whirled round. "He just completely railroaded me! Why can't I stick up for myself, Sam?"

Her steward drew in his chin and looked at her through the dark pebbles of his eyes. "No idea, Missus. All's I can say is 'e seems a wee bit too slick for mine. Likes getting 'is own way."

"I'm not interested in any stinking May Day fair – I need to …" she gestured wildly, "speak up or something."

"Shoulda just said you didn't wanna go."

Jessica snorted. "That's the trouble, I *never* say what I want. Especially when it involves these two – they need some fun in their lives." Jessica glanced fondly at her children. "Mary, you didn't seem all that enthusiastic. Don't you want to go?"

"There's something about him, Mummy," Mary said, childishly insightful. "First it was the fair, and now we're going to his house too. Seems he's trying very hard to be our friend."

"A bit too hard," Jessica agreed, impressed by her daughter's acumen.

"Mary's being silly," Thomas informed them.

"Your sister's entitled to her opinion, Thomas."

"Even if it's wrong?"

"Opinions are just views of things. They're neither right nor wrong. Now, both of you run inside and do the washing up. One of you washes – the other dries and puts away."

Mary turned, without another word, towards the garden door. Thomas sighed petulantly but followed.

"I don't like 'im meself," Sam stated as he and Jessica returned to the stable. "Thinks 'e's Errol bloody Flynn."

**

Jessica closed the journal. She had been sitting by the empty fireplace in the bookless library for a long time and was starting to feel cold. With a soft groan, she stood, stretching and rotating her shoulders.

She'd been avoiding visiting the German. Marg said he'd asked about her and although the older woman hadn't commented further, Jessica read the suspicion on her face.

Had he told Marg they'd parted on less than friendly terms? *Bloody rude if he had*, Jessica thought. She hadn't seen him for several days and it was true, his future was in doubt. But her remark, *if you get home*, had been unnecessary. He'd been nothing but polite to her, yet she had behaved like a schoolyard bully.

Anyway, she justified herself, fully recovered, he could be

very dangerous. She must tread warily.

I could go see him now or... or I could go work in the garden.

She was still considering when she looked up and gasped in surprise.

A pretty young girl stood staring into the depths of a roaring fire. Now she slowly turned and an unearthly thrill ran down Jessica's back as the girl returned her astonished gaze. A foggy confusion, like waking with a fright, washed over her, and Jessica felt woozy.

The girl was petite, small-breasted and slim-hipped. She had dark hair curling riotously around her face and beautiful, warm brown eyes. She wore a gown of soft, mint-green fabric in the Empire style. As Jessica's eyes returned to the girl's face, she found she was being similarly examined.

But when the girl's eyes moved down and came to rest on the book in Jessica's hand, there was recognition in her expression and Jessica's blood ran cold.

Oh, God! Jessica's eyes bulged. *You're Alexandra! This* is *your journal!* Jessica's heart was pounding and her skin prickled; she felt as though the very hair on her scalp was standing upright.

Afraid to look away lest the girl vanish, and uncertain what else to do, Jessica attempted a smile.

Slowly, hesitantly, Alexandra's lips twitched... then she was gone.

***

Over the next week, spring progressed through the last days of April and the trees in the orchard lost their blooms in a blizzard of pink and white petals. The new fruit appeared, hard, green little nubs where the flowers had been.

Elsewhere the estate was returning to life after the dormancy of winter. On her knees in the kitchen garden, Jessica inspected her new seedlings. They shivered delicately in the afternoon breeze.

Mary and Thomas were playing some kind of game behind the stables, their shouts and laughter brought a smile to their mother's face as she flicked a snail away from her young plants.

Towels and sheets snapped on the washing line. It was a homely sound and Jessica sat back on her heels, looking up at the bright April sky.

A party of swifts swooped and circled, calling and chasing one another round the garden.

A long, narrow shadow fell over her and Jessica recognised Sam's lanky form.

"How they looking?" he asked nodding at the young plants. He extended a hand to help her up.

"Well," she brushed the dirt off her knees. "They're coming along."

"They the seedlings Marg gave you?"

"No, she gave me those turnips and beets." Jessica indicated two neat rows of lush reddish-green leaves. "These, and the cabbages over there, I sprouted from seeds."

Jessica gathered her weeding tools and dropped them into a bucket. "I'm done for the day, I think. Time to start preparing tea."

Sam pulled the pitchfork from where she'd jammed it into the ground, and they turned together toward the stables. "Missus," he said, and she groaned inwardly at his tone. "I wanna talk to you about Anton."

Surprise, surprise. "What about him?"

"'E said you've 'ardly spoken to 'im for nearly a week. I'm wondering if there's summat wrong."

I agreed to feed him, not entertain him. "Nothing's wrong – busy, that's all."

"Jessie," Sam halted her with a hand on her arm. "'E's just a lad. Just a young fella, a long ways from 'ome. We're all 'e's got."

Why's that my problem?

Jessica didn't give voice to her thoughts. She walked ahead, aware that her steward was following her into the stables. He propped the pitchfork against the wall, took the bucket from her and sat it on a bench. Turning, he regarded her critically.

"What?" Jessica demanded.

Sam shrugged and pulled out his tobacco pouch. "'E likes you, you know. Enjoys your company and I suppose 'e's a bit bored now 'e's on the mend."

"I'm not running a guest house. Besides, he's our enemy – let's not forget that!"

"He's not our enemy –"

Jessica rounded on him, mouth open to protest but he cut her off with a raised hand. "'E's *not* our enemy. The country 'e were born in 'appens to be at war with the country *we* was born in. People ain't enemies – politicians are."

Jessica sighed heavily. *There was a simplistic logic in that.*

"Anyways," Sam began rolling a cigarette, "'e was saying that when 'e's feeling better, 'e wants to 'elp out around 'ere."

Jessica turned away, ostensibly to brush the dirt off her work trousers. "We don't need his help. Besides, I –"

"We need all the 'elp we can get – especially *free* help."

She gestured impatiently. "Of course we need help! But what you're saying is –"

"What's wrong with 'im 'elping out? 'Specially if Bright 'n' Sons's wantin' more milk off us. Besides, we're feeding 'im, 'e might as well earn it like the rest of us."

The colour was rising on Jessica's cheeks. *Sam's right, but I don't want some bloody Kraut working in my dairy.* She opened her mouth to protest.

"Now Missus," Sam patted the air, a fresh cigarette held between thumb and index finger. "I know what you're thinking, but what 'arm can 'e do? Why not put 'im to work?"

Her cheeks puffed out in a petulant exhale.

"Fact is," he went on, "once 'e's recovered, what're we gonna do with 'im? Can't send 'im anywhere without incriminating ourselves."

Jessica leaned a hip against the workbench and folded her arms. "Should've thought of that before," she muttered sourly.

"We wouldn't've done owt differently," he responded. "You're only against the idea because you don't trust 'im. Give 'im a go – 'e's a farm boy, 'e'll know what 'e's doing."

Jessica pushed away from the bench and strode to the door, pausing on the threshold. "I'll think it over. We've plenty of time – he's still weak as a kitten."

"But getting stronger every day!" Sam called cheerfully, as Jessica strode away.

Chapter 8

Jessica moved quietly about the German's room so as not to wake him. Marg had earlier brought his breakfast; two slices of toast, cheese, a fried egg and tea, which he'd managed to finish, and Jessica was collecting the empty dishes. She was pleased he'd been able to eat his food – this time last week he couldn't have managed half that amount.

She knew she should apologise to him but while he was asleep she could avoid it. Jessica collected his empty plate and cup, ensuring they didn't clink together, then paused. Marg hadn't shaved him recently and the stubble on his cheeks and chin lent him a rugged appearance, although his expression was softened and unguarded in sleep.

Very attractive, her mind registered. Jon's face had been so familiar to her that she couldn't know if he was attractive or not – although others said he was. Anton was very attractive – but young. While Jon had been older than her by two years, this fellow was younger, twenty-three or –four perhaps?

She turned, then did a double take. She could swear she'd seen a dog in the corner of the room. She looked again but saw only a shifting shadow caused by the curtain moving lightly in the morning breeze. She shivered, *someone dancing on my grave*.

Jessica crept from the room and the German continued to sleep.

***

It was early evening when Jessica knocked softly on his door. If the Gerry was sleeping, he wouldn't hear the knock and she could continue to avoid him.

"*Ja*," came the response. She exhaled resignedly through her nose.

He was propped on pillows reading a newspaper by lamplight, and when she came in he lowered the paper and smiled, evidently pleased to see her.

He'd been freshly shaved and was well on the road to recovery. His face was filling out and the dark shadows ringing his eyes were fading.

"Good evening, Frau Barrow," he said, folding the paper. She saw his eyes skim over her appreciatively, then he frowned. "You are tired. Why do you not sit for a moment? Talk to me."

Jessica smiled faintly. She pulled over Marg's chair, and allowed herself to relax. "I am tired," she admitted with a sigh that morphed into a yawn. "I came earlier to collect your breakfast dishes – you were sleeping."

Jessica glanced at the folded newspaper on his lap. A fragment of the headline was visible, *London bombed; House of Commons...*

She saw him follow her gaze to the paper. "It is a terrible thing, *ja*? I am sorry for it."

"You've nothing to be sorry for." She wasn't sure how to address him. Using his name didn't seem appropriate. "Wars are not fought by people like us," she went on, feeling magnanimous. "They are fought by generals and politicians. We are just the pawns they move around their chess boards."

***

Anton inhaled slowly, thoughtfully; there was a faint smell of lemon verbena about her and he liked it. "We are all *entbehrlich*," he said. "That is how you would say when something is not needed."

"Expendable?"

"Oh, *ja*. Expendable – I am remembering more English every day." He indicated the newspaper. "This is good practice."

Frau Barrow nodded. She got up and went to the window.

Anton could see the evening sky appeared bruised – mauve streaked with magenta. The window was open a couple of inches to admit a freesia-scented breeze. Frau Barrow pushed it wide and braced her elbows on the ledge.

She was wearing a skirt and blouse. Her legs were bare, and as she leaned on the window-ledge, her skirt rode tantalisingly high.

Frau Barrow was blessed with slender, shapely legs and a deliciously curved arse. He was appreciating her rear view when she suddenly turned and caught him.

Quickly lifting his eyes, he felt the heat creep into his cheeks; an answering colour flooded her face before she turned away.

***

Jessica turned suddenly. A little thrill ran through her as she surprised the captain admiring her backside. She saw him flush slightly and as her own cheeks grew hot, she glanced quickly away, thinking wearily, *How lonely we both must be.*

"I'm sorry," she blurted, to cover the momentary awkwardness. Her blush deepened. "I shouldn't have said those horrible things to you the other day. I'm not normally such a bigot."

She looked at him and he met her eyes. "I am also sorry. It was very... unthinking of me to speak the way I did. I should be more considerable."

Jessica smiled but didn't correct him. She returned to the chair and sat on its edge, leaning forwards. "You speak English very well, you know." She indicated the copy of F. Scott Fitzgerald's *Tender is the Night* on the table by his bed. "Have you been reading that? It's a classic but I've never read it."

"I am reading it, but very slowly. Frau Clay brought it."

He smiled at her; he had a beautifully formed mouth and the unbidden thought popped into her head, *Who is the girl that kisses that mouth?*

Afraid her thoughts would show on her face, she leaned back in the chair and gazed through the window. The sky was moving through shades of lavender, purple, violet. Before she could stop herself, she said, "Tell me about your family... your wife."

His smile turned coy. "I have no wife. I have... I suppose you might say, a sweetheart. Her name is Natalia. My parents live in the countryside, they have a small farm with *Kühe...* cows."

"Cows," she repeated, smiling.

"Oh, *ja*! But they do not have many. Their main work is *der Hopfen.*"

"*Der Hopfen?*"

He frowned, as if considering, searching for the word. "*Der Hopfen* for *das Bier.*"

"Oh, hops!" Jessica was surprised. "They grow hops to brew beer?"

"They grow *der Hopfen und* they sell it to the ones who make the beer. I am fortunate, this way, because my parents... they are farmers... they live in a rural area. Only our cities are being bombed by your planes."

She watched him as he spoke, but saw no malice. She thought, *We can speak frankly. Our countries are bombing one another – it's no secret.*

"What is your family like?" she asked.

He shrugged one shoulder. "They are not unusual. My parents have been married about thirty-five years *und* there is my sister *und* me. There was another – a boy – but he drowned in a lake when he was five years old."

Jessica made a sympathetic sound. "Do you remember him?"

He shook his head. "No, I was a baby. I am the youngest child. My sister, Brita, is older. She is married *und* I am *ein Onkel*. Brita has a small girl *und* a smaller boy."

"And your parents, have they always worked on the land? Is it a good living?"

He gnawed his lip uncertainly. "A good living?"

"I mean – well, farmers here are not particularly wealthy. Do farmers earn good money in Germany?"

He seemed to think before responding. "It is not a bad living. My parents are comfortable, but they are not wealthy people. Why?"

"Because they were able to send you to America. My parents could never afford that."

"They paid my fare but I did not arrive in New York with money in my pockets. I had to earn it – I found a job the first week I was there."

"So soon?" She was impressed. "How did you live until then?"

"That is the real story." His face grew animated. "I have a friend – Josef. He lived in the village near my home in Germany, *und* we went to school together – we grew up together. Josef's family moved to New York. We stayed in contact *und* a year later he invited me to stay with his family."

"What an opportunity!"

"Oh *ja*. My parents used their savings to pay my passage on the ship. They hoped I would go to the university."

"But you didn't?"

He grinned, somewhat sheepishly. "I learned to fly instead. My mother cried but my father was proud. When I wrote to tell them I had a job flying aeroplanes she changed her mind – especially when I sent home money to repay my fare. When I returned to Germany, I spoke English well *und* was a pilot, they thought I was a hero. I was not a hero but it..." he broke off and eyed her rather self-consciously.

Jessica waved for him to continue.

"It made me popular with the girls." He shrugged and grinned shyly. "I liked that, of course. That is when I met Natalia. She is Josef's cousin. She lives in Frankfurt... or she did last time I heard."

Jessica was aware of an uncomfortable shift in her stomach. *Surely I'm not jealous because this young man, a virtual stranger, has a sweetheart? What a foolish lonely woman you are, Jessica Barrow!*

She realised he was regarding her curiously. "What about your parents?" he asked.

"My father owns a shop – a grocery shop – in Leeds," she replied. She was feeling relaxed, comfortable. "They are not wealthy by any means, but they were comfortable until the war. These days nobody has any money and Dad lets people buy things on account. He knows they'll never pay."

"But he will do this anyway?"

Jessica nodded. "He's a generous man."

The German shifted in the bed and she said, "Do you need another pillow?"

"*Nein danke.*"

They fell silent for a moment, then she asked, "Do you have grandparents?"

"A grandmother on my father's side *und* that is all. Both my grandfathers were killed in France in the last war."

"Oh."

He gestured resignedly. "It was war."

Jessica nodded as the sounds of a childish squabble somewhere in the house filtered up to them.

"If I don't get involved, they usually sort it out themselves," she said hopefully and he laughed. He had a wide, expressive mouth and he laughed easily. *He's had a happy life*, she decided.

And suddenly Mary's voice rose in a torrent of abuse at her twin, which was followed immediately by a loud bang. Jessica made a rueful face. "Maybe I *should* get involved."

She got up and dragged her chair back to its place by the wall and went to the door. Pausing with her hand on the knob, she turned towards him. "It's nice talking to you," she said truthfully. "Good night."

He smiled. "I enjoy talking to you too. *Gute nacht,* Frau Barrow."

Chapter 9

"So, what made you become a pilot?" Jessica had a pile of mending to do – mainly tears in Thomas's clothes. The children were at school and Marg and Sam were in Wolstone. The empty old house was a lonely, creaking place, so Jessica took her sewing box upstairs and sat with the German. "Were you one of those little boys obsessed with aeroplanes?"

"Oh, *ja!*" He laughed, looking very young. He was out of bed, sitting in a chair, wearing Jon's pyjamas and green tartan dressing-gown. "Do not all small boys dream of flying? I always wanted to. When I went to the United States, my parents expected I would study English at the university. Perhaps I would become a doctor or..." He made a rueful face. "I left the university after only a few months *und* went to the flight school. I had a job *und* nearly all my money was spent on lessons. After I became a pilot I found a job with the United States Mail Service. I flew the mail all over America. There were very big arrows made of concrete across the deserts for the pilots to follow."

Jessica was astounded. "Concrete arrows, across the United States?"

"Oh, *ja*, everywhere. It is true! But when war came, they removed many of them." He winked conspiratorially, "They do not want the enemy following the arrows to the cities, you see."

She laughed. "No, I suppose not." She squinted as she threaded a needle. "Were you kicked out when the war was announced?"

He nodded. "Suddenly I was no longer welcome. The United States government ordered me to return to Germany or they would send me to an internment camp." He gave a light, humourless laugh. "It was not a difficult decision."

Jessica found the tear in Thomas's trousers. She settled the garment across her knee and set to work. "Your parents would have been glad you were home."

"*Ja* – as was the Luftwaffe, when it discovered I was a pilot."

Jessica raised her head and studied him. He said, "I was summoned to the Luftwaffe headquarters *und* recruited immediately." He shrugged, adding meaningfully, "When my government requests you do something, it is expected that you do it *und* be proud to do it. They call it *Pflicht* – an obligation. *Es war meine Pflicht...* It was my duty as a German." He opened his hands helplessly. "You see, I did not choose to be your enemy."

She felt him watching her with an odd, almost expectant, expression on his face.

"I know," Jessica admitted, gently, "and I understand."

He visibly relaxed.

"How old are you?" she blurted, suddenly. "I mean..." The blood rushed to her cheeks and she leaned over her stitching to hide it. "You look so young yet you've done so much."

"How old are you?" he countered.

She raised her head to find him grinning wickedly.

It was infectious and she grinned back. "That's not fair, I asked first."

"Oh, *ja*. So you did, *und* I am rude to ask a lady's age."

"Oh, *ja*," she mimicked, tying off her needlework.

He laughed. "I am twenty-five. I have been flying planes for almost six years, nearly two with the Luftwaffe. I am Hauptmann Anton Vogel. Hauptmann is what you call Captain."

Jessica smiled. She was feeling light and girlish. "Captain Vogel, I am Jessica Barrow. Most people call me Jessie." She held out her hand. "Pleased to meet you."

He took her hand. "*Und sie,* Frau Jessie." He said her name with a soft *J* sound and she thought it sounded nice.

Having finished her work, she gathered her things, preparing to leave.

"It was good talking with you," he said, sincerely, smiling, "*und* tomorrow, you will tell me more about yourself?"

She stood beside his chair, considering. "Captain, when did you first meet my children?"

"Please... do not be concerned."

"Just tell me when you first met them." Her tone was cautiously neutral.

"They found me in the stables... I do not remember it clearly. They called Herr Clay."

"So how long were you out there before they found you?" She folded her arms across her chest and studied him.

***

Anton thought Frau Jessie was trying to look fierce but it wasn't convincing; she still looked pretty. He controlled his expression and said, "I do not know. I was not well."

Jessica made an irritable huffing sound. "Well, there's nothing to be done about it now." She moved to the door but turned unexpectedly and caught a forgotten smile on his face.

"What?" she demanded.

Anton couldn't prevent his smile widening. "You think they all keep the secret from you."

"Why is that funny?"

"Because they did not want to; it was me."

At her quizzical look, he explained. "I am young enough that Herr Clay *und* his wife would want to care for me, *und* your children – they think we play an exciting game. But I feared you – perhaps," he added cocking a single eyebrow, "I still do. A mother alone – you might want to..." he gave a quirky one-shoulder shrug and grinned villainously, "bloody well kill me when you have the chance."

She seemed amused but forced her face into a stern expression. "It's not polite to remind me I said that. Good night, Captain Vogel," she said.

"*Gute Nacht*, Frau Jessie."

***

"It was very odd," Olive said over the phone a week later. "They flew past – you would've heard 'em too. Then, nothing."

Jessica sat on the telephone stool in the hall outside the kitchen. "Yes, we heard them. Were you in the cellar?"

"Aye, and right crowded it were too, what with Mrs Burnside and the four little ones."

"Four! I thought she had three."

"Carol, two months last week. Wonder what they were doin' just flying over. Reckon we've got 'em scared."

"If they were scared they wouldn't be coming at all."

Olive didn't seem to be listening. She continued, almost talking to herself, "The Luftwaffe has thrown everything at us and there's nowt left."

"Mum, that doesn't make sense. They wouldn't waste all that fuel if they didn't have good reason. Anyway, they're still testing the Messerschmitt... who knows what's –"

"They needn't bother," Olive assured her. "That Messerschmitt they shot down a while back – took it to some secret location, they did. Studied it from top to bottom. Won't be long till we can build our own just like it. Anyway, war's been going more than two years already – can't last much longer!" Olive finished with bravado and Jessica smiled to hear it.

Olive's voice faded into the background as Jessica's mind returned to her chat with the German captain the other night. It disconcerted her because she liked him; she found him interesting and intelligent – and attractive. If they'd met under other circumstances...

Lucifer's balls! she thought. *What if that was the plan all along; send a handsome officer to England, find some silly, gullible local, befriend her – make her feel pretty – spin wild tales about technology and fighter jets, trusting all along that she would tell her friends and family.*

Is this the new German style of warfare? The New Model Army of the Third Reich?

"Don't you think? Jessica?" Olive broke into her thoughts.

"What? Sorry, I –"

"I said, I wondered whether they might billet some child evacuees with you. You've so much room there, and Mary and Thomas could make new friends."

"You were just telling me that the war can't last much longer."

"But what if it does?" Olive pondered. "They're still evacuating children from big cities. Broughton Hall has been classified as a reception zone – they could send one or two kiddies to you."

"I suppose. Do you have to put your name down or do the children just get billeted?"

"I don't know – billeted, I should think."

"Interesting." *How long before the Kraut was discovered, then?*

"What about a farm girl?" Olive went on, seemingly oblivious to her daughter's distraction. "City girls are signing up to work on farms... they help out and learn the ropes in exchange for bed and board, sometimes a small wage. You're always needing an extra pair of hands."

"But I don't need an extra mouth to feed, Mum. And I already have Sam and Marg on the books, remember?"

"Oh, aye. So you do."

A door banged upstairs and Jessica heard childish chatter echoing down the hallway. "Mum!" Thomas shouted, running up to her. "Oh, sorry," he whispered, as he saw her on the telephone. "Is that Granny?"

Jessica put her hand over the receiver. "Yes. Want to say hello? Just a minute, Mum. Thomas wants to talk to you."

"All right, love. Where's my little man?"

"Here, talk to Granny and hang up when you're finished."

Thomas took the receiver. "Hello Granny," Jessica heard him say as she pushed open the kitchen door.

"Oh, God!" She rushed to the range. "The soup!"

Fortunately, it was only simmering and hadn't boiled over. Stirring it with a large ladle she found it had thickened nicely.

Grasping the pot by its two handles, she moved it across the plate and away from the heat.

Her new concerns about the Gerry were gnawing at her. It was one thing while he was confined to that room, but once he was recovered and moving about...

What am I going to do with him then? I suppose he could help Sam with the cows – he's a country boy after all.

"Mum," Thomas burst into the room. "Granny says she and Grandad might come visit."

Jessica's mouth went dry. She swallowed. "Really? I've been trying to convince them to come for ages. What did you say to her?"

"I told her it was quiet here and the planes only fly over – they don't drop bombs on us. Hullo, Mrs Clay."

"Hullo, Tommy," Marg said, coming through the garden door.

"Morning, Marg," Jessica said. "I'll put the kettle on. Thomas, you didn't say anything to Granny about Mr Bird, did you?"

He shook his head. "Nah-ah. Mr Bird is *our* secret."

"Good lad." Jessica put out two cups while Marg picked up a tea towel and began drying the breakfast dishes.

"Besides," Thomas went on, "Granny won't like Mr Bird."

Jessica glanced over her shoulder, her expression carefully blank. "No, I don't expect Granny would like Mr Bird. That's why we can't tell her."

"Granny loved Daddy. She won't like Mr Bird being our new daddy."

"Thomas!" Jessica gasped, whirling about to face her son. "Mr Bird is *not* your new daddy! Why would you even think that?"

Thomas's eyes grew wide in alarm. He glanced towards Mrs Clay and back to his mother. "Because Jack Ramage said one of the Yanks staying at his house is his new daddy. He even sleeps in Jack's mum's room."

Behind her, Marg snuffled with suppressed laughter. Jessica looked her son sternly in the eye. "Jack shouldn't have told you his mum's private business."

"But Mum –"

"And you shouldn't be repeating stories you hear at school."

"I do 'ope, young laddie," Marg interrupted. She'd contained her laughter and now her tone was all seriousness. "I do 'ope you don't talk about things what goes on around 'ere."

Jessica nodded adding, "You know that if –"

"Mummy, you *told* me," Thomas rolled his eyes and adopted a tone of exaggerated patience, "if anyone finds out about Mr Bird they will take him away. I haven't forgotten, you know."

"Good. Now –"

"Besides, Jack's mum's gone all religious with that Yank. Jack says sometimes in the middle of the night she yells out, *Jesus, Mary and Joseph!* Jack says it keeps him awake!"

Marg burst out laughing while Jessica's mouth dropped open in shock. "Thomas!" she cried, but his mind had already leapt to a new topic.

"Can I go upstairs and see Mr Bird?" He ran to the hall door without waiting for her response.

Jessica adopted a firm tone and asked, "Have you mucked out the henhouse yet?"

Thomas faced her, his lower lip sliding out.

"It's your main job, so I would like you to go and do it, please."

Reluctantly, the child turned back, muttering to himself and Jessica distinctly heard, him say, *Lucifer's balls!*

"Thomas! Where'd you get that from?"

His expression turned mutinous. "Where do you think, Mummy?"

"Don't be cheeky. You're not to say it."

"But you don't mind me saying *okay*."

"That's different."

"Can I see Mr Bird after the henhouse?"

She inclined her head.

"Goodie!" He dashed around the table and shot out into the yard, the garden door banging behind him.

Jessica poured out two cups of tea and met Marg's eyes through the steam. "Children talk... I'm that worried about someone finding out."

"I know," the older woman said, "but if they know the importance of it – children also love secrets."

"But they're all repeating things they hear the Yanks say. Just imagine if they pick up some German phrase..." Jessica rubbed her forehead worriedly but Marg didn't seem too concerned.

"We'll be all right. They're sharp kiddies you 'ave." Marg took a sip from her cup and chuckled delightedly. "Who woulda thought it, eh? Marjory Ramage taking a Yankee lover. Not worried for 'er reputation, I'll give 'er that!"

Jessica grimaced. "If anyone finds out about our Mr Bird, my *reputation* will be the least of my worries." But she too grinned then. "Marjorie Ramage and a Yank. Well good luck to her!"

Marg gave a snort and sipped her tea. "Reckon you'd be the envy of the county if it were found out *our* fella's such a looker!" Marg wiggled her eyebrows, sobering quickly at Jessica's frown. "Anyway, you probably should 'ave a chat with 'im about 'ow 'e can be 'elping out. On the mend 'e is. Won't be long before 'e's up and about."

Jessica sighed. "I know. I'll talk to him this afternoon. For now, though," Jessica rose and put her empty cup in the sink. "I've got washing to do. Thomas slipped in the paddock yesterday. The only pair of trousers he has, without holes in them, is caked with mud – again!"

***

Later, Jessica was elbow-deep in filthy water. Thomas's trousers had dried out so she could brush off the worst of the mud. Now, she leaned over the stone trough, scrubbing the stains from the knees before she could throw them in the copper with the rest of her washing.

The trousers had started life made of heavy drill cotton, but were now so thin and worn that she wondered how much more of Thomas's mistreatment they could take.

The steam coming off the water dampened her face; her hair clung in tickling tendrils to her cheeks. Groaning, she straightened, massaging the small of her back, and wiped the hair from her face with her shoulder.

"*Gut* day to –"

With a small cry of alarm, Jessica spun around. The sopping trousers in her hand sprayed an arc of water over the man standing behind her.

"Captain Vogel! What the hell!" Her heart thudded in her chest and she took an involuntary step backwards. Clutching Thomas's sodden trousers defensively to her chest, she spoke evenly, "What are you doing here?"

He retreated, hands up innocently. "I am sorry... I –" reaching cautiously towards her, he plucked the trousers from her grasp and threw them back into the trough. "You are all wet, now." He smiled, disarmingly handsome, which unnerved her all the more.

"How long...? You scared the life out of me! Are you feeling better?" The front of Jessica's cotton dress was wet and clingy.

Deliberately raising his eyes to her face, he said, "I did not intend to surprise you. I wanted to say that I am much improved. I would like to be useful."

Feeling exposed, Jessica grasped an old towel and crouched to mop the floor, tutting at the muddy water puddled on the flagstones. The captain was wearing Jon's pyjamas and slippers but he was shorter than Jon and the slippers were too big, the pyjamas too long; he'd rolled them up at the ankles.

"I was going to talk to you about that," she said. Floor dried, she rose to face him, towel held before her. He was only a couple of inches taller than she was. He wore Jon's green tartan dressing-gown, belted at his waist. He hadn't shaved but it looked like he'd combed his hair.

It was the first time they'd stood face to face. But for his recent illness, during which he'd lost considerable weight, he would be strongly built, athletic – yes, that was it! He had the posture and proportion of an athlete.

They must train them hard in the German military, she thought, uncomfortably aware of her defencelessness.

"It's good that you're feeling better," she said, rattled.

"Oh, *ja*." He smiled, though she noticed how he leaned his left shoulder against the door-frame, favouring his broken ribs. "This fact is pleasing to me too."

"And you found me..." she began. *He must have been wandering about the house alone! And now he's outside – in the wash-house. Had he been spying?*

"Frau Clay told me I would find you here," he said, quickly, as though reading her thoughts.

"I was going to talk to you," she repeated, flustered. "I was wondering how you're feeling and whether... whether you'd want to..." *earn your keep... pay your way... move out.*

Jessica was foundering but he spoke calmly. "I thought I would visit you this time."

She could find no deceit in his face. *Perhaps he'd been selected for this mission for his excellent acting skills*. Her heart was gradually slowing. *Don't let them see you're vulnerable.* "Well," she said, brightly, "what do you think you can do?"

He folded his arms across his chest. "Help here," he made an expansive, one-handed gesture, "something useful. I am stronger each day. There must be something."

"Yes, Marg mentioned that."

Jessica returned to Thomas's trousers. She took them from the sink and tossed them into the copper, intensely aware that the German continued to stand behind her – the hairs on the back of her neck stood up like tiny spines.

Dear God he could thrust a knife into my back at any moment.

Jessica wheeled around. He hadn't moved but his gaze was fixed on her bottom. Raising his eyes, he smiled, unrepentant, and added, "If you think of something..." he pushed away from the door and went to leave.

Was it possible he meant no harm? "Captain Vogel?"

He turned. His face was open and friendly.

"Perhaps you could help Sam in the dairy?"

"I can... I was raised on a farm, as you know. I am good with animals... cows."

"Yes. That's what I was thinking. Very well," she nodded more or less to herself. "I will speak with Sam; he'll find something for you."

He nodded. "That would be *gut*."

"But now," she went on, "you should go back to your room."

He inclined his head obediently and left her. She watched him return to the house and disappear through the garden door.

He *was* getting stronger every day – that was the trouble.

Chapter 10

British engineer, Frank Whittle, had been obsessively working on a design for a jet-propelled engine. In Europe, Hitler's engineers were similarly at work.

As a result of each nation's military intelligence, a race to develop the first jet-powered, high-speed aircraft was underway.

Germany had won that race with the launch of the Messerschmitt 262, Sturmvogel, baby of Wilhelm Messerschmitt. The Messerschmitt was capable flying up to 100 miles per hour faster than the most advanced aircraft available, and could destroy an R.A.F. bomber in a single pass.

That March evening, when English anti-aircraft guns took aim at two German planes, they had unwittingly brought down one of the first Messerschmitt 262s built. Blasting holes through its fuselage and fuel tanks, they effectively destroyed the fastest aircraft on earth as it streaked across the English night-time skies – it had been a remarkably lucky shot and the gunner responsible admitted he'd simply pointed his gun and fired.

"'E were goin' that fast," Bert Carlton told the local paper, "ah couldn' even see t'bugger."

At the same time, a second Luftwaffe plane had been shot down. Of the three Germans captured, the one who was evidently a bomber, was assumed to be from the Messerschmitt. The German airmen failed to disabuse their interrogators of the mistake, and Hauptmann Anton Vogel had parachuted, seemingly undetected, from the remains of the Messerschmitt somewhere over the West Yorkshire dales.

***

Six weeks later, the German officer was well enough to venture downstairs for his first supper in the kitchen with the Englishwoman and her children.

Still somewhat unnerved by the German's presence, Jessica invited Marg and Sam to join them round the kitchen table for a simple meal consisting of a small ham and roasted vegetables. The Yorkshire puddings made from National Flour didn't rise as they would normally but were suitably stodgy.

Marg contributed a rhubarb and apple pie – its crust made from finely crumbed stale bread mixed with butter and pressed into the pie pan.

Sam commented on the captain's recovery, agreeing that an extra pair of hands in the dairy would be invaluable. "Provided you take care not to over-exert yourself."

"Of course," the captain agreed, "but I am getting stronger each day." He turned to Jessica, adding, "I know you are sharing your food with me – I must contribute to my keeping."

"You're too thin, not strong enough yet," Marg said before Jessica could respond.

"You worried about your family at home, lad?" Sam interrupted.

They'd finished dinner and Jessica was serving the pie. Looking over her shoulder, she said, "Your parents will be wondering where you are, I suppose, Captain?"

The German nodded as Jessica passed him a plate. "I expect they will be. I cannot stay here forever. I understand the risk you are taking."

"If you're thinking of leaving, lad, I'm not sure 'ow we could do it or where you'd go."

"Oh, *ja*," he agreed, "but it is not possible to stay here."

The three adults nodded sagely but Thomas, who'd been enthusiastically applying himself to his dessert, now spoke up. "But isn't this Mr Bird's home now?"

"This is *not* Mr Bird's home," Mary countered firmly.

The boy's alarmed gaze moved from his mother, to Marg, Sam and back to his mother as Jessica said gently, "He can't stay here – it's too dangerous for him – and us."

"Your mother is right," the captain said quietly. "*Und* my parents... they will be thinking..." he raised his eyes to Jessica. "But there is no way that I can write to them."

Jessica drew in her breath to speak but didn't know what to say.

"Anton's right," Sam said. "'Is parents'll be thinking the worst 'as 'appened to 'im. But for 'im to send a letter..." he left the sentence hanging.

"Let's not spoil a nice evening with this talk." Marg interjected. "Why don't we 'ave a little chat about it later, eh?"

Jessica swallowed a mouthful of pie. The rhubarb was tart, sweetened slightly by the apples. "All mail to and from England is being checked. I've heard there are twenty-odd censor stations operating right across the country... checking everything coming in and going out."

None of the adults around that table were incognisant of the consequences should they be discovered harbouring an enemy officer.

Thomas's face was reddening. "But –" he began and Jessica feared a tantrum was about to erupt.

"Let me talk with your mother, young man," the captain interrupted. "Then we will decide what can be done."

Jessica smiled placatingly at her son. "There you go. Now, finished your pudding? Good. Put your plate in the sink, then you and Mary should finish that jigsaw... it's been on the dining-room table for two months."

Thomas brightened immediately, as Jessica knew he would, while Mary regarded her suspiciously, as Jessica knew *she* would.

"Can't we stay and talk to Mr Bird too?" her daughter asked.

"Perhaps Mr Bird might help with the jigsaw later." Jessica glanced at the German who nodded agreeably. He probably didn't know what the word *jigsaw* meant. "Now, off you go." She waved the children away.

The adults waited at the table until the children had gone, then Jessica rose and put the kettle on the hob.

Turning, she found three sets of eyes on her, waiting expectantly, and while the captain's expression showed moderate concern, Marg's eyes were slightly narrowed, anticipating Jessica's next move.

Only Sam seemed relaxed, and he addressed Jessica, "I can see we've got a bit of a problem, so why don't you tell us your thoughts, love."

Jessica busied herself taking out four mugs and scooping tea into the teapot while casting about for the right words. Their eyes were boring holes in her back and she could guess what each person was thinking.

The Gerry wants me to help him get home – which is impossible. Marg wants him to replace her lost son – also impossible, and Sam just wants to keep the peace, equally impossible.

As for me? I want him out of my house before the authorities find out, but I don't know how or where.

She was standing with her back to them, one hand on her hip, the other on the edge of the bench when the kettle began to boil.

Relieved to have some legitimate activity, she took up a cloth and removed the kettle from the hob.

Marg and Sam allowed him into our lives, but he's living in my house and has somehow become my burden. I'm the one at risk here.

The steam rose round her face as she poured the water into the pot. *This man is my enemy*, she grumbled to herself. *Why should his welfare be my problem? I could – I should – contact the authorities. That's what P.O.W. camps are for.*

She returned the half-empty kettle to its normal position at the back of the range. *I'll explain it to them. He won't be mistreated*

– he'll even be able to write to his parents. Sam's pragmatic enough but I need to convince Marg.

Turning, with the teapot in her hands, she found Marg staring sullenly at her hands and Sam watching his wife with a rueful expression.

But the German's eyes were steady on Jessica and her defiance melted immediately at the understanding on his face.

Jessica took the teapot to the table and brought over the cups. Before she could resume her seat, the German touched her arm. It was gently done, just his fingertips, but she flinched as though burned.

"It is all right, Frau Jessie," he said softly. "My being here is dangerous for you. I understand that you need me to leave."

"It's not that..." she began. "Christ!" She dropped into her seat. "It *is* that! It's exactly that!" Not brave enough to speak directly to Marg, she turned to Sam. "Sooner or later someone will find out he's here. Do you have any idea what will happen?"

"He'll be sent to jail!" Marg snapped.

Sam spoke calmly. "He'll end up in a prisoner of war camp and 'e'll be all right for it."

"They'll let him write to his parents," Jessica added.

"Excuse me..." the man in question interrupted as they discussed him. "It would seem better for all concerned," he said, "if I were to return home."

Jessica snorted rudely. "So you can get yourself another Messerschmitt and go dropping bombs on innocent people again?"

Marg gasped and Sam cleared his throat uncomfortably.

Bloody hell! I said that out loud! Jessica was mortified as all eyes rested on her burning face.

The room fell into an awkward silence and the captain stared into his cup.

Jessica felt the weight of Marg's glare heavily on her and

dared not raise her head. "How could you say that?" the older woman whispered. "How could you be so unkind?"

"Because it is true." The German answered softly and Jessica looked up. The captain's eyes passed over each of them in turn. "That is what they will want of me. I am *ein Flieger*. I am *ein Hauptmann*. It is my job..." his cloudy blue eyes met Jessica's hazel ones. "I will not be given a choice."

The intensity of his gaze caused Jessica's heart to stir. "Captain Vogel," she said contritely, "I'm sorry. It was very unkind of me to say what I said."

He smiled crookedly. "Oh, *ja,* perhaps. But your thoughts must always be for your children."

So damn understanding. Now I feel worse.

He was watching her from across the table and Jessica couldn't look away.

Sam noisily cleared his throat, "Anton, look," he began and the captain turned to him. "I know a man –"

"Sam..." his wife suddenly cut him off. "I'm not sure –"

"I don't see as there's owt else we can do."

Jessica saw Sam hold his wife's gaze for several moments, the two engaging in the kind of wordless communication only those that have known each other many years can do.

Finally, Marg drew in her breath and made a gesture of resignation. Sam returned his attention to the young man beside him at the table.

"I know a man – Dick. 'E's got a fishing trawler – takes it out of Whitby. I'm wondering if we could talk 'im into taking you 'ome."

She saw a flicker of hope briefly light the captain's face but it was quickly extinguished as the German's knowledge of geography seemed somewhat better than the Englishman's.

"I am afraid that this idea may not work very well, Herr Clay. The North Sea is very wide. It is not like the English Channel –

it is many miles *und...*" he paused, his expression both regretful and wary, but Jessica knew instinctively what he was thinking because her thoughts ran similarly.

"And your U-boats are regularly blowing up our ships, including fishing boats." She carefully modulated her tone and while she sensed Marg stiffening, both Sam and the captain nodded, accepting, pragmatically, that she was right.

"Aye," Sam conceded, "and Dick's unlikely to put the trawler at risk like that."

"What about ..." Jessica began hesitantly. "No, that won't work."

Three sets of eyes were on her. *You've opened your mouth now – you might as well say it*. "This may be a really stupid idea," she hedged, "but a large part of France is German occupied, right? What if the captain could get across the channel? Sneak in via one of the German-held ports?"

Jessica knew Marg would be obstinately opposed to all suggestions but as her idea was not immediately discredited, she was heartened to continue. "If we could get a boat... I don't know how but there must be people who sail back and forth... like... smugglers?"

"It ain't the seventeen 'undreds, love," Marg said. "Even if there *were* smugglers, you'll 'ave an 'ard time of it finding one. They're not like to advertise."

"We do 'ave smugglers," Sam piped up. "We've still got supplies going back and forth to France. Someone's moving them."

"But how to contact this someone?" Jessica mused.

Nobody spoke. They'd all run out of ideas, so they sat for a long time in silence, sipping their tea.

***

Jessica was in bed, propped on pillows, reading from the

memoir. It was late at night and the rain beat against her window in a relentless torrent while the wind clawed and howled around the house. At least in weather like this there should be no planes flying over. It was the only consolation because Jessica hated storms.

A particularly strong gust of wind rattled the glass in the windows. Jessica peered over the top of the old journal, worried that the frames – originals from Broughton Hall's construction – would not hold. Silly, of course; the house had withstood centuries of brutal Yorkshire weather.

She turned up the wick in the lamp next to the bed and returned to the journal.

Jessica read by lamplight for quite a while, until finally her eyes began to smart. She reached for her little bookmark Mary had made her – a strip of card to which a dried dandelion had been pasted – and slipping it between the pages, closed the memoir. Though her eyes hurt, she didn't feel tired. Her bedside clock read ten past eleven o'clock.

I need a cup of tea.

With that thought in mind, Jessica got out of bed, slipped into her dressing-gown and, grasping her lamp, made her way out of her room and down to the kitchen.

Broughton Hall was dark and decaying during the day. By night it was very unnerving, with its shadowy nooks and mysterious corners – food for a fertile imagination!

Something banged outside in the buffeting wind and Jessica started. Light from the lamp leapt like a living thing on the wall beside her.

You don't need a fertile imagination in this weather! she told herself. The creepiest section of the house, she felt, was the corridor to the kitchen with its two descending left turns and flights of stairs. She navigated them quickly but carefully, holding the oil lamp high and ignoring the shadow creeping along an inch behind her.

Entering the kitchen, Jessica gave a relieved sigh but immediately choked on a cry of fright. The garden door stood open framing the silhouette of a man leaning against the jam.

He turned at the sound of her behind him.

"Wha–what are you doing here?" Jessica demanded angrily. Her heart was racing so fast she was breathless. "You scared the life out of me!"

The German made an apologetic face. "*Entschuldigen...* I did not mean to frighten you."

"Well, you did. What are you doing up?" She pushed past him to shut and bolt the door. "The wind is ferocious tonight."

"Oh *ja*," he agreed. "I could not sleep. I –"

So, you thought you'd go prowling around the house! She waved a dismissive hand, adding, "I couldn't sleep either." She was being unreasonably short – she knew it – but he'd scared her half into next week. *Shouldn't be down here anyway!*

Jessica put the lamp on the table and busied herself with the stove, poking the dusky coals back to life. "I was going to make tea."

Tea was in short supply and she resented inviting him to share what little she had, but good manners prevailed. "Would you like some?"

He eyed her doubtfully. *He still doesn't look well*, she thought, shamefacedly. *All hollow cheeks and bags under his eyes.* "Why would you ask me that?" he countered. "It is plain you do not –"

"I'm making a pot," she snapped. Embarrassed by her rudeness, she turned her back on him and filled the kettle at the sink. "You're welcome to share it with me." *He knows I resent him, but it's worse because he knows I haven't got the guts to say it to his face.*

"Thank you," he said, softly, and sat at the kitchen table while she faffed around at the stove to avoid his gaze. She could feel his eyes boring holes in her back.

Why don't I ever speak my mind? And if I did, what would I say?

"What are you not saying to me?" he asked suddenly and heat flooded her face. "It is obvious that you... er... the word...

He's a bloody mind reader! "Lucifer's balls!" she cried in frustration whirling to face him. "Resent! Resent is the word you're looking for and *yes*! I *resent* you!" She turned back to the stove, wishing the kettle needed attention but it didn't. She ran her hands over her face, breathing hard.

The kitchen was silent but for the cheerful bubbling of water slowly coming to the boil.

His chair scraped on the flagstone floor. "Thank you but I do not think I shall take a cup of tea."

"Captain Vogel!" Jessica exhaled heavily in frustration and turned to face him. Horribly humiliated by her rancour, she said softly, "I'm sorry. I've been... My children have better manners than I have. Please," she waved at his chair. "Sit. Please. I'm asking you to stay."

"Frau Jessie," he looked weary, "you do not want me here... this is all right, I understand." He smiled wryly, "I do not want me here either."

Taking a deep breath, she opened her mouth to respond just as the kettle came to the boil. Gratefully, she turned away, saying, "You're right – sit down, Captain Vogel – I don't want you here." She was surprised to hear a soft chuckling behind her and realised the ambiguity of her last statement.

Outside, the wind continued to howl and the house continued to creak and rattle but Jessica no longer heard it. The kitchen was warm – it felt like a cocoon. The captain was smiling at her as she brought the teapot to the table. His was the sort of face that easily slipped into a smile and as she placed the steaming pot between them, she felt herself relaxing. By the time she sat and poured a little of the tea into her cup to test its strength, her hands were steady and her heart had resumed its normal rhythm.

She felt him watching as she poured the tea into two cups. He asked, "Do you often have difficulty sleeping?"

"It's funny," she answered, "I never used to. But these days – milk?"

"*Ja. Danke.*"

"Sugar?" He shook his head and she passed him the cup, saying, "Captain, look, let's speak plainly."

"I wish you would."

Her head snapped up and he met her gaze almost defiantly.

"What's that supposed to mean?"

"It means," he said, patiently, "that you never say what you really want to say. You should be honest because we both know the situation. I want to go home." His shrug implied this last was obvious. "You want me to go – anywhere. I am not wrong, no?"

Jessica drew a slow breath through her nose, inclining her head in cautious agreement.

"*Und*, there is another problem, *ja*?"

She cocked an eyebrow. "Which is?"

"We are both afraid that I will be discovered."

This time she nodded with certainty. "And the longer you're here, the more likely it is that one of the children, or Sam, Marg or I, may inadvertently let it slip."

"So what can we do?" Anton sipped his tea, watching her over the rim of his cup.

"I don't know."

"What will your government do to you if they find me here?"

Jessica grimaced. "Nothing good, but I'm not sure. I heard about a woman who was married to a German man," she said, relaxing further into her chair. "When war was declared, he was supposed to go to an internment camp but instead they moved to another town where she tried to hide him. Eventually the neighbours found out, she ended up in jail and her husband was sent to the camp anyway."

"Terrible things are happening all around Europe."

They regarded each other through the steam coming off their cups. "I do not want to bring your family into danger, but I do not know what to do."

They fell into silence. Jessica was intensely aware of the captain's eyes on her as she drained the dregs in the pot, sharing it between them. The howling of the winds outside showed no sign of abating; she decided to tell him about the journal and the latest she had read.

"It sounds very interesting," he said sincerely. He put his mug on the table. "This Alexandra, she was born here, in this *Haus*?"

Nodding, she said, "But I don't think she lived out her life here. I believe she married and lived with her husband."

"Yes, I remember you read it to me. Do *you* find these things interesting?"

"I didn't think I would, but... Captain Vogel," Jessica paused. She was about to confide in him – tell him about the ghostly girl she'd seen. *What are you doing?* her brain demanded, *he's not your friend!*

He looked at her, expectantly. His face was still hollow but once it filled out a bit more, he will be very handsome. As though sensing her thoughts, he smiled gently at her and Jessica felt a softening within.

God, I'm lonely... The thought crossed her mind before she knew it was even coming. She blinked away the stinging behind her eyes and blurted out, "I think I've seen her ghost! Oh, God!" she gave a nervous little titter. "Do you think I'm crazy? I'm not crazy... I was probably dreaming."

She was rambling, the words tumbling out of her, but he wasn't laughing. He was watching her from those bluish-grey eyes of his and she noticed for the first time how nicely shaped his brows were. *You really are crazy, Jessica Barrow!* She told herself. *You're sitting at the kitchen table, in the middle of the night, drinking tea with a Luftwaffe fighter pilot and telling ghost stories!*

As he continued watching her, she found his uncritical gaze disarming. All Jessica needed was for him to think she'd taken leave of her senses. She forced herself to pause and draw a breath, then, "I'm sorry. I'm blethering like a mad-woman. I obviously dreamed all –"

"No!" His hand shot out and impulsively touched hers across the table. "You are not this mad woman."

She looked down in surprise. It was a nice hand with clever looking fingers but he retracted it immediately, self-consciously. "In my *Haus*," he continued enthusiastically, "when I was a boy, there was an old man that I would see. Sometimes he would be on the stairs, *und* other times I would see him in the living room."

"Did anyone else see him?"

"Oh *ja. Meine mutter...* my mother, she would see him from time to time, but not my father. He did not."

"Why do you think he came to you?"

"I do not know, but I think I have seen your woman too. I got up one night to use the bathroom. It was dark in the hall, but I saw... I *know* that I saw a woman... younger."

"A girl?" Jessica whispered, remembering the dark-haired girl she'd seen.

He frowned as he considered, "*Ja*, but older than a child. A young woman in a long..." he indicated his ankles.

"Dress? Skirt?"

He nodded.

They listened to the wind outside for a moment, then he asked, "What is your word for, *Friedhof*? Is it cemetery?"

"Cemetery?"

"When people are put in the ground when they die."

"Oh buried! Yes, cemetery. Why?"

He shrugged one shoulder. "Perhaps, if there is a cemetery near here, there might be people from this house buried."

Jessica looked at him with interest. "There is a chapel... about fifteen minutes' walk through the forest."

He looked at her and smiled. "We could go *und* see."

This time she laughed out loud. "Not right now, no."

Grinning, he said, "Oh, but you are not adventurous, Frau Jessie!"

"You've got that right! You sound just like my husband. Jon used to say..." Her voice drifted off and she stared into her empty cup.

His kind killed my husband. The words she'd shouted at Sam came back to her, along with the old man's response, *His kind killed my boy*!

The clock in the hall struck one – she didn't remember hearing it strike midnight but it must have while they were talking. "I think I'll be able to sleep now."

"Frau Jessie," he reached for her hand again but she pulled away. He looked mildly hurt. "Frau Jessie, it is war *und* it is terrible. Men kill each other. I can no more apologise for the things my country has done, than you can for the things your country has done."

My country is not murdering a generation in cold blood. She knew he read the thoughts on her face.

There was an appeal in his eyes as he said, "Please do not judge the German people by the crimes of their leaders."

She stared dumbly at him for several heartbeats, then with nothing to say, she resolutely collected their cups and took them to the sink. He brought the teapot and left it on the side.

"*Gute nacht,* Frau Jessie. *Schlaf schön.*"

By the time she turned to respond, he'd already gone.

Chapter 11

It was Saturday, the third of May, and Jessica was not looking forward to the day ahead. Later that morning, Robin Tyler was due to pick her and the children up to take them to the May Day fair and Jessica could see no way of avoiding it.

The clock in the hall was chiming seven o'clock as she passed it on her way to the kitchen. Entering the room, she was surprised to find the captain peering into the firebox, stirring the coals to life.

Jessica paused indignantly on the threshold. *What's he doing making himself at home in my kitchen?* Such resentment made her feel churlish. *Probably trying to be helpful.*

"*Guten morgen*, Captain," she said, hoping she sounded cheerful.

He turned and smiled at her. He hadn't shaved; the light-brown stubble on his chin lent him a rugged look. He seemed pleased to see her. "*Guten morgen*, Frau Jessie." He gestured towards the stove. "I hope you do not mind. I want to be more help now that I am feeling better. *Und* I will be working with Herr Clay today."

"I see. How is your breathing, are you still coughing? Are your ribs still sore?"

Confused ridges formed on his brow. She repeated. "Are you still coughing?"

"Oh, *ja* – little. But much better, *danke*."

"And here..." she pointed to his left side. "Your ribs? Are they still bruised? Is it tight when you breathe?"

He looked baffled and she realised she was asking too many questions.

He guessed, "You want to see er... *Prellung*... the colour?"

"Colour? *Prellung* does that mean bruise? Yes, are they still *Prellung*?"

He gave her an odd look but nevertheless tugged the shirt out of his trousers and began unbuttoning it.

"I don't mean –" Jessica began, before her throat constricted. She was unprepared for the sight of a young man's bare, muscled abdomen displayed in her kitchen. Unabashedly, he opened the shirt, turning to show his left side.

Jessica's cheeks flamed. Something low down in her stomach tightened and she stammered, "Um... I hadn't... didn't mean..." She gave up.

Adopting a professional attitude, she edged closer to examine him. His skin was yellowing as the extensive bruising over his ribs was healed.

"Does it hurt? Here?" She touched lightly.

He gave a sudden yelp and jumped away. She looked up in alarm to find him grinning and hunched protectively against the wall.

"You're ticklish!" she announced, unable to suppress the grin creeping across her face.

"*Kitzlig*," he agreed.

"Ah, now I know that you'd best watch out!"

"Oh, *ja*? You?" His hand shot out to prod a finger into her side. Jessica leapt aside with a startled cry.

"That's not fair!" She turned away from him, secretly enjoying the childish game but unsure how to play.

"Frau Jessie?"

She was too embarrassed to look at him. "Button your shirt."

"Frau Jessie?"

She cautiously turned and he lifted her face with a finger beneath her chin.

The intimacy of his gesture caused her heart to flutter like some silly adolescent's. Raising a single eyebrow, he searched her face. "You are... what is it you say when your face goes red?"

"Oh for God's sake, Captain Vogel!" Jessica slapped his hand away. He began to laugh and it was impossible to feign irritation when she felt so young and playful. "Embarrassed is the word!"

"Oh, *ja*, I remember! You are embarrassed!" He stopped laughing, but continued to grin at her, and she couldn't prevent the silly smile spreading across her own face.

"Yes, you idiot – I'm embarrassed, as you well know. Button your shirt – your ribs look fine."

Turning, she picked up the kettle but he caught her arm and took it from her. "Why are you embarrassed?"

She watched the movement of his shoulders as he put the kettle under the tap. "Because I... since my husband, I've... I'm not used to seeing a man, naked."

He slid a sly glance over his shoulder; his eyes glistened with mischief. "Have you not seen me without my clothes? When I was ill?"

"*I* couldn't do that! Sam and Marg bathed you and dressed you. You are a..." She bit back the words before she revealed how lonely she often felt, how vulnerable she was, and how attractive she found him. She felt desperate and pathetic. Besides, he was the enemy and every moment he spent here, beneath her roof, endangered her family. "It was not appropriate," she finished lamely.

He put the kettle on the hob then rested a hip against the bench. "Frau Jessie, I understand your feelings. I am a stranger – a man – in your *Haus*." He looked pensive. "You know, I have not seen my girlfriend for more than a year. It is difficult. I do not know when I will see her again. I do not think she is my girlfriend after so long."

Jessica relaxed slightly but kept her distance.

"A year?"

"Natalia lives in Frankfurt *und* I am... was based in a town where they build..." he wavered, regarding her speculatively. "It is a... an old sand mine... in the middle of Germany. Far from

Frankfurt." He turned away, ostensibly to check the kettle's progress.

Jessica realised with some surprise that he'd been talking about the factory where the Germans were building their fighter jets. He was based there because he'd been testing them.

"What is the Messerschmitt like?" she asked softly. "I mean, as a pilot – are they *really* that advanced?"

For a moment, she thought he wasn't going to respond and was mildly insulted. *I can be trusted. I'm British – unlike him! He's the enemy and acting as though* I'm *the untrustworthy one.*

The sudden stab of shame was so intense she gasped. *My God! What a bigot I am!*

The captain was regarding her with interest. Finally, he nodded slowly. "The Messerschmitt is incredible," he began. His eyes shifted out of focus, as he went on, "So powerful that you must increase the fuel carefully at first to allow her engine to gradually gain speed. It is difficult, but when she is in the air she is unlike any other machine."

"Because she is so fast?" Jessica asked. His ordinarily attractive face was illuminated into a masculine beauty by his passion for this plane.

"*Ja*, but it is more," he said, reverently. "Her sound is different too because the engine is behind the pilot. Also, she is smooth... such an advanced machine that I... I trusted her... I trusted the technology."

"You sound like a man in love."

He gave a short laugh, his focus returning to the room. "We have a saying, if you see a white plane, it is American, if it is a black plane, it is RAF. But if you see no planes at all, that is the Luftwaffe."

Jessica smiled despite herself, but he went on with a rueful expression. "*Sturmvogel* is very good in the air; it is the landing that is difficult. She is too fast and does not reduce speed easily.

She is difficult to land."

"Try crash-landing, then," Jessica remarked flippantly.

His face hardened and his eyes locked with hers.

"I'm so sorry," she whispered, contritely. "That was thoughtless."

He shrugged one shoulder, as though to dismiss her apology, but Jessica went on, "This war is changing everyone. We're all different; we're all ruining one another." She took a deep breath and changed the subject. "Of course you must miss your girlfriend. I'm certain she will wait for you."

Jessica realised she meant it – who wouldn't wait for him? She sighed, "I would have waited for Jon ..."

I missed Jon – miss him still, she thought, miserably. *No, that's not right. He loves her... Probably plans to marry her. I didn't love Jon... No, that's not right either. I did love Jon – he was kind, gentle... I loved him...*

The unwelcome thoughts were like a punch to the stomach. Jessica swayed on her feet and the tears welled in her eyes. *I never loved Jon! We cared for each other... we had children and I loved for him for it... just not like that.*

***

Anton saw the grief rise on her face. A single tear dribbled down her cheek; she put her hands to her face and turned her back to him.

He watched helplessly, wavering between going to her and allowing her space. He liked this young woman, though he recognised her uneasiness around him, he also understood her attraction to him. For wasn't he attracted to her for the same reason? That they were both alone and lonely?

Was this the reason he felt compelled now to draw her to him and give comfort?

He argued with himself until her hunched and shuddering

shoulders forced his reaction.

***

Jessica felt his hands on her, gently turning her to face him. Pulling her into his arms, he rubbed her back, soothing, murmuring softly into her hair. Jessica's hands rested lightly on his hips and she wept against his chest.

They stood for a long, *long* time, until she grew calm, until she realised that he was holding her. Immediately she put her hands up between them but she didn't push back, merely looked at him and found him watching her.

His eyes were the colour of summer storm clouds, and slowly, his hands moved to frame her face, thumbs smoothing the tears from her cheeks.

Jessica stood quite still, as the thought sprang into her mind, *He's going to kiss me!* She held her breath. *He's going to kiss me and... Lucifer's balls! I want him to!*

She gaped at him, knowing all the while that she should shove him away. *God, what are we doing?*

Suddenly the captain seemed to shake himself, as though emerging from a dream. He dropped his hands, and took a quick step backwards. His face registered his surprise. "Frau Jessie, I am sorry, I..."

He hadn't seen it coming either.

Jessica spun away and began setting out the children's breakfast dishes. Her hands fluttered over bowls, plates, cups, mugs, spoons – *where are the spoons?* Anything to avoid looking at him. *He's the enemy, enemy, enemy... you stupid, woman! Desperate, lonely, pathetic woman!*

Aware that he continued to stand irresolutely behind her, she fussed round with her head in a cupboard, praying he'd leave the room before she turned and threw herself at him.

Christ, he's younger than you, you foolish bloody –

"Frau Jessie," he said softly. "I think I will go to see Herr Clay."

"Oh... good. Good idea, Captain."

Idiotic woman!

She heard him move to leave and almost panicked as she remembered. "Captain!" she stalled him.

He turned expectantly. "*Ja?*"

"Um... One of the neighbours, Mr Tyler is coming this morning. He is taking me and the children out for the day. Please stay out of sight."

"Oh." A shadow crossed his face. "*Ja*, of course."

"Do you understand? Don't let him see you!"

He sighed. He sounded weary. "*Ja. Ich verstehe.*"

***

Jessica sat in the front seat beside Robin Tyler as he navigated the narrow Wolstone lanes. They were clogged with cars and delivery vans, while boys pushing barrows of produce wove between skipping, excited children and strolling adults.

"We may have trouble finding a spot to park the motor," Tyler murmured, narrowly missing two men unloading a large wooden crate of cabbages from a lorry.

Mary and Thomas were in the back seat chattering like magpies. They were so excited that Mary had even put aside her grudges.

Jessica smiled to herself, remembering how, as Tyler had pulled up the drive in his shiny new Jaguar, Sam had leaned against that great gnarly oak tree, rolling a cigarette and muttering, "Errol bloody Flynn 'e ain't, an' I don't see 'ow a pensioned soldier can afford a fancy new motor like that. Someone tell 'im there's a war on!"

Jessica took a deep breath, the smell of new leather in her nostrils. *I wonder what the captain would make of Mr Tyler.*

Probably agrees with Sam that –

"Penny for them?" Tyler broke into her reverie.

"Sorry?"

"You're smiling to yourself," he said, eyes on the road. He glanced briefly across at her. "I said, penny for them – for your thoughts."

Jessica flushed and laughed lightly through her nose. "I was just thinking what a nice day it is," she said, weakly.

He leaned forward to look up at the sky. The clouds were lowering, there was a hint of rain in them. "Really?" He shot her a quizzical look.

"I mean, nice outing – we don't get out often, do we kids?"

"No, Mum," they chorused dutifully from the back seat.

"Ah, here we are!" Tyler braced an arm on the seat behind her and looked over his shoulder, reversing neatly into a tight space.

He shut off the engine and Thomas reached immediately to open the car door. "Wait!" Jessica snapped. "I don't want you two running off into the crowd. Stay close, and if you happen to get lost come back to the car. Got that?"

"Yes, Mummy!" Mary agreed.

"Will there be donkey rides?" Thomas wondered aloud.

"Did you hear what I just said?"

"Yes, Mum," Thomas said, with exaggerated patience. "Did you hear what *I* just said?"

"Don't be cheeky. Yes, I did hear what you said. We'll have to see."

Unlike market day, during which Wolstone bustled with farmers and livestock, the May Day fair was a different kind of assault on one's senses. It was an explosion of colours, smells and sounds. Food stalls were selling everything from pork-pies to stick-jaw toffee – a rare treat considering that sugar, although not yet rationed, would soon be, and was in short supply. Jessica gave the children each a penny and advised, "Make the most of it!"

Someone had set up a DECCA portable record player and Gertrude Lawrence was singing *Mad about the boy...* while group of people danced.

Tyler offered Jessica his arm and the pair leisurely followed the flow of the crowd, while the children ran ahead.

Jessica craned her neck, trying to keep them in view, but eventually gave up. Tyler said, "If we lose them in the throng they know where to go."

He bought Jessica a slice of Beltane cake and they continued to drift towards the town centre. There the May Pole stood, at least ten feet tall and topped with a large floral offering to the Gods and Goddesses of fruit, flowers and fertility.

Just then, Thomas and Mary came running up. "Mum!" Thomas cried, his jaw bulging with toffee. "The parade is starting – the Jack in the Green's coming!"

Gertrude Lawrence was drowned beneath the beat and strain of traditional drums and pipes. As the parade approached, the crowd rippled and buzzed with excitement, then suddenly a great cheer rose.

"Here he comes!" Mary shouted. "Tommy, let's go up the front!"

Jessica watched her children disappear between the bodies lining the street. The float carrying the Jack in the Green came closer and the roaring of the spectators swelled to deafening proportions.

Hanging back against the brick façade of a building, Jessica and Tyler watched from a distance. It was difficult to see very much over the heads and flat-caps. She doubted Tyler could see anything, even though he was several inches taller than she was.

The captain's not much taller than me – he wouldn't see a lot either. The thought was in her mind before she even realised it. *Stop thinking about him!* she ordered herself. *You're here having a nice day out, with an English gentleman, enjoying a traditional English festivity. Forget the bloody Kraut!*

So, she did, putting all thoughts of the German determinedly aside. At that moment, the clouds parted and, as the excitement of the crowd became contagious, Jessica laughed from sheer happiness and the life-giving warmth of the spring sunshine in her face.

"You're very happy," Tyler shouted, leaning close to be heard over the beat of the drums.

"I am! It's such a beautiful day I feel I can put aside all my cares," she shouted back.

The noise of the crowd swelled to a crescendo as the procession drew closer. Tyler's lips were moving, but she couldn't hear a word over the racket.

"What?" She edged closer, "I can't hear a –"

"I said," he caught her chin in his hand, his face very serious, "What sort of cares do you have? Anything I can help you with?"

Jessica felt the tell-tale warmth spread up her neck and into her cheeks. "Everyone has cares, Mr Tyler." She smiled, brightly, hoping he didn't notice her rising colour. "But today is so lovely I'm putting all mine aside."

Tyler studied her face for long seconds, finally he smiled. "You're beautiful when you blush."

Jessica's first thought was to pretend she'd not heard, but she couldn't remember receiving a compliment from a man. Certainly, Jon had never complimented her – they'd grown up as brother and sister – and Jessica had never had a serious boyfriend. Now as Tyler bent towards her, she didn't know what to do, other than watch with a mix of trepidation and surprised interest, as he gently brushed his lips against her hot cheek.

At the same time, he dropped his hand from her face. Pressed against the wall by the crowd, she couldn't move, so she continued to stand there, hands hanging uselessly at her sides. His arm snaked out and his fingers loosely curled around hers. His pleasant face was alight with all the excitement of the occasion, as the Jack in the Green rolled by, trailed by a procession of devotees dressed in garlands.

Jessica remained frozen in place, her heart beating in time with the parade drums and feeling as light as a young girl.

As the crowd began to thin, Thomas and Mary returned at a run. "Mum, did you see that?" Thomas gasped. "Did you see the Jack? He was sitting up on top of a pile of flowers."

"Yes, I saw," Jessica replied, though in truth, she'd been only vaguely aware of the passing parade, so absorbed had she been in Tyler's profile, limned against the bright colours of the crowd and carnival.

Two men in one day, Jessica mused in wonder, *although the captain didn't kiss me, he'd thought about it. I wonder what –*

"Mum did you see the lady doing tricks on the pony's back?" Mary asked.

"Oh, yes," Jessica responded distractedly. "Very nice."

***

As Tyler's motor sped through Wharferidge and on to the lane towards Broughton Hall, he threw the occasional smiling glance towards her. Inexperienced as she was with men, Jessica didn't know what to think.

He obviously likes me. Do I like him or am I just feeling flattered? I don't know... perhaps if I get to know him better...

It was dusk as they pulled in front of her porch. The children were asleep in the back of the car. Thomas lay sprawled along the seat while Mary was squashed in the corner, her head resting on the padded wall.

Tyler shut off the engine and turned to Jessica. "I know we talked about going to see the Fresian horse but..." he glanced over his shoulder at the sleeping children, "I think we can do that another day, don't you?"

Jessica nodded. "I think so." Her eyes were drawn to a movement beyond him. *Did a curtain just twitch in the parlour window?* Her blood turned cold. "All right, sleepy-heads," she said in a loud voice. Both children stirred and Mary yawned.

"We home, Mummy?"

Tyler got out of the car and was coming round to Jessica's side. Without waiting for him, she threw open her door and leapt out, then quickly opened the rear door. "Out you hop, Thomas," she said brightly.

Thomas was still half asleep as she reached in and lifted him out with a grunt. *He's heavier than last time I tried to lift him.* "Here," Tyler held out his arms, "I'll carry him in for you."

Oh, Christ, don't come in the house!

"No need," Jessica dropped Thomas onto his feet, effectively jolting him awake. "He can walk, can't you, love?"

"Yes, Mummy," he responded, automatically.

Mary had let herself out the other side and had come round. Reading her mother's thoughts, she grasped her brother's hand. "Let's go, Tommy. Maybe Mrs Clay left our jammies to warm by the stove."

As the two children made their way up the steps to the front door, Thomas drawled in a sleepy voice, "Do you think Mr Bird is waiting for us?"

Jessica's breath hitched. She stood beside Tyler in the lavender evening, watching as the children hauled themselves wearily up the steps. Light spilled onto the porch as they opened the door.

"Mr Bird...?" Tyler asked with a small smile.

She waved breezily, "Oh that's... Mr Bird is Thomas's... er... one of his teddy bears."

"They're good kids."

"Oh yes, they are. Well –" She stuck out her hand. "I've had a lovely day, Mr Tyler, and I know the children –"

"Jessica," he interrupted her. "I'll apologise – if you want me to – if you think that kissing your cheek was a bit forward, but," he shrugged, "you're beautiful – I couldn't help myself. I hope you didn't mind?"

Her hand was still extended, and now he took it and looked down at her work-roughened fingers. She followed his gaze.

Things move quickly in wartime, her mother had once told her. *I met your father in nineteen fourteen. Married him two months later, just before they shipped him off to France.*

She searched the face of the man standing before her. Even in the dark, she could see the hope in his eyes. *He likes me,* she thought. *Fancy that!*

"I didn't mind." She answered truthfully. "It was just... unexpected. I'm not used to flattery, Mr Tyler."

"You have to call me Robin, and it wasn't flattery. I meant it."

Jessica's neck was prickling. Someone was watching. "Robin, I –"

"I'd like to kiss you again," he said quickly. "Properly." His gaze was intense, searching. "May I?"

"Um..." She must have had a gormless look on her face, for he laughed lightly and tucked a stray hair behind her ear.

"I'll take that for consent." He bent his face towards her.

His kiss was not unpleasant – in fact it felt very much like kissing Jon, except that Robin tasted of ale and toffee. His lips were warm and soft, not too insistent, but she sensed he wanted more.

Drawing back, he scanned her face. "Is it too soon, Jessica? I know you must still grieve your husband."

"Well..." she started, but too late. He pulled her to him and kissed her again. This time he was more demanding. She allowed him to part her lips, and her arms, hanging limp at her sides, edged up of their own accord until her hands rested lightly on his sides.

"*Mum!*"

Jessica leapt as though scalded. Robin released her and she looked up to find Mary on the porch, hands on hips and glaring down at her with all the outrage an eight-year-old can muster.

"Coming..." She threw an apologetic grimace in Robin's direction and fled up the porch steps.

Closing the front door, she leaned against it and exhaled gustily, waiting until she heard the car door shut and the engine start.

Mary stood in the hall, her small face pinched and angry. "What were you *doing*, Mummy? If you want to kiss someone, why does it have to be Mr Tyler? I don't like him."

"Neither do I," added Thomas, coming out of the parlour.

Jessica regarded her children, sadly. *They miss their father.* She felt unhappy and confused – which was probably not the way you should feel after a handsome man has just kissed you and told you he finds you beautiful.

She sighed, "Go put your pyjamas on."

They turned away and Jessica remained where she was, leaning against the door, listening to the car's engine fading into the distance.

Suddenly she felt heavy and tired but she needed to prepare something for tea. She was about to push away from the door when a shadow emerged from the parlour. In the dimness of evening, he was a silhouette before the golden glow from the room behind him.

His voice was an accented whisper. "I do not like him either."

***

The evening was chilly for late spring and even though the day had been warm, the stone of Broughton Hall cooled quickly. Jessica had Alexandra Broughton's memoir in one hand, a cup of cocoa in the other; the children were in bed and the captain had been invited to have supper in the cottage with Sam and Marg.

Jessica was alone and happy to be so. Relaxed on the couch, feet extended towards the fire, she'd been reading Alexandra Broughton's journal for some time when she closed it and placed it on her lap.

The girl was in the grip of an unrequited love, even though she knew the object of her adorations was utterly unsuitable.

Lost in her thoughts, Jessica started as the parlour door swung open and a man stood on the threshold.

"Good heavens, Captain, you scared the life out of me!"

"I am sorry," he made to step further into the room but paused. "I have returned from the cottage. Do you wish to be alone?"

"No, please." She waved at the chair across the fireplace from her. "I didn't expect you back so soon. Did you enjoy your meal?"

The German officer sat. "Frau Clay made a pie. It was very good."

He was tired, she could tell because his accent was always thicker when he was tired. *He is still convalescing*, she reminded herself with some surprise. *He never says anything but he's not back to full strength.*

Nodding towards the book on her lap, he said, "Have you read more? What is happening?"

"Alexandra is in love with a man who is very unsuitable. She will never be allowed to marry him."

"Ah. Unsuitable lovers are the most tempting, *ja*?"

Jessica regarded him curiously, wondering if he was referring to Robin Tyler but his expression seemed innocent enough. She turned away and stared into the flames.

Finally, the captain said, "Has this made you sad?"

She chuckled, a little embarrassed, and looked across at him. "I know I'm being silly, but I feel sorry for her. She loves him so much – even though they have no future together."

The captain stretched his legs out before the fire and sucked in a deep breath. His breathing sounded slightly raspy. *Must be cold outside*, she thought, as she watched the dancing flames again.

"We must continue reading. Perhaps she does marry this man." He grinned. "Perhaps he will carry her away on the white horse!"

Jessica smiled and bowed her head in agreement. "I didn't know you were such a romantic." When he merely shrugged, she said, "Who knows? Maybe she wins him in the end. Here," she rose and handed him the journal. "Read it for yourself. Goodnight Captain."

"Süße Träume, Frau Jessie. "

Chapter 12

Jessica stood at the garden door, absently looking outside as she finished doing the washing up. The crimson evening sky was casting an eerie orange glow over everything – a storm was brewing.

Ordinarily she would have asked Thomas and Mary to help with clearing the dishes but this night she was loathe to interrupt the game taking place on the kitchen table. Her children had dragged Jon's oak shove ha'penny board out of the sideboard in the dining room and, after a quick ten minute run-down of the rules, had challenged the German captain to a winner-take-all contest.

The *all* that the winner would take consisted of a tin of fruit Thomas had won off his friend – the one with the billeted Yanks – in a similar game. Thomas, as current champion, had invited contenders, and his sister and the captain were quick to take up the challenge.

Jessica smiled as the opponents battled it out, each shove resulting in either cheers or groans, depending on whose turn it had been, and the result.

Captain Vogel and Mary were united against Thomas's arrogance, but once the reigning champ had been defeated, the battle turned serious between the two remaining competitors.

The Captain was either genuinely hopeless at the game, or was delivering a remarkable performance as someone *seemingly* hopeless at the game, for Mary consistently chalked up her three points, and, in a final play-off, won the tin of fruit.

She held it between two hands and examined the coloured label. "I don't even know what that is, Mum," she said pointing.

"It's a pineapple," Jessica responded. It was sad that in these times of war and rationing, most English children didn't know what a pineapple was. "And that," she added, gesturing with the cup she was drying, "is a banana."

Mary held the tin out to her mother. "Can you open it, so we can share?"

"That's very generous of you, love." Jessica had avoided looking at Thomas since he'd lost the champion's title, but now she glanced his way and saw his little face brighten.

"I do not need to share this fruit," the captain said. "I will go for a walk outside."

"No!" Thomas cried.

"We want you to share with us," Mary added, but the captain shook his head.

He was about to respond when a loud rapping on the window startled them all. Reacting with military swiftness, the German leapt into the corner of the kitchen, beyond view of the window.

The rapping came again and Jessica was about to lift the edge of the curtain when Sam's voice called out, "Missus! You there?"

Both she and the captain exhaled in relief, while the children visibly relaxed in their chairs.

Jessica threw open the garden door.

"What on ear –" she started.

"Missus..." Sam panted, coming into the kitchen. He'd run from the stables, and blew into the room on a violent blast of wind. "It's Norma... she's trying to drop 'er calf, and 'aving a right difficult time of it, she is."

"Oh lord, so soon?" Jessica grabbed her cardigan from the back of a chair and followed Sam outside. "You kids stay here," she threw over her shoulder and pulled the door closed behind her.

Sam was already halfway down the path. He beckoned urgently and she ran to catch up. He shouted something over his shoulder but the gusting wind whipped his words away.

"What?" she cried, jogging to catch up.

"She's struggling," he repeated. "I think the calf is too big, or not positioned right..."

They arrived at the stable to find Norma lying in a circle of light from a lamp hung on the wall. She was panting, her gentle eyes glazed and rolled back with pain. The stall had been filled with fresh straw that was now wet and filthy. The air was humid, smelling strongly of blood and urine and cow breath.

Norma was groaning and heaving, her legs working restlessly in the hay. Part of the water sack trailed from her nether regions, deflated and glistening wetly.

Sam crouched beside the cow's head. "Aye, you're very brave, ain't you girl."

"How long has she been like this?" Jessica stared fearfully at the struggling animal.

"Labour started about eight hours ago. The sack started showing about two hours ago but it 'asn't moved since." He stroked Norma's face tenderly with his calloused hand. "If we need to 'elp 'er, we probably should get to it."

Jessica met the cow's frightened eye. Her own eyes stung with sympathetic tears. "The trouble is knowing the best time to help her and when it's too late."

At a sound behind them, they both turned to find the German standing there. "Or," he said, "when it is too early."

That's right – his parents have kuhe, *as he calls them.*

"My father always says," he stepped into the stall, "that you should only help the *Kuhe* when you can see three things. Either the face *und* two front feet, or the tail *und* two back feet."

"You done this before, lad?" Sam asked.

"Oh, *ja*. But there are times when it does not go well."

As though she understood his words, Norma bellowed painfully and Jessica's gut twisted. "Three things," she repeated.

"Do you want me to look?" the captain volunteered.

"Sam? Do you think –?"

"Aye, if the lad's got experience in this. I'm 'appy to let 'im."

Anton squatted at Norma's side, running a gentle hand along her belly, moving slowly towards her tail. He didn't speak, but Jessica read the concern in his eyes. *More grey than blue in this light. Why am I even thinking about that now? Ridiculous woman!*

The German captain moved behind the cow and made an examination beneath her tail.

"*Sehr gut*, I cannot do more now... I will need to wash first. Hot water... soap."

"I'll wait here for you." Jessica stroked Norma's head as the captain nodded and left them. Norma groaned again, and heaved, painfully and ponderously, to her feet.

Jessica pressed her knuckles to her teeth and gave a sympathetic sob. "Oh God, Sam. She's in too much pain!"

"She's in labour, lass."

"No, it's worse... I've seen cows in labour before. This is worse."

They watched helplessly as Norma paced about the stall, swaying on her feet, the yellowish sac trailing from her. Then, with a great huff, she dropped heavily to her knees in the straw, and flopped down, rolling clumsily onto her side. The whites of her eyes were showing and her hooves pawed at the straw. Bulges rolled and rippled across her distended abdomen.

Frustrated by her helplessness, Jessica went to stand at the stable door. The wind was thrashing the trees, and leaves and twigs were blowing about the yard. She could feel the static in the air – the storm was almost upon them. *Come on Captain, what's taking so long?*

To her relief, she heard the pounding of boots along the path from the house. The German officer arrived at a run, all but crashing into her as she hovered in the doorway.

The captain dashed to the stall and was immediately on his knees beside the cow, and as Sam held her thrashing rear legs, the German made a further examination.

"Oh, *ja*," he muttered, then sat back on his heels. "There are *four* things." He looked across at Sam. "Four feet."

Jessica groaned dismally.

Sam said, "All right. 'Ave you seen this before, lad?"

The German nodded grimly. "The... er, *Kalb*... it will need to be turned. It will be difficult ... The cow, she will be ..." he didn't finish for Norma had kicked his hand away in an effort to get back on her feet, but this time she flailed about, unable to stand.

"Go back to the 'ouse." Sam told Jessica. His voice was firm, his face grim. "Go put the kettle on, stay inside. We'll do what we can."

***

Jessica paced back and forth in front of the stove. The weather howled round the house, clawing at the stonework, battering the windows. Eventually, her anxious tread wore down even the children who begged her to sit.

"What's up with this weather?" she demanded in frustration. "It's driving me insane."

"Miss Haberfield talked about it at school," Mary informed her. "She says it's normal for spring – it's called a haster – nothing to worry about."

"Well, Miss Haberfield doesn't have a labouring cow in the stables," Jessica retorted, irritably.

Over the course of the next two hours she made cups of tea that she didn't drink and attempted a game of shove ha'penny that she couldn't concentrate on. She wandered about the house, refilling the oil lamps and checking the windows were all closed against the rain. Finally, worn out with worry and unable to find adequate diversion, she sat at the kitchen table and gnawed a hangnail.

Mary and Thomas were, in the way of most children, easily distracted and the kitchen soon rang with their chatter and laughter and the clatter of the ha'pennies sliding along the game board, or occasionally falling to the floor.

And Jessica, in the way of stressed parents, fretfully watched the clock, and the longer the wait, the more convinced she became that the situation would not end well for Norma. Her heart ached with empathy for the poor creature. As a woman experienced in the pain and fear of childbirth, she felt an innate feminine bond with the cow.

Suddenly overcome with melancholy, her eyes welled. She blinked quickly against the inexorable rush of emotion.

My children are growing up without a father. I will grow old without a husband. Adolf Hitler is hell-bent on taking over Europe. Young men and women are sacrificing their lives in defence of our country. And I'm weeping because there's a poor cow dying in agony in my stable.

In her self-absorption, she was unaware that her children had fallen silent until Mary put her hand over her mother's.

"Mummy, it'll be all right."

Jessica gave an involuntary sob and a tear splashed onto the table.

At that moment, the garden door crashed open with a blast of cold, wet air and Sam burst in. "She's all right!" he announced without preamble, adding, "and we 'ave a fine baby boy, Missus."

Jessica had bounded to her feet when Sam came in, now she slumped, weak with relief, against the cupboards.

"I didn't know that cow was so important, Mummy," Thomas said.

"Neither did I." Jessica sniffed, laughing and weeping together. She pulled a hanky out of her sleeve. "Where's Captain Vogel?" She wiped her eyes and blew her nose.

"Still with 'er. 'E'll be in soon. I'd best be getting back out there to 'elp 'im tidy up and 'elp Norma get settled."

"Can we come and see the baby cow?" Thomas asked.

Jessica deferred to Sam. "Pr'aps tomorrow," he said.

"She's very tired, Thomas," Jessica added. "She's worked hard to have her baby."

"And she doesn't need you running around like an eejit," Mary added for emphasis.

"Stop picking on me!"

"Leave 'er be tonight," Sam halted the budding dispute. "You can come down tomorrow." He turned to Jessica who was blowing her nose. "Anton did well. It were all 'is work. 'E'll be in shortly."

***

Half an hour later, the children were upstairs getting ready for bed and Jessica stood alone by the kitchen window. The rain was streaming down the darkened glass; the flickering lamplight behind her turned the window into a black mirror. In it she saw the cupboards, the kitchen table with the remains of a shove ha'penny game scattered across it and a bright pink Carr's biscuit tin.

Suddenly, her eye was drawn to a reflected movement in the corner. Whirling about, she was certain she'd seen a black and white dog but in that moment, the garden door flew open and the captain stood on the threshold.

"Good God!" Jessica grabbed a handful of his shirt and dragged him inside, slamming the door firmly behind him. "Look at the state of you!"

The captain's shirt, arms and hands were caked with blood, cow dung and other, indiscernible filth. And, besides that, he smelled like it too, but he grinned at her, showing even white teeth, and blew at the hair hanging over his eyes.

"She is not out of danger – the next few days will tell, but she lives, *und* the baby too."

"Thanks to you – thanks *so much* to you!"

He shrugged shyly and looked away. "I must wash... could you," he held up his bloodied hands, "*Vielleicht*, could you help, please? I do not want to touch anything."

"Yes, of course. Come upstairs, I'll light the boiler."

He followed her upstairs to the bathroom. In the corner was the cast-iron water boiler. A bucket of anthracite sat beside it – fortunately anthracite wasn't rationed, so the Broughton Hall inhabitants continued to enjoy the luxury of hot water.

Jessica allowed the boiler fire to go out during the night although it wasn't fully dead yet. She dropped a scoop of anthracite lumps through the lid and returned the fire to life.

Opening the tap over the bath, she released the hot water in a steaming jet into the tub.

"It is *gut, ja*, this hot water. It is for the kitchen also?"

"Yes. We – Jon and I – put the boiler up here so it could gravity-feed the kitchen too; such a luxury! Now arms up... let's get that shirt off."

Recalling her previous embarrassment, he grinned playfully and raised his arms, exposing the waistband of his trousers. Her eyes were involuntarily drawn to his naked abdomen and fine trail of light-brown hair.

Reddening, she looked up and found his eyes on her and her cheeks grew hot. "I'm sorry, I meant..." she stammered, while he continued to grin at her. "Put your arms down, Captain," she snapped, taking refuge in irritability. "I'm so used to my children... I forgot myself."

He dropped his arms and began unbuttoning his shirt while she leaned over the bath, testing the water temperature.

"It is all right, Frau Jessie," he said, behind her. She could hear the rustling of his shirt and felt the air move as it dropped to the floor. "I like to tease you."

"Well don't!" She wondered how much of his familiarity was due to seeing her kissing Robin Tyler. *He thinks I'm loose, but I'm not.* More composed, she straightened and looked at him.

He stood before her, naked to the waist but for the dog tags hanging about his neck. His recent illness had certainly stripped meat from his bones, but only seemed to add definition to his silhouette. He had the proportions of an athlete. "Saving cows makes you cheerful," she observed.

He shrugged one shoulder and smiled. "Of course. Are you not cheerful?"

"Yes, I am." She dropped her gaze to his feet. He was still wearing his boots. "I'm relieved and very grateful to you. Here," she indicated the three-legged stool behind him, "sit here. I'll help with your boots."

He obeyed, and she knelt before him, working at one set of laces. They were wet and tight but loosened with a little effort and he raised his leg to help her.

"You do not like me teasing you," he commented, as she started on the second boot.

"It's not that I don't like it." As she spoke she picked at the lace; it was tighter than the first. Eventually the knot worked open, "I just don't expect it. I mean," she looked up at him, "you *are* German, after all."

He reached down and removed the boot himself. "What does that mean?"

The captain's eyes were more grey than blue and regarded her narrowly. She couldn't tell if he was angry. She edged back on her heels to search his face.

His expression was inscrutable. "It's just that," she explained, "we English, we think... well, Germans are not known for a sense of humour."

"Oh," he rose and looked down at her. "I see. In that case, I would say that you English do not know we Germans very well."

Was he standing over her to intimidate? If so, it was working. She got up and shut off the bath taps. "Perhaps that's true," she said over her shoulder, "but most English people have never met a German person. The thought of meeting one is truly terrifying."

She straightened to find him watching her with interest. "I can understand how that could be. Now, Frau Jessie," his hand moved to the buttons on his trousers, "you must leave the room because I am about to take off my trousers *und* as I am not wearing underwear you will see *mein Schwanz und* that would be truly terrifying."

***

Jessica heard the laughter and sounds of cheer as she approached the kitchen. She pushed the door open and found Sam and the children seated at the table. Marg was removing the steaming kettle from the hob.

"Cuppa, Missus?" she asked.

Jessica held up the bottle she'd collected from the cabinet in the parlour. "I thought we might celebrate with something stronger. I've been saving it." The bottle of Tokay had been brought from Slovenia by a friend of Jon's. "Jon kept it for a special occasion, but I think we should open it and make tonight a special occasion. You two can have cocoa," she added to Thomas and Mary.

"Ooh, I 'aven't 'ad a decent glass o' anything in an age," Sam said. "Where's Anton?"

"Upstairs... having a bath."

"'E were right in it, you know. Bloody filthy business it were, too. Did a marvellous job, 'e did. Reckon 'e mighta done it before."

While they were talking, Marg took four short glasses from the cupboard and put them on the table, pushing aside the remains of the board game. She poured two cups worth of milk into a saucepan to heat on the range for the children's cocoa. "'Is parents keep cows," she said.

"They also grow hops for beer," Jessica added.

At that moment, the door opened and the man in question came into the room, freshly scrubbed and wearing a clean pair of trousers and shirt.

In the flickering lamp light, Anton's face looked drawn and tired, but he raised his eyes to Jessica's and she drew in her breath. *My God, he's handsome...* She mentally shook herself. *He's also three years younger than me and...* and *he's the enemy*!

Somehow the fact that their two countries were at war didn't seem to carry as much weight as it once did. Jessica smiled at him – probably the first genuine smile she'd given him. *I smile so rarely these days.*

His lips gave a slight twitch in response.

Jessica uncorked the bottle and poured four glasses of Tokay.

Chapter 13

It was raining – had been for days; steadily streaming down the panes of glass and flooding the garden with life-giving spring showers. Jessica rose from her bed, and went to look outside. By the colour of the sky she could tell it was late afternoon but strangely, she felt no compunction at having slept through the day.

The colours of the garden were bright and glistening wetly; a trickle of water snaked along the stone window-ledge, like mercury.

Jessica turned away. Moving to her door, she stepped into the hallway. An unfamiliar, patterned rug ran along the floor. It felt plush and expensive beneath her bare feet as she made her way towards the stairs at the end of the corridor.

Her hand trailed lightly along the wall as she walked; she noted how clean and fresh the plaster seemed, not scuffed and worn as she knew it.

At the stairs, a border collie dog waited. Its tail swung lazily from side to side, its mouth open in a wide canine grin.

"Jemima?" Jessica was surprised at the sound of her own voice, as if her tongue didn't work properly, the word clumsily formed as though she was unused to speaking but even so, the dog knew her name and trotted forwards, stopping at the library door.

Unthinkingly, Jessica went in, halting in mild confusion.
Where did all these books come from?
She drifted about the wood-panelled room, pausing before a wall consisting entirely of works bound in fresh red, blue and green leather. The rows reached as high as the ceiling and spanned wall to wall – neat, orderly lines of reference and classical literature.

Jessica's fingers rippled over the texture of their spines:

the ancients, Sophocles and Pliny; the classics, Chaucer and Shakespeare; modern works by Richard Graves, Mary Ann Hanway, John Shebbeare. The sciences were represented: Professor Hugh Jones, Jan Czekanowski, *L'Histoire naturelle* by Georges Buffon, their names illuminated in gold lettering beneath her fingertips.

Moving away from the shelves, Jessica was strangely unsurprised to find she was not alone.

The girl sat in a chair by the window, one leg folded beneath her. She wore a dress of green wool, her hair was a cloud of unruly brown tendrils reaching below her shoulders and her eyes, a warm, darkly-fringed brown, regarded Jessica curiously.

"You're Alexandra, aren't you?" Jessica said.

By her expression, Jessica thought Alexandra couldn't hear her, but the girl's eyes locked, without fear, on her own.

"Jessica..."

"You know my name?"

"Jessie..."

"Alexandra...?" Jessica moved a step closer to the girl.

"Frau Jessie...?

***

Jessica felt as though she'd fallen from a great height to land with a thud on her bed.

Her eyes snapped open and she gasped – a shocked, squeaking sound – at the face hovering over her in the pearly light of early morning.

"Frau Jessie... I am sorry to startle you..."

"Captain Vogel!" Jessica gasped, clawing the bedclothes modestly to her chin. "What is it?"

"I am sorry..." he said again and retreated a step or two from the bed. "I needed to awaken you. It is Thomas. Come quickly... he is unwell."

All thoughts of modesty flew out the window, as Jessica leapt from the bed and reached for her dressing-gown in a single movement.

The German turned away and she followed, belting the robe as she went. She made to turn towards her son's room but the Captain said, "No, this way."

Jessica's heart began to hammer in her chest – a mother's intuitive warning, "What's he doing in your room?" she demanded. Without waiting for an answer, she hurried to the bed where the child lay sleeping. His arms were flung out, his face flushed, the traces of tears on his cheeks. "What have you done to him?"

Even as she said it, she knew it was unfair. The boy was sleeping but why he was in the man's bed was another matter and Jessica felt sick.

"Thomas," she said gently, touching her son's shoulder. "Thomas, love. Wake up... it's Mummy."

The child stirred, his swollen eyelids fluttering and opening a crack. "Thomas, what's wrong?"

"Mummy?" he murmured. "I feel sick."

"Can you get up? Let's get you back to your own bed."

The child's face crumpled and he began to cry.

"Oh, love, you're burning up. What is it?" Jessica cried. She tore back the bedclothes and pulled him towards her.

"I have a sore throat," Thomas rasped. "Here …" he indicated his glands.

"I can carry him to his room," the captain offered, stepping closer.

"Move back!" Jessica snapped. "Stay away from my son!" She held Thomas's perspiring body. "Come on, love. Let's get you to your room."

Thomas was only eight but he was a sturdy little boy and a healthy weight. Jessica grunted with the effort of helping him get up. With not a glance at the man standing unhappily behind her, she carried her son out of the room.

***

"Spring cold," Marg asserted, "'e'll be all right with a bit of rest."

Jessica sighed. She was sitting on the edge of her son's bed. "Hear that?" she addressed Thomas. "Mrs Clay says you're to stay in bed."

"All right," Thomas agreed. Evidently he was too poorly to put up an argument.

Jessica waited until the older woman left the room then, casually tucking the blankets around her son's chin, said, "Love, tell me something. Why were you in Mr Bird's bed? Did he... invite you? Was it his idea?"

For an agonising moment the boy didn't respond, "You're not in trouble," she added, gently. "I just want to know."

"Is Mr Bird angry with me?"

"No, why would he be angry with you?"

"Because he didn't know I was there. He woke up with a surprise and asked me what I was doing."

Jessica puffed out her cheeks in a relieved sigh but for her own peace of mind, she repeated, "So Mr Bird didn't ask you to go to his room?"

The child shook his head.

"And he has never come into your room, during the night or... or any time?"

"No, Mummy." Thomas's damp little face gazed anxiously at her, his eyes glistening with tears. "He's angry, isn't he?"

"No, love, he's not angry. But I just want to know, did you go to his room because you felt sick?"

The boy nodded.

Jessica was vaguely aware that Marg had returned with a

steaming cup of lemon tea sweetened with honey. "There, there little fellow," the older woman soothed. Thomas shuffled up in bed and received the mug. "This'll make it all better."

***

Jessica left Thomas sleeping peacefully. She'd been in to check on him earlier and was satisfied to find he'd eaten the food she'd taken him. Collecting the empty dishes, she softly closed the door and leaned against it.

It had been a busy day; she felt she hadn't had a moment to sit and catch her breath.

What next? she thought, wearily. With a gusty sigh, she pushed away from the door, knowing that *what next* was an apology.

She found him sitting at the kitchen table, a pot of tea and two cups before him. He looked up as she came in and proceeded to pour the tea, pushing a cup towards the empty place closest to the range where she generally sat.

The kitchen felt close and she was a little clammy. *Guilt will do that*, Jessica thought contritely as she stacked Thomas's plate and cup in the sink.

Pushing up the sleeves of her worn cardigan, she sat and stirred a small amount of milk through her tea.

"Captain," she began, eyes on her cup.

"Is he all right?" the German interrupted.

She nodded and raised her eyes to his face. "Yes, thank you. It's just a cold. Look... I must apologise. This morning, I –"

He held up a hand. "Frau Jessie, please do not."

"I feel terrible. I wouldn't let you speak and I jumped to – I jumped to the wrong conclusion. An appalling conclusion. It was very insulting to you and I am sorry."

"You are a mother."

Jessica felt her ire rise. "Why do you have to be so bloody

understanding all the time?" she demanded.

He gestured undecidedly. "My mother would have acted the same way with a stranger beneath her roof."

Jessica lowered her eyes, tracing the pink roses around the rim of her teacup. "Every day, Captain," she said softly, "you become less of a stranger."

"I am happy to hear it. *Und* while we are being honest, I want to tell you that I owe you a great debt."

She lifted her head and it was his turn to look away as he spoke. "Had you not allowed me into your home, I would surely have died. Had you turned me over to your authorities, I would be a prisoner – if I were still alive. But neither of these has happened, thanks to you."

Jessica exhaled wearily. "You're as good as a prisoner here. You can't go anywhere."

He pushed his chair back and went to look out the kitchen window. "But I am alive *und* I can *hope* to see my family again."

Turning suddenly, he leaned against the sink. "This morning when I came to wake you, you said *Alexandra* in your sleep. Were you dreaming? Did you dream of the girl in the book?"

"Oh, yes!" In the flurry of the day's events, Jessica had completely forgotten. "Yes, I'd been dreaming that I was in the library and Alexandra was there. I was trying to talk to her."

Captain Vogel nodded with interest. "Perhaps we should read more of her story."

She nodded in return. "Perhaps we should. When shall we go to the cemetery?" she asked, suddenly. "I'm keen to see if we can find any Broughtons there – perhaps even Alexandra's grave."

"Whenever you like. It would be interesting."

Jessica sipped her tea and observed him momentarily. "You speak English very well, you know."

The captain smiled. "Most of the time. Sometimes it is easier to read English than to speak it, particularly when I am tired."

"I've noticed. When you were unwell, you spoke slowly and your accent was stronger." Jessica rose and looked out the kitchen window. Summer was nearly upon them; evenings were longer, slower to slip into dusk. The sky was bruised; shades of lavender and lilac, shot through with ribbons of pink.

"Do you think I will soon sound like Herr Clay?"

Jessica gave a short laugh. "I doubt it." As she continued to watch through the window, the night closed in, and the colours shifted, deepening to purple and violet.

The captain came to stand behind her. The life radiating from him caused her skin to prickle with intense awareness. How comforting it would be to lean back and rest her weight against him, to feel the solid security of a man's strength supporting her.

"I enjoy talking about the diary with you," Jessica said, impulsively. Instantly her face grew hot.

Shaking off her foolishness, she turned abruptly and caught a strange, thoughtful look on his face. But it passed so quickly it could have been the shifting light from the lamp on the bench beside her.

"Let's go to the cemetery early tomorrow," she suggested, "before anyone is up."

He nodded. "All right. But now, I will check Norma *und* her baby." He moved away and Jessica resisted the urge to follow him into the lovely soft night.

At the garden door, the captain paused, head cocked as the sound of engines vibrated on the edge of their hearing.

The low drone seemed to reverberate and expand as it drew closer.

I wonder how he feels hearing those.

"*Gute nacht*, Frau Jessie," the captain said, breaking into her thoughts.

"Good night, Captain. Please lock the door when you come back in."

He nodded and went outside, closing the door softly behind him. She watched briefly from the window. He moved along the path, a colourless shade blending with the thickening shadows of the night, then she turned away.

Without warning, the kitchen exploded.

The intensity of the blast blew the window inwards and Jessica was thrown like a rag doll across the room. Unconscious before she hit the ground, she lay in a twisted heap as the world erupted in light and shattering glass around her.

Splinters of crockery, plaster and wood fell like rain over her insensible body.

Chapter 14

Broughton Hall shook on its foundations. The ground beneath the house trembled and heaved with the impact.

Jessica lay groaning, partially buried beneath the wreckage of her kitchen.

Her ears were ringing – an eerie sound layered over the silence of a night in shock. Slowly, she came to her senses, watching in dizzy detachment, as red and gold lights danced over the kitchen walls.

Pushing to all fours, coughing and choking on dust and wincing at the splinters of glass beneath her hands, Jessica gazed about in bewilderment.

What the hell just happened?

In a sudden rush of awareness, she remembered the planes flying over – the last sound she'd heard before …

"*The children!*" Jessica cried. Clambering to her feet, she staggered under a wave of dizziness and momentary panic as she wondered how much of her home remained beyond the kitchen.

Just as the thought entered her mind, she heard screaming, thumping echoing through the house.

She exhaled in relief, then, *Glass on the floor!*

Jessica leapt towards the door as Mary and Thomas burst into the kitchen, barefooted, wearing only their pyjamas. They flung themselves into her arms. "You're all right!" she gasped, frantically examining faces, arms, legs. "You're all right! Stand still – there's glass!"

But they were bawling, their eyes wide with fright. "What happened, Mummy? What was that noise?"

"I don't know! I think it was a –" she hated to say the word. "I don't know."

"Mummy, a fire!" Thomas was pointing behind her. Jessica turned to the glassless window and saw spears of flame thrusting into the night sky; gold sparks shooting upwards from the rubble that had been the stables.

"Oh, God!" Jessica's stomach rebelled and she swallowed the urge to throw up. *The captain... Norma*!

Grasping each child by an arm, she forced them down, "Under the table! Don't move until I get back!" She scrambled cautiously over the rubble to the garden door. It hung precariously on a single hinge and fell as she grabbed it, banging resoundingly as it hit the floor. "I'm serious," Jessica shouted at her children. They were hugging each other, their faces white with shock. "Don't move a muscle!"

Jessica ran out into the yard. "*Captain*!" she screamed. "*Anton...*!" The stable was ablaze. She got as close as she dared, shielding her face with her arms. There was no sign of him.

Panicking, she ran, skirting the flames and heat. From within the inferno came a crash of timbers as the roof collapsed, sending a geyser of sparks into the night sky.

"Missus!" A dark shape loomed through the flickering light.

"Sam!" she gasped, rushing towards the old man. "The captain... Norma – they're in there!" Her face hurt and her hands shook uncontrollably as she clutched at her steward.

"Norma's not in there," Sam yelled above the roar of the fire. "Anton knew that. Where–?"

"Over 'ere!" The shout was barely audible over the scream and thunder of the flames. Sam and Jessica flew to where Marg knelt beside an inert body.

"'E's alive," Marg gasped, as the pair dropped, panting, to their knees beside her. "Knocked out, I think."

The German was lying face down, half buried beneath the mud and dirt thrown up in the blast. He groaned as his senses slowly returned, coughed and groaned again.

Sam rolled him over and helped him sit up. "Anton? You 'ear me?"

Jessica held her breath as the captain blinked dazedly at the three faces before him. Slowly he seemed to be regaining consciousness and his eyes locked with hers.

"*Meine Liebling...*" he murmured, suddenly pulling her into his arms. He buried his face in her neck and her arms went around him. Clinging and bunching the back of his shirt in her fists, she sobbed into his chest.

***

At length, the captain and Jessica drew apart. Pushing back, he smoothed Jessica's hair from her brow and wiped the tears from her grimy face. "*Es ist in Ordnung, meine Liebling, es ist in Ordnung...*"

Jessica gazed at the German officer. His eyes were dark pools reflecting the leaping flames behind her. "I thought..." she croaked, "I –"

She was suddenly aware of Sam and Marg beside them, exchanging surprised looks as she and the captain held each other.

"Let's get inside," Sam said, glancing nervously over his shoulder. "Won't be long before someone from Jackson's 'Eath comes investigating that blast. Let the stables burn – can't do nowt about it now."

Marg helped Jessica haul herself up while Sam supported the captain. They quickly made their way back to the house where, in the jumping glow of the stable fire, Jessica saw the children still huddled beneath the kitchen table.

They began wailing when they saw her but Jessica held up a staying hand. "Don't come out!" she ordered, hearing the crunch of broken glass beneath her shoes. She realised that the captain's arm was about her waist and felt the loss of it as he released her. "I'll get your slippers," she told the twins.

"I'll go," Marg volunteered. "Poor little lambs," she added, hurrying away.

Sam had gone outside. He returned with a broom and bucket and began sweeping up the shattered glass and crockery.

"Jessie, Anton, you sit, both of you," he insisted and Jessica complied, dropping with nervous exhaustion into a chair. Her hands and knees were still trembling and beginning to sting from the dozens of glass-splinter cuts. She examined her hands, turning them over and back, avoiding the captain's gaze.

Something had passed between them. In the aftermath of fear and destruction, in the intense relief that the other was unharmed, something had passed between them.

And now, bewildered and self-conscious, Jessica couldn't look at him.

**

Anton was equally disconcerted and continued to stand irresolutely by the range. Marg returned with the children's slippers, a bottle of Dettol and a handful of cotton balls. "'Ere you go, lovies."

Mary and Thomas gratefully took their slippers and scrambled from beneath the table, rushing at their mother.

Anton was feeling shaken and vague. His skin tingled with Frau Jessie's proximity but such was his confusion over the situation that he couldn't look at her.

"Anton, sit!" Marg ordered and, thankful of the distraction, he obeyed. "Let me look at you in the light."

"Mummy, your hands!" Mary exclaimed. "And Mr Bird, your face is bruised and you have a big cut right here –"

"All right, little miss, out of the way," Marg scolded gently. She dabbed antiseptic on Anton's wounds, while behind her, Sam swept the remains of the wreckage into a bucket, raising a cloud of dust.

While all this was going on, a group of men from Jackson's

Heath arrived. Having heard the explosion and seen the flames colouring the sky, they'd climbed the orchard wall and come to help. Fortunately, Thomas spotted them in the firelight before they got to the house.

Sam and Jessica intercepted the group and confirmed that everyone at Broughton Hall was well and safe.

From the kitchen, Anton could hear raised voices cursing the Luftwaffe, before they made a final grumbling inspection of the ruined stables.

After the men returned to the village, Anton helped Sam secure the garden door in some temporary fashion; more permanent repairs could be made in the light of day. They removed several wicked glass shards still wedged in the window frame, and made a temporary window covering by nailing a few planks over it.

It was all that could be done for the time being.

***

Sometime later, the six residents of Broughton Hall sat nursing warming cups of cocoa. Jessica had taken surreptitious peeks at the captain over the rim of her mug and was upset by the bruising on his face. *But he's alive*, she told herself, relieved. She refused to think about the tide of emotion that had swept over them, and their desperate, unthinking embrace beside the devastation that was her stables.

Occasionally, she felt his eyes on her but couldn't meet them. Whatever had passed between them, he must have felt it too, and Jessica was confused and unsettled.

Eventually, the tumult of the night's events waned. Thomas was snuggled on the captain's lap, his tousled head nodding against the man's shoulder, while Mary yawned on her chair and rubbed her eyes.

Jessica took the children upstairs and tucked them safely into their beds; the cocoa had warmed and calmed them.

She returned to the kitchen as Sam said, "That were a bomb, weren't it, Anton? Dropped by accident?"

The German shook his head solemnly. "I do not think it was an accident – we..." he stumbled slightly on the word, but carried on, "we have specific targets – targets that do not include country houses. It was not a bomb; sometimes smaller incendiaries are dropped to light the pilot's way. I believe it was one of these that hit your stable."

"I see," Sam said, grimly. "Makes sense, I suppose. Unfortunately for you, you were outside at the time."

"I was checking Norma."

"Thank God she wasn't in the stables," Jessica spoke, for the first time allowing her eyes to meet the captain's."

"None of the beasties were in the stables," Sam said. "Even Mary's pony was turned out in the paddock, the nights getting warmer an' all. But Norma's youngster don't seem all that interested in feeding like 'e should. Keeping an eye on 'im... Thought it'd be easier if 'e were near the cottage."

Jessica frowned. "Is something wrong with him?"

"Don't think so," Sam replied, "I'm sure 'e'll be fine. But the little fellow's 'ad a tough start to life and..." he shrugged.

"I see." Jessica knew she should worry over the calf but after the events of the night, found she was simply exhausted. "I'll go see him tomorrow morning."

Marg lightly touched Jessica's arm. "'E'll be fine. Sam's just a fusspot. Now," she turned to her husband. "Time to go 'ome, Samuel Clay, it's past three and you need your beauty sleep."

The couple departed and Jessica put the mugs in the sink while the captain secured the fire in the range for the night. He escorted her through the creaking old house and up the stairs, pausing outside her door.

"I apologise," he said soberly. "You were hurt *und* frightened. The children..."

She waved his comments aside. "You did nothing wrong."

"My countrymen caused this – damaged your home, destroyed your stables. *Und* besides that, I fear … it's a matter of time before I am discovered here. My presence is putting you in danger." He gestured helplessly, "At least, Norma *und* the pony had been moved."

Jessica smiled wryly. "Well, it could've been worse. You were hurt more than any of us."

They each held a lamp, and in the flickering light, the wounds on his face were thrown into ghastly relief. "I hope you won't be scarred," she said, adding to herself, *His face is too beautiful.*

Without thinking, she extended a hand to lightly touch the nasty lump rising below his left eye but he caught her fingers and turned her hand over in the light to expose the half-dozen angry little cuts on the back of it.

"I am sorry," he repeated. Then slowly, tentatively, he raised his eyes to hers as he lifted her hand to his lips.

He tenderly kissed the back of her hand and she watched, heart pounding, as he turned it over and pressed his mouth into the cup of her palm.

She gasped involuntarily at the spark of electricity that shot through her, but before she could react further, he folded her fingers, safely sealing in his kiss.

Releasing her hand, he stepped back. "*Schlaf schön*, Frau Jessie."

Jessica stood stunned, pulse racing, and leaning against her door as he turned and strode decisively up the hall. He disappeared into his own room and closed the door without a backward glance.

Chapter 15

The next morning, Jessica awoke to the sound of voices. The late spring sun was pooling on her bedroom floor, showing up the faded and threadbare patches on the carpet.

She stretched and yawned, listening to see if she could identify the owners. One of the voices had the lilting, sibilant sounds of a child, while the other had the deeper tones of an adult male.

Glancing at the clock on her bedside table, she exclaimed, "Lucifer's balls!" and leapt from the bed. "Damn!" She hopped up and down, trying to get her feet into her slippers, while reaching for her dressing-gown. Coming suddenly and fully awake, she realised one of the voices was Thomas's, while the other... she dashed to the window. A new Jaguar was parked by the porch. "Lucifer's great hairy balls!"

Rushing from her bedroom, she barrelled along the hall, plunged down the stairs and threw open the front door.

Thomas was standing with the visitor – a man, leaning against the handrail, arms folded across his chest. They both looked up in surprise as she burst, puffing, onto the porch.

"Mummy! I was just telling Mr Tyler about the explosion last night."

"Morning, Jessica," Robin said, his eyes sifting over her. She suddenly realised that her hair must be sticking up at all angles and her dressing-gown was hanging open to reveal her thin cotton nightdress. She quickly belted her gown and came down the porch steps, raking her fingers through her hair.

"Young Tommy's been filling me in on all the excitement."

"Has he?" Jessica levelled a significant look at her son. "I hope he hasn't been boring you with all the tedious details? Seems we were bombed last night – surely a mistake. Can't imagine the Luftwaffe considering our humble home a strategic target," she repeated Sam's words with a wry smile.

Robin's eyes slid to Jessica's hands. "The Germans left their mark on you, then?"

Jessica's face coloured guiltily as her mind immediately flew to the captain's lips on her palm. "Oh... glass..." she stammered. "The kitchen window was blown in."

"Can I see the damage?"

Thomas's eyes suddenly grew wide with alarm. Jessica spoke calmly, "Thomas, take Mr Tyler round the back... show him the stables."

As the pair disappeared round the side of the house, Jessica whirled about, *Please God, don't let him be in the kitchen*! Tripping on her slippers, she bumped clumsily against the door, regained her balance and bolted back through the house, past the staircase, down the long hall... left turn... four steps... left turn... four steps... past the telephone table...

Bursting into the kitchen, she surprised the German taking the kettle off the hob. "Upstairs!" she gasped breathlessly and leaned on the back of a chair. "*Now!*"

He responded without question, leaping past her mere seconds before Thomas trotted cheerfully through the broken door with Robin Tyler behind him.

The man seemed surprised to see her. "Well, here you are again!"

"Oh..." Jessica waved breezily towards the range. "I forgot the kettle was on..."

"I'll have a cup if you're offering," Robin said, cheerfully inviting himself into the room. His head swung up and round as he stepped through the splintered ruins of the door and frame. Then he headed over to the window and rapped on the boards nailed over it. "Whew... bit of damage."

"Could've been worse." Jessica moved about the kitchen taking out cups and saucers. *We're going to have words about this,* said the glare she shot at her son.

"Will you rebuild the stables?" Tyler sat himself at the table and watched as she poured the boiling water into the teapot.

"God, Robin, I've hardly had a chance to think about it."

"I'll check it out later – see what we can do. Any livestock in there?"

"Mr Clay had moved Norma to the woodshed so she was all right," Thomas piped up.

"Sugar?" Jessica interrupted before Thomas could say anything else.

"One please – provided the stone walls are intact, it may be just a matter of putting on a new roof. I can organise a work party, if you like."

"That would be fun," Thomas began. "It was lucky that –"

"Thomas, go see what Mary's doing please." Jessica brought the teapot to the table. "Tell her Mr Tyler's here and I want you both ready for school before I make your breakfast."

"Okay, Mummy."

"Okay?" Tyler asked. "What's that mean?"

"The Yanks say it," Thomas informed him proudly. "Means all right."

"Off you go." Jessica made a shooing gesture and watched her son leave. *I must get dressed.* She was feeling rather exposed wearing only her nightdress and dressing-gown.

Tyler waited until the boy left the room before getting up from his chair. He came round the table to take her in his arms. "Jessica..." His mouth had come down on hers before she knew it.

Twisting out of his grasp she took up the teapot, pouring the tea so she didn't have to speak. But he wasn't deterred. He stood beside her, stroking her cheek, "My sweet. I only found out this morning. You must have had a nasty fright. Why didn't you call me?"

"I'm all right." Jessica took a step to the side, ostensibly to reach for her own cup, but she was feeling naked and uncomfortable. *And he's so... patronising.*

"I would've come straight away."

"I'm all right," she repeated. *I shouldn't have let him kiss me.* "Don't let your tea get cold."

He looked as though he was about to say something else but thought better of it and returned to his chair. She felt his eyes on her while she busied herself at the sink. *He means well. I shouldn't be so rude to him, but... oh, Christ, how to get rid of him?*

"I was about to make the children's breakfast – I need to get them to school." She hoped this would be his cue to leave and glanced at him over her shoulder. His expression was speculative, but then he smiled. "I only popped over to make sure you're all right. Dad and I heard the blast but had no idea where it'd come from. Harry Woods came over this morning to drop the paper in – told us it was the Hall. Are you upset with me for not coming sooner?"

She dried her hands and came over to the table feeling contrite. He wasn't a bad man, and if it weren't for that bloody Kraut hiding upstairs she might even be happy to see him. "I'm not upset with you, Robin. I'm just a bit... flustered. I'm sorry."

Bloody Kraut, she reaffirmed even as the thought of the captain caused her palm to tingle.

"Perhaps I'll share some porridge," Tyler suggested, reaching for his tea. "Would that be all right?"

No, it's not all right. I have a fucking German officer upstairs and you're scaring me more than he does!

"Of course, Robin," she said, pleasantly. "I know the children enjoy seeing you." *At least Thomas does.*

He grinned and settled back in his chair.

He doesn't look anything like Errol Flynn.

"Please give me a moment. I must get dressed."

***

Tyler stepped over a charred beam and stood looking up at the smoke-blackened stone wall. As he moved, puffs of ash swirled round his feet. "I don't know how sturdy it is," he called to Jessica. He thumped a stone wall experimentally with his fist. "You can see how the mortar's been burned..." he poked a finger into the space between two stones and scratched. "See how it just crumbles?"

Tyler dusted off his hands and kicked at a rafter that lay smouldering amid the devastation. "If you ask me, you should demolish it and rebuild – I couldn't vouch for its stability."

Jessica sighed, as he returned to her. "Nice to have the money." She glared accusingly at the twisted ruins of her butter churn and milking equipment. "I don't even have the means to earn a living now."

"I'm sorry, my sweet, I don't know what else to suggest. Whatever happens, don't let the children play in this mess. It could all come crashing down at any moment."

She sniffed back the emotion building in her chest. "Thank God the animals weren't in there. And Jon's car – Sam keeps it down at the cottage." *How am I going to rebuild this? How am I going to earn a living? What am I going to do? I'm not going to cry...*

Tyler took her shoulders and pulled her into his arms. "You're being so brave."

The luxury of a consoling embrace was irresistible. She allowed him to hold her while he made soothing sounds and stroked her hair.

Finally pulling away, she tugged a hanky from her sleeve and blew her nose. "I'm sorry, Robin," she said thickly. Her throat was aching. She swallowed hard. "It was just such a shock."

"You have my shoulder to lean on, whenever you need it."

"Thank you." She smiled and took a fortifying breath. "I'll be fine now."

"I know you will – but remember, I'm just down the lane."

And too close for comfort, Jessica thought wryly.

***

Before he left, Robin managed to extract a commitment from Jessica that she and the children would visit Krijger the following Saturday.

The children ran around the corner of the house, to where his Jaguar was parked in the driveway, while Robin strolled casually beside their mother. Pausing once the children were out of sight, he said seriously, "Jessica, I feel I've rushed you – it wasn't my intention and I'm sorry." He gave a nervous little chuckle and went on, "I'm not sorry I kissed you, mind, but I'm very aware that you're … you will be grieving your husband. You have so much on your plate. But, I want you to see me as a friend. I'm here for you – whatever you need." He paused, searching her face and wondering why she averted her gaze.

"Thank you, but I have Sam and –"

"An old man," he snorted contemptuously. He gently held her chin and forced her to look at him. Softening his tone, "You must know I want to get to know you, be part of your life – yours and the children's. I know it's early days yet, but," he released her and made an open-handed, helpless gesture. "It's how I feel."

Jessica nodded, and chewed on a hangnail.

Robin went on, "The other evening, after the May Day fair, you were … you seemed receptive. But this morning …" he shrugged, searching for the words. "Jessica?"

***

Jessica felt a pang of suspicion. Something wasn't quite right.

Tyler seemed pleasant company – she could do worse than spend time with him, but not the way he apparently wanted, and so soon.

"Jessica...?" he was watching her.

"Robin, look, I do enjoy your company, but let's get to know one another first. *Okay*?" It was a feeble attempt to lighten the mood, but it worked.

He smiled. "Okay. Well," he drew himself up, "I'd better get going."

Thomas and Mary were waiting beside the Jaguar. Jessica heard Thomas giggle at the brotherly peck Robin placed on her cheek, but Mary frowned thoughtfully.

Once Robin was gone, Jessica felt she could breathe again. "Right you two," she addressed the twins, "get your satchels. Bus'll be here any moment."

Thomas took off at a run towards the back of the house but Mary walked beside her. "Mummy, what's going on with Mr Tyler?"

"Nothing," Jessica responded. "We're friends, that's all."

Her daughter's expression suggested Mary wasn't buying that for a moment. She said, "He likes you but I don't think we should be his friend. I don't trust him."

"What if *I* like him?"

Mary narrowed her eyes. "You don't. I can tell."

Jessica chuckled and dropped an arm around Mary's shoulders as they turned towards the house. "Oh, you can tell, can you?"

Mary stopped and glared mutinously at her. "Don't poke fun! I can *tell* he likes you and I can tell something else too. He's up to something. He seems to be in an awful rush to be our friend and I don't trust him."

With that she ducked from beneath Jessica's arm and ran to catch up with her brother.

***

"It's not connecting." Jessica was sitting at the telephone table in the hall.

"That's normal, though," Marg said from the doorway, a tea towel in her hands. "If they took a battering last night it may be some time before the lines 're up again."

"I suppose." Jessica got to her feet and followed the housekeeper into the kitchen. "I'm making a few loaves today – hopefully a week's worth – I'd better get started."

"I've cut some rosemary you can put through the dough," Marg offered. "Take away the blandness of that bloody 'orrible flour. Where's Anton?"

"Helping Sam finish the milking – he had to wait until Robin left." Jessica grunted, as she hefted a bag of the grey, national flour towards the table. She placed a measure into a mixing bowl, added water, fresh yeast, a bit of butter, then began turning the ingredients with a hand.

Marg finished tidying the kitchen and went outside, returning a few moments later with the rosemary.

"The milking has to be done by hand now the equipment's gone." Jessica said dismally. She turned the dough onto the table and began kneading. Marg sprinkled the herbs over it as Jessica went on, "I've told Mary and Thomas... they'll have to help." Her words fell into the rhythm of her work. "There're too many cows for... two men. I can help in the ... mornings. The children... can help after school."

She blew at a wisp of hair falling over her forehead. "I'll have to... see if anyone has... milking equipment... going cheap."

Marg hung the tea towel on its peg to dry. "Perhaps Sam can ask at Bright and Sons when 'e delivers the milk tomorrow."

"Shit!" Jessica paused in her work. "We lost the steam engine too. Even if we had milking equipment it'd be useless without the engine. Replacing that's the priority."

Her chest tightened with emotion again. If she gave in, it

would become insurmountable; collapsing into a weepy mess was a luxury she couldn't afford.

She dragged in a breath and continued her kneading.

It was three hours before the men finished the hand-milking. Jessica was taking the bread from the oven when Sam and the captain arrived, stinking of milk and cow dung, sweaty and hungry. Sam complained his back was giving him merry hell, but they were both cheerful.

Jessica ordered them to the wash-house to clean up. By the time they returned she'd put out plates of hot, fresh bread, cheese, boiled eggs and cups of tea.

They fell ravenously on the food and Jessica asked her steward about enquiring at Bright and Sons for a cheap steam engine and possibly some milking equipment.

He nodded, cheeks bulging with food and took a sip of tea to wash it down. "I reckon if they don't 'ave nowt themselves, they might know someone who does. Can't 'urt to ask."

The two men continued eating, chatting companionably between mouthfuls and laughing over the captain's near miss, when Hedy Lamarr lifted her tail and emptied her bowels at his feet.

Jessica was leaning against the bench, teacup in hand, when she caught herself chuckling as Sam described the scene. She allowed the laughter to come and soon she was wiping tears from her eyes. She couldn't say whether they were tears of mirth, grief or exhaustion.

Yet as she met the gleaming, blue gaze of the German captain, her heart lightened.

"Eh-up," Sam said, rising and clapping his flat-cap on his head. "Better get this milk off."

"Ask about the engine," Jessica reminded him.

"Will do."

Jessica pushed the splintered remains of the door to. Turning, she found the captain putting the lunch plates in the sink.

"Herr Clay asked me to move the cows to the pasture at the back," he said. "I shall do that now *und* then I must cut off that branch hanging over the wash-house."

"Thank you, Captain."

He went to step past her but paused. "It will get better." He gave her shoulder a light squeeze. "We will make certain of it."

Jessica stood in the kitchen with the reassuring pressure of his hand lingering on her shoulder, long after he'd gone.

Chapter 16

Summer arrived at Broughton Hall. It brought warm golden days and balmy pastel evenings.

One such evening, after the children had gone to bed, the captain asked for a sheet of paper and a pencil. Jessica poured them each a short glass of Jon's Tokay and sat opposite, watching as he sketched by the rosy twilight filtering through the boarded-over kitchen window.

"Herr Clay could get these parts from the village." He indicated a series of rods and bolts, coming into black-and-white relief on the page.

"What is it?" Jessica asked.

He smiled, without lifting his eyes, and continued his work. "A butter churn."

"Really?" Jessica leaned forward for a closer look. "What would we use for a bowl?"

"We have wood."

"But wood leaks."

Now he looked up, eyes dancing, "Oh, *nein*, because we make the boards narrow *und* fit together like this," he demonstrated with his hands flat, index fingers pressed tightly together. "Before using it, it must be soaked in water to make the boards swell *und* push together even more." He grinned at her, "Do you see? Water fit."

She gave a little laugh. "Water *tight*."

"Oh, *ja*. Water tight."

When he smiled like that, she felt a lessening of her troubles. "You look like you've made one before."

"I made one for my mother, then later when my sister married *und* moved away, I made one for her too."

"So it will work."

He made a smug face. "Of course."

Jessica continued to sip her Tokay as the captain completed his drawing. Finally, he laid down the pencil and raised the glass. "*Prost*!" He took a sip. "This is *gut, ja*. It was your husband's?"

"Yes."

"Where did you meet? Your husband *und* you?"

She regarded him curiously. "Why do you want to know?"

"Because I have what is called an inquiring mind."

"Or because you are what *we* call a nosy-parker."

He laughed lightly. "Then I am this nosy-parker because I have an inquiring mind."

She finished her Tokay, then poured another measure for herself and topped up the captain's glass. "Jon and I did not have a conventional relationship. Jon was born in nineteen thirteen, just before the last war. His father volunteered early and went to France. He died horribly of nephritis – caught in the trenches. His kidneys failed. Anyway, Jon was raised by his mother."

Jessica sat comfortably in her chair. "I don't recall meeting Jon – it's like we always knew each other. His mother worked in my father's shop, in Leeds – when he could afford to employ someone. When the Depression hit, Dad kept her on, though by then he couldn't afford it."

"A good man."

"Hmm. Anyway, every morning, she would walk Jon to school, then come to the shop to work. Each afternoon she collected him and they went home together."

Jessica paused to sip her drink. "One day, she didn't arrive at the shop."

"She was ill?"

"She was hit by a bus. She'd just dropped Jon at school and was coming to work."

They were silent for several minutes, while Jessica stared into the deep amber colour of her Tokay. She heard the captain gently place his glass on the table.

The silence continued and Jessica felt a certain peace settle over her. The summer weather had arrived; the animals overnighted in the fields and she had months to decide how she would shelter them during the winter.

"My father," she continued, eventually, "brought Jon into our home. He was only eight – same age as Thomas and Mary are now. We grew up as brother and sister."

She drained her glass but continued to hold it. "Of course, we weren't brother and sister, so everyone joked that we would marry – Mum and Dad's customers, friends, everyone. As we got older it seemed less of a joke and more serious. People stopped saying, *when you get married*, and started saying, *when are you getting married?*"

She shrugged ruefully. "Poor Jon. He never stood a chance. They put so much pressure on him that I think, in the end, it was easier to go with it."

"He would have loved you though. Who would agree to a marriage otherwise?"

"A man with an overwhelming sense of gratitude," Jessica responded evenly.

He cocked his head and studied her. "You think he married you because your parents gave him a home?"

Jessica nodded. "I *know* he did. But we were good together. We were..." she looked away, searching for the right expression. "We were best friends."

He nodded thoughtfully. "I see this might be so. But I look at you now... I see a strong woman, a kind woman, a *good* woman. I think he saw these things too, *und* I think maybe he said, oh, *ja*, here is the mother of my children."

Jessica felt the warmth spread up her neck to flood her cheeks and was grateful for the gathering darkness in the kitchen. Rising, she took the empty glasses to the sink and busied herself rinsing them.

Finally, she turned. He was watching her with a vague smile on his face.

"I'm going to bed, Captain," she said, adding, "Thank you for all your help – I don't know what we'd do without you."

"Frau Jessie, you would be all right. I make it easier, that is all, *und* I will continue to do so. I do not forget that I owe you a great deal. *Gute nacht.*"

***

Jessica was smiling to herself as she went into her bedroom. She was still smiling as she climbed into bed and didn't notice the border collie dog sleeping before the empty fireplace with its head on its paws.

***

As June progressed, Jessica had begun rising at four o'clock. Dressing in Jon's clothes that she used for gardening, she crept downstairs in the opaline morning light. In the kitchen, she poked the fire to life and filled the firebox with coals to start heating the range.

The kettle was simmering on the hob, and Jessica was slicing bread when behind her, the door swung open.

As the captain came in, a ripple of happiness ran through her. He looked tired but he smiled at her, running a hand through his bed-tousled hair.

"*Gut* morning, Frau Jessie."

"*Guten morgen, Hauptman*," she responded.

He went to the window and examined the palings Sam had boarded over it after the explosion. "I was thinking that I could take glass from another window *und* fit it here if you would like. What do you think?"

She was melting dripping in a frying pan, swirling it around to coat the base. "I hadn't thought about it. But, I wonder if it would be better to keep it boarded up for now."

He glanced quizzically at her over his shoulder.

"Oh, don't get me wrong," she said quickly, "I miss the light coming in, and it's a good idea, but I've been concerned that anyone coming to the garden door could look in and see you here."

His expression changed with understanding. "You are right, *und* I did not think."

Dropping two slices of bread into the pan, she left them sizzling in the dripping and rinsed her hands under the tap. "Don't worry," she advised, reaching for a towel. "I have plenty of work for you to do."

His voice lowered. "You do know that under the Geneva Convention, it is illegal to put prisoners to hard labour?"

Her head lifted in surprise but she found him grinning at her. "Hmph!" she snorted, and flicked her towel at him, catching him with a snapping sound across his thigh.

"Oh! *Und* now the prisoner is subjected to brutality!"

Without warning, his hand shot out and snatched the towel from her. Twirling it menacingly, he began to advance upon her.

"*Eek!*" she yelped, and leapt behind a chair while he continued towards her, twirling and snapping the tea towel threateningly with every step.

Breathless with laughter and conscious of the children sleeping upstairs, she pressed herself into a corner. Her eyes darted towards the garden door, the broom cupboard, the hallway and back, searching for escape, but she was well and truly cornered.

The captain obviously realised it too for his grin became victorious. He paused three feet in front of her, "So Madame, you have heard about the relentless, conquering nature of the German forces." He exaggerated his accent, and cocking an eyebrow, continued to taunt her with the twirling towel. "Now you will experience it!"

His hand moved so quickly that she didn't see it, but she saw the towel lash out and felt its brief sting as it cracked against her thigh.

"*Ahh!*" she squeaked, shaking with silent laughter and twisting to escape as he took another step towards her.

Snap!

"*Captain...! Enough...!*" Her sides were hurting with the effort of trying not to laugh.

"*Oh nein. Das ist nicht genug!*" He too was breathing hard, his face alive with the game. He took another step, and twirled the towel in a manner indicating it was going to be a big one. "*Ich bin für dich gekommen!*"

Jessica didn't understand a single word, but understood the tone. He paused, a mere step in front of her, the towel moving ominously, his expression wolfish.

Without pausing to think, she snatched the end of the towel. Rather than seizing it from him, she used it to pull him towards her and before he realised what she was about, she'd thrust a hand beneath his arm.

Instantly, he dropped the towel, jumping away from her as she chased him back across the kitchen. "*Kitzlig! Oh, ja... Kitzlig!*" she taunted while he attempted to protect his ribs from her tickling.

Eventually, they both collapsed against the bench, laughing and catching their breaths.

"Frau Jessie..." he gasped. "You are very unkind!"

Before she could respond, a cloud of acrid brown smoke billowed through the kitchen.

"Lucifer's balls!" Jessica leapt to the hob and dragged the frying pan from the range. The bread was like charcoal; flicking at it with a finger, she groaned. "Damn. Pan's burnt too."

He was peering over her shoulder so she angled the offending article to show him. "Someone's going to have to scrub this," she declared, glancing significantly at him.

He removed imaginary headgear with a flourish and swept the floor in a very courtly bow. "*Zu ihren Diensten, gnädige, Madame.*"

"Whatever that means," she responded. "Now, will the brave German officer – who squeals like a girl when tickled – please take his seat? His breakfast is ready."

***

Jessica's step was light as she followed the captain outside. She tried to avert her gaze as they passed the scorched stone and crumbling timbers of the stables, but her eyes were inevitably drawn to the devastation and her feet slowed.

Even the surrounding ground bore the scars with its potholes and lumps, and bright new grass sprouting in spiky patches.

"Frau Jessie..." The captain waited a few yards ahead. "Staring at it will not make it better."

"I know." She sighed and continued towards the paddock, beyond the rubble, past the woodshed adjacent to the wall bordering the village of Jackson's Heath.

Some twenty cows were milling about waiting for them; three were tethered to the fence and Sam was already sitting on an upturned bucket, milking the first of them. The grass was ankle deep and damp with dew. As Jessica came through the gate, her outdoor shoes were immediately soaked, as were her socks.

"Who is this *hübsches junges Mädchen*?" the captain asked, as they approached.

"Ah, good morning," Sam greeted them. "This is Carole Lombard – one of my favourites."

Jessica accepted a bucket from the captain. "They're all your favourites." She sat behind one of the other tethered cows and set to work. "This is Thelma, I think. Am I right?"

"Nope," Sam replied without looking up. "That one's Bette Davis. You can tell by the beauty spot she 'as beneath 'er eye there."

The captain and Jessica exchanged a smile. "Which one is yours, Herr Clay?"

"I'm with Anita Page – she's got the gentle, sad-looking face."

"It's all beyond me," Jessica remarked.

The captain said, "I have not even heard of these ladies."

Jessica was surprised. "Didn't you go to the cinema when you lived in America?"

"Oh, *ja*, but not often – ahh, do not flick your tail at me, Frau*lein* – before I worked for the postal service, my English was not good. Watching a movie was difficult."

Sam stood and stretched his back. "All done, lassie." He untethered Carole and sent her off with a slap to her rump. Reaching for the next in line, he asked, "But you went?"

"Occasionally. There was a young lady I spent time with. Sometimes on Friday night we saw a film."

The jolt of intense and unreasonable jealousy took Jessica by surprise; her treacherous mind wandered, visualising a laughing, carefree American girl with movie star looks on the arm of a handsome young pilot.

She didn't like it at all. As the two men continued talking, her eyes moved to the middle distance and she tried to think of other things, *What shall I prepare for tea tonight? How can I get some shelter built for the animals before winter? That looks like that horse Robin rode over here that day when...*

"Lucifer's balls!"

At Jessica's sudden exclamation, both men turned to stare at her. "Captain, get down! Lie among the cows!"

"Jaysus! What's that bugger doing 'ere?" Sam growled as the German threw himself flat in the grass between the cows.

Tyler hadn't seen them as yet. He was mounted on his horse, walking casually up the driveway. Ordinarily the stable would have hidden them, but as it was now, Jessica had a clear view of the visitor – as he had of them.

She jumped to her feet and flew through the gate, past the ruined stables and down the side of the house to intercept the visitor in front of the porch.

Sam strode purposefully behind her, not bothering to hide his displeasure.

Tyler reined in before the porch steps, just as Jessica arrived, blowing hard. Shading her eyes from the sun rising behind him, she greeted her visitor in what she hoped was a welcoming voice. "Good morning, Robin, what a lovely surprise."

Robin Tyler considered her from his saddle. "Really, Jessica? You could at least pretend to mean it."

Jessica flushed guiltily while Sam said directly, "What brings you here this morning, Tyler?"

"Thought I'd offer my help with the milking. I know you're doing it by hand and –"

"That's kind of you, Robin," Jessica began, "but –"

"S'all under control," Sam interrupted, curtly. "We're just about finished."

Tyler looked across to where the cows could be seen in the paddock and Jessica's heart nearly stopped. "Honestly, Robin," she called his attention back. "It really *is* under control. Sam and I take care of the morning milking and the children help us in the afternoon after school. It's working quite well."

The visitor regarded her speculatively, and in that time Jessica wondered at the intensity of his gaze as his eyes lingered on her before shifting to Sam. *He knows we're up to something*, she thought with alarm. Then, *Oh, God, please go away!*

"Not only that," she went on cheerfully, "but Sam spoke with the overseer at Bright and Sons and they think they can find us an old engine and milking equipment. We could buy it – dirt cheap! We'll be up and running properly in no time."

"How cheap?"

"Well," Jessica tried to keep the nervous tremor from her voice. "They said we could probably have it for a couple of days' worth of milk."

He stared down at her from the saddle, thoughtfully rubbing his chin. His stubble sounded scratchy against the leather of his glove. "Seems a bit rich to me. Perhaps if *I* were to speak with them..."

Sam snorted. "You'd be wasting your time."

Tyler blinked and slowly turned in Sam's direction. "Only offering to help." His mouth twisted unpleasantly. "I've got a bit of influence, you know."

Jessica felt Sam bristling beside her. "Thank you, Robin," she said quickly, "but we're happy with the deal, honestly. We're just waiting for them to get back to us."

Tyler faced her; chewing his cheek thoughtfully. Eventually he nodded. "Very well. I can see you're busy. I won't hold you up any longer." He wheeled the horse round and reached down to lay a comforting hand on Jessica's head. She resisted the urge to duck out of it. "Don't be cross with me for feeling protective of you. I'll try to stay away until you call me, but *you* must promise that you will. Do we have an agreement?"

Jessica bowed her head – as much to remove his hand as to express agreement. "We do."

"Good!" He gathered his reins. "I'll be off then. See you tomorrow." He tugged at the front of his riding hat and clicked to the horse.

"Tomorrow?" Jessica called after him.

"Don't forget!" he shouted over his shoulder. "Saturday. You're bringing the children over."

"*Blast!*" she cursed under her breath, as he trotted out of sight.

Sam and Jessica stomped back to the paddock. The captain, who'd watched Robin leave from the security of the steward's cottage, arrived at the same time.

Irritated and afraid, Jessica turned on him. "You can't be here!" she cried in a hoarse whisper. "That's two near misses in a week. I'll end up having my children taken away from me... I'll be thrown in jail... I – Oh, God!" She hid her face in trembling hands, controlling herself with deep breaths.

Marg had followed the captain back to the paddock. Now she stood with one hand on her hip, the other on the young German's shoulder, her mouth a grim line.

"What are you looking like that for, woman?" Sam demanded. "None of us can 'elp it if the bastard won't stay away!"

"And he won't," Jessica wailed.

"Enough!" the older woman snapped and Jessica felt the power of her glare. Addressing both her husband and employer, Marg said, "Finish the milking, then all of you come down the cottage. This needs sortin'!"

At that, she turned on her heel and waddled indignantly back to her home.

***

"I'm sorry, Captain," Jessica murmured, an hour later. The three were in the cottage, sitting at the kitchen table, while Marg stood over them with hands on hips.

"Now," the older woman said taking a seat. "Seems we 'ave a problem. Jessica, love, why is this fellow 'anging around so much?"

"That's not 'ard to figure out," Sam grumbled, "sniffing around like a bloody dog on the scent."

"Samuel Clay! You're not 'elping!"

"Robin says he feels protective of me." Jessica said.

"Well, I reckon 'e –"

"Sam," Jessica held her ground, "we came to an agreement this morning. I promised to call if I need his help, and he agreed to stay away."

"Is 'e trying to court you?" Marg asked directly.

Jessica felt her face grow hot and looked away.

"Pretty pleased with 'imself, 'e is!" Sam's tone was contemptuous. "But I reckon it's more than that. I was in the front room 'ere the other day. You know it looks out onto the Leeds road? I 'eard voices and there was young Thomas, just off the school bus, and this Tyler fellow asking 'im questions."

If Jessica's face had been burning moments ago, all the blood drained from it now. She gaped at her steward. "Why didn't you tell me?"

Sam gestured dismissively. "Weren't nowt to tell. Lad did nowt wrong... I went out and told 'im to come inside and that were the end of it."

The captain had been silently following the discussion. Now he spoke up, "I must leave." Jessica saw Marg open her mouth to protest, but the captain continued hurriedly, "I am a danger to this family. *Und* it is dangerous for me. To be discovered here would be –"

"You've nowhere to go and you're not turning yourself in so be quiet about it." Jessica snapped forcefully, startling herself with her vehemence.

"There must be another way." Marg said, frowning. "Sam, perhaps –"

She broke off abruptly, and all four froze, not even daring to breathe as they listened to the sound of running feet outside the cottage.

Jessica's eyes met those of the captain's. He started to rise when Marg motioned everyone to remain seated. She went to the back door. "Who's there?" she called in a deceptively cheerful voice.

"Mrs Clay, it's me." It was a child's breathless voice.

"Mary!" Jessica rushed to the door as Marg opened it. "What is it?"

"Mummy – thought you'd be here," Mary said.

Thomas, hopping anxiously from foot to foot behind her added, "We just missed the school bus!"

"Damn!" Jessica turned to her steward who'd pre-empted her request.

Nodding, Sam reached for the car keys. "Come along, I'll drive yers."

***

"The accelerator. The brake. This one is the clutch. You will remember with practice."

Jessica sat in the driver's seat of Jon's Daimler. The engine was idling roughly in the Broughton Hall driveway; the captain sat beside her pointing out the car's vitals.

"Now, of course," he said, "first thing is to look around you."

"Then what?"

"You did not look."

She glanced across at him – he jerked his chin in the direction of her mirror. "Look!"

"*Jawohl, Herr capitan!*"

He glared at her and muttered something that sounded rude. But the guttural nature of his language often sounded rude. She narrowed her eyes at him. "Did you just swear at me?"

"I might have. You will not know, so every time I speak to you, you will wonder. I suggest you do as I tell you to avoid it."

His face was entirely deadpan but she was learning to read the glisten of mischief in his eyes – bluer than grey today, reflecting the summer morning sky. She cleared her throat and glanced in the rear-view mirror, adjusting it to suit.

She looked at him, and he inclined his head, "*Und* the

window."

She obeyed.

"*Und* over the shoulder."

Twisting, she glanced over her shoulder.

"Anything coming?"

"Sam is walking along the drive with a rake."

"He is not in a car?"

She smirked at him, "No."

"He is not close enough that you will hit him?"

Jessica sighed. "No."

"Very well. You may begin."

"Um..." She paused, trying to remember.

"Clutch... gear... foot off the brake *und gently* press the accelerator while you *gently* release the clutch."

"Clutch..." she depressed the pedal. "Gear..." she manhandled the stick attached to the steering column and the car's engine changed pitch.

"Now slowly..." he cautioned. "Accelerator *und* clutch together."

Jessica complied. The car jerked, coughed and died.

"This is normal. Let us try again."

Jessica stalled the car another three times before she could get it to bunny-hop along the driveway. Each time she grew more frustrated, and each time the captain bade her try again.

"You know," he told her, "I did this when I was learning to fly."

"Aeroplanes have clutches?"

"No. No clutch, but they have gears. You can stall a plane in the air."

"That'd be a lot more dangerous than in a car. Did you ever stall a plane?"

"Oh, *ja*. It was part of our training. *Und* remember, I was a test pilot – it was part of my job to test that the engine *would* restart after stalling."

She looked at him in surprise. "Obviously, it did restart."

"Obviously..." he nodded pointedly at the ignition. "Again."

Fifteen minutes later, she was driving up and down the driveway, successfully negotiating bumps and pot holes, and braking before the porch stairs. She began by making seven-point-turns, then driving back towards the gate where her seven-point-turn graduated to a five-pointer, and then back down the drive again.

Eventually, Jessica was driving up to the house without stalling. She carefully braked, performed a three-point-turn and returned to the gate.

She beamed across at him as they bounced along the driveway and was ludicrously pleased by the smile on his face.

"You're proud of me," she stated, grinning as she pulled into the car spot outside Sam's cottage.

"*Ja.*" It was all he said, but he smiled at her and a little thrill ran up her back. "Your next lesson will be on the road. I will not be coming with you."

***

Returning to the kitchen, Jessica and the captain found the children sitting at the table. Mary was reading *Raggedy Ann's Lucky Pennies*, while Thomas was using his worn-down crayons to fill in his colouring book, with imaginative colour combinations.

Jessica watched the captain stand over Thomas's shoulder for a moment before pointing to a picture of a man walking a dog. "Why is that man green?"

"He is a Martian," the boy replied, "of course!"

"Oh, *ja.* That was my mistake. It is obvious now."

Mary glanced over the top of her book. "Tommy's just being silly. There's no such thing as Martians."

"Why not?" The captain took a seat beside her. "There is a planet called Mars. Would you say that the people living there are Martians?"

Mary's face turned thoughtful, then she eyed him sceptically. "You're poking fun at me."

"No. Not at all. They would be Martians."

"Have you flown there in your plane, Mr Bird?" Thomas piped up.

"No. My plane cannot go that high."

"Don't forget, we're going to Mr Tyler's today," Jessica interrupted. She bent to stack some items in the ice-chest, then straightened and closed the door.

"Do *I* have to go?" Mary inquired. She exaggerated a pout. "I don't want to."

"Yes, you have to go. Mr Tyler wants to show us his Fresian – he thinks you, particularly, will be interested."

"Well, I'm not," Mary declared rebelliously.

"Will you drive us there, Mummy?" Thomas asked, his head bent over his colouring book. She glanced at the captain, then back to her children. "I don't think I'm ready for that yet. Perhaps another time."

Mary looked up. "Is she ready, Mr Bird?" Her eyes narrowed cunningly. "I'll go if Mummy drives us."

Jessica interrupted. "I could drive, but if I get us all killed don't come crying to me."

She saw the children exchange amused looks. "Okay, Mummy," Thomas conceded. "Maybe Mr Clay should drive us."

Mary made a contemptuous sound in her throat. "Which means Mr Tyler will drive us home, and that will give him another excuse to come snooping round."

Jessica shot a look at the captain, then back to her daughter. "What do you mean?"

Mary's expression suggested it was the most obvious thing

in the world. "Why do you think he comes over so often?" she demanded. "You think it's because he likes you – but he doesn't, not in *that* way."

Jessica felt her cheeks grow hot and avoided the captain's gaze. Forcing herself to concentrate on Mary, she questioned, "Why do *you* think he comes here?"

The girl sat up in her chair, evidently pleased that her opinion seemed important. "I think he's one of those whatchercalls, the home something."

"Home Guard?" Jessica suggested.

"Mm-hm. I think he's one of them. And I think it's strange that he showed up at the same time Mr Bird came."

Jessica's stomach dropped. She glanced towards the captain, but he was watching Mary with a thoughtful frown.

While they were talking, Thomas had continued his colouring. Without pausing in his work, he said, "Jack Ramage said his grandad is a Home Guard. He said they were looking for a Gerry who jumped out of a plane."

Now Jessica was beginning to feel ill. The captain caught her eye; a quick shake of his head warned her to say nothing, as Mary said, "People don't jump out of planes, silly."

"They do!" Thomas insisted. "They found this thing –a par-shoot."

"A parachute," Jessica breathed. Her heart began pounding and she dropped into a vacant chair.

Thomas continued, "Jack said his grandad told him the par-shoot was found hidden in some bushes. He said, 'Hey, Tom, you better watch out for Gerries. They cook people in ovens and eat them.' Then he says there are Gerries near Broughton Hall, and he goes, 'Hey, Tom, you live at Broughton Hall! Watch out the Gerries don't getcha.'"

Jessica sat very still and forced herself to breathe normally. She was vaguely aware of the captain's hand on her shoulder, as though to calm her. With a deep intake of air, she asked, "And what did you say?"

"I said there were no Gerries at Broughton Hall, and he said, 'There are too,' and I said, 'There aren't and even if there were, they wouldn't be in my Mum's bed,' and everyone knows there are *Yanks* in *his* mum's bed!"

Jessica felt the captain chuckle with amusement beside her. To cover her discomfort, she addressed her son, "Now, Tommy, I –"

"Frau Jessie, I do not think this is what we need to talk about." The captain turned to Mary, who had been watching her brother with a thoughtful expression on her face. "What do you think about this?"

"Oh, you're ready to listen to me?"

"Don't be rude," Jessica admonished.

Mary made an impatient huffing noise. "I don't *know* anything. But I'm guessing, because Mr Tyler was waiting when we got off the bus the other day. He asked Tommy about Mr Bird."

"What did he ask?" The captain's tone was one of calm inquiry.

"He asked Tommy if he had a teddy bear called Mr Bird. I don't know why."

Thomas had laid down his crayons and was following the discussion with interest. "And I told him I have lots of teddies and they have different names."

"Then what did he say?" Jessica demanded.

Thomas's face took on a hunted expression. "He asked if he could come over and see Mr Bird."

"What did you say to that?"

"Mummy!" Thomas's chin began to quiver.

"Why are you being so mean?" Mary demanded. Jessica realised, guiltily, that her tone must have been rather abrupt for

Mary to defend her brother.

"I'm sorry, Thomas. You're not in trouble. I just need to know." She moderated her voice. "Sweetheart, what did you tell Mr Tyler?"

"I didn't tell him anything. Mr Clay came out and told me and Mary to come inside because Mrs Clay had made scones and they were still warm."

Jessica sat back, relieved.

"Mummy?" Mary's voice was a thin thread. "Can we please tell Mr Tyler I'm sick and we can't go over?"

Jessica too, was tempted to beg off, but if they didn't go today Robin would insist on another day. Before she had a chance to respond, the captain said, "I think it would be best if you go. Be careful of what you say, *und* Tommy," the boy looked across at him, "take one of your teddy bears with you *und* tell Mr Tyler that you brought Mr Bird to show him."

***

Sam drove the Daimler into the drive of the old farmhouse. Jessica, in the front beside him, looked out at a double storey house, constructed from local Yorkshire stone with a slate roof. Symmetrically designed, it had a green front door between two green-framed windows, and three windows upstairs. Large tubs of purple lavender sat either side of the door, alive and buzzing with bees.

"Pretty," Jessica observed. She and the children climbed out of the car, and Jessica leaned into the window, "Thanks for the lift."

"Do you want me to come collect you in, say, an 'our?" Sam asked.

"I don't think so. It's a nice day, we can walk home."

"If I don't collect you, it gives 'im a reason to drive you 'ome."

He was right. Jessica was about to respond when there was a shout behind her.

"Jessica!" Robin had emerged from the house and was coming towards her, a welcoming smile on his handsome face.

"Here 'e is! Errol bloody Flynn," Sam mumbled, and she laughed.

"I'll see you at home." She turned to meet their host.

***

An older man, presumably Robin's father, rose from a rattan chair. He'd been sitting on the edge of the porch, in the shade cast by the house, as the June afternoon was warm and bright.

Albert Tyler was a tall, spare man with bristling grey eyebrows and a close-cropped grey beard. He had a kindly face with an intelligent twinkle in his eye and Jessica immediately warmed to him.

Robin introduced her and the children to his father, then ushered them into the house for a cool drink. The entry hall was shadowy after the glaring sun outside and Robin led them into a tidy little sitting room saying, "Dad makes his own lemonade. You'll like it... nice and refreshing."

"Then can we go and see the horse?" Mary asked.

Evidently Robin took her question as eagerness to admire his Fresian, but Jessica knew better. She dropped a hand lightly on her daughter's shoulder. "Just be patient, Mr Tyler's being very hospitable."

Albert came in behind his son. "Not to worry, young lady. Krijger's not going anywhere. Too busy out in that paddock tucking into a bucket o' chaff."

"Take a seat," Robin urged them, "Dad'll keep you company. I'll be back in a moment."

Mary smiled politely and took a seat beside her brother on a two-seater brocade couch.

Jessica looked round the room. There were two single chairs by the window or another two-seater, to choose from. She selected a chair closest to her children while Albert took the other chair.

"So," he addressed Jessica, "how long've you lived at the Hall?"

"My husband and I bought the place in nineteen thirty-nine," she explained. "I fell in love with it. We planned to restore it – over time. Of course, it needs so much work – but that's the only reason we could afford it."

"Big place for the two of you cheeky monkeys."

Thomas squirmed delightedly at being addressed, while his sister sat very upright in her seat, her face revealing nothing.

Jessica smiled indulgently. "They love having the space to run around."

"And that explosion the other night... Rob said it were a bomb?"

"Took out the stables, did I tell you Dad?" Robin said, coming into the room carrying a tray bearing a jug of lemonade, glasses and a plate of Digestives.

"Bomber on its way to Leeds or Sheffield, no doubt. Must've got its directions mixed up."

"Odd, don't you think?" Albert said thoughtfully. "Out here in the middle of the dales, no lights or nothing."

"That's what I thought," Jessica said. "I'm no expert. My steward, Sam Clay, he agrees, it's odd."

"Gerries can't read their own gauges," Robin quipped, with a wink in Mary's direction, but she didn't respond.

"Mary..." Jessica gave her daughter a significant look. Mary offered their host a weak smile.

"What's that green stuff in the jug?" Thomas piped up.

"It's mint." Jessica responded, tightly.

"Urgh!"

"Don't be rude. I'm sorry Robin –"

"It's all right... Not to everyone's taste," Robin smiled at his young guest and passed him a glass. "No mint in yours. Now, Mary, you having mint?"

Mary nodded, and Jessica glared at her. "Could you please answer Mr Tyler."

"I'm happy with mint, thank you Mr Tyler." She took the proffered glass.

"Mummy, I forgot to bring Mr Bird!" Thomas cried suddenly, his face stricken. "I was supposed to bring –"

Jessica interrupted urgently. "That's all right, love. Robin, Tommy wanted to show you his teddy bear." She shrugged helplessly. "I don't know why. He just said –"

"I told you," Thomas accused. "And you –"

"Shut up, Tommy!" Mary said. "Nobody's interested in your stupid toys."

"Stop it!" Jessica hissed. "I'm sorry Robin – they've been at each other's throats all day." Jessica made a rueful face, while admitting to herself that Mary's grumpy attitude had effectively diverted attention from the non-existent teddy bear.

"Not to worry." Robin poured another lemonade and handed the glass to Jessica. "You can introduce me to Mr Bird next time." He poured two further glasses and gave one to his father and took the other for himself. He sat on the empty couch. "So, have you decided what you're going to do about the stables yet?" he addressed Jessica.

Swallowing a mouthful of her drink, she said, "I must do something – the animals will need shelter for the winter. Fortunately, I don't have too many cows and we've only the one horse. Sam says it looks sturdy enough – I may only need to put a roof on it."

"We've got a barn here that's a deal bigger than we need." Albert said. "The sheep winter in it but there's plenty of spare room. We could probably house half a dozen cows. The original owner of this land had a bull and twenty or so cows on the property."

"But that was years ago, Dad. Is it the same barn?"

"Yes, I think it is. They built 'em solid those days."

"How old is this place, Albert?" Jessica asked. "I wonder if it's older than Broughton Hall."

"Well," he responded, absently stroking his beard, "I don't think it's older, probably about the same age. My parents, Rob's grandparents, bought this place off some fellow called Steven Jackson – claimed to be some great nephew of the original owner. They used to own all the land that's now Jackson's Heath. The whole estate ran from the wall bordering your orchard, right down that slope to Blackwood Lane."

"Huge," Jessica remarked.

"Sure was. But large parcels of it got sold off over the years. Jackson's Heath was the first to go – sold to the Broughtons. Farm land, it was at the time, and the young fellow, Sir Simon Broughton, bought it and built a handful of cottages. Put tenants in them. Over the years it's grown with more cottages... eventually became a village in its own right."

Jessica leaned forward in her seat. "The Broughtons don't own this land anymore though, do they?"

The old man shook his head. "Nah. Broughtons don't even exist anymore. Pretty much died out after Joseph Broughton. He never married, never had children. End of his line, although I suppose there are cousins around somewhere."

"Joseph. That name rings a bell. I think that's who we bought the place from."

"Joseph Broughton has a lot to answer for, he does. Bled the place dry. It was a prosperous estate, but he was a gambler – blew the lot. Born in your house, he was."

Frowning, Jessica tried to remember what she'd read in the

memoir. She vaguely recalled Alexandra's brother's name was Simon. She said, "Wasn't there a Spanish connection? Didn't Sir Simon spend time in Spain?"

"Oh aye! He were a doctor during the Napoleonic Wars. Married some Spanish lass and ended up living in Spain."

"So there's no grave or anything for him in the Broughton cemetery?"

"Nope. You'll find others there, though."

"Are these people who lived in our house?" Thomas asked.

"Yes indeed, laddie!" Albert Tyler said. "Sir Simon and... now what was her name? Maria! That's it! Maria – they had several children, and their children had children, but they all lived in Spain. It wasn't until the grandson, Andrew, came home to take up his inheritance that any of them came back. That would've been around the early eighteen eighties – place'd been empty for ten odd years after Sir Simon's sister died – you'll find her in the cemetery. Margaret I think they called her."

"I've heard of her!" Jessica felt a surge of excitement as parts of the diary came alive in Albert's explanation. "Didn't she live in the house alone for years?"

The old man inclined his head. "Sure did – Rob, pour us another, will you?" Albert held his empty glass to his son who dutifully filled it. "Now, Andrew came home with his wife, and his two sons – I would've been about eight years old at the time. I remember him restoring it beautifully, must've sunk a fortune into it. Fortunately, Jackson's Heath was thriving and the estate was raking in the rent, but there was a lot to do – that old woman had lived there so long, she never noticed the place practically falling down around her. Regular Miss Havisham, she was!"

"Who's Miss Havisham?" Mary piped up, showing interest for the first time.

"Character in a book," Albert told her. "You're a bit young just yet but in a few years, you make sure you read *Great*

Expectations. Right, so, where was I?"

"Andrew Broughton returned from Spain and restored the property," Jessica said, eager to continue.

"Good-oh. Andrew's son, Francis, maintained the place and it continued to do well. When he died, in the nineteen twenties, his boy, Joseph, inherited."

Robin cleared his throat. "Joseph was the gambler, right Dad? You knew him."

"Poor chap went to France in fifteen. He made it back but he was never the same. I knew him for a time – always had this shocking cough. People said the mustard burnt his lungs out; he didn't talk about it. Never married, spent most of his time in Leeds. Had a penchant for cards – illegal tables, you know? Fell out with his dad over it... especially when he started losing.

"Things were manageable while Francis was alive. When he died, there was no one to hold the reins. First he sold off Jackson's Heath – most of the tenants bought their cottages at rock-bottom prices. Next went the land." He gestured towards Broughton Hall. "Your property once ran down past your steward's cottage to the Old Leeds Road. When the government was talking about upgrading the highway ten years back, Joseph went to them and offered his land up."

"He could've waited," Robin said dryly. "Would've got a better price."

"Probably, but the Hall was mortgaged to the hilt – he were desperate for the money. Government got itself a bargain! Poor old Andrew Broughton would've turned in his grave. All that love and effort restoring the place only for his grandson to let it go to ruin again."

"And all these people are buried in the cemetery?" Jessica asked. "I could go there and see the graves?"

Robin made a snorting sound. "You could, but why you'd want to is beyond me."

"I find it interesting," Jessica said, mildly affronted. "It *is* my house, after all."

Albert shot his son an injured look. "I find it interesting too, and I don't live there."

"What else do you know about the family, Albert?" Jessica asked.

"Mum, can you and Mr Tyler talk about this another time?" Mary prompted. After a brief spark of interest, she'd become bored again. "I'd like to go see Krijger."

"I'm with you, Mary," Robin said, rising from his chair. "If your mum wants to stay here and talk, I'll take you down to see him."

"No! I'll come," Jessica said quickly, unwilling to give Robin a chance to question the children.

***

Krijger was, as Robin had claimed, a magnificent beast, glossy black with a stocky, muscular frame. At about sixteen hands, he was an imposing sight, yet possessed of a sweet and gentle nature.

Jessica smiled as Mary's eyes popped with wonder. The girl approached warily, but was soon giggling with pleasure as the large stallion whuffed and snorted into her hair.

"He's a gentle giant," Robin observed. "The Friesians originated in Friesland, in the Netherlands."

"Do you ride him?" Mary asked.

"No. Only my father does. Krijger's a mild-mannered chap right now, but he's a one-man horse. Not fond of anyone else riding him."

"So I wouldn't be able to?"

"Afraid not, young lady."

Mary looked disappointed, but seemed happy soon enough when Robin passed her an apple, explaining, "His favourite."

***

Robin offered to drive them home, as Jessica knew he would. She insisted they walk simply because the day was so beautiful, even though Thomas pouted most of the way – he loved Robin's fancy modern motor.

Mary was satisfied that they were leaving. On the way home, she'd complained to her mother, yet again, that she didn't trust Mr Tyler, although she conceded that meeting Krijger had made the visit tolerable and that Mr Tyler's father was very nice.

For the most part, Jessica was oblivious to her children's chatter. She was too caught up in the Broughton history Albert had shared.

She couldn't wait to tell the captain about it and read more of the journal.

***

After tea that evening, the twins sat in the parlour practising their reading from a book they'd brought home from school. As the evening was mild, Jessica hadn't lit a fire. She threw open the window and a gentle breeze whispered into the room carrying with it the perfume of the wallflowers she'd planted in tubs below the window-ledge.

Jessica was darning a pair of Thomas's socks in the hopes that he would get another few months out of them, while the captain sat opposite repairing the seam on his trousers.

At first, she'd been amused by his ability to sew; Jon and her father had agreed that work with a needle and thread was women's work. But the captain explained that while living alone in America, he either learned to do his own repairs, or wear clothes with missing buttons and torn seams.

She smiled to herself as she watched him now, frowning over his work. *What a beautiful-looking man*, she thought. His hair had fallen over his forehead and as he blew it out of his eyes, he glanced up and she was caught watching, a forgotten smile on her face.

He smiled in return, then continued his work.

Tying off her stitching, Jessica took up another sock, and realised what a pleasant domestic scene the four of them made. Although her heart still grieved for Jon, just having a man in the house made her feel less alone, less vulnerable.

And feminine, the word popped into her head. *Jon never made me feel feminine – or attractive. We were like brother and sister. Jon and I...* Jessica sighed. *We should have stayed brother and sister.*

Suddenly Mary burst out laughing, teasing Thomas over something he'd misread. He, in his turn, pinched her knee – right in the ticklish spot causing her to squeal and kick out.

They both tumbled to the carpet giggling and wrestling and Jessica knew that she would never regret marrying Jon. *He gave me these two.*

Much later, after she had tucked the children into their beds and kissed them goodnight, she returned to the parlour to find the captain reading the children's school book.

"Entertaining?" she asked. It was starting to grow cooler outside. She closed and latched the window before resuming her seat.

"It pleases me," he said, flipping the pages over, "that I find this book so easy to read. When I was first learning English, I found even these difficult."

"You speak very well, though." She reached into her sewing basket and took out one of Thomas's shirts. "Captain, are you still interested in the history of this house?"

She hated to think he may have grown tired of it. She'd been enjoying sharing it with him, as if by sharing the diary with another person, she was not merely a lonely woman desperate for any kind of diversion.

But he nodded enthusiastically. "Oh, *ja*. What have you learned?"

Such a small thing, but it pleased her immensely. She filled him in on her discussion with Albert Tyler.

By the time she finished, he was sitting forward in his chair, elbows on his knees, hands dangling between them. "This is very interesting because it confirms what we know from the journal."

He yawned, covering his mouth politely.

"I suppose so. You're tired?"

Nodding, "*Ja*. I helped Herr Clay move the broken beams and clear the fallen stones from the stables today. Then we did the evening milking."

He stretched. Jon's shirt was too big for him and sat on him like a shapeless bag. It tantalised Jessica, knowing as she did, what was beneath it.

"Herr Clay says he can find what I need to make the butter churn."

"Never mind that," she said looking at his hands. "Are your hands sore from milking?" she inspected the thickening calluses on her own hands.

"*Ja,*" he said. "But they are getting hard... these lumps. It is *gut*."

She took his hand. It was ridged with calluses. One of them seemed to have split and bled recently.

"It is not *gut*. Come and let me bathe these for you before they end up infected – then you wouldn't be able to do anything."

He followed her obediently to the bathroom and sat on the stool she indicated while she bent over the boiler, stoking it to life. She felt his eyes on her – she often did as she went about her business. She felt admiration in the way he watched her, and knew he was probably aware she found him attractive in turn. Jessica swallowed a sigh – they were both so lonely.

They could be such a comfort to one another if they... she

forced her thoughts away from that path for it led to certain trouble.

As the boiler fired, Jessica opened the mirrored cabinet on the wall and took out Dettol and a fresh towel, turning abruptly she caught his eyes on her hips.

Slowly, seemingly without any discomfiture, he raised his eyes to her face. "Frau Jessie," he said matter-of-factly "I think you have a very nice arse."

He didn't seem uncomfortable, but Jessica couldn't say the same. Confused in the face of such open admiration, she stood irresolutely before him, the disinfectant in her hands.

With a half-laugh of disbelief, the heat rushed straight to her face. "Captain..." her heart was pounding and she was afraid it showed through her cotton blouse. "Captain, please behave yourself," she said in censorious tone. "I am going to put this on your hands. It will sting, but I am going to do it regardless of your flattery."

Turning away, she opened the tap on the boiler and ran a basin of warm water. He watched wordlessly as the Dettol was added, filling the room with its distinctive anti-bacterial smell.

Kneeling before him, she took one of his hands and dipped it in the water. He winced at the sting and made to pull his hand away but she held tight. "Stop it!" she ordered, adding, "you big baby."

Irritability was a safe refuge from the distraction of being close to him. Patting his hand dry, Jessica took the other and administered the same treatment. This time he didn't try to pull away but bared his teeth at her in a pained grimace.

"What a carry-on! And you, a brave Luftwaffe Captain, and all. You ought to be ashamed of yourself." When he grinned at her, she added, "What would Herr Göring have to say?"

"Herr Göring would be glad it was me *und* not him."

"Hmph!" She got to her feet and busied herself tidying things away while he rose and waited. "Off to bed now."

He smiled at her. "*Gute nacht*, Frau Jessie, *und* thank you for taking care of me."

He made to leave the room, but turned back. "Let us get up very early tomorrow... before the milking, before anyone will be on the road, *und* go to the cemetery."

Her eyebrows rose in surprise. "You seriously want to find the graves?"

"Oh, *ja*. I think it would be interesting."

"All right, then." She smiled, absurdly excited.

Chapter 17

The sky was still dark and the earth vibrated with pre-dawn magic as the couple picked their way along the forest path. The sound of their footfalls was deadened by years of accumulated leaf debris. The smell of wet earth pervaded the air and the leaves of beech, silver-birch and pine dripped with early morning dew, rustling and shivering, as little grey squirrels darted along the branches and hid within the foliage.

Jessica and Anton stepped carefully, round and over fallen logs and tree roots, holding branches aside for one another and following the trail only vaguely visible in the shimmering early morning.

The sky was gradually lightening, shifting seamlessly through shades of blue and lavender and rose.

Eventually, the forest gave way to a path bearing the rut-marks of hay carts and other farming vehicles, and not too much further, it forked.

Jessica led them to the left and they soon arrived at the churchyard, as the first golden threads of sunrise slipped between the trees, promising yet another beautiful summer's day.

As they approached the gate, the captain pushed it open and Jessica stepped through. He went to follow and was trapped behind. "This is very odd," he commented, in a hushed voice. "We do not have these in Germany."

"It's called a kisting gate, although people tend to call them kissing gates... for obvious reasons."

He smirked at her. "Because you have me locked here and could kiss me if you chose?"

Is he teasing me? It always feels like he's teasing, but he doesn't smile when he teases... maybe that's just his way.

She gave herself a mental shake. *He's a handsome young man, grateful because you've taken him in. Don't read more into it than that*! "That's what they say," she responded at last. "But kisting gates are generally found in graveyards, not usually popular with courting couples."

She stepped through and heard the gate click behind her as he pushed it open and followed.

The cemetery was unkempt. Grass and weeds grew in tufts around headstones that were grey and green with lichen and age.

"Where do we start looking?" she wondered out loud, gazing round.

"Anywhere."

He began wading through the morning-damp grass, pushing tussocks aside so he could read the dates on headstones. Jessica did the same, *Cuthbert, nineteen twenty-three, Jackson nineteen twenty-nine, Jackson nineteen thirty-six – not so long ago.*

The rows of monuments were arranged in vague lines; she moved back a couple of rows, *Banyon, Stiles, Sharples...*

Suddenly he called out and her head shot up. The captain was waving at her. "*Komm her!*"

Hurrying over, Jessica ignored the dampness seeping through her shoes from the wet grass. She came up beside him and looked where he indicated. "Broughton," she read. "Francis Dudley Broughton. Born September eighteen sixty-four, died, June nineteen twenty-five." She met the German officer's eyes. "This would be Simon's great-grandson. Does that make him Alexandra's great nephew? Great-great-nephew?"

He didn't respond. He was crouching beside a much older looking stone a row away. Looking across, he asked, "The man mentioned in the journal. What was his name? The step-brother in Margaret's letter."

Jessica cast her mind back. "Patrick, I think. Patrick Washburn."

The captain nodded and pointed with satisfaction. "I think we have something here, *ja*? Look."

He read from the inscription, "Sylvia Atherton, nee Washburn. What does *nee* mean?"

"It means formerly – that was her name before she married."

"Then she was a Washburn. Born July seventeen ninety-one, died September eighteen sixteen."

"How strange," Jessica murmured, thinking. "Alexandra's journal named her step-sister as Maeve."

But suddenly she knew and let her hand drop onto his shoulder. "Oh, she was the maid!"

He gaped up at her. "The maid?"

"I read about her, in the journal! I'm sure it said, *bastard half-sister.*"

Jessica's hand still rested on the captain's shoulder as she gazed at the headstone. "Sylvia Washburn. She was Alexandra's step-sister, or *half*-step-sister."

A sense of connectivity with the former resident of Broughton Hall seeped through her.

The captain rose to his feet and she let her hand fall to her side as she glanced towards the eastern sky. Soft summer clouds floated white and gold – the day had officially begun. "We should be getting back. Besides," she added, "the cows'll want milking."

They turned together, making their way singularly through the kisting gate, retracing their steps through the clearing and into the screening security of the forest. "We must come back," the captain said, holding a branch aside for her to pass. "I think there will be more Broughtons, or even Washburns there."

He pronounced Washburn as Varsch-bourne and she looked at him. "The way you say that name... Is it a German name?"

"Oh, *ja*, I think it could be old Saxon."

"That would make sense." She stepped over a protruding root. "The Saxons came to England around the seven-hundreds, if I remember my school history lessons correctly. Does," she tried to pronounce it the way he had, "varsch-bourne mean anything?"

"It means fast moving stream. It is not, what you would say, a noble name. But these Washburns were wealthy, *ja?*"

Jessica nodded. "And titled. From what I've read in the journal, Alexandra's step-brother was an earl. They're very high ranking – wha –?"

He had suddenly grasped her hand and was urgently dragging her off the path, pulling her down with him behind a thicket of hawthorn.

"What is it?" she whispered, wrinkling her nose at the overpowering smell of the hawthorn blossoms.

"A man coming!"

Shit! Jessica's heart began pounding as she peered through the shrubbery and recognised Albert Tyler, strolling along the path they'd only recently been walking on. He was about ten yards away and would soon be upon them. She could hear him humming a little tune to himself as he drew closer. *How could he not have heard us?*

"He'll see us!" she breathed. She started to move further into the hawthorn where its lower branches brushed the ground.

"Lie flat," he ordered, crawling in behind her. "Face down!" She obeyed without question, prostrating herself in the forest debris, averting her nose from the mouldy smell of decaying leaves.

The captain lay close beside her, half covering her, neither daring to breathe as the older man ambled past.

When at last Albert disappeared from view, and was, hopefully, out of hearing range, the pair cautiously crawled from the undergrowth.

Jessica's clothes were stained from lying in the muck. When she was able, she sat up and looked down at herself. Her blouse was wet and clingy with mud and slime. "Urgh, disgusting!"

He grinned, his eyes sifting over her, and reached over to

pluck a hawthorn blossom stuck to her forehead.

"Why did you say to lie face down? Look at the state we're in now." She picked at the leaves in her hair.

"Faces are white. They are more easily seen than hair *und* clothing. Come..." He pulled her to her feet. "We must go quickly."

They hurriedly returned to Broughton Hall and discovered that the children were still in bed. Quietly, they made their way upstairs. The captain went to the bathroom to stoke up the boiler while Jessica went to her room to fetch clean clothes.

By the time she went to the bathroom, the captain had gone to his own room. The heat coming from the boiler was warming the room and Jessica opened the tap to fill the bath and hurriedly stripped out of her filthy clothes.

The German was evidently giving her some privacy for she had time to quickly wash. Jessica was just stepping out of the bath when there was a light rap at the door and a whispered, "Frau Jessie? Are you finished?"

Wrapping herself in a towel, she crossed to the door and opened it a crack. "Nearly, oh... you're freezing!" She could see him shivering in his wet, muddy clothes. She stepped back, opening the door fully. The cold morning chill in the hallway made her shiver too. "I'll get dressed in my room."

He glanced at the raised bumps on her arms. "No... I can wait –" She grabbed him and pulled him into the room, closing the door after them to keep in the warmth.

"Turn your back, Captain, and wait while I get dressed. It's too bloody cold to stand out there while you're wet!"

He did as instructed, turning politely away as she dropped the towel and quickly slipped into her clothes.

He stood with his back to her, facing the boiler, and she saw his body relax in the warmth. But she sensed his awareness of the towel dropping to her feet, and heard him draw in his breath at the knowledge she stood naked behind him.

The faint rustling of her clothing and snap of elastic as she dressed sounded loud and sibilant in the small room and she remembered how the captain had kissed her palm.

She'd been slightly embarrassed facing him the morning after, but he'd behaved as though it had never happened. Granted they'd both been somewhat distressed that night. They had both needed comfort and it had seemed natural to find it in one another but –

Suddenly Jessica heard him give a soft grunt and the damp shirt clinging to his back showed a tensing of his muscles as he seemed to writhe.

"All right, Captain," she said. "You may turn round now."

He whirled about and Jessica was alarmed at the look on his face. Squirming as though something extremely disagreeable was beneath his clothes he gritted his teeth and frantically tore the shirt out of his trousers. Fumbling, clumsy in his urgency, he fought to undo the buttons.

With a strangled cry, he lost patience, and pulled the shirt over his head. Something plopped onto the bathmat.

Jessica gaped in bewilderment, while he stood very still, eyes like great grey pools in a pale face.

Together, they peered down at the glistening bluish grey slug that fell out of his shirt.

"*Verdammte Scheiße! Eine Schnecke...*" he growled, shuddering in horror.

"It's a slug!" She laughed in surprise. "I've no idea what you just said, Captain, but I'm guessing it wasn't polite!"

He was breathing hard, his eyes wild. "Oh, *nein*. A slug, eh? That is what you call this... this..."

She bent down to pick up the offending creature and held it in the palm of her hand. "Some men are afraid of spiders. You, it appears, are afraid of slugs."

He edged away from her, watching as she opened the bathroom window and tossed the mollusc to the grass below. "I have not liked them since I found some in my bed," he made a face of disgust. His accent was stronger after his ordeal. "My sister had played the joke on me."

Jessica latched the window and turned back to where he stood, naked to the waist and looking somewhat traumatised.

She felt the blood race through her veins at the sight of him. He'd filled out since recovering from his illness, and his physique had become lean, muscular and well-proportioned from his work with Sam.

Athletic – he didn't look like a footballer or swimmer, he wasn't lean enough to be a runner, but he was clearly athletic. Either way, she shouldn't be staring at him like a starving dog drooling over a bone.

To distract herself, she impulsively reached for his dog tags. He froze as she held the small aluminium disks in her hand, trying to read the markings.

"It is encoded," he told her. "No identity details are shown."

"So your name won't be there?"

He shook his head. "But you can see other things." He pointed, "This number is my personal number."

She nodded, noting that there were other decipherable details, such as *Haupt*, which she guessed was his rank, and *Luft w* which needed no explanation.

"If you decide to murder me *und* bury me in your garden, you will need to dispose of these."

She dropped the tags and they slapped against his bare chest, and before she could stop herself, she reached out a hand and cupped his cheek, feeling the raspy stubble there against her palm.

"Aw, it's all right, Hauptmann Vogel, you are quite safe. The slugs won't kill you and neither will I." She gave his cheek a playful pat and bent to gather her dirty clothes, including the shirt he had discarded. Straightening, she found him watching her, his mouth grim, though his eyes glistened with humour.

"It is not something to laugh at," he said, adopting an affronted tone. "These things, these slugs … they are evil things, dangerous things."

She laughed again. "They are only a danger to my vegetable patch. I will have your breakfast ready when you come downstairs, Captain, and I trust you will recover from your nasty fright with no lasting damage."

***

Jessica was still smiling as she laid the table with bowls and spoons and began preparing the children's porridge. Thomas came in rubbing his eyes. "Mummy, you were making a lot of noise this morning. Where did you go so early?"

She stood over the range, stirring the porridge. "Did you hear me go out?"

"Yes. And Mr Bird too. I heard voices."

No point denying it, she thought as the captain strolled into the kitchen. His hair was still damp from his bath and he was wearing fresh clothes.

"Mr Bird and I went for a walk. We didn't want to wake you so we didn't say anything."

Thomas made a snorting noise and pulled out a chair. He sat with a huff and rested his chin in his hands. "Elbows off the table please," Jessica said, spooning porridge into his bowl. "Captain, take a seat if you want your breakfast."

"I was awake. You could have come in and checked but you were being mean."

"*Danke*," the captain said, as Jessica filled his bowl. "We did not know you were awake."

"But I *was* awake," Thomas insisted reproachfully.

Jessica glanced at her son. "Well, we weren't to know that. Now, eat your breakfast."

Mary chose that moment to arrive. Yawning, with her hair sticking up like a crest and the belt of her dressing-gown trailing on the floor.

"Mummy's mean," Thomas told his twin.

Mary wrinkled her nose at him. "And you're an eejit." She dipped her spoon into her porridge.

"I am not an eejit!" Thomas shouted, lashing out. He whacked his sister's arm causing her to drop the spoon. It fell, splattering porridge on the table and floor.

"Thomas! *Das ist genug!*" The captain took a cloth from the sink and began cleaning the mess on the floor.

"Don't, Captain! Thomas, you clean that up this minute," Jessica snapped but her son leapt off his chair and ran from the room.

"You're not even going to check to see how badly hurt my arm is?" Mary demanded.

"He hardly touched you," her mother stated. "Don't carry on about it – eat your breakfast."

Mary gave a pained sigh, but took up her brother's untouched spoon and obediently returned to her bowl. She quickly finished and put her bowl in the sink.

"I'm going to get dressed, Mummy, then I'm going down to see Spencer."

***

"So we are still friends, young man?" the German asked earnestly. He held his hand out to the small boy who shook it, nodding grimly.

When Anton had first asked Thomas to join him outside, he feared he would be met with sullen petulance. But the boy had responded well and had eventually accepted that next time his mother and the captain went for an early morning walk, Thomas would be invited.

"Why did you go for a walk?" He asked, moving quickly to his more pressing subject. The man and boy were strolling up to the paddock where Mary's pony was kept. Spencer had a cut on his leg that the captain had been tending.

"Your mother wanted to show me the old cemetery beyond the forest. It has a pretty chapel."

Thomas readily accepted his friend's explanation, and as they approached the paddock, they saw Mary some twenty yards away. She started towards them, Spencer following, his great gentle head bobbing with his stride.

"What's wrong with Spencer?" Thomas asked.

"He has hurt his leg," Anton replied. "How is the leg this morning, Mary?"

"Better, I think."

Spencer was a small, rotund pied pony wearing the kind of laconic expression that suggested he wasn't the district's most shining equine example. But for all that, he was a mild-mannered horse who was eager to please his young mistress.

Anton and Thomas stood watching while Spencer readily trundled around the paddock, following Mary even though he favoured his wounded leg.

Thomas leaned towards him and whispered from the corner of his mouth, "Spencer always seems to have this daft look on his face."

Anton snorted with humour as the boy went on, "Don't tell Mary I said that. She thinks he's *awfully intelligent*!" He mimicked his sister's voice causing Anton to laugh out loud.

Mary came over. "It's bleeding again, Mr Bird," she pointed at the horse's injury. "See?"

Anton knelt to remove the bandage he'd applied the day before. The wound wasn't deep, it was a cut that had taken off a half-inch strip of hair and skin just above the fetlock joint. A thin line of blood seeped from it.

"Why won't it heal?" Mary asked.

"It will eventually, but we must keep it clean. We do not want it to get... er... what is it when a cut gets –"

"Infected," Thomas supplied.

"Oh, *ja*. That is it."

"Do you sometimes forget words?" Mary asked curiously.

"*Ja*. Sometimes it is hard to remember all the words I know."

"I think you speak English really good," Thomas stated.

"*You* don't," his sister observed, "you should say, speak English really *well*."

Thomas ignored her. He said, "It'd be hard to know all our words. Can you teach us some of yours?"

"*Ja*, I can do that."

"*Ja* means yes," Mary said. "And you call Mummy, Frau Jessie. What does Frau mean?"

"Frau means what you would call a married lady. It is like saying Missus." Anton wasn't paying too much attention to the conversation. He was leaning over, running his hands down the rest of Spencer's leg, checking for other injuries. Satisfied, he straightened and caught both children exchanging smug smiles.

"*Was ist?*"

"That means what is it?" Thomas told his sister.

Anton regarded them archly. "Very good. But what is funny?"

"You like our mum." Mary said. It wasn't a question, and it was delivered with conviction. Frau Jessie had warned him that Mary could be direct.

"She likes you too," Thomas added and to Anton's annoyance, he felt the blood rushing to his cheeks. "It would be all right if you kissed her. Mr Tyler kissed her and we didn't like him doing that. But if you kissed her that would be okay." Thomas paused to stare into the man's face. "You're going all red, Mr Bird," he declared, and the twins erupted into giggles.

"Enough, Thomas," Anton grumbled with feigned anger. "It is very dangerous to laugh at air force officers."

The boy pursed his lips in an unconvincing attempt to contain himself. Anton went on, "Can you go to the house *und* ask your mother for a large bowl of warm water *und* put some salt in it?"

"*Ja*, Mr Bird."

"*Danke, junger Mann.*"

He watched as the boy skipped away to the house. "You do like my mum, don't you?" Mary said, behind him.

He turned to face her. She was regarding him with interest and he wondered at her acuity.

"*Ja*, that is true. I think your mother is a very kind lady. She took care of me when I was unwell. Now –" he returned to the horse, but the girl wasn't finished with him.

"My mother doesn't have many friends. I think it's nice that you like her – so long as you're going to stay here."

"Mary –"

"I won't say anything about kissing," she interrupted, eying him with an expression that was more mature than her eight years warranted. "And I'll tell Tommy to shut up, he can be so childish sometimes."

The girl didn't see the smile that crept across Anton's face for she'd knelt to look at her horse's leg.

"Mr Bird?"

He turned to look at her. Her little face was serious.

"I don't want you and Mummy to be friends – not if you're going to leave one day."

Anton stared at the girl. She regarded him solemnly and said softly, "You *are* going to leave, aren't you?"

Equally solemn, he nodded. "I cannot stay here." After a moment, he added, "Would you like me to stay?"

There was a long pause before she whispered, "Yes, and

that's the problem. You won't."

***

Later that day, Jessica was kneeling in the kitchen garden. The seedlings she'd planted several months ago were approaching maturity. Her cabbages had formed hearts and the carrots, turnips and potatoes were growing well, as evidenced by the lush tops sprouting like verdant fountains from the ground.

She scrambled across to where the peas were strung on wires and rifled through the vines, picking the fattened pods. There would be enough for two meals and she was smiling with satisfaction when a shadow fell over her.

The captain was standing with the late afternoon sun haloing him. He dropped to a crouching position and absently pulled out a few straggling weeds.

"I spoke with Tommy this morning."

"So I understand." Jessica continued her work, picking and dropping the pods into a basin. Recent rains had been good for the garden; there was an abundance of pods ready to burst. "I don't know what you said to him but he seems quite happy now."

She didn't want to meet his eyes; they'd be blue, she knew. In the clear afternoon light, they were always blue.

"I had to promise to take him next time we go for a walk."

"I suppose it wouldn't hurt," Jessica said.

"*Ja*. Also, Mary's horse's leg is slowly getting better."

Jessica paused to swat a bug from her face, wondering at the captain's small talk. He wasn't normally given to idle chatter. "My children can be trying but you're good with them," she said, spotting another peapod. She picked it and dropped it in her basin.

"They also," he broke off to cough lightly. "They said that you like me. I told them that I like you too," he added quickly. "They remind me of my sister's children. They too can tease a person."

Jessica sat back on her heels and cocked her head on an angle. "Well, they're right, Captain. You are likeable – not nearly as fearsome as I first thought." She laughed to cover her discomfort. "And my children like you too. They don't like Robin Tyler."

"No. *Und* they did not like that he kissed you."

"Neither did you, apparently." She boldly met his eyes.

Now, he was grinning at her. "Oh, *ja, das ist richtig*. I did not like that at all." He shrugged. "But I already told you that."

Absently, the captain plucked a stray leaf from the ground. He offered it to her and she took it in her gloved hand. It was a dried rose leaf, crisp and curled on the ends.

"I want you to know, Frau Jessie," he said soberly, "that you have shown me much kindness. I owe you a great debt that I hope I will one day be able to repay."

Slightly embarrassed, she studied the rose leaf. "You already *are* repaying me, you just don't realise it. You've changed me. I have learned that I am stronger than I knew. I can cope with things that happen round here..." She gestured expansively to encompass her small farm, then emboldened, looked at him. "You're helping round the property so much. I don't know what I will do without you."

It was his turn to look uncomfortable and she glanced away to save him. After a moment, he pushed to his feet. "*Nun, ja*! I can see Herr Clay's ladies are ready for milking. I will go now."

As he turned to leave, she felt his hand linger lightly, for the briefest second, on her head. She knew that in the sun, her hair would be warm and burnished like polished bronze. She wondered what prompted him to touch it, then suddenly, as if realising what he was doing, he snatched back his hand and strode briskly away.

Chapter 18

Thomas knelt beside Anton, watching as the man pushed an axle through one side of a wooden tub. To the axle, he attached a handle at a right angle, then sat the entire tub on a frame that would enable it to turn like a hamster wheel when the handle was cranked.

"See?" Anton sat back. "You try."

Thomas grasped the handle and cranked, his face lighting up as the mechanism moved, causing the tub to spin. "We can make butter!"

Anton indicated the opening, turning the barrel so that the hatch rested on top. "In here, you put the cream *und* the salt. Then turn this handle until you cannot hear the cream. This way you will know the butter is ready, *ja*?"

"Shall we try?" Thomas jumped up. "I'll ask Mummy for the cream and we can see if it works."

As the little boy ran to find his mother, Anton carried his contraption to the garden tap and filled it with water. He hunkered on the cracked flagstones, watching lines of water bleed through minute gaps between the wooden slats. Gradually the seepage stopped as the wood swelled, forcing the panels to seal.

He looked up as he heard her approach. She stood looking down, a thick copper plait falling over her shoulder.

"Thomas says it's ready." She was eyeing the barrel-shaped machine on the ground before him.

The captain made a hopeful face, "Let us try it *und* see."

"All right," she turned. "I have a tub of cream in the ice box. I'll go and get it." She disappeared into the house, while he turned the handle on his churn ensuring it was adequately sealed.

Jessica returned shortly carrying a ceramic bowl covered by an enamelled plate. Thomas was beside her, a serving spoon and salt cellar in his hands.

"Does it leak?" the boy asked.

The captain shook his head and grinned up at them. "She is ready."

***

Jessica stood by as the captain opened the latch and emptied the water out of the barrel. Unguarded in concentration, she saw his face was less angular; he'd lost that drawn, pinched look he'd had a few months ago.

A few months! She was shocked and had to think for a moment. *It's now almost July. He's been here more than three months!*

Suddenly he glanced up and noticed the look on her face. Cocking an eyebrow, he said, "Frau Jessie? The cream now please."

"Yes, sorry. I was just thinking... It doesn't matter. Here," she thrust the basin at him. "Let's see how it goes."

The captain allowed Thomas to spoon the cream into the opening of the tub, and Jessica followed it with the prescribed amount of salt. "Mr Bird, can I turn it?" Thomas begged.

"Of course." The captain gave the handle several experimental turns before saying, "Off you go, *junger Mann*. It will take a long time."

"I can do it," Thomas insisted and started work.

After ten minutes, Thomas had grown tired of churning and the captain had taken over. By the time Jessica returned to her ironing, they were taking turns although she suspected the captain would do most of the work.

***

That evening, Jessica served fresh butter with warm bread and home-made soup for dinner. Thomas bragged to his sister about the achievement, exaggerating his contribution to the work effort. Jessica met the captain's eyes over her son's head.

"Thank you," she mouthed, smiling at him. Speaking aloud, she said, "Thomas, don't you think Mr Bird did a wonderful job to make the churn?"

"Oh, yes," the boy enthused. "It worked perfectly, Mummy."

"Good, because I've made pancakes for afters using the buttermilk. What do you think of that?"

Both children leapt from their seats cheering. The captain joined them, grasping their hands and dancing about. *"Pfannkuchen, pfannkuchen!"* He chanted and the children followed.

Jessica was laughing, "Righto, you lot, settle down. Finish your soup first."

She joined them at the table, remarking at how quickly they finished their meals, wiping their bowls clean with chunks of buttery bread in anticipation of a rare treat for pudding.

***

Being summer, the evening lingered long and warm. After tea, the children went down to the cottage to visit Sam and Marg while the captain and Jessica remained in the kitchen.

Jessica got up to put a saucepan of milk on the range. The afternoon sun was seeping through the open garden door, shimmering through the shapeless summer frock she wore. Anton's eyes sifted appreciatively over her trim lines.

He knew his thoughts were inappropriate. Knew also, that the unfamiliar stirring beneath his ribs was futile.

God help us, he thought, noting irrelevantly that he still thought in his mother tongue. *This is not going to end well.*

Even so, his eyes lingered on her bare legs, pale-skinned, with a scattering of freckles. Her calves were slender, her feet long and narrow. She wore slippers that looked hand-knitted with soft, leather soles. His mouth twitched at how charming he found that.

Natalia had always insisted on wearing the latest fashions; even about the house she ensured her hair was carefully styled, her skirts impeccably tailored, the seam up the back of her nylons perfectly straight.

Frau *Jessie doesn't even wear nylons – I don't expect they are easy to come by these days – but she is natural and unpretentious. How do they say unpretentious in English?*

She turned suddenly, the saucepan of steaming milk in her hand and caught him watching her. He might have been embarrassed but the nature of their friendship had changed, subtly, indefinably, and if she noticed him admiring her, he no longer cared. She was attractive and caring, and now that she had learned to trust him, she was no longer so guarded.

No, this is definitely not going to end well, he thought again.

Jessica approached the table and he pushed the cups towards her, first one, then the other, as she poured.

He stirred a spoon of cocoa into one cup, as she put the pan in the sink. He slid the cup to her side of the table, before attending to his own.

"What were you thinking?" she asked, suddenly, as she took her chair. "You had an odd smile on your face."

She has changed – not so shy anymore. "I was thinking about Natalia – er, *meine Freundin.*" It was the truth – of a sort.

***

Jessica was aware that the German's eyes had been following her as she moved about the kitchen. It used to embarrass her, but this evening she felt warmed by it. As she turned, she caught a hint of a smile on his face – prompting her to ask the question. But his answer had sent a jolt of realisation through her. *His girlfriend, of course!* she thought, feeling foolish.

"You must miss her," she said, as much to punish herself as

to create conversation.

"Oh, *ja*. I sometimes wonder what she is doing."

He seemed tired; his accent was always stronger when he was tired. It sounded like he said, *I voonder vhat she iss doingh.* She thought it made him sound young – and he was young – even if he was an experienced pilot. She was closer to thirty than his age of twenty-five.

Sipping his chocolate, he said, "This is very *gut*. Creamier..."

"I used the last of the buttermilk. Gives a more intense flavour."

"Oh," the captain said, somewhat distractedly. He seemed to be thinking carefully. Finally, he said, "Frau Jessie, I do not think about Natalia often any more. You remember, I told you that I have not seen her for more than a year?"

"You did say that." She looked through the open door to where the evening sky was slowly turning mauve.

He went on, hesitantly, "I have thought recently that... I wondered why I cannot remember her face."

Jessica's breath caught in her throat. She forced her eyes to focus on a swallow swooping and circling above the ruins of the stables just visible beyond the washhouse. The distinctive streamers of its tail seemed a bit longer than others she'd seen. *It's a male*, she thought, although she couldn't remember how she knew that. "It's hard to recall the features of someone's face," she said softly. "I have photographs of Jon, but..." She turned to him. "Did you carry a picture of Natalia with you in your aeroplane?"

The captain shook his head. "*Nein*."

Jessica held her chocolate mug in both hands, resting it against her lips. She didn't know what to say; she knew that servicemen generally carried pictures of their sweethearts with them. She let her eyes meet his and the expression there prompted her to speak. "You don't seem... you're –"

"I have changed."

She didn't speak. Instead, she drained the dregs of her chocolate, but continued holding the mug for the comfortable residual warmth in the stoneware.

"I have changed in many ways." He looked at his hands, clasped loosely on the table. "I will return to Germany one day, Frau Jessie. It is my home *und*... I don't know when... or how... when the war ends, perhaps sooner. I must go home. But I am changed. If I go home before the war is ended... I do not want to fly anymore – not for the Luftwaffe."

She gaped at him. "But Captain that is what you do. I mean," she huffed, in a humourless laugh, "it's not that I want you dropping bombs on people, but... won't your government insist?"

He shrugged one shoulder. "*Ja*. Of course."

Jessica saw the shadow cross his face. "You would miss it – flying, I mean. And you love the Messerschmitt."

He nodded. "The Sturmvogel is a magnificent machine. A dangerous machine. If she were in full service today, the war would be nearly over – at least for your country."

Jessica stiffened, but he quickly reached across the table to grasp her hand. "*Nein*! Do not look me like that – it is true."

"You are *losing* this war!" she snapped, pulling her hand away.

"I have read your newspapers."

"So you know the truth – not those lies *your* government tells!"

His eyes looked more grey than blue as he narrowed them at her. "Oh, *ja*... I know the truth. *Und* I can tell you that this war has not yet been decided. But if the Messerschmitt had been in service two years – less, one year – this war would be over for England."

Jessica made a derogatory sound but he ignored her and continued. "The first Messerschmitt, the one-zero-nine, was in production in the thirties. I know this because I have flown her. She was a fighter plane but not as sophisticated or as fast as the two-six-two. *This* Sturmvogel could change the war – if she were ready."

"Well, thank God, she's *not!*"

He made a gesture conceding the point.

"Perhaps if –" she went to say something else and he cut her off.

"Frau Jessie – please let us not talk about this. We will never agree."

"I just wish you would understand; they are telling your people lies, your politicians and that Adolf Hitler. It's all lies. And you are killing millions of innocent people – in your concentration camps. You know this?"

"*Und* what can I do about it?" he demanded angrily, slamming his hand on the table. She drew back in shock. "Even if I were not here," his gesture encompassed Broughton land and beyond, "if I were home, what could I do but accept *und* obey?"

His voice was bitter and resigned, and Jessica realised he was very aware of what was going on.

But he looked at her, his eyes holding hers. She saw the appeal in them and began to feel churlish for arguing with him. "Captain," she rose from her chair, collecting their empty mugs. "Let's go to the cottage and see what they're all up to down there."

***

The morning had started out sunny and bright, but as the sun slowly moved overhead and began to lower towards the westerly horizon, Anton thought the gathering clouds heralded a summer storm that might force him to lay down his tools.

He was perched on the ridge of the stable roof, having finally completed the skeletal structure of battens and rafters. Sam had located a company that specialised in salvaging reusable building material from the rubble remains of bombed houses.

The steward had traded half a dozen cans of milk for a load of roof shingles. They had been delivered the previous day, while Anton had hidden indoors. He hated such subterfuge, but there was no choice. When he emerged later, he looked the materials over with satisfaction and began planning the repairs.

Now he reviewed the first stage of his work. Tomorrow, weather permitting, he planned to begin hammering the shingles in place over the frame.

From where he sat, he could see across Broughton land, beyond the scraggly old orchard, towards the village called Jackson's Heath. Behind him were the paddocks where Jessica's cows were lounging in the summer grass, in the almost mesmerised state cows adopt when chewing their cud.

A flash of green to his right caught his eye and he turned just as Jessica appeared with her empty washing basket. He watched as she went to the clothes hoist, untying the pulley and swinging the line low enough for her to gather in the washing.

She was wearing a sheer summer frock in a shade of mint that, albeit faded, perfectly suited her autumn colouring. He knew that in her pragmatic way, this was not by design. It had been a warm day and the dress was probably the most practical she had for the work she'd planned.

He watched as the hem of her dress flapped round her thighs in the breeze as she reached to unpeg her washing. To his eye, she was beautiful in an honest and artless way, and he enjoyed watching her in her unguarded moments.

But she was inordinately reserved and blushed a pretty colour if she caught him looking at her.

Suddenly, as though she sensed his eyes on her, she turned. It would have been a normal response for him to wave at her, or smile at least. But he didn't, and nor did she. They simply regarded each other.

He watched as her hand came up to brush the stray hair from her face while the other flattened her billowing dress.

He knew she'd been afraid of him when they'd first met. He, himself, had been wary of her – for good reason. He'd been weakened with injury and illness and was entirely dependent on her for his recovery and refuge. Yet, as she gradually relaxed around him, he discovered a caring, intelligent woman hidden behind a shy façade.

And he had opened up to her too, being honest with her about who he was, what he was – her enemy, the means by which his country was attempting to crush hers.

Strangely, he'd wanted honest communication between them right from the beginning. It was as though, in his growing regard for her, his deepening feelings were inevitable.

The sun made a last valiant effort to break through the clouds, and, for a moment, her hair shone like copper shot through with sparks of cinnamon and strands the colour of rich, dark ale.

All this had transpired within seconds, but he felt his heart had stood still for long, long minutes. As a dark cloud suddenly obscured the sun, the spell was broken. Jessica unpegged the last of her washing, bent to pick up her basket, then returned to the house.

Anton felt as though he was awakening from a sleep. He dragged himself back to awareness that he was precariously straddling the gabled peak of the roof, which at this point was no more than rafters and battens. Over the coming days, he would finish the repairs and add the flashing along the top to seal the ridge.

The stables would be ready for winter. As it was, Mary's pony was housed within its roofless walls for the protection afforded from the wind.

He drew a deep satisfied breath and, as the first fat drops of summer rain began to fall, he decided his work was done for the day.

**

Jessica hung up the telephone and returned to the kitchen. She'd heard the planes go over the previous night and was relieved to hear from her mother.

"Are Granny and Grandad all right, Mum?" Mary asked, scraping the last of her breakfast from the bowl.

"They're fine. But Grandad's working too hard. Granny's making sure he takes his pills. The planes went somewhere else last night... Sheffield, she thinks. They have that steelworks there. Eat up, Thomas, or you'll be late for the school bus."

"Where's Mr Bird?"

"He's helping Mr Clay load the milk cans into the car. Finish your porridge."

"I have."

Mary was taking her bowl to the sink. "Mum, can you tie my hair back?"

"Come here then."

Mary had the brush and elastic band with her. She passed them over her shoulder and Jessica dragged the brush through the tangled strawberry-blonde strands in long, rapid strokes, smoothing it into a single bunch and securing it with the elastic band.

"All done, now don't miss the bus!"

**

Jessica waved the children off from Broughton Hall's front porch. The sky that morning was a clear blue with only a single fluffy, inoffensive cloud. It promised to be a perfect summer day.

The captain will be able to finish the stable roof, she thought, as her eyes slid to the left of the driveway, to just beside the steward's cottage. He and Sam were there, prattling on together, as they hauled the great vats of fresh milk into the Daimler's boot.

In recent days, Sam had sat beside her as she practised her driving, taking the milk to Bright and Sons herself. And with each trip she grew more confident on the lanes and roads of Wharferidge and Wolstone. But today she'd opted to remain at home and catch up on a few chores.

Suddenly Sam gave a shout of laughter and she saw him slap the captain's back in some shared humour. Sam and Marg had certainly adopted him as a son, and the captain, in his turn, seemed fond of the older couple.

As though he knew she were watching, Captain Vogel closed the boot of the car and raised his head to meet her eyes.

The look that passed between them caused her heart to swell and an odd thrill rippled through her. It was magnetic, a connection at some boundless level that imbued her with a sense of lightness and warmth.

That I should feel this way, while my country is at war and everyone is facing grief and hardship, is shameful, but I can't help it.

Tearing her eyes away, she bent and took up the cane basket at her feet, descended the porch steps and turned towards the orchard.

***

The apples were clean-smelling, firm and damp from overnight dew. The morning sun hadn't yet reached the orchard so the air was still cool; Jessica buttoned her cardigan and began her work. It was still too early in the season for the apples to be properly ripe, but there might be some she could gather for an apple pie.

As she worked, Jessica checked each apple for suspicious

holes or signs of worms, discarding those that may be inhabited, placing the ones suitable for cooking in her basket.

Moving about the trees, pulling branches down for easier access, she welcomed the sense of well-being passing through her. Breathing deeply of the apple-scented air, an illicit contentment expanded her lungs and seeped throughout her body. It flooded the tips of her toes and warmed her cold fingers, as she plucked the apples from their stalks.

A clear, repetitive bird call echoed through the still morning and Jessica spied a sweet little brown thrush, with a speckled breast, standing on the leaf mulch about ten feet from where she worked.

"Hello, that's a pretty song. Looking for some breakfast?" Jessica selected a suitably wormy apple and tossed it near the bird.

A dreamy enchantment seemed to permeate the estate, and Jessica responded with a breathy, off-key song.

"An apple for the teacher, that seems the thing to do, because I want to learn, about romance from you –"

"Frau Jessie?"

She turned with a start to find the German captain standing some three yards behind her. His gaze held hers for several heartbeats while she watched the play of thought ripple across his face.

She saw wonder and pain, delight and grief.

Then, finally, she saw resignation, followed by a wordless question.

Without being entirely aware of it, she took a step towards him.

He accepted her movement as consent and bridged the gap between them.

***

Anton didn't know why he followed Jessica to the orchard. Only minutes before, he'd been helping Herr Clay with the milk cans, but as he'd straightened, he'd seen her across the morning-damp lawn, standing on the porch, her eyes on him.

A look had passed between them; something intangible, yet compelling. It caused his breath to hitch, and his better judgement failed him.

Herr Clay had climbed into the driver's seat. Slamming the Daimler's door, Anton turned away as the car bounced down the driveway. He didn't question his actions as he walked unthinkingly, deliberately across the lawn.

He left boot prints in the wet grass behind him. They traced a direct line to the remains of a short flight of steps down to the old orchard, where the gnarled stumps of long dead apple and plum trees kept a silent vigil, like soldiers in formation.

It was beyond here that he went; where the lichened, ancient stone wall marked the border of Broughton land with Jackson's Heath; where the newer trees, the self-seeded and the suckers, grew in a haphazard stand; where he could see the twitching of leafy, heavily-fruited branches as the ripe fruit were selected and plucked by an unseen hand.

He approached, becoming aware of her voice whispering among the branches, gentle and cheerful; he didn't know to whom she was talking, and just as he wondered, she began to sing – a little tunelessly, but her happiness warmed his heart.

Anton rounded an apple tree that was clad in bright summery green; she didn't hear his step for her song continued – some popular American tune he wasn't familiar with – growing clearer as he drew closer.

And then there she was.

The morning sun had not yet warmed the air and little puffs of steam issued from her lips. Dew dripped from the trees and sparkled, jewel-like, in her hair. The dampness caused the tendrils about her face to frizz and stick out.

Breathing steadily, he watched her for a moment as she examined the fruit, passing over the immature, dropping the ripe ones into a basket slung over her arm.

She was unknowingly beautiful, and his heart gave a lurch. He knew he should turn away. But then, he'd known for a long time that he ought to have risen from his bed late at night and crept into the darkness and out of her life. He had done neither, and now...

Anton stepped forward, "Frau Jessie?"

Her song broke off and she turned with a jerk. A flush of happiness washed over her face but she quickly controlled her expression, her lovely hazel eyes regarding him serenely.

Something unexpected and unwanted had grown between them, uncultivated and free of circumstance, it had sprung of its own accord – like these trees, self-sown, self-sustaining and fruiting.

Jessica had evidently felt it too, and in that moment, the German captain knew a grief so intense that he wanted to weep – for they were worlds apart, sworn enemies. They had no right to each other.

But she took a step towards him – a single step that changed everything and he knew they were both lost.

***

In the split second it took for the captain to reach her, Jessica had dropped her basket, oblivious to the apples that spilled onto the wet grass. She automatically raised her face to meet his mouth as his arms came around her.

He kissed her with an intensity for which she was unprepared. They staggered heavily against the solid trunk of a tree, their mouths fused with a desperate passion, a hungry delight that left her insensible to the world beyond the seclusion of the orchard.

His lips were hot and demanding, and Jessica replied with equal fervour. As the world shrank to a fresh, verdant haven, they clung to one another with a ferocity that left them both breathless.

His hands roved over her back, down to the low curve of her spine, around her hips, drawing her hard against him.

She pressed forwards, responding with an urgency born of a truth too long denied.

A sobering truth, as finally, he raised his head. She felt him pull away from her and looked up. His cloudy blue eyes searched her face. His fingers gently traced the curve of her jaw and cheek. His thumb brushed her swollen lips.

Jessica found she was trembling while her heart was pounding beneath her ribs. Pressing her palms against his chest, she felt his own hammering in time.

In the long moments that followed, she stood within the circle of his arms, hidden in the sheltering embrace of the apple trees, while the truth lay exposed between them; an impossible, hopeless reality, too distressing to be spoken in words.

The German captain's face was filled with pain. As Jessica gave an involuntary sob, he pulled her against his heart, holding her in his arms as she rested her forehead against his collar.

Chapter 19

Jessica sat on her bed, staring at the pair of shoes she'd kicked off as she'd come in. One was upright, ready for the insertion of a foot, while the other lay on its side, heel towards her so she could see the caked earth and leaf debris on its sole.

Under any other circumstances she would never have worn her outdoor shoes through the house – but evidently she had. Evidently, because she had no memory of returning to the house, much less finding her way upstairs and to her room, nor could she remember what she'd done with her basket of apples.

All she could remember was the stricken look on the captain's face as she'd twisted away from him and taken an unsteady step backwards. His arms had dropped to his sides and he'd watched helplessly as she turned away from him.

"Frau Jessie..." he paused and she heard him draw in his breath. "I am sorry."

At this, she turned to face him, back straight and nostrils flaring in an effort to breathe evenly. "Yes, captain, you are sorry. But I allowed it... You are a handsome young man and I am a foolish, lonely widow. Let us forget this happened."

She'd felt his eyes following her as she strode back to the house.

Now, she stared at her hands where they lay loosely clasped in her lap. *What the hell do I do now?* she wondered. While neither had acknowledged the growing accord between them, they had, by tacit agreement, presented as friends.

Now, though, everything had changed, for in those brief moments beneath the apple tree, they had exchanged a physical dialogue. If they were not lovers, they were not merely friends either.

Yes, she'd told him to forget that it ever happened, but in truth, could she?

Could we be lovers? The thought came without prompting and refused to be allayed, just as she accepted now, without denial, that she loved him. *It will be hard enough to see him leave when all this is over, without being his lover too.*

She sighed again, a ragged exhalation filled with pain. But the ache in her chest was not going away. He'd fired a need, low down in her belly. It smouldered and boiled, fanned into a bright glow whenever he looked at her or inadvertently touched her. Now, after kissing him, she was on the brink of combustion.

Not even Jon made me feel so alive and so... she searched for the right word ... *attractive. He makes me feel attractive and sensual... and desired!*

A sob escaped her but she immediately shook herself. *I will not cry, not now, because I know there will be a million and more tears shed before this is over.*

It was not even nine o'clock, yet she felt she'd lived an entire day already. She got up and drifted to the window. Her bedroom overlooked the front yard; the porch was down and to her left, visible when she pressed her face to the glass. Immediately before her was the ancient oak tree with its massive trunk and heavy, weather-beaten limbs. As she watched, the captain came into view behind a wheelbarrow. It was piled high with roof shingles for the stables, a hammer and tin of shingle-nails balanced on top.

He continued across the drive, towards the stables, and out of her sight.

Jessica sighed and swallowed the emotion welling anew in her throat. She turned away; there was too much work to be done for her to linger here. Nor could she afford the luxury of grief for something that could never be.

She squared her shoulders and left her room.

***

Anton slumped heavily against the apple tree watching Jessica rush away from him. As a gentle morning breeze stirred the leaves above him, he felt the cool dampness of her tears on his shirt.

He felt like weeping, himself, for the pain he'd caused her and the pain he'd caused himself. Why had he gone to the orchard? Why had he followed her, taken her in his arms and kissed her? Why had she let him? They had responded to one another with a passion that was overwhelming.

Between them, they had held a match to a dormant cognisance and it had ignited like a bonfire the moment their lips had touched.

Of course, they could have continued to deny it, allowing it to smoulder beneath the surface of their daily lives until he could leave her. It would then have gradually cooled and inevitably died.

That would have been the sensible option.

No such sanity had prevailed.

With a grunt of uncommon ill temper, Anton pushed away from the tree, his foot bumping against something small and hard that rolled away from him.

Squatting, he gathered the apples that had spilled across the ground, then carried the basket back to the house.

The garden door was propped open with a chair, the kitchen within was dim, silent.

Anton went inside, quietly placed the basket of apples on the table. He guessed she was upstairs and considered – for the briefest of moments – going to her. But the need to hold her would not be stilled, the raging desire so newly awakened within him continued to burn. She had told him it couldn't happen again.

It would be more than stupid to go to her room – it would be dangerous.

So, he retreated to the comparative safety of physical labour.

***

Jessica was unaware that Sam had returned from Wolstone until she heard the Daimler pull up beside the wash-house. She'd just taken a pot of stewed apples from the range and set them aside to cool. The pastry for her pie could be made later.

Earlier, when Jessica had come downstairs from her room, she'd been gratified to find the basket of apples on the table, even if, knowing the captain had brought them, poked at the raw wound in the region of her heart.

The Daimler's engine shut down. The door slammed and not long after, her steward came loping into the kitchen. She hadn't expected to see the captain come in behind him.

Over Sam's shoulder, her eyes met the younger man's blue ones and a million silent words passed between them – words of apology, regret and sadness. But there was also understanding, warmth and affection. She smiled at him and her heart swelled as he returned her smile. *We'll be fine*, she thought, *whatever happens now*.

"I asked Anton to come in with me," Sam was saying, "interrupted his work, I did, 'cause I've got summat you both need to 'ear."

"Shall I put the kettle on?"

"No. Shouldn't take too long." He pulled up a chair and indicated with a gesture that Jessica and the captain do likewise.

Once they were settled, he turned to the captain. "Anton, what did you do with your parachute? The night you were shot down, where did you leave it?"

"After I landed, I did not have much time. I cut the lines *und* gathered it. I buried it as best I could."

"You also 'ad them broken ribs... wouldn't've been easy," Sam commented, thinking. When the captain didn't respond, he added, "Come down quite a distance from your plane, that right?"

The captain nodded. "Over that way." He pointed towards

Jackson's Heath. "In a field on the edge of the forest. I buried the parachute there."

Sam nodded. "Aye, well it were found, and guess who it were reported to?

"Christ, not Robin?" Jessica guessed, aghast.

"Yup."

"That doesn't mean..." she paused, "Captain, if you were so close to the village, why did you come here?"

"There were too many cottages – too many people. I hoped I was not badly injured *und* could hide somewhere until I recovered."

"So you came here?" Lingering emotion after the episode in the orchard made Jessica's tone sharper than intended.

"I..." He sighed, "I was not thinking clearly."

"Of course you weren't, lad," Sam threw an admonishing glance in Jessica's direction. "Anyway, turns out it were found and taken to our friend. Now," Sam paused significantly. "Robin Tyler, I 'eard down at Bright and Sons this morning, is an investigator with the Security Service."

"What!" Jessica cried. "Since when?"

"I didn't know such a role existed, myself," the older man said. "But apparently, it does and 'e's it. 'Is job is to investigate unusual sightings, or anyone be'aving suspiciously. This morning, when I dropped off the milk, Georgie Bright was talking to Jeremy, the stonemason from Jackson's 'eath. Jeremy reckoned that it were 'is dad what found the parachute and took it to the 'ome Guard. They reported it, and because our chap Tyler 'ad a relative living so close, the case were assigned to 'im."

Jessica started to feel ill. "When did all this happen?" She kept her gaze firmly locked on her steward, not daring to meet the captain's eyes.

Sam, the bugger, apparently knew exactly how her thoughts ran and spared her nothing. "Around the time 'e took you and the children to the May Day parade."

The time Robin kissed me. The flush started on her chest and moved rapidly up her neck.

The captain noticed and made a snorting sound. She glared at him and he grinned in response. "I said I did not like him."

"Shut up!"

That made him snort again.

"Sam," she said, "does this mean Robin suspects we know something? Is that what they're saying in Wolstone?"

"*They're* not saying that, *I* am. There's a reason the bastard's been sniffing around 'ere, being all friendly-like, and there's a reason 'e were questioning young Tommy."

"What are we going to do?" She fidgeted with a cup left on the table after breakfast. *If the captain's discovered, if I'm found to have concealed him, they will lock me away – I will lose my children!* She spoke carefully, "If Robin suspects, it's only a matter of time before..." she looked at the captain.

"I must leave." He reached across and took her hands in both of his. Her heart leapt at the contact and she stared down at their clasped fingers.

The gesture was more than a comforting touch from a friend, and its significance was not lost on Sam. He scratched his chin and said, "Hmm."

The captain released Jessica's hands and sat back decisively. "I will hand myself in."

Jessica drew in a quick breath but the older man cut her off.

"No," Sam responded firmly. "They'll want to know where you've been all this time. Won't be 'ard for them to figure it out, then Jessica will be in all kinds o' strife."

"I can say I held her against her will."

"And allowed me to go out visiting the neighbours, freely driving myself about the countryside and going to May Day fairs?" Jessica made a scornful sound. "As if they'd believe that!"

"Look," Sam interrupted, "you can't turn yourself in and you can't claim you 'eld Jessica and the children against their will. Facts are, 'e only suspects – 'e 'as no evidence and no way of proving it if 'e can't find you. We 'ave the advantage because we know what 'e's about. Just stay out of sight and given time, 'ope it'll blow over."

"Robin's not going to let this go," Jessica said dismally.

"Probably not, and we'll need to come up with summat." Sam agreed. "But for now, I gotta get back to work." He rose, pulling his tobacco pouch from his pocket as he strode outside.

"So I must," the captain said, rising. Jessica's eyes followed him as he moved towards the door, but suddenly he paused. Turning, he said, "Frau Jessie, I am sorry for what happened in the orchard but... I do not know how to say it; I find that I care for you but I have complicated things between us."

She looked away, unable to meet his gaze.

He spoke slowly, trying to find the right words. "I know you are afraid," he said gently. "*Und*, these are dangerous times, but... even knowing it, I cannot help how I feel. If you truly wish it, I will not touch you again – not that I do not want to," he added roguishly.

"I don't know what I want," Jessica murmured softly. "I..." she sucked in a breath and ran her hands through her hair making the short pieces at the front stick up. "I'm afraid of so many things."

He stepped closer but she refused to look up at him. "Tell me," he said, "do you honestly want me to stay away from you?"

In her head, the answer was *yes*, but in her heart... Raising her eyes, she said, "God help us all, Captain, no. I don't want you to stay away. But I like you and I don't want my feelings for you to grow stronger. So, despite what I want, we cannot become involved. It will only be more painful when eventually you go."

She added in a whisper, "And it's obvious that you *must* go."

He extended a hand and lightly stroked her cheek, then on impulse, bent and pressed his lips to her forehead, firmly and lingeringly. Jessica closed her eyes, savouring the touch of his warm breath on her face.

"Then it is for the best, *mein Schatz*."

He was gone before she opened her eyes, and she sat for several minutes thinking over Sam's report. Despite her better judgement, whenever she thought about the captain's admission that he cared for her, her heart rode on a tide of dreamy happiness.

If only he were not the enemy... But *if only* was futile.

"Okay." She spoke out loud, as though to lend herself strength, and getting up from her chair, she went to check her stewed apples. She stirred them with a wooden spoon and inhaled the sharp-scented steam.

"Let's take every day as it comes," she told the fruit.

Chapter 20

It was another clear summer morning and Anton felt uplifted as he dressed, made his bed and tidied the few items that belonged to him about his room.

"*Guten morgen, Herr* Bird," Thomas greeted him, as Anton came into the kitchen. The two children were sitting at the table in their school uniforms, loudly scraping up the last of their porridge with their spoons.

"*Guten morgen,* Tommy *und* Mary," he responded, brightly. Anton was growing inordinately fond of these children and it was a sentiment foreign to him. He'd never been overly interested in children. Not even his sister's offspring instilled him with any great desire to have his own.

But these two, he rather liked. Mary was intelligent, wise beyond her years, and Tommy had an enquiring mind coupled with a natural ability to remember things – a talent that evidently extended to languages. When at first the boy was speaking German to him, Anton assumed it was mere mimicry. Yet as the child's vocabulary expanded, Anton began actively teaching him.

Anton believed that children could do worse than be multilingual – indeed most people in Europe had more than one language.

"Mummy will be upset if she hears you two speaking German," Mary pointed out. Unfortunately, she was right. Jessica would probably see value in her children learning a second language, provided it was not German.

"Mummy's just being silly," was Thomas's determination and Anton privately agreed.

"Where is she?" the captain asked, filling the kettle.

"Out at the hen-house collecting eggs," Mary responded, glaring at her brother. "It's about the only chore Thomas has, but he's too lazy to get out of bed in time."

"I'm not lazy!"

"Yes, you are!"

"You're the lazy one, you –"

"*Das genügt!*" Anton put the kettle on the hob as Jessica returned. She stood outside the door, toeing off her boots before coming into the kitchen with a basket of eggs. Meanwhile Anton got out the crockery for Jessica's and his own morning cups of tea.

"There." Jessica put the basket down in front of her son. "When you get home from school this afternoon, you will weed the kitchen garden to make up for it. Morning, Captain," she added, seeing Anton for the first time. "Mary, keep making faces at your brother and you can help him! Captain, sit down and get out of the way!"

Anton made a face of solidarity with the children and hurried to obey. Mary giggled and Thomas leaned conspiratorially towards him and whispered, "Mum's grumpy this morning."

"And like to get worse if you don't get a move on." Jessica was packing sandwiches into paper bags and thrusting them at the twins. "Look at the time – the bus'll be here any moment!"

Both children jumped off their chairs, grabbed their bags and made a dash for the door.

Jessica turned to the captain. "I was thinking –"

"Good morning Mr Tyler!" Mary's bright voice filtered in from outside.

***

Jessica and the captain froze, listening.

"Good morning, young lady, young man. Is your Mum inside?"

Thomas didn't miss a beat, "She went down to the hen-house. You can look for her if you like..."

"God bless his little heart," Jessica murmured, turning, "Quick! Upstairs –"

But the captain had already vanished through the hall door.

Jessica followed, in case Robin came into the kitchen. She and Anton ran up the stairs as quickly and lightly as possible. While Jessica paused on the landing, Anton continued along the hall and into his room. He smiled encouragingly at her before softly closing the door.

Jessica went into her own room, going directly to the window. It looked down on the drive where Robin's motor was parked out the front. *How the hell did we not hear him pull up? Sneaky bastard!*

She stood anxiously, counting the minutes, then, undoing the top buttons on her blouse, she left her room.

Robin was just returning up the path from the hen-house when Jessica came outside. She was buttoning her blouse as she saw him. "Oh, hello," she said, feigning surprise and quickly fastened the last button. "What brings you out and about this early?"

"Friendly visit. Thomas said you were down at the hen-house. I've been looking for you."

"I was down there but managed to get muck all over my shirt." She chuckled self-deprecatingly. "Had to go and get changed. Did the children get on the school bus, do you know?"

He glanced in the direction of the drive, although it wasn't visible from where they stood. "I assume so, they told me where I could find you, then dashed off."

"Good-oh..." Jessica paused. He was obviously waiting for an invitation to come inside. Containing a sigh, she waved towards the garden door. "The kettle's just boiled. Would you like some tea?"

Say no, say no!

"Lovely, thank you."

She felt his eyes on her back, heavy and penetrating, as she poured boiling water into the teapot. When she turned, he made no effort to pretend otherwise. Instead, he indicated the two cups the captain had laid out only minutes earlier.

"Expecting me, were you?" It was a casual question delivered with his most charming smile. He couldn't know what Jessica had learned about him; her senses were on high alert. She arranged her face into what she hoped was an open and friendly expression and spoke lightly. "Unfortunately, I'm not psychic. I usually put a cup out for Marg. She often stops for a chat before she goes upstairs to tidy up."

"As yes, if only we *were* psychic," he said.

Jessica smiled politely, pouring the tea while he watched and absently fingered a teaspoon. Intensely aware of his eyes burning holes in her back, Jessica felt the air grow thick and tight round them.

She'd already inquired the reason for his visit – it would be rude to ask again – yet something was up and the longer he sat watching her like this, the more uneasy she felt.

Casting about for something to break the tension, she said, "Do you know if the telephone lines to Leeds are down? I can't get through to my parents."

Inane, perhaps, but it broke the rigid silence and he responded genially enough. "No, I haven't heard about any problems. I called Leeds only last night and everything was working."

"My father has been ill lately. It's hard to know what to do for the best. I could go over to see them, I suppose but I'm loathe to use the petrol."

"How long since you've heard from them?"

"A few days."

"Unusual?"

"Not really. But I worry about Dad's health and all. Perhaps I'll give it a couple more days."

He nodded thoughtfully and they fell silent again. Jessica suspected that he was trying to unsettle her. It was working.

She concentrated on sipping her tea and breathing evenly although her heart was pounding so hard she could almost see it leaping beneath her blouse.

"Jessica," Robin began suddenly and she nearly choked.

Here it comes... Oh, God, help us! She opened her face innocently and looked across at him.

"I don't mean to alarm you," he went on.

She laughed, hoping it didn't sound contrived. "Whenever someone says that it's impossible not to be alarmed."

His smile seemed forced. "Well, I don't *want* to alarm you but there have been reports of a stranger roaming hereabouts – No, let me finish," he added at her quick intake of air. "It has only been a rumour. I just wanted to let you know, since you're alone here with the children."

"I'm not really alone. Marg and Sam are –"

"An old man and woman in a cottage down the drive." His mouth twisted derisively.

"Hardly what I'd call helpful if someone came creeping into the house late at night."

Jessica frowned thoughtfully. "How serious are the reports?"

He studied her for several long moments before appearing to make a decision. "A parachute was found... a month or so back. We suspect –"

"A *parachute*?" she interrupted, fearfully.

"It was found in the forest behind Peter Edmonds's place."

"Peter Edmonds?" She could feel the back of her blouse becoming damp. "I don't think I know him."

"Doesn't matter if you know him. He found a parachute in his field – someone had tried to bury it – didn't make a good job of it."

"Seems very odd. What would a parachute be doing out

here?"

He narrowed his eyes and watched her unwaveringly. Jessica tried very hard not to squirm.

Finally, he said, "Jessica," his tone was firm, carefully modulated. "I came to warn you. You may remember, a while ago, two German planes were shot down."

"Oh, yes, my mother telephoned the next morning. She was very excited; told me the searchlighters found the crew." *Stop blethering, you idiot!*

"They found three crewmen. We suspect... there is reason to believe there was a fourth. When the others were questioned, they insisted there were only the three of them but..." Robin shrugged. "We didn't believe them – especially now, since finding the parachute... It's Luftwaffe."

Jessica didn't have to feign her agitation. She said, "You think there's a, a –"

"A German – yes, in the area."

She dragged in a ragged breath. Her hands were trembling so badly she clasped them firmly in her lap beneath the table. "Why do you keep saying *we*?" she asked, ingenuously. She was beginning to feel dizzy. "Are you with the Home Guard?"

"No, but in times like these we all like to know who's about, don't we?"

She nodded her agreement and tried to breathe evenly.

He went on, "When the parachute was found, we knew for certain there was a fourth man. *Jessica*," he stressed her name. "You *must* contact me immediately, if you see anyone, a stranger roaming the area, anything suspicious or unusual at all." His eyes bored into her. "It's your *duty*, Jessica, as an Englishwoman. If you see anything or... you *know* anything."

He suspects!

Suddenly she drew in her breath indignantly. "The bloody Germans killed my husband, Robin! Of *course* I would report anything I saw." She hoped her tone was edged with just the right mix of resentment and anxiety, but couldn't resist adding, innocently, "But shouldn't sightings be reported to the Home Guard?"

"Report anything you hear or see, any concerns, directly to me."

He rose and, relieved that he was leaving, Jessica rose with him. But instead of moving directly to the door, he took her hand and pinned her beneath his heavy gaze.

Don't let them see you're vulnerable, Jon's words echoed in her brain as she held Robin's stare.

Unexpectedly, his manner became more personable. "Jessica, I'm sure you know I'm very fond of you and the children. Why don't the three of you visit next Sunday?"

She tried not to grimace. "Robin, I …"

He smiled persuasively. "Lunch?"

"I'm not sure –" She gave a slight tug of her hand but he wasn't relinquishing it just yet.

"Twelve-thirty?"

"I –"

"My father would love to see you. He's so excited about your interest in the Broughtons." Finally releasing her hand, Robin turned to the door. "Twelve-thirty," he repeated, and was gone.

***

Anton was listening from the hall. He wondered how much Tyler knew and how much was mere guesswork. The man was dangerous! He could easily trap Jessica, intimidate the children into saying something incriminating – and that demand framed as an invitation to lunch... Anton clenched his fists.

Waiting impatiently, Anton knew what trepidation felt like. He counted interminable seconds before he heard the garden door close and Jessica's relieved exhalation.

***

The kitchen door burst open and Jessica gasped in surprise. "For God's sake, Captain!" she cried in a hoarse whisper, a hand going to her throat. She was leaning against the door through which her visitor had just left. Pushing away, she abruptly crossed the floor and grasped the man by the elbow and marched him into the hall. "What if he comes back?" she hissed. "Stay here!"

Releasing his arm, she shoved passed and strode up the stairs and down the hall to the parlour where she could watch Robin's departure from behind the curtain. Only when the fancy green Jaguar turned out of the driveway did she relax and feel as though she could breathe again.

The captain was lurking in the doorway. "You can come in now," she said slumping onto the couch, chafing her cold hands. "That was horrible! He knows something, I'm certain of it." She gazed up at him, her face pale. "Is there any way anyone could have seen you working in the paddocks or – Lucifer's balls!"

She jumped to her feet and grabbed his forearms. "Captain, tell me. When you were ill, when you were hiding in the stables, did you go outside at all – at night?"

His expression grew quizzical. Slowly shaking his head he said, "Unless I was um... *geistig verwirrt...* er raving. I do not remember doing so. Why?"

"Thomas saw someone, a man, lurking round the stables late one night. He said it wasn't Sam – he also said it wasn't you. But... please say it was you. Try to remember!"

"If it were me, Tommy would know. If he saw someone in the dark, it was not me."

Jessica felt her insides grow cold. "He would've said if it was Robin. So, if it was not you, and it wasn't Sam or Robin... Who the bloody hell was it?"

They wordlessly stared at one another and Jessica's knees

grew weak. She dropped bonelessly onto the couch again and he sat beside her.

Leaning forwards, elbows on thighs, hands dangling, he said, "Whoever he was, if he knew about me, I would not be here now."

"That's true. But if it were someone who suspects you're here..."

"He would have searched the property."

"Hmm," Jessica said, thoughtfully, faintly relieved. He was right: If there were even a hint that she was harbouring a fugitive, a lynch mob would have combed the place from top to bottom.

An unexpected bang from another part of the house caused them both to jump.

"Mornin'... Anyone around?" Marg called out from the kitchen and Jessica finally relaxed.

Chapter 21

"Mummy … wake up!"

Jessica stirred and blinked open her eyes. The room was shrouded in grey, the sky beyond her window was heavy with leaden clouds. She groaned and rolled over.

"Mummy, you awake?" It was Mary's voice, questioning, with a slight hint of worry.

Jessica groaned again. She felt exhausted, and for a moment, she wondered why. Then she remembered the late night spent working through her accounts, straining her eyes in the inadequate lamplight while unseasonably icy winds had lashed the house with relentless rain and hail.

"The Scots call it a blirty," Sam had informed her the previous afternoon as the driving rain had hammered on the new stable roof.

"Mummy?"

"Yes, Mary," Jessica murmured. "I'm awake." She slowly rolled over, then suddenly sat bolt upright. "Bloody hell! What time is it?"

"It's not late, Mum." Mary responded. "It's not even six."

"Late enough! That sky's black as gunpowder. You should've woken me sooner." She slid out of bed and reached for her dressing-gown. "The cows need milking. Have you eaten?"

"Mr Bird made toast for Tommy and me, then we all went down to the paddock and helped Mr Clay with the milking. Mr Clay says another blirty's on the way."

"Terrific!" Jessica grumbled, shoving her feet into her slippers and combing her hair with clawed hands.

"Mummy, I would've let you sleep longer – Mr Bird said you were working late last night – but there's water in my room."

"What do you mean there's water in your room?"

Mary shrugged. "I think it was the storm last night. Mr Bird had a look at it and he thinks there's a hole in the roof."

"You'd better show me."

***

Jessica stood in a corner of Mary's room, peering at the ceiling. When Mary had said there was water, Jessica had assumed a trickle, easily repaired. But this was something different.

The ceiling was saturated in a patch, roughly two feet in diameter, causing the area to sag precariously. A steady dribble of water was tinkling into a tin bucket on the floor beneath it.

"Lucifer's balls!" Jessica growled irritably. "As if we don't have enough to worry about."

"Mr Bird said he could get into the ceiling to see how bad the damage is."

Jessica sighed resignedly. "I hope it's something that can be fixed easily. We haven't an unlimited supply of money."

"What about Daddy's insurance?" Mary asked.

The insurance company had paid out on Jon's policy, but claimed that as Jon had chosen to enlist, rather than wait to be conscripted, he'd contributed to his own death. Under such circumstances, they would only pay fifty per cent of the benefit.

Bitterly disappointed, Jessica had paid a lump sum off her mortgage and kept a small nest egg for emergencies. It was one of the reasons she was up late the night before, poring over her books.

"Daddy's insurance won't last five minutes at this rate!" she snapped in frustration.

Mary's face had looked hopeful. Now it fell and Jessica, immediately contrite, lightly touched her daughter's cheek. "Don't worry, love. We're lucky we have the money – many don't. Off you go – I need to get dressed. I'll see you downstairs in a few minutes."

***

Later that morning, Anton found Jessica standing on a step-ladder in Mary's room, gingerly poking the wet plaster with her fingertips. Even the slightest pressure caused the soaked plaster to give like a sponge.

Anton watched silently while she stretched upwards to examine the damage. He'd already made his inspection, and stood back now admiring the creamy flesh around her belly button as her knitted top rode up. Realising he was behaving unchivalrously, he averted his gaze.

"It's pretty bad, isn't it?" she said. He came forward and offered his hand as she climbed off the step-ladder.

"It could come down any moment," he agreed.

Jessica tugged her clothing into place. "I'll ask Sam to go up on the roof to look at it straight away."

"You should not ask an old man onto the roof."

"Well, *I* can't do it – and neither can you. You're still getting over broken ribs, remember?"

"The water is coming from a hole that may be repaired from inside. *Jedenfalls*, I am recovered enough to fix the stable roof."

He watched her expression change in the face of his logic.

Mary had taken out the full bucket and the steady, metallic *plinker-plinker-plinker* of dripping water into the empty one filled the room. "You did fix the stables, didn't you? Very well," Jessica conceded. "Marg'd kill me if Sam fell off the ladder or something."

He chuckled, "Oh, *ja*, she will be not pleased."

***

Jessica watched Thomas hop about with excitement as the captain ascended the ladder. "Please Mummy, *please* can I go up too?"

"No, love." Jessica was holding the ladder, peering into the darkened space above. "I don't want you making holes through the ceiling with your feet."

"I wouldn't," the boy implored. "I could help … I could hold the lamp and –"

"No, Thomas! I won't tell you again!"

Mary was sitting on her bed, watching. She made a derisive noise. "You can't help. You'd only be in the way."

"Both of you be quiet. Captain Vogel, can you see anything?" Jessica called into the attic.

There were various bangs, scrapes and muffled bumps coming from overhead. "Not yet," he responded, "nothing but … urgh, *Spinnen*!"

His head appeared in the hole above them. "*Phht* …!" he swatted at a spider's web sticking to his hair. "Many *Spinnen*. Can I have the lamp, please?"

"I've got it!" Thomas cried.

"Just pass it to him," Jessica said, as the boy quickly climbed several rungs of the ladder. "Here Mr Bird."

The German took the lamp and vanished into the cavity again. A pale-yellow glow was visible through the hole, leaping and bouncing as he moved about, and Jessica heard him make a low whistling sound through his teeth.

"There is a room here. Frau Jessie," his head suddenly appeared again, "you really must come *und* see this."

"Let me!" Thomas started up the ladder again.

"Thomas!" Jessica barked, "What did I tell you? Stay here and hold the ladder, please. Mary take the other side and neither of you move."

Jessica saw Mary poke her tongue out at her brother but was tired of scolding them. She started up the ladder. At the top, she held the edges of the hole and pushed off the last rung. The captain stood, stooping uncomfortably, in a space between two wooden roof beams. Dust floated and glittered in the lamplight.

Jessica scrambled through the manhole as the captain took

her arm to help. The roof was so low that fully upright, the top of her head was brushing the beams. It was even lower towards the edges where it angled down to meet the floor.

She'd imagined having to step carefully, balancing on the joists supporting the ceiling below, but to her surprise, she found herself in a large space with a proper floor.

"It's an attic." Someone had gone to the trouble of creating a serviceable room. As the captain held the lamp high, its light stretched, fading into the dark depths some twenty yards from where they stood.

"*Ja, und* look at this." He swung the light about, guiding it around the small room. "These things are not yours, no?"

Jessica gazed about in astonishment. "No." There was a collection of trunks, boxes and crates piled against a far wall. "I had no idea all this was here. And there's room for me to store some of Jon's old things."

Looking up, she saw the clay tiles of the roof. They seemed to have been attached to slats of wood that were themselves supported by trusses and beams. In their angles and crooks were centuries of brittle, abandoned bird nests and derelict spider webs.

"I wonder what's in the trunks," she mused.

"We can open one to see, but first …" he moved forward, carrying the light into a corner, "I think this is where the water is coming in. Come, look."

Jessica followed him down the centre where the roof peaked, then they both dropped to their knees and crawled into the space near the floor. As they approached the corner, she saw what appeared to be a cascade of daylight streaming through the roof.

He pointed. "The roof is broken."

"Broken? Some of the tiles?"

He nodded and crouched lower, bringing the light closer to the floor and indicating a gap between the wall and the attic floor. "See there – that is where it dripped onto the plaster of the ceiling below."

"Can it be fixed?" Jessica asked.

The beam of light swung upwards. "Oh, *ja*, but not from in here."

"Damn!" She watched as he reached up to examine the damage.

"You see this? I must go onto the roof to replace these tiles." He turned to look at her. "Do you have a … er, is called –"

"A ladder?"

"*Ja*, a ladder, but big."

"Sam'll have one. We need to work fast though – another storm's coming."

***

Jessica followed in the bumpy wake of the old car as Sam drove straight round the back to the stables. He was just getting out as Jessica arrived.

"How'd you go?" she asked.

He opened the passenger door and took out a box. "There were a chap in Wolstone I spoke to … didn't 'ave the right kind of roof tile – sold out. Reckons all these old places 'ave been losing their rooves in the storms. Gave me these shingles, though."

She peered into the box. "Will they hold?"

Sam made an uncertain face. "They're temporary but better than nowt. Reckons 'e can't guarantee them and we'll need to replace them soon as we can. Right flimsy they are," he weighed the box in his arms doubtfully. "But there were nowt else for it. We need to get that 'ole fixed. Right quick too," he added, searching the sky.

The dull grey morning had steadily descended into an eerie purple afternoon with blue-black clouds hovering low in the sky. More threatening clouds rapidly piled over the Pennines, promising further unseasonal hail and wild winds.

"I'll find the captain," Jessica said, "if you can fetch the ladder."

Jessica was heading towards the garden door when the wind suddenly picked up. It was an icy blast that clawed at her hair and took her breath away. As she approached, the door opened and the captain took her arm, bustling her into the kitchen and closing the door after her.

"You'll have to go up straight away," she told him apologetically. "This wind … another storm is coming."

Mary and Thomas were sitting at the kitchen table. They had the pieces of a jigsaw puzzle spread across it and the box, showing a coloured picture of a kitten dipping a paw into a fish bowl, sat at one end.

The captain stood by the stove, patiently allowing Jessica to tug a woollen cap over his head. "It's freezing out there," she told him.

"If Mr Bird doesn't get up there before the storm," Mary stated, "my room will be completely flooded!"

"I've told you a million times, Mary," her brother admonished, "don't exaggerate!" Jessica and the captain exchanged smiling glances as the two children erupted into giggles.

"A trillion, billion times," Thomas embellished to his sister's increased merriment.

The captain laughed, causing Thomas to add, "A trillion, billion, *zillion* times!"

"It is funny, *ja*!" the German said, grinning at her.

"*Ja*!" both children agreed.

"Yes, very funny, and don't say *ja* in front of *any*one!" Jessica turned to the captain, "And don't you encourage them. If they start spouting German at school or in the village, we'll all have a great deal of explaining to do."

The German was suitably admonished, but she saw him share

a look of solidarity with the children. It warmed her heart, while it saddened her at the same time.

Suddenly the garden door flew open and Sam and Marg blew in."

"Blimey Teddy, but it's windy out there!" Marg gasped. "Nearly blew me eyebrows off!"

Both children laughed again and Sam turned to the other man. "You ready, Anton? Ladder's outside."

"Don't let 'im up there, Anton," Sam's wife warned. "'E's way too old to be climbing up ladders, the silly apoth!"

"There is no question of who is getting on the roof!" The captain looked up from the box of tools Marg had dropped on the bench."

"I'll go up too, Mr Bird!" Thomas leapt from his seat. "I can pass the tools to you."

The captain ruffled the boy's hair. "That would be most helpful but perhaps another time. I need you to help Herr Clay hold the ladder."

***

The wind was worsening and the first drops of rain were falling as Anton squatted on the edge of the roof. From where he was positioned, at the south-eastern end of the house, he could see several chimneys, the sloping sides of the roof, and the gutters and downpipes running along the edge. Beyond and below, were the washhouse, stables with its new slate roof and other outbuildings. Water lay in puddles in the garden beds Frau Jessie had been slaving over; he hoped her efforts would not be destroyed in the coming storm.

Anton had a rope tied round his waist. Now in position, he pulled it in, lifting, as he did so, a bucket containing the tools he'd need.

Jessica had suggested putting the repairs off until later,

regardless of the leaky roof, but with the amount of water seeping into the ceiling, there was a real risk of it caving in all together – the repairs couldn't be delayed.

Anton hauled the rope until the bucket rested on the roof beside him. He leaned over the edge of the gutter to where Sam, Jessica and Thomas stood, shielding their faces from the rain and squinting through the growing darkness.

Waving to indicate all was ready, Anton set to work.

***

Jessica stood beside the ladder, watching, but as sporadic drops of rain began to fall, she swallowed nervously. "Sam, I really think we should call him down. This isn't safe." Yet even as she spoke, she knew that any more water in the roof could be disastrous. *He's up there now. Fingers crossed the rain holds off ... just a few minutes.*

Thomas and Sam were holding the ladder, one side each, and Jessica stood beside them. All three craned their necks skywards, watching as the captain perched two storeys up, carefully examining each tile for signs of damage.

"I found the broken ones," he called down. "There are three or four." They could barely hear him over the increasing wind.

Jessica cupped her hands round her mouth. "Fix them quickly. The rain is getting heavier." *I don't like this*, she thought, adding to Sam, "I want him down from there as soon as possible."

"Don't we all, Missus."

***

The rain was beating metallically against the lead flashing on the peak, several yards above him. The roof was slick with water running into the gutters and gurgling through the downpipes.

The damage was confined to a group of interlocking S-shaped clay tiles. They were head-fixed with timber pegs and the gaps between were filled with lime mortar.

Anton's inspection revealed that three tiles had broken – probably in the explosion back in May – and the mortar between had crumbled and fallen out leaving gaping wounds, through which rain and wind found easy access.

He selected a clawed hammer from the bucket and levered up the damaged tiles. The wind had increased; it tore his shirt-tail from his trousers. The rain was falling steadily; already the hat Frau Jessie had made him wear was sodden and felt like wet plaster pasted to his skull. The engorged clouds threatened to burst at any moment and release a violent torrent over him. Anton bent further over his work, hurrying to get it done before the storm hit.

"Captain Vogel," Jessica called from below. She was standing some yards from the house, the better to see him, pointing towards the sky behind him. "I think you should come down. I saw lightning …"

Following her raised arm, he saw the storm front approaching in a great boiling thunderhead. In that moment, a gust of wind blasted him sideways. He heard Jessica's shriek as his foot slipped and he momentarily lost his balance.

The roof had become a deadly cascade of water and the thick clouds had turned the afternoon into a dirty crimson night. The hammer's wooden handle was greasy with rain and, as he recovered his balance, it slid from his fist.

"*Achtung!*" he shouted, leaning precariously over the guttering.

"Whatchit!" Sam cried. With a surprisingly strong thrust, he shoved Thomas aside so forcefully that the boy was flung a good four feet and hit the ground hard just as the hammer thunked into the earth only inches from where the lad had stood.

Peering over the edge of the roof, Anton watched as Frau Jessie checked her son was unhurt. Then she cupped her hands around her mouth. "Come down, Captain!" she called. "It's not safe!"

But Anton couldn't stop now; the crumbled remains of the tiles had fallen away to reveal a gaping hole into the roof. Nothing would prevent the rain from pouring into the ceiling.

He ignored her directive and took a shingle from the bucket.

***

Thomas watched Mr Bird moving about high above him. He looked like a large crow outlined against the purple storm.

When Mr Clay had shoved him aside, Thomas had been momentarily winded. Apart from that, he was okay. He took a minute to catch his breath and in doing so, noticed a set of car headlights bouncing along the Leeds road beyond the trees. He watched curiously; during the day you couldn't see the road from the house, but in the dark …

Suddenly Thomas's eyes bulged.

***

Jessica's neck was starting to hurt but she continued to stare up at the man on her roof. She stood, shivering and blinking against the steadily worsening rain, watching the captain work – an indiscernible shadow hunched against the weather.

"One is done," he called down. "Two more to go!"

"Mummy," Thomas said tugging her sleeve. "There's –"

"Just a minute, Thomas. Hurry, Captain! I …" the remainder of her words were drowned in a rumble of thunder that seemed to roll up the slope from Jackson's Heath.

"Mum," Thomas said again. "Mummy!"

"Wait, Thomas!" Jessica snapped, distractedly. "Mr Bird's nearly finished."

***

Thomas wasn't interested in Mr Bird. He'd been watching the car bumping and jouncing over the potholes in the lane. As it approached Broughton Hall's driveway it reduced speed. The headlights swung in a wide arc.

Thomas screamed.

***

At her son's shriek, Jessica finally looked around. His eyes were fixed on the gate, arm outstretched, pointing. "Someone's here!"

"*Oh, God*!" Jessica shoved past Sam, grabbed the ladder and started up. "Captain!" She shouted, waving frantically, climbing higher, "Captain! Get back! Hide!"

"Wha –?" Sam began, then, "Saints preserve us!"

***

Anton, engrossed in his work could hear nothing but the wind howling about his ears. The rain was streaming over his face and blurring his vision. He'd just wedged the second shingle in place when he heard Jessica's scream and lifted his head.

***

Robin Tyler pulled his car up the Broughton Hall driveway. The rain was sheeting in the car's headlamps as he swung the wheel round. Coming to a stop, he pinned the old steward and the boy in parallel beams of light. He clambered out of the car, running forward, shouting, "What the hell're you two doing out here?"

That's when he saw Jessica, stepping off the last rung of a ladder propped against the house.

***

She was slicking the rain out of her eyes with dripping hands as Robin bounded up to her; his shoes slipped and he stumbled slightly on the sodden grass.

His shoulders were hunched against the wind and rain; the collar of his sports jacket was pulled up around his neck.

"What're *you* doing 'ere?" Sam demanded, one hand to his head holding down his flat-cap. He raised his voice to be heard over the wind.

"Don't tell me you stood holding the ladder while a woman climbed up it?" Robin bellowed. "Why weren't you up there?" He gestured angrily towards the house, his tone was scornful.

Jessica saw Sam bristle with fury. "I insisted, Robin," she leapt in before Sam could respond. "As Sam's employer, I –"

"What sort of man are you? Robin continued, derisively over the howling wind.

"For Christ's sake, let's get out of this weather," Jessica shouted. In that moment, a great fork of lightning split the sky and illuminated the yard in brilliant, false daylight. Jessica dared not look up at the roof, as the thunder crashed across the paddocks.

Thomas ran towards the house and Sam and Jessica followed. "You're not leaving the ladder there, are you?" Robin called after them. "This wind could bring it down – straight into a window."

"Go inside, Tommy," Jessica shouted over the gale. "You go too," she told Sam. Eyeing him firmly her expression said, *leave it to me.* "Tell Marg that Mr Tyler's here and to put the kettle on," she added. Her steward threw her a hard glare as he obeyed.

Robin was already working the pulley rope and unlocking the ladder's extension mechanism. He slid the upper section down and lifted it away from the house, dropping it with a clatter, barely audible over the storm. Jessica stood by, watching helplessly, her heart in her mouth. "Come on," she shouted above the din and shoved him unceremoniously towards the house, ostensibly to get him out of the weather, although she relished the physical violence of it.

A sharp jag of lightning lit up the sky again and was followed immediately by a detonation of thunder that sent a shudder through the ground.

Forcing her mind away from the man trapped on her roof, Jessica plunged into the warmth of the kitchen and slammed the garden door shut behind her.

Chapter 22

Thomas and Sam burst into the kitchen with enough time for Marg to put the kettle on the hob and send Mary to fetch towels before Tyler and Jessica arrived. Jessica immediately took Thomas by the arm and led him upstairs to change his clothes.

The house was in night-time darkness as they carefully mounted the stairs without lamps. On the landing, Thomas turned to her, his young face wet with rain and pale with fright. "Mummy," he began, but she quickly shushed him and bustled him into his room.

"Don't say a word," she whispered behind the closed door. "He'll be all right, we just need to stay calm. We can't ask Mr Tyler to leave … Mr Bird must hold on tight."

"But Mum, what if Mr Tyler stays all night?"

"He won't," she assured him. "It's only until the storm eases. And we have to be hospitable – it will be suspicious if we send him away in this weather."

She noticed Thomas was shivering and began undressing him, realising that she was shivering too. "Come on, get out of these clothes, put on your pyjamas and dressing-gown, then go downstairs. Act like nothing unusual's going on. Can you do that?" While she spoke, she was fumbling with his sodden clothes.

He was trying to help but his little fingers were stiff and icy.

"Damn it!" she growled, her own fingers were next to useless "Arms up for dip'n'bread …" He lifted his arms and she peeled the top layer of clothing over his head, then started on his trousers.

His skin was so mottled with cold that it looked almost blue. "Now, I'm going to get changed," she told him. "Put on your dressing-gown and meet me in the kitchen. Remember, not a word!"

He made a gesture of zipping his lips.

Dropping a quick kiss on his wet head, she rushed out of the room.

Jessica arrived back in the kitchen just as Marg was pouring cups of tea for the adults and warm milk for the children. Thomas and Mary were seated at the table beside Sam who'd removed his coat and shirt and was sitting in his singlet with a towel draped over his shoulders and crossed over his chest.

The tension in the room was so thick that Jessica decided Robin must be completely insensible not to feel it. Hopefully, he put it down to the frightful storm raging outside – which would be partly correct.

Marg's mouth was compressed to a firm line and her gestures were stiff and jerky as she poured the tea. Robin stood before the range. The door to the firebox was open and his clothes were gently steaming. As Marg opened her mouth to offer him milk for his tea, the thunder crashed directly over the house and the garden door rattled.

She gave a startled cry and dropped the milk jug, breaking stoneware and splashing milk across the kitchen floor. Sam and the two children were so desperate for diversion that all three leapt as one to clean up the mess while Marg's stricken eyes met Jessica's over their heads.

"Ooh, I just 'ate thunder!" the older woman murmured.

Jessica drew a deep breath and affected an air of relief. "It's good to be out of those wet clothes." She seated herself at the table. "Sam, come sit down. We've worked hard enough for one day. Let the kids clean that up."

Mary was wringing out a cloth and wiping up the milk while Thomas swept the broken crockery into a small dustpan. *If Robin knew them better he'd immediately suspect something was up*, Jessica thought, watching their industry.

Jessica feared that Robin sensed something wasn't right. He was observing each of them in turn, his expression speculative.

Don't be silly. He's not suspicious. It's just your own guilty conscience.

"So," the object of her cogitations came over and took a seat at the table. Marg poured his tea and brought a fresh jug of milk. "What were you doing up there on the roof? You could have picked a better day for it."

Jessica stirred her tea. "We sprung a leak in the storm last night. Mary had water dripping from her ceiling this morning so Sam and I went into the roof and found broken tiles."

"Right," Robin nodded his understanding, "thanks," he added, as Marg banged a cup of tea before him.

Jessica continued. "We knew more storms were coming; if we didn't get it fixed there'd be serious damage." *Shut up. Don't over talk*, she told herself sternly.

"Did you get it fixed after all that?"

"Oh yes! I was just coming down as you pulled up."

"As to that," Sam said. He'd been blowing over his tea, now he placed the cup on the table. "What brings *you* out in this weather?"

"Being a good neighbour … checking to see how you all got on." Robin glanced towards the window, still boarded-up after the bomb blast. Sheeting rain washed loudly over it. "I'd hate to think of my old Dad with no one bothering to check on him."

Jessica felt Sam's dislike of Robin creeping like a heat haze over the table. The feeling was probably mutual. In the warmth of the stove, the wet clothing was making the kitchen too humid and steamy for comfort. *If only the rain would stop and Robin could go.*

Fear for the man on the roof, as well as her family's safety, had Jessica's nerves jumping. She remembered reading about soldiers required to stand motionless for hours on end, who would imperceptibly wriggle their toes within their boots to keep their blood flowing.

Adopting that practice now, she straightened her shoulders, pasted a smile on her face and concentrated on keeping her body still. Her toes wriggled in her slippers, while she pointedly avoided looking towards the door every time a blast of wind shook it on its hinges.

A dazzling flash of lightning threw day-bright slivers of light through the boarded window. Almost immediately, the thunder crashed again. Even the cups on the table rattled and as the tremors slowly echoed into the distance, Mary's soft weeping was the only sound remaining.

"Come 'ere, little love." Marg held out her arms and Mary crawled onto the woman's lap and buried her face in the large, soft bosom. Jessica watched nervously as Marg stroked the girl's hair and exchanged a worried glance with her husband. "I just 'ate this weather," she repeated. "'Ad me awake all last night, it did."

"I understand, Mrs Clay."

Smarmy. Jessica thought. "Robin," she said. "Does your father have the electricity connected? We don't have it here, although I have the telephone. When the electricity came through, the previous owners couldn't afford it."

"Dad has it; Jackson's Heath was connected about eight years ago. My father was one of the first." He smiled at her.

Errol Flynn has nicer teeth – must be those pure Tasmanian waters.

"Some of the villagers were suspicious," Robin continued. "Thought their houses would explode or burn down or something ..."

Jessica nodded, encouragingly. "But not your dad ..."

"No, not him! My old man loves anything new." He gave a delighted little chuckle. "When he read about those new ballpoint pens the airforce was trying out, he wrote to the chap who invented them, somebody called Biro. This fellow worked at a newspaper in Hungary. Dad asked if he could buy one straight from him."

Thomas sat up, all ears. "What did the airforce try out, Mr Tyler?"

Jessica's heart leapt into her throat. "Thomas, don't interrupt, please."

"It's no bother, Jessica. Boy has an enquiring mind." Robin turned back to Thomas. "The airforce is testing a pen with a continuous flow of ink. No need to keep filling it."

Jessica smiled as Robin looked round at the adults. She wondered if he noticed how they were all trying to look interested despite the palpable tension in the room.

He seemed thoughtful, but went on with his story. "This fellow reckons that they last about two years without needing to be refilled."

"Then what?" Sam asked. "There's some special kind of ink to refill it?"

"You throw the thing away. Buy a new one."

"Just like that?" Thomas was excited. "Mum, can I have one? My birthday's coming up!"

"Might be a bit difficult with a war on," Robin responded for her.

"Your birthday's five months away," Jessica said. "I think you've started something, Robin." The smile she levelled on her son was pleasant enough, but her eyes bored into him and spoke clearer than words. *Be quiet now*!

She knew that Thomas was quite familiar with that expression. The boy sat back in his chair and applied himself to his milk, and just as he did, an explosion of hail clattered against the window boards, and the gathering round the table fell silent again.

Chapter 23

"Thomas, wait here!" Jessica whispered close to her son's ear. They were standing on the front porch beside Mary, Marg and Sam, shivering in the icy aftermath of the storm.

The garden was a mess of wind-blown twigs and leaves, and though the rain had eased, large puddles were visible in the bouncing twin beams of light as Robin's car negotiated the flooded driveway.

After almost two hours of howling winds, rain and hail – during which the three adults and two children of Broughton Hall had known moments of desperate, escalating fear – the vicious summer storm had finally abated enough for their visitor to take his leave.

Exhausted with worry, they all knew there was no time to waste. Immediately Robin's headlamps veered onto the lane, Jessica turned decisively to her son. "Watch the drive. Make sure the car doesn't come back. Yell out straight away if it does. Good boy."

Turning, she grasped her daughter's hand, "Mary, come with us. Sam, Marg, let's go."

Jessica dashed back through the house, her daughter, her steward and his wife following closely behind. In the hall, within earshot of Thomas on the porch, she paused and took Mary by the shoulders. The girl's face was pale and tear-streaked but she nodded when her mother said, "Stand here and listen for Thomas. If he shouts, run – fast as you can. Come and warn us. Understand?"

"Yes, Mummy," the girl answered solemnly.

The adults hurried out of the garden door, sloshing through puddles and storm debris. The night was black with boiling, purple storm-clouds and the wind continued to thrash the trees in the nearby forest.

Jessica glanced uncertainly about. Her eyes were wide and wild; she squinted through the dark, into the gardens, along the shiny wet paths and bedraggled shrubs, dreading the thought that a man's broken body might be lying somewhere.

How could he have possibly survived that storm, perched on the roof?

"He's not 'ere that I can see," Sam said, reading her thoughts.

That was something. But if he's still on the roof, what state is he in?

Marg held the lamp while Jessica and Sam dragged the ladder over. Constructed of wood, it was water-logged and heavy and they were breathing hard by the time they got it in place. They worked the pulley to extend the top section and secured it firmly on its iron hooks.

"Anton!" Sam called. "You there, lad? Can you 'ear me?"

The three held their breaths, listening intently. No response came from above. "Captain?" Jessica called, a little louder.

Still no sound but the dripping and creaking of the trees, as their branches swayed and leaves rustled in the wind.

"All right." Jessica held out her hand. "Give me the lamp." Marg automatically obeyed.

"No! I'll go." Sam moved, grasping the ladder.

Jessica shouldered him out of the way and already had her boot on the first rung when he grabbed her upper arm. "No, Missus, I'll not allow it"

"Sam Clay," his wife admonished. "Stop trying to be chivalrous, you silly old goat."

Jessica turned on him. "Sam, let go of my arm!"

Shocked by the vehemence in the two women's voices, Sam relented.

Jessica, one hand holding the lantern, the other grasping the side of the ladder, started up.

Past the first-floor windows, she climbed, the lamp swinging with each rung she trod. The wind was buffeting her about but she was undeterred. One boot followed the other, pushing higher with each step.

The couple on the ground receded into the shadows behind her as the swaying light tracked her progress.

At the top, she held tight with a one-handed grip, stabilising herself. The wind irritatingly fanned the hair across her face.

Jessica hung the lamp from a hook at the top of the ladder, but it was virtually useless. Tucking the hair behind her ear, she leaned over the guttering and squinted into the darkness.

"Captain!" she called. *God, what's happened to him?*

"Captain!" she repeated, louder, feeling the panic rising in her breast. Her heart was beating too fast – it was making her hands shake, or it could be the cold wind. Her fingers were so bloodless and numb she couldn't tell.

From where she stood on the ladder, she could see up the steeply pitched roof to the ridged gable peaking above her. It was sealed by a wide strip of lead flashing that glistened wetly.

With a juddering breath, she realised there was nothing else for it. She would have to climb onto the roof itself, and crawl along, hoping to find him.

With frozen hands, Jessica couldn't be certain that she had a good grip on the roof. Her boots were slippery on the ladder, but she gritted her teeth and pushed up to lay over the edge of the roof. The guttering was pressing against her abdomen and she could feel her pulse beating violently in her neck and temples.

Groping with her foot, she felt for the top-most rung, bore down and slithered the rest of the way onto the roof. *Oh, God ... Oh, God ... Oh, God ...* her mind chanted but she lay still for a moment, focusing on her breathing, fighting the fear threatening to overwhelm her.

After a pause, she mustered the strength to push herself further up. Fortunately, it was slick with rain and she slid easily.

Then, with a deep, steadying breath, she inch-wormed along the tiles.

The rain continued, and though not the torrent of the past hours, it was enough to soak through her clothes and plaster her hair to her skull.

Jessica had shimmied some half-dozen yards before she paused to catch her breath. Limned against the bruised sky were the stacks of Broughton Hall's multiple chimneys. There were at least four that she could see; there would be more but … one seemed to have an unnatural bulge at its base.

Sudden hope flared to life. "*Captain*!" she cried. "*Anton*!"

Was it her imagination that made the lump appear to move?

She called again, and this time she knew for certain. Her relief was so intense that she felt momentarily faint.

"Anton! Don't move! I'm coming!"

With renewed determination, Jessica bent her knees and broke into a commando crawl on her belly along the edge of the roof. As she got closer, she could see the silhouette of a man hunched into himself.

Christ! If he moves he'll fall!

"I'm coming," she panted, "don't move!"

Nearing the chimney, she could see him clearly now. He seemed unhurt but was trembling fitfully and obviously soaked through to the skin. She drew even with him but he was huddled about three feet up the slope of the roof, sheltering against the base of the chimney.

Far below, Sam and Marg's upturned faces shone like pale disks. "He's here," she called and faintly heard their relieved exclamations.

Now she began the most dangerous section as she slowly, slowly inched her way up the greasy tiles to where the captain huddled in the forty-five degree angle formed between the roof and the chimney.

Jessica's boots scrabbled for footholds and she scraped her hands painfully, groping for grooves and crevices to grip.

Her shoulder muscles were screaming by the time she pulled herself up beside him. The whiteness of his face turned to hers. "F-Frau ... J-J-Jess ..." he stammered, through chattering teeth. "V- vhat are ... vhat are you d-doing hier?" His accent made him almost incoherent.

"God, Captain!" she cried, she threw herself against him in a tumult of madness and relief. As the wind and rain continued to beat steadily, she kissed him hard, almost angrily. "Are you hurt?" she demanded, between kisses, "Are you all right?" Without waiting for a response, she kissed his eyelids, his cheeks, temples and nose, finally returning to his mouth.

His skin was like ice, his lips trembled and his body shook violently. He gasped against her mouth unable to return her kisses but clinging to her in a desperate frenzy. With an almighty crash above them the skies shattered and pelted them in a renewed shower of hail.

Jessica pressed her face into Anton's neck and he cupped his hand protectively over her head. They were pressed against the chimney stack, as frozen pellets clattered on the roof round them, stinging the backs of their necks, their arms and hands, like fierce little darts.

After what seemed like minutes but was, in reality, only seconds, the hail gave way to rain and the pair raised their heads to look at one another.

Jessica framed his face between her hands, turning it back and forth, peering at him. His face was ghostly in the darkness. *It's a wonder he's not dead from exposure.*

His movements were slow and clumsy as he took her hands from his face and although his grip was weak and he shook uncontrollably, he said, "I-I am f-fr-freez-ing ... but I am al-all right."

***

Jessica had no idea how they managed to get off the roof. Her memories of the entire event were a blur of frigid temperatures, fear and fatigue, but later, as she stood looking down at the sleeping man, she was aware of a strained muscle in her neck, and a weary heaviness in her arms.

She recalled her desperation when he began to slip into a hypothermic stupor. She rubbed his face, chafed his hands and berated him furiously for being a stinking Kraut.

Sam and Marg had dragged the ladder closer to where she was positioned, and she harangued and hounded him inch by painfully slow inch, to the edge of the roof.

Jessica had a tight grip on his shirt, even knowing that if he were to fall she couldn't prevent it.

She bellowed at him, slapped him, forced him onto his belly and, leaning precariously over the guttering, guided his boots onto the ladder.

It had been excruciatingly slow; then came the tremendous relief as her feet touched the squelching mud at the foot of the ladder. Her knees had buckled and she'd crumpled onto the sloppy ground, aware only of being bundled into a warm blanket.

The captain had fallen the last few rungs into Sam's waiting arms and was half-carried, half-dragged into the kitchen. After the bitter conditions on the roof, the room seemed oppressively hot and Jessica gasped, swaying on her feet and clutching the back of a chair to steady herself. Sam and Marg took the captain directly upstairs.

Earlier, in what Jessica considered a moment of old-school resourcefulness, Marg had thrown a brick into the firebox. It had subsequently been removed and wrapped in a towel and placed at the foot of the captain's bed to warm him.

Jessica's clothes clung like an icy sheath. Upstairs, Marg peeled them from the younger woman's motley-blue skin, while down the hall, Sam was doing the same for the captain.

The children were in the kitchen, charged with the task of watching a pot of soup on the range. Marg had told them to push it away from the direct heat as it began to bubble but under no circumstances should they lift it.

Jessica shivered in layers of clothing – nightie, cardigan, socks – as Marg pulled back the bedclothes. "Get in!" she ordered and Jessica complied. The blankets were tucked round her shoulders and beneath her chin. "Be right back," the older woman said, leaving Jessica curled in a tight ball on her side, shivering fitfully, her breaths coming in dry gasps.

It seemed a long time, but was only moments, before Marg returned with a steaming bowl of soup. Mary followed close behind.

"Get in bed with your mum," Marg directed. "Cuddle 'er close … warm 'er up with your body."

Mary obeyed immediately. Heated from standing over the stove, the child snuggled close to her mother, and at long last, Jessica began to thaw, her muscles gradually relaxing, loosening, unfolding, and finally she lay still.

As Jessica's tremors eventually subsided, Marg approached the bed with the soup. "Time to eat. It'll do you good, then you can sleep, lass."

Mary crawled away from her mother as Jessica shuffled to a sitting position, pillows wedged behind her, the meal tray on her lap.

Marg said, "If you're all right, I'll go check Anton."

Jessica nodded, too involved in the soup to speak. She ate enthusiastically, scraping the last of the meat and carrots from the bottom of the bowl, before snuggling down, exhausted.

She was vaguely aware of Mary taking the tray and tiptoeing from the room.

**

The following morning, as Jessica stood beside the captain's bed, she knew that her fear for him had been more than simply concern for a fellow human being. This young man had become more than that to her, more than it was safe to admit. That morning, nearly two months ago, when he'd followed her to the orchard and kissed her, she'd known then that he meant more to her than he should.

At the time, she'd scolded herself for being a silly, lonely widow, and she'd told him it would never happen again. But now, as she stood watching him sleep, a tenderness swept over her. The urge to touch his cheek, the rough stubble on his chin, the softness of his lips, was almost overwhelming.

How could it be that a good man like Jonathon Barrow had not inspired the affection in her that she now felt for this man – this sworn enemy? But sworn enemy or not, this man was kind, gentle, funny, intelligent. Sam and Marg loved him. Her children loved him.

Foolish woman! She grumbled reproachfully. *At his earliest opportunity, he will go home – he* must *go home for all our sakes, and you will never see him again.*

The knowledge sent a searing pain through her heart.

She swiped the tears away with her sleeve, and found the German's eyes on her. Although fatigued, they were clear and greyish-blue in the pearlescent morning light.

They gazed at each other for several aching heartbeats. Then he smiled, despite his cracked and rain-scalded lips.

The tears sprang anew into Jessica's eyes. She scrubbed them away with an embarrassed huff but they kept coming.

"Frau Jessie …" his hand extended from beneath the covers; she grasped it without thought.

She meant only to hold his hand, enjoy the vital warmth of it but she slowly brought it to her lips.

Then, with an involuntary sob, Jessica dropped to her knees

beside the bed and laid her head on his chest, revelling in the steady heartbeat beneath her ear, the feel of his arm going round her, holding her against him, gently stroking her hair.

"I owe you my life – again," he whispered and she heard the smile in his voice. "I am a German officer – your enemy. You have, once more, betrayed your country. I must inform you, madam, that your behaviour is unacceptable."

***

It was close to midday when Anton came to full wakefulness. He was tired and vaguely dizzy, but apart from that, he felt all right.

All right, that was, until he tried to get out of bed. He groaned audibly as he forced his tortured muscles into movement.

Dressing slowly, he noted the purpling bruises on his legs and arms and the stiffness in his shoulders when he slipped into his shirt.

His quadriceps screamed as he made his way down the great staircase and hobbled along the hall towards the kitchen. He hoped to find Jessica there; he wanted to talk to her, thank her … more than anything, he wanted to touch her.

***

Jessica was sitting at the table with Sam when the captain came in. Immediately she retreated to the range while her steward guided the younger man to a chair before returning to his own. "How are you, lad?" Sam asked. "Bit of an ordeal, eh?"

The captain nodded. "I," he croaked. His throat seemed dry and raw. He swallowed and tried again, "I am fine."

Jessica peered into the stewpot – it was simmering cheerfully. She felt hot and self-conscious; her heart had begun racing the moment the captain stepped through the door.

She felt him shoot a brief glance at her. "I am bruised, *und* I am sore but I am fine," he said, adding, "I was able to fix the roof before the worst of the storm came."

"Well, that's good," Sam said, "job well done, lad, well done. Nearly cost you dear, but it's all good now."

There was silence in the room, during which Sam fidgeted awkwardly. Suddenly he rose, "Righto, back to work – you rest today, Anton."

Jessica remained by the stove for some moments after Sam left.

When the captain had appeared in the kitchen, her instinct had been to rush at him and feel the strength of his arms going about her. But her natural reticence would never allow so demonstrative a reaction.

Instead, she'd gone to the stove – it was safe there – and she could ladle him a bowl of stew. The emotions welling in her chest threatened to erupt in the form of full-blown weeping; an utterly foolish display of sentiment that could only lead to further grief.

Swallowing hard, she gave herself a good mental shake. The stew was ready. She moved it off the heat and ladled a serve into a bowl.

She felt the German's eyes following her. As she placed the bowl before him, he opened his mouth to speak.

"Captain," she interrupted, then paused awkwardly, "I feel I –"

"You want to tell me that you love me." He spoke plainly, but there was mischief dancing in his eyes. She noted they appeared more grey than blue in the dimness of the kitchen. There were dark smudges of fatigue beneath them.

Jessica's face grew hot. She made an embarrassed huffing sound. "That isn't what I wanted to –"

"You kiss me like you love me." Now he grinned at her, pale and disarmingly handsome, adding, "It is all right, you know, because I love you too."

Uncertain how to react, she dropped into a chair and retreated behind humour. "I suppose you say that to all the girls."

Adopting a serious expression, he said, "Oh, *ja*, but not in English."

She suddenly broke into laughter, but it was laughter tinged with nervousness. He watched her, a faint smile lurking round his mouth and when finally she sobered, her eyes were glistening.

"No, Captain," she stated firmly. "I am fond of you, but it is not love. And with that out of the way, I want to thank you for fixing the roof and ..." she gestured expansively, "all the work you do round here. Now, I want you –"

"I think I am recovered enough." He waggled his eyebrows suggestively.

Jessica's lower regions tightened and her mind whispered wickedly, *God, I really do want him!*

The thought shocked her. She'd never felt the like before, but her mind raced ahead, *If he touches me now I think I will die.*

Once again, she chose the path of humour. "I am a widowed mother of two impressionable young children. I am also older than you. I suggest you collect yourself, Captain, and behave as befitting an officer of the Imperial German Flying Corps and not make indecent propositions."

"*Die Fliegertruppe? Nein*, we have not been called this since nineteen eighteen. I am as you say, off the catch."

"Off the hook. And you still shouldn't make indecent propositions."

"So are you saying, no?"

She nodded but he drew in his breath, and rising from his chair, came purposefully round to her side of the table. Reaching down, he handed her to her feet and stepped her back against the wall.

His arms went about her and he bent his head to hers, kissing her deeply. A sigh escaped her and she swayed into him.

"Ah," he whispered against her mouth. "You see, this is why I do not believe you."

All of a sudden, he released her and seemed to rock on his feet. "I think I need to eat something," he murmured.

She laughed. "That's what I've been trying to tell you."

***

The blood was throbbing in her veins as she pushed him back into his chair. Placing a spoon before him, her emotions were laced with regret, for she and the captain were rushing headlong into extremely dangerous territory.

"Eat, Captain." She was grateful that he was feeling weak – she was feeling weak herself, but for other reasons, and she did not trust herself. "I must bring in the washing before it rains again."

With that, she fairly bolted through the garden door and outside where the fresh, after-storm air soothed her heated skin.

Chapter 24

It was a hot sticky night and the air felt thick as Jessica drew a deep, thoughtful breath. She rested Alexandra's journal on her lap as she read by lamplight; the flame flickering within its glass casing was eerily reflected in the blackened parlour window.

The captain had passed a succession of particularly exhaustive days helping Sam haul round and cut up the many trees uprooted in the storms. They would fill most of next winter's firewood needs but the work was punishing and backbreaking and Jessica knew the captain did most of it, being the younger man.

It was Friday evening; she and the children were due at Robin's for lunch on Sunday and she wasn't looking forward to it.

Jessica had gone to bed earlier, but too restive for sleep, she'd wandered downstairs wearing only her nightdress and wrapped herself in a crocheted rug. Folding her legs beneath her, she'd opened the journal and begun reading.

That had been over two hours ago, and in that time the words on the pages had revealed the love between two young people blossoming into something beautiful and passionate.

Over the course of reading the diary, Jessica had sensed the growing accord between Alexandra and the young man she was enamoured with. It was uncanny how it reminded her of her own growing feelings for the captain, feelings that she'd been trying to suppress.

Just as Alexandra Broughton had fought to suppress her growing desires, seemingly because she believed they would lead to certain grief, Jessica knew her desires for the German captain were similarly futile.

As she read, her skin began to prickle. "This is impossible," she said aloud, staring at the page.

She read it again:

That morning in the orchard, it was like a spell had been cast over us, for in the midst of yet another disagreement, he had turned on me and I'd feared I'd lost his friendship forever.

But as the cows in Jackson's paddock lowed gently nearby, he took my shoulders and pressed me against the trunk of an apple tree.

He kissed me.

Oh, God, how he kissed me! I hadn't known such kissing existed. It made my head spin and the earth stand still. I shamelessly clung to him, opening my mouth beneath his lips and kissing him in return!

Jessica sat very still, her fingers touching her mouth. She skipped back to read the line again.

...as the cows in Jackson's paddock lowed gently nearby, he had taken my shoulders and pressed me against the trunk of an apple tree...

She stared at the page with her mind swimming. That morning in the orchard, when she and the captain had kissed ... was it fanciful to say that she too felt a spell had been cast over them?

She shook herself. *Don't be ridiculous*! But was it any more ridiculous than seeing ghosts? Suddenly, her head shot up and she spoke out loud. "Lucifer's balls!"

Closing the journal, she quickly opened its front cover to where the letter from Margaret lay folded beneath. She spread it out on her lap, eyes skimming to the bottom of the page.

"Meggie, please take this journal home to Broughton Hall." Pressing the well-loved book into my hands, she added, "It's for the lady... you know of whom I speak. Keep it safe for her. Let her find it... somewhere..."

Jessica was trembling as she laid the journal on the seat beside her. There was no doubt in her mind that she was *the lady*, but why did Alexandra want her to find the diary? What was she trying to tell her from so long ago? What could be so important that she left a journal? Why did she continue to walk these old halls?

"All right," Jessica took herself in hand. "What do we know? Alexandra was in love with a man considered inappropriate." She counted off a finger. "We know that he led a very different life than she did – diametrically opposite, in fact." She counted another finger. "Her family would not approve," at this Jessica snorted and acknowledged with a wry twist of her mouth that there were definite parallels between Alexandra's love affair and Jessica's confusing relationship with the German captain.

"But why leave me the diary?" Her words sounded empty in the silence that followed.

Despite the warm night, a chill rippled up her spine and she knew. It was like a bell chiming in her head!

"*Bloody hell...*" Jessica breathed, as she suddenly realised the implication. "*I* am the ghost, not her! Alexandra sees *me* – in her world *I'm* the ghost! Oh... My... Bl –"

***

"Frau Jessie?"

Jessica gave a startled yelp and leapt off the couch. Anton stood in the doorway wearing pyjama bottoms and Jon's dressing-gown, hanging open.

"I am sorry ..." he hesitated on the threshold. As she'd jumped up, the rug had dropped, unnoticed, to the floor. She stood before him in her nightgown, the lines of her nakedness beneath shown clearly in silhouette by lamplight behind her.

Anton flushed and shifted uncomfortably, closing the dressing-gown and averting his gaze. *Scheiße, er war geil!* His body reacted with a painful tightening. He snapped, "Cover yourself!"

Jessica snatched up the blanket but seemed too excited to care that he was angry. "Captain, you'll never believe it!" She hugged the crocheted rug to the base of her throat where her pulse was thudding. "I can't believe it myself!"

He stared at her in disbelief, his chest rose and fell rapidly. "*Was?*"

She didn't appear to register his clipped tone. "I'm the ghost."

Anton shrugged slightly. "*Nein.* I did not just frighten a ghost."

She made an impatient sound. "Not now! In the journal – I'm *the lady* she talks about."

"*Ja*, we knew this." He felt uncommonly irritable.

"But it's more than that. I thought I was seeing Alexandra's ghost, but *I'm* the ghost – she sees me!"

"Can you not both be ghosts? You exist in different times, but you return to her world, *und* the reflection of hers comes to you." He cocked his head to one side to illustrate the simplicity of his argument.

***

Jessica was confused. The captain was usually interested in Alexandra's story but tonight he appeared short-tempered, distracted. Jessica wasn't even certain that he was listening to her.

Suddenly, he sighed and indicated the couch. "Sit *und* tell me."

She sat obediently, thrown by his coolness, then a thought occurred to her. "What are you doing up?"

He dropped to a chair opposite and leaned against its padded back. "I think you would find this strange but," he chewed the inside of his cheek hesitantly, "perhaps not so much."

"What?"

"I was sleeping. I thought I heard a voice. I thought you were standing over my bed *und* calling my name, trying to wake me. When I looked –" he made a quizzical gesture with his hands, "there was nobody there."

"So you came down here?" Jessica stated softly.

"I was going to the kitchen … I heard you talking to yourself." He smiled at her and she sucked in a breath.

How attractive he is. The play of light threw the planes of his face into sensuous relief. *He looks … seductive … sinful, like he's aroused.*

The captain was watching her steadily; she knew he read the thoughts and emotions there. Suddenly spotting the journal on the floor, he reached for it.

"What part did you read?" he flicked absently through the pages. It seemed he was trying to distract himself – and her.

"Captain," Jessica said carefully. He shifted and adjusted the folds of the dressing-gown over his lap. Jessica swallowed hard. "They kiss in the apple orchard!"

He pulled back and his eyes bored into hers. "*Was?*"

"Alexandra and her lover."

The captain's jaw tightened. He exhaled slowly.

She said, significantly, "Their first kiss was in the *orchard*."

"I see."

"Do you? There is a parallel."

He got up.

Jessica's eyes followed him.

***

Cursing colourfully in his mother tongue, Anton stared into the empty fireplace.

"Captain," Jessica said, behind him. "It's –"

Anton rounded on her, his accent thickening with his

frustration. "Jessica! What do you want from me?"

Her mouth fell open in surprise. He'd never used her first name in such an angry growl like that, but he was too upset to be sorry.

"You stand before me," he flicked a hand at her, "wearing not enough to cover yourself. You tell me not to touch you, but you look at me like … I have told you what I feel for you," he cried in frustration. "I agree to … I *try* to …" his voice trailed off and he stood in the middle of the floor breathing hard.

Anton was at the limit of his English; his vocabulary had no previous experience of this kind of discussion.

Forcing himself to calm down, he made another attempt. "I try to *do* as you ask, but then you tell me these stories of lovers *und* kissing like you are trying to … *what*!" he cried, unhappily. "What are you trying to say?" He broke off with a sob of exasperation.

Turning, he leaned his forearms on the cold mantelpiece and the room fell silent but for his ragged breathing.

***

Jessica stared at his heaving back for several long moments. She'd never seen him like this before and it shocked her. At length, she got up from the couch and gathered the rug modestly about herself.

"I am sorry, Captain," she said softly.

His shoulders moved as he drew a shuddering breath, muscles bunching beneath the dressing-gown.

She swallowed uncomfortably. "I apologise because I have been thoughtless and you probably think I've been teasing you – it wasn't my intention. You're … young and healthy. You have …" *God, this is embarrassing.* "You are an attractive man," she whispered, burning with mortification.

"I enjoyed it when we kissed," she went on, although her

throat felt parched. She swallowed again. "But it frightened me too because … because of the way you make me feel."

The captain slowly turned to face her but didn't respond. He looked weary and cautious.

"I have so often," she continued, "wanted to go to you … just to have you hold me. But that would be selfish because I – we … I'm so afraid of my loneliness. I'm afraid of falling in love with you and of how it will be when you go."

Her voice caught on the lump in her throat. Unable to meet his gaze, she took an unsteady breath and whispered, "I'm afraid of myself and what I want."

She waited for his response. The lamplight created leaping shadows that seemed to shift and take shape. She blinked them away.

Yet the hairs on the back of her neck spiked at the sudden chill in the air and she dragged the rug tighter round her shoulders, watching his face as he digested her words.

And in that instant, she knew without doubt what she wanted. *For once in my life I don't want to play it safe.* One way or another, the captain will leave here, and in the decades of struggle and rebuild following the turbulent years of war, she would remember the time she lived purely for the moment.

But she had confessed her fears and desires, and he had not reacted. He simply stood there, his face impassive.

Why doesn't he say something?

***

Anton watched Jessica struggle with her admission. He understood her fears, and though he wanted her, he enjoyed the purity of their friendship too; it would change irrevocably if they gave their desires free rein, particularly if she had any lingering doubts.

But he also recognised her loneliness and how she longed

for companionship. How could he reassure her that their parting would be as painful for him as it would be for her?

He couldn't, because Anton was an adventurer – willing to risk an unknown future to savour a moment wholly in the present. It was a quality recognised and capitalised on by the Luftwaffe for it made him energetic and daring – a formidable combination.

Anton didn't question the strength of his feelings for Jessica. Accordingly, he accepted the grief their inevitable separation would bring; it was a price he would readily pay to enjoy whatever time remained to them.

But he respected that she was different, and in the midnight silence, he waited. She'd opened herself to him, laid her fears before him. Now she must be clear about how far she would go.

He waited for her to say the words.

***

Long seconds ticked by during which the captain didn't speak. Finally, Jessica sighed with resignation, drew the ends of the rug tighter and turned towards the door.

She froze in awe. The shade of a lovely young woman drifted silently from the room.

Alexandra!

Jessica whirled around to face him. "Did –"

"I saw her too."

***

Later, neither could have said who'd made the first move. But suddenly she was in his arms, his mouth coming down hungrily on hers.

A moan escaped her and the rug slipped from her shoulders.

His hands framed her face, trailed along the sensitive skin beneath her ear, brushed against the side of her breast until his arm slid around her waist and pulled her hard against him.

Jessica could feel the need in him as he held her and her stomach clenched urgently. His lips moved across her cheek and jaw and he whispered, "You are afraid of what you want."

Then as he nipped at the skin between her neck and shoulder, he murmured, "Are you not afraid of me? What *I* might want?"

She pulled back to search his face and boldly whispered, "What might you want, *Herr Hauptmann?*"

His breath was a humid whisper as he replied, "I want to take you to my bed." Her head lolled back as his lips traced the curve of her throat, "I want to kiss you here," he cupped an aching breast and teased the nipple against his palm, "I want to touch you here," he pushed into the junction of her thighs and she whimpered against his mouth, "I want to penetrate your body, little by little," he plunged both hands into her hair and shifted against her hips, "*und* I want to move within you, deeply *und* slowly until you cry out …"

Jessica writhed with a sinuous, primitive instinct and he sighed against her ear, "*Und* then I want to spill inside you, *und* hold you until your breathing slows *und* you sleep in my arms."

Suddenly he released her and stepped away and she dropped weakly onto the couch, breathing hard; her limbs throbbed in time with her pulse.

She stared up at him and found him watching her steadily.

Finally, he spoke, "It is true, Frau Jessie." He was standing before her, smilingly sadly. "I want to make love to you. I have tried not to want you but I find it difficult to be near you *und* not want you. *Und, ja,* you tease me with your kisses *und* your body, but we cannot look at this like it will last forever. Do we take pleasure in each other while we can, or do we not? For me, I would rather have you one night than not at all."

He stepped towards her again and leaned over her to pluck a tendril of hair from the corner of her mouth and she was caught in his blue gaze.

"Now, I have told you what I want *und* what I would do should you allow it. You have told me your fears but you have not said what *you want*. You must be certain *und* say it clearly. I will ask you once *und* if you say no, I will not ask again. But if you agree, you must know that it will change everything between us. So now I ask you. Will you come to my bed?"

Jessica's body was taut and vibrating. Her throat was dry and parts of her were throbbing. Finally, she found her voice. "You don't fight fair, Captain."

He made a wry face. "I am trying to be fair."

"And you're a bloody German."

He grinned. "Oh, *ja*, I am that."

"We are enemies."

"Only outside of this house."

"And if you don't take me to your bed now, I will kill you."

He saluted her with a finger to his brow. "*Jawohl*!"

Chapter 25

It was a shrill sound, relentless, insistent and coming from downstairs.

"Frau Jessie ... the telephone."

The words, accented in guttural tones, were whispered so close to her ear that her hair stirred with his breath. She rolled onto her back and extended her arms above her head in a languid, catlike stretch. He was lying on his side, propped on one elbow, watching her.

As the ringing stopped, Jessica burrowed further beneath the blankets, luxuriating in the warmth of shared body heat.

She was drifting once again towards sleep when her senses stirred and a delicious sensation spread through the lower part of her body. Surfacing to wakefulness, she opened her eyes. It was still quite dark outside; the captain hovered above her in the pre-dawn light.

"Mmm," she moaned, arching into his touch.

He removed his hand and she immediately felt its loss. "Don't stop ..." she sighed, but he smiled and leaned forward to press a soft kiss to her lips.

"*Guten morgen,*" he whispered against her mouth, then drew away to look at her.

"Good morning, Captain ..." Jessica flushed self-consciously. She felt lazy and sensuous but the captain's touch beneath the blankets had ignited a restless spark between her thighs. Her head lolled to the side and she returned his gaze.

Jessica thought he looked young and vulnerable – and something else. His feelings for her were clear on his handsome face.

She cocked an eyebrow at him. "Captain, are you all right?" she teased.

He nodded. Deflecting her attention, he asked, "Are *you* all right? You have no regrets?"

"No," she said firmly. And it was the truth.

"*Sehr gut*. In that case ..." he gently pushed her back against the pillows and rolled onto her, taking his weight on his elbows, he covered her mouth with his own.

She felt him rising against her groin and her hips instinctively pushed up to meet him while her arms clasped behind his back, holding him to her. He shifted slightly to part her legs and she sucked in her breath in anticipation.

The telephone screamed through the house again and they sprang apart as though burned.

"Shit!"

"*Scheiße!*"

Jessica leapt naked from the bed, wildly searching for her nightgown and snatching it from where it lay crumpled on the floor.

Flinging open the door, she ran down the hall, praying the children were still asleep.

She took the stairs two at a time, made a sharp left turn, more stairs, stubbed her toe and arrived breathless to pick up the receiver.

"Hello?" she gasped down the line, plopping onto the telephone stool.

There was no sound from the other end. "Hello ..." she repeated. "Hello?"

She put the receiver down and sat waiting in case it rang again.

"No one there," she said as the captain arrived. He was dressed only in pyjama bottoms and in the grey of morning he looked ghostly pale. He'd collected her dressing-gown from her room.

She rose as he held it for her.

"Christ, it's early," she murmured, belting the gown. "I'd

better –"

"Mummy? Where have you been?"

Jessica froze on the spot, her guilt rising immediately. "What a question!" she laughed dismissively but Thomas wasn't fooled. "I've been in bed, where else? I came down to answer the telephone but there was nobody there."

"I went to your room. You weren't there and that was probably Granny trying to ring you."

"Thomas –" Jessica began.

"Granny was on the telephone!" he insisted.

"Perhaps." Jessica fought to regain control of the situation. "But she'd hung up by the time I answered."

"Because you weren't in your room," the boy cried, his voice faltering. "You hadn't slept in your bed."

"Come on, Tommy," the captain said, gently. He made to usher the child away. "It is too early to get up. Go back to bed *und* your mother will telephone *deine Großmutter* later."

"No!" he shoved away from the German, "I want to talk to Granny now. She'll know what to do."

"What to do about what?" Jessica asked, perplexed.

"You and Mr Bird!" he cried. "You're just like Jack's mum."

Jessica's stomach slipped and she felt sick. Thomas's face was flushed, his mouth quivering. "That's not true, Thomas," she said forcing herself to remain calm. She put a conciliatory hand on his shoulder. "Now, why don't you let Mr Bird take you back to bed and –"

"Why don't you!" he shouted, jerking away from her. Jessica turned a horrified face towards the captain as the sound of her son's feet pounded up the staircase.

***

The fire in the boiler roared and Jessica poked at it with an iron rod. She slid open the vent, allowing it to breathe before shutting the hatch on the flames.

Warm air filled the bathroom and while waiting for the water to heat, she stripped off her nightdress and stood naked before the mirror, looking at herself in a way she hadn't done in a long time.

She noted the weariness round her eyes and the first crows' feet in the outer corners. She saw how her eyebrows needed tidying and there were more freckles on her nose since the last time she'd looked.

There were faint lines round her mouth; evidence that her expression was too often turned down. She used to smile all the time but it seemed such a long time since she'd had a reason.

Until now …

Her brow puckered and something inside her chest felt tight. She was afraid to frame the words, as she recalled Thomas's anger. She didn't want to remember her son's fierce little face as he shouted at her and ran away. She'd taken a step to go after him but the captain had stayed her with a light hand.

"Let him go," he said, gently. "Let him think it out in his own time, then talk to him quietly when you are both not so emotional."

So, she had come to the bathroom instead.

Please let me savour the feeling of being loved … just for one day … she thought, looking at her plump lips, reddened from beard stubble; they looked like she'd been eating ripe raspberries. Her hair was a cloudy mess and her eyes had that hooded, sensuous look of a woman who had been thoroughly loved.

She took a step backwards and looked further down.

Her breasts were small and sagged slightly after having fed two babies, but the nipples were rose-coloured and stood up expectantly. There was a small purpling bruise above the left one. Jessica touched it with a fingertip, feeling the slight tenderness and recalling the flood of desire as the captain had closed his mouth over her skin.

She ran her hands down her sides – rationing and worry had stripped pounds from her and her fingers rippled over her ribs before she splayed her hands over her stomach. It was flat enough though the faint silver marks of her pregnancy snaked over her hips.

Had the captain noticed them? He hadn't said anything if he had.

Jon had once commented that he found them unattractive but without them he would not have his children. Jessica had never been sure how to take that remark. It had not been a compliment, but neither had it been an insult. Regardless, she'd been self-conscious when undressing in front of him after that.

The mirror wasn't long enough to show further down her body, but Jessica didn't need to see her thighs to be aware of the slight chafing, the discomfort there, and the slick, pearlescent fluid that had dried and made the skin feel tight.

The captain had made good on his promises – all except one, for precaution's sake.

It had been a long time since a man had held her in his arms – indeed, until last night, Jon was the only man ever to do so.

And Jon had been gone two years now.

She thought she should feel ashamed of her behaviour but she did not – she was too much in love to feel shame, and she was too afraid of an uncertain future.

Love was stronger than fear, but uncertainty was the world she lived in.

***

Later that morning, Jessica was in Mary's bedroom folding clean washing when the child came in.

As her mother dumped the freshly laundered clothes on the

bed and began folding little skirts and jumpers, Mary took up a pile of underwear to put in her drawer.

Jessica glanced briefly at her daughter's stern face and deflated. It wouldn't be hard to guess what she was thinking.

She'll talk when she's ready.

"Mummy?"

That was sooner than I thought! "Hmm?"

"Mum, Tommy says you didn't sleep in your room last night. He said you slept in Mr Bird's room."

Jessica continued her work as calmly as possible, yet Mary's expression was combative; Jessica felt the child's eyes burning into her.

"Is it true? Tommy says you're just like Jack Ramage's mum with that Yank."

Pausing in her work, Jessica regarded her daughter steadily for several heartbeats before reaching for Mary's hand and pulling her down to sit on the bed beside her. "Yes, Mary, I spent last night in Mr Bird's room, but it's not like Jack Ramage's mum because Mr Bird is not replacing your father, and you and Tommy know that."

"Mrs Ramage knew the Yank wasn't staying forever, but then she got all upset when he left and Jack told Tommy –"

"First, we're not talking about Mrs Ramage. Secondly, nobody will ever know about Mr Bird but us. He will *never* replace your father and …" Jessica blew out her cheeks in frustration.

She's only eight, for God's sake! What am I doing to her?

"Look, we all love Mr Bird, but –"

"Mum," her daughter interrupted. "I'm not like Tommy. I understand these things."

If I smile now, I've lost her.

"What do you understand?" Jessica asked evenly, watching Mary closely as the child considered her answer.

At length, the girl conceded, "Well, I don't know *everything.*

But I *do* know this isn't good."

Jessica breathed carefully and modulated her voice. "What don't you think isn't good? Do you think we like Mr Bird too much?"

Mary was quick to respond. "Yes! That's exactly the problem."

Jessica nodded sadly. *I see where this is going.* "He *must* go home, love."

"But if he likes us and we like him, why can't he stay?"

"It's not that simple. You know there's a war on."

"Yes, Mum," Mary said with exaggerated patience. "The goodies against the baddies."

"There's more to it than that."

"Miss Haberfield says it's simple."

"Your teacher? Well, Miss Haberfield is sort of right. But you know the reason we don't talk about Mr Bird is that people will think he's with the baddies. It's why he can't stay with us."

"Then if he is leaving, why don't you sleep in your own room?" her daughter demanded, mutinously.

Lucifer's balls I should send this child to law school!

"Mary –"

"Don't tell me I'll understand when I'm older," Mary cried, suddenly. Her face was growing pink and her eyes were beginning to well. "The only thing I need to understand is that Mr Bird is leaving." She tried hard to compose herself. "And it seems to me," she added in the strangely adult tone she sometimes adopted, "that you need to understand it too."

Jessica stared uncomfortably at her daughter, momentarily lost for words.

Mary wasn't finished. "Tommy loves Mr Bird. He's frightened because he doesn't understand what's going on. He hears everyone talking about Mr Bird leaving but then you and Mr Bird... Tommy's confused. He thinks now that Mr Bird is going to stay. He loves him, but …" Mary scrubbed at her eyes as the tears began. "I won't. I'm *not* going to love him. I *know* he's not going to stay. I *won't* love him! And I don't want *you* to love him either."

Mary lost control then and Jessica bundled the child into her arms. The girl's breath was hot as it bloomed through the wool of Jessica's cardigan.

"Shh …" she soothed, not knowing what else to say. She held the child until the girl's wiry little arms relaxed their tight grip.

"Tommy was frightened when he saw you weren't in your bed," Mary murmured.

"Frightened?" Jessica pulled away in surprise. "Neither of you have reason to be frightened."

"Yes, we do … because we loved Daddy but he still … he went away … and … when he went away … he … I …" Mary clutched her mother again in renewed sobbing. "Daddy's never … coming back," the child wept. "And neither will Mr Bird …"

***

Jessica was on her knees beside the rows of carrot and turnip tops inspecting them for storm damage. After the recent rains the ground was sodden – perfect for loosening the soil. Her mind drifted as she dug the ground around the vegetables.

I can't do this to the children, she thought.
I've only been thinking about me, but it's about them too.
I can't do it – to them or me.
I'll tell him … later.
I must be honest with him.
It can't go on – we made a mistake.
I'll tell him tomorrow.
No, he'll wonder why I won't sleep with him tonight.
But I want to sleep with him tonight.
I'll tell him this afternoon.

"Frau Jessie? Why are you sitting out here in the wet?"

She looked up at the handsome face above her. His brow was furrowed with concern but his eyes held genuine affection. For an instant, she remembered his hands on her, and his mouth. Her lower regions tightened with desire. *I've got to nip this in the bud. I need to do it now.*

She stood up and faced him – which she could. *He is not as tall as Jon. He is slighter but stronger – handier round the place than Jon too. How would Jon and I ever have restored this old house, with Jon unable to tell which end of a hammer was the handle?*

She realised the captain was watching her, trying to read the thoughts running rampant in her head. His hand hovered momentarily, like he wanted to touch her, then thought better of it.

"I'm all right," she said finally. "It's just that I still can't get through to Mum and Dad."

"Ah." He looked unconvinced.

"I don't know if it's the telephone here or … I don't know how it works. How would we know?"

He gave his distinctive one-shoulder shrug. "I do not know. I am going to cut some wood. I promised Frau Clay."

He went to move but she thrust out a hand to stop him. "Captain, we need to talk."

Apprehension flickered across his face. *He knows.* Jessica turned away. "Meet me in the parlour where it's quiet."

***

Anton waited patiently while Jessica changed out of her work clothes. He knew what was coming, and her reasons, he assumed, would include her inability to commit to something so fleeting and temporary; she was not the type of woman to engage in a short-term affair. He should have known …

Now she sat on the couch and Anton, sensing her distance, chose a chair by the writing desk in the window.

He listened quietly, saw how tightly clasped her hands were in her lap. His heart ached as her words came out, clumsy and full of regret, but assertive.

***

Jessica couldn't meet the captain's eyes as she talked. When at last she could look at him, they were blue, she noted, like the summer sky visible through the window over his shoulder.

He was silent for a long time. "Is that it?" he asked, finally. "I gave you the choice last night. You have changed your mind so soon?"

She understood what he was saying, but for the sake of her children – and herself – she had to stay firm. Her children's fears had driven home the reality of the situation.

"Last night," Jessica said sadly, "was ... special. But in the light of day ... Please," she begged softly, "don't make this harder than it already is. I hadn't considered the children. I'm ashamed to say that I was caught up in the moment with you – I only had thoughts for myself. I didn't think about how this might affect them."

"Frau Jessie," his voice was gentle, reasoning. "We spent last night together, *und* it was a beautiful thing. We did it, each knowing the consequences. There is no shame in two people taking happiness where they find it ... especially in a world such as this."

"I am not ashamed, but it's too simple to say we are two people taking happiness. There is more than that between us and you know it. It's hard enough to think about your leaving, imagine if we... if I allowed myself to fall in love with you. You said it yourself – this can't last forever."

"You accepted that last night."

Jessica sighed dismally. "Last night was magical," she conceded, "I have no regrets, but it can't happen again."

She got up and felt his eyes following her to the door. She closed it behind her and marched resolutely through the house.

Out in the wash-house, she leaned heavily over the copper. The soft warmth of evening floated through the door on a honey-scented breeze. She tried to breathe evenly, tried to keep her emotions in check.

At length, Jessica pushed away from the copper. Her hands trembled as she tucked the hair behind her ears. She mopped her eyes on her sleeve.

I can't think about this anymore. It's done. I won't think about it again.

***

Anton sat alone in the parlour for a long time. He turned his chair to face the front garden where the late afternoon shadows were closing in. A mere twenty-four hours had changed his life. This time yesterday, he had felt like a young man playing at being in love. One day later and he knew he wasn't playing.

Last night, he and Jessica had made love with a tenderness and passion he'd never known with Natalia, nor the other two women he'd slept with.

But of course, those two girls had been attracted by his dashing pilot's uniform and daring reputation. His couplings with them had been clumsy, hurried exchanges – one in a storeroom, the other in an aircraft hangar.

Natalia was – he could say it now because he had a proper experience with which to compare it – Natalia was unresponsive, more interested in ensuring her make-up was not smudged by his kisses or her carefully set hair was not flattened on the pillow.

He understood Jessica's anxiety and her children's fear of losing someone important to them. But that did not make his own grief less profound, because Jessica's reasoning did not make sense to him; her children were already attached to him – and he to them.

Anton grunted irritably. Jessica was deluding herself if she thought denying herself, and him, the comfort of each other would make their inevitable separation more bearable. Yet she had made her decision and he had no choice but to live with it, along with the clenching pain beneath his ribs.

As he watched, the sun shifted behind a cloud, shrouding the garden in dull, evening light. *To start and end in the same position*, he thought, miserably, *but to have a life-changing experience in-between was* … he sighed and rose to stand in the window.

A flock of small orange birds with black-and-orange-speckled heads was flitting among the shrubs. He raised his face towards the soft evening sky.

As a pilot, he'd learned to read the clouds. The clouds he saw now lay in flat, horizontal formations. Stratus, they were, and stained with gold stripes from the sun settling somewhere beyond the horizon. Too high to signal further rain, in months to come they would bring snow.

Anton shivered involuntarily.

Jessica was afraid of falling in love and the subsequent grief when they parted. For him, it was too late; last night had sealed his fate. Anton had already resigned himself to the inevitable pain of loss, but rather than avoid it, he wanted to make the most of his time with this small family while he could.

He wished it were otherwise, but the fact remained – he did not belong here. Even after the war, Jessica would be ostracised, or worse, for her relationship with him, however brief, if it ever became known. There could be no future for them … anywhere.

Perhaps she was right.

He sighed sadly and looked to where the birds had been.

Bramblings – that's what Herr Clay called them. Cute, busy little bramblings.

Anton remained in the window long after the birds had flown away. But he had wood to chop; he would need to take a lantern.

Chapter 26

Robin and Albert met the Daimler as Jessica pulled up before the old house with the green door. The tubs of lavender were as she remembered them but as summer had crept along, they had become woody and tired, where previously their bright purple heads had been alive with bees.

The younger man came round to open Jessica's door. "Twelve-thirty! Right on time and look at you," he declared, cheerfully, "driving yourself round like you were born behind the wheel!"

"Hello, Robin," Jessica got out of the car. The children were slamming the back doors as they let themselves out.

"It's good that Mummy knows how to drive now, isn't it?" Robin addressed Thomas. "Who taught her?"

"Sam," Jessica leapt in before her son could respond, "Mr Clay taught me, didn't he, love?"

Thomas nodded vigorously, "Yes, and now she drives all over the place."

"She does not," Mary contradicted. "She doesn't have enough petrol."

Robin laughed, "None of us has enough petrol. Come, let's go in where it's cooler." He turned towards the porch, while Jessica made warning eyes at her children behind his back.

"Lovely to see you again," Albert Tyler took her hands as she approached. "When Rob said you were coming, I was thrilled. I've something exciting for you."

Jessica followed Albert into the sitting room. When she'd visited several months ago, the windows had been open to the fresh spring breeze. Today, the room was shady and cool. A plush grey cat occupied the prime position on the window-seat.

Thomas spotted the cat and immediately rushed to it, while his mother and sister shared a couch. "Oh, I love cats. What's his name? Can I pat him?" He squatted beside the laconic feline.

"He is a she, young man," Albert told him. "Her name is Alice and you may pat her. She will let you know when she's had enough."

As if on cue, Alice opened a cool green eye and inspected Thomas, noted his eagerness to be friendly and endured exactly six gentle strokes before contemptuously flicking her tail at him.

"I think she's had enough," Thomas decided, wisely backing away.

Albert laughed. "Not the most patient of cats, but certainly one of the most queenly. You're lucky you got to pat her at all."

"Oh dear," Jessica said, with a short laugh, "I can see who runs this place."

She hadn't noticed Robin leave the room, but he returned now, tea towel over his shoulder. "I've just checked the joint – I managed to get a piece of beef. Probably wants another fifteen minutes."

"Perfect," Albert said. "That'll give me time to show Jessica what I've got." He reached for a large, yellowing envelope on the table beside his chair. "Found these the other day – thought of you immediately," he said, passing it to her.

Jessica eyed the packet curiously. It was weighty, its opening flap was tatty, the strip of glue was brittle and flaky with age.

Albert gestured with his chin, "Go on – open it."

Sliding off the couch, Jessica knelt and up-ended the envelope, spilling the contents onto the rug. An assortment of small pictures fell out – some old sepia photographs, but mainly hand-painted cards showing various landscapes, houses, people and animals. Jessica's heart skipped a beat. "Is this ...?" she selected one at random – a watercolour of a splendid, sprawling mansion, "What is this?"

"Remember I told you about Meg, the old woman that lived in your house?"

"Sir Simon's half-sister?"

"The very one. These pictures belonged to her sister, Maeve. Now Maeve was a bit of a rebel for her day. She travelled extensively, refused to marry … even took lovers," he glanced quickly towards the children, but both were distractedly sifting through the pictures scattered on the floor.

Clearing his throat, Albert continued, "Maeve liked to do a bit of painting – not bad at it either, by the looks o' these. When she died, back in …" he frowned, thoughtfully, "early eighteen fifties, I think, well, these found their way back to Broughton Hall.

"When Andrew Broughton returned from Spain and restored the old place, he found them and put them aside."

"Andrew's grandson," Jessica said, "Joseph, he was the man we bought the Hall from." Her hands were trembling with excitement. *Surely this isn't … Surely these aren't …*

"These are some of Maeve's paintings along with a couple of old photographs – more recent, you know? The family kept them. When Joseph fell on hard times, he knew I was keen on the history of Wolstone and the Broughtons and all. He offered me the lot for a couple of pounds."

"Oh, my," Jessica breathed in awe. She gazed at the eight by ten card she still held in her hand. It showed a huge, stately mansion basking in an early morning sun. Its stone seemed to glow with a pink and gold lustre, while a magnificent, coloured dome rose in the centre. A long, double-storey gallery stretched between two three-storey wings.

It nestled within perfectly tended gardens, and the marble fountain in front of the portico was so clearly depicted, with jewel-like drops of water sparkling in the sunlight, that Jessica imagined she could hear it tinkling. "But …" she started in confusion. "This isn't Broughton Hall."

"No," Albert agreed. "It's Waterville Place, seat of the Earls of Thorncliffe. Maeve was the earl's sister. Lord Patrick

Washburn." He nodded toward the pictures on the floor. "There's a few pictures of him in there."

"Step-brother, to the Broughtons," Jessica said.

"Yes, of course. That's the earl's connection with your place."

Jessica shuffled the pictures round – there must have been close to thirty of them, all beautifully rendered, capturing a fleeting moment, frozen forever.

"Here, Mummy." Mary held a watercolour towards her and she took it, drawing her breath in slowly, appreciatively. *Blonde hair, green eyes ...* She knew immediately who this was.

Patrick Washburn stared out of the card. Dressed in a snowy white shirt, a black waistcoat, with some golden thread glistening through it, topped with a green brocade coat. His trousers were black and his long slender legs were encased in thigh-high black boots. He was an imposing figure, very charismatic. Though he seemed to be formally dressed, unusually for the times, he was not wearing a neckcloth.

Beside him, was a woman; Jessica immediately knew it was Alexandra, with whose image she was familiar. Alexandra was wearing a beautiful gown of emerald-green silk.

"Good heavens!" Jessica looked up at Albert Tyler. The old man's face was alight with pleasure. "These are beautiful."

"I knew you'd enjoy them. Let me make a gift of them to you."

"Oh, Albert, I –"

"Don't say you can't, you *must*. This one here doesn't care for them." He thumbed towards Robin, reclining disinterestedly on the couch. "I'd like to know they mean summat to someone." He jerked his chin at her, "Go on, take 'em. They belong at the Hall."

Robin rose then. "I'll check on the roast. Should be done by now. If you're keeping those, Jessica, best you put them away and don't forget them when you leave."

"Thank you so much, Albert. You've no idea how much I'm going to enjoy going through them. I'm simply fascinated by Alexandra's story."

"Especially the diary," Thomas piped up suddenly. "She's always talking about it to the captain."

Jessica's heart stop beating for a second and she froze. She could see Robin, from the corner of her eye, pausing on his way from the room. She tried to adopt a casual expression but Robin wasn't looking at her. His speculative gaze rested on Thomas, and he turned slowly, coming to stand over the boy.

Thomas gazed up at the man with a mixture of guilt and fright on his small face. "And who is the captain, young man?"

Jessica heard Mary slowly draw in her breath. Thomas said nothing but his eyes filled with tears as they stared fixedly on the man leaning over him.

Robin had arranged his face to look friendly, although Jessica saw every fibre in his body was tense and alert – like a predator that had scented his prey. He bent slightly from the hips to peer into the child's face. "Thomas? *Who* is the captain?"

Thomas's chin quivered and Jessica wanted desperately to pull him into her arms but she knew, instinctively, that any movement from her would seal their fates as the story would come spilling from her frightened son.

Thomas had proven himself a quick thinker in the past. *Please let him think quickly now!* Jessica prayed. *Oh, god, he's too young for this!*

"Thomas, you can tell me." Despite the mildness of his tone, Robin's body language was distinctly menacing. Albert shifted uncomfortably in his chair and even the cat raised her head, sensing a change in the atmosphere.

Thomas's face reddened, he swallowed hard, working to control himself as he murmured, "He's m-my f-father, sir."

And then the small boy burst into tears.

Jessica exhaled in a rush and pulled Thomas into her arms. Holding him tightly and making soothing noises against his hair, she glared at Robin over her son's head.

"Rob!" Albert said accusingly. "He's a child, for God's sake!"

Robin ignored his father. "Your husband was not a captain, Jessica."

How does he know that? Jessica wondered but her thoughts were interrupted by a clear little voice.

"That's right, Mr Tyler. Our father wasn't a captain." Mary's small face open and innocent, although Jessica recognised the glimmer of defiance in the girl's eyes. "But Mummy used to tease him and call him the captain – it was a joke and Tommy and I used to laugh at them."

She glanced at her mother. Jessica was still kneeling on the floor, gently rocking Thomas's juddering body in her arms. "Mummy, I'm sorry, but Tommy and I were spying on you the other day when you were talking to his picture – it's on the table in the dining room, Mr Tyler," Mary added. "She always talks to it."

Jessica thought she was going to pass out. *I should never have put them in this position!* She wanted desperately to clutch both children to her and run from the house, but Albert stepped in. "Robin, we were having a lovely time and now you've upset everyone. Sometimes he's too direct, laddie," the older man addressed the back of Thomas's head, but his eyes held Jessica's. "Doesn't realise how gruff he sounds. Doesn't mean anything by it."

Now Albert turned to his son, "Rob, go serve the dinner. We'll be in shortly."

Chastened, Robin left the room, while his father looked Jessica in the eye over her son's head. "He's concerned about these reports he's heard – maybe you've heard them too. About a–" he glanced at Thomas, still hiding his face against Jessica's blouse, "a stranger … lurking about."

"A German," Jessica supplied, adding truthfully, "I've heard the rumours, Albert. Believe me," she lied firmly, "if I thought some Gerry was prowling about our place, Robin'd be the first person I'd call."

Albert nodded, apparently satisfied. By now, Thomas had recovered and pushed away from her. "All right now, young man?" Albert asked, getting to his feet.

Thomas nodded, mopping his eyes on his sleeve.

"Good-oh," he ruffled the boy's hair. "Let's go and see if that son of mine has served up lunch. Nothing like a hearty meal to cheer you right up."

***

Robin proved himself a passable cook. As Jessica and the children relaxed and put the earlier issue behind them, the gathering round the table tucked into baked turnips, roast beef and Yorkshire pudding. Robin had even gone as far as making a respectable spotted dick for pudding, although it was unavoidably light on currants, which didn't detract from the children's delight.

After eating, Thomas and Mary went outside to visit Krijger. Albert was busily washing up while Robin made tea.

Jessica held her cup in both hands, as though warding off potential approaches from Robin, but she needn't have worried; he seemed to have something else on his mind and her skin prickled with foreboding.

She felt him watching her thoughtfully before speaking. "Jessica," his tone was pleasant but his brown eyes held hers firmly. "You know you can trust me, don't you?"

Her heart began to pound at once. She tightened her hold on her teacup and opened her eyes innocently. "Of course, Robin."

He rested a hand on her knee. *Thank god I wore slacks*, she thought as she stared down at his fingers. They were soft, not work worn and strong like the captain's. Two or three hairs sprouted from each knuckle, not unattractive or excessively hairy by any means, just typical man's hands. Yet the captain's hands were more attractive, square and long-fingered with blunt tips. *Musician's fingers,* the thought occurred to her. *Well, naturally – Germans are brilliant musicians –*

"Jessica?" Robin gave her knee a slight squeeze.

She exaggerated a jump, a foolish little giggle and brushed his hand away. "That tickles."

"We need to talk." He ignored her attempt to lighten the heaviness that was thickening the atmosphere.

"Oh Robin, thank you so much for the lovely meal. And the pudding … It's been so long since –"

"I think you know what I'm about to say," Robin sliced through her remark. His expression was grim, determined – he wasn't about to be distracted. "And I don't think you're as silly as you're trying to pretend. There are rumours going round – rumours about a man seen working on your property."

"Of course there's a man on my property – you've met Sam. He's been –"

"Jessica!" Robin's hand returned to her knee and this time the grip was not playful. "Don't treat me like a fool. A young man – fit and strong. Someone has been hand-milking your cows, your stables were repaired, and I do not believe for a single moment that you climbed onto the roof of your house, in a storm, while that steward of yours held the ladder."

Playing the innocent young mother clearly wasn't working. Jessica drew a long, fortifying breath and taking his hand, emphatically removed it from her knee.

"Don't touch me like that." She rose and stood before the cold hearth. Adopting the stance that always worked when asserting herself with the children, she bunched both hands on her hips and spoke with a tight jaw. "Why don't you say what you want to say instead of making these half-baked accusations? What are these rumours? That I've had a man do work on the house?"

Suddenly inspired, she added, "Are you suggesting that I have a lover? Because if you are, I'll have you know –"

Robin got up slowly. "That's not what I'm saying. But I have to tell you there are several reports about a man –"

"Robin! I am a widow with two young children. For you to suggest that I would bring a man into my house –" she made a face of outrage. "How could you think such a thing?"

"Jessica, for Christ's sake – it's not that! Look," he reached over and took her shoulders. "There are rumours in town... Wharferidge, Wolstone – you're running that place on your own. Delivering milk, every morning without fail, without mechanical equipment – the chaps at Bright and Sons were wondering, that's all."

"Well, if they bothered to come out at five in the morning to see me and Sam milking by hand, I suppose they'd have nothing to gossip about, would they?" She shrugged away from his hands. "Or perhaps they should come over in the afternoons while my eight-year-olds manage the evening milking – gaggle of bloody busybodies, they are!"

"Please, Jessica." Robin shook his head in frustration. "I'm trying to say ... I want you to know that," he paused, then seemed to make up his mind before going on, "if there's anything you need to *tell* me, I suggest you tell me now before –"

She glared at him, "Before what?"

Robin sighed, and moving away, went to look out the window to where the Daimler waited with the afternoon sun reflecting off its roof. "There wouldn't be talk ..." he hesitated. Jessica sensed he had something on his mind and was working out how best to phrase it.

Eventually he turned to face her. "They wouldn't talk if they thought ... if you and I were together." He paused, adding with a significant look, "I *can* help you, Jessica."

Jessica's shock was genuine. She gaped at him. "Are you serious? Are you *seriously* offering protection from village gossip in return for –"

"Listen to me!" He held his hands up as though to pacify her. "They're saying you are hiding someone – and there's evidence, circumstantial I know. But facts are, a German pilot parachuted into the area some months ago; he was never found."

"But –"

"The cows, the repairs, the work … things don't add up, Jessica!"

"Christ, Robin! I've explained –"

"I'm willing to overlook certain things … accept that perhaps your steward –"

"I can't believe you're saying this!"

"*You* can't believe …?" Robin shook his head in bewilderment, his mouth turned down. "Jessica," he said with exaggerated patience. "You must know that I … I'm quite attracted to you. There are things I could do for you – even if you *did* know something. I could help you."

Jessica felt the heat flood her face. "I see," she hissed. "You're offering to protect me in exchange for … favours?" She sneered at him. "I may be alone, Robin, but I'm not desperate. I don't need your *protection*."

He opened his mouth to speak but she wasn't finished. "Is it so hard to believe a woman can survive without a husband? I'm working my bloody arse off! You wouldn't question a man, would you?"

"Calm down! I'm only telling you what people're saying."

"And turning it to your advantage."

"That's not fair."

"Isn't it?" She glared at him challengingly. "If there is a German lurking about the dales, why aren't you out there with the Home Guard, hunting him down instead of propositioning me?"

Robin looked sheepish but not repentant. "These days everyone's doing what they can to survive. No one would judge you if you took... certain measures to protect your family."

"*Certain measures!*" Jessica couldn't believe what she was hearing. "*Certain measures* that include sleeping with a man I don't love so he can shield me from gossip?"

"Jessica – " Robin took a step towards her but she held up a staying hand.

"*Certain measures* doesn't include being blackmailed into your bed," she snarled.

"Nor does it include harbouring the enemy!" Robin shouted.

The words hung in the air and seemed to suck all the oxygen from the room. Hearing them aloud filled Jessica with such terror, that it was easy to appear speechless with outrage.

When Robin spoke again, his tone was measured. "If you are, Jessica, now's the time to tell me."

In that instance Jessica recognised the grave danger she was in. Additionally, she understood that if she turned the German over to him, Robin would protect her – for a price.

Nevertheless, she didn't consider her response and her outrage was unfeigned.

"I am an Englishwoman," she ground through gritted teeth. Her hands shook as she gathered her handbag and the packet of pictures Albert had given her. "My husband died in the service of his country. Don't you *dare* speak to me like that ever again. And furthermore," she straightened and faced him, "you and I – it was never going to happen Robin – *never*! Especially in return for your *protection!*" She spat the word contemptuously.

"What's going on here?" Albert stood on the threshold, tea towel and plate in his hands.

"I'm leaving, that's what. I'm not going to stand here and be insulted and … and … *blackmailed*," she spluttered, glaring at Robin, before looking at his father. "Thank you for everything, Albert. I really enjoy talking to you and thank you for …" she held up the packet of pictures. "Now," she marched to the door, "I'll fetch my children and be gone."

Robin reached forwards, attempting to detain her. "I'm not your enemy Jessica."

"Leave me alone!" she snapped, stepping aside and brushing past Albert.

The older man stared at her then levelled an accusing gaze on his son. "Rob –"

"I'm not trying to harass you, for God's sake," he barked. "I'm trying to *warn* you!"

She whirled to face him, hoping that he would see her fear as umbrage. In any case her fear was making her strong.

"Warn me about what?" she demanded. "That the men in town don't believe a woman can survive on her own? That she's incapable of milking a cow? Climbing a ladder? Hammering in a nail? And I won't be sleeping with you just so you can tell them to mind their own business. I can bloody well tell them myself!"

Robin's face flushed with anger, his mouth became a stern, white line as he strode towards her and grasped her elbow, hard enough to make her yelp. "I'm trying to bloody warn you, you stupid woman!" he shouted into her face. "They think you're hiding that German fugitive! If that's true –"

"Let me go, Robin. Right now!"

"Let her go, Rob."

"Stay out of it!" Robin threw at his father. He gave Jessica's arm a shake. "I can help you! I can –"

"*Let. Me. Go!*" she growled through clenched teeth, trying to jerk her arm away from him, and hurting herself in the process. "I swear if you don't let me go I'll call the Home Guard out on *you!*"

"You can try!" he sneered, although he released her.

"So you *are* with the Home Guard. I don't know why you don't just admit it – every other man is proud to do his duty. Everyone in Wolstone is talking about someone – I've learned not to care. But if you *ever* try to blackmail me … if you accuse me of *any*thing, you'd better have the evidence!"

With that, she stormed out of the house. After the cool shade of the house, the warm afternoon sun hit her full in the face, momentarily blinding her. Forcing herself on, she marched towards the car.

"*Thomas! Mary!*" she shouted. "*Come here now!*"

"Is that a challenge?" Robin stood by the front door, arms folded over his chest. He was regarding her through dangerously glinting his eyes. "You're behaving very guilty for an innocent woman."

By now Jessica had the Daimler's door open. She threw her handbag and the packet of pictures onto the seat and spun round to face him just as the children came running. "Get in the car," she ordered. "I *am* innocent, you bastard, and if you ever come near my home again, or speak to me or my children I *will* go to the Home Guard, the police, even the army, and report you."

He smirked at her. "Report me, if you like, they'll only issue a warrant to search your house."

"Good! Maybe then you'll leave me alone." She got into the car and slammed the door shut. The Daimler's engine fired and she threw the car into gear.

Perhaps it was the devil in her, or her newfound confidence, but without her even thinking about it, she vigorously unwound the window and leaned out. "And if you ever thought for a moment that I might be tempted to sleep with you," she allowed her gazed to sift condescendingly up and down his frame, "I'd rather sleep with Adolf Hitler and his entire band of madmen before I'd let you even hold my hand!"

Immediately she said the words she wished she could take them back. Robin's face darkened with a terrifying fury and she realised she'd just made a great mistake. He was her enemy now, and he would not stop until he'd found out everything he could about her and her family.

With nothing else for it, she slammed her foot on the accelerator. The Daimler's wheels kicked up gravel before they gained traction. Jessica last saw Robin in the rear-view mirror standing in front of the green door, watching her.

The expression on his face made her stomach convulse.

Chapter 27

Sam and Anton were leaning against the wash-house wall, catching the watery, early December sunlight, and enjoying a moment's peaceful companionship. Time had marched on and the year seemed to have passed in the blink of an eye.

The relationship that had sprung from an unlikely friendship between an Englishman and a German had grown into something resembling father-son closeness. Natural perhaps, for the older man had lost his son, while the younger was missing his father.

Sam was rolling a cigarette; they both watched Norma and her calf enjoying a cloudless winter morning. The calf, named Basil after the actor that brought Sherlock Holmes to life, frolicked about the glistening grass, while Norma contentedly munched hay from a broken bale along with the rest of the recently milked herd.

Anton bent to inspect a wooden crate sitting at their feet. It was filled with a peaty smelling earth and he poked a gentle finger at the white, velvety hoods pushing through the dirt.

"What's mushroom in German?" The older man asked and ran his tongue along the edge of his tobacco paper.

"*Ein Pilz.*"

"Do you –"

At the sound of breaking crockery both men raised their heads. "Came from the kitchen," the older one said.

Anton straightened. "*Ja.* I will go see she did not hurt herself."

"I'll be in when I finish this." Sam struck a match and lit his cigarette. "We can tell 'er then."

In the kitchen, the captain found Jessica squatting on the floor collecting broken pieces of a china soup tureen. He went to the broom cupboard and took out a hand-held pan and brush. Squatting beside her he swept up the smaller shards.

"Thanks." She offered a brief smile.

Getting up, he tipped the contents of the pan into a bin. "You are tired?" He held the pan and brush, one in each hand to prevent himself reaching out to touch her.

***

Jessica's skin prickled with the captain's nearness – it had been almost two months since their night together but she was no less sensitive to him. She nodded, crouching to look in a cupboard. "Didn't sleep well."

She rootled round, coming out with a large ceramic basin. "I loved that tureen." She shrugged. "No point crying over it."

Last night, Jessica had made soup from the remains of a lamb shank. Now cooled, a quarter-inch layer of dripping had formed a solid crust on the top. The captain watched – hip resting against the table, arms folded over his chest – as she scooped out the fat, putting it aside to use later, then ladled the soup into the basin.

"Why did you not sleep well?"

She had her back to him, but he would have heard the fatigue in her voice. "I don't know … just worried, I suppose."

Up-ending the soup pot, she poured the last dregs into the basin. The empty pot went into the sink. Anton pushed away from the table and opened the tap, filling the pot with water. Elsewhere in the house, the boiler fired into life. He took up a scourer and began scrubbing at the cooked-on line round the rim.

Jessica bent to put the soup basin in the ice box. Straightening, she stood watching him for a moment, distracted, gaze softening. *What a beautiful looking man, he is.*

"*Was ist es?*"

When his eyes met hers, a little thrill shot through her; he was smiling, one eyebrow raised in enquiry.

At a sound behind them they both turned. Sam was stamping mud from his boots on the threshold. "If they're mucky you can leave them outside," Jessica called.

The steward complied, toeing his boots off at the door and entering in his socks. "Did the lad tell you what's been going on?"

"No."

She smelled Sam's freshly smoked tobacco as he passed her and pulled out a chair. The captain, tea towel in hand, gave the pot to Jessica to put away.

There was an unconscious domesticity in their actions that clearly wasn't lost on the older man. She saw Sam smile to himself before he spoke. "At Bright and Sons this morning, a couple o' the chaps were talkin' about Tyler going round asking questions and saying stuff."

"Oh, yes?" Jessica took the flour bin from the cupboard and cleaned a section of the table. "Has Robin been talking to other people?"

"Well, yes 'e's been talking *to* other people, but 'e's been saying stuff about *you*."

A scoop of flour in hand, Jessica paused and stared at him. "About me?" At Sam's nod, she snorted contemptuously and measured several scoops of flour into a bowl and added salt. "Stuff like what?" The men's eyes followed her as she mixed the dry ingredients with a wooden spoon.

"Usual stuff like 'ow you're managing a big place like this, 'ow you've built up that milking herd. Stuff like 'ow it in't right that a young woman would live out 'ere with only children and an old couple for company."

Jessica took out a jar of yeast, measured the required amount and added it, along with warm water from the kettle. Stirring, she considered Sam's words. "So," she said, tipping the mixture onto the table, "what do you think he was really saying?"

"It is what he was *not* saying that matters," the captain said.

"Aye. Lad's right. Think about it: Tyler's putting it out there that there's work around 'ere that a woman on 'er own and a pair of oldies couldn't be doing."

"He's been carrying on about this for months," Jessica remarked, unimpressed.

"But he is keeping the story alive," the captain said. "Giving enough information for people to form their own conclusions."

"Dangerous," Sam agreed, nodding. "More dangerous than accusing you outright of summat because 'e's planting the seeds – they're coming up with the story themselves."

"Christ, I'm sick of that man," Jessica cursed, floured to the elbows now.

"Aye, but that ain't the worst of it."

"There's more?" She continued kneading, but looking up, caught the two men exchanging glances. Sighing irritably, she snapped, "Just tell me!"

"Nigel Bright swears some bloke told 'im 'e saw a man sitting up top of the stables a few months back. Would've been around the time Anton fixed the roof."

Jessica's kneading came to an abrupt halt and one floury hand rose to brush the hair away from her eyes.

The German captain was casually leaning against the bench, still holding the tea towel, and looking infuriatingly calm. Turning to Sam, Jessica said, "What did you tell them?"

He grinned. "I told them some returned soldier was passing though on 'is way 'ome to York. Said 'is name were Richard Marsh, and you offered 'im bed and board if 'e could fix your roof. 'E stayed for a couple of days, did the work, then moved on."

Jessica hadn't realised she was holding her breath until she exhaled in a great gust. Understanding dawned and she nodded slowly, a small smile tugging at her lips. "And his name – Marsh – common Yorkshire name." She punched the air out of her dough. "You're a clever man, Mr Clay! Glad you're on my side." She went on with her kneading.

"Ahem," Sam coughed, slightly embarrassed. "Righto." He nodded and left the kitchen, stooping to pick up his boots as he went. "C'mon Anton."

***

That evening, Jessica found time to be alone. The children were in bed, the captain was at the cottage with Sam and Marg – Jessica had the place to herself. She sat in the peaceful ambience of the parlour where the fire had burned down to a glowing mound of orange coals.

A lamp on the table before her threw a dancing circle of yellow light round much of the room, although the corners remained shadowy. She'd swept her long hair round her neck and over one shoulder as she leaned over the Yorkshire Post. Dated 9 December, 1941, the headline WAR IN THE PACIFIC! screamed at her.

Sam regularly brought papers from Wolstone after taking the milk to Bright and Sons; the luxury of time to read them was rare. Jessica had put on her nightdress and dressing-gown, poured a small measure of Tokay and settled in for an evening's quiet time.

She was reading an article describing how the United States had officially entered the war after the Japanese bombed the U.S. Pacific Fleet in Pearl Harbor. She hoped now that America had joined in, there might be a quicker end to it.

Unlike many Britons, whose only experience with American people were the soldiers billeted in their homes – *overpaid, oversexed and over here* – Jessica trusted that the United States army could do more than simply produce illegitimate children. She had faith in their resilience, their fortitude and their alliance. Ever since Hitler had threatened to blow up the U.S. aid ships plying between North America and Britain – when the Americans had thumbed their noses at the German menace and continued delivering supplies to England – she had placed her confidence in them. Now she read the article with a sense of hope.

Additionally, she was outraged that so many people had been killed. Not just servicemen and women, but islanders, civilians, innocently going about their daily lives, when the Japanese bombing raids had struck. Yet now, in the aftermath of President Roosevelt's declaration of war, she allowed herself a moment's optimism.

So absorbed was she in her reading, that she was unaware of the man standing silently behind her.

*****

It was late when Anton left Sam and Marg's cottage. Instead of coming directly up the drive and entering the house through the front, he circled round the back to make a final check that the cows were safely locked in the stable for the night. His breathing created plumes of fog and his hands were freezing as he tested the iron bolt on the twin doors. It felt like a block of ice, wet and slippery, and he shivered as he glanced into the overcast night sky. Despite the cloud cover, it would be a cold night leading to an icy morning.

There was a muffled snuffling and the movement of contented, heavy bodies settling into warm hay coming from within the barn.

Satisfied that all seemed secure, he continued round the wash-house and through the garden door into the kitchen. Pausing momentarily by the stove, he thawed his hands on the residual heat coming from it, while he wondered what the time was – he didn't own a watch, not since his had been irreparably damaged that night he'd parachuted to the ground, some – he counted backwards through the months on his fingers – nine. Nine months ago, he'd found himself here, in this old, yet beautiful home. *Her* home.

His mind shifted to Jessica. He loved her and it made him feel alive to think of it, even if he was powerless to control his own destiny. It seemed that he'd loved her since the moment he'd opened his eyes and found her leaning with concern over his bed, copper hair falling about her lovely face like a silken veil. And despite not knowing where he was or what would happen to him, he had placed his life in her hands.

That she had grown to love him in return was no comfort to him because she was fiercely determined to deny it, building some impenetrable wall round her heart, protecting both herself and her children.

Even though he understood her fear of the future, Anton was an adventurer by nature, preferring to enjoy the present while the future took care of itself. The one night he and Jessica had spent together would never be enough for him. But she'd made her decision and in the intervening months, they'd circled one another cautiously, not risking even a small, inadvertent touch.

Anton stretched his arms overhead, feeling the flexing and contraction of the muscles across his shoulders and back. He worked hard – he always did: turning the animals out into the fields in the mornings; mucking out the barn after their overnight stay; sawing and pruning the trees in the orchard for winter; chopping wood; and carrying out any number of maintenance tasks. He didn't mind the work, in fact he welcomed it.

His arms dropped heavily to his sides and he pulled out a chair, happy to sit in the darkened kitchen for a moment before going upstairs to bed.

No, he didn't mind the work because it distracted him from his homesickness, and it helped Jessica. He wanted to help her. She'd saved his life, she'd fed and clothed him, she hadn't turned him over to the authorities, in fact she was standing firmly against them, denying their well-founded suspicions – and he'd fallen in love with her.

Anton's exhalation was a breathy, humourless laugh. By working hard, he was contributing what he could, earning his keep in some small way; paying his debt.

Yawning, he acknowledged that the hard work had other rewards too, for he fell into bed each night, exhausted and ready for sleep, the easier to forget that she slept only a few doors down the hall, the easier to ignore the relentless physical need of her.

At length, he rose and made his way from the kitchen up the hall towards the great staircase, and it was there he paused, hand on the newel post.

A pale puddle of yellow light was seeping round the parlour door.

Without thinking, he went over and pushed it open.

Anton stood for several heartbeats, taking in the sight before him.

Jessica, soft and warm in a white cotton nightdress and pale blue dressing-gown, was seated at a table, newspapers spread over its polished surface. The lamp on the table splashed yellow light over her shoulders and highlighted strands of gold in her autumn-coloured hair. Her back was to him and so engrossed was she in what she was reading, she seemed unaware of his presence.

Holding his breath lest he startle her, he was free to admire her slim silhouette, her sensuous femininity and her air of innocence, despite her motherhood. His pulse quickened and his senses stirred. He must have made some muted sound for she turned to see him standing there behind her.

**

It had been the faintest of sounds: a breath, the movement of a foot on carpet – no more – that caused Jessica to glance over her shoulder. The captain stood in the doorway, disarmingly handsome in the subdued lamplight. Absently, pulling the folds of her dressing-gown securely around her, she watched as he moved further into the room, closing the door behind him to prevent the warmth escaping.

Within the circle of lamplight, she realised he saw the look on her face. Pausing, cocking his head to the side, he said, "*Was ist?*"

"Here." She indicated a newspaper and pushed it towards him as he approached.

"War in the Pacific," he read, then settled his blue-grey gaze on her. "America?"

Nodding, she pushed to her feet. "Do you want to read these?"

"Not now." His words were simple, but by his expression, she thought he seemed distracted, and her heart skipped a beat.

Jessica began gathering the papers, shaking them into order and folding them. "What do you think it will mean?"

He pursed his lips thoughtfully; his eyes followed her as she stacked the papers into a neat pile. She turned away, but continued to feel his eyes lingering like a warm caress on the back of her neck.

He wanted her. She felt his need calling to her, an urgent, primal compulsion, drawing her to him. She heard him drag in a shuddering breath, seemingly forcing himself to concentrate.

"I do not know," he said, his accent heavy. "It is bad, of course, America *und* Japan. This war will get worse before it gets better."

Jessica turned her head to speak but his eyes were on her mouth. A delicious warmth settled in the pit of her stomach; a liquid heat seeped lower. The captain's gaze dropped to the décolletage of her nightgown and Jessica flattened her palms on the table to steady herself.

***

"Don't you think this could end it sooner?" Jessica asked

him. She was leaning over the table. Anton saw the round outline of her hips and bottom through her dressing-gown. He'd been abstinent for so long – honourably keeping his distance, as she'd requested – and now his head was beginning to swim.

He tried to focus on her question. "I think probably not," he said. "This is a different war within a war." Her hair was pulled over one shoulder. He moved, involuntarily, to finger the coppery threads and heard her quick intake of air. He saw her hands move, flutter uselessly, fidgeting randomly with items on the table.

The sight of her there, lovely in white and blue, smelling of freshly-baked bread and lemon verbena, was too much for any man to bear. His hands ached to take her by the waist and turn her to face him. The urge to kiss her, plunge into her was overwhelming.

He felt his desire growing, an insistent throbbing that caused his blood to boom in his ears and his senses to whirl.

He edged closer – he couldn't stop himself.

***

Acutely aware of him behind her, Jessica shuffled papers and moved the lamp uselessly round the table. She could feel the heat coming from him like a pulsing electrical charge. Naked under her nightdress, she felt sensual and parts of her began to ache in time with the beating of her heart.

Nerve endings stretched tight were vibrating; it was all she could do not to cry out when he lightly touched her hair.

But then he pressed his mouth to the nape of her neck. Jessica's skin rippled, shivering as his lips followed the curve of her neck, sliding upward into her hair while his hands stroked the delicate spot beneath her ears. She straightened, closing her eyes, going limp against him as he ran his hands over her shoulders and down her décolletage.

Inhaling deeply, expanding her lungs; her breasts filled his hands. Her body moved without conscious control, her bottom pushed back, seeking and finding the hard ridge behind her.

His breath was hot against her cheek. A hand left her breast to splay over her belly, then move lower, lower still, cupping her intimately through the cotton of her nightdress.

She whimpered, breathing hard, moving wantonly against him.

He whispered something indiscernible, sipping at her throat.

Jessica's senses were reeling, her mind incapable of thought. She vaguely heard him murmuring in her ear … asking something … She was trying to gather her thoughts, when he groaned, "God, I need you!"

She exhaled in a rush, "Captain …!" Eyes closed, head spinning, she was oblivious to everything but the emphatic throb between her legs.

Mouth against her throat he gasped urgently, "If you want me to stop … say it … you *say it now*!"

"Captain …" Her mind was a whirl of colour and sensation. She felt, with detachment, the back of her nightdress and dressing-gown ruching upward. His insinuative fingers burned a path up the back of her thigh, over her round buttock, hand hot and firm on her naked skin.

Then a fumbling behind her … The metallic hiss of his zipper.

"Frau Jessie," his voice was gravelly, strained, "If you do not say it …"

Jessica was almost weeping with indecision. His arm banded round her waist, held her firmly against him. Her hips moved of their own accord, innately meeting the questing, silken-skinned probing at the junction of her thighs.

And the slow, deliberate, gentle parting, guiding … he exhaled heavily.

"*Jessica*!" His voice was throaty, passionate, aggressive

enough to startle her.

"Oh, God!" she sobbed, her mind fogged with desire. Mustering every ounce of willpower, she stumbled, feeling the swish of air and fabric around her calves as her clothing fell back into place. "I can't! *We* can't!"

Dropping weakly into a chair, Jessica covered her face with her hands, breathing hard, willing her heart to return to normal. "I'm sorry ... Captain, I'm so sorry."

He had moved away, turned his back and was adjusting his clothes.

He's going to hate me ... he'll think I'm a tease – and he would be right! But I can't be intimate with him, only to lose him. I am not Jack Ramage's mum!

Filled with shame and remorse, Jessica remained, elbows on the table, head in hands, even after he bent towards her and whispered, "It is all right, Frau Jessie. I want you, but I will not seduce you into my bed this way."

A short time later, she heard the front door softly close and knew he'd gone outside into the cold night. Only then did she rise and take the lamp by its handle. The swollen ache between her legs testified that she was both a coward and a fool.

***

It had snowed overnight and the landscape glistened like mother-of-pearl in the pre-dawn light. Icicles hung from the boughs of skeletal trees and dripped sporadically with soft plopping sounds. When the sun came up, the icicles would grow slick and steadily begin to trickle. But soon the days would be so freezing that the icicles would remain dry and solid.

Anton grunted irritably as a cold drop struck his cheek and slid down the collar of his shirt. He hunched his shoulders at the discomfort, continuing his way across the paddock to where Sam had noticed, yesterday evening, a broken gate.

Before the cows could be released into the paddock for the day, it must be fixed, and Anton, unable to sleep, had decided to get up and repair it before the constant need to keep one eye on the driveway pressed upon him.

Aware that Robin Tyler was closely watching Jessica's family, Anton couldn't afford to become complacent as he moved about the property. Unlikely that Tyler would be watching at this hour.

Anton had collected a variety of tools in anticipation of the job. As he arrived at the broken gate, even in the gloom of early morning, it was evident by the hairs trapped in the splintered wood, that one of the cows had rubbed against it and the rusted hinge had given way. The gate hung precariously by its top hinge.

He crouched by the bottom hinge and, selecting a tool, began unscrewing what was left of it attached to the frame. His fingers quickly grew numb, losing dexterity in the biting cold. The screwdriver slipped and he cursed descriptively in his first language.

Shaking off the bead of blood that welled out of the cut, he watched it splash onto the fresh snow, instantly blooming then freezing, leaving a bright stain on the otherwise pristine ground.

Just then, he heard the crunch of footsteps behind him. Sam, he knew, would be eager to get the cows milked and outside so the stables could be mucked out. Expecting to see the old man behind him, Anton was slightly taken aback to find Jessica with a steaming cup in her hand.

Wordlessly, she handed him the tea. He put the tool down and gratefully accepted it, holding it in both hands to thaw them. "*Danke.*"

She nodded, and for a moment she looked as though she wanted to say something but changed her mind. Her eyes were dull with fatigue and he suspected she hadn't slept any better than he had.

"What happened?" she spoke at last, indicating the red

blemish on the snow with a jerk of her chin.

"Nothing serious. I slipped with the … this." Unable to remember the word for it, he indicated the tool with his boot.

"Screwdriver."

"Oh, *ja*." He sighed wearily. "Screwdriver."

He looked across the field to where the seamless undulations of the wintry landscape were slowly emerging from the grey, half-light of dawn. Sipping the scalding tea, he wondered, *Why does she continue to stand there? Perhaps because she knows we need to talk. She is braver than I am.*

"Captain …" Jessica began hesitantly. He didn't turn to look at her, but his skin tingled with her proximity. "I am …" she exhaled a gust of steam, "I am quite embarrassed about last night. I … I feel I have … um … led you on. Do you know what I mean by that?"

He nodded. He still wasn't looking at her but he could feel her eyes on him; could feel the tension coming off her in waves. He wanted to reassure her, but he didn't know what to say – wasn't certain that he had the vocabulary. This was a conversation he'd never had in his native language, let alone in English.

Jessica's booted feet shuffled like she was considering going back to the house. Finally, looking at her, he said, "I also want to say things. Please be patient while I find the words."

Stepping backwards, she leaned against the fence post and shoved her hands deep into her cardigan pockets, as much to prevent them fidgeting, he suspected, as to warm them.

"Frau Jessie," he started, paused uncertainly, took a sip of tea as though to fortify himself, then continued, "it is I who should apologise. You were in *der salon*. You were alone *und* reading the newspaper. I was the one who interrupted you. You did not *lead me on*. You wanted to talk … You asked me questions. I lost myself."

She opened her mouth to speak but he cut her off. "*Ein*

Moment, please … I have made love to you *und* I wanted to do so again. I wanted you so much that I …" he shrugged, helplessly. "Perhaps I tried to tease you into it, I do not know. You have told me how you feel, yet I …" He frowned, searching for the word. "I took advantage – I think that is how you say it. I am a grown man. I should have more respect for you – more control of myself."

He gestured towards her. "You did nothing to be embarrassed by. I was what I think they say, carried off with the moment."

***

"Carried away," Jessica corrected gently. His usually excellent grasp of English seemed to be failing him. *Perhaps he's tired. He looks as though he didn't sleep well.*

"*Ja*. I was carried away, I was …" he paused and the colour rose in his cheeks, "I was as a man is when he wants a woman badly *und* I pressured you."

Jessica suppressed an inappropriate urge to laugh. "You were horny, Captain? I think that is the common term for it."

He responded quickly, "*Ja*, I want you. But I will not force myself on you. You have told me your fears *und* I should not have put you in such a position."

Jessica did laugh then, a small, rather embarrassed giggle. "Captain, I could have stopped you any time but I didn't. It was wrong of me to let you think –"

He gestured dismissively. "I touched you … as I agreed I would not. It will not happen again."

But I wanted you to touch me – and more! Jessica's treacherous mind screamed just as her lower regions began throbbing again with the memory of his intimate caresses.

While they'd been standing together, the morning sun had risen like a thin gold line on the eastern horizon and as Anton shifted from one foot to the other, a splash of watery light fell across his head, shooting pale sparks through his hair.

Easy to forget, as he stood before her squinting in the early light, and looking heartbreakingly young, that he was a fighter pilot, a captain in the Luftwaffe, a member of Göring's elite flying squad.

He flew the formidable Junkers, Dornier and the Messerschmitt – the *Sturmvogel.*

Stormbird ...

The word came to her unexpectedly and the tears suddenly sprang into her eyes. *My Stormbird.*

He was looking out over the field again and she surreptitiously swiped at them before he turned back. "It will not happen again," he whispered.

Now it was Jessica's turn to look away as she remembered backing into him, the hardness of him behind her. The heat flooded her face and she leaned against one of the wooden uprights, between which were strung lines of wire, hoary with frost, to fence in the cows. The wood was slick and wet, the post capped with snow and she felt its cold through the wool of her cardigan.

She heard his soft laughter and shot a sideways glance at him. With a roguish grin, he said, "Oh, *ja*, you were horny too. *Und* you fought against a natural urge." He stepped closer to her and her stomach quivered as his breath warmed her ear, "I spent a long time out in the cold waiting for *mein Schwanz* to cool. If you ever decide to stop denying yourself the satisfaction of my body, you must tell me immediately. My toes were nearly frozen solid when I returned inside."

Her eyes widened in surprise but she didn't know whether to be shocked by his words or amused by his honesty. She stared at him, doing neither.

He grinned disarmingly and gave a one-shoulder shrug. "I am sorry, but that is the truth. Now," he tossed the cold dregs of his tea onto the snow and handed her the mug, "Go back to the house where it is warm. I must finish this gate."

He turned away, effectively dismissing her, but she knew intuitively that he was as upset as she was and attempting to cover it. For a moment, she studied the lean curve of his back as he bent into his work.

Then she turned away.

Chapter 28

Later that night, after the day's chores were done, the fire roared in the grate in the parlour and Jessica sat on the settee, a child on either side. She listened as they took turns practising their reading.

From time to time, she glanced across the room to where the captain sat reading yesterday's Yorkshire Post. On the table beside him was Alexandra's journal. The red, leather cover was faded and scuffed and Jessica marvelled, yet again, at how well preserved it was given its years underground.

"Mummy," Mary interrupted her thoughts. "Why are you going to Wolstone tomorrow?"

"I have to see the bank manager – I want to talk to him about the mortgage on the house."

"Can I go too?"

Jessica shrugged. "You can, but you'll be bored."

"I'll wait for you at the market," Mary explained brightly. "Peggy Walsh is going to be there. She's the one Tommy likes."

"I don't like anyone," Thomas insisted, though his flushed cheeks suggested otherwise.

Mary chortled. "See how red he's gone? He's lying! He's liked her for ages. Anyway, he hangs around that Jack Ramage all the time. No wonder Peggy doesn't talk to him!"

"All right Mary, enough now," Jessica said. "Don't pick on your brother."

"Why not? He's an eejit!"

"Mary," the captain had turned in his seat and had levelled a steady blue gaze on her. "It is unkind of you to speak like that. But you are a smart girl – kindness is part of being smart, *ja*?"

He spoke assertively, in a voice that accorded no argument and Jessica was reminded that he was a military officer. Mary's lower lip hung out and she stared at the floor between her feet.

"Okay?" the captain asked, his use of the American idiom caused Thomas to giggle, but the German's gaze did not waver from the girl.

Finally, she nodded. "Okay." She looked up to meet his stare and he held out an arm to her. Without hesitation, Mary rose and went to him but her eyes filled with tears and she pressed her forehead into his shoulder. The captain curled his arm about her waist.

"What should you say?"

"I'm sorry, Tommy."

Thomas appeared uncertain how to react. First he stared at the captain in surprise, then his expression turned to bemusement as he looked at his sister. Eventually, he said, "It's okay, Mary."

Jessica was watching the captain curiously. The children loved him. No wonder Mary was afraid of losing him. They were not even six years old when their father left. This man is the father they are afraid to become attached to.

"I think I'll go to bed now," Mary said. She wished the adults a good night, offered her twin a brief smile, then taking one of the lamps Jessica had prepared, left the room.

Thomas yawned. "Think I'll go too. I want to help Mr Bird make the butter in the morning."

"*Vielen Dank. Du bist ein guter Junge!*"

"*Ja, ich bin!*" Thomas responded cheerfully and Jessica suddenly felt sick.

"For God's sake Thomas, don't you dare speak like that outside of this house!"

"I won't, Mum!"

"And what do you think you're doing teaching the kids German?" she rounded on the captain who responded with an unrepentant smile.

"It is good to know a second language."

"Not during these times, it's not!"

"I apologise." He inclined his head, conceding the point and the thought crossed her mind that only a few brief months ago she would never have asserted herself so forcefully.

In any case, normally, she'd have agreed that a second language was good, but the ease with which German phrases seemed to flow so casually from her son frightened her.

Lucifer's Balls! Another thought occurred to her. "Thomas! Don't, whatever you do, say anything in German to that Jack Ramage!"

"I won't, Mum," he assured her. "Anyway, I don't like Peggy Walsh!"

Exasperated, Jessica wagged a finger at him. "Pay attention to –"

"He understands, Frau Jessie." The captain's tone was gentle but persuasive.

She held her arms out to her son, "Come on then. You want me to tuck you into bed?"

"I want Mr Bird to tuck me in." Thomas's request took Jessica aback. She glanced at the captain, who shrugged and nodded.

"Very well, then," Jessica waved. "Off you go."

"Piggyback!" the boy demanded. Before Jessica could intervene, the captain had swung her son onto his back and was marching up the stairs.

Following behind, Jessica met Mary coming from the kitchen with a glass of water. "Thomas is getting too attached," Mary declared sagely.

"So are you," Jessica returned. "You went straight over when he asked you to."

Mary snorted. "There must be a way for him to stay, Mummy."

"There isn't love, and you know why."

"Well, then, he needs to go now!" The child's face was set in stone.

"He probably can't until the war's over."

Mary shook her head obstinately. "That'll be too late." She gave her mother a knowing look and pushed past, continuing up the stairs, directly to her room.

In Thomas's room, Jessica found the boy climbing into bed, while the captain stood by and held the bedclothes. He pulled them round Thomas's chin. Jessica approached and kissed the child's forehead.

"Good night, love."

"Good night, Mummy. Good night Mr Bird."

"Good night," the captain responded dutifully in English.

They left his room together, and Jessica poked her head around Mary's door as they went past. Mary was already in bed pulling the blankets up.

She went in and kissed her daughter good night and closed the door behind her.

Jessica and Anton didn't speak until they were back in the parlour. She resumed her seat but he remained standing. He said, "She is afraid of getting too close to me."

"Yes."

"As are you."

Jessica didn't respond.

"It is all right, Frau Jessie." He smiled gently and supressed a yawn. "I must check the cows, then I will go to bed. *Gute nacht, meine Liebe.*"

Jessica watched him leave and sighed wearily. How easy it would be to fall into his arms. How easy to accept the comfort of his companionship, the warmth of his touch. Yet she couldn't do it.

I'm too much the coward. Too afraid to of a future without him.

The temptation to relive that unforgettable night in his bed was ever present, but was it wise to succumb to it? This whole saga with the captain, without doubt, would end in the breaking of her heart. If she was destined for this pain anyway, why resist the intimacy they both craved? Keeping him at arm's length, denying them both, had not assuaged the feelings she had for him.

Meanwhile, her refusal was hurting them both and suddenly she realised why. Though she desired him, what she felt for him was not merely sexual. It was genuine affection, not to be satisfied by a fleeting physical joining. It was more than that.

Despite everything, she was in love with him.

Jessica was startled from her reverie as a log shifted in the grate and a small eruption of sparks flew up the chimney. She yawned and stretched, feeling the muscles in her shoulders tighten and release. With a soft grunt, she pushed herself off the couch, banked the coals in the fireplace for the night, and went to bed.

Chapter 29

Jessica awoke feeling groggy, unrested and faintly troubled. The winter sky outside her window was dark, the clouds laden with snow and her room was so cold her breath fogged before her face. She shuddered and burrowed deeper beneath the bedclothes.

She was just drifting back to luxurious sleep when a bump somewhere in the house brought her to full wakefulness. Mary's voice, raised in some dispute with her brother followed and, dreading the thought of mediating a juvenile squabble, Jessica pulled the bedclothes over her head with a groan.

Any moment now, one of her children would burst into her room demanding she reprimand the other.

She groaned, feeling the tension of the day ahead weighing on her as she remembered that she had to go into Wolstone.

If only I could hide here all day.

The thought was tempting but impossible and as Mary's voice drew closer, Thomas could now be heard arguing in his defence. Jessica was bracing for the inevitable confrontation when the captain's quiet, accented tones intervened and she immediately felt her muscles release.

Funny how one's perceptions can be conditioned, she thought abstractly. All her life, she'd been taught that Germans were ugly, ignorant and brash. Their language was guttural and their manners abrupt and cold.

For fifty years, the world had viewed the German population as a single, loathsome culture. Nazis were to be feared, the Third Reich a machine built for terror, Germany's leaders and its civilians of one bent; murder and destruction.

Yet, the man in the hallway, effortlessly controlling her riotous children, was as removed from her preconceived beliefs as it was possible to be.

He was kind, intelligent and beautiful of face and form. He

was gentle and generous, and beyond that, he seemed as opposed to his leaders' behaviour as the rest of the world.

Sighing with resignation, Jessica climbed from her bed and shivering, quickly put on her dressing-gown and slippers.

"What's going on?" she demanded, throwing open her bedroom door.

Three faces greeted her with varying expressions. Mary's was red and outraged. Thomas's was red and indignant. The captain was leaning casually against the frame of the bathroom door, arms folded across his chest, smiling indulgently.

"Mum! Thomas said –"

"Mum! Mary said –"

"Stop it, both of you!" she glared at each child in turn, then faced the captain. "What's going on here? You tell me!"

His glance took in both children, then he grinned at their mother. "Mary said Thomas likes her friend, but Thomas claims –"

Jessica sighed. "Not this again!"

"It is all right," the captain said. "Thomas believes Mary is mistaken."

"I'm not mistaken," Mary insisted, "he's lying!"

"*Nein*, now. You must not say this of your brother."

Suddenly the shouting between the twins erupted again. Jessica threw a pleading look in the captain's direction and he responded.

"*Stille!*" The captain's order rang out above the squalling children, shocking them into silence. "*Das genügt!* There will be no more of this. Go downstairs now *und* do your chores. Thomas, go see to the hen-house *und* Mary go to Herr Clay *und* collect the cream for the butter."

Both children stared wide-eyed at the young man and neither moved. While Thomas appeared stunned, Mary's expression was belligerent. She opened her mouth to speak and was immediately met with the captain's most authoritative, stereotypically German command, "*Schnell*!"

The twins scrambled to obey, while their mother stood watching, a hand against her mouth to stifle her giggles. As the pair disappeared downstairs, she turned and met the captain's gaze. He arched his eyebrows at her and she relaxed against the wall, laughing openly.

"Well-handled."

He grinned. "It worked when my mother did it, *ja*? Do you want to use the bathroom? I have lit the boiler, it should be warm for you."

Jon never once lit the boiler! She felt her eyes well and for a moment his expression changed. He put a hand out as though to touch her, before reconsidering and retracting it.

"Thank you, Captain. That's very thoughtful."

He regarded her narrowly. "Is everything all right?"

"Oh yes, everything's fine."

He made a sceptical face and she gave a little laugh. "Well, it's just that … you've come to mean so much to us. We'll miss you horribly when this … when it's over and you're gone."

He grinned sardonically. "We will all grieve our separation – it is too late to prevent that now."

"I know!" she cried in frustration. "That's the trouble: my children adore you, you're the father they lost. You're the son Sam and Marg lost."

"*Und* you?"

Her eyes dropped. "You know the answer to that."

They momentarily fell silent, until he said, "So playing-it-safe has got you nowhere."

"One of us must look to the future," Jessica responded stubbornly. She folded her arms and leaned against the wall.

He stepped closer and took her by the shoulders. "*Meine liebe*. Tell me what has *really* upset you?"

She shrugged his hands away impatiently. It would do neither of them any good if she were to admit her feelings for him now. "I don't know ... I don't *know!* Something came over me that night we went to bed. For the first time in my life I lived for the moment. Yet to continue physically with you ... I am not a woman who can continue such a relationship without becoming emotionally involved."

"We won't be continuing – you have made your decision," he said dispassionately.

"I have," she lied firmly. "But ... fact is Captain, you're a virile young man – you have physical needs. While I'm ... I'm just some foolish, lonely widow. I went outside my boundaries with you. I risked everything: my self-respect, your respect, my children's ... all for a man who will inevitably leave."

He took her hands and raised them to his lips. "You think I only want you to satisfy my needs? That is insulting. I would not care if I never made love to you again," he kissed her knuckles. "Do not misunderstand me, I want you – I want you very much. But I want you as a man who loves you, *und* if I am never to touch you again, I will accept that ... *und* still love you."

Her eyes filled again at his words but she blinked the tears away.

"As for taking a risk," he continued, "I loved you before that night. I love you now. *Und* long after I have left you, I will continue to love you."

Jessica sniffed and swallowed.

"So you see," he said simply, combing the hair from her temples with his fingertips. "No risk."

"Bringing you into my home was a risk."

Grinning, he said, "*Nun, ja*, you did that."

"I went to bed with you and," her colour heightened, "it was impulsive and ... you were lonely. I told myself that it was natural, that you were far from home; you needed companionship, then I tried to forget about it."

"What is wrong with you?" he demanded, suddenly angry.

She recoiled. "What?"

"I did not rape you, Jessica!" he added, in a frustrated growl. "You came willingly to me because we *both* needed love. We were *both* driven by our passions *und* did not think beyond that night. *Ja*, I must leave but while I am here, why can you not accept that something is growing between us *und* enjoy it? It is more than loneliness!"

The bitterness in his words instantly dried her tears.

"But it's pointless," she persisted, aware that she was being dreadfully self-absorbed.

"*Und* I will tell you something else." His voice was gentler now. He took her hands again. "When I was ill *und* first saw you leaning over my bed all angry *und* afraid, I knew then that you would become dear to me."

Jessica stared at him in wonder. "I don't understand."

He shrugged a single shoulder, smiling wryly. "Of course you do not, but I loved you from the first day I saw you. *Na, sicher*," he admitted with a glimmer of humour, "at first I just wanted to have you in my bed because you are sexy. Then it became more. I will grieve you no less when I leave."

"I didn't know." Jessica felt humbled, confused and warm all at the same time. "I was so afraid of you and so afraid of the situation … I just wanted you gone."

"*Ja, ja, ja*," he waved impatiently. "I could see that, but you were very sweet all the same. I looked forward to seeing you each day. And when you did not come I missed you *und* your sexy arse."

Jessica snorted. It was all she could manage with a blocked nose.

He leaned close to her ear. His warm breath stirred her hair. "Frau Jessie, you have a *very* sexy arse."

She flushed and thumped him playfully on the arm. She could see the juddering rise and fall of his chest, his eyes were clear and honest – grey in the dim light of the hall.

Lost in her own misery, she'd not considered what it must be like for him. He was in a hostile, foreign land, hundreds of miles from his friends and family. He would have known moments of incredible fear and loneliness, and yet all she could think of was how hurt she will be when he goes home.

Wouldn't this fear and loneliness drive him to seek comfort in my bed? Her traitorous mind whispered.

"Jessica," that was twice he'd used her first name and it got her attention. "I know what you are thinking, but I will tell you this." He took her face between his palms, forcing her to look at him. "I have fallen in love with you, *und ja*, I want to sleep with you – every night. But if we are never to be together that way again, it will not change my feelings for you. I would even say that I would prefer we never touch again if it means you will believe me. It is going to kill me to leave you, but we know there is no alternative."

He leaned in then, and lightly kissed her lips before releasing her face and stepping back. "Frau Jessie, I suggest you now use the bathroom. I will make you a cup of tea, then you must find your pretty smile to take to your bank manager."

She groaned. She'd forgotten all about that.

Chapter 30

"Well, Mrs Barrow," George Hammersmith said, pensively. His round-rimmed spectacles slipped to the end of his nose, as he squinted at the insurance papers Jessica put before him. "Says here your husband contributed to his own death; they didn't pay out the full sum."

He raised his head and pushed his glasses up his nose. "Were you aware?"

She nodded sadly. "Of course. I've already paid a lump sum off my mortgage, but now I'm wondering, if I pay off this much," she pointed to a figure on the page, "how much my monthly repayments will be reduced to."

Mr Hammersmith's smile was syrupy sweet. "Now, Mrs Barrow, of course we can calculate this for you, but surely you have a father, an uncle … We'd be very happy to explain everything to –"

"Mr Hammersmith," Jessica interrupted, firmly. "I have been running my business and raising my children – alone. I have been making my mortgage payments – alone. You will deal with me, you will respond to my request and you will not be condescending about it."

The bank manager pulled in his chin and sniffed disdainfully. Jessica asked, "Now, when can I expect to receive my information?"

"Well, we'll need to –"

"This week will do nicely, thank you."

Jessica rose, extending her hand.

Mr Hammersmith looked at it reproachfully but reluctantly shook Jessica's hand before escorting her from his bank.

Out on Boroughgate, Jessica was trembling with her own audacity. Angry and perspiring, despite the chill afternoon wind, she strode briskly across the road, into the market square and down New Market Street where Mary's friend's mother ran a little tearoom.

Mary and Peggy Walsh were huddled together for warmth on the footpath just as a light snow began to fall.

"Oh, here's Mummy," she heard her daughter say.

"Hello, Mrs Barrow," Peggy said. She was a pretty little thing with blonde hair tied in bunches and a rose complexion.

"Hello Peggy. Ready, Mary?"

Mary nodded and said goodbye to her friend. Jessica turned and marched angrily down the narrow lane; Mary jogged several paces to catch up.

"What's the hurry, Mummy? Can we go –"

"We're going straight home," Jessica said. "I've had enough for one day. Let's get in the car before –"

"Jessica! What a lovely surprise."

Lucifer's balls!

Robin Tyler stepped onto the cobbled lane, blocking Jessica's way. "Hello Mary," he added.

Mary didn't respond and for once Jessica overlooked her daughter's rudeness. "Going somewhere in a hurry?" Tyler smiled arrogantly.

Smarmy bastard! Jessica offered a watery smile. "Yes we are, Mr Tyler, so if –"

"Mr Tyler is it? I thought we were friends."

"And I thought I'd been perfectly clear on that score," Jessica retorted. "Come on Mary."

Jessica took her daughter's hand and made to go round him but he moved with her, further blocking the lane. "Ah yes, you did express your preference for Germans."

Stunned, Jessica stared at him.

"If I recall your words correctly," he sneered, "'I'd rather sleep with Adolf Hitler and his entire band of madmen …' So, how's that working out for you, hmm? Slept with any Germans lately?"

Jessica felt herself grow pale. "You're disgusting."

Tyler laughed, "Hostility will get you nowhere."

"Let us pass," she hissed.

With a derisive smile, he stepped casually aside. "I'm watching you, Jessica," he whispered into her ear as she shoved past him. His warm breath against her hair made her skin crawl.

"I told you I didn't like him," Mary commented. "Right from the start, I said –"

"Not now, Mary." They arrived at the car just as the snow began falling in earnest.

***

Jessica felt physically ill in the aftermath of her confrontation with Tyler. It was the last thing she needed after that chauvinistic bank manager. Her stomach was churning and she was shaking so badly that her foot bounced on the clutch. The car slipped and skated precariously on the icy road as she fought with the wheel, navigating the twisting, undulating lanes of Wolstone and the narrow bridge into Wharferidge.

The engine screamed as she struggled to balance the accelerator and clutch, and suddenly, just outside her front gate, the car stalled. Rather than restart it, she steered by momentum to the shoulder of the lane.

"Stay in the car," Jessica threw over her shoulder and clambered out. The road was slick with snow and ice and her feet slid beneath her. Lurching drunkenly to the side of the road, she collapsed to her knees in six inches of fresh powder.

Damn them! Damn every bloody man to hell! Anton bloody Vogel, George bloody Hammersmith, Robin bloody Tyler, even Jonathon bloody Barrow for leaving me in this mess!

"Mum!" Jessica heard Mary's distressed cry but didn't respond. Her stomach was roiling, reacting disagreeably with the acidic taste of anger and fear. Her breathing was coming in hard gasps but she felt starved of oxygen. Leaning over, she scooped a handful of snow and pressed it to her hot forehead, sighing with the relief it brought, and waiting for the nausea to pass.

Behind her, a car door slammed but she didn't have the presence of mind to think about it.

It was some time before she became aware of a burning numbness in her fingers and she realised she was kneeling on the verge, her clenched hands were buried in the icy drift.

Rubber-booted feet were running across the road and Marg shouted her name. Jessica dazedly looked around. Marg stood over her while Mary waited across the road with Thomas.

"She's all right," Marg called to them. "Go back to the cottage – one of you get a blanket ready, the other go get Mr Clay – he's in the woodshed. Tell 'im to come collect the car."

The children ran to obey without argument, while Marg crouched and wrapped her arms around Jessica's shoulders. "Come on – up you get. Can't stay out 'ere all afternoon."

After a moment, Jessica settled a little. She was shivering more with cold than fear and anger now. "Oh Mah-Marg," she stammered through chattering teeth. "I d-d-don't kn-know what came o-over me – I just ..." Jessica allowed herself to be led across the road, through the gate and along the path to the cottage.

"It's all right. Let's get a hot cuppa into you." Marg directed her into the kitchen. It was blessedly warm, and she dragged a chair toward the range and deposited Jessica onto it. Only then did the younger woman realise that the captain stood in the corner, his expression grim. One hand was stuffed deep in his trouser pocket, the other was clutched tightly in Mary's little paw. Thomas came forward with a red tartan blanket and wrapped it round his mother's shoulders, as Marg put a steaming cup of tea before her.

"What happened?" Marg pulled a chair close to Jessica's and

dropped onto it. "What's going on?"

Jessica gave a dry sob and let her head fall into her hands. "He knows …" her voice was muffled against her palms.

"Mr Tyler was at Wolstone." Mary explained. "Mummy argued with him."

"What about?" Marg pushed.

Jessica gulped loudly. "The captain." She lowered her hands and raised fearful eyes to the man in the corner. "He knows you're here. I'm *sure* he does."

The captain seemed outwardly calm, though his jaw was clenched and his eyes glittered with anger. Jessica recognised the irony of her situation: this man was not her enemy. That honour was shared jointly by the Englishman threatening her and the bank manager treating her like a useless female.

And suddenly, she decided, whatever the cost to herself, she would allow herself to love this young man. He'd come into her life and done more to help and support her than anyone else. He cared for her family and he cared for her. She sensed their time together drying up; every moment she deliberated was a moment she would regret for the rest of her days.

Robin Tyler might claim he was only doing his job, but his aggression, his thinly veiled threats and his attempts to extort sex from her were not part of it. And yet this German, from whom Tyler purported to protect his country, had never harmed her or threatened her or her children in any way.

Her eyes locked with his and for a moment the room and turmoil fell away and she wanted nothing more than to have him hold her.

All three adults in the room started as the door suddenly opened and Sam approached the range to warm his hands.

"Told 'er yet?" he asked. When no one answered he looked around and met his wife's glare. "What?"

"No, we haven't told her yet, you silly git."

"Christ! What now?" Jessica demanded, looking from Marg to Sam and back. "What else can possibly happen today?"

The older woman took a breath. "Jessie, while you were out, your parents arrived."

***

Jessica's first reaction was relief since she hadn't heard from her parents in almost a week. But the relief was quickly followed by yet another clenching of her stomach.

"Granny and Grandad are here?" Thomas did a little jig of excitement and dashed towards the door.

"Stop right there, my boy." Sam grasped the child's collar. "Sit down and be quiet while we talk to your mum."

Jessica's head began to spin and a great chasm gaped at her feet – a vortex threatening to suck her down to oblivion. Remembering the tea, she took up her cup and drank deeply, allowing the dry flavour of the tannins to soothe her frayed nerves.

"Did they see you?" She addressed the captain. He shook his head.

"Anton and young Tommy were in the stables when they pulled up," Sam said. "Fortunately, I 'eard the car. I told them you were out … Suggested they come down 'ere for a pot o' tea while they waited but they insisted on waiting at the 'ouse."

Jessica's eyes met the captain's. "If they go into your room … is there … have you left anything lying around … men's things they might see?"

The captain exhaled slowly and nodded. Jessica closed her eyes in a weary, extended blink. When she opened them again she looked at Sam. "What did you tell them?"

"Nothing." He smirked at her somewhat sheepishly. "Your father is unwell. I 'elped them into the 'ouse, stoked the fire in the parlour and left them. Sorry."

"No, that's perfect. Thank you."

Jessica drained the remaining mouthful of tea in her cup, took a deep breath and felt herself mildly restored. "Right then," she said with false cheer, "no point putting it off."

"Will you be all right?" Marg asked, worry lines ridged her brow.

Jessica got to her feet with a humourless laugh. "We'll see, won't we? Anyway, I'll have to tell you about my disagreement with Robin Tyler later. Kids," she held out her arms, "come on. Let's go see Granny and Grandad."

The children jumped up eagerly, and she added, "Not a word about Mr Bird until I've told them privately, you hear me?"

They nodded vigorously and rushed to the door.

"What do you want me to do?" The captain spoke softly behind her. He looked worried and apologetic.

It's not his fault – neither of us chose this. I need to apologise to him, and tell him how I feel. But it will have to wait.

After everything she'd been through today, with more waiting for her up at the house, the realisation that he must leave, and the sooner the better, struck her like a blow to the heart. She had wasted so much time.

Resolutely and regardless of her audience, she strode determinedly towards him. Taking his face between her palms she kissed him firmly on the mouth.

He stood very still, arms at his sides and Jessica felt courageous, full of purpose, as she drew away. "Wait for me here. Let me break it to them gently." She drew a deep breath and added, "They loved Jon very much. To them, you are the enemy – a callous murderer. You, *personally*, probably destroyed their friends' homes and places of work. My parents will not be pleased to meet you."

He nodded and slipped his hands into his pockets.

"But *I* love you." She looked about the small kitchen. Sam

stood passively, leaning against the table while Marg smiled with satisfaction. Her children watched on – both were smiling, but that could be because they were eager to see their grandparents. She turned back to the man who'd come to mean so much to her and whom she was determined to defend. "I love you, and they are just going to have to accept that."

***

Her father had lost weight. That was the first thing Jessica noticed. The second thing was that her mother was tired and seemed to have aged ten years in the year since she'd seen her last.

"Has it really been that long?" Jessica asked, turning from the hearth, having thrown a fresh log on the fire.

"Aye," Eric said. "And too long. Look at the size of these piglets."

"Not piglets anymore, Grandad," Thomas declared from his grandfather's knee.

"No, you certainly are not. Your old Grandad can't hold all your weight now. What's your mum feeding you?"

"Bricks!" Thomas giggled, but slid off the elderly man's lap.

The children were overjoyed at seeing their grandparents again, and the pleasure was returned. But Jessica could see the worry in her mother's eyes whenever Olive looked at her husband.

Before leaving the cottage, Marg had pressed a recently baked loaf into her hands. Jessica now served it sliced and spread with soft, creamy butter, and as her parents complimented the freshness of both, she wondered what they'd say if they knew the butter had been churned that very morning by a Luftwaffe captain.

The incongruity of it made her smile darkly to herself but her mother picked up on it straight away.

"You're happy to see us, are you love?" Olive asked. "But I suppose you've been asking us to come for so long …" She left the remainder of the sentence hanging, as though not entirely sure of their welcome. Jessica wondered if her mother sensed her anxiety.

"I'm glad you're here," she said, taking a seat opposite. "I worry every time those planes go over. But after all the times I've been asking, *begging,* you to get out of Leeds, why now? They say the worst of the bombing's over."

"Aye well," Olive swallowed a mouthful of bread. "It's your father. I was always keen to get away but who could drag him out o' that shop?" she smiled warmly at her husband.

"It's my health," Eric supplied making a contemptuous face. "Doctor reckons it's the dust and smog – all that rubble, you know? Air's thick with it … lungs full of congestion."

"Is that it?" Jessica asked, cynically. "You've given up smoking, have you?"

Olive grunted. "As if that's ever going to happen. It'll be the death of him, I keep telling him but he won't –"

"If it's good enough for Doctor Ross to smoke it's good enough for me. Besides, it's the rubble lying about what makes the congestion," Eric insisted.

"All right you two." Jessica laughed at them but it was without humour for the seriousness of her father's condition was plain with every wheezing breath he took. *Wait till they find out about the captain. He's going to have a seizure!* "So are you here to stay? What's happening with the shop?"

Her parents exchanged a glance and some wordless communication seemed to take place. Jessica was struck with a momentary sadness; how she envied the intimacy of a relationship with such discourse.

"Jessica, I'm sorry to tell you, love," her mother said. "The shop was destroyed. Took the edge of a hit a couple of weeks ago – they were probably aiming for the railway station. The gas cylinders out back went up. Most of the house was burnt to the ground before we knew owt about it."

Olive's voice was steady but Jessica sensed the emotion beneath the words. She glanced at her father and thought his eyes appeared wet. It was, after all, the house he'd built for her mother after he'd returned from the Great War.

Jessica asked gently, "What about the shop – the stock and all?"

Her mother gave a resigned shrug. "Most of the foodstuffs, cans, non-perishables and so on we've stored in the hole under the counter. No one'll ever know they're there."

"We didn't like to display everything anyway," her father put in. "With people on rations an' all, weren't fair."

Olive continued, "We got what we could out of the house; a few clothes, my mother's locket and wedding ring. They said in the Yorkshire Post that it's helpful to have bags packed with valuables, clothes and things, in case you need to evacuate in an emergency. I'd already done that so your father just loaded them into the car and we got away. The roads were a mess. A brick wall'd come down and we got diverted towards Beeston – near the Ridgely's place, so we stayed there until the road cleared."

Jessica wanted to weep. The house and business had been her father's pride, they were everything he owned. She herself had worked in the shop as a child. And the rear residence was the only home Jessica had known until Broughton Hall. It was certainly the only home she'd ever known her parents to have. Every penny they owned was in those walls.

"What about Scaramouche?" Thomas asked suddenly.

"Yes, what about Scaramouche?" Mary echoed. "Did you bring him with you?"

Jessica had forgotten about her parents' Yorkie – a scruffy little stray that had wandered into the shop several years ago.

Enquiries in the neighbourhood turned up nothing so Scarry had joined the family.

Eric's face fell, and he rubbed Mary's back between her shoulder-blades. "Not good news, I'm afraid. Scarry ran off in all the confusion and we couldn't find him."

"Did you look?" Thomas demanded, accusingly.

"Of course we did; we looked everywhere."

"He was gone, love," Olive said gently. "Probably found himself another family."

Neither child seemed satisfied. "Anyway," Jessica said quickly, "we're glad you're here. You might've lost your home and your little dog, but you have your lives."

She regarded her father's downcast face. "At least you have that, Dad," she insisted. "This is your home, however long you need."

"Forever," Thomas added helpfully, while his mother wondered how on earth they were going to react when they found out about the captain. Particularly in view of their extensive loss, and evidently, Mary was wondering the same thing. Her eyes bored into Jessica's and her little eight-year-old face spoke as eloquently as a grown woman's: *He needs to go.*

But first he needs to meet my parents, Jessica thought with dread.

"Well, come on kids,' she said brightly. "I've got a couple of jobs for you."

***

Mary was assigned a position at the bench to peel potatoes; Thomas was seated at the table to shell peas. They were so obediently industrious that Jessica knew they were worried too.

Thomas looked up at his mother. "Where are Grandad and Granny going to sleep?"

It was a good question. The obvious room was the captain's,

as it was furnished with a double bed. The only other room was used for storage and assorted junk. It was filled with things that had belonged to Jon's mother, or other items she and Jon had never needed enough to unpack.

The room also contained an ancient single bed; Jessica's childhood one. It had been earmarked for Mary, but sagged so badly in the middle, Jon had condemned it as scrap that would deform his daughter's young spine.

Jon and Jessica had invested in two new beds for their children; the old one was relegated to the junk room.

"I suppose we could move Mr Bird into the junk room," Jessica said, thoughtfully. "That old bed will be uncomfortable but rather *he* sleep on it than Granny or Grandad."

"When are you going to tell them about him?" Mary asked, without looking up from her work.

Jessica sighed. "I can't put it off, can I?"

Both eight year olds raised their heads and observed their mother. "No," they said in unison.

"Do it now, Mum," Thomas urged. "Get it over with – that's what you tell me about my chores."

She smiled wanly. "And I'm always right, aren't I."

He grinned at her. *He's going to break some hearts one day.* "Not always, but this time you would be."

"Righto," she said, resolutely. "Can one of you go down to the cottage and ask Mr Bird to come up? All of you wait in here until I've broken the news ... Until I know they've got used to the idea."

They nodded solemnly and she felt a twinge of guilt that such young children were forced to live with so much responsibility and subterfuge. *Still, as Jon's children, they're probably relishing the intrigue and adventure.*

She'd already left the room when she thought of something else. Turning, she stuck her head back into the kitchen. "No matter what you hear – and there might be yelling and tears – stay in here and keep Mr Bird with you. All right?"

"Okay, Mum," Thomas agreed.

Mary snorted at the Americanism, and said, "*Yes*, Mum."

***

There was yelling.

Demands for explanations, admonition and oft repeated, *How could you?* and *What could you be thinking?*

And there were tears. Floods of them – her mother sat weeping into a hanky, while her father vented his grief, his anger on behalf of his friends for all they'd endured, everything they'd lost: their home, their livelihood … "*Scaramouche*!" he ended on an anguished cry, the little dog's disappearance being the final straw.

Jessica sat mired in wretchedness while her father's wrath crashed over her. She'd never known Eric Bentley to raise his voice and she stared at the floor between her feet while guilt and defiance competed in her stomach. For it was true, what her father said, every word of it.

Including the final insult; an elderly man, destitute of everything – including his dignity –left to beg charity from his widowed daughter.

"*Damn those bloody Gerries*!" he thundered, his breathing coming in rasping gasps, his fists clenching and unclenching. "Damn their black souls to hell, bloody Nazis, bleeding Nazi *bastards*!"

It was the worst language ever to pass her father's lips, and it continued; a long stream of vitriol, punctuated by hacking coughs that caused the broken veins in his cheeks to turn purple and his lips to tremble.

He paced from fireplace to window, door to table, back to fireplace – up and down, back and forth. Jessica sat, head in hands, willing it to end, and accepting that it only *would* end once her father had exorcised from himself all those weeks of accumulated heartache, fear and loss.

"What did I go to war for?" he demanded in an agonised voice. "What did we fight for? My mates were dying all around me and we swore we'd never go to war again – *ever*! *Why?*" he demanded, leaning over her. "Answer me that! Why are we at war now? Because of those bloody German bastards, that's why! Evil's what they are!" he shook his fist in the air. "*Plain evil*! Bombing us out of our homes … And what about your own husband? Poor bloody Jon. Killed – *drowned*," he added for gruesome affect, "because of a bleedin' Kraut U-boat!"

He broke off to cough and struggled to catch his breath. Olive looked up at him, her face awash with tears, "Eric, love, you're going to have a stroke if you don't calm down."

But Eric obviously had no intention of calming. While his wife shook with silent sobs, he was clearly making damn sure his daughter knew where he stood on the matter.

Horrified, Jessica sat weeping into her hands while her father paced, coughed and grew purple in the face.

"You're harbouring a *Nazi*!" he bellowed. "The *enemy*!" he paused to cough. "Not enough that he killed your husband, left your children fatherless, but it's *illegal*! They'll take *your children away,* you realise that? They'll *lock you up*! Is that what you want? What do you think of that, eh? Still willing to take care of your bloody Gerry friend?"

Finally, Jessica had had enough. She leapt up, her face distorted by grief and anger. "That's it, Dad!" she shouted, stamping her foot in frustration. "You've said your piece … it's nothing more than I've tormented myself with all along. *Yes*!" she screeched, "the Germans killed Jon. *Yes*, they destroyed your home and business. *Yes*, they killed Marg and Sam's son – yet Marg and Sam can put this hatred behind them. We *have* to," she cried, "otherwise we'll carry it from generation to generation." She paused, gasping for breath.

"He's decent," she went on, composing herself, "well-educated. He has helped me ... without him I'd have lost everything ... I couldn't have kept the cows, or milked them! I'd have had no income. I wouldn't have been able to pay the mortgage ... we'd *all* be homeless!"

She broke off to swallow. Her nose was so blocked with tears that she couldn't breathe properly. Her throat felt raw, her head was pounding.

"He didn't ask to be German," she drew a ragged breath. "He didn't want to join the Luftwaffe but he was conscripted – just like our boys. He's living here ... and now so are you ... that's the end of it. We've all got to live with it."

"What about the children?" Olive's reddened eyes were raised to where Jessica and her father stood toe-to-toe, breathing hard. "Has anyone considered the children?"

"Oh Mum," Jessica exhaled with a humourless laugh. "They love him! They're his strongest champions."

"Jessica!" her father's bark interrupted a brief lull in the shouting. "He is a young man, a Nazi –"

"He's not a Nazi, there's a difference."

Eric dismissed her comment with a gesture. "He's a filthy Kraut! You're a married woman. Let me speak plainly. Young men have appetites ..."

Jessica groaned.

"They have urges! He's in the *German* military – they're brutes! I've seen them ... back in sixteen. They take what they want – by force, if necessary. I'll bloody kill him if he's laid a hand on –"

"Dad, for Christ sake...!"

Jessica's cheeks were flaming. She'd turned away from her father, ostensibly in disgust, but felt her mother's eyes on her.

The older woman compressed her lips contemplatively as the flush extended into Jessica's hairline.

"If he's touched a hair on your head, Jessica," Eric continued, "I swear to God it will be the last time he –"

"Enough!" Olive interrupted. She had scrunched a sodden handkerchief in her fist and was glaring at Jessica, a knowing look on her face.

Oh, God, Jessica's heart sank, *she'll never forgive me!*

"Enough you two," Olive cried, impatiently. "The young man is here and there's nowt we can do about it so Eric, you can pull your bloody great head in. Jessica is a young woman, alone, trying to raise her children. This man was wounded and deathly ill – what would you have her do? Throw him into the gutter? What if it were Jon and a German woman found him? Would you want her to throw him out? Turn him over to the authorities? Is that the way you want the world to be? If so, you're not the gentle, compassionate man I married."

"That's not fair," Eric protested. "This man is our enemy. I fought against –"

Jessica opened her mouth to speak but her mother wasn't finished. "You think I'm happy with this?" Olive demanded of her husband. "I'm no happier than you but we're at war and nothing is fair! We lost our home and business. Jessica lost her husband, the children lost their father, and this young man was conscripted and forced away from his home. That's not fair either." She raised a trembling hand and pinched the bridge of her nose. "No more shouting – I'm getting a headache. I'm sure, given a choice, he'd rather be home with his family. Jessie's right; at least for now, we have to learn to live with this."

"He can't stay," Eric stated stubbornly.

"So what are you going to do?" Olive cried, blowing her nose. "Turn him in? Betray your daughter?"

Eric suddenly wilted. He dropped weakly to the couch beside

his wife, elbows on his knees, hands dangling. The rasping of his laboured breathing filled the room.

Exhausted, standing alone in the middle of the parlour, Jessica watched her parents unhappily. She'd let her father down in so many ways. If he even suspected she'd willingly gone to bed with the German – God, it didn't bear thinking about!

Lucifer's balls, what if they knew I was in love with him? It'd kill Dad.

"How long has he been here?" Olive interrupted her thoughts.

Jessica took a seat opposite, grateful for a relatively calm, sensible question. "About ... Late winter? Early spring, I think. Shortly after he was shot down."

"Messerschmitt, you said?"

Jessica nodded.

"Probably lying," Eric grumbled.

"*Messerschmitt*? Oh, Christ!" Olive pressed the balled hanky to her mouth. "They shot down a Messerschmitt ... months ago. He's the missing pilot!"

"Yes," Jessica confirmed, flatly.

"They've been looking for him ... Jessie, what have you done?"

"That's the limit!" Eric stated decisively. "The authorities need to know! They've been knocking on doors ... hounding innocent people ... all the while," he paused, shaking his head in disgust, "my own daughter ..."

The room fell silent but for the gentle crackling of the fire. The fight seemed to have drained from all three and they sat, exhausted with grief, anger and fear, and the knowledge that the unthinkable was a reality: harbouring the enemy, in a time of war, was among the greatest of crimes.

Long minutes ticked by, during which each sat in the loneliness of his or her own thoughts. Finally, Olive dragged in a deep breath. "Jessie love," her voice was strained and barely above a whisper. "Since this young man is here, at least for the time being, perhaps," she drew another breath and threw a cautious, sidelong glance at her husband. "Perhaps, it's time we met him."

Jessica shot a furtive look towards her father but he was still staring at his hands hanging limp between his knees. Turning back to her mother, she smiled gratefully and nodded.

***

The captain was seated at the table, a child cuddled beneath each arm, when Jessica went into the kitchen. Sam and Marg were also there, offering grim-faced support against the unavoidably audible shouts and accusations coming from the room up the hall.

The children rushed to their mother and she clasped them against her while her red-rimmed eyes rested on the captain.

"They have asked to meet you."

He nodded, adding with a glimmer of dark humour, "Is your father armed?"

She smiled weakly. "Pistols at dawn, he says."

"I am sorry you faced that alone."

Jessica gestured dismissively. "There was no other way to do it. My father would've dropped dead on the spot had you just strolled in." She gently put the children aside and searched their faces. It was only then she saw their tear-stained cheeks. "Stay here with Mr and Mrs Clay. It's going to be all right. Granny and Grandad just got a fright, that's all."

"Will they make Mr Bird go away?" Thomas asked fearfully.

God, I hope not! She forced a smile. "No, of course they won't. They just need to get to know him, that's all. Like we did." She ruffled his hair.

Mary, too astute for her age, was eyeing her sceptically but refrained from commenting.

Jessica and the captain left the kitchen together. In the privacy of the darkened hallway, they turned to each other and embraced. "No matter what they say," Jessica assured him, "be gentle with them. My father fought in the last war, as yours did. It's hard for him and they've just lost their home and business in the bombings. They're in pain and they're grieving. Let them get to know you – they'll have questions. Just be honest."

"About *every*thing – you *und* me?"

"I hope he won't ask," she shrugged ruefully. "But I think so."

"Will *you* be honest?"

She gazed at him uncertainly for a moment. "I'm being as honest as I can – I'm being honest with you. Let that be enough for now."

He nodded and wordlessly took her chin in his hand and touched his lips to hers in a gentle, lingering kiss. "I love you," he said when he drew back. "They cannot change that."

How easy it would be to melt against his chest and forget all her worries. Instead, she forced herself to pull away. "Come on. Let's get this over with."

Jessica pushed open the parlour door and preceded the captain into the room.

"Mum, Dad … This is Hauptmann Anton Vogel. Captain, my parents, Eric and Olive Bentley."

Her parents rose and stood side-by-side. Olive's eyes were wide and curious while Eric's were narrow and disapproving. His jaw was clenched, his lips compressed into an angry, bloodless line. Both brazenly scrutinised the young German, taking in every detail from head to foot.

The captain clicked his heels and dipped his forehead in a very formal, imperial acknowledgement. Such blatantly Germanic behaviour wouldn't soften their attitudes towards him, but Jessica understood the statement he was making: he was German and unashamed.

He waited impassively, hands hanging loosely, as their eyes sifted over him.

Subconsciously, Jessica moved impartially aside.

The silence in the room was thick with accusation and challenge. Such was the tension that all four started when a log popped in the fireplace, spraying orange sparks over the tiled hearth.

Finally, just as Jessica thought she could stand the strain no longer, her mother spoke.

"Jessica says you speak English."

"Yes."

"You flew aeroplanes for the United States postal service."

"Yes, that is correct."

"Are you a Nazi?"

"Mum –" Jessica began.

"Frau Jessie, it is all right. No, Ma'am, I am not a Nazi."

"Yet you ..." Olive's voice trailed off hesitantly.

"I am not a Nazi," he repeated evenly.

The room fell silent again.

Then Olive continued, "My daughter says you have helped her round the property." Rather than being a question, the statement seemed almost conversational.

The captain appeared to relax slightly. He cast a warm glance at Jessica, the significance of which, she feared, was not lost on her mother. He said, "I am glad I have been able to help. I owe her my life."

Olive nodded, seemingly satisfied with the young man's responses. Jessica was afraid her mother, if only with a mother's instinct, would guess there was more between her daughter and the German officer than either might readily admit.

God, he's smiling at her! Does he realise he weakens knees with that smile?

Jessica exhaled, relieved and turned to her father. "Well, Dad?" she implored. "Haven't you anything to say?"

***

Eric dragged his gaze away from the young Kraut to look at his daughter. Her mouth trembled slightly and her work-worn hands were clasped so tightly that the knuckles were white. But it was the appeal in her face that almost broke his heart.

Returning his attention to the German, his eyes went immediately to the man's hands. They were as work worn as Jessica's; the nail on his left thumb was a purple bruise.

Eric'd heard about the German military. Heard how upright they were, hardened, well-trained, disciplined. Evidently this young man was no exception. He seemed taller than he was for he carried himself confidently, a fine specimen with squared shoulders, straight back and a clear, intelligent, blue-eyed gaze.

The kind of man a father would be proud to show off down the pub – if he were a good English lad. Judging by the look that passed between him and Jessica, he had obviously enchanted her. But there was no getting away from it, this man was his enemy.

Eric opened his mouth, yet nothing came out; it was the first time, in Eric Bentley's life, that the power of speech utterly failed him.

"Eric?" Now his wife was looking at him.

Eric drew in a wheezing breath, filling his lungs to capacity. He felt the tightening, the rattling congestion that caught in his throat. He must not cough, must not show any form of weakness.

Exhaling carefully, with three sets of eyes levelled on him, Eric said, "I thought you Aryans were supposed to be taller than that."

Chapter 31

Jessica dared not leave the captain alone with her parents so she went to the door and called down the hall for the children. Returning to the parlour, she urged Olive and Eric to resume their seats on the couch.

She waved the captain towards a chair and he sat obediently as both Mary and Thomas bounced into the room. They ran immediately to their German friend who welcomed them with wide arms.

"They love him," Jessica said, by way of explanation to her parents.

Eric made a derogatory sound while Olive smiled at her grandchildren. Trusting the adults would be civil in front of the children, Jessica left briefly to return to the kitchen.

Marg had made a pot of tea and laid a tray with cups, a milk jug and plate of lemon biscuits.

"Sounds all quiet in there now," the older woman observed, placing a stack of plates on the tray beside the biscuits.

"So far so good." Jessica took up the tray as Marg held the door for her. "Wish me luck!"

"He's our friend," Thomas was assuring his grandparents as Jessica returned to the parlour. "Please don't make him go away, Grandad!"

Eric sighed heavily and rolled his eyes.

"Grandad's not going to do anything like that," Olive answered, "Are you?" she eyed her husband significantly.

"That all depends," Eric grumbled without elaborating.

***

Olive got up and poured the tea and Jessica gave the first cup to Eric. When Jessica handed a cup to the German, her back was to her father, but Olive saw the look they exchanged as he took the cup.

She decided that the byplay between the German and her daughter was honest and caring. There was no doubt Jessica was in love – or thought she was. The German apparently returned Jessica's affection. Whether their relationship was physical, Olive couldn't know, but she hoped it wasn't.

Olive's heart ached for her daughter, and the futility of her feelings for this young man. Jessica had never felt real love; Olive had known full well that Jon had married her daughter out of a sense of duty. And Jessica had known it too, even if she'd seemed happy enough.

Now, though … Olive studied the German, noting the unconsciously intimate smile he settled on her daughter, and shook her head sadly.

"Show us your dog tags!" Eric ordered suddenly and Olive flinched at his rudeness as he thrust out his hand.

***

Jessica watched the captain wordlessly reach into his shirt and take out his dog tags. Slipping the chain over his head, he dropped them into Thomas's waiting hand.

"Here, Grandad," Thomas crossed the floor, aluminium discs swinging from his index finger.

Eric took his glasses from his breast pocket and perched them on the bridge of his nose. Holding the tags up to the yellowish lamplight, he squinted at the embossed script before raising his head and observing the captain over the rim of his spectacles. "What's this?" His tone was accusatory. "I can't read this!"

"It's encoded, Dad."

Jessica's father glared at her. "I can see that! *Why* is it encoded? What are you lot hiding?" he demanded of the German. "Why is your name not here?"

The captain gave a one shoulder shrug. "It is what they do. I do not know why. But you can see my rank, my company. That number is my personal number. The Luftwaffe could identify me by that number."

Jessica saw her mother's mouth tighten at the captain's accented pronunciation of the word *Luftwaffe*. Her father's expression remained belligerent.

"Hmph!" Eric said, and handed the tags back to Thomas. "Now what?"

"Now what?" Jessica repeated in confusion. "What do you mean, now what?"

"Well, for starters, where will your mother and I sleep?" Eric's face suddenly darkened and he regarded the captain through narrowed eyes. "Are you sharing my daughter's bed?"

"Dad!"

"Eric!"

The two women were aghast, while Thomas and Mary stared goggle-eyed.

"What kind of question is that? And in front of the children?" Olive snapped.

Clearly unrepentant, her husband retorted, "It's a perfectly legitimate question, especially since these children live beneath the same roof. Well?" he turned back to the German. "Are you sharing my daughter's bed?"

The captain's lips twitched but he responded evenly, "I would like to, Herr Bentley, but she will not allow it."

Jessica groaned while her mother drew in a sharp breath.

Eric, meanwhile, flushed hotly right into the balding spot above his forehead. Levelling a murderous glare on the young man, he snarled, "You think it's acceptable to speak about my daughter like that?"

"No, I do not. But you asked me a question *und* Frau Jessie told me to be honest with you."

Olive made a choking sound and Jessica was surprised to

find her mother stifling a laugh. "Oh Eric, give over, love. Stop interrogating the young man like that. Jessie, what *are* we going to do about the sleeping arrangements?"

"I thought the captain could move into the storage room – my old bed's in there – we just need to clear out the boxes of junk. We could put them in the ballroom – it's never used for anything. Then I thought that you and Dad could have the double bed at the end of the hall."

"Is that where *he's* been sleeping?" Eric indicated the captain with a jerk of his chin.

"Yes, Dad," Jessica said with exaggerated patience, "that's where *he's* been sleeping."

"Mum, when are we having dinner?" Thomas suddenly piped up. "It's getting late."

"Mrs Clay's knocking together a rabbit stew. That all right?" she asked her mother.

"Perfectly," Olive stated firmly.

***

The four adults and two children enjoyed a hearty winter meal before Jessica instructed her parents to relax by the fire, then she, the captain, Mary and Thomas went upstairs to the spare room to start clearing out the boxes.

As soon as they were out of hearing range of his grandparents, Thomas began bouncing joyously about. "Mr Bird, you can stay!" The boy apparently considered the matter resolved. His mother had said she liked Mr Bird, his grandparents had come to live with them and all was right in Thomas's world.

"Nothing's changed! He can't stay," Mary asserted quickly. Jessica saw her daughter throw an apologetic glance toward the captain. "I'm sorry, Mr Bird, but it's true."

The man in question nodded but said nothing while Jessica stacked a box on top of the one he was already holding.

"Everything's changed!" Thomas insisted. "Mary doesn't know what she's talking about."

"Thomas," Jessica said. "Mary's right – nothing's changed, but we can't talk about it now. Take that bag to the ballroom then come back and get these ones." She bent to pick up another box. This one was light enough for Mary.

"But you told Mr Bird you loved him!"

Jessica straightened, glaring at her son. "That's –"

"It is true," the captain weighed into the discussion. He stood patiently with his arms out as Jessica built a tower of boxes on them. "You did say you loved me."

"*Phht!*" She blew the hair away from her face. "All right, I said it. Now get back to work!" She suppressed a smile as her son and the captain exchanged triumphant grins, then added, sternly, "Both of you, take that stuff to the ballroom. Now."

They disappeared from the room and she heard the tramp of their feet along the hall and Thomas's lilting, excited voice. Turning to Mary, she went to hand her a box but the look on the girl's face halted her.

"What are we going to do?" the child demanded.

Jessica sighed, "Mary." The girl stood with hands on hips, glaring at her mother. "You were right," Jessica said. "Nothing's changed. He still has to go."

"So why did you say it? Why did you say you loved him?"

"I said it because it's the truth – and don't say anything about your father! I'll always love him – he was your daddy. But he's gone, Mary, and we're not. Mr Bird has helped us, and he –"

Mary's eyes widened in amazement. "I never said anything about Daddy!"

"Here!" Jessica thrust the box into Mary's hands. "I know you didn't." *It was my own guilty conscience,* Jessica chastised herself. "God, Mary!" She swung away, unable to face her daughter's accusatory face. "You're a child for heaven's sake and these are adult problems. They shouldn't involve you."

"But they *do* involve me, don't they," her daughter's incongruously mature voice said. "You're feeling guilty, *that's* got nothing to do with me."

Mary turned and stomped off down the hall.

"Lucifer's balls!" Jessica growled.

"Mummy, you said I wasn't allowed to say that, so how come you say it all the time?" Thomas enquired pleasantly behind her.

"Because I'm a bloody grown up, that's why, and I can say whatever I like!" She turned and met her son's glistening brown eyes. He, at least, seemed very happy with the way things were working out.

"Mary will come round," he stated, as though he'd read her mind. "She's always too serious about stuff."

As the captain came back into the room, she directed him and Thomas to the remaining boxes for removal and put all other thoughts from her head.

***

It snowed overnight.

Next morning, Jessica stood in her bedroom window gazing out at the seamless, icy landscape. The lawn was a glistening, rippled blanket, the driveway a crease running through it and the ancient oak tree, just to the right of her window, clawed at the sky with gnarled, witchy-fingers while its craggy boughs strained beneath a thick, white mantle.

The entire garden, everything beneath her and as far as she could see, was a work of art, a masterpiece in white and grey.

Even the sky was grey; there'd been no dawn this morning for the sun had risen behind a leaden bank of clouds, portending further snowfalls. But it held a loveliness all its own, and Jessica was drawn to it.

She exhaled in a sigh that left a patch of fog on the window, and turned away.

Downstairs, Jessica poked at the firebox in the range, fed it a few sticks and a log, then, taking Jon's big woollen coat off the hook, opened the garden door and pushed her feet into her wellies.

The air was crisp, icy and burned her lungs, but it was clean. The wood smoke that generally hung like a pall over the entire county seemed to have lifted overnight, and despite the brittle cold, she moved off, strolling unhurriedly along the path between the house and the washhouse, beyond the shrivelled remains of last summer's vegetables, past the hen-house, round the stables.

And then she paused.

Jessica had no idea where she was headed, knowing only that the silence of the snow-covered panorama beckoned with an offering of peace, a place where she could still her mind and lay her fears aside – if only momentarily.

She resumed her walk and her boots crunched on the virgin snow, sinking some three inches deep, up to four or five in some spots. Suddenly, a splash of colour off to her left drew her attention and she stopped in her tracks, inhaling in wonder.

Starkly purple against the brilliant white of the snow, were the first crocuses of spring.

But it's not even January! Jessica thought in wonder.

Crouching beside the bold patches of colour, she gently stroked a delicate, cupped petal with the tip of her finger. It trembled beneath her caress and she withdrew her hand. These spring flowers were a miracle of winter, a mistake of nature, yet the vibrancy of their exquisite colour lifted her spirits.

She was vaguely aware of the sound of boots on the snow somewhere behind her. Sam, no doubt, of the same mind – to enjoy the fresh morning before the round of daily activities began.

But the boots were drawing closer, then they stopped beside

her and she knew, by the tingling of her skin, by the singing of her blood, that it was not Sam.

The captain hunkered beside her and she looked across at him; every nerve in her body twitched with the urge to reach out and touch him. His eyes were fixed on the plants in front of them. She studied his profile: the strong jaw with its morning beard stubble; the wide mouth; long straight nose; and clear eyes fringed with honey-coloured lashes, framed by honey-coloured brows.

Then he cocked his head and met her eyes with his steady blue gaze and he smiled. "What is this … er, this here?"

She dragged her eyes away from his face to look where he indicated. His finger dipped gently into the golden heart of the flower. "What do you call this part?"

"That is the stamen."

"The stamen? Sta-men." He tested it on his tongue. "That is dangerously close to a rude German word," he said, with a smile.

"What do you call it?"

"This, or the rude –"

"That!" Jessica, laughing, pointed to the crocus.

"We say *das Staubblatt*. Do you know that it is a prize of great value in some countries?"

She frowned. "No. Really?"

"Oh, *ja*. You have heard of *der Safran?* I think you say it, saffron."

"I have heard of saffron."

"*Der Safran ist das Staubblatt* of the male crocus plant. Very valuable in countries like India or China."

"Are you telling me that I have a small fortune growing wild on my land?"

"If you have a market for it. So …" he reached for her hand and rose, pulling her to her feet, then stood facing her. Her hand was growing warmer in his and she wished he would continue to hold it but she had no right to expect anything of him.

His eyes were a smoky shade of blue and there was an intensity in them as he looked at her. With the same gentle touch he'd applied to the flower, he lightly brushed a strand of hair from her face and allowed his fingers to slowly follow the line of her cheekbone and down, tracing the curve of her jaw, leaving a tingling trail along her skin.

At her chin he paused and she drew a shaky breath. She felt mesmerised, weak at the knees and trembly all over. Her lips throbbed, quivering with each intake of air. His mouth hovered only inches from hers.

She could so easily lean into him.

"So," he said again, adding in a whisper, "you love me."

It wasn't a question. She continued to stand spellbound beneath his gaze, their breaths coming in little puffs of fog that blended before their faces and dissipated in the icy morning air.

"Come," he took her hand, "I want to show you something."

***

Anton had slept badly. The single bed was old, small and sway-backed – still he'd slept in worse places, the cold concrete floor of an aeroplane hangar, for example. When he did finally manage to sleep, he'd been plagued by vivid dreams of an older man with a great mane of blond hair, sitting in a winged chair in the corner of the room, reading a book by the flickering light of a candle. Upon waking, Anton found no one there.

The final time he woke, the sky was marginally lighter and there were birds singing nearby. The room was freezing. He rose and dressed quickly – and as he did so, he happened to glance out the window.

Jessica was strolling, in no great hurry, over the thick blanket of fresh snow. The blue of the greatcoat and bright copper of her hair stood out boldly against the glistening white landscape.

She was beautiful and she loved him; she'd finally admitted it.

Anton's heart swelled and he smiled to himself as he continued dressing. *Scheiße,* it was cold!

As he buttoned his shirt, he watched her natural grace as she drifted aimlessly across the snow. When he'd first met Jessica Barrow, he'd been overwhelmed with lust. His hands had itched to touch her; he'd ached with longing. He thought he'd never survive the forced abstinence of illness and convalescence.

He had wanted her. And the wanting was enough to drive him to distraction, indeed he'd questioned his sanity as he eagerly anticipated her visits. Once recovered, he'd offered to help her – *wanted* to help her, protect her and nurture her.

And then there were her children. Anton had been happy to play *Onkel* when visiting his sister but felt no great attachment to Brita's children.

But Mary and Thomas, *Jessica's* children, were different. He liked them. Stranger still, he enjoyed their company.

His own behaviour was a mystery to him. He'd tried to convince himself that he was infatuated with their mother and that a lively tumble with her would disabuse him of such sentimental notions. He didn't expect to be *in love* with her. The night he had taken her to his bed had confirmed everything!

Anton had expected that a quick and cheerful, mutually satisfying roll between the sheets would get the pretty widow out of his system and prove that it was lust not love. But he'd been surprised by how much he'd wanted to linger, hold her, to take his time with her. And afterwards, as she'd drifted into a sated sleep, he'd laid propped on one elbow watching her.

It was a revelation to him, that what he'd initially considered a purely sexual fascination, was in fact something more substantial. He was in love with her – a state of affairs that was both unwelcome and inconvenient. *Das wird nicht gut enden.*

This will not end well, was one of his mother's favourite expressions.

And as Jessica awoke the morning after, and rolled over to smile at him, he was overcome with such emotion, that he'd kissed her so she couldn't see the welling of his eyes.

Dummkopf! He had behaved with less sense than a horny fifteen-year-old boy in the throes of first love and now it was too late. Their time was running out.

Shaking off his thoughts, he finished dressing and quickly trotted downstairs to catch up with her.

"Come," he said now, taking her hand. "I want to show you something."

***

They left the crocuses behind and the captain continued to hold her hand as they skirted the garden and outbuildings. Jessica knew he was leading her towards the orchard but she couldn't fathom why. The time-worn steps that led to the fruit trees lay buried beneath a blanket of snow. Rather than inadvertently slip on them, they followed the bordering stone wall and arrived among the trees from the opposite direction.

Releasing her hand, he pointed.

The headstone over the small grave had been cleared of brambles, and even with the covering of snow, Jessica could see the ring of stones outlining the spot where a dog had been buried more than a hundred years ago.

She turned to look at him, but he was standing, hands in pockets, looking down at it.

"Do you tend this?"

He shook his head. "*Nein*. Mary comes every week."

Jessica nodded to herself. "I didn't know." She turned away, drifting towards the apple trees, taking a thin whip of a branch in her hand to examine its buds. They were hard, tightly wrapped little nubs awaiting the warmth of the spring sunshine, some months away yet.

"Frau Jessie?"

She let the branch spring out of her hand and faced him. He was right behind her. Now he placed two hands on her shoulders and pushed her gently back until she reclined against a hoary, low-hanging branch.

"Is it true?" he asked, his voice barely louder than the breeze that stirred her hair. "Do you love me?"

She smiled and he seemed to hold his breath, releasing it in a cloud when she said, "Yes. I love you."

He kissed her then, leaning half over her, one hand at her waist, the other cupping her cheek. He kissed her lingeringly, lovingly, in a manner not engineered to result in a passionate conflagration, but rather was a yielding to the impossible – plans they could not make, promises neither could keep, but was nonetheless real, intense and enduring.

Undoing the top button on her thick coat, his icy fingers traced the line of her throat, causing her skin to ripple, and moving closer, he pressed his lips to the warm pulse that throbbed with her precious life.

Jessica gasped as he bared his teeth and gently grazed the sensitive places below her ear while other parts of his body responded firmly against her hip.

Even so, she knew he would not seduce her into his bed with passionate kisses and intimate touches. He would wait for her to come to him of her own accord, and if she didn't – she knew he would accept her choice.

As if to confirm her thoughts, he stepped away.

"I have loved you many months, *meine Liebe*," he said, "*und* much as I am happy that you feel the same way, I am sad too."

She tilted her head, quizzically and he went on. "I know how I can get home – I should say I *think* I know a way. It might even work," he added, with a wry smile. "We must talk with Herr Clay, *und* we cannot wait – Robin Tyler is too suspicious."

All the while he'd been talking, Jessica felt her stomach clench and a lump grow in her throat. "We cannot do anything yet. We must talk about it and make plans."

Jessica's heart sank. "Already," she whispered. "I've only just … It's only now I've admitted …" she reached out and grasped a handful of his clothing, pulling him towards her.

"I have wasted too much time worrying about the future. And now it's on my doorstep. Don't say you warned me!"

He smiled and bowed his head to hers, and she revelled in the feel of his arms coiling about her as he covered her mouth with his own.

Jessica didn't know how long they'd been in the orchard – it seemed like hours, yet no time at all. They sat beneath the craggy trunk of an old, old tree, and it was a wondrous thing, to be like this, with a man as a companion. Hidden among the trunks and boughs, they allowed their passions to rise and their love for each other to bloom. Much as they needed physical fulfilment of each other, their contentment was in their togetherness; their pleasure was in their undisturbed exploration of an embryonic love.

The hour spent holding one another in the grey morning, among the drifting snowflakes, would stay in their memories longer than any heated, hurried tryst.

Besides that, Jessica's children, and now her parents, shared the house. Perhaps this was all they would have of each other – stolen moments; secret smiles.

The simple delight of kissing and touching was new to Jessica. It was a joyous amatory concord that could be savoured purely for itself, without the complexity of sexual culmination.

Any intimacy between Jessica and Jon had always taken place in the bedroom and always led to sex – a marital duty performed and accepted.

But this tender communion with Anton was different. They were loving one another in ways she'd never known; talking, sharing thoughts and ideas, often falling silent to merely hold one another and wonder at the beauty surrounding them.

And as the dry flakes of snow settled on Jessica's forehead, Anton lightly kissed them away, trailing his lips down the narrow slope of her nose to her mouth, where he remained, clutching her to his breast until their hearts pounded together.

At length, Jessica became vaguely aware of movement nearby. Opening her eyes, she gently pushed him back. "Captain, shhh. Turn very slowly. Look behind."

They both sat curled into each other at the base of the tree, as a doe and her fawn pawed at the snow, clearing it away so they could nibble at the milky-white shoots of new grass on Jemima's little grave.

Chapter 32

Jessica was moving as though a weight had been lifted from her shoulders as she made her way back to the house. She and the captain had parted ways at the orchard, he to help Sam with the morning milking and she to prepare the children's breakfast before school. Only a couple more weeks and they would be on their Christmas holidays.

As she pushed open the garden door, she was met by a hail of cries. "Mum, where've you been?" Mary demanded, while Thomas wailed about missing the school bus.

"What time is it?"

They ignored her question but she shot a look at the clock and her heart sank. She'd been outside with the captain longer than either had realised.

"Where were you, Mum?" Mary asked again. "We looked everywhere and couldn't find you."

Jessica's lips tingled guiltily. "Obviously, you didn't look *everywhere*."

"We saw the bus go past," Thomas informed her. "About five minutes ago."

"Are you ready for school? Have you had breakfast?"

They both nodded, and Mary added, "Granny made toast."

"Where's Granny now?"

"Upstairs with Grandad. He's been coughing badly this morning. He said some rude things about Mr Bird being too lazy to dust his room."

Jessica made a tutting sound. "Well, never mind. Run out and get in the car, I'll be out in a moment and drive you to school."

She dashed upstairs and down the hall to her parents' room. The door was open so she tapped on the frame and stepped inside. Her father was sitting in a chair by the empty fireplace while her mother made up the bed. "The children said you weren't well,

Dad. Is there anything I can do?"

"You can tell that bloody Kraut to clean up after himself, that's what you can do! Place is full of dust!"

"Eric, not now, love."

"The children said you'd been grouching about him. It would be nice if you didn't. This is an old house – it's dusty everywhere. Look," she changed the subject, "they've missed the school bus so I'm going to drive them. I'll be quick – Sam needs the car to deliver the milk."

When neither responded, she made to leave but her father mumbled something faintly audible. The words she did detect were unpleasant so she turned to him. "Do you have something to say, Dad?"

"They couldn't find you, Jessie." Her mother said, fluffing the pillows. "And they couldn't find Mr Bird either." Olive didn't meet her daughter's eye, but Eric did. He glared at Jessica over his red-tipped nose.

"Were you off somewhere with that Nazi?"

"He's not a Nazi."

"What were you doing with him? You'd better not be consorting in any –"

"Dad!" Jessica snapped. "He wanted to talk about an idea he has that may help get him out of England."

"A bullet to the brain'll get him out of England!"

"I don't have time for this." Jessica whirled on her heel and ran downstairs and out to where the children waited in the car.

***

The Daimler's tyres were slipping on the icy surface of the road as Jessica drove. She wasn't an experienced enough driver to handle the car well in such conditions and was crawling along at a snail's pace with the steering wheel in a death grip.

"Mum, there's the bus," Thomas said, pointing past her ear

from the back seat.

She'd been so focused on the road immediately ahead that she hadn't seen the lumbering school bus in the distance. Now she had an idea. "How about we catch up and I drop you where you can get on it?" she suggested.

They readily agreed, which she supposed was a comment about her driving. She braved it out for another two minutes, finally catching, then perilously overtaking, the bus. A group of children waited by the following bus stop, stamping and blowing into their hands.

"There's Peggy," Mary said. "She's the one Tommy fancies."

"Do not!"

"Do so! Michael told us."

"Michael's my friend, he would never tell if I said not to."

"Hmph," Mary said triumphantly. "Sounds like you do like her."

"Righto, you two," Jessica interrupted, steering the car on to the shoulder.

Both children hopped out, and she watched until they were safely on the bus before pulling away.

While negotiating the slippery roads, Jessica had been distantly aware of something sliding around on the floor of the car. Now, as she pulled up Broughton Hall's drive, the thing slid out from beneath the seat.

"I'd forgotten about you." She reached across the seat for the packet of pictures Albert Tyler had given her. With all that had happened over the past days, she'd completely forgotten it.

Jessica was slamming the car door when Sam came out of the stables, wiping his hands on an old rag. "Back just in the nick o' time," he said. "Gotta get this milk out."

"Sorry Sam, I had to drop Mary and Thomas at the bus stop," she explained, starting towards the house.

"Aye, I know," he said after her. "Your mother told me when

she come out 'ere to collect Anton."

Jessica whirled about. "She came out to … Jesus! What does she want with him?

Sam smirked and held his hands out helplessly. "What can I tell you – 'e's a good-looking feller."

"Very funny, Sam!" Jessica huffed, marching up the drive and round the side of the house. *Probably questioning him about our whereabouts this morning*, Jessica grumbled to herself. She strode through the garden door and stopped dead at the sight that met her eyes.

For there, at the kitchen table, sat the captain and her mother, sharing a pot of tea, the last threads of laughter dying as they both looked up to see her in the doorway.

"What's going on?" Jessica demanded, eyes going from one to the other.

"Now, Jessie, love," her mother got up. "You look cold and worried. Sit down – there's a bit of tea left." She virtually pushed Jessica into a chair and busied herself at the range.

Behind her mother's back, Jessica glared at the captain, mouthing the words, *What are you doing?*

He smiled innocently and looked up as Olive turned back with a cup in her hands. She resumed her seat and pushed the cup towards her daughter.

"Anton and I have been getting to know one another, haven't we, love?"

"*Ja,*" he responded dutifully.

"What's going on?" Jessica demanded. "I know you're up to something, Mum, so out with it."

Olive adopted a hurt expression, but before she could respond, Anton spoke. "Your mother asked me if you *und* I are lovers."

Jessica felt her eyes bug out and hot blood rushed to her cheeks.

"I told her the truth," he went on, and Jessica felt dizzy as that same blood suddenly drained away to leave her cold and pale. "I told her that I had made an inappropriate ..." he sought help from his new friend.

"Proposition, love," Olive supplied while Jessica narrowed her eyes. *He doesn't need help with his English*, she thought suspiciously.

"I had made an inappropriate proposition," he explained, "which you quite rightly refused. Since then I have behaved myself *und* you have been polite enough to pretend that I never asked."

Relief perhaps, overwrought nerves certainly, caused Jessica to burst out laughing, to the bewilderment of the other two. They exchanged convivial glances and as Olive leaned across the table to gather the used cups, her eyes lit on the envelope Jessica had dumped on the table.

"What's that?" she asked, nodding towards it.

Jessica sipped her tea. "It's a stack of watercolour paintings and some old photographs the man up the lane gave me."

"Robin Tyler?" The captain's face immediately darkened.

"No," she said quickly. "His father, Albert. He's quite nice, and he's lived round here all his life. Mum, he knew the Broughtons when he was a child and has an interest in the history."

"Oh, I see." Olive evidently didn't share her daughter's enthusiasm but the captain did.

"Have you looked at them?" he asked.

She slid the packet across the table. "I've seen a few. Have a look. A lot of the paintings were done by Maeve Washburn, she was Alexandra Broughton's step-sister. Mum, Alexandra grew up here. The paintings are fascinating – people, houses, animals. A couple of really old photos too."

Anton had up-ended the envelope on the table and the cards and photographs spilled out in a scattering of black-and-white and coloured images.

He moved them about, selecting randomly for closer inspection.

Olive came round the table to stand behind the captain to look at the pictures. Jessica wasn't quite sure what to make of her mother's apparent acceptance of the German. Everything seemed amicable, so perhaps Olive would be able to convince her husband to pull his head in a bit. "Look at this one," Olive said, reaching over the captain's shoulder. Anton put his picture down and looked at the one Olive held.

"It is Broughton Hall," he said. "Frau Jessie, look at this … it is beautiful."

Olive passed the watercolour to her daughter and Jessica exhaled slowly. "My God," she whispered in awe, for before her was Broughton Hall in all its eighteenth-century splendour.

Standing there, in the kitchen of that old house, she was immediately transported to a graphic dream that, until that moment, she'd forgotten.

The estate was depicted as though the painter was standing beside the gardener's cottage. The sky was a perfect blue above billiard-table-green lawns that were divided by the formal driveway. It swept an elegant arc to the right, beckoning the beholder towards the gracious, stately old home.

In the left of the painting, Jessica recognised the majestic oak tree, whose enduring strength, over a century later, provided winter refuge for squirrels and birds, and verdant summer shade.

"My God," Jessica repeated, "how I wish I could restore this place."

The three in the kitchen fell into a thoughtful silence just as Marg came bustling through the garden door.

"Ready, love?" Marg asked.

"Blimey!" Jessica exclaimed. "Is that the time? Marg and I planned to get into some serious baking."

"Perhaps Anton and I will take these into the parlour?" Olive suggested gathering the pictures.

***

Hours later, Jessica was tired, her shoulders ached from kneading bread and her head was pounding with the echo of angry words – the result of yet another argument with her father.

It had been a long day and now she sat between the captain and Sam at Marg's kitchen table, while Marg stood at the bench cutting turnips and carrots for soup. The knife chop-chopped steadily in the background and Sam quietly rolled a cigarette.

Jessica hoped this discussion wasn't going to take too long – she couldn't imagine the captain had anything that could genuinely help his cause.

"As we know, parts of France are under German occupation," he began. "I know someone in France who may be able to help me get to France."

"Is that this Josef, you told me about?" Jessica asked, stifling a yawn.

"No. Josef is in New York, but he knows this person in France – I once did him, I think it is as you say, a favour. I was thinking about these connections, who knows who – like that. I remembered this man, Peter, *und* what I did for him. If I could get a message to Peter, I am certain he would help me."

"Do you think," Sam paused to lick the edge of his cigarette paper, "that this Josef would write to him?"

"*Ja*, I *know* he would if I asked."

Marg continued her work as she spoke. "Say Josef writes to this Peter chap," she said pragmatically, "we still have the problem of getting a Frenchman to help you. How would we do that?"

The captain made a dismissive gesture, "Josef is German *und* my friend. Peter is Dutch."

Jessica watched absently as Marg continued chopping.

"That's all very well," Sam said eventually, "but, Anton, lad, we need to be realistic. These are people you *used* to know. War changes things."

The captain smiled patiently. "Josef is a *very* good friend – I have helped him in many ways. If I ask, he will help me, *und* he will write to his friend."

Jessica snorted impatiently. "You're planning to ask a boyhood friend to write to someone you hardly know, to agree to something very dangerous. Why would a Dutchman, living in German-occupied France risk helping a German? The Dutch hate the Germans."

"Anton, love," Marg said, continuing her work. "Jessie's right. It would be suicide if 'e were caught."

"Josef is Jewish."

Everyone froze. Even Marg's knife was silenced while Jessica closed her mouth.

In the weighty silence that followed, Anton added softly, "As is Peter."

"How …?" Jessica started, but her voice trailed off.

"Peter was living in Amsterdam," the captain explained. "His wife *und* daughter got out *und* went to relatives in France at the first signs of trouble. Peter, I do not know why, he waited behind. Around the time I was ordered to leave America, Josef received a letter from Peter's wife, begging him to help get Peter out of Amsterdam."

"And?" Sam prompted, waving his unlit cigarette.

"Josef told me what was happening *und* asked me to contact his cousin Natalia when I returned to Germany."

At the mention of his girlfriend, Anton's eyes met Jessica's. She was leaning forward in her chair, staring at the young Luftwaffe pilot, completely stunned. This was the last thing she'd expected. *Weren't all Germans anti-Semitic?* He smiled gently at her, as though reading her thoughts, but carried on speaking.

"When I returned to Germany, I told Natalia about her cousin's friend. Natalia's father owned a freight transport business *und* regularly used a cargo plane – it was an American Douglas DC-3, similar to the one I flew for the U.S. Mail service. She hired it in the company's name – it would not attract attention. That night, I flew Natalia *und* myself into Amsterdam, illegally, of course. We had arranged to meet Peter at a private airstrip owned by a Jewish business man. From there I flew into France, *und* landed in a field outside of Nancy. We stayed only long enough to say *auf wiedersehen* to Peter, then we flew directly back to Germany. We returned the plane before we roused suspicion. Bad enough that I flew beneath air traffic radar, had I been caught ..." he shrugged one shoulder. "I wasn't. The next week, I received a letter from the German authorities. They said they understood that I was a pilot *und* I thought then that I was discovered. But the letter said they knew I had arrived from America *und* ordered that I present myself immediately to the Luftwaffe. I was to be trained to fly *die* Junkers five-two, transporting troops *und* supplies across Europe. Soon after, I was trained to fly *der* Dornier three-three-five, *und* I became a fighter pilot."

The three round the table sat in stunned silence as the captain ended his story. He sat back in his chair, as though awaiting a jury's verdict.

Sam exhaled in a long whistle. Marg seemed to shake herself and remember the knife still in her hand. She placed it on the cutting board and distractedly paced the small kitchen.

Jessica simply stared at him in wonder. *He must be the farthest thing from a Nazi there is*. At length, she reached across the table to touch his hand. "You took a very great risk, Captain. You endangered your life, risked your freedom – you'd surely be in a German prison now if your government knew what you did."

"He'd be dead," Sam stated flatly. "Nazis would've been

merciless."

"Josef was my friend." It was a simple statement but carried all manner of feeling.

"But this Peter wasn't," Jessica said, reasonably.

"No, he was not. But it was enough that Josef was. Still is." His voice was barely above a whisper.

Now Jessica nodded. Her head was spinning with everything that had happened over the last couple of days, and now, she digested this last with a combination of hope and sadness.

But then something else occurred to her and she noted it with a mixture of smugness and anger. "My father constantly calls you a Nazi, and you've said nothing to defend yourself."

He smiled at her. "What would I say?"

"Tell him your childhood friend is Jewish; that you risked your life to rescue another Jew."

To her astonishment, he began to laugh. "Frau Jessie," he said. "When Josef asked me to help him, I was helping a friend. I am Catholic, Josef is Jewish; the government told us we were different but *we* never thought it so. We were just boys who grew up together."

***

Not long after, Sam walked them to the door and held it open as Jessica slipped into her coat. She watched as the older man pulled the younger one into his arms in a shy, masculine embrace. "You're a good lad, Anton. A brave, good lad." He clapped the captain's back then released him with a sniff. Passing the back of his hand over his eyes, he said, "Well, we'll talk more about this tomorrow, figure a way to contact this Peter chap. Getting you to France might be possible, but for now … off with you both! Milking to be done in the morning and them lasses wait for no man."

The captain pulled Jessica's arm through his as they crunched over the crisp ground. It was cold, the night still and moonless. The air felt sharp and dry in her lungs as she breathed.

"He's right." Jessica spoke in a whisper, the night being so quiet.

"Hmm?" The German was lost in thought.

Pausing, she tugged gently on his arm and forced him to stop beside her. "What Sam said: you're a good man."

"There are many like me, you know." He smiled and tucked her arm more securely through his own. "We are not all Nazis, but where I come from it is wise to keep your politics to yourself. If I were discovered to be a Jewish sympathiser, I would be sent to a concentration camp *und* my family with me. To protect my family is one of the reasons I flew with the Luftwaffe. A refusal would be unpatriotic *und* very suspicious."

Jessica detected bitterness in his voice. She knew her father's attitude was not uncommon although she was embarrassed he'd proved himself such a bigot. No different, she supposed, from her own attitude when she'd first met the young pilot. But now she was proud of him.

She turned to him to say as much, just as his mouth met hers.

They stood together in the dark, huddled for warmth and the love of one another. When he finally released her, she was trembling from more than the cold.

"You are freezing," he said, chafing her hands between his own. "It will be warm in the kitchen." He curled his arm round her, hugging her to his side as they walked.

She felt him slide a sly sideways glance at her and looked over at him. "May I sleep in your bed tonight?" he whispered. "Mine is very uncomfortable, you know. I am certain yours would be much more to my liking."

She thumped his arm playfully as he reached past her to push open the garden door. The warmth of the kitchen flooded over them.

"Nice try, Captain," she said with a laugh, "but with my parents here, you're pushing your luck."

"Oh, *ja*, I did think this might be the case." He ushered her ahead of him, murmuring against her hair as she passed, "But you know that I am very daring!"

***

Their evident intimacy caused the couple seated at the kitchen table to fall silent and Jessica knew instinctively that her parents had been discussing her and the captain. Olive looked guiltily away when Jessica glared at her.

"Sit please, Captain," Jessica instructed. "I think my parents will be interested to hear what you told us."

From the corner of her eye she saw her father stiffen in his seat but refused to look at him – he was no doubt throwing dirty looks at both her and the German. "You seem awfully pally-wally," Eric commented dryly. "Has Hitler surrendered in the last hour and –"

"Lucifer's balls! Dad, give it a rest." Jessica pulled up a chair beside the captain and turned to him. "Do you want to tell them, or shall I?"

Anton frowned uncertainly. "I did not know we were telling them."

"That'd be bloody –"

"Enough, Eric!" Olive said irritably. "I would like to hear. If you're not interested, take yourself to bed."

Eric snorted rudely but remained in his chair.

"The captain knows somebody in France. We think it's probable that he'd be willing to help get him across the channel."

Her father snorted again. "What a surprise! The Kraut knows somebody in German-occupied France. How lovely! You could have a nice little reunion with all your Nazi chums in someone else's country. Pick right up where you left off."

"That's it!" Jessica cried. "I've had your bigotry up to here, Dad." She indicated her forehead with a vicious stab of her finger. "If you knew –"

"Frau Jessie," the captain's voice was firm. "No."

She turned on him. "Why? You should be –"

"No." His eyes bored significantly into hers before he pushed back from the table and, to Eric's outrage, clicked his heels in a very imperial, formal bow towards Olive. Then dropping a light kiss on the part in Jessica's hair, he said, "*Gute Nacht, mein Schatz! Schlaf schön!*"

"It doesn't seem such a guttural language when he speaks it," Olive observed, as the young man closed the door behind him.

"Bloody Kraut!" Eric grumbled, "Bloody rotten Nazi bastard!"

"He's not a Nazi, Dad."

"They're all Nazis. Can't help it – brainwashed is what they are!" Eric slammed his hand on the table for emphasis. "And what's with him kissing you? What's going on? You better not be playing the whore for him or so help me –"

"Right, I've had enough!" Jessica got up, face flaming. A clammy sweat had broken on her nape from the warmth in the room, embarrassment and anger combined. "I'm not putting up with this from you in my own home."

Eric also got up and faced her, "But you'll let that filthy –"

"Shut up!" Jessica cried, fists clenched at her sides. "Just shut up, Dad! I'm a grown woman. If I want to play the whore with the entire bloody county it's no concern of yours."

"My grandchildren are in this house too," Eric shouted, "or have you forgotten about them in your dizzy little love affair."

"Your grandchildren adore him!" She shot a glance towards her mother. Olive had a look of abject horror on her face as her daughter and husband bellowed at one another. "And if you cared to look at your own wife, you'll see she likes him too."

"Don't bring me into this," Olive interjected defensively.

"And you know why?" Jessica went on. "Because she looks beyond all the prejudice and extremism of war and can see that he's a decent man."

Jessica flung herself across the kitchen to lean over the sink. She'd never, *ever* stood up to her father before and she didn't know whether to feel proud of herself or to throw up. Breathing hard and shaking, she felt herself edging towards hysteria and worked to contain her emotions.

But Eric wasn't finished. He prodded a finger into her shoulder. "Your mother can't see beyond his handsome face and deceiving manners. But *I* won't be suckered in by his nice-boy behaviour. He's a Kraut and that's all I need to know."

Finally, at the end of her tether, Jessica faced her father – no less incensed but more under control. "Dad, I love you, you're welcome to stay here as long as you need to, but the captain is also here and until we find a way to get him out of England, this is where he's staying. Now – *no*!" she threw up a quelling hand as Eric opened his mouth. "Let me finish. It's nobody's business if the captain and I are lovers, but I will tell you this – if only to put an end to your crude speculation. He and I have formed a *special* friendship. I won't deny that he has asked me to share his bed and – *Dad I said, let me finish*! I said *no* and he accepted graciously. He told you that but you won't listen. I *am* attracted to him. We care about each other – a lot. If things were different: if he were not German, if I were not English, if we weren't at war – there it is.

"And let me tell you something else," she went on. "He is *not* a Nazi – he's the farthest thing from a Nazi. Why he doesn't want to talk about it is his business. But please, for my sake, I'm not asking you to like him, but *please* stop calling him a Nazi."

With that, Jessica marched across the room and wrenched open the door. She saw her parents exchange a bewildered look just before she flung herself into the hall and slammed the door behind her.

Chapter 33

He was passionate, tender and patient – all the things I knew he'd be. I went virgin to his bed, with little to no understanding of what would happen, only the vaguest notion of how the act of love between a man and woman was consummated. I went to him knowing only that I wanted to be his in every sense of the word.

There was pain when he first entered me – he knew there would be and was gentle and loving, and afterwards, he rocked me in his arms and held me against his heart as I wept from sheer joy.

He, himself, was not unmoved by the love between us for even through the darkness I could see the glistening of his eyes as he lay above me and kissed me to sleep.

Warm and sated, we dozed briefly in one another's arms, before waking to make love a second time – a bitter-sweet coming together tempered by the knowledge that in only a few hours he'd be riding away. And, if the first time, he was gently considerate of my virginity, this second, he was thrillingly hedonic.

He was an experienced lover, and I an enthusiastic confederate. He took me with a savage, unbridled urgency, rendering me breathless. And when I felt him shudder and release, I prayed there would be a new life within me – a child created in a kaleidoscopic explosion as primordial as time itself – to sustain me over the months, perhaps years, until he would return to me.

Was it truly possible to love as I did? How was it possible to be so loved? Please God, let me be worthy of this incredible, surprisingly sensual, beautiful man.

Jessica closed the diary and let it rest on her lap as she stared into the glowing fireplace. The passion between Alexandra and her lover was wild and uninhibited – fired with the kind of intensity most women only dream about. Certainly, Jessica herself had not experienced such a conflagration in her husband's embrace.

But that night with the captain …

She drew in her breath. Alexandra's forthright descriptions had left her with an abstruse longing. As though every nerve in her body was coiled tightly, trembling and ready to explode at the slightest touch.

If he were to walk into the room …

She physically shook herself.

I am lonely. I spent one night with the man and … It's only natural to feel this way – I'm young, after all. What I'm feeling is normal for a healthy young woman. Just as he is a virile young man – he, likewise, will have needs.

And there is no crime in it, her changeable mind pointed out. *We're both consenting adults, with normal, healthy appetites – the need for companionship and sensual expression …*

She shook herself again. *But then to lose it … to lose him …*

No. That would be worse than never having him at all.

***

Jessica came slowly awake to the sound of her children's voices lifting lightly over the strains of a Christmas carol. She rolled over in bed and sighed a puff of fog. *Lucifer's balls, it's cold!*

The song outside her door began again, the melody unmistakable but … the words. She cocked her head, the better to hear her children sliding fluently through the unfamiliar phrasing.

Stille Nacht! Heil'ge Nacht!
Alles schläft; einsam wacht
Nur das traute hoch heilige Paar.

Holder Knab' im lockingen Haar,
Schlafe in himmlischer Ruh, schlafe in himmlischer Ruh.

Smiling, she listened as the final line tailed on a lower resonant note, their pure voices fading out together. A moment's pause, then a tentative knock on the door.

"Come in," she called, wriggling to a sitting position and scrunching her pillow up behind her. Thomas and Mary burst into the room in their pyjamas, dressing-gowns flying.

They bounded towards her and landed on their knees on the bed. "It's Christmas!" they announced together.

"Did you like our song, Mummy?" Thomas asked, face alive with excitement.

"Yes I did."

"We've been practising for days to sing it for you," Mary said.

"Jessica yawned. "Aren't you clever for remembering all that?"

"Yup!" Thomas agreed. "Mr Bird said there is a lot more to it but we couldn't have learned it all."

"We couldn't wait to sing it for you," his sister added.

"Then, all I can say is you did very well, but don't let anyone *ever* hear you sing it."

They both made derisive faces – one of those rare moments when the twins looked alike, prompting their mother to laugh and say, "All right, I know!"

"We can also say, *Frohe Weihnachten*," Mary told her. "That means Merry Christmas."

"*Und ein gutes neues Jahr*," Thomas said. "Do you know what that means?"

"I don't know. Why don't you tell me?"

"It means, and a good new year."

"That's lovely. Come here for a hug then." And as they both

threw themselves against her, she held them tightly, breathing deeply of their warm, flannelette smells. Over the top of their heads, a movement by the door caught her attention. The captain stood leaning in the door frame, arms folded on his chest and a gentle smile on his face as he watched the interaction between Jessica and her children.

Their eyes met for only a moment, but it was enough. They exchanged a smile, then Jessica pulled away from her children, kissing each on the top of the head. "Now," she said, glancing at the bedside clock. "It's not even five … why are you up so early?"

"Because it's Christmas!" Thomas stated, adding, "*Obviously*!" It was his new favourite word.

"Isn't it obvious, then, that it's way too early?"

"No!" They both responded and Mary said, "Come on, Mum. Get up … let's see if Father Christmas has been."

Her heart sank, *Bloody hell, I meant to put their presents under the tree last night*! And to make matters worse, the captain pushed away from the wall and said, "*Ja*, let us go see what *der Weihnachtsmann* has brought."

She tried to catch his eye, to warn him, but he had held his hand out to Thomas – who ran eagerly to him – while Mary gathered Jessica's dressing-gown off the end of the bed and stood waiting with it.

"Come, Tommy," the captain said politely. "We men shall wait in the hall while your mother gets out of bed."

***

Some days ago, the children had dragged Mr Bird into the forest late in the afternoon, when the half-light of dusk enabled him to move relatively freely about the property. The crunching of the snow beneath their boots joined the chorus of evening birdsong, as the twins eagerly trotted ahead, skirting trees and lifting their knees high to wade through mounds of the soft, virgin snow heaped in gullies and ditches, and at the base of trees.

At length, they had selected a suitable pine branch and their adult companion had sawed the branch through, warning them to stand clear as the wood splintered and the branch fell to the frozen ground with a dull thud.

***

As evening became full night, Jessica and her parents went onto the porch to wait, stamping in coats, mittens and boots until three shapes detached from the shadows of the distant trees, dragging a sturdy pine branch behind them.

The decorations were wooden figures: angels, drums, stars, tin-men, which had been Eric and Olive's gift to Jon and Jessica the first Christmas after they'd married. Having prettily adorned each year's tree for the past decade, the wood had become dry and brittle, the bright red, blue, green and yellow paint was now faded in parts, chipped and flaking in others.

They were a symbol of a world that was not such a violent place, when times were not so severe. Marg brought in a great jug of mulled wine. Even Eric had unbent enough to smile and lend his slightly off-key baritone to all the traditional songs, while his grandchildren decorated the tree and danced joyously about the room.

***

Now that Christmas morning had arrived, the children bounded excitedly down the hall towards the stairs. Jessica dreaded what was about to happen when Thomas and Mary saw the Christmas tree bereft of gifts. They ran ahead, pausing at the top of the stairs.

"Come on, Mummy, come on Mr Bird!" Thomas cried.

"Hurry!"

"We are coming," the captain said, laughing.

Satisfied, both children plunged down the stairs and Jessica took the opportunity to grasp the captain's sleeve. "Captain! I –"

He turned and took her hand off his arm. Raising it to his lips, he said, "Frau Jessie, do you doubt *der Weihnachtsmann?*" His eyes were twinkling as he playfully nipped her index finger. "For shame!"

"What's this racket!" The door to Eric and Olive's room down the hall opened. The captain continued to hold Jessica's hand but Jessica pulled it free.

"Oh, Dad, the children are –"

She broke off as a pair of childish shrieks drifted up the stairs.

"Well, it seems Father Christmas has visited," Olive said. Belting her dressing-gown, she pushed past her husband. "We'd better go see."

Now the captain grasped Jessica's hand again and gave a gentle tug. "*Na komm schon!*"

***

Father Christmas had indeed visited, and in confusion, Jessica studied each of the adult faces about the room but none was giving away the secret.

The children were impatiently hopping about the tree while the captain stirred the fire to life.

Jessica realised there were several gifts she hadn't prepared herself – gifts that for the most part were, by necessity, practical. Socks and bolts of fabric smelling strongly of smoke and dust, with which to make clothes, cards of wool and tins of jam, all likely salvaged from the remains of Eric's shop.

Each child received a book; faded and smoke damaged, nonetheless they hugged the books to their chests with delight.

When Thomas opened a package to reveal a brand-new

cricket ball, he gazed at its gleaming red surface as a though it were a religious artefact, while Mary received a sketch pad and selection of coloured pencils with equal enthusiasm.

Finally, two long, thin parcels remained, roughly the shape of foot-long broom handles. Each child tore the paper off to reveal a stick of rock, pink and shiny outside, white on the inside with the words Blackpool in red type running through the middle. A faded grey and white photograph of the famed Blackpool Tower wrapped around the middle of each stick.

"Looks like Father Christmas visited the kiddies in Blackpool, and picked up a couple of souvenirs before coming to Broughton," Olive said archly, while both Mary and Thomas exclaimed over the rare treats.

Somehow the gifts Jessica had managed to scrape up over the course of the year had found their way beneath the tree too and she narrowed her eyes at the captain, he being the only other person who'd known where she'd hidden them as they'd been stored in his room.

However, some degree of collusion must have taken place between the captain and her parents since their contributions were also beneath the tree.

The only gift missing was the one Jessica had set aside for the captain. It was a new shirt of his own – not a second-hand one of Jon's. She'd asked Marg to purchase it from the Wolstone market, since a widow buying a man's shirt would certainly occasion more gossip than any town could handle!

"Well," she said, uncertainly, "there is still one more gift. Father Christmas left it in my room. I'll just go –"

"I'll get it," Mary jumped up. "Where is it?"

"In my wardrobe. You'll find it in the market bag at the back."

Jessica's pleasure in her children's joy as they opened their gifts was heightened by the captain's rather humble happiness when he opened the bag containing his new shirt. In these times of austerity, such an item was a luxury indeed. Its significance was not lost on him, nor was it lost on Eric who harrumphed and glared his displeasure. His frown lines deepened as the young German, glassy-eyed with emotion, pecked his daughter's cheek in gratitude.

Olive cleared her throat loudly and elbowed her husband in the ribs.

***

Christmas Day was a celebration, a day in which the inhabitants of Broughton Hall made a valiant attempt to set aside differences and enjoyed a time of peace and laughter.

Marg and Sam arrived and joined the gathering round the infrequently used dining table in what, Marg decided, must have once been a very grand, formal dining room. By silent, mutual agreement, they had all dressed in their best for the occasion. Jessica was saddened by the fact that even Thomas's best pants were patched at the knees and short at the ankles, although the captain was wearing his new shirt. He was freshly shaved and Marg had evidently trimmed his hair.

The table, a beautiful mahogany piece – which had been Jon's mother's and the only item of furniture he'd kept after she died and he'd moved in with Olive and Eric – was laid with Olive's best china and silverware, rescued from the destruction of her home.

A fire danced in the rarely used fireplace, while Marg brought in the meal: a small ham surrounded by an assortment of roasted vegetables grown in Jessica's garden. She had harvested them just before the first snowfall, and cooked them that day, with a generous serve of bread sauce – Marg's specialty – followed by a plum pudding made with the few remaining plums Jessica had collected and preserved from last summer's crop. They ate well, savouring the meal in a mood of hope and gratitude, and

Jessica was relieved when even her father relaxed and conversed relatively congenially with the German.

***

Unlike the Great War of almost thirty years ago, there was no repeat of the legendary Christmas truce of 1914. Instead, the guns continued to blaze, the bombs rained from the skies and the horror of violence and destruction hung like a pall over Europe. But for the group gathered round this table of celebration in rural West Yorkshire, for a few hours at least, the outside world ceased to exist.

***

After the meal, Olive and Marg volunteered to do the washing up. The children, Eric, Sam and the captain moved to the smaller, cosier parlour, while Jessica took the opportunity to go outside onto the porch for a moment's solitude in the twilight.

Despite the low cloud covering, the evening air was cold and brittle. Jessica shivered and pulled her cardigan tighter as she hugged herself. The crisp evening was welcome after the humid closeness of the kitchen, while the vegetables roasted and the plum pudding steamed.

The dining room had become cloyingly warm during the meal.

I'm sure that chimney is not drawing properly, Jessica thought, remembering. *Seemed way too smoky to me. Just another job to add to the list.*

It was growing dark. Golden light was spilling through the parlour windows onto the porch; she could hear the subdued chatter of her family, weary after the day's excitement.

A robin called through the purple evening. Its song was wistful, almost sad, but Jessica smiled to herself at the little bird's persistence. While most of her garden birds migrated south over the colder months, these steadfast little creatures huddled in plump pairs in their grassy nests, awaiting the coming of spring.

Jessica exhaled a plume of fog. With no breeze to disperse it, it lingered momentarily before her eyes. *I wonder if I could blow a fog ring, like Dad used to blow smoke rings from his pipe?*

She made several attempts before abandoning the idea, just as one of the great twin doors behind her edged open and for a moment she was bathed in rich warm light.

There was no need to look round. She knew instinctively who stood behind her; her skin tingled and her blood pulsed just that little bit stronger.

The captain came silently, two steaming cups in his hands. Wordlessly, he handed her one and she inhaled long, savouring the sweet, spicy fragrance of mulled wine.

She smiled her thanks and took a tentative sip. *Perfect drinking temperature.* She sipped again and closed her eyes briefly with contentment.

"Frau Jessie?" His voice was soft and she thought she detected a certain hesitation. Opening her eyes, she found him gazing at her, a small parcel in his hand wrapped in newspaper and tied with twine. "I have a gift for you. It ..." he looked hopeful and boyishly shy. "Please ... it is not much. I ... I made it for you. I worked on it in the evenings I spent with Herr *und* Frau Clay."

Her heart swelled as she took the small package. He held her cup while she unwrapped her gift.

The captain seemed inordinately fidgety and she realised that he was nervous, and perhaps, ashamed that he had neither money, nor opportunity with which to buy things. *How emasculating that must be*, she thought. For a man such as he, an adventurer, educated, energetic and confident, to be so constrained must be incredibly difficult – particularly after the excitement and danger of his flying career, to be reduced to living off the charity of strangers, with no freedom to come and go as he chose.

Additionally, she was, through her brief experience in his arms, aware he was a highly sexual man. Yet even those fundamental human urges had been stymied by her reluctance to involve herself to a greater extent than she already had.

This small gift, more than anything else, convinced her of the urgency for him to leave Broughton Hall.

He'd not uttered a single word of complaint or recrimination against her country or the restraints under which he lived. He'd shown himself both willing and capable of contributing his share of work towards running Jessica's small farm. Yet he was in reality little more than a prisoner.

But she loved him. And he loved her in return, and the tears sprang easily into her eyes as she opened the package to reveal his gift. It was a calf, hand-carved from a small piece of wood and polished smooth to capture a delicate face, knobbly juvenile limbs and a gentle eye. The little figure showed not only a certain skill as a craftsman, but a sensitive observation of a baby animal in all its gangly, clumsy innocence.

In the dim light, she could see he'd coloured it with something and, reading her expression, he said, "Beetroot juice. Frau Clay helped me to draw it out *und* use it as a dye."

"It's lovely, Anton," she said, unaware that she used his first name. She held the gift to her heart. "I will treasure this forever."

"She is yours, of course, but if you do not mind, I would like to name her Lil." At Jessica's quizzical look, the captain went on to explain, "Lil Dagover is a German actress. I have enjoyed many of her films, *und,*" here he paused and waggled his eyebrows, "she is very attractive."

Jessica grinned. "Well, it would be unacceptable for any cow on this property not to bear the name of a famous actress. Lil she is, then."

He returned her mulled wine and though it had cooled, it was still warm enough to enjoy. Jessica took a large sip, and swallowed, sighing happily. "Do you have mulled wine in Germany?"

"Oh, *ja*." He brightened enthusiastically. "We call it *Gluhwein.*"

He pronounced it, *gloo-vine* and she repeated it, asking, "Is this gloo-vine made the same way?"

"I think perhaps we use more orange *und* lemon *und* there is another spice we use that I cannot taste here."

"What is it?"

"Ah … I only know the German word. It is *Kardamom*."

"Cardamom! That's what we call it too." She took another sip and said, pensively, "Yes, I could see how cardamom would be nice. Unfortunately, those sorts of things are just not available these days."

Jessica turned away to rest her elbows on the balustrade and look out over the darkening garden and driveway, just as the snow began to flurry about – too light yet to fall. Several flakes drifted onto her hair and sat glistening like tiny stars among the copper strands.

"Pretty," he said, simply, touching them with a finger.

"Hardly!" she huffed, self-consciously. "The damp makes my hair go all frizzy."

"What is this frizzy? It sounds unpleasant. The damp makes your hair curl here *und* here." He indicated her temples which, to her mind, were the worst of the frizziness.

She playfully swatted away his hand. "My hair has always been the bane of my life. It's uncontrollable when it frizzes like this, and the red doesn't look nice with any other colour – clashes with everything."

"*Nein, nein. Das ist nicht wahr*! This colour is all the passion of fire *und* complements the jewels of the earth."

Jessica made a face. "That's a bit poetic."

"Not poetry, *die Geologie*. The colour of your hair, the heat of it, is bright like copper – a natural element. The jewels of the earth are its companions – the green emerald, the blue sapphire, the golden topaz. You were given the gift of fire to accompany the tone *und* beauty of these jewels. But you do not allow the fire to govern you – which is fire's nature. You force yourself to be gentle *und fügsam.*" At her inquiring expression, he added, "I think it is as you say docile. But you can be hot *und* blazing with passion. You have all this inside you – this I know from experience," he added in a devilish whisper close to her ear, "but you fight it. You lose so much by not giving in to it."

Flushing, she pushed him aside. "Are you *still* trying to get me into bed, Captain?"

Her attempt at humour worked for he grinned, heartbreakingly handsome in the deepening violet of the winter evening. "I had not planned it this way, but if you think it might it work …"

She laughed, but he added soberly, "No, Frau Jessie. The truth is I like to tease you, *ja*, but I am not trying to get you into bed."

"Thank you," she said, vaguely wistful, but he wasn't finished.

"*Doch,* if you were to change your mind …" he laughed lightly and pulling her against his hip, planted a smacking kiss on her temple. "*Frohe Weihnachten, meine Liebe.* Now," he released her abruptly and handed her his empty cup. "I must check the animals are secure for the night."

Chapter 34

Jessica tore her eyes away from Alexandra's memoir. Marking her page, she placed it on a table beside her and rested her head on the back of the sofa. She'd been sitting in the parlour for so long, enthralled in her reading, that her neck and back had grown stiff.

Massaging the bone round her eyes, she exhaled in a long, ragged sigh, then resolutely returned to the journal, re-reading Alexandra's words.

Simon once explained to me why the heart pumps blood around the body. "It is the blood that transports the oxygen we breathe and keeps the body alive," he'd said. "If the heart stops beating, the blood stops flowing – we die."

I know this to be true, for in that second, that infinitesimal moment when I learned of their treachery, I died. Although it was only for a moment, I know I died for my heart stopped, my blood slowed and my body grew cold.

They carried me to my bed, and as my heart sullenly, stubbornly, maliciously resumed its rhythm, I wished that it had not, for the pain was beyond endurance.

It was a pain so great, so consuming, that there was nothing left in me for any other emotion; no anger, no shock, no disgust at what they had done, just this searing white blade of agony, plunged between my ribs and twisted into my very soul.

And my traitorous heart kept beating, kept pumping my blood, and I, to my great despair, remained alive.

Disturbed and mildly distressed, Jessica thought about Alexandra's outpouring of grief, wondering at how upset she felt over an event that had occurred more than one hundred years ago.

Her heart hurt and her throat ached with the force of her sadness.

Such perfidy, treachery and deceit; it was a strangely surreal experience to read about events that had occurred in this house so long ago.

Jessica had known an almost maternal affection for the young Alexandra growing to womanhood within these very walls. Yet she also experienced an odd sense of connection with the girl through the parallels of their lives.

Hadn't they both given their hearts to the most inappropriate men?

In Alexandra's case, her family, her structured Regency world, her society would never allow such a match.

Jessica sighed again. The world may be one hundred years older, yet the same restrictions applied to her.

But Alexandra had been happy. She'd been describing an idyllic summer filled with love and happiness and then, out of the blue, in the turn of a page – a confession.

In the utterance of a single sentence, in this very parlour, the revealing of a betrayal of such weight that the walls ought to weep.

Alexandra's world had collapsed.

Just as Jessica's could do any moment. Just as Jessica's will eventually.

It was as Margaret had written in her opening letter, *This is a fascinating, sometimes painful, sometimes joyous story*. The disclaimer was there, but until now Jessica hadn't thought about it. Nor had she expected to become so involved.

***

The following morning Jessica was in the kitchen early. She poked the stove fire to life and set to work kneading a large amount of dough, separating it into four round shapes and continuing to knead each in turn.

The vigorous activity left her arms satisfyingly achy and took her mind off Alexandra and the uncanny mirroring of their two worlds.

Turning at a sound behind her, she found Mary, knuckling the sleep from her eyes, the belt of her dressing-gown trailing on the floor.

"What are you doing up, love?" she asked, as her daughter pulled a chair close to the warmth of the range and plopped herself onto it.

"I could ask you the same thing," Mary responded with a sleepy smile. Jessica raised her eyebrows and Mary added, "I heard you coming downstairs earlier, but I went back to sleep for a bit. Then I woke up again and decided to get up."

"Do you want a cup of warm milk? I'm making myself one."

Mary nodded and yawned, watching as her mother put the milk on the range. "It's your birthday next week," Jessica said. "With everything that's been happening I almost forgot." She grinned at the child. "That would be unforgivable, wouldn't it?"

"I'll be nine." Mary smiled and drew in her breath, thoughtfully silent for a moment. "Things are not good, are they? Not much to celebrate."

Jessica felt a stab of sadness. Almost-nine-year-olds shouldn't have such worries. Mary continued, "Mum, it's getting more important for Mr Bird to leave us. I mean … I don't trust Mr Tyler – you know I never have – and I get this feeling that Mr Bird will have to go *really* soon."

Jessica was pouring the warmed milk into two cups. She came to the table and placed a steaming cup before her daughter, then took the seat opposite. "Yes, he will. We'll need to prepare ourselves to say goodbye. Although," Jessica added cheerfully, "it'll be a happy goodbye because he'll be going home – back to his family."

Mary looked doubtful. "Do you think we'll ever see him again?"

Jessica blew on her milk and didn't meet her daughter's eyes. "Probably not."

Mary sat quietly for some time, sipping her milk. Finally, when she spoke, her voice was a mixture of sadness and fear. "Will he drop bombs on us again Mummy, do you think?"

"What a question!" Jessica exclaimed, adding a little laugh for effect, but truth was she wondered that herself. As a trained fighter pilot, the captain's skills were invaluable. What government would not take advantage of them? But Mary was watching her, eager to be reassured. Jessica hesitated, uncertainly.

"I will never drop another bomb."

Whirling round, Jessica saw the captain standing in the doorway. He was wearing his outdoor clothes and holding the oil lamp he used in the stables during milking.

Stepping into the room, he said, "Mary." He pulled over a chair and sat, looking directly into the child's eyes. "When I dropped bombs, I was doing what my country asked of me *und* I thought it was right. I will never do it again – that is my promise to you. *Und* if I am fortunate enough to fly a plane again," he glanced towards Jessica and said significantly, "I will not be doing so with the intention to cause harm."

He patted Mary's knee and looked across to her mother, and said, "That is my promise to you too."

"Thank you," Jessica said, solemnly rising, "And now, would either of you like some breakfast?"

But Mary was yawning. She slid off her chair and put her empty cup in the sink. "Mum, I think I will go back to bed. Just for a little bit."

Jessica nodded. "All right. Do you want me to wake you at six?"

Mary shook her head. "Thomas always wakes me." She took

a step towards the door but paused. Changing her mind, she threw herself against the captain's chest and kissed his cheek. "We will miss you, Mr Bird."

***

"Shall I make some tea and toast?" Jessica asked after her daughter left.

Anton nodded, watching her move about the kitchen. She'd pinned her hair up this morning – a sure sign, he was learning, that she was tired and couldn't be bothered brushing it out. His eyes caressed the line of her neck below the knot of hair at her nape, roving lovingly along the curve of her spine, to her slender waist where her hips flared beneath her old woollen skirt. He allowed his gaze to soften, imagining, remembering, the roundness of her bottom and how it felt in his hands. It wriggled delightfully with effort as she sliced the coarse bread.

In that moment, his heart swelled to become almost painful. How he wished he could buy her a lovely new skirt – one with those box-pleats like Natalia had worn the day he'd accompanied her to a friend's wedding.

He sighed. Natalia.

He thought of her so infrequently these days. If he ever made it home … *when* he got home, he would break it off with her. Though they'd been lovers, they were not officially engaged; there was no formal arrangement between them. Too much had changed. *He* had changed. He wasn't the same man who had proudly stood for the photographer beside the shiny new *Sturmvogel* in his dashing jet pilot's uniform.

He'd had two copies of that photograph printed; one he'd sent to his parents, the other to Natalia.

But war changes people. War changes everything.

"Anton?" Jessica rarely used his first name, and it surprised him back to the kitchen where it was warm and the smell of toast filled the air. She was looking at him oddly. "Are you all right?"

He smiled and nodded. "I am all right. I was just thinking …" he absently rubbed his chin, rough with his overnight beard, and didn't complete his sentence.

Jessica continued to watch him for a moment before she turned away, setting her loaves on a shelf to prove. It was a while before either of them spoke and in that time Jessica had made a pot of tea and they were both buttering their toast.

"You look tired," he said, taking a bite. "You are yawning. Are you sleeping well?"

"I didn't sleep well last night. I was reading the journal …"

He nodded to prompt her. "And it made you sad?"

"*Ja*," she said unthinkingly. Language was contagious.

"How much have you read of it?"

"Quite a bit. And last night I read about something terrible – a most horrible betrayal. I doubt Alexandra ever recovered."

He looked at her and saw the grief on her face – she was very involved in this journal. He wondered if it was healthy. "Why does it make you so sad?"

She shrugged. "I don't know. Perhaps because she loves this man so much and yet … and yet it was always impossible and now … she bears this great scar across her heart."

Anton didn't know what to say. He finished the last of his toast and got up, taking his plate to the sink.

"Captain, I know it's foolish, but it does upset me," she said. "Don't look like that. I feel so close to her," she continued. "And it happened here, in this house."

"It does not mean you should grieve over it."

"I know, but I feel … it's like … "

She didn't finish but he knew what she wanted to say. Coming to stand behind her chair, he massaged her shoulders and neck, feeling the knots and tightness beneath his hands. She bowed her head and he ran his hands up the muscles, pushing his fingers into the hair at the base of her skull, loosening the tenseness there.

How he would love to lay her across his bed and soothe her worries and cares away. He said, "You cannot change anything that has happened just as you cannot change what the future has planned."

She groaned and leaned back, resting her head against his stomach. Her face was turned up to him, eyes closed.

Leaning down, Anton kissed her lips, upside down. He gently drew her lower lip between his teeth.

Jessica breathed deeply through her nose, filling her chest, her breasts swelled beneath her jumper. Impossible to resist, Anton ran his hands down her décolletage to cup them.

She lifted her arms in a sinuous stretch, arching further into his hands. "Mmm, Captain," she sighed languidly, against his mouth. "I think I'm going to fall asleep."

Suddenly he burst out laughing. "*Und* here I am making love to you … most inadequately it would seem."

He removed his hands and her eyes fluttered open. She grinned up at him, "I'm sorry … I'm just so tired and your hands felt so good."

Holding his palms out, he said, "My hands are at your disposal, *mein Schatz*. But first, they must tend the cows."

He opened the garden door and a rectangle of yellow light splashed across the path outside. The sky over his shoulder was still dark, with only the faintest trace of morning outlining the eastern horizon. With a final, loving smile, he was gone.

***

It wasn't until later that night, after the children had gone to bed and the day's chores were done, that Jessica found time to sit in the parlour with the packet of pictures Albert Tyler had given her.

The captain was visiting Marg and Sam, and Olive was quietly knitting on the other side of the fire. The steady clack-clack of her knitting needles made a pleasant, comforting sound that reminded Jessica of winter evenings in Leeds, when as a child, she'd been awed by the speed with which her mother's needles worked. Olive could sit, seemingly lost in thought, staring into the distance, not even watching her own fingers as they flew, and the balls of wool tumbled across the floor.

Jessica smiled to herself and observed the familiar, closely tucked-in position of Olive's elbows, right index finger extended with the wool wrapped around, its tension controlled, feeding into the next stitch, and the next, and the next … click-clack, click-clack, click-clack.

Mesmerising, hypnotic … Jessica felt her eyelids droop, a forgotten hand lying on a watercolour image. She made no effort to prevent the heavy relaxing of her weary muscles.

"Never thought I'd see it," Olive said suddenly and Jessica was jerked out of her doze.

"What?"

Her mother looked over. "Your father and the captain – if they're not exactly friends, seems they're getting along well enough."

"Tolerating each other, most like."

"Yes, that's probably it."

"Where's Dad now?"

"At your steward's cottage with him."

"Oh?" Jessica wasn't terribly surprised.

"Hmm," Olive looked down apparently concentrating on her knitting. Knowing that her mother could knit without looking, Jessica suspected that Olive had something on her mind and was trying to figure out how best to say it.

While she waited, she glanced at the picture beneath her hand. It was a beach scene with a small, single-masted ship tossing on a wave.

"Anton is very helpful round the place," Olive commented. "What will you do once he's gone?"

Jessica suppressed a bitter snort. "I'll have to work round it, won't I."

"Will you, though?"

Frowning, she said, "What do you mean? Of course I will – it's not like I can afford to employ someone."

"It'll be tough." Olive got to the end of her row, but instead of turning it, she wound up the ball of wool and pushed the needles through. "Tough, particularly if you care for him."

"What makes you –" Jessica began.

"Oh, come on, Jessie love." Olive interrupted. She placed her knitting in the basket by her chair. "You fancy yourself in love with him. But how can you be certain it's real? How do you know you're not just lonely? Jon's been gone a couple of years now and –"

"I don't want to talk about this." Jessica rose and taking the poker, jabbed it sharply into the fire to turn the logs. Golden sparks exploded and flew up the chimney.

"Don't be defensive. I'm not judging you … not now that I've got to know him. He's a right winning lad, and it's only –"

"Stop it, Mum." Jessica's face was burning. She kept her back turned.

"It's only natural," Olive finished stubbornly, "that a young woman like you would … Oh, I don't know. We never talk about these things but you must miss –"

"All right! That's enough." Jessica straightened and replaced the poker on its hook. "You're my mother and you're embarrassing me."

"I'm just saying that you're young. You must be missing –"

"What's got into you?" Jessica turned back to her mother.

"Nothing." Olive was all innocence.

"You think I'm missing sex. There!" Jessica added defiantly.

Olive smirked. "I was thinking more about companionship, but if you're honest about it – you probably are."

Jessica plopped down on the couch and stared thoughtfully at her mother. "Are you telling me to sleep with the captain?"

Olive adopted a scandalised expression. "I'm not telling you anything of the sort."

"But you wouldn't condemn me if I did." When her mother didn't reply, Jessica added, "Well, you've changed your tune since your little tête-à-tête with him."

Olive sighed resignedly. "No, love. I've changed my tune since I've seen how happy you are whenever you're with him. Now, don't look like that! I've seen you two laughing together, I see him helping you in the kitchen, and outside with the cows and chickens … you make such a –" Olive broke off abruptly, and Jessica realised her mother was about to say the unthinkable.

Olive seemed to shake herself. "Oh, God! It's not fair that he's –" and once again she stopped.

Anything she said would appear such a betrayal of Jon, Jessica thought.

"He's off limits." Jessica finished for her mother. "It was hard losing Jon – he's the father of my children. But he was also more like a brother to me. We loved each other, in a gentle, homely kind of way. He felt sorry for me and grateful to you – you know that's the truth. It was never this raging, fiery passion where we couldn't keep our hands off one another."

Not like with that German. Olive didn't say the words but they were written clearly on her face.

For a moment, Jessica lost herself in the memory of Jon's lovemaking. Though tender and considerate, it was so perfunctory as to be almost choreographed – a duty. A duty fulfilled once she fell pregnant, and after the twins' birth, and the desire to conceive had been removed, it had continued in response to a basic physical urge and nothing more.

"And the captain?" Olive said, at last, breaking into Jessica's thoughts.

Jessica's face was so hot she felt perspiration prickling her lip. She gave an embarrassed little laugh. "You're my mother – I can't discuss this with you. Anyway, I'm not sleeping with the captain."

Olive raised a single, curious eyebrow. The question, *why not*, hanging in the air between them.

"Too meaningful," Jessica whispered, her mind returning to that exquisite night in the captain's arms, and the numerous other occasions when she'd almost lost control. The urge to touch him was a constant physical pull within her. Every time he looked at her, she felt a clenching down there, a hot ache that surged upwards causing her breasts to tighten and her pulse to race.

The heat in her cheeks had seeped down her neck, but she forced herself to look at her mother. "He's … a very passionate man, and he's constantly teasing me, making me laugh."

"Does he pressure you for sex?" Olive asked. Her tone was cautious.

Jessica shook her head. "No. But he makes me feel pretty and desirable … if things were different …" She exhaled heavily. "But they're not. This is the way it is and," she gestured helplessly, "that's all. It works well for us to be friends. It'll hurt less when he leaves if we're just friends."

"He's attracted to you, you know." Olive spoke matter-of-factly. "I can tell."

"He's lonely and missing his family, nothing more –"

"No. It *is* more –"

"He has a sweetheart back in Germany."

Olive was about to say something but she stopped and closed her mouth.

"It's true." Jessica raked her fingers through her hair. "It's true. Her name's Natalia – he's told me all about her. They're expected to marry – she's the one he'll be going home to."

"And what are you meant to do?"

"I don't know, Mum!" Jessica cried, suddenly growing exasperated. "That's why I can't have a physical relationship with him. You think I'm wrong? You think he should stay here, marry me, get a job and all that? He'd fit right into the community, wouldn't he! They'd welcome him with open arms and make him feel right at home!"

"Jessie, love –"

"Or maybe I should just make the most of having a handsome, sexy man in my house and fuck him like we haven't a care in the world!" Jessica broke off, breathing hard and on the brink of tears.

Olive frowned. "Don't speak like that," she said gently.

"How should I speak then?"

"Not like that. I don't want to hear you talk like that."

"It's how I feel. If he were American no one would bat an eyelid."

Olive snorted derisively. "That's not true. When the Yanks were billeted round Leeds, the women who –" she broke off suddenly, head cocked to the side. "They're coming."

Jessica heard it too, the low timbre of male voices and heavy footfalls in the hall. The door swung open and Eric entered, the captain following.

"Bloody cold out there," Eric declared, going straight to the fire and holding his hands to it.

The German, however, immediately sensed the tension in the room and hesitated just inside the door.

Jessica smiled reassuringly at him, but she groaned inwardly as Olive said, "I understand you've a sweetheart back home, Anton."

The young man bowed his head slightly in acknowledgement. "*Ja*, that is right. A childhood friend."

"Will you marry her when you return to Germany?"

"Mum, please don't –"

Eric had turned his back to the fire and was watching the scene with interest, while the captain seemed to consider the question. Finally, he said, "Natalia *und* I spoke briefly about this before I joined die *Luftwaffe* – mainly because a marriage between us would make our families happy. But when a man returns from war, he is often changed. The things that had once been important may no longer be so."

He shot a glance at Eric, who nodded imperceptibly. He added, "I do not know what I want any more." Daring to look towards Jessica, he smiled sadly, then, "That probably does not answer your question, Frau Bentley."

"No," Olive said, softly. "That answers my question perfectly."

***

Later, Eric was lying on his back, hands clasped on his chest. It was his preferred sleeping position but Olive hated it. She thought it made him look like he was practising for the day they measured up his coffin, and after thirty-two years of marriage, she'd never got used to it.

She lay on her side facing him, but she wasn't asleep. Her mind was going over her conversation with Jessica.

"What is it then?" Eric asked suddenly.

"I thought you were asleep."

"How can anybody sleep with that racket going on?"

"I haven't said a word," Olive said, disgruntled.

"Not out loud, but I can hear your mind working at a million miles an hour." He turned his head and peered at her through the dark. "So, what is it?"

Olive sighed. "It's Anton. Eric, I think he loves Jessica."

"I know."

"I mean *really* loves her."

"I know."

"What do you mean, you know?"

"I've seen him looking at her, and I know what makes a man look at a woman that way."

He suddenly looked away from her, closing his eyes as though trying to hide.

"Eric Bentley, are you blushing?" Olive propped herself on an elbow.

"Go to sleep."

"You are, aren't you?" She extended a hand. "Your cheeks are hot!"

He swatted her hand away. "Go to sleep."

She chuckled to herself but lay down beside him and closed her eyes.

His voice was a whisper but she heard the words clearly enough. "I know because I've looked at you that way most of my life."

Chapter 35

It was early afternoon on New Year's Eve and Jessica sat in the Daimler, outside the Wolstone grocers on Kirkgate, engine running and gnawing a hangnail. She'd never got over hearing Nigel Bright and Lillian talking about her all those months ago, and had to force herself to go into the shop.

Engrossed in thought, she was unaware of the man approaching until his knuckles rapped on the window.

Jessica's head snapped round in surprise.

Albert Tyler bent at the waist, and peered in at her. "Afternoon. Lost in thought?"

She shut off the engine and wound down the window. "Hullo Albert. Yes, I was trying to remember what I needed," she prevaricated. "Left my shopping list at home."

"Ah. Then how about half a pint while you think about it?" he nodded towards the Black Horse Hotel just up the road, and opened the car door without waiting for her response.

Jessica got out, dragging her handbag off the seat.

"Saw you sitting there," Albert went on, "and it reminded me of the, er ... disagreement you and Robin had a few weeks back. Meant to come see how you were."

Albert held the door and ushered her ahead of him into the pub's lounge. "I'm excited, you know, that someone other than myself is interested in Broughton history."

Jessica brightened and chose a table beside the fire and waited as Albert went to the bar. "Looked through those old pictures yet?" Albert asked, as he returned with two halves.

"I've had a quick look. I want to go through them in more detail – try to match houses and faces to the places and names in Alexandra's memoir."

"Aye," he said and raised the beer to his lips. He took a long pull and sat back with a satisfied sigh. "Robin wouldn't be too happy with me coming into town for a drink – not in the middle of the day. Always so worried about what people might say."

Jessica nodded and sipped her beer. "Well, it's after midday. I reckon we're all right." She put her glass on a coaster and said, "So about those Broughtons – how much do you know of the ancestry? Where does Francis fit in?" She wiped away a beery moustache with the back of her hand. "We … I found his grave in the churchyard near Broughton Hall."

Jessica wondered if she'd imagined Albert's expression tightening. "Francis Broughton was Andrew's son." Albert flipped over a coaster and drew a pencil from his shirt pocket. "It all started with Sir Simon."

As he spoke, Albert sketched a family tree. "Simon was your Alexandra's brother. He and his wife had four children. The eldest was Dudley. He married, and his eldest was Andrew." Albert drew connecting lines on his diagram. "Francis Broughton was the generation after. Dudley, Andrew, Francis – in that order inheriting the baronetcy."

"I see."

"Andrew – he were raised in Spain – was the first to come home to Broughton Hall … early 1880s. Place'd been empty since the aunt, Meg, died ten or so years earlier."

Albert laid down his pencil and rotated the coaster towards Jessica. "Spent a small fortune restoring that place. Made a few changes too, a ballroom and such. Held some fancy parties there, he did."

Jessica's head was spinning. She sat back in her chair and stared at Albert's drawing. Parts of a puzzle were dropping into place with such clarity that she fancied she heard the metallic clicking sounds.

"Dudley, Andrew, Francis," she repeated. "And then Joseph, whom my husband and I bought the place from."

Albert drained his glass. "Aye," he stifled a belch.

"Tell me," Jessica said. "What do you know of Alexandra after she moved away from Broughton Hall?"

"Ah, Alexandra." He frowned thoughtfully. "What I learned when I did me own research, was that she moved to the south – somewhere near Exeter, if memory serves. Lived with that earl."

"Patrick? He was her stepbrother."

"Aye. From the bits I found out about him, he were quite the soldier. Had a reputation for daring – when he weren't getting into trouble with the ladies, that is. Decorated several times though, including Waterloo, but quit soldiering a year or two later."

"And Alexandra?"

Albert shrugged. "Not much to tell but that she eventually ended up living in his thumping big mansion down in Devon – being his step-sister 'n' all, I suppose it made sense."

Jessica frowned, thinking and piecing together the details she'd read in the journal. "Interesting," she murmured.

"There were rumours, of course."

"Like what?" Jessica raised a curious eyebrow.

Albert shrugged. "Just rumours – he were a big-knob down there in Devon. Right popular with the common people he were. Because o' that, there were rumours that he were in with the local trade."

"Local trade?"

Albert drained the last of his beer and put his glass down with a satisfied sigh. "Same trade what's been carried out along the coasts of England for centuries – going on still, I'd reckon. Smuggling," he said, in answer to her puzzled look.

"Really?"

"Oh aye, o' course. Nothing substantial were ever pinned on the earl himself, mind, but the trade were rife down there. No way he couldn't've known. You want another?" Albert asked indicating her glass. Jessica shook her head. "Righto. Back in a sec."

There's a reason I found that journal. Jessica thought. *There's a reason I'm visited by Alexandra's shade.*

"It's all starting to make sense," she murmured to herself. She took a sip from her glass as Albert returned and settled into his chair.

"Listen," he said. His expression had grown serious. "I don't mean to upset you, and I love that you're interested in the Broughtons – talk about them all day I could, but there's summat I need to say while we have a moment to ourselves."

Intrigued, Jessica leaned forward in her chair.

Albert took a deep breath. "There are stories going 'round about you."

It seemed to Jessica that the room suddenly grew warm. Working to control her emotions, she laughed lightly. "I wouldn't take gossip seriously."

Albert laid a gentle hand on her arm and Jessica felt the blood drain from her face at his expression. "I think you should. It were Mick, a fellow down at Bright and Sons. Reckons he saw a stranger – young chap – untangling a cow from a hedgerow down by the Leeds road some time back. One o' your cows, on your land."

"There was a … a –" she groped for the story Sam was putting about.

"Another time, about a month later. He pulled up the drive to see that old steward of yours about your milk – reckoned he saw the same young fellow working on the roof of your stables."

While Albert was talking, Jessica felt her hands grow clammy and her left knee jittered uncontrollably beneath the table. She tried to shake her head in denial but found herself paralysed as Albert went on. "I know your steward set up that tale about some returned serviceman, but Jessica," and here he paused significantly, "the men making these claims – all they've got are suspicions and circumstantial evidence, but it's enough for them.

"I – Albert, I don't know what –"

"Look, take this how you will: we English got a duty to protect what's ours. My son is doing his duty – woe betide anyone Rob finds not doing his or her duty too." Albert's expression was grim.

He watched her for a long moment and Jessica tried not to squirm. He said, "There ain't no sympathy for Gerries anywhere in England. And as for anyone harbouring them … well, fraternising with the enemy is worse than *being* the enemy if you get my meaning." He shook his head. "Robin's got a job to do and he's got his suspicions too. If it turns out he's right, if he finds a Kraut lurking anywhere in his jurisdiction … th'authorities know there's a Kraut on the loose and they want him badly. Rob's job is to bring him in, and Rob knows his duty." Albert stared hard at her. "We *all* gotta do our duty, Jessica."

Jessica felt sick but she drew a deep breath and swallowed the large lump in her throat. "Thank you, Albert, for the beer and … the history …" She rose unsteadily. "I'd better be on my way. Happy New Year, Albert."

***

Albert watched through the pub window. Jessica seemed to have forgotten about going into the grocer's and was in a hurry to get away – even stalled the car.

Turning back to his beer, Albert reflected unhappily on what he'd told her; he liked Jessica, liked that she was trying to do her best.

But he wasn't a stupid man, and Rob was convinced she knew something about that Kraut. Albert didn't want to believe it. For now, a warning was all he could give her. He hoped it was enough.

***

Jessica drove home from Wolstone with her mind buzzing and her hands trembling. She turned in her gate just as her children trotted over and jumped in the back seat for the fifty-yards ride to the house.

"Where've you two been?"

"We've been down at the stream. It's frozen solid," Thomas told her. He was sitting forward, his arms resting on the seat behind her.

"Sit back, please. That's nice, isn't it," she responded, absently.

"No, it's not. Jack Ramage has skates. One of the Yanks made them for him last year. Do you think Mr Bird would make some for me?"

Jessica met her son's eyes in the rear vision mirror as she pulled up beside the stables. "Mr Bird has enough to do without making skates for you." She turned off the ignition.

"You're such a git, Tommy!" Mary said throwing open the car door. "All you think about is yourself!" She got out and slammed the door shut and ran into the house leaving her twin to stare after her for a moment before breaking into laughter.

"What's got into her d'you think?" Thomas pushed open his door but Jessica turned round in her seat and levelled a stern gaze at her son.

"Remember, Mr Bird's leaving us one day, probably soon. You need to get used to his not being around."

All mirth fell away from the boy's face and he gaped at her. "But he's not *really* leaving? Mr Bird loves us and we love him – we're his family."

"We're *not* his family, and he's not a pet we can keep. He has a home and his real family waiting for him."

Jessica watched the harsh realisation dawn on the boy's face. It occurred to her that over the course of the last ten months, Thomas had not accepted that the captain could leave – unlike

Mary, who had understood all along and steeled herself for it.

Thomas's small face crumpled and he flung himself out of the car and ran to the stables where he expected to find Mr Bird.

Pity we can't all be as strong as Mary about this, she thought, entering the house by the garden door.

Her mother was standing at the range, stirring a pot of something that smelled rich and meaty. As Jessica came in, Olive turned and smiled, "Braised rabbit for dinner?"

"Perfect," Jessica responded. "Where's Dad?"

Olive tapped the spoon on the side of the pot and placed it on a saucer. "Brace yourself ... He's down in the stables with Anton. Been down there for a while – thought they must've killed one another it were so quiet. I crept down to make sure and they were each sitting on a hay bale having a right old chat."

"They were never! It was amicable?"

Olive nodded archly. "Seemed to be. Right, that looks about done." She took the pot from the heat and removed her apron, draping it over the back of a chair.

"Hmm." Jessica watched abstractedly and made an instant decision. "Let's go join them, shall we? I have something to share with you all."

***

Eric and Anton sat on opposite bales of hay. Mary's pony was wuffling gently in a stall beside the German airman, while Jessica's cows shuffled about within a railed enclosure at Eric's back.

"Well, I don't have to like it, and I certainly don't approve," Eric said. "Jessica has never stood up to anyone in her life, but she stood up to me to defend you." He looked the other man up and down, his expression disdainful. "You look like a bleedin' movie star – is that why they sent you? Is it a plot to capture England via the hearts of its women? Are there more of you out there set to overrun us?"

Anton snorted humorously. "I was not sent by anyone, there are not more of us *und* I did not set out to capture anyone's heart."

"You've clearly captured one – two if you count my wife's. Olive was always the first to condemn you Krauts, now she's defending you along with Jessica!"

"Your daughter has captured *my* heart."

Eric narrowed his eyes and exhaled long and slow. "Don't play with me, boy!"

"I would not dream of it."

"You think you're very clever, don't you, with your winning smile and smart tongue?" Eric's voice was dangerously low and he leaned forward on his hay bale. "I don't know what you're up to, I don't know why you're here, but I'll tell you one thing – I don't trust you! If I suspect you're not who you say you are, or that you've touched a single hair on the heads of my grandchildren, or that you are compromising my daughter – if I even *imagine* you're lying to me or intend to do my family harm, I will kill you with my bare hands. Am I understood?"

While Eric was speaking, Anton was watching him steadily. The man meant every word, and though he was older and neither as strong nor as fit as Anton, he had passion and righteousness on his side and that made him dangerous.

"Am I understood?" Eric asked again.

But Anton had had enough of the man's stubborn prejudice. "*Jawohl*," he grunted curtly.

The older man muttered an explitive and glared at the German. "Insolent bastard! How is it you speak English so well, by the way?"

Anton rolled his eyes and opened his mouth to reply, but the Englishman cut him off with a scornful gesture, "Oh, don't tell me you lived in America. I've heard all about that! I'm not interested in the romantic tale you spun for my gullible daughter.

I want the truth."

"You have the truth."

Eric growled low, "The *truth*, you sodding Nazi!"

Anton gritted his teeth. He was genuinely angry now and breathing hard through his nose. "All right," he said tightly, "It may have escaped you in your ignorance, that the English language is based on the German ... Did you know that?"

Eric glared at him with hatred in his eyes but Anton wasn't finished with him yet. "It is easy for us to learn your language ... but you English," he went on contemptuously, his accent growing more guttural, "are so disdainful of anything beyond your shores, it is a wonder you have any international capability at all!"

While the German was speaking, the blood was steadily draining from the Englishman's face. His chin was pulled in, his mouth a tight, white-lipped line. "How dare you ..." he growled, clenching his fists, as though imagining them wrapped round the German's throat.

"Oh, I dare because I am *German*, you fool!" Anton felt all the anger and frustration within him bubble to the surface and explode from him in a stinging tirade over the man sitting opposite, wrapped in his cloak of bigotry and scorn. "We are more advanced than you," Anton stated proudly. "We have mastered science, medicine *und* engineering. We have grown from financial ruin *und* military subjugation – imposed on us by *you und* your American friends – to become a power before which you tremble. We are the master race!"

Anton leaned further forward. His countenance was a fearsome distortion of his good looks and he was so close that his breath was hot on the other man's face.

"Wir sind die Zukunft, du verdammter Narr! Zu deinem Unglück bin ich in deine Tochter verliebt!"

***

Eric knew a moment of genuine alarm at the wildness in the young man's eyes and the contained power exuding from him. He was strong, athletic … and the stream of vitriolic foreign language, enunciated with such biting fury, was no doubt some kind of threat.

As the German continued to glare menacingly into his face, Eric forced himself to remain still; refusing to be intimidated, even though he was facing a trained military officer, disciplined and dangerous, and who was, Eric realised with shock, laughing at him so hard that his eyes were streaming.

"Did you like that?" Anton asked, sitting back and wiping his eyes, his accent considerably diminished. "It is what you wanted to hear, *ja*?"

He rose suddenly and clapped Eric companionably on the shoulder. "I understand, you are suspicious, fearful *und* protective of your family. But let me tell you something."

Eric was too stunned to react as the German dropped to a crouch before him, bringing their eyes level. "I am not *up* to anything *und* I have been honest about who I am *und* why I am here. I am very fond of your grandchildren *und* would defend them against anyone wishing them harm. Further," here the young man paused, swallowed and drew in his breath, "I find myself in love with your daughter, it is inconvenient *und* I wish it were not so. If she would allow it, I would spend every night in her bed, but she will not allow it *und* I accept her decision. That is all the truth I have to give you.

"Now," he continued and Eric watched in stunned silence as the German pushed to his feet and strode to where Spencer's head hung curiously over the half-door of his stall. Giving the horse a friendly rub on the nose, "It is time I fed the animals. But for your information, I am not a Nazi, you limey bastard!"

The German disappeared down the end of the barn, beyond the lamplight, where he melted into the shadows.

Eric could hear things being moved about and the sound of animal feed being poured into a drum. Swallowing the lump that had risen in his throat, he allowed that he'd been quite daunted by the other man's attack. But while Eric was not about to admit he'd contributed to it, in the end, as it turned out, the smart arse had been poking fun at him.

"Hullo Grandad!" Young Thomas flew into the barn and rushed up to him. The boy's eyes were wild and he appeared agitated. Eric held out his arm and curled it round the boy's waist.

"Been out playing, have you?"

"Yup! The stream's frozen and we could walk on it."

"You want to be careful with that. I knew a chap once who –"

"Where's Mr Bird?"

Eric contained a derisive grunt. *Everyone in this bleedin' house is besotted with that Kraut!* "He's down the end getting the animal feed ready."

"Thanks Grandad!" And he was off, disappearing into the shadows.

Eric cursed *sotto voce*. What was it about that Gerry that was so damn engaging? His wife, daughter and grandchildren all loved him. Besides that, but he found himself, albeit reluctantly, believing the young man genuinely cared for Jessica and the children.

"Doesn't mean I have to like him," Eric muttered, grumpily. "Called me a limey bastard!" To his chagrin, he felt his lips twitch.

"Who called you a limey bastard?" Olive came into the stables, Jessica behind her.

"No one."

"That's an American term, isn't it Dad?" Jessica sat on the German's hay bale while Eric made room for his wife beside him.

"Apparently. I think it were one of the Yanks what come into the shop one day and called it me."

"If the cap fits," Olive started.

"Wear it." Jessica finished, with a chuckle. "You are, by the way, a limey bastard."

"Who is a limey bastard?" the German reappeared, carrying a tub of chaff. He opened Spencer's stall and the pony snorted at him in greeting.

Even the bloody pony loves him! Eric grumbled privately.

"Someone called Dad a limey bastard."

"Oh, *ja*?" Anton came out of the pony's stall and threw the bolt home. "Is that an English term? Is it nice?"

"It's American, I think," Jessica supplied, innocently. "It's not meant to be nice, but in this case, I think it's rather funny."

The German leaned casually against the wall and seemed to be thinking. Nodding thoughtfully, his eyes met Eric's and he grinned. "Well then, perhaps it was not meant as an insult."

Eric watched, dumbfounded, as the captain returned to the shadows to continue his work.

***

In the barn, at the end of the corridor where the last stall was used for storage, Thomas sat on an upturned bucket. When Mr Bird returned after feeding Spencer, he pulled up another bucket and sat opposite. He did not pressure him, or ask any questions, he merely adopted the casual attitude of one man sitting quietly with another.

At length, Thomas sniffed and wiped his nose on his sleeve. "Mr Bird, Mummy said you really *are* going to leave us."

It wasn't a question, but Thomas nevertheless expected an answer.

"Did you not know?" Mr Bird asked, softly.

Thomas shrugged, and studied his foot, scuffing stray pieces of straw about the cobbled floor.

"You know, I will not ever forget you," Mr Bird said. "We will always be friends *und* one day, perhaps, when our countries like each other, I will come *und* visit you. Or," he added, "you may come *und* visit me."

"What is your country like? My teacher says it's dark and cold. She says that people are kept in sheds and they are starving and that your leader is cruel to people."

"Ah, your teacher is mistaken. We do have a leader *und* he can be cruel but in times of war many leaders are cruel. The people in my country live in houses, like you. We have big cities, also like you, *und* we have countryside, like you."

Here he broke off and Thomas glanced up to find Mr Bird's eyes focused on a point in the distance. When he started to speak again, Thomas felt that Mr Bird had forgotten about him.

"My country is beautiful." His voice seemed quiet and dreamy. "It has tall sharp mountains that reach into bright blue sky. In the winter, everything glitters in white – it looks like a wedding cake with pretty gingerbread houses. In the summer, the mountains are a blue-grey colour; they poke up out of fields of green, with flowers that grow wild. They are yellow *und* red *und* the cows *und* sheep wander across the fields through these flowers. You can hear the bells the animals wear round their necks, always clanking in a sound that … I do not know the word for it, but it is a sound, you would know anywhere – it can only mean cows."

"Cowbell," Thomas whispered.

***

Anton's gaze shifted and he met the sad eyes of the boy before him. "Cowbell," he repeated. "*Ja*. The sound of the cowbell is music to me."

They fell silent for a time, then Thomas spoke, "Maybe I will come and visit you one day, Mr Bird. When I am grown up. Will you remember me?"

Anton felt a tightening in his heart and a wave of emotion, such as he'd never felt with his sister's children. Impulsively, he opened his arms to the child who instantly rose and threw himself against his chest. He hugged the boy close, his chin resting on the warm, tousled head. "Of course I will remember you. Impossible to forget you."

Chapter 36

The night was crisp and still. The sky arched above her like indigo velvet, encrusted with diamonds, and somewhere in the distance an owl hooted. The sound fell flat, smothered by the thick layer of snow. Jessica shivered and tucked the edges of the crocheted blanket beneath her knees. She felt warm enough, on her seat on the front porch, although the wet chill from the stone beneath her feet, crept insidiously up her ankles and calves.

A splash of warm, golden light, from the parlour windows behind her left shoulder, puddled on the porch. From time to time, there rose a childish squeal of delight coupled with Eric's lower tones, as he lamented his evident lack of success in a ferocious contest of shove ha'penny; a high stakes game with egos and bragging rights on the line.

Olive had been in the kitchen, having volunteered to do the washing up after tea. As the front door opened behind her, Jessica continued to gaze into the deepening shadows, and her mother's light footfall sounded on the stone.

"Well, that's done." Olive handed a cup of tea to her daughter, then pulled a chair over to sit beside her. "All tidy."

"Thanks, Mum." Jessica held the cup between two hands and watched the steam rise and bloom into a cloud, before dissipating into the frosty night air.

"You're worried aren't you, love?"

"Of course." Albert's warning three days ago had been playing on her mind. It was what she had already feared, but the verbalising of it had sent an icy tremor through her. She'd finally repeated it to her parents and the captain earlier that evening while the children were having their baths.

"Still an' all," Olive went on, "forewarned is forearmed."

Jessica nodded and took a tentative sip of tea. It was scalding; she decided to give it a few minutes to cool.

"This really is a beautiful house," Olive said, arching her neck to look up at the old stones above them. "And despite the work it needs, you took it on. One day it will be paid off. In the meantime, you can gradually repair, rebuild, replant …"

"It was supposed to be a joint effort." Jessica said, softly. "I was the one who fell in love with it but Jon agreed – he *promised*. We'd hardly been here eighteen months when he left."

"Well, love, the war came. Besides that, I don't remember him making any promises about restoring it."

Jessica gaped at her mother in disbelief. "We were married, Mum. That's a promise. He didn't have to agree to buy it, but he did. He knew the work we had ahead of us and he took it on with his eyes wide open."

"But the war –"

"He wasn't conscripted," Jessica argued unhappily. "He volunteered. He *chose* to leave his children. He *chose* to leave me with this place, with all the work it takes just to keep it from falling down."

"I think you're being unfair to him. You wouldn't expect him not to defend his country."

"He never could do any wrong in your eyes, could he?" Jessica tested her tea again and found it a bit cooler. "Let's be honest, shall we?" she continued. "It was the adventure that called him, the excitement. Not the opportunity to fight for his country. You should've seen him the day he left. Skipped off this porch like a child going to a party. I suppose he thought his salary and the amount I could make from the cows would keep us going. He never expected to die; that's what ruined his plans."

"But there was the insurance money. Jon told us about it. See? Always thinking ahead."

"Oh, Mum!" Jessica exhaled sadly. "Yes, there was the insurance, but the company disputed it. They said Jon had knowingly placed himself in danger. Had he been conscripted, had he gone because the government called him up, it would've been entirely different."

"So, did you get any money at all?"

"Some. Not enough to pay out the mortgage. I was able to reduce it quite a bit and keep some cash aside for urgent repairs."

"Oh," Olive murmured.

"As for the captain," Jessica swallowed a mouth full of tea. "If not for him I'd have been ruined. The work he's done round here ... well, there's no way I could've afforded that. And another thing –"

Olive sniffed. "I don't remember asking."

"In the ten months he's been here, he's done more work round the place than Jon did in eighteen months – and that's the truth of it," she added.

She saw her mother's mouth open in protest, close, then open again. She said, "You're really in love with him, aren't you?"

"What's that got to do –"

"It's not a criticism," Olive said quickly. "It's an observation, and I'll admit, he's a fine young fellow – easy to see why he'd turn your head. But Jessie, he's *dangerous*!"

"You think I don't know that?" Jessica felt the frustration rising in her chest. "But what can I do? I didn't choose this situation. I couldn't turf him out, I couldn't report him ... He was wounded, we thought he was dying. What would you've done?"

Olive patted the air, as though warding off her daughter's attack. "I don't know what I would've done," she admitted, "But I wouldn't be going to bed with him – that much I *do* know."

Jessica eyed her mother narrowly. "What's that supposed to mean?"

"It means exactly as I said. Have you," Olive asked, in a carefully moderated tone, "gone to bed with him?"

"We're not discussing this. I've told you before."

Jessica moved to get up but her mother threw out a hand to

stall her. "So you have, then."

Sighing, Jessica slumped back into her chair and stared into the darkness. In the near distance, just beyond a small stand of birch, was the steward's cottage. If she squinted, Jessica would just be able to make out the lights from Marg's kitchen flickering between the branches. Come spring, the cottage would be hidden behind a screen of lush greenery.

The captain was down there. He regularly had dinner with Marg and Sam, lingering afterwards, and Jessica believed it was as much to give her some peace and private time with her children as to remove the burden of having to feed him.

These days, avoiding her parents was probably another reason.

At length, she turned towards her mother. The older woman's face was partially illuminated by the warm glow from the parlour window. The light was at Jessica's back, her face in shadow, providing a modicum of cover as she said softly, "Yes. We spent one night together."

Jessica heard Olive suck in a sharp breath, yet her mother remained silent. Jessica continued, "I realised the next morning it was a mistake because ... because I felt so vulnerable, so afraid of losing him. We talked about it. I told him we could never be like that again. He accepted my decision."

Jessica fell silent, watching her mother gaze into the night. Olive's voice was gentle when she asked, "Have *you* accepted your decision?"

Jessica's mouth fell open. "I made it, of course I accept it."

Olive looked at her and shook her head. "That's not always the case, is it? There's a lot of affection between the two of you. An obvious ... intimacy. Your father ... he's a man after all. He might not've picked up on it. He suspects something's up and it hasn't endeared Anton to him. If he knew for certain ... I expect he'd rather think you'd been raped than believe you went willingly into a German's bed."

"Dad needs to mind his own business."

"Your welfare, and the children's welfare, *is* his business," Olive pointed out gravely.

Jessica snorted. "We're not in danger from the captain. We're in danger from our own kind – Robin and the Home Guard. Ironic isn't it?"

***

Just then, a door banged down at the cottage, and the crunch of boots on fresh snow drew closer.

"What about the warning that man gave you?" Olive asked, changing the subject. "What are you going to do?"

Jessica shrugged. "I don't know."

Olive's eyes lingered on her daughter a moment longer as the German mounted the porch steps.

Sadly, Olive turned away. "Good evening Captain," she said cheerfully.

"*Guten Abend*," he smiled at her and for a fleeting second, Olive wondered what it would be like to be young again. "I heard voices," he went on. "Are you not cold out here?"

His breath hung in a fog before his face as he spoke. Olive felt his eyes on her, though she knew he was intensely aware of Jessica sitting beside her. It was like an electrical current sparking between them.

Yes, Olive thought bitterly. *You love her in return. What a travesty!*

***

"Captain?"

Jessica awoke suddenly to the unmistakable feeling of the side of her bed dipping as someone sat on its edge.

Silhouetted against the moonlight beyond her window, was

the outline of a man. "Captain," she repeated. "What is it?"

At the sound of her voice, the visitor slowly turned and she saw his face. Thrown into gruesome relief by the light and shadow of the night, she recoiled at the sight of a horribly disfigured man.

Her eyes widened and the breath froze in her lungs.

"I'm sorry," he said, and to Jessica's horror, he shifted to appear off balance and she realised that he was not only missing half his face, but he was also missing an arm. "I'm sorry, Zan," he repeated.

In a panic, Jessica's legs scrabbled up the bed, her back thumping loudly against the bedhead. She could feel the weight of him pinning down the blankets as she tried to scrunch herself as far from him as possible. "He won't marry you," he said, leaning closer. He extended his arm, a hand, long white fingers. She felt the weight of it on her leg through the blankets. "There's nothing else you can do."

Jessica screamed.

***

She awoke with a fright, bathed in sweat and heart racing. Lying for a long time staring at the ceiling, she waited for her heart to gradually slow. It was a week into the new year and the night was still and silent; not a breeze stirred the trees in the garden, not an owl hooted and the moon was absent. The paddocks outside her window were shrouded in an impenetrable black veil.

It was a night for sound sleeping, yet there was tension in the air, a pervasion of something unnamed and arcane, seeping into every crevice, gap and nook in her room.

Perhaps it was the last thread of the nightmare that had woken her. Yet even now, the room seemed to vibrate with a presentiment, a premonition that wrapped icy fingers round her heart, squeezing with increasing pressure.

"Alexandra, is that you?" Jessica breathed into the darkness. She didn't expect a reply, and received none, but the sense of threat lingered. Alexandra never came with such a malignant sensation. This presence, neither growing nor receding, was just there; an expectation, or a foreboding.

Jessica lay in bed, tense and alert. Something was about to happen, something ... fearful.

"This is ridiculous!" Muttering to herself, she threw back the bedclothes and swung her legs over the side. Her feet groped for her slippers and she pulled on her dressing-gown.

The hall was black as pitch. The feeling of apprehension stayed with her and the floorboards beneath her feet creaked loudly as she crept downstairs and into the kitchen.

It was still warm from the coals glowing in the firebox. She poked them to life and was about to reach for a saucepan when she froze.

Someone was behind her!

"It is only me," came an accented voice and she exhaled in a huff. "Blimey, Captain, you scared the life out of me!"

Turning, she found him standing in the door through which she'd just come. He was wearing his pyjamas and dressing-gown and she cocked an eyebrow at him. "You can't sleep either?"

"*Nein*. I have been in the parlour reading the journal – I heard a noise *und* came to look."

"I feel like ..." she paused, "I had a nightmare, I was going to make some warm milk. Join me?" She took the milk jug from the icebox and he nodded and sat at the table.

"Frau Jessie, I have been thinking."

"Hmm?" she said, over her shoulder, pouring milk for two into the saucepan and placing it on the hob.

"I was reading the journal *und* I think that your life is being guided by Alexandra. She is guiding you through her memoir *und* her visits to you."

Jessica snorted and he looked bewildered. She glanced into the saucepan to check the milk's progress before coming round to take a seat opposite him.

"Why do you laugh?"

"Because you're trying to woo me into your bed."

For a moment, he looked genuinely surprised, but then he smiled and shrugged. "Oh, *ja*, you have little faith in me. I promised you I would not try to seduce you *und* I mean to keep my promise." He made a dismissive gesture. "*Nein*, I was thinking that there are many similar things between your situation *und* Alexandra's."

"Like what?"

"Like how she is prepared to fight her family for the man she loves – you have done that for me, I know."

She smiled sheepishly at him as he got up to check the milk. "I knew it!" she said. "You're still trying to win me over –"

"*Nein, nein!*" Now he spoke impatiently, pouring the milk into two cups. He turned to her. "You are mistaken. I am pointing out similar things – not trying to win you to my cause." He passed one of the cups to her and resumed his seat. "I have already won that war." He grinned briefly, and here, in the lamplight, with the day's stubble on his chin and a villainous glint in his eye, she decided he was the most disarmingly beautiful man she'd ever seen and her heart skipped a beat.

Shaking off the thought, she said, "Don't look at me like that!"

His grin widened. "Frau Jessie," he broke off to sip his milk, "What is it with English women? Do you think all men want is to take you to bed?"

She shrugged. "That is what we are taught from a young age."

"Well then, little English girls are taught incorrectly." While they'd been talking, he'd been staring into his cup. Now, he looked up and met her eyes. All humour had gone from his face.

"I am content to just be with you – I do not need you in my bed."

"Oh that's a lie, Captain!" She laughed bitterly. "You've already had me in your bed and you'd have me again were I willing!"

"This is true. But you miss my point. I *want* you in my bed, of course I do. But if it cannot be, then I am content to just be with you – like now," he gestured to indicate the room, the solitude of night and their cups of warm milk.

They were silent for a long time, both lost in private thought.

"Why can you not sleep?" he asked, finally breaking the silence.

"I don't know … I feel strange, nervous. Like something's about to happen and I don't know what."

He nodded and drained the last of his milk. Rising, he placed his cup on the sink, then turned and held out his hand. "Come with me."

She responded automatically, rising and taking his hand. "Where are we going?"

"Not to bed," he replied, with a sardonic smile. She felt a perverse stab of disappointment and allowed him to lead her up the hall and into the parlour, where the banked coals were glowing in the grate and the journal was on the table. His place was marked with a scrap of paper.

Hands on her shoulders, he pushed her gently onto the couch. Taking the crocheted rug that Olive had left on a chair, he draped it round her, picked up the book and opened it at his marker.

"There. Read it, *und* tell me you see the similarities."

"I already have."

"Ah," he crouched before her then and took her face between his palms. "Then read anyway until you can sleep. *Gute Nacht, mein Liebster.* "

He bent to kiss her but she pulled back suspiciously, "What did you just say?"

Grinning like a small boy caught doing something naughty, he whispered, "I said good night my lover, for that is what you are."

Then he kissed her, deeply and slowly. Her body was quick to respond with a longing for him that was a physical ache. But her parents and children were sleeping upstairs and they both knew this was all they would ever have.

He was the first to pull away. Pushing to his feet, he gently stroked a knuckle against her cheek before leaving her alone.

***

Jessica couldn't read any more. Her eyes were hurting from the effort of reading by the lamplight, and her throat ached with unshed tears.

The chapter the captain had given her was the chapter in which Alexandra and her lover first declared their passion for one another, one gentle spring morning in the orchard. Jessica had forgotten how enchanted she'd been when she first read this scene.

But why Jessica felt like weeping, she didn't know. Was it for the beauty of their budding love? Was it for the futility of the love between herself and the captain? Could it be because the relationship between her and Jon had never had an opportunity to bloom into the kind of love Alexandra described?

Friends for too long, she and Jon hadn't known how to be lovers.

Perhaps it was all these things … perhaps none. Maybe she was just tired, emotionally as well as physically.

Jessica passed the back of her hand over her eyes and yawned. It was warm in the parlour, the crocheted rug the captain had tucked round her was cosy and comforting. *I could probably sleep now ...* But the prospect of returning to her cold and lonely bedroom was unattractive. She swung her legs onto the couch and stretched out with her head on a cushion.

She was asleep immediately.

***

Suddenly, the silence of the night was shattered by a loud hammering on the front door. It was quickly followed by a strident shout, "Jessica Barrow – open this door!"

Jessica's heart leapt painfully, then began racing. Her eyes darted about with confusion. The banging on her door grew more insistent and a man's voice bellowed, "*Jessica Barrow! Home Guard! Open up this instant!*"

At the same time, streamers of torchlight flashed through the parlour window, dancing over the walls, streaking the furniture and finally, coming to rest on Jessica herself, pinning her, white-faced and frozen in terror, in its bright, dazzling beam.

Chapter 37

Bewildered, Jessica stumbled into the entry hall. The pounding on the door caused the heavy wood to shudder in its frame. In her fright, she fumbled with the bolt, taking skin off her knuckles. As soon as the bolt shot aside, the banging ceased and the door crashed open.

A crowd of men in Home Guard uniforms shoved past, slamming her indifferently against the wall. They fanned out, into the parlour and across the hall into the formal dining room, while others marched down the passage towards the kitchen.

Jessica's knees were trembling so much they threatened to give way just as Robin Tyler strode up to her and grasped her roughly by the wrist.

"Robin!" she gasped, trying to prise his fingers off her arm. "These men …" Her heart was racing. Her mind was a swirling mass of confusion and questions. "Who … What …?"

Robin didn't answer. He marched into the parlour, hauling her after him. When she staggered, he dragged her across the rug.

"Robin, please!" she cried frantically. "You're hurting! What's going on?"

But Tyler, apparently, wasn't in the mood for answering questions. "Where is he?" he demanded, giving her wrist a rough jerk. She felt the bones flex painfully.

"Who …? Robin, for God's sake …!" Jessica begged. "You're hurting me!"

"I'm not an idiot, Jessica. Where've you hidden him? Search upstairs," he ordered the men tramping roughly through her house. "Search every bloody room! He's here somewhere!"

More men were barrelling through the front door, while others, it seemed, had broken in through the garden door. Many carried torches; beams of light chaotically striped the walls and ceiling. Strangers tramped through her kitchen and down her hall, calling to one another in the darkness.

The house echoed with bangs, crashes and the drumming of heavy feet. Jessica felt the panic building in her chest, rising into her throat. "Who are these men …? Robin – wha –"

"So many questions, Jessica." Tyler still had her by the wrist. Now he shook her violently, and she yelped with the pain. "I'm the one with questions. Now, where is he?"

"I don't …"

Tyler jerked her towards him and her neck snapped with an audible crack. Leaning over her, his mouth an ugly gash in the lamplight, he snarled into her face, *"Where is he?"*

From elsewhere in the house came the shouts and bangs of Tyler's men as they tore through rooms, cupboards, wardrobes. Jessica's head was reeling, her fingers were growing numb from his grip on her wrist.

The men on the stairs were brandishing weapons: someone had a cricket bat, others had iron bars, but as a pistol glinted dangerously in the torchlight, Jessica turned into a madwoman.

Oblivious to the pain in her arm, she twisted round and attacked Tyler with her free hand. Screaming like a banshee, she clawed and tore at his face, kicking his shins with her slippered feet, fighting to free herself.

"You bring a gun into my house?" she cried, incredulously, thrashing about like a wildcat. *"Let me go! Let me goo!"*

Suddenly Mary's shrill squeal rose above the cacophony of crashing and bellowed orders and the pounding of boots in the rooms above.

"*Mary*! My children …!" Jessica screeched hysterically, "The children!" Terrorised, she turned to her captor and in a moment of dementia, bared her teeth and sank them deep into the hand gripping her arm.

With a howl of outrage, Tyler released her but only long enough to pull back and slap her hard across the face. Jessica's legs buckled and she tasted blood. An instant later there was a searing pain in her scalp; Tyler had a handful of her hair wrapped about his fist. Now he wrenched her back to her feet.

"*We know he's here ...*" he roared, inches from her face. "*We know you're harbouring a German pilot – and when ...*"

Her scalp gave way as she tore free of him. Glancing fearfully over her shoulder, she saw him staring, open-mouthed in shock, at the auburn strands wrapped around his hand.

She dashed for the stairs. Starting up, she saw her mother appear on the landing above. Olive was wearing her nightgown, her hair in rollers. In one hand, she wielded a heavy china jug. Both children were hugging her, eyes wide, thin little arms clutching at their grandmother's waist. "What is the meaning of this?" Olive demanded imperiously.

The men continued to shove past, heedless of the elderly woman and small children.

"Mummy!" the children wailed as they saw her. Jessica staggered up the stairs, dizzy with pain, and nearly lost her balance as Mary and Thomas flung themselves at her.

Olive pushed past and started down the stairs, meeting Robin half way. "Are you the leader here?"

"Yes, Ma'am. I have an order to search this house. Out of my –"

"We got 'im!"

The shout rang out and Jessica's stomach turned to water.

"We got 'im, Mist. Tyler!"

Jessica slumped heavily against the wall on the landing, sheltering a child beneath each arm. She felt weak and dizzy and was gasping for breath. She slid to her knees.

"There's a man 'ere, Mr Tyler ... in the bed!"

"Good work, Stanley," Robin clapped a tall man on the back.

Jessica raised her head. No more than five feet from where she knelt, trembling, with her children, two Home Guards stood in the hall, torches aimed through the open door of the Luftwaffe captain's room.

***

Jessica's world shrank inward, fading at the edges until she was aware of nothing but her own erratic breathing and the pain in her scalp. She experienced a slowing of time, a moment perhaps, when all she could hear was her own blood pounding in her ears. She was aware of being intensely cold. *Shock. I must be in shock*, she thought with detachment.

And something's wrong with Thomas and Mary. The children were unnaturally still, huddled against her. Jessica's mind reeled. *They're so quiet ... too quiet.*

Jolted back to reality, she found herself kneeling in the hall, her children's white faces staring at the German's door. Robin bounded up the remaining stairs and pushed past. Olive came to stand beside her, a steadying hand resting gently on her shoulder.

The sounds of destruction, elsewhere in the house, were gradually easing as the news of the discovery filtered through.

The fugitive had been found. There was cheering. More men were mounting the stairs. They crowded onto the landing, squeezed into the hallway, eager to witness history: the capture of a dangerous Luftwaffe pilot.

They were laughing, congratulating one another as they stood about. From where Jessica crouched on the floor, she could just make out Robin, through a forest of dark trousers, in the bedroom door, his torch trained on a point within the room. Suddenly, he turned on his heel and strode towards her.

Legs moved aside as he approached. A calmness, borne of capitulation, washed over her. She boldly raised her eyes. The look on Robin's face told her everything as he smirked contemptuously, victoriously, down at her. "Come with me."

This moment, she knew, had been inevitable since the day the

German had parachuted into the field beyond her garden, since the second he'd opened his eyes, opaque with pain and illness, and she had taken pity on him and helped a fellow human being.

In the interminable seconds that followed, she painstakingly unwound her children's clinging arms, and rose on unsteady legs. Dazedly, she followed, like a condemned man on his way to the scaffold.

Robin's swagger was triumphant and he accepted the nods and slaps of approval from his men as he passed. Approaching the bedroom, he gripped Jessica's upper arm and escorted her along. The men crowding the doorway to catch a glimpse of the prisoner stood back deferentially – men she recognised from the dairy, from the Wolstone market, even the doctor. She saw the derision in their eyes … felt their contempt burning holes right through her.

Robin unceremoniously propelled her ahead of him, into the darkened bedroom. Taking a lantern from one of his men, he held it high and gave the bed a hard kick with his boot. "Get up!" he ordered.

The pain from Jessica's scalp was making her dizzy.

Slowly, the dormant form stirred, rolled over and blinked up them. His eyes slid to Robin standing self-importantly beside her.

Jessica swayed on her feet.

"Oi, what's all this ruckus, then?" Eric Bentley queried, rubbing the sleep from his eyes. He pushed stiffly to a sitting position. "Jessie, love, what're you doing wakin' your old man in the middle o' the night like this?"

But Jessica was beyond response. Her eyes rolled back in her head and she collapsed in a dead faint on the floor at Robin's feet.

Chapter 38

Thwarted, Robin's fury knew no bounds.

He shouted at his men, "Search the house again! The outbuildings, that cottage down the drive. Scour the whole bloody estate – top to bottom!"

Robin's men dragged Sam Clay and his wife from their bed and sent them up to the Hall. They appeared bleary-eyed and white-faced in the parlour where Robin directed the elderly couple to sit and be quiet. Clay had always treated him with disdain, now Robin was revelling in his power over the man.

Jessica's children immediately cuddled up to Clay's wife. Robin had tolerated the children to ingratiate himself with Jessica, although he found the boy irritating and the girl precocious. Now, they were satisfyingly subdued, their faces ghostly above their dressing-gowns.

Turning his attention to Jessica's father, Robin stood intimidatingly over the man. Eric Bentley responded sullenly to his questions.

"Took a sleeping pill," the man told him. "Been struggling to sleep."

"If you're so ill, why are *you* the one sleeping in that cramped bed while your wife's in a comfortable bed in another room?" Robin reasoned, pacing the floor. He dragged a hand through his hair with mounting frustration.

"Not that it's any business of yours," Eric retorted angrily, "but we sleep in the same bed until my coughing starts up. Then I go to another room. It's not unusual for us to sleep separately … been doing it for months now."

Robin grunted with annoyance. He could hear his men milling about on the porch, smoking cigarettes and muttering discontentedly between themselves.

Jessica was sitting with her mother. The older woman was

dabbing Dettol on the raw wound where her hair had been wrenched out. Robin refused to feel remorse over hurting Jessica: treasonous bitch deserved all she got.

Her mother glared at him. He curled his lip at her and turned away. Weary and disappointed beyond measure, Robin was nevertheless convinced the German was here… if only he knew where.

He studied Jessica again. She was white as a sheet and seemed genuinely bewildered. So did her parents and that elderly couple from the cottage.

But one of them knew something – surely.

Her parents. Robin turned back to scrutinise the father. Could he possibly be the stranger reportedly seen doing odd jobs around the place?

Robin snorted to himself. No, Eric Bentley was an old man. A *sick* old man. But he *might* be hiding something … someone was!

He puffed out his cheeks in frustration. There was nothing to be done about it now – it was almost three in the morning. Those fellows outside had day jobs to get to in the morning.

Smarting with loss of face, Robin approached Jessica and thrust a finger an inch from her nose. "This isn't over!" he growled. "I know you're harbouring the German and I *will* find him. And when I do …" he paused significantly, glancing at each of the stricken faces round him, "and when I do you can kiss your precious children goodbye."

Marg Clay gasped. Mary gave a sob and turned into Marg's bosom. Eric opened his mouth, "You –"

"Get of my house!" Jessica hissed, revulsion for him clear in her face.

"Oh, I'm going – but I'll be back," Robin snarled, then with an ugly twist to his mouth, added, "What … nothing else to say? No further questions, Mrs Barrow?"

With a great effort of will, Jessica held his stare and drew in a slow breath. "Just one. Why don't you go fuck yourself?"

***

He'd gone and taken his thugs with him and Jessica was dizzy with relief. Mary darted to the parlour window. She knelt on the window seat, watching the last of the raiders leave the property then drew the heavy blackout drapes across. Turning, she nodded at Marg.

"Eeyup there Sam, let's go," Marg said.

Thomas was jiggling with excitement. He leapt off the couch and dashed out of the room, following his sister and the older couple.

Jessica was staring after them in surprise when her mother spoke. "How are you feeling, love?" Olive put the Dettol aside.

"I have a headache, and ..." Jessica rotated her shoulder. "I think I strained my arm when he dragged me into the parlour."

"Bastard!" Eric declared. "Bloody bastard, barrelling in here like we had Hitler, Mussolini and the entire bloody crew sitting down to tea."

"I cleaned most of the blood away with the Dettol," Olive said. "If we arrange your hair carefully, we could cover the bald spot."

A door banged somewhere towards the kitchen and Jessica started nervously, but as she recognised the children's running feet, she relaxed.

"So where –" Jessica broke off as the captain was dragged into the parlour by a triumphant child each tugging an arm.

He stood, still dressed in pyjamas, looking down at her for several heartbeats and Thomas and Mary danced around him as though he were a Maypole. "He's safe! He's safe!" they chanted.

"Hush, now," Olive said.

Jessica felt the weight of Eric's eyes on her as she, heedless of anyone else in the room, purposefully rose off the couch and threw herself into the German's arms.

He caught and held her, his head bowed to hers, hand stroking her back as she broke into gulping sobs.

At length, the captain guided her to the couch. He sat and she nestled under his arm avoiding the steely gaze of her disapproving father.

Sam stoked up the fire and they each took a moment to steady themselves. Thomas and Mary cuddled their grandparents on another couch, Sam and Marg sat on chairs, and Sam said, "All right you two, before you bust a foofer valve, you'd better explain how you managed to spirit Mr Bird away."

Thomas was only too eager to share his story. He had been woken, he described gleefully, by the voice of a small girl calling his name. "She said, *Wake up Tommy, wake up now!* I thought it was Mary, but there was no one there. I rolled over to go back to sleep but then she said, *Tommy wake up and hide Mr Bird. Hide him now!*

Thomas shrugged as though disembodied voices were common occurrences for him. "I think it was that girl I sometimes see. So, I got up and went into Mr Bird's room. I said, 'Get up quick, Mr Bird. You must get into the attic.'"

By that stage, the men had arrived and were pounding on the front door. Mary had emerged dazed and blinking into the hall. Immediately realising what her brother was doing, she dragged the step ladder from among the items stored in the ballroom, and with help from the two children, the German pilot climbed into the attic and closed the hatch behind him. The ladder was returned to the ballroom, and the children flew back to their respective beds, to await whatever was to happen next.

"Such brilliant little people!" Marg gushed, hugging the children tightly. "While that horrible man was wrecking your house, Jessie, Mary whispered to me that Anton was in the attic."

"So you knew he was safe all along?" Jessica asked in surprise "I should send the lot of you to Hollywood. Make a fortune with those acting skills!"

"We didn't know for sure," Mary qualified. "Turned out he wouldn't've been safe because those men looked inside the attic too. Mr Bird went up onto the roof and hid there."

Thomas jumped in. "He told us to wait until the men left then get the ladder and put it where we had it last time he was on the roof."

Still snuggled beneath the captain's arm, Jessica twisted round to look at him. "What did you do?"

"When we fixed the roof, *und* Herr Clay could not get the right tiles, I knew I could push through them from inside."

"Flimsy," Sam explained. "Those shingles we got were only temporary, remember? Being night, there'd be no light to show a hole."

"God, yes." Jessica breathed. "I'd never've thought of that."

"Hmph!" Eric shifted uncomfortably "Well, I've just about had enough of this. We're all lucky we weren't murdered in our beds!"

Jessica felt Anton adjust his position. He dropped his arm from her shoulders, and she, considering her father's disdainful expression, sat up.

"Mr Bentley," the captain said and Jessica noted how carefully he spoke, the better to minimise his accent. "Mr Bentley, I would like to thank you for what you did, going to my bed. It was very –"

"Didn't do it for you," Eric snapped. "Did it for Jessie and the children. For all I care you could –"

"Dad, *please* …" Jessica implored.

Her father's expression effectively finished his sentence, although the captain accepted Eric's attitude with a solemn nod. "Whatever your reason, I thank you because Frau Jessie's safety and that of her children is important to me."

"If it were that important you'd –"

"Dad, for God's sake!" Jessica got up and went to her father. "You're a bigoted old fool who's just done something heroic and clever. Don't ruin it. Just accept our appreciation." She kissed his brow while Eric grumbled something under his breath and seemed, albeit reluctantly, to acknowledge the captain's gratitude with a short jerk of his head.

Satisfied, Jessica turned to her children. "All right, it's been a big night but the excitement's over. Better go back to bed for a couple of hours."

"But Mummy," Thomas protested, "I want to tell you something."

"Can it wait until morning?"

Thomas shook his head.

"What is it then?"

"Remember the man I saw that night from my room?" He paused expectantly. When Jessica nodded, he went on, "Well he was here tonight. He was the one Mr Tyler called Stanley."

Jessica sighed wearily. "Must've suspected something and was having a snoop around. At least that mystery's solved. All right, kids," she said, briskly. "Off now."

"It's almost time to get up anyway," Mary reasoned.

"So you *want* to start your morning chores?"

"No!" they cried in unison.

"Right, off you go then."

With that, the children said their goodnights. Marg and Sam decided to leave too, with a promise to return in the morning to help clean up.

"Do you think the children are all right?" Olive asked.

"You saw them," Jessica said. "It's been a terrific game. Wish I could say the same for myself," she added, eyeing her trembling hands.

"Jon's children for sure," Eric quipped.

"Garden door's been kicked off its hinges," Sam told her, getting up. "I'll fix it as best I can. We can look at it properly tomorrow."

When finally, there were only Jessica, Anton and Jessica's parents in the parlour, Olive yawned and turned to her husband, "All right love, we should go back to bed too."

She gave his arm an experimental tug but he resisted. Jessica saw the suspicion in his eyes as he regarded her and the captain. "What are *you* doing?" he addressed Anton.

"I was planning to return to my bed, Mr Bentley," he responded, eyes gleaming. "But if you prefer it to your own, I suppose we could trade places." He threw a jaunty wink in Olive's direction.

Jessica saw her mother flush like a girl while her father grunted, "We're going to bed."

***

Bending intensified the throbbing pain in Jessica's skull, but she did so anyway, picking up the crocheted rug. Straightening, she was taken aback at the look on the captain's face.

"What is that?" he queried darkly. He was frowning, his accent more defined. He pointed to her hair, "There is blood. What did they do to you?"

Jessica's hand automatically flew to the wound on her head. "Nothing serious ..."

"Come here," he demanded.

"I said it's nothing. Go to bed."

He edged closer and gently lifted aside the sticky, tangled strands of her hair. Jessica winced and bit her lip against the pain. She heard his quick intake of air and he stared into her face. "They pulled out your hair?" he asked incredulously.

She laughed nervously. "No. Robin was holding my hair. I

ran away from him so technically, I pulled it out."

His eyes glinted dangerously. "I will kill him."

"No you won't!"

"I am going to kill him!"

"No. You're not! I've taken care of you and nursed and loved you. You do something like that – they will shoot you where you stand and all my work will be for nothing!"

He folded his arms belligerently over his chest, but she grasped his face between her palms. "Captain, I'm serious. Look at me! I'm all right – everyone is all right. Go to bed – it's almost four. We'll talk in the morning."

His smoky-blue eyes had been focused on a point over her shoulder, refusing to meet her gaze. Now they shifted to her face and slowly he nodded.

Releasing him, she retrieved the rug again and proceeded to make a comfortable nest of cushions on the couch.

"What are you doing?"

Without responding, she lay on the couch and tucked the cushions and rug about herself.

"Frau Jessie? What are you doing?"

"I'm going to stay here. I don't feel like going to bed." She smiled up at him. "God, you must be cold. Did you go onto the roof in just your pyjamas? Barefoot?"

He smirked and held his arms out helplessly. "The children did not give me time to get dressed. Move over."

"What?"

"If you are sleeping here, then I will stay with you. It may be the only opportunity I ever have to hold you to sleep."

***

Eric coughed, tossed and turned; coughed some more and tossed and turned some more. Olive, in her typical fashion was fast asleep. Lucky for him his wife had always been a good solid sleeper – not that that was such a good thing when the air raid sirens were blaring and the woman slept right on through them.

But out here, there were no air raid sirens – only a bloody Kraut. A *Luftwaffe* Kraut just to make it worse! That he seemed friendly enough was beside the point. *Must be because he was educated in America*, Eric decided. *No German school could have produced such a* ... Eric hated to say the word *decent*, even in the privacy of his own thoughts, but it nearly came out despite himself.

Didn't matter anyway. The terrifying events of the night could be laid entirely at that bastard's feet, and still Jessica defended him.

And what's with that attitude of hers? Eric had never known his daughter to be so argumentative, so opinionated and rebellious. Teutonic, that's what it was and no prizes for guessing where she picked that up!

Eric coughed again. A dry, painful, hacking that ensured sleep would remain elusive. He decided a cup of tea might do the trick. He could also get stuck in and clean up the kitchen before Jessie got up. Poor love, quarrelsome though she was, she was still his daughter and was doing it tough.

So it was, Eric found himself in the kitchen at 4.30 am. That old steward of Jessie's had managed to cobble together some kind of door to keep the cold and damp out. Aside from the broom cupboard, whose contents were strewn across the floor, the kitchen wasn't too badly off.

He stacked the mop and brooms, dusters and buckets back where they belonged while the kettle gurgled on the hob, and by the time he closed the cupboard door, it had boiled.

Eric made tea-for-one in the little single-serve gadget Jessie had. Shaped like a spoon with a mesh lid, it held enough tea leaves for one cup. He only half filled it – *things were getting out of hand when rationing interfered with a man's cuppa.* Stirring it absently like a spoon, he wondered whether that gang of thugs had damaged anything out the front. *Car's out there – they better not have touched it! Better check – look through the window.*

Unhurriedly, Eric made his way from the kitchen, up the two short flights of stairs, and along the hall towards the parlour. The door was partly closed, which he thought odd, but he pushed it open without thinking any more of it. The sight that met his eyes caused his cynical old heart to turn over in anguish.

There, on the couch, cradled in the German lad's arms, his daughter slept. She looked warm, untroubled and comfortable, but more than that, in the restful nature of sleep, the expression on her lovely face was one of peace and security.

Eric gazed down at the sleeping pair, marvelling at the evident love between them – for it was written plainly on both their faces. If previously he'd had reason to doubt the sincerity of the Kraut's affection for Jessica, in this unguarded moment, he could not. He also realised that he'd never witnessed such sentiment between Jessica and Jon.

What he could not know, was how far this relationship had progressed. Eric hoped to God they were not lovers, but he wouldn't be betting on it.

And suddenly he knew the kind of pain only a parent knows; the despair that comes with the knowledge that one's child is about to be grievously hurt, because there was no possible way the German could remain here. Eric felt an unwelcome tightening in his chest at the thought of his daughter's imminent grief.

How cruel, that she lost her husband, her children their father, only to find what purported to be a deep and clearly reciprocated love for a man who was …

Eric couldn't even think it any more. Jessica loved this man and it seemed that they were good for one another. He exhaled sadly, and in that moment, the Kraut's eyes flickered open and he squinted up.

The two men studied one another for several heartbeats, until the captain's expression grew defiant. He brushed a light kiss against Jessica's temple, and she felt the touch, murmured something in her sleep and snuggled further into his embrace.

Eric sighed again, but this time it was a sigh of resignation. Accepting defeat, he nodded briefly, and strode from the room.

***

Jessica first became aware of being cold, which was quickly followed by the crick in her neck when she tried to snuggle down in search of warmth. It seemed to her, in the drowsiness of sleep, that she was lying in an unusual position and when she attempted to move, she gasped at the surprising sharpness of the pain, and her hand shot up to massage her neck. She realised that she was lying on a couch, head at an odd angle on the armrest, being spooned by a warm body – a warm, *male* body, given the rigid pressure, nudging insistently against her bottom.

As though answering some primitive call, a warm, restless sensation seeped through her, pooling deep in the junction of her thighs. She resisted the urge to push back on him and forced herself, instead, to come fully awake.

One of his arms was under her, the other over her, holding her close against him; she opened her eyes to find she was in the parlour, the fire had burned out and she and the captain were cuddled together, covered inadequately by the crocheted rug.

With a rush, the events of the night before, the terror, the destruction, her children's screams came back. Her children! Oh, God … eight year olds who had outsmarted Robin Tyler and the Home Guard! She smiled to herself, but it faded as she recalled the captain staying with her, spending what remained of the night on the couch with her, and she felt the rise of his chest against her back as he stirred and yawned.

Rolling over in his arms, she was nose-to-nose with him on

their narrow cot. Her movement caused him to quickly draw breath, his eyes were heavy-lidded, he licked his lips.

She could so easily kiss him – it was her first impulse, the only thing she wanted to do, and she saw the answering thought flicker across his face. But he would not initiate it, she knew – it was too dangerous, so early in the morning, the two of them wrapped tightly together like this … and she was trying to ignore the firmness now pressing against her stomach and the ache in her loins.

"*Guten Morgen, meine Liebe.*" He smiled, and adjusted his position slightly. She supressed a shiver but the expression on her face gave it away. "I apologise," he said, "It is … er, it cannot be helped, I am afraid. It is the morning salutation."

I must get up," she said decisively.

"*Ja*, you must, right away, before I forget my manners."

Jessica laughed lightly through her nose, grateful of his easy banter. He moved back as best he could in the small amount of space, and pushed onto one elbow, while she continued to lie beside him.

Looking down at her, his cheeks coloured slightly. "Please, Frau Jessie, do not make me ask again." Adding with a suggestive cock of one eyebrow, "Unless, of course, you intend to offer relief."

It was her turn to flush. Stammering an apology, she quickly slid off the couch, while he swung his legs to the floor, and sat with the crocheted rug over his lap.

"Oh dear," she swayed, pressing a hand to the side of her head, and wincing at the sharp pain.

"*Was ist es?*"

"I forgot the cut on my head and stood up too quickly … bit dizzy, that's all."

"Are you all right?"

"Yes, yes. Don't get up, Captain," she turned to look at him and grinned. "Whatever you do …"

"Frau Jessie," he flushed self-consciously, "I have been walking on three legs since I first met you."

She laughed out loud then. "You're a wicked man!"

"Oh, *ja*," he drawled, and let his eyes drift slowly over her, causing a shiver to run along her spine. "I am very wicked, *und* I am having very wicked thoughts right now so …" he jerked his chin towards the door.

"All right, I'm going!"

***

"I still say we should call his bluff," Eric said.

The morning after Tyler's raid, Anton and Jessica, Eric and Olive sat round the small table in Broughton Hall's kitchen. The children were busy in the parlour playing Snap, leaving the adults to discuss the events of the previous evening. Eric was all for reporting Robin Tyler and his men to the authorities. "A formal complaint. It's not right, what he did … barging in to someone's house and smashing it up like that. Over officious is what it was."

"The problem though," Jessica said, "is that he was right to do it. The captain *is* here, after all."

"But he don't know that!"

Olive made a popping sound with her lips. "Calling his bluff is all very well if the risk isn't so great. But the risk is *very* great – what if the bluff were to backfire?"

Until now the captain had sat quietly listening and considering each opinion. To the others, his face gave nothing away, but Jessica was now familiar with his various expressions and subtle nuances. She could easily read his unhappiness.

Finally, he cleared his throat and three sets of eyes swung in his direction, as though they'd all been waiting for him to speak.

"I think," he said slowly, his voice soft, his accent heavy,

"I think it would be best for all concerned if I go somewhere …" Jessica opened her mouth to speak but he cut her off with a gesture. "There must be somewhere I can hide … Somewhere I –"

"Anton," Olive interrupted and her voice was firm and even. "I think that might be for the best, but we would need –"

"Mum, no!" Jessica felt her stomach twist.

"Jessica, you can't put the children through another night like last night."

"Your mother is right, Frau Jessie."

"No, you're both wrong. Think about it – Mary and Thomas were the sane ones last night. It was a game to them … it –"

"Jessica!" Eric said tightly. "Last night may have been a game to them, but if it happens again, if that Tyler fellow finds the captain, losing their mother won't be a game. Seeing him dragged off to a prisoner of war camp won't be a game." Eric glanced toward the captain and the two exchanged a nod of understanding. "Much as I hate to admit it, they *are* fond of him."

"Frau Jessie," the captain said gently, reaching across the table to take her hand. "It would not be my choice to leave you *und* the children like this, but can you not see there is no other way?"

Jessica was staring at her hand clasped in both of his. In her head she knew he was right – they all were – but in her heart she wished it were not so.

Yet it was so, and she raised stricken eyes to meet his, then glanced quickly to her father, her mother and back to the captain. Slowly, recognising the futility of their situation, she nodded.

Withdrawing her hand from the captain's she sat back in her chair and watched the emotions play over his face. She saw fear and anxiety, sadness and uncertainty – all the emotions she knew would be on her own face. But they had no choice. "Very well. If that's it, then that's it."

"We need to plan this properly," Eric said. "We need to consider all the options and carefully map everything out."

"He could go to Leeds," Olive suggested. "A person could get lost in a big city like Leeds."

"He wouldn't last five minutes with that accent." Her husband dismissed the idea.

"The captain can do an American accent," Jessica told them.

"Provided I am not required to speak more than one sentence," he said with a mirthless laugh.

"Look," Eric said, "I think we all agree he has to go. Let's start with that." When no one objected, he got up from the table. "For now, I promised Sam I'd accompany him in picking up a load of anthracite."

The captain pushed his chair back. "*Und* I must do the milking."

***

The first signs of approaching spring would be in the orchard, Jessica reasoned. She could tell how close spring was by the size of the tight little nubs on the branches of the trees. So after tidying the mess Tyler's men had made, after clearing up after breakfast, after hanging washing on the line in the vague hope the sun might steam some dampness from it, she drifted down to the edge of her land where it bordered Jackson's Heath.

The sky was the shade of bright blue peculiar to winter, accompanied by crisp, cold air. The garden glistened wetly in the sunlight; fresh snow made a distinctive squeaking sound as it compacted beneath her feet.

Jessica's wanderings brought her to the broken steps into what remained of the once lovely family orchard. The snow had melted in patches and the steps looked treacherous so she skirted round the edge to avoid them.

It was still possible, without much imagination, to identify where the original lines of trees had stood. Jessica paused before another tree; the tree where the captain had kissed her for the first time. He had kissed her most passionately and Jessica had responded with a fervid eagerness that Jon had never sparked within her. Indeed, her own reaction had excited her even as she chided herself for her foolish attempt to assuage her loneliness.

She reached for a branch, whip thin and nobbly with immature buds. It flexed easily as she pulled it round to examine it.

Jessica had suspected, even then, that her feelings for the German were more than the lonesome musings of a desolate, single mother approaching middle age.

Admitting to herself that she had fallen for the man did her no good. It was a fast path to grief, as Olive was wont to say, because to engage in any sort of liaison with the German airman was more than socially unacceptable – in this time of war, it was downright treasonous.

Jessica released the slender branch and watched it spring away with green suppleness. Spring was a way off yet. It would be possible for the captain to take a boat across the channel but it would be foolish to do so before spring – the narrow strip of water being perilous at the best of times.

But they couldn't wait until spring – they had to act urgently, and the chill that ran up her spine was fear: Robin Tyler would not wait until spring.

***

Later that day, they started planning. The first discussion was about who would accompany the captain, because he clearly couldn't go alone. Marg and Olive were not considered, while Sam was deemed too indispensable in the dairy. That left either Eric or Jessica.

Olive looked doubtfully at her husband. "In this weather, the cold and all, I don't think you'd get five miles up the road before you coughed yourself to death."

While the captain sat at the table, eyes down, a troubled expression on his face, the four other adults turned to Jessica.

She swallowed hard before speaking. "What about the children? I can't just leave them."

"Their grandparents are here," Marg pointed out. "So are Sam and I. You know they'll be all right."

Jessica was watching her father, noting the tightness round his mouth. "What do you think, Dad?"

Eric shrugged grumpily. "I should be the one to go. Your place –"

"You know you can't go," Olive interrupted, "so just leave off. Jessica," Olive turned to her daughter, "I think Marg is right. You're the obvious choice to go. We'll take care of the children."

"And when Robin Tyler comes snooping round?" Jessica asked. "He won't be looking for any of you – it's me he'll want to talk to."

"She's right," Eric muttered.

"Can't be helped." Sam's voice had a ring of finality about it.

"We can put around the story that you're ill – in bed with summat," Marg suggested.

Sam rose, tobacco pouch in hand. "That wouldn't deter 'im. I'm going out for a smoke and to lock up the stables. When I get back, we'll talk about when they'll go."

"Well, that's decided, then." Olive said. "Jessica'll be going. Now we need to figure out the details."

Eric nodded, "We can't afford to wait. Last night was proof of that."

"But where?" Marg added. "We still don't know *where* they'll go."

"Where doesn't matter, as long as it's away from 'ere." Eric spoke evenly, aware that his words were harsh but the truth couldn't be avoided.

Chapter 39

Among other things, white flour was not so much rationed as banned. For the twins' birthday cake, Marg was only able to buy the national flour. She sieved it through the remains of Jessica's last pair of nylon stockings to separate the bran.

"At least the chickens will enjoy that," Marg grumbled, glaring at the greyish husks and pouring them into a bag.

"Did you get enough sugar?" Jessica asked. She was leaning over Marg's shoulder as the older woman assembled the ingredients for the cake.

"Traded some eggs," she replied. "Norma Cotter's daughter is diabetic. Never use all their sugar ration, but love the eggs. She trades them whenever she can … Rubs lard over them. Reckons it 'elps preserve them."

Jessica nodded. "It would be good to get more sugar if we can. Start stocking up now for next summer. I'd like to make jam. So much of our fruit was wasted last summer."

"Hmm." Marg measured out the precious sugar. "Just enough," she said with satisfaction. "Now, butter."

"Here." Jessica had brought a plate of butter fresh-churned that morning. She put it on the bench beside the mixing bowl. Marg measured by eye and cut the amount she needed.

Normally very chatty, Marg was strangely quiet and Jessica noted the thoughtful ridge on the woman's brow and the irritable way she blew a wisp of grey hair from her face. The butter and sugar were being pummelled in her mixing bowl rather than creamed.

"Marg," Jessica was hesitant, but she couldn't let it sit. "Something getting to you today?"

"Hmm?" Marg had one sturdy arm wrapped round the mixing bowl, the other whipped the wooden spoon with uncommon aggression.

"Marg, what's wrong?"

Marg's cheeks puffed out in a gusty exhale and abruptly laying down her spoon, she continued to stare into her mixing bowl.

Jessica persisted. "Marg?"

Finally, the older woman raised her eyes and, frowning, drew a slow, deep breath. "Sit down, love."

Jessica obeyed, watching uneasily as Marg took a chair opposite. "What is it? What –?"

"Jessie, I'm worried that …" she gnawed thoughtfully at her upper lip while Jessica felt her heart move into her throat.

"You'd better tell me. Is it … it's Robin Tyler, isn't it?"

Marg shook her head. "No, but … God, Jessie. I've caused this … I 'arried and guilted you into taking Anton into your 'ome … I don't know what we'd 'ave done with 'im if you'd refused. But now … I didn't think for a minute 'e'd come to mean to so much to you – to all of us."

Jessica watched in dismay as the other woman struggled to find the right words to explain. "Just out with it, Marg," she urged, attempting a lightness she didn't feel. "You've got me all worried."

"Your father was down 'ere the other day with Anton. They seemed to be getting along all right. Not exactly amicable, mind, but they're tolerating one another."

"So?" Jessica gestured with her palms up. "That's hardly cause for concern."

"Sam'd brought a few of the papers in – the Yorkshire Post, the Sheffield Telegraph and that other one from Leeds."

"The Intelligencer?"

"No, that weren't it." She shrugged. "Not important, but the papers were sitting on the stool over there and your father started flicking through. 'E comes across this article. There's this village in France, prob'ly similar in size to Wolstone. Well, a woman from the village were accused of fraternising with the Germans."

Marg raised her eyes to meet Jessica's. "Love, she were a young woman, from a good 'ome an' all. The villagers, they dragged 'er from 'er 'ouse, shaved 'er 'ead, stripped 'er naked and paraded 'er round the town centre."

Jessica stared mutely down at her hands, clasped in her lap. Marg reached over to touch her lightly on the upper arm. "Love, do you understand? This woman … even 'er family did nowt to 'elp 'er. Just stood by with the entire village – children included, jeering 'er, throwing muck at 'er."

Finally, Jessica looked up. "That's France. Of course, neighbours are turning on each other, no one trusts anyone. But this is England. Things are different here."

"'Ow do you figure that?" Marg retracted her hand and stared at the younger woman. "They're no different 'ere."

"France is occupied by Germany. There's more ill-feeling there. Nerves are stretched to snapping point. It's not like that here."

Marg shook her head, sadly. "It's no different 'ere. People are angry and frightened. Think about all we've been through: 'ouses bombed, people killed … love, 'e's come to mean a lot to all of us … 'e's like a son to me and Sam … but I'm that worried. Honestly, if we don't get 'im out of 'ere soon … I'd 'ate to think what'll 'appen if anyone found out 'e were 'ere."

"Dad never said anything to me. If it were that bad he would've said something."

"He never said owt to you. But 'im and Anton talked about it and 'e agreed to do whatever 'e can to 'elp. We're running out of time," Marg said emphatically. "Who knows 'ow long we've got before that bastard Tyler comes sniffing round again. Your father doesn't want to worry you, but it's urgent now … we've got to do summat soon."

Jessica stared at the other woman for several heartbeats.

Marg was leaning against the table. She had creases in her face that Jessica hadn't noticed before. They were thrown into strong relief with the intensity of her anxiety.

Finally, Jessica nodded. "So, what you're saying is –"

"I'm saying …" Marg exhaled suddenly and it was like a sob. "I don't know what I'm saying. Perhaps it's already too late. Oh, Jessie, love, there's talk in Wolstone … whispers and rumours … we need to get 'im away from 'ere."

"I know – and we're going to … soon."

Suddenly Marg lurched forward and took Jessica's hands in a crushing grip. "We can't wait!" she gave Jessica's hands a quick, tight shake to emphasise her point. "Don't you see? It could already be too late! Every moment we delay could be disastrous!"

***

That afternoon, Jessica stood at the range in her kitchen. A casserole simmered gently on the hob and she was stirring it absently, a slow automatic rotation, as she rolled an idea around in her mind.

"Mummy!" Thomas shouted, as he barrelled through the door. "Mummy you'll never believe it!"

He was followed by Mary, whose expression said quite clearly that her mother *would* believe it.

"What won't I believe?" Jessica asked. She tapped the spoon on the edge of the casserole pot and rested it on a plate.

"Mummy, Granny says that Mrs Clay has made us a birthday cake."

Mary snorted. "That's not so unbelievable."

"It is, Mummy, isn't it, because we don't have the ingredients."

"It's hard to get the ingredients," Jessica said. She moved the casserole away from the heat. "Mrs Clay has been stocking up for you. You'll need to thank her very much."

Both children nodded eagerly and as Olive and Eric came into the room, Jessica added, "And it was wrong of Granny to spoil the surprise."

"What surprise?" Olive asked innocently.

"The cake," Thomas told her. "Granny, it was *supposed* to be a surprise."

"Where's the captain?" Eric interrupted, his eyes on his daughter. "I 'aven't seen 'im all afternoon."

"Well, after cutting wood for the kitchen fire," Jessica replied, "he went down to the east field to bring the cows up for the night." She glanced at the wall clock, adding, "Should be back by now, though. I told him we're having an early tea for the children's birthday."

There was a brisk knock on the garden door followed by Marg's bright, "Halloo … Anyone 'ere 'avin' a birthday today?"

Thomas and Mary bounded to the door as it opened and Sam ushered his wife through with great ceremony; she carried a plate covered by a large enamel basin, held before her like she was balancing the crown jewels on a cushion.

Suddenly the kitchen erupted into cheerful chaos. Marg placed the plate on the table and despite Mary and Thomas's pleas, she refused to unveil it just yet. "After you've 'ad your tea," she insisted, laughing and playfully slapping their questing hands away from the plate.

Jessica took Sam aside. "Where's the captain? He should've finished by now. I told him to come straight back."

"Back from where?"

"The stables, of course. It doesn't take *that* long to put the cows away for the night. Do's a favour? Pop down and tell him to hurry it up."

Sam frowned but Jessica turned away, she was taking plates out of the cupboard and trying to dodge the children who were jumping excitedly about the room.

***

Marg was rootling round in the sideboard for enough cutlery for eight people when her husband leaned over her shoulder.

"You seen Anton about?"

"Not for hours, come to think of it." She straightened, one hand full of knives, the other holding forks. "I thought 'e were upstairs."

"Jessie thinks 'e's putting the cows in."

Marg met her husband's brown gaze. He had two vertical lines between his brows. "The cows're still in the paddock," she whispered. "You don't reckon 'e's taken off, do you? Saving us the –"

"No. Not on the kids' birthday. Summat must be up."

"But what?" Marg gestured helplessly, still clutching the cutlery.

Sam rubbed his whiskery jaw. "I dunno." He exhaled. "I better go out and see what's to do."

"I'm coming with you." Jessica, said, overhearing. She untied her pinny, and dumping it on the bench, followed her steward out the door into the darkening yard.

***

Broughton Hall in the first week of February: the evenings still closed in early as the sun drew its arc toward the western horizon and dipped below the ridge of trees bordering the estate. The air was brittle and the clouds piling in the sky suggested more snow to come. Jessica stood by the eastern paddock, arms resting on the top railing as the cows milled towards the gate.

The captain was nowhere to be seen, but farm animals know routine and the cows were crowded round, waiting and swaying their heavy heads.

Sam unhooked the gate and swung it wide. Without prompting, the small herd moved as a tide towards the stables where they would be warm and secure until morning.

After the last of his girls lumbered past, Sam closed the gate and strode up to Jessica. His mouth was a grim line. As he approached, Jessica went to speak, he gave a tight, almost imperceptible shake of his head.

"Come, Missus," he said and his voice sounded incongruously cheerful. He turned purposefully in the direction of the stables and Jessica followed.

The interior, since its repair and rebuild, was like a large barn with several cordoned off areas for equipment and feed. The large open area in the centre comfortably housed the cows, with enough room to move or lie down. Towards the back were two remaining stalls. One was Spencer the pony's private quarters and the other was generally used for calving or any cow needing separation from the herd. It was currently empty and it was to this stall that Sam guided her.

Here, he turned, eyes bright and vigilant, he said, "We were being watched out there. Didn't you see the motor over by the lane and the two men sitting on the wall near the forest?"

Jessica frowned and shook her head. "No."

"It's my guess," Sam went on, talking close to her ear to avoid shouting above the lowing and shuffling of the cattle, "that Anton 'as either been caught, or 'e got wind o' summat and is 'iding out somewhere."

Jessica felt her stomach turn over. "Surely if he were caught, they would've … we'd know about it. Robin would've come banging on the door straight away."

"Aye, you'd think so, wouldn't you?" He thought for a moment. "Where d'you think Anton'd go if 'e 'ad to 'ide?"

"I've no idea. He wouldn't be familiar with …" Her voice trailed off and she looked at Sam. "The forest! Along the path to that old graveyard. We walked there one morning. I'll bet he's hiding along there somewhere. You know the path that starts at the edge of the garden beyond that old oak tree?"

"If there are men crawling around 'ere in full view, you can bet your life there'll be others hiding in the trees."

"So, what do we do?" Jessica was trying to contain the panic rising in her chest.

Sam pinched the bridge of his nose, thinking. "I don't know."

"Lucifer's balls!" Jessica cursed in frustration.

"Look," he lightly touched her arm, "let's go back to the 'ouse and act like nowt out o' the ordinary's 'appening. If 'e's not back soon we … well, we can't really go looking for 'im without rousing suspicion."

"Not if we're being watched." She made a sound of frustration and stamped her foot like a petulant child. Panic was giving way to anger – and she preferred that! "Damn them!" She slumped against a wall and chewed at her lip. "Damn them all to –" Suddenly fired with anger, she pushed away from the wall. "I'm not standing for this, Sam. This is my home – my children's birthday!"

"Missus! Jessie –" he reached for her but she was already marching past the cows.

"Jessie!" he called in alarm. "What are you doing?"

She whirled about to face him. "I've had enough, Sam! I can't move in my own bloody house for fear that Robin Tyler and his gang of thugs are going to burst in on us again."

Jessica stormed out into the descending darkness, and without pausing, marched along the path, veered past the washhouse, kitchen garden, and the house itself. Aware that if she hesitated for even a second she would lose her nerve.

She ignored the burst of festive laughter from within the house, and continued down the side, along the eastern border where the forest crept close to the craggy ancient oak tree standing vigil over the driveway.

There was no fencing or stone wall here; she knew she could

proceed directly into the forest and she did, her outdoor boots pounding the frozen ground as she plunged determinedly into the woods.

"Robin!" Jessica screamed at the full pitch of her lungs and a cloud of steam exploded from her. She fought the thick undergrowth, lifting her knees high as she stepped over weeds and crawling brambles. "Robin Tyler! I know you're here! Come out you bloody bastard!"

"Jessie!" Sam was puffing to keep up with her but she continued crashing through the undergrowth, following the tree line.

"Sam," she turned briefly, "he's in here somewhere ... I'm fed up with –"

She stopped with a gasp as a man rose up from the scrub before her.

Squinting through the dark, she immediately recognised one of the sons from Bright and Sons. "Nigel!" She exclaimed. "So you're here too!"

"Now, Mrs Barrow, we're only –"

"Don't you, *now Mrs Barrow me*!" She clouted him over the head hard enough to make her palm sting with the impact. "How ... dare... you ... stalk ... my family!" She punctuated her words with slaps that, for the most part, only connected with his raised arms as he fended off her attack.

"Jessie!" Sam caught up with her and grasped her flailing arms.

"She's bloody mad, she is!" Nigel declared, as Sam pinned her arms at her sides.

"What's all this commotion, then?"

All three turned as Robin Tyler spoke behind them. He was leaning casually against a tree, arms folded over his chest, watching the scene with a look of amusement on his face.

"What's all this commotion?" Jessica repeated, incredulous.

She fought to free herself from Sam's restraint. "What's all – Sam for Christ's sake let me go! You've got a bloody cheek spying on me and my family like this – Sam I said, *let me go!*"

"Not until –"

Jessica shrieked in fury. "*Bloody let me go!*" Adrenalin lent her strength. She twisted and wrenched out of her steward's arms, then breathing hard and trembling with the intensity of her anger, Jessica clenched her fists and marched up to Robin.

He, to her satisfaction, was no longer looking so arrogantly relaxed.

"Jessie …" Sam's voice was low, a warning tone that she waved aside.

"I will not have you spying on my children and me. Take your men and go!" Jessica spoke in clipped tones, holding her temper tightly under control. Pointing in the direction of the road to Wharferidge, she snarled, "Get off my land."

Robin pulled himself up to his full height and glared down at her. "This is not your land. This is crown forest and we suspect a fugitive's lurking about. It's –"

"*My* land," Jessica said through gritted teeth, pointing to a spot over Robin's shoulder, "extends to that stream. There! Twenty yards from where you're trespassing. Now, get *off my land*."

"I'm on official business," Robin sneered at her. "I've got every right to be here if I think the safety of our community is compromised. I can search your house if I want."

"You've already done that!" she snapped, viciously. "Or have you forgotten your midnight raid? Rousing elderly people from their beds! Terrifying children's all in a day's work for you!"

"And I'd do it again if I saw fit," Robin shouted, exasperatedly.

Jessica shrieked like a wildcat and threw herself at him, determined to rake the smug look from his face. Both Nigel and Sam leapt towards her, each grasping an arm and hauling her back. "Get off my land!" she screamed. "*Leave us alone you bastard* ... It's my children's birthday and we can't even have a little party without you stalking around!"

"Robin …" Nigel said. He sounded weary. "Come on, let's leave 'em alone."

Jessica wilted in Sam's arms. It seemed Nigel felt it too, for he dropped her arm and stepped aside, being sure to keep out of her reach. "Come on, mate," he repeated. "Nowt's going on 'ere, not tonight anyways," he added, eyeing Jessica with a wary, sidelong glance.

Jessica glared at him. "Not tonight, nor any other night except for when gangs of thugs storm into my home!"

"Jessie, enough," Sam said softly, still holding her arm. "They're going now," he said, adopting a warning tone.

"Christ, Sam, *let me go!*" Jessica shook her arm free from her steward's grasp and folded her arms belligerently across her chest. "If I see you here again, Robin Tyler, prowling through the bushes and peeping in windows, I'll report you to the authorities and see what they make of that. You won't be so pleased with yourself then!"

"Just try it!" Suddenly Tyler was before her, leaning into her face. "We're watching you for a reason – you can play Little Miss Innocent all you like, we're gonna get you and – *oomph*!"

Jessica shoved him, two hands on his chest, as hard as she could. Tyler staggered backwards and it was her turn to advance on him. "You just try it! You –"

"Come on," Sam took her arm again. "We're going, Tyler. I'm taking Jessie back to the 'ouse. You and your men'll be off this property in five minutes, got that? You reckon there's a stranger 'round 'ere? Well, I got a nice sharp pitchfork and I'm ready to defend this place if I find 'im. A man could make a mistake in the dark! So take your pack o' bullies and get gone!"

***

Jessica was still breathing hard when she and Sam returned to the stables. Both realised she was in no state to face her children so she sat on an upturned bucket, hunched into herself and trembling with the shock of her own behaviour.

Sam paced back and forth, his boots shuffling awkwardly through the straw on the floor. His flat-cap was in one hand while the other raked through his sparse hair. Finally, when Jessica felt more under control, she said, "He's still missing."

The steward nodded. "At least we know Tyler ain't got 'im – 'e wouldn't be prowling around if 'e 'ad. Still, we've –"

"What's taking you two so long?" Eric appeared in the door, silhouetted against the wintry, night sky. "The twins are eager to …" his voice faded and he stepped closer, peering into his daughter's face, then to the man standing beside her. "What's going on?"

"The captain's missing," Jessica said.

"And your daughter's just given what-for to the 'ome Guard and Robin Tyler," Sam added, and as Eric's face suffused with angry colour, the steward gave a brief synopsis of the events of the past fifteen minutes.

Fifteen minutes, Jessica thought, as she listened to Sam speaking. *Only fifteen minutes but so much has happened.*

Finally, Eric came over and put his hand on her shoulder. "Brave Jess, eh?" He gave her shoulder a brief squeeze, "I'm proud of you, love, standing up to them thugs, but now we gotta go inside. The children are asking after you and –"

"But he's still out there somewhere, Dad." She raised distraught eyes to his.

Eric sighed and drew his lips into a taut line. "I know, Jessie, but we can't go looking for him. Come on, up you get. Behave normally, don't let the children see you're upset."

"There's no 'iding the fact 'e's missing," Sam said.

"No," Eric conceded, "but let's not worry anyone. There's

nowt we can do but trust he's well-hidden and'll make his way home when he can."

Unless he takes the opportunity to leave, Jessie thought, fearfully.

"We'll tell the kids 'e's minding a sick cow or summat," Sam added.

Jessica nodded, reluctantly. She accepted her father's help getting to her feet, then the three returned to the little party in the kitchen.

Chapter 40

Jessica couldn't sleep and wasn't trying to. She'd begun her vigil by the window in her bedroom, pulling over a chair and huddling beneath a blanket to watch and wait.

He'll come home – he must! If he can possibly come home, he will ...

And even as she kept telling herself this, a dreadful thought came to her and would not be put aside: what if Robin Tyler *had* captured him and said nothing to see if she would give herself away? What if he was continuing to observe her, to build a case against her?

Alternatively, what if the captain had decided to leave? Would he really go without saying goodbye? After everything? What if an opportunity had arisen and was too good to pass up?

As dawn approached, Jessica grew more anxious, and in her anxiety, her fevered imagination created a range of scenarios, each more worrisome and impossible than its predecessor.

What if he'd been a spy all along? Flattering her into his bed? Waiting for the right moment to reveal his true, perfidious intent ...

Oh, God! She inhaled on a sob and buried her head in her hands.

Suddenly she stiffened. Holding her breath, she took her hands from her face and clutched the blanket to her throat. It wasn't a noise she heard, not exactly – it was a feeling – a skin-rippling sensation. Someone, some *thing*, was moving behind her.

Slowly, she turned.

Through the dark, she could just make out her door slowly swinging open.

Jessica's knees were trembling as she, without a sound, slipped to the floor and huddled, a formless shape, in the shadow of the wall beneath the window. Holding her breath, she waited for whatever – human or otherwise – was about to reveal itself.

Jessica's room was dark except for the pewter-grey dawn beyond the window, above where she crouched, ice cold but sweating, her heart pounding in terror.

When the outline of a man filled the space made by the open door, the effort of containing a terrified scream made her dizzy.

Silently as a cat, he slipped into her room and closed the door behind him. He was vaguely limned against the night-blue of the wall, hunched, treading lightly … he crept towards her bed.

Why am I hiding? she questioned herself. *I've let my imagination run amok, yet nothing has changed …*

Jessica watched wide-eyed with horror. The intruder leaned over her bed and found it empty. She heard him inhale in slow contemplation, and when he straightened she recognised his silhouette immediately.

Oh, God, she thought. *What was he planning to do?*

Yet, as she watched, the man dropped to sit on the edge of her bed with a sigh and a little moan that sounded like grief.

Nothing's changed, she insisted. *They've got you spooked!*

Slowly drawing in her breath, she swallowed and tried her voice. "Captain?"

It was little more than a whisper but he leapt to his feet, peering through the dark. "Frau Jessie? *Mein Schatz*, I have –" At the weary pain in his voice she didn't hesitate.

She launched herself off the floor and into his arms. He caught her, held her in a desperate embrace as she sobbed into his neck with relief and the lingering threads of fear. "I thought …" she began, but he was kissing her cheeks, her neck, her forehead.

His hands framed her face as she clung to him. "You were gone," he gasped against her temple. "I thought they had arrested you because of me."

She heard herself mumbling incoherently, clutching at him,

kissing him desperately in return.

It was a frenzied, animalistic clawing at one another in the aftermath of fear and worry, and she was insane with it.

They were both swamped by their emotions, and as panic gave way to relief, relief gave way to passion. They staggered together and tumbled onto her bed, hungrily and urgently touching one another and devouring one another.

Jessica was breathing hard, arching into him as his weight came down on her. His hands were on her face, in her hair, grasping her breasts. He was rough and demanding and she met him with a savagery of her own, pushing up his shirt to viciously rake the skin beneath.

"You frightened me," she gasped accusingly.

His breath was hot on her face. He was murmuring foreign words in her ear. A calloused hand rucked up her nightgown, his fingers grazed the sensitive skin of her inner thigh. Then, as his palm cupped her, sending an electric charge through every nerve ending, Jessica gave a sharp cry.

They didn't hear the door open.

"Jessica …" his voice was a low groan against her mouth, "Jessica …"

The bedroom door closed with a soft click.

Jessica started in fright. The captain leapt to his feet, dragging a sheet protectively over her. Adjusting his clothes, he turned to face the intruder.

The light of a single candle momentarily blinded them to the prowler's identity.

"What the bloody hell's going on here?" The candle was placed on a table and Olive stood in the middle of the room, hands on hips, mouth set in a stern line.

***

Jessica's mother had just caught her in bed with a man and

Jessica felt like a teenager. Under other circumstances she would have been mortified. But the incongruity of the situation struck her as ludicrous, for there she was, a grown woman, discovered in *flagrante delicto* with a Luftwaffe officer, and he completely cowed by a five-foot-two elderly Englishwoman.

As the captain stammered a very embarrassed and nonsensical explanation, Jessica began to laugh and once she started she couldn't stop. The floodgates holding back all the fear, the helplessness and rage of the past months burst open. She curled onto her side, hugged her pillow and allowed herself to lose control.

"I'll deal with you later," Olive snapped at the German. Eyeing him up and down she added, "At least you've still got your trousers on. That's summat, I suppose."

Beneath her mother's acerbic gaze, Jessica finally grew calm. She sat up on her bed, clutching her pillow, and mopping her damp face with the sleeve of her nightgown.

Olive stepped closer. "Just what do you think you're doing? What if the children walked in … or your father?" Olive grimaced. "God knows the truce between those two is tenuous enough without this." She flung a disdainful hand at the storm-tossed bed.

"Frau Bentley –"

"Captain," Olive levelled a steely gaze on the German. "I'm sure you've had a trying experience over the past hours – there'll be time enough to tell us all about it in the morning. Please go to your own room now."

He turned to Jessica. Her body was hot and throbbing with a need that would not be assuaged – her mother had seen to that. "Go to bed. We can talk tomorrow."

Cupping her cheek, he leaned in to kiss her forehead, despite her mother's disapproving eyes boring angry holes in his back. *"Gute Nacht, mein Schatz."*

"My God, you smell!" Jessica recoiled.

"And you didn't notice before?" Olive muttered sardonically.

"I was hiding in the woods. There were those … *die Schnecke*." He screwed his face up and Jessica laughed.

"Oh yes, slugs. Terrifying creatures – worse than Robin Tyler." She reached up to stroke his cheek, disregarding her mother's impatient snort, "Better wash before you go to bed. *Gute Nacht*."

***

Olive waited until she was alone with her daughter. She pulled a chair closer to the bed and opened her mouth to speak.

"I love him, Mum." Jessica spoke before her mother had the chance to say anything. One side of her face was lit by the flickering candle, the other remained in shadow, but she knew Olive would see the truth in her words. "I love him in a way I never loved Jon. If it's hard for you to hear that, it's even harder for me to say it."

Her mother drew in a breath. "I know. I never saw you like this with Jon – nor he with you. I wished it were different, you know." Olive's eyes looked damp in the candlelight. "From the day I met your father there was this … spark. It was a physical pull between us. We had to be together … couldn't keep our hands off each another. We married as soon as we could."

Jessica nodded and her mother went on, "I despaired that there was nothing like that between you and Jon. I wished you could experience that kind of love. Then when we arrived here and I met Anton I saw it. Immediately."

Olive put a weary hand to her forehead and sighed sadly. "Oh Jessie love, *why* did it have to be him? It's impossible and dangerous and, oh my goodness, if your father had walked in and seen –"

"We hadn't done anything."

"You were about to."

"Mum –"

"Jessie, I know you think I'm an old prude, but honestly it wouldn't have worried me at all except that your children are sleeping only yards away and your father up the hall. He'd kill the man and be a national hero for it!"

Olive fell silent, and Jessica, accepting the truth of her mother's words, picked absently at a thread unravelling from the embroidery on her nightgown.

The sickle moon had drifted beyond the frame of the window and the sky was just beginning to lighten. It was that time of early morning, just before dawn, where the trees and forest creatures shook off the night and began a new day, and it hung like a damp, pearlescent shroud over the world.

Olive drew a deep breath, patted Jessica's legs through the sheet and got up. Both women were cold and tired and Olive bent to retrieve Jessica's blanket from the floor.

"We'll talk more in the morning, love," she said, tucking the blanket round her daughter's shoulders. "We won't mention this to your father, of course, but ..." Olive looked sympathetic and she cleared her throat before going on. "He has to go. Now we know we're being watched, it's more urgent than ever."

***

"I had finished cutting wood and went to put the cows away for the night. It was only luck that I was walking along the edge of the forest instead of out in the open."

The children had been seen off on the school bus and now the six adults were standing round Jessica's kitchen while Anton filled them in on what had happened during his twelve-hour absence.

As he explained, he'd been attracted by the strong scents of the freesias growing wild along the edge of the forest. Their perfume was a signal that spring was imminent. Even though it was February, the evenings were still closing in early and despite their bright colours, the little flowers were difficult to see through the gathering dusk.

Anton had followed the path to where Jessica's mowed grass gave way to an untidy weave of ivy and undergrowth. The flowers bobbed on their grassy stems and as he'd squatted to inspect them, he'd heard the unfamiliar voices, snarling, *sotto voce* in heated disagreement.

Anton froze; the voices were close, to his left, among the trees. The tone was angry, the hissed words fired so fast he could recognise only sporadic mentions of, *Jessica Barrow* and *Sam Clay*.

"It was fortunate," Anton told his audience, "if they had not been arguing I would not have known they were there *und* would have walked right into them."

Realising they had not seen him, Anton had immediately ducked into a clump of low lying hawthorn where he crouched, ears straining and heart racing.

"That you, Jack?" At a voice behind him, he'd stopped breathing, not daring to look around. "Seen owt yet?"

Anton drew in a raspy breath. "Nope," he replied gruffly, hoping to Christ he'd adequately mimicked Sam's accent.

The other man didn't seem to notice anything amiss. He acknowledged Anton's response with a grunt, then added, "Aye well, I'll go up t'other side an' 'ave a look."

He moved away and the captain exhaled in relief, giving thanks for Tyler's men's lack of training and professionalism. Unwilling to risk his luck a second time, Anton turned and plunged deeper into the woods, veering well away from where he'd heard the voices.

The only path he was familiar with was the cemetery path. He found it easily and followed it for about ten minutes – until he was a safe distance from Broughton Hall.

Eventually, he'd scrambled under a thick dogwood tree and into a tangled clump of ivy beneath. Only then did he relax. Evening had given way to night; it was growing darker and colder. Anton was grateful he'd grabbed Jon's heavy coat off the hook by the garden door as he'd gone outside to tend the cows.

He wrapped it tighter about himself, smiling at the faint puff of lemon verbena that rose from it.

Jessica.

Anton paused in the telling of his story. He wouldn't share how the thought of her caused his heart to clench, how afraid he'd been of what may be happening back at Broughton Hall.

As he huddled on the forest floor, his mind ran amok with worry: were they raiding her house again? He considered, as he had many times, turning himself in. Would that help? He could not see how he could fix things – they would still arrest her for harbouring him all this time.

Jessica had turned his emotions inside out. He loved her in a way he'd never loved anyone – not even Natalia.

And he had loved Natalia. Until meeting Jessica, he'd thought that was all there was to it. But to be *in* love … Now, that was quite different – and it's what he felt for Jessica. Anton was in love and it was something special, some indefinable ember that glowed in his very soul.

Sometimes the desire to fold her in his arms was overwhelming, and not just for the sexual release he needed – although that was certainly part of it.

No, it was more. It was a physical hunger, a yearning to be close to her, to hold and shelter her, an instinctive masculine impulse. Was he being a chauvinist?

Smiling to himself, he accepted that the urge to defend her and provide for her family bordered on the primitive, though she was an independent woman, raising her children alone. If he wasn't feeling so emasculated by his current situation, he'd have laughed.

Instead, he exhaled in a sob of grief and burrowed further into the folds of the coat. It was going to be a long night.

Anton shook off his memories and resumed his story. He'd slept, he told them, for how long, he had no idea. It was still dark when he awoke, though the forest seemed to be trembling with anticipation of a new day; the birds and creatures were emerging from their nests and dens, stretching, yawning, ready to begin their ritual of survival.

It was the cold and damp, rising off the ground and through the coat, that had awoken him. Slowly, as the blood began to flow through his numb limbs, he crawled from beneath the tree. His hair was wet, the coat was slimy with forest debris, but his clothes were reasonably dry underneath.

Slowly, cautiously, Anton made his way back to Broughton Hall. He was relieved to find it peaceful; perhaps Tyler and his men had been only watching the house, not planning another raid.

Anton let himself in through the garden door. Going immediately up the hall, he checked the parlour first in case Frau Jessie was sleeping on the settee – as she often did. Finding the room empty, he crept upstairs and along the hall to her door.

He was cold, but he was trembling more out of fear that she'd been arrested. By now the man he'd spoken to, who'd taken him for someone called Jack, might have realised his mistake and raised the alarm.

Anton slipped into Jessica's room, edging carefully, silently, to her bedside. He could have wept when he found it empty.

"And that was when you called out," he said, and his eyes locked with Jessica's, intense as he recalled the ensuing explosion of passion between them.

***

"Ahem," Olive coughed loudly and Jessica jumped, startled as though her mother had interrupted them all over again. "Which brings us to where we are. Robin Tyler may be here any moment. He's not likely to be sent away so easily again."

"He came here? To the house?" the captain asked.

"Not exactly," Jessica replied. "I'll tell you later."

"He'll be on the warpath for certain now," Eric said, leaning back in his chair.

"We're going to have to act – fast," Jessica said, authoritatively. "The captain and I will make our own way. If Sam drives us to Leeds, we can take a train to the south. Provided the captain doesn't speak, we should be all right."

"It's a thought," Eric agreed, considering. "Then, what will you do? Come home?"

"Of course not!" Jessica glared at her father.

"She could 'ardly leave a German officer at large, could she?" Marg said with wry humour. "No telling what 'e might get up to!"

"Why not?" Eric countered stubbornly, overlooking Marg's humour. "Worried 'e might be blown up in an air raid? That Luftwaffe … Indiscriminate's what they are."

The captain gave a snort of laughter, and Eric frowned at him. "That weren't meant to be a joke."

Olive sighed. "Eric, can we please try to sort this out without the smart remarks?"

"What if Tyler comes looking for you?" Sam asked Jessica. He was leaning against the bench, a cigarette paper balanced down the seam between two fingers, shredding just the right quantity of tobacco along it. He didn't look at her as he spoke, concentrating on the quick and dextrous movement of practised fingers as they rolled the perfect shape.

"We could say I'd gone to visit my cousin Sadie in Glasgow. She's just had a baby."

"We could," Sam licked the edge of the paper and sealed his cigarette. Now, he looked up. "Bastard's likely to drive up north to bring you back."

"Still," Marg said, "it's a good option."

"I'll only be gone a few days," Jessica added.

"You shouldn't be going at all." Olive spoke softly but decisively. The five adults in the room stared at her in surprise."

"You were all for it a couple of days ago," her husband pointed out. He leaned forward. "What's changed?"

Olive didn't reply. Jessica saw her mother's eyes were on Anton and knew all too well what she was thinking.

If her father had cared to, he could've guessed by the way Jessica blushed and the captain stared at his feet. "Anyway," Eric said, ignoring everything his wife *wasn't* saying, "Jessica's the only one who can go – we've settled it," *for better or worse*, his expression said.

Marg cleared her throat. "What's the go then, eh? Sam'll drive 'em to Leeds and drop 'em at the station? They'll need overnight bags, money ... owt else?" she asked, looking round.

Jessica and Anton glanced at each other. "I do not have anything that belongs to me," he smiled. "I travel light."

At his words, Jessica felt a twinge of grief. Of course, he has nothing – even more reason for him to leave; it's just further evidence that he doesn't belong. "You have your Christmas present," she said simply, "and take as many of Jon's clothes as you need."

"What about the children?" Olive asked her daughter. "Will you say goodbye to them or ...?" She opened her hands in a questioning gesture.

"I've thought about that. It might be best if I don't tell them. We'll leave while they're at school so they're not distressed watching us go. I've asked too much of them already – I keep forgetting they're only nine – they're still babies. I can't expect them to go to school and behave as if nothing's going on at home. If we leave tomorrow, Friday, they'll have the weekend to get used to the captain being gone. Hopefully, I'll be home by Sunday night."

The room was silent as everyone digested that. Jessica heard a bird singing loudly outside in the kitchen garden and was surprised to realise spring was coming.

She felt she'd spent the year submerged beneath the sea, suddenly bursting to the surface, wide-eyed and gasping for air, to find the world was just as she'd left it, while she was changed in every way.

"So, you'll get off the train," Sam said, breaking into her thoughts. He was fumbling round in the breast pocket of his flannel shirt, looking for matches; a sure sign he considered the conversation almost over. "Where will you go from there?"

Jessica smiled, "Oh, I know exactly where we're going." She looked up at the German captain. He was leaning casually against the wall, watching her steadily. "We're going to Devon. We're going to an estate called Waterville Place."

***

All that day, Anton waited for an opportunity to speak with Jessica alone. Her confident statement that they would go to Waterville Place intrigued him, but more than that, he wanted to apologise.

After the meeting in the kitchen had broken up, he loitered in the corner while she talked to Marg about preparing a bag of food to take with them. Sam had grasped his elbow and, giving him no chance to resist, almost dragged him outside. "Milking to be done," the steward had reminded him and Anton had obediently made his way to the stables. Once there, however, Sam indicated an upturned bucket with a brusque, "Sit."

Curious, the captain obeyed and listened with a certain

pride, as Sam, on a hay bale opposite, filled him in on what had happened the night before, how Jessica had confronted Robin Tyler and attacked one of his men.

He smiled. "She is brave."

"That she is. But it's even more important now that you go, son," the older man said. "They know you're 'ere – I'm certain of it – they're closing the net on 'er. So I'm asking you, don't linger. Let 'er 'elp you to Devon or wherever it is you're going, then send 'er 'ome. If they discover 'er missin' there'll be 'ell to pay."

Anton nodded. "I will."

"Good!" Sam braced his hands on his knees and pushed up. "Let's see to the lasses, then," and with that, they began the day's chores.

Later, after Sam and the Daimler had disappeared down the lane towards Bright and Sons, the car loaded with a dozen cans of fresh milk, Anton had gone back to the kitchen garden. In recent days, he'd been digging and clearing a new plot so Jessica could plant additional summer vegetables. He was standing by, inspecting yesterday's work when he remembered Sam's words.

Tyler and his men could be watching the house at this very moment. It was unlikely they'd come up this way since that was clearly trespassing, and unless they did come this way they wouldn't see him here. But Anton was unwilling to take the chance, especially now they were preparing to leave. He sighed heavily and returned to the house.

His desire to talk with Jessica was even more urgent after learning of the way she'd attacked Tyler *und* his *Schwein*. She was both brave and foolish and he felt like a coward for hiding in the forest while she defended her home and children.

He searched all the likely locations but couldn't find her anywhere, so occupied himself in the parlour, kneeling on the hearth and sweeping out the remains of last evening's fire, scooping the ashes into a metal bucket ready for the compost heap near the kitchen garden. He was busily resetting the fire when he heard a thumping coming from upstairs.

Following the sound, he discovered Jessica, or rather Jessica's bottom half, standing on a ladder at the end of the hall, her top half swallowed by the dark mouth of the attic.

"Frau Jessie?" he called up, one hand steadying the precariously rocking ladder. Her legs were bare beneath her woollen skirt, the skin lightly freckled. She wore short socks and scuffed shoes and he smiled, thinking how Natalia would not have been seen dead without her nylons and high heels. Then again, Natalia wouldn't be climbing ladders either. He resisted the urge to caress the firm calf before his eyes and said, "What are you doing *und* can I help you with it?"

She glanced down at him. She had a scarf wrapped round her head to hold her hair back. "I put some of Jon's stuff up here. There's something I think might be useful."

Her feet moved past his face as she climbed the remaining steps on the ladder and pushed herself into the attic. Her face appeared above, peering down at him. "Come up, you can help me."

He followed her up the ladder and crawled across the dusty floor to where she sat with a small trunk. He'd seen it before, noticed it when he was hiding from Tyler a few nights ago. By the time he settled himself beside her, the lid was pushed back and Jessica was elbow deep in it, rummaging, searching for something at the bottom.

"Ah!" she said with satisfaction, extracting a box fashioned from dark, highly polished wood. It had an intricate design carved into its lid with inlays of mother-of-pearl. Anton had seen boxes like this before and felt a twinge of trepidation as she placed it on the floor between them. "They were Jon's father's," she explained, "from the Great War, but I'm certain they're in good order."

She flicked the latch and reverently raised the lid to reveal a pair of Webley Bull Dog pistols.

Anton exhaled in a whistle of appreciation as he gazed at them. The compact little guns were laid in a neat linen-lined box. Never having had the opportunity to examine such weapons up close before, he gazed at their smooth, curved grips, low-slung trigger rings and the distinctive short barrels that gave them their name. They were a magnificent pair, but … he looked at her, ridges of concern on his brow. "Why did you get these out?"

"You *do* know how to fire a gun don't you, Captain?" she asked, sardonically.

He made an impatient gesture with his hand. "What are you doing with them?"

"We can take them with us!"

He sighed. "*Meine Liebe*, we cannot take these."

"Yes, we can. They're mine."

"I mean we *should* not take them with us. We cannot use them, it could be …" he searched for the English word, unable to remember it, settled for the German, *"Katastrophal."*

She didn't understand the word so ignored it. "How else do we defend ourselves?"

"A man with a gun is more likely to be shot than a man without a gun."

"But –"

"If I am caught, regardless of whether I am armed or not, I will be taken. The only difference is whether I am taken alive or dead. If I have a gun," he jerked his chin towards the box, "it reduces my chances of remaining alive. It will be no different for you. If you are armed –"

"I thought that if we had one each –"

"No," he said gently. "It is best we are unarmed."

He saw the worry on her face and added, "I think you are

being very brave, but I am certain that we should leave them here. It is too dangerous."

Jessica sighed and nodded, reluctantly, and he thought she suddenly looked worn out. He gathered the box, secured its lid and returned it to the trunk, covering it carefully with assorted pieces of clothing and personal effects that he assumed had been her husband's.

"Now," he turned to her, "we are alone here so this is a good place to talk."

She lifted an eyebrow.

"Frau Jessie, Herr Clay told me what you did last night – the way you attacked Robin Tyler *und* the other man."

He saw her deflate as if to say, *oh that.* Continuing, he said, "*Meine Liebe*, I am proud of you, how strong you are, but you must not put yourself in danger like that – let me finish!" He saw she wanted to interrupt and took her hands from where they were picking at a fold in her skirt. Holding them between his own for emphasis, "You have children, you have responsibility. Please, do not make enemies of these men."

"I couldn't help myself," she admitted. "It was out of character for me, but … I'm exhausted, Captain. I'm frightened and tired and I'm very, *very* angry."

He sighed, sadly. "It is another reason why we must not take the guns. *Mein Gott*, I love you – I cannot allow you to be in more danger than necessary."

As he moved to stroke her face, she tilted her head so her cheek rested in his palm. "I wish it could be different," she murmured, turning to press her lips to the cup of his hand.

Drawing in a long breath, he said softly, "I want to sleep every night with you in my arms. I want to wake every morning *und* make love to you. I want us to make brothers *und* sisters for Thomas *und* Mary." He smoothed a stray tear from her cheek with the pad of his thumb. "I do not ever want to leave this place.

I want to help you care for your farm. I want to help you restore this old house." He spoke slowly and gently, his voice barely above a whisper. "We could live quietly here, but they would never allow it."

She sniffed and drew a steadying breath. "You would leave your family for this?"

"I want you for my family – you *und* your children."

"They'd never leave us alone."

"No. Not here, *und* you would not be welcome in my country either."

"It would be the same in America, or Asia or even Australia … There is nowhere we could go where we could live in peace."

He shook his head and swallowed the painful lump in his throat. "So now, *mein Schatz*, we leave tomorrow *und* we take no guns. The worst that would happen if we are discovered, is that they arrest us both. Perhaps they would release you. Or perhaps – which is the best end for us all – I will successfully escape *und* you return home safely."

He pulled her into his arms, cupping her head against his chest, and they sat quietly for a long time. Anton closed his eyes and listened to her soft breathing. He wanted to ask her about Waterville Place, but the moment of solitude, rare minutes when there was no possibility of intrusion, was too precious. He could ask later.

For now, he would just hold her.

Chapter 41

Olive realised her daughter was determined to make sure the children didn't notice anything out of the ordinary that evening. To that end, the captain was dispatched to Marg and Sam's cottage to eat with them, as had become their Thursday evening routine.

After dinner, suspecting nothing, Thomas and Mary took their school books into the parlour to practise their reading by the warmth of the fire. Eric followed them and read the local papers, while Olive helped her daughter to do the washing up.

Jessica hadn't spoken with her parents about the events planned for the next day, but Olive saw the tension round her mouth and the way her eyes appeared to focus on some point in the middle distance, thinking, checking off a mental list.

The last plate dried and put away, Olive measured five cups of milk into a saucepan and put it on the range to heat up. "Why don't you go sit in the parlour, love," she suggested, looking over her shoulder. "Listen to your children reading."

Jessica hadn't responded but she disappeared, and Olive considered how hollow the old kitchen suddenly felt.

Turning, she leaned against the range, feeling its warmth seeping through the back of her slacks. Odd how she'd never felt entirely comfortable in this room. Olive prided herself on being too pragmatic for superstitious fancies, but there were times when she could swear she was not alone, even when she knew there was no one else there.

There was also that time she thought she'd seen a black and white dog asleep on the hearth but it turned out to be just the play of light and shadow over the mat.

Suddenly the garden door opened and Olive started, hand flying to her throat. "Oh, it's you," she said. "You're back early."

Anton closed the door after him.

"I'm heating milk, would you like a cup?"

He nodded, "*Danke*."

Olive wondered why he continued to stand there watching as she measured the additional cup of milk and added it to the saucepan. He seemed unusually awkward, tired, and she raised an inquiring eyebrow. "Said your goodbyes down there, did you?" she guessed, noting by his grim expression that she was right.

He nodded again and gave a one shoulder shrug. "I ..." he paused and looked at her sadly. "I feel I am saying goodbye to family. These people have been good to me."

Olive nodded and said lightly, "I suppose it will feel strange. You've lived here almost a year. But just think, soon, God willing, you'll be back home with your *real* family."

He smiled weakly and Olive was satisfied he hadn't missed her point. "Oh, *ja*," he said. "But you will know, Frau Bentley, that the love one feels for family is different from the love one feels for ..." he paused uncertainly, his brow furrowed.

"A lover?" Olive finished for him. And when his eyes met hers, she said, "Oh yes. I know that you and Jessica were lovers, even if only briefly. My husband doesn't know, not for sure." *He'd kill you if he knew for sure.*

"Frau Jessie *und* I ..." again he paused as though he didn't know what he wanted to say.

Olive was more astute than she ordinarily let on. Again, she supplied the words, "Only the once. Thank God my daughter had the good sense to nip it in the bud before it got out of hand."

He looked confused by the idiom but she ignored it, saying, "Thank God you were not the type to ..." This time it was Olive who ran out of words.

"Force her? I am no rapist, Frau Bentley. Nor am I a barbarian, despite what you might think of my country."

"I never said you –"

"You never said but you always thought."

"That's not fair."

He shrugged. "It is not fair that any of us judges the other. Take off my uniform *und* I am a man just as any other. I enjoy the warmth of family, I like to laugh, I enjoy reading *und* helping things to grow in the garden – except Brussels sprouts. You see, I am just like anyone else, *und* I love your daughter. I would never harm her or her children. If I could, I would stay with her, help her *und* love her for the rest of our lives – the milk." He indicated the stove with a jerk of his chin. The saucepan was about to boil over.

Olive leapt to the range and removed the pan just as the milky froth surged upwards. Anton took out the cups and queued them in readiness.

She watched him surreptitiously as she poured. If she'd thought he was attractive when she first saw him, in recent weeks, he'd continued to fill out and was quite disarming. His eyes were a changeable blue-grey, intelligent and humorous, his nose was long and straight, his lips full and … Olive blushed to think of it but the word that came to mind was *sensual*. Not for the first time she wondered what it would feel like to be kissed by lips like those. *I've been reading too many of those novels.*

She couldn't blame Jessica. She must be terribly lonely, and this man has been good to her.

"I will take these with me now," he volunteered, managing to grip the handles of four cups in long fingers. "Will I come for the others?"

"No, I'll bring them," Olive said, finishing pouring and taking the pan to the sink for rinsing. Ordinarily she'd put a sprinkle of nutmeg on the milk, but they'd learned to go without once their small supply had ended. Olive missed having nutmeg on warm milk.

***

Anton toed the parlour door open and went in with the milk, pausing before Herr Bentley, who took one with a murmured, *thanks*, Jessica, who searched his eyes and smiled, and finally the children. Mary and Thomas were sharing the settee. They made room for him between them, so he obligingly squeezed in while they placed their milk on the floor, well away from their feet as they'd been taught.

"Mr Bird?" Thomas asked. "The gov'ment makes us close all our curtains at night so the Gerries can't see our lights from the sky. Could *you* see the lights when you were way up there in a plane?"

"Yes, it is true." Anton was warmed by the boy's use of the word, Gerries. Thomas evidently did not consider his house guest to be one of them. "When you are in a plane – especially over a place like this where there are no cities, light can show up very bright. When there is snow, the light is reflected *und* it is even brighter."

Thomas looked impressed. "Mummy, why do you think Mr Tyler and the other men are only coming at night? If they're looking for Mr Bird, why don't they come during the day?"

"Good question, love," Olive said. She had come in quietly and handed the captain his cup of milk, then had taken her own and sat beside her husband.

"They came that night because they wanted to surprise us," Jessica replied. "But they are there during the day too. Remember Mr Tyler was down by the gates when you got off the school bus that time?"

Thomas nodded and blew on his milk.

"They are trespassing," Mary interjected, pleased with her knowledge of the word.

Thomas nodded again, apparently satisfied, and returned to his school book.

***

It wasn't common for Mr Bird to help him collect the eggs from the hen-house in the mornings. He was usually busy with the cows. Regardless, Thomas was grateful of the help because he'd been reluctant to get out of bed this morning and was now late for the school bus.

His mother had been in a fun mood last evening and allowed him and Mary to stay up nearly an hour after their usual bedtimes. Maybe it was because he had been reading to Mr Bird from his school book.

Mr Bird seemed very quiet today. He was normally pretty chatty but this morning he wasn't. Maybe he was tired too.

The hens had done well. Thomas groped about in the straw, gathering a handful of eggs and putting them in the basket Mr Bird held. He was about to return to the house when Mr Bird suddenly pulled him into a tight hug.

"Ich werde dich vermissen," he was murmuring over Thomas's hair as the boy fitted his head neatly beneath the German captain's chin.

Thomas was bewildered, but allowed the captain a moment before the older man released him. "You have not taught me that one. What does it mean?"

"It means," Mr Bird seemed to hesitate, then said, "it means you are a good boy."

"No it doesn't," Thomas declared. He'd learned enough of the language to know that wasn't what had been said.

"Ah," Mr Bird rose to his feet, "you are too clever for me. Come, let us take the eggs to your mother."

By the time they returned to the kitchen, Mary was waiting at the door with Thomas's satchel. "We're going to miss the bus," she told him, accusingly. "Let's go."

But Mr Bird had other ideas. He grasped Mary in a quick, firm embrace and said, *"Hab einen schönen Tag."*

Thomas thought it was odd behaviour, and evidently Mary

did too. Thomas watched as his sister pulled away and stared hard into Mr Bird's eyes.

Mummy was standing by the door with a strange look on her face. Stranger still was the long look Mary gave her mother, seemingly making up her mind about something. Then the strangest thing of all: Mary kissed Mr Bird quickly on his cheek and flung herself away without saying anything to him.

"Come on, Tommy," she snapped, nudging Thomas's satchel with her toe. "Let's go."

Mary's eyes looked a bit watery and Thomas thought she might have got some soot in them from the kitchen fire. It sometimes happened if Mummy was using wood instead of briquettes. Thomas followed his sister down the drive. She was walking quickly, head down.

"Mary," Thomas did a couple of skips to catch up. "What's, *you're a good boy in German?*"

She stopped abruptly and rounded on him, "Shut up!"

Thomas's mouth fell open. "Wha —"

"Never mind, you're a *good boy*, how about, you're an *eejit*!"

***

Jessica stared out of the Daimler's window as Sam slowly navigated the car through the streets of Leeds. Rows of houses, neat lines of suburbia, would unexpectedly give way to an impossible devastation. The alleys, buildings and lanes that had formed the comfortable landmarks of her childhood were virtually unrecognisable, many were unpassable, piled with rubble and indistinguishable mounds of blackened bricks and twisted metal.

Then just as quickly, the orderly lines returned, vegetables grew in the front gardens, washing was strung across the lanes.

There were streets where only a single house remained — its blacked-out windows seemed bewildered and apologetic beside its collapsed neighbours. Here a single wall teetered precariously, there an upstairs bedroom appeared untouched: bed, dressing-table, slippers on the mat, displayed like a theatre set, the missing fourth wall offering audiences a sly glimpse into a family's private life.

Jessica had been very familiar with the area surrounding the station – her parents' home and shop being in the vicinity. But as the car bounced over pot holes and obstructions, she struggled to reconcile the tidy neighbourhood of memory with the splinters of glass and tile, the webs of metal wrought by heat and violence, and piles of smashed bricks. And lying like a blanket over everything was a thick mantle of reddish grey dust.

Brick dust: ruined homes and shattered lives.

The morning was sunny, promising a pleasant winter's day. As they passed a street that had evidently attracted considerable Luftwaffe attention, children played in the rubble, picking their way over and through it, on their way to school, hiding from one another, laughing.

For them, it was an adventure. Their parents were emerging, blinking in the sunlight from the black caverns of cellars, the only habitable parts of their former homes. These small underground spaces were previously deemed suitable only for rats or storage. Now, they were dank rooms crammed with the most valuable, or serviceable, items a family could salvage.

The captain was silent. Sam had felt it best that he remained out of sight, at least until they had arrived in Leeds where unfamiliar faces didn't draw so much attention. The German was curled in the Daimler's spacious back seat footwell, beneath Jessica's feet, with a blanket over him. Sam had told Jessica to pull the blanket over her knees. No one carelessly glancing into the car would notice the mound beneath her feet.

Once they were in the thick of Leeds, a young man dressed in simple clothes, like everyone else, would not be out of place –

they'd probably assume he was a young soldier on leave, visiting his sweetheart.

"*Whew*," Sam whistled through his teeth. "You wouldn't think they got out of it lightly 'ere but apparently they did. They reckoned Sheffield an' Manchester copped it worse."

"I couldn't imagine anything worse than this," Jessica murmured.

"At least the trains are still running 'ere." Sam craned his neck to see round a lorry in front of them. "They still 'aven't repaired York Station since it were bombed out."

Jessica felt the captain move uncomfortably and just for an instant, the old resentment of him rose to the surface.

"You can come out now, Captain." Her tone was sharp but she resisted the urge to add, *and inspect your handiwork*. She moved her legs aside; he crawled out and slid onto the seat beside her.

***

Anton didn't speak. He just breathed and sat looking out of the car window; there was nothing he could say. To be at ground level, amid the destruction his work had wrought, was a surreal experience. If he'd been able to articulate his thoughts, he'd have said that this destruction was no different from the destruction he'd witnessed in his own country. He'd have pointed out that patched clothing and flapping-soled shoes was a uniform common to children across Europe. That the adults here wore the same grey, weary expressions as those in Berlin, Kessel and Hamburg.

But he, in a previous life, was Hauptmann Anton Vogel, and he had, with his own hand, released the bombs that had dismantled these peoples' lives. He was looking directly into the faces of children whose futures were altered as night after night, he had prowled the skies above their beds.

It was a sobering thought.

The politicians will eventually announce a victor; the history books will record the stories of bravery and stoicism. But here, at street level, there were no winners and bravery was just endurance in another guise.

Anton did not have the words to express his thoughts, and the man and woman in the car with him wouldn't have wanted to hear them if he did.

So, he sat wide-eyed and mute, as Herr Clay steered the car across the River Aire and into the crowds along the approach to Leeds City Station. From here, the car slowly crawled along, slower than walking pace, then slower still.

Ten minutes … fifteen, twenty minutes of going nowhere, and eventually Herr Clay turned to look over his shoulder, arm stretched along the back of the seat. "Missus, I reckon you both might be better off walking from 'ere. Summat's blocking the road – accident p'raps. What do you think?"

Frau Jessie had seemed increasingly fidgety in the back seat. "Anything's better than this snail's pace," she snapped. "Captain? You ready? Remember," she added curtly, unnecessarily, "don't say a word – even to me if there's anyone within earshot!"

Anton nodded, acquiescent although the bitterness in her tone made him want to shout, *You're doing this to my country too!* But he held his tongue, and since the car was already at a standstill, he opened the door to the traffic and stepped out into the central business district of one of the largest cities in England.

Looking about, a German fighter pilot amid the chaos and devastation he'd helped to create, he did not feel proud, but he would not feel ashamed either. Feeling slightly dazed, Anton waited, on the footpath for Jessica.

She was still in the car, leaning over the seat, talking to her steward and the thought crossed his mind that she could so easily slam the car door shut and leave him there.

For a moment, he held his breath and then he saw her give

the man's shoulder a friendly squeeze before she grabbed the rucksack she'd brought with her and climbed out onto the road.

Sam wound down the car's window and leaned out. "Lad, c'mere."

Anton braced his forearms on the window-sill and leaned into the car. He noticed immediately the dampness round the old man's eyes.

"You've come to mean a lot to us, Anton," Herr Clay said. His voice was rough and his throat worked as he swallowed. "To all of us – especially the Missus there," he added, jerking his chin to where Jessica stood looking anxiously up and down the road. "You've been good to 'er and you've been like a son to Marg and me, a father them children don't 'ave. We'll all miss you but we need to part as enemies. When you get back to your own country, you do as they tell you. Don't be an 'ero, don't try to stand against them. You go back and do your duty and you be safe."

The old man sniffed and gulped. "An' when all this's over and done, you find some way of lettin' us know you're all right." He gripped Anton's hand where it hung loosely over the sill of the car. "Do as they tell you, you 'ear me, now? You be safe!"

Anton nodded and felt the emotion rise in his own chest. He swallowed hard. The man suddenly gripped his hand, put it to his lips and pressed a firm kiss to it, before almost flinging the hand away in his grief. "Go!" he said. "Go now and take care of 'er."

A break had opened in the traffic ahead and as the car behind used its horn, Sam acknowledged the driver with a quick wave and roughly shoved the Daimler into gear.

It lurched forward and Sam drove on without another glance.

Chapter 42

It was a short walk up Boar Lane to the station. Jessica walked briskly, eyes down. The captain, carrying the rucksack, walked silently beside her. To any casual onlooker, they would present as an energetic couple from the country attending to business in the city. She was slim and pretty, with a cascade of auburn hair and a light step. He was only an inch or two taller but carried himself in an upright fashion that implied strength and a military background.

Look more closely and the observer would see the creases etched into the young woman's face, how her mouth was set in a grim line, how faded were her blouse and woollen slacks, the patches in the coat draped over her arm and the scuffed walking shoes. The young man at her side was handsome although his expression was equally bleak, his eyes a dull grey-blue with traces of sadness round them.

But no casual onlooker would notice this couple, for everyone on that street walked with same weary resignation, wore the same patched and faded clothes, with the same disenchanted mien. All had suffered hardship and loss.

So, Jessica and Anton moved freely, blending with the foot traffic and drawing no particular attention, on their way to the station.

Once inside, she hissed, "Stay close," and they stood among the crowd and gazed up at the timetable. She felt him edge closer to her side. They'd just missed a train so the next one would have to do. Jessica read through the list of stops: Wakefield, Sheffield, Derby, Leicester and on to London.

"The next train doesn't leave until half past one." She glanced at him, adding, "Nearly four hours away."

Now he looked at her and gave a rueful smile. There was something in his expression and she felt a pang of contrition.

"Look," she said softly, reaching for his hand, "I'm sorry. I was very short with you before. It was the shock of seeing it all … I shouldn't blame you."

He leaned close to her hair, pressed his mouth to her ear, "But Frau Jessie," he whispered, his breath warm on her neck, "I have contributed to this. You should blame me, just as I would blame you if we were standing in Pariser Platz."

Pulling back, she searched his face for a glimmer of his usual humour. It wasn't there, but he gave his one-shouldered shrug and planted a quick, defiant kiss on her mouth.

"You're right, I suppose." She smiled at him and spoke in a bright voice, "Well, let's buy our tickets."

They were holding hands while they queued at the ticket office. At length, a woman wearing too much rouge on her cheeks called, "Next," in a weary voice. The counter was highly polished, the effect of thousands of coat sleeves. Jessica added her own as she leaned on it and asked to buy two tickets for the next train to London.

"Yer'll be waiting a while," the woman said. She said *waiting* in the distinctly Lancastrian way: hanging on the 'g' at the end of 'waiting'.

"That's all right," Jessica assured the woman. "We'll have a cup of tea –"

"Yer'll be wanting more'n a cuppa, love. Next train's fully booked – all them troops what's going back t'front. Not even standing room left."

"But …" Jessica shot a glance at the captain waiting quietly at her shoulder. "My husband here, he's with the …" she couldn't bring herself to say air force, "the army … needs to get to London as soon as –"

"Yer not 'earing me, love. Fully booked. 'E's not t'only fella lining up t'take 'is shot at Mr 'itler. I can sell yer a couple fer t'morra – departing ten aft' eight. Got nowt earlier."

Jessica thought quickly. The woman's accent gave her an idea. "What if we caught a train to Manchester and went from –"

"Nope. It's t'overflow from York station we got 'ere. They're all going to Manchester or coming 'ere. York Station … part of it's still out of action so …" The ticket seller shrugged and glanced pointedly over Jessica's shoulder, "If yer can't make up yer mind, at least stand aside an' let me see't next customer."

Forced into making a quick decision and realising that the tickets for the following day would probably sell quickly, Jessica purchased two seats on the 8.10, Saturday morning train to London.

Outside on the street, she faced the captain, a little bewildered and uncertain of their next move. Neither had foreseen this circumstance, though Jessica berated herself. "I should've known," she grumbled. "It was in the papers – York Station bombed."

"It cannot be helped." The captain squinted into the sunlight. "We need somewhere to wait."

She nodded, thinking. "Mum and Dad's shop isn't far from here."

"Was it not destroyed?"

"I'm pretty sure Mum said most of the stock had been stored in the basement. That means something's still there."

"The stock?" He looked confused.

"In the storeroom," she explained. "Even if the shop isn't standing, the storeroom will be all right. It's not big, but we could stay there overnight. We'd be safe, hidden."

While they stood on the footpath, a young woman passing by glanced admiringly at the captain.

Yes, Jessica thought, *he was attractive with his blue eyes and tousled hair, but he was also the woman's enemy – had she known it – and according to the authorities, highly dangerous.* Jessica snuffed a laugh.

It was nearing midday and the sky was a clear, bright blue with small, puffy clouds floating innocuously high. But a cool breeze was picking up – a reminder that spring had not yet arrived. Jessica shivered and taking his hand, said, "Come on. Let me show you where I grew up."

***

Jessica led a zigzag path along the backstreets, heading away from the station. Anton looked about with interest – these houses were vastly different from those of his own country. These were double, occasionally, triple-storey brick structures, lined up in neat rows with non-descript façades and empty-eyed windows.

People living in the big cities of Anton's country tended to inhabit apartments in large, gothic style buildings. He thought this English housing was dated and a waste of space, but he wouldn't say so to Jessica, whose step had quickened as she trotted lightly across the road.

"It's just up here," she told him. "On the corner." He wondered at her eagerness to see her parents' house given that it would almost certainly be a ruin.

And then suddenly they were on the flagstone footpath before what had once been a red brick shop. Jessica visibly deflated and she stared at the remains of the building, with its window boarded up with salvaged timber.

The front door was in place, and the wall adjoining a property to the left – an abandoned bakery – appeared solid and unharmed. The wall on the right, overlooking a side street, was a pile of crumbling, blackened bricks.

Someone, probably the authorities, had secured the property for safety purposes, but it was otherwise exactly as Olive and Eric had left it, some two months ago.

***

Jessica glanced up the street. But for an elderly woman walking a dog at the far end, there was no one around. Squaring her shoulders, she said, "There used to be a spare key hidden in the garden." Approaching the door, they saw the lock was broken and Jessica added, "Don't think we'll be needing it."

She tried to open the door but it seemed to be wedged tight against its broken frame. The captain lent his shoulder to it as Jessica shoved and finally it gave with a sharp creak and splintering of wood. The bell above it, that over the years had announced countless customers, was strangely intact. It gave an incongruously cheerful jangle as they stepped in to what remained of Eric's livelihood.

Fine ash and brick dust swirled about their feet and the bell tinkled, as the captain pushed the door to behind them. They moved into the room.

Jessica stared dismally at the blackened beams and collapsed shelving. Dust and ash created a ghostly world of grey emptiness, while a gaping hole in the ceiling allowed a crepuscular beam to filter through the motes floating in the air. It splashed in a weak puddle on the floor.

A cool, spring breeze whistled through an open wound in the wall. The side street beyond was visible; a bus lumbered by.

"Do you think people have been in here?" the captain asked.

"Hard to say." She jerked her head towards the bare shelves lining the walls. "Dad kept those well-stocked. And those," she added, indicating the display cases that had served as the main counter. "He kept a lot of stock in the storeroom, and he said he'd taken most of the rest down from the shelves after the explosion. Everything else he took to our place."

The captain nodded and she wondered abstractedly if he realised she'd referred to Broughton Hall as *our place*. It seemed natural, but was of no consequence anyway.

"What is through there?" He was pointing towards a charred

wooden door behind the counter, which was hanging by a single hinge.

"That was where we lived. It leads into the kitchen and sitting room. The bedrooms are upstairs ..." Jessica went over and gingerly moved the door to peer round it.

The kitchen was relatively intact, and the sitting room beyond, but she saw the burnt remains of the staircase. The landing at the top was entirely gone and the fire had evidently destroyed the roof, for the afternoon sky could be seen through its blackened ribs.

"The bedrooms *used* to be upstairs."

She sighed sadly and he touched her arm gently. "Frau Jessie ... I am –"

"Don't say you're sorry, Captain," she snapped. "As you said before – this is war. This is what happens." She turned and slid past him.

The floor was gritty beneath her feet as she shuffled about, taking in the blackened remains of her parents' lives.

"Where is this storeroom?" he asked suddenly. "Should we –"

He broke off at a brisk knock on the front door and a sprightly voice called, "*Yoo hoo!*"

Jessica leapt in fright, hands flying to her mouth, eyes wide.

"Hello in there!" the woman persisted, "This is private property ye know."

There came the sound of a grunt; the door shuddered as the woman gave it a shove and suddenly the bell announced she was in the shop.

She was a rotund woman with crêpey skin and the fine lines typical of a smoker round her lips. Under one arm she held a Scottie dog and Jessica recognised her as the woman she'd seen up the street earlier. She also recognised her as one of Olive's friends and the neighbourhood's most unremitting gossip.

Jessica's heart sank, but realising there was no escape, she boldly faced the intruder. "Hello, Mrs Markham."

The woman gazed short-sightedly at her. "Tha' you, Jessie?"

Jessica stepped closer and Mrs Markham's face lit up, "Oh, 'ullo, love!" she cried and suddenly the little dog was squashed between the two women as Mrs Markham caught Jessica in an enthusiastic embrace.

It squeaked and the woman stepped back quickly, "By gum, it's good t'see ye."

Behind her, the breeze blew through the open door setting a cloud of choking dust and ash into a mini tornado. "Eeyup, love," Mrs Markham spoke to the captain, "Tha' wind's fair parky. Put wood in't 'ole, aye?"

Under any other circumstances, Jessica would have laughed at the captain's expression. It was a mixture of confusion and alarm as Mrs Markham, whether by cunning or habit, slipped into the local dialect.

Jessica suspected the former – people were inordinately suspicious of strangers these days and Mrs Markham may be the local bletherer but she was no fool. Jessica quickly moved to shut the door, saying above the jangling bell, "Oh, this is Anthony – my cousin … Dad's side … from up Inverness way."

"Oh, aye?" Mrs Markham regarded the captain curiously. "Gradely one, int 'e? Yer da's family, eh?"

The captain levelled his most charming smile on the older woman, stepped forwards and politely held out his hand, "Pleased to meet you, ma'am."

Mrs Markham all but blushed like a teenager. She continued to hold the German's hand, openly scrutinising his face. "Nowt o' yer da in 'im what ah can see. An' tha' accent in't like no Scot ah've ever 'eard."

"Anthony spent time in Boston – with my cousin Sadie's friend." Jessica grimaced internally at the ridiculousness of her explanation.

Finally managing to extract his hand from Mrs Markham's grip, the captain stepped back and grinned.

God, he's gorgeous when he does that, Jessica thought. And at Mrs Markham's girlish giggle, Jessica realised the captain was deliberately distracting the older woman.

"Anthony's on his way home," Jessica supplied, "On leave from the er … army." She clamped her mouth shut. *Don't waffle*, she told herself.

"Oh aye?"

"Aye," the captain confirmed, imitating Sam's tone.

"Well, good luck, t'ye lad. Sooner we gi' tha' fugglin' bugger o'er't wa'er a good skelpin' t' be'er we'll all be!"

Despite not understanding a word the woman said, the captain nodded solemnly and muttered, "Oh, aye."

Mrs Markham looked Jessica up and down. "You're lookin' well, Jessie, all things considered." She glanced at the captain again, eyes narrowing, and murmured, "Cousins eh? Right, well … yer 'eadin' back t'old 'ouse o' yers?"

Nodding vigorously, Jessica said, "Oh yes. Anthony and I've had a couple of errands to run in Leeds and, er, Dad asked us to pop in … just to check on the place."

Mrs Markham looked archly at the vacant shelves. "Nowt much left, eh? Couldn't imagine why Eric'd think there were owt to check."

Jessica shrugged. She could feel the captain's discomfort beneath Mrs Markham's hawkish gaze. He smiled again, but to lesser effect this time and Mrs Markham said, "Hmm, wouldn't 'ave taken ye fer a Scot."

"Well, then, Mrs Markham," Jessica said brightly, "hate to hold you up." Jessica moved towards the door.

The captain stepped over a fallen beam and pulled the door open, the little bell tinkled merrily.

All but shoved onto the footpath, Mrs Markham hoicked her dog further under her arm and looked back at Jessica. "E's a right winnin' lad, tha' one, Jessie, love," she said with a nod towards the shop, "an' ye can put out word 'e's yer cousin an' all but it won't do ye no good. No'ne could deny yer findin' 'appiness where ye can. God knows Jon's been gone awhile now, eh? But if ye're 'iding th'fact 'e's a Yank – 'e might as well *be* a Yank an' tha' lot ain't too popular 'round 'ere. I'd be sendin' 'im on 'is way soon as ye can, aye?"

"Thank you, Mrs Markham." Jessica was already back in the shop, edging the door closed. "In that case it may be best if you don't say anything about him."

"Aye, love, you know me," Mrs Markham made a gesture, as though buttoning her mouth. "Steel trap."

Jessica smiled and closed the door. The bell jangled as Jessica muttered, "Steel trap, like hell!"

"She is a …" the captain frowned, unable to think of the word.

"She's a gossip," Jessica said.

"She does not believe I am American."

Jessica snorted. "Probably not, and she doesn't believe you're my Scottish cousin either. She thinks we're lying … suspects we're up to something."

The captain smiled ruefully. "She is right."

Jessica was leaning against a display case. Grunting irritably, she pushed away from the rickety cabinet. "You're not helping. She'll have people crawling all round here in no time. Come on …" she said, and he followed as she hurriedly stepped over shattered bricks and a chair with only two legs.

The counter had been a long, L-shaped cabinet with register and display case situated at the bottom horizontal of the L. Along the top had been trays, angled to display rows of ladies', men's and children's singlets, socks and underwear. At one time, nylon stockings and make-up had also been displayed here, beside spools of cotton, cards of wool, pins, sewing kits and knitting needles.

The longer vertical line had formed a longer display case with tinned vegetables and preserves, packets of biscuits and jars of sweets arrayed within. Other trays had contained tinned chocolates and trinkets but in the last year or so, due to rationing, these displays had rapidly dwindled and Eric had been unable to replenish much of his stock.

Along the wall behind the counter, was a hip high bench. Above it was shelving, and below were more cupboards. It was one of these cupboards Jessica went to now. Crouching before it, she opened the twin doors and peered in.

The captain, standing behind her, leaned over her shoulder. "It is empty."

Jessica smiled cunningly. "That's what you're meant to think." She opened the cupboard doors wide, and explained, "When Mum and Dad bought this place, before they built the shop and the house upstairs, there was a really old house here – some merchant's place."

She hooked her fingers under the overhanging lip of the cupboard's floor. "The original house'd been built years ago – sixteenth century. It was virtually a ruin, which they planned to pull down so they could build on the land."

While she'd been talking, the captain squatted beside her and could see that the floor of the cupboard was hinged. "Where we're sitting now was about where a fireplace had been. When the old house was knocked down," Jessica continued, "they found this underneath the hearth."

She gave a push and the floor of the cupboard lifted like the lid on a trunk. "Pass me that, will you?" She indicated a lump of wood that turned out to be a chair leg. The captain complied and Jessica used it to prop open the lid, then she sat back, gesturing for him to look in the cavity.

The captain peered into the black hole beneath the cupboard. "*Was ist das?*"

Jessica grinned at him. "It's a priest hole. Dad thought it would be a secure way of storing cash and stock, so he had the cupboards built over it. This cupboard has a false floor. Underneath is the perfect hiding place."

The captain stared at her. "What is this priest hole? I have not heard of such a thing."

"I'll explain later. For now, we need to hide in it before Mrs Markham sends the entire Leeds constabulary over."

"Is it large enough? It does not look large."

"It'll be a tight squeeze – lucky neither of us is big. I'll go first. There's a hurricane lamp and matches – Dad put stuff in there in case he couldn't make it to the bomb shelter out the back. Hop out the way."

***

Anton edged aside and watched as Jessica reversed into the cupboard. "Best to go backwards," she advised. "Find the ladder with your feet."

She quickly disappeared into the gaping hole. After a moment, he heard a metallic rattle followed by the strike of a match and suddenly the small room beneath the cupboard was lit by a jumping yellow light. "Come on down, Captain!"

"*Jawohl.*" He turned as Jessica had done and slid his legs over the edge and into the hole. Initially his feet found only air; with a guiding nudge from Jessica's hand, he located the ladder. That was all he needed and soon he was standing on an uneven bricked floor some six feet below the opening.

It was indeed a small space, a square measuring no more than eight feet by eight feet. Anton watched as Jessica climbed back up the ladder and pulled the cupboard doors to, but not closed. "There is no airflow down here," she explained. "If someone comes, we can quickly shut the cupboard doors, pull the floor down and blow out the lantern. They'll never know we're here."

"*Wie genial*," he breathed in wonder. "This is very clever."

"Well, it was a matter of life or death back in the fifteen hundreds. Now," she held the lamp up and the shadows fled to the corners of the small room, "let's see what we have here."

The light of the lamp revealed shelves stacked with a variety of cans and glass jars. Jessica peered closer and read the labels. "Apples, potatoes, plums, cabbage ..."

"*Und* this," he held a can-opener under the light."

"Perfect! We'll be needing that."

Beside her, the captain drew in his breath. "Frau Jessie?"

"Hmm?" she responded absently. "Oh my – strawberry jam!"

"Frau Jessie," he repeated. "I think you should tell me why we are going to Devon. Why do we not go to Dover or another port? Something that is closer to Calais?"

Jessica slid a sly look in his direction, a tin of jam in her hand. "We're going to Devon," she said, with a secret smile, "because Alexandra Broughton told me to go there."

Chapter 43

Jessica and Anton sat side by side on the floor of the priest hole, backs propped against the brick wall, with a row of shelves over their heads. The floorboards of the shop above were their ceiling; thin threads of grey light filtered down to them. They were wrapped in their coats and sharing the sandwiches Jessica had brought from home.

At the bottom of her rucksack, beneath where the packet of sandwiches had rested, lay the journal. Dusting the last breadcrumbs from her hands, Jessica now extracted the old book and turned to a page towards the end of it, marked by one of the pictures from Albert's envelope.

"Should you have brought this?" the captain asked. "What if it is lost?"

"I thought of that, but I've finished reading it and there are sections we might need to refer to."

"All right, so then you must tell me, why are we going to Devon?"

"Because there's an entry in the journal where Alexandra talks about the smugglers on the coast of Devon. This is the part I want to read to you. Look!" Her eyes grew bright and she shifted to kneel before him. "You need to understand the map of Devon. It has water on two sides – the Bristol Channel on the north, and the English Channel on the south. Alexandra's stepbrother, Patrick, his home was south of Exeter, near Sidmouth, on the coast."

The captain nodded patiently and Jessica realised he was probably very familiar with the English coastline – no doubt he'd flown over it more times than he could number.

"Apparently," she went on, "there are caves near Sidmouth where they kept these boats called gigs. They're what the smugglers used."

Now, she held up the card from the collection of pictures Albert had given her. The picture showed a short, pebbly beach beneath a line of cliffs. On the water, not far out, was a small wooden boat with a single mast. Its sails were furled, and it rode at anchor on the tossing waves of a grey sea.

"See this?" Jessica asked.

She gave the captain time to examine the picture before she turned it over.

There was writing on the back. The ink was faded but still legible.

Smuggler's gig. Sidmouth, 1834

Jessica waited as the captain read the inscription and sat silently, apparently thinking. "But that was so long ago," he said at last. "This was –"

"We are in the middle of a war, Captain, if you haven't noticed," she grinned at him. "What happens during war? Smuggling!" she responded excitedly to her own question. "We know that there are smuggled goods entering Britain from France all the time. Doesn't it stand to reason that the same routes would be used? And if they are …" she gestured to indicate an inevitable conclusion.

"You are thinking …"

She grinned. "I'm thinking that one of these boats could take you to France!" She moved to settle more comfortably beside him. He looked doubtful but seemed to be considering her words.

Opening the journal at the place she'd marked with the card, she said, "I found this …it's one of the last entries Alexandra wrote. She must've been staying at her stepbrother's house in Devon – he was the earl and from the description his place was a mansion. Now listen, I'll read it to you."

I saw her last night. It was at the Coachman's Rest, an inn in Astor with a reputation for whispered conversations and shady business. She was there: Kat Wheeler. I recognised her from Sylvie's wedding, although she had changed over the years and was now rather plump. I would know her anywhere by the hatred in her eyes whenever she looked at me.

Well, it's hardly my fault! I know Patrick dallied with her many years ago, and after he put her aside she hated everyone, however loosely connected with him.

Certainly, her father bears no such grudge. John Wheeler loves Patrick as an overlord and friend. I think Patrick respects him in return. There is much private discussion between the two during our visits to the inn, and a group of scraggy-looking fishermen regularly join in.

These men, local rumour has it, are engaged in an obscure kind of fishing business. One that, by prior agreement, can provide certain shipments: quality brandy or cigars for the discerning gentleman, silks and Venetian lace for the ladies.

And while I know Patrick is not directly involved, he turns a blind eye to his tenants' alternative industries, "A man must earn a living," he says. "Not everyone enjoys the privileges we do."

John Wheeler's devotion to me stems from one incident. John came banging on the servants' door one evening. The excise men, he told me, wild-eyed and panicked, as we sat in the kitchen – much to Patrick's cook, Monsieur Chartrain's disdain – were chasing him down. It would be all over for him, he said. A dance at the end of a rope for sure!

Patrick was abroad and not expected home for the night, but I acted decisively – I knew instinctively what he would have done.

After hiding John beneath a bench in the observatory, I waited in the parlour for the message from the butler, Leonard.

It came soon enough. The excise men were at the door wishing to speak with the earl.

That evening, I charmed and entertained as never before, though my knees trembled beneath the dining table and my clammy hands could barely hold my wine glass. After the excise men had eaten like a plague of locusts and drank their fill, they performed a rather apathetic search of the guest wing.

When they expressed ridiculously overblown appreciation for Patrick's brandy, I had Leonard bring a cask up from the cellar for them. They rode away, all smiles and satisfied that they had done their duty.

Since that night, John Wheeler has been my unwavering champion. So much so that I have been granted status as a 'friend'. Before leaving Waterville that night, he leaned close to my ear and said, Dear lady, you have proven yourself most gracious, most daring. If you are ever in need of assistance from me or one of my associates, you must only say these words, "I expect to see the early crocuses." Upon recognition, the associate will reply, "I don't think they are out yet."

Over the years, I have never had cause to call upon the crocuses, although I have, from time to time, overheard them mentioned – particularly in the Coachman's Rest. I will never forget John's words to me though, for if I have not ever needed to say them, there are others who will. So, I consign them to memory and record them on this page now.

Jessica looked expectedly up at him. "That's why we're going to Waterville Place. The way Alexandra wrote that – I'm sure she was writing that information for me – telling me there'll be smugglers in the district. The hard part'll be finding them."

The captain nodded thoughtfully. "This would seem … " he paused thoughtfully. "It seems how you would say a long bow, *ja?*"

Jessica drew back. "What do you mean, a long bow? It's clear she's talking to me. This whole journal has been for me. I'm the lady she has mentioned several times."

He shrugged one shoulder. "I agree, but I am not certain that – "

"Captain, I *am* certain and that's why we're going to Devon."

His expression was doubtful but he didn't persist. Instead he said, "Even so, Alexandra would not know if the trade continued to this day. We do not either."

"That's true, Captain," Jessica said, closing the journal, "but it probably is, and it's our best chance."

She fell silent for a few minutes, thinking. Then, "I find it strange, rather unnerving that I see Alexandra. And she's aware of it too – enough to write to me. And she *is* writing to me, I'm convinced of it."

He shrugged, and she went on, "Sometimes I feel we are small parts in a large machine – the parts of a plan greater than ourselves. Do you think that's strange?"

Anton shook his head. "That you see ghosts? You are asking a German this? I do not think it strange. There are many rumours in Germany about secret government experiments that –"

Jessica waved her hand dismissively. "Oh, we've all heard those stories … they're not strange, they're barbaric! Horrible experiments conducted on –"

"No!" he cut her off, irritably. "This is different. These are experiments that are …" he gestured impatiently. "It is rumoured that there is a machine called *die Glocke* – in English this means *the bell*. There are men of science working on this … it is *eine Wunderwaffe.*"

"All right. What is a vunder vaffer?"

"It means, literally, wonder weapon."

Jessica blithely raised her eyebrows. "Really?"

"Do not look like that! My government is spending much money on this *Wunderwaffe*. According to the rumours, the men of science have built a machine that moves through time."

She stared hard at him and felt the smile tugging at her mouth. "You really believe this? A time machine?" He glanced at the floor and she gave his arm a playful thump. "You do, don't you?"

He flushed slightly and looked sheepish. "Well, you are the one believing in messages from a girl who lived more than a hundred years ago."

Jessica sniffed. "*Touché*."

She hugged her knees, feeling the captain's arm go around her shoulders. She leaned into him. His breath was warm on her hair.

"Captain, none of this is coming out right but I *must* believe. I have to because otherwise, I wouldn't have a clue what to do next."

"I know what you are saying," he whispered. "*Und* I know we are here to protect your family *und* help me find my way home – even though you will never know if we have been successful."

She lifted her head to look at him and he lowered his gaze to hers as she spoke. "I'll have no way of gauging our success. This journey is dangerous and I'll never know if –"

He kissed her, hard and demanding. She curled further into him, the moment sweeping her away. In the privacy of this small room, there were no children to consider, no frowning parents, and the warmth of her desire for him began low in her stomach and bloomed out like ripples on a pond.

Raising his head, he whispered, "If I can get a message to you, I will."

"But –" she began, but he was kissing her again, a hand cupping her jaw, his arm holding her to his chest.

Suddenly he broke away.

"Capt –"

"*Ruhig!*" he whispered suddenly, pressing his fingers to her lips. "*Shh!*"

Holding their breaths, they strained their ears for a repeat of the sound the captain had heard. Through the silence, the creaking protest of the damaged door and the jangling bell filtered through to them down in the priest hole.

"Blast!" Jessica cursed, but the captain was already up the ladder, soundless as a shadow, pulling the cupboard doors together.

Standing below, holding the lantern, Jessica's recent rush of warm passion gave way to cold, fearful adrenalin. "Hurry!" she whispered, reaching up as he passed her the chair leg they'd used to prop up the cupboard floor.

She waited only long enough for his feet to be back on the floor before she ever so gently lifted the glass cover on the lamp and blew out the flame.

***

The darkness swallowed them instantly. Jessica still held the lamp by its handle and the puff of smoke from its extinguished wick drifted in the air.

Please don't let them smell it!

Not daring to move, Jessica and the captain stood stock still in the inky blackness, listening to the various scrapes and bangs overhead. Ever-so-fine lines of rubble dust streamed between the gaps in the ceiling and powdered their hair. Jessica scrunched her eyes tightly against it.

Two male voices became audible as the intruders moved about the shop. The captain slipped an arm about her waist. Pulling her close to his hip, he gave her a reassuring squeeze.

"This the place? You're sure, sir?" The words were easily discernible, directly above their heads. The two men were evidently standing beside the counter.

"Yes," the second man responded.

"Looks like someone's been in 'ere, but were it 'er? Tha' old woman coulda been mistaken, d'yer think?"

"Poppy Markham's known Jessica all her life, she's not likely to be mistaken." The second man spoke with authority and Jessica stiffened, instantly recognising the voice. She swayed slightly; the captain's arm tightened about her.

"Search this place – top to bottom," Robin Tyler ordered. "Doesn't look like they're here, but see if you can find some indication of *why* they were here and *where* they've gone."

"Aye, sir," the other man responded and the two hiding in the priest hole heard his footsteps moving off.

Alone now, Tyler snarled a curse and there came a thumping sound, as though he'd lashed out at something with his boot. Another ribbon of silt cascaded onto their heads.

Jessica hissed softly and slipped away from the captain's arm. She dropped to the floor, trembling all over and not entirely from fear, for at the sound of Tyler's voice she'd known such fury that she could have cheerfully wrung his neck.

Jessica noticed that the man with Tyler was questioning politely, speaking respectfully. Clearly, Tyler was not some ordinary man who had gone home to his father's farm and was doing his bit for his country. Robin Tyler was more than that, and he was tracking them in some official capacity.

Oh, my God! Jessica felt the blood drain from her face. *He has lied to me all along*!

***

Anton remained standing, as Jessica dropped and crouched on the floor. He rested his fingertips lightly on the top of her head, absently stroking the silky threads of her hair, grainy with dust, as he closed his eyes, the better to hear what was going on above them.

He recognised Robin Tyler's voice immediately, and felt Jessica stiffen at the same time. Anton had long suspected Tyler was not what he claimed; he was more, and hearing the deferential way in which his companion spoke, Anton was now convinced. Tyler was someone important, probably working for the government – and dangerous.

A series of bangs came from elsewhere in the building; Tyler's man conducting his search. Tyler himself seemed to be searching, judging by the shuffling and scraping coming from above.

He was not military; that much Anton knew – he had watched the man through the windows at Broughton Hall often enough in those early days when Tyler had been visiting Jessica, attempting to woo her. There was no rigid discipline about him, no straight-backed posture that seemed inherent in those who'd served in the armed forces.

No, Tyler was something else, and a worm of suspicion slithered into Anton's mind. The British knew what they had when they'd shot the Messerschmitt down. The most advanced fighter jet of its time had crashed in their backyard and they wanted the pilot, wanted to squeeze every last piece of technical information from him.

Anton could understand that; he'd have done the same if the situation were reversed. They would have known immediately that they hadn't captured *all* the Germans that night. But evidently, having interrogated their prisoners and satisfied themselves that none of them knew the detailed workings of the *Sturmvogel*, they'd realised their mistake: they'd lost the Messerschmitt pilot.

Booted feet circled the display case above their heads. Tyler was behind the counter, right by the cupboards, and Anton heard each door being systematically opened, its interior inspected.

His fingers continued to stroke Jessica's head, absently noting the raised, crusty patch where Tyler had torn out her hair. Anton's skin tightened angrily as he felt it, but suddenly he froze. Neither he nor Jessica dared to breathe as their cupboard was opened.

"Find anything?" Robin's voice was so close that it came as a shock, and the pair in the hole jumped as though burned. Anton felt Jessica's hand clutch at his in the dark.

"Nowt." The reply came from elsewhere in the room above them.

Tyler grunted and Anton, standing only inches from the other man, felt cold sweat dribble down his back.

"Well," Tyler's feet scraped on the gritty floor as he moved, "we know they've been here, I suppose the key to it is, why?"

There was a soft bang as the cupboard doors were closed, followed by the clump of boots and a trickle of dust through the floorboards. "D'yer think they mighta bin lookin' for owt in partic'lar? Summat 'er old man left 'ere or …?" The voice trailed off uncertainly.

"No." Tyler's response was absolute. "They were looking for shelter … perhaps not realising how bad the damage is. It's my bet they're in Leeds somewhere."

"Or they coulda gone back t'Broughton 'all."

"No. They're here all right – and thanks to Poppy, we've a decent description of him."

"Why d'yer think they're 'ere in Leeds?" the other man asked, reasonably. "What could they be lookin' for, d'yer reckon?"

Robin gave a huff of a laugh. "A train, of course."

Chapter 44

They know what he looks like! Well, not exactly. They've only Poppy's verbal description but … "Oh, God." Jessica murmured, resting her head against the wall of the priest hole.

Neither Anton nor Jessica would take the chance of lighting the lamp again and so, long after the jangling of the bell signalled Tyler's departure, they huddled together in the dark silence beneath the abandoned shop.

"He'll be at the station tomorrow," Jessica whispered, anxiously. "Watching, waiting for us. What are we going to do?"

Anton didn't answer immediately. Then, "We could hope he does not board the train."

"What good is that?" Fear and frustration were making Jessica irritable. "We still have to catch it if we're to –"

"Oh, *ja*, we will catch it, but what if not from here? What if we go to another station … further down the line?"

Jessica felt like her brain was frying. She opened her mouth to dismiss his idea as foolish, but his words, spoken softly and reasonably, gave her pause. Forcing her mind to focus, she recalled the stops listed on the board at the station. The next one had been … what?

Think, Jessica! She closed her eyes, picturing the information board … *Wakefield, Sheffield, Derby* …

"Wakefield," she said, excitedly. "Not too far. It's only about …" thinking quickly, "eight miles."

She shifted to her knees before him in the dark, "We can take the bus!"

"From where?"

"Right outside the door!" She grinned and pointed towards the side street to their right, although he wouldn't see in the darkness. "The stop's only a few yards from the corner."

"Then we –" he broke off and they stiffened at a new, strange sound filtering through the floor above. It was a faint scratching, snuffling sound.

"What's that?" Jessica whispered, edging closer to the captain.

She felt, rather than saw, his shrug. "The rats you have in this country must be very large," he replied softly.

"You think it's an animal?"

"It sounds like it."

"But –"

There came a faint thud, as though something was bumped, followed by a plaintive whining and scratching at the floorboards above and silt sifted onto their heads.

"You have *die Füchse* here … in your cities?" His voice registered his surprise.

"*Die Füchse?*" Jessica repeated in confusion, then, "The fox … foxes. No – I mean, yes but not this bold, not …" her voice faded, listening to the sounds of clawed toes, padded feet, and she gasped. "Oh, my God! Scaramouche!"

"*Was ist …?*"

"Scaramouche – Mum and Dad's dog!" Jessica scrambled to her feet and immediately began climbing the ladder. "Light the lantern."

The captain leapt up beside her, his hand on her arm, "*Nein!* Frau Jessie – it could be … *eine Falle, eine –*"

"It's a little dog, Captain!" She pushed up the floor of the cupboard.

He stood below, looking up at her whispering urgently. "What if Tyler is here too?"

Jessica paused, briefly, and peered down at him through the dark. "Pass me the chair leg – we didn't hear the bell or any footsteps … I'm sure it's all right – light the lantern." She took the lump of wood from him and propped up the cupboard floor, then stepping up to the last rung, she eased into the cupboard, as light flooded the small room behind her.

Slowly, cautiously, she opened the cupboard doors.

As though blasted by an explosion, Jessica was almost thrown backwards down the ladder in surprise. A small, scruffy creature had launched itself at her.

Catching the frenzied animal, she laughed with joy as the little dog wriggled and whimpered with sheer delight in Jessica's arms. "Oh Scarry, how good it is to see you – you dear, dear little boy! Oh, God …!" recoiling she held him away from her, "you stink to high heaven – what've you –!"

"Here," the voice behind her said. Anton stood with arms raised. "You must come back inside."

Closing the cupboard doors, she turned awkwardly on the ladder and held the filthy scrap out with her hands around his ribby middle; his stumpy legs paddled the air.

The captain took the dog, tucked him under an arm and reached up to help Jessica negotiate the ladder.

Finally, back on solid ground, she stood before him. Scaramouche had got over his initial excitement, although he was overjoyed at being reunited with his old friend. The captain was still holding him, but now the dog was all tongue and slobber, pushing away from this stranger to reach the only familiar person he'd seen in weeks.

Laughing lightly, the captain said, "He wants you."

Overcome with emotion at seeing the loved pet thought lost, Jessica took the dog and hugged him to her chest, despite his smell. "Oh, Captain," she murmured, "you can't understand how much it means to know he's still alive. I wonder how he survived?"

When the captain didn't respond, she looked across at him. He was watching the dog, his face a mixture of concern and that indulgent expression common among dog lovers. He glanced up and met Jessica's eyes. "Now what?"

She shrugged, apologetically. "Well, we can't leave him behind."

He smirked resignedly. "No, I did not think we could."

***

"We need to get some water," Jessica said the next morning. The trio had passed an uncomfortable night sitting on the floor of the tiny cellar – there being not enough room to lie down – and were breakfasting on a shared can of Spam and water crackers from Eric's supply on the shelves. "We need something to drink and we need to wash Scarry to make him presentable. There's a tap out the back; I could get water, though it will be freezing."

The captain was chewing his food, apparently deep in thought and watching Scaramouche swallow his share of the tinned meat. "This could work," he said. "They will not be looking for two people *und* a dog."

"No." She looked across at him. His face was unshaven, and his eyes, in the yellow glow of the lamp were more grey than blue. He looked rugged, dangerous. "And they won't be looking for a man alone with a dog."

The captain regarded her with interest. "What are you thinking?"

"We already have the train tickets. Captain, if you take Scaramouche, assuming he's clean, that is," she added, glancing affectionately at the scruffy animal sitting between them, "you could board the train. You wouldn't need to speak to anyone, you wouldn't be questioned, you just show your ticket and get on."

The captain was staring at her uncertainly. "You could go home," he said, then looked down at Scaramouche. "But –"

Jessica frowned at him. "Of course I wouldn't go home!" She was surprised, slightly offended, that he thought she could abandon him so easily. "Who would help you when you got to London? You can't speak to anyone. And there's Scarry – what would you do with him?"

Jessica ruffled the dog's fur and immediately regretted it. Holding her hand at arm's length, she made a face. "Urgh, Scarry we really must get you bathed! No, Captain. I'll catch the bus to Wakefield, as we planned, and meet you on the train there. Save me a seat, eh?"

***

An hour later, Scaramouche was relatively clean, albeit the poor little scrap was shivering and dripping. Jessica, having found a packet of Velvet soap in their hole and an old metal bucket in the shop, had taken the dog out to the tap.

The captain had followed her outside, both stepping carefully over and round the rubble and destruction. Anton took the opportunity to find some secluded place behind a tumbled brick wall to relieve himself. As soon as he disappeared back into the shop, Jessica did the same, noticing with some amusement that Scaramouche followed, finding a suitable wall to cock his leg against.

It was still very early, the sky only just beginning to lighten at its eastern fringe. Jessica worked fast, steeling her heart against Scarry's whimpering protests. "I know you're cold, boy, I know. But we must get you clean. You can't come with us otherwise." Miraculously, he was still wearing his collar but she hadn't been able to tell earlier for the matts and muck in his coat.

Scrubbing, lathering, rinsing, then doing it all again, she worked hard and quickly got the dog clean.

"At least he smells like soap now and not whatever filth he'd had all over him," she said, passing Scaramouche down the hole to the captain's waiting hands. "Thank God he's only small!"

***

Later that morning, the captain stood before her in a beam of light filtering through the gaping hole in the shop wall. Casting a critical eye over him, she inspected his clothes, hair and face. "You're dusty and you're unshaven." She made a tutting sound. *The stubble makes him look sexy – a problem if it draws attention to him. If Robin were to question the right people, they might remember seeing him.* "Robin has a description of you but hasn't actually seen you," she thought out loud, licking a finger and smoothing his hair into place like she did Thomas's.

He squirmed under her ministrations and it tugged at her heart. *Thomas did that too.*

"I am ready!" He made a grab for her hands. "I am ready, *ja!* Stop making the fuss." She stepped back and he continued to hold her hands, gazing at her. "I am ready and you cannot make me look any cleaner."

"Yes, Captain, you are ready," she agreed, noting that his accent seemed more pronounced. *He's worried*, she realised.

Pulling her hands away, she glanced at her watch. "Seven thirty-five – time you two got a move on."

"What time will you leave?"

"I'll be able to see the bus coming up the road from the door. I'll wait inside until I see it, then run out to the stop."

Scaramouche sat at their feet, looking up, back and forth between them, tail gently swishing. He was dry now, a pretty little dog who, albeit on the thin side, was showing no other signs of living rough and fending for himself these past weeks.

The captain drew a deep breath and crouched. "*Komm her, mein Bürschchen.*"

Scaramouche went happily into his arms and obligingly held still as Jessica tied a length of cord to his collar. She'd found it attached to the blind that had once hung in the shop window but now lay battered and broken on the floor.

The captain held the makeshift leash. "Well? Do I pass for a Yorkshire man?"

"Almost."

"By gum," he mimicked Sam, in a strong German accent.

Nervous laughter bubbled up in her. "By gum, yourself. Don't you go trying that in public. Now, do you know where to go?"

"*Ja.*"

"Good, here's your ticket. When you get to Wakefield, don't move from your seat. I'll find you, all right?"

He nodded solemnly. "Be careful."

"Of course, now," she leaned in and kissed him gently on the cheek, "go!"

As she stepped away from him he reached out and curled an arm about her waist, pulling her to him. Scaramouche danced round their feet as the captain kissed her properly. "I will see you soon," he said, releasing her.

Saying nothing, she watched him as he looked cautiously up and down the street, before stepping onto the footpath, the little dog trotting along beside him. She thought he looked for all the world like a young returned soldier taking his dog for a morning stroll.

And she breathed a sigh of relief.

***

But it was not over. Jessica had to make her way to Wakefield, and while the captain could move about relatively anonymously, she could not. This was her neighbourhood – she'd grown up here, she was well known. The captain was only in danger from Robin and his offsider, thanks to Mrs Markham's description.

After he left, Jessica went back, down into the priest hole and raided the stock on the shelves. First, she ensured the journal was tucked safely at the bottom of her rucksack, then she piled an assortment of goods on top; tins containing meat, vegetables, fruit, a packet of Digestives and a tin of Spam. She had just enough room left for her coat, rolled up in a tight bundle.

Returning upstairs, she sat on an overturned wooden crate and looked about the damaged room that used to be her family's life and home. She didn't have time to think … or feel. When she got back to Broughton Hall, she would ask her father if he planned to rebuild, although at his age and with his failing health, it was doubtful. Pity.

They still owned the land, though. Eric had made the final mortgage payment only five years ago. One day it would belong to Jessica – but she didn't have time to think about that either, or wonder what she would do with it.

Nor did she want to. With luck, Eric had years ahead of him.

Wandering to the door, she tugged it open to the cheerful jangling of the bell and the scrape of warped wood on linoleum floor. The street was empty but for an elderly man carrying a string bag and a woman pushing a baby's pram. She checked her watch – five past eight. Anton's train would soon be pulling away from the station. *Damn! Where was that bus?*

Jessica huffed impatiently and turned back into the shop, leaving the door ajar behind her.

Just as she did so, she heard the rumbling of a large engine and the grind of heavy gears. *It's coming*! Her stomach leapt in relief. With a final glance round her father's ruined livelihood, she hiked her rucksack over her shoulder and stepped through the door.

The aftertaste of Spam rose into her mouth.

Robin Tyler stood, arms folded, lounging against a street pole. "Good morning, Jessica. Strange the people you bump into, isn't it?"

***

Every fibre of Anton's being urged him to the station by the quickest, most direct route, but caution, intuition – whatever it was – suggested otherwise. He couldn't tell whether he was being followed – he couldn't tell if he wasn't. Applying the self-discipline impressed on him by the German military, Anton, at the first intersection, led Scaramouche down a narrow side street, the opposite direction from the station.

With no way of tracking the time, he set a pace, walking with a rhythm that counted the minutes forward from the time he'd left Jessica behind. As he walked, he chanted in his head, *eins, zwei, drei, vier* ... all the way to *sechzig*, counting to the beat of his boots. Folding a finger into his palm, he began again, *eins, zwei, drei* ... thus he kept track of the time.

The lane was cobbled, lined with blank windows and closed doors. In the distance, where it formed a T-junction with the main road, he could see a boy standing beside a stack of newspapers, mouth moving as he called out the morning's headlines to passers-by. Occasionally someone stopped to buy a paper.

Scaramouche scampered cheerfully at his side. Resilience ... both animals and humans were innately resilient but reluctant to call on such reserves. Only during times of duress: natural disasters, wars ... those were the times when people showed their strength and resourcefulness. And their resilience.

When he had folded ten fingers into his palm, Anton knew roughly ten minutes had elapsed. The lane behind him was empty; he felt it safe to assume he was not being followed. Now, he turned his measured pace towards the railway, exiting the lane and joining a stream of servicemen and women heading in the same direction.

The closer he got to the station, the thicker grew the pedestrian traffic until he was forced to scoop Scaramouche into his arms and weave through the swarm of humanity. He heard the cacophony of sound before he saw its cause – cars and lorries tooted at one another and adults called to children. Somewhere a dog was barking and on a corner, another boy was selling newspapers. He had a bundle tucked beneath his arm and was shouting something that was indiscernible until Anton drew closer, "*Japanese air strikes against New Guinea ... Japs threaten Australia ...*"

Anton held Scaramouche closer and melted into the crowd milling about the station.

A train had only just pulled in; its human cargo was spilling onto the platform and flooding towards the gates, moving as a tide through the building.

Groups of small bewildered children with pasty, tear-streaked faces, waited. Their names and addresses were printed on tags and pinned to their coats; they gripped miniature suitcases and occasionally a teddy bear or rag doll. Evacuees from London, Anton deduced. He'd seen the like in Berlin and Munich – terrified children relinquished into the care of strangers, embarking on a new, hopefully safer, life in the country while their parents remained in the cities.

Now he waited among the heaving throng where he and Jessica had stood the day before. Staring up at the departure board and wedging Scaramouche more securely under his arm, he took out his ticket and checked the platform number against the board.

Uniformed men and women stood with family members in varying degrees of grief, excitement and anxiety. Shouldering his way through them, Anton arrived at his designated platform. The clock showed 8.05 am. He had five minutes to spare.

Anton's ticket indicated carriage three, compartment two, seat seven. The train rocked gently side-to-side, belching spasmodically – as though catching its breath after its long haul through field and dale to the north. Carriage five was written in gold paint on the carriage in front of him. Adjusting Scaramouche's position, he ignored the pounding of his heart and set off down the platform, edging through the crowd and reading the carriage numbers as he went.

Carriage three.

A group of people milled about waiting to board. Anton nudged past a couple in a tight embrace and strode confidently towards the uniformed conductor waiting by the door. The man was checking tickets as passengers clambered up the two rungs into the carriage. Anton's heart began to beat faster.

Fool, he berated himself harshly. *You have a ticket – board the train and don't draw attention to yourself.*

Nevertheless, he tightened his hold on the little dog who'd begun to squirm and caught a whiff of the soap Jessica had used on him that morning. There was comfort in the warmth of Scaramouche's fur and wriggly body and Anton composed himself.

The boarding line had stalled. The conductor was holding a ticket, pointing something out to a passenger.

Red-faced, the passenger was gesturing wildly and as Anton watched, the conductor roughly shoved the passenger aside, thrust the ticket into his hand and turned to the next in line.

The Luftwaffe had taught Anton to be disciplined, poised and controlled under the most harrowing of circumstances, but strangely, the prospect of being interrogated by a harried public servant caused the sweat to break on his lip.

The conductor was an older man with a grizzled grey shrubbery of a beard. The shrubbery parted in a greeting that revealed a set of badly stained teeth. Anton supressed the urge to physically recoil, as he remembered the English were known for the poor quality of their teeth. *Jessica's weren't like that*, he thought, noticing how the thought of Jessica seemed to settle his nerves.

Where was she? Did she meet the bus?

"Mornin'" the man said brightly. "Giz a look 'ere." The German captain tried to look as though he understood what had just been said and offered his ticket to the man's waiting hand.

"Off to London, are ye?"

"Yeah," Anton responded. He'd decided his American accent was better than his English one.

"Yankee are ye?"

"Yeah," Anton said again. *Why wasn't the man giving back the ticket?*

"No luggage?" The conductor tipped his head to look at the ground around Anton's feet. "Where's yer bags?"

"My wife has my bag." Anton smiled pleasantly. "She is meeting me in … Wakefield." Praying the pause was indiscernible; Anton hoped the man didn't notice his cautious pronunciation of *Wakefield*. His mouth automatically wanted to shape the word, *Vayke-feeldt*.

He glanced at Scaramouche. "She's bringin' the bags and yer've got t'dog. Seems odd but …" the man shrugged and handed back the ticket. "On yer get. Enjoy yer trip."

Anton nodded thanks, tucked the ticket into his pocket and climbed onto the train.

He easily located his compartment. A young woman in an army nurse's uniform was already in there. She smiled as Anton settled into the seat opposite, arranging Scaramouche on his lap.

"Ooh," the woman said, leaning forwards. "A right bonnie wee laddie, eh."

Anton had no idea what she'd just said but he nodded and smiled in response.

"Wass 'is name, then?" she asked.

"Scaramouche."

"Ooh, an' 'e's a lovely fellow an' all," she said, scratching behind Scarry's ears. "Where ye off to, then?" She tucked a stray curl behind her ear and gazed at him. Her hair was straw-coloured and shoulder length, pinned curls framed her face in a style reminiscent of the German actress, Ilse Werner. Anton thought she looked pretty.

"London."

"Aye, London. So," she stuck out her hand, "Frances, but me friends all call me Frankie."

"A pleasure to meet you … Frankie," Anton said, uncertainly, adding, "Tony."

"Y' 'merican, Tony? Aye, I knew yer weren't from 'round 'ere."

Anton nodded.

"Ye off 'ome, then? To the States?" She didn't wait for his response. "They're sendin' me –"

The compartment door slid open and three women in WRNS uniforms bounced in, noisy and bubbling with excitement.

"Oh, 'ello love!" A buxom brunette plopped onto the seat beside Anton, and pressing closely against him she cooed, "An look, girls, he's got his little dog with him."

"Ain't 'e gorgeous … the little dog, I mean," another one said, dropping onto the seat beside Frankie. Her companions shrieked with laughter.

"Daisy didn't mean that, love," the first one assured him. "She meant you, all right."

Frankie had sat back in her seat and was eyeing the newcomers resentfully. Anton met her gaze and smiled ruefully.

"Wass yer name, 'andsome?" a third one questioned. She'd squeezed herself between Anton and the window and was fondling Scaramouche's ear.

Before he had chance to respond, two men paused outside the window and peered in at them. They stared intently at Anton before studying each of the women. They conferred briefly with one another, then moved on. "How odd," Frankie murmured. "Do ye think they're lookin' fer a seat?"

"P'raps they'll join us," the brunette beside Anton suggested. "I'm Betty and these are Daisy and Kate," she added for Anton's benefit.

"Pleased to meet you," he said uncertainly. Nothing in his Luftwaffe training had prepared him for a situation such as this and he was immensely uncomfortable.

"A Yankee!" Daisy declared. She was ferreting about in her handbag, pulling out a tatty-looking novel. "What you doing up north?"

"I have been visiting friends. Now I am returning to London."

"Shipping you out are they, love?" Betty asked.

"Yeah," Anton agreed. It sounded plausible enough. "I will be meeting my division in London." None of them seemed to notice anything odd about his accent.

"Ooh, I do love Yankees," Daisy sighed her face becoming wistful. "Remember those Yankees in Leeds what took us driving, Betty?"

Betty rolled her eyes. "This one's better looking."

"You weren't so fussy at the time," Kate quipped and the three burst into gales of laughter again.

Just as Anton was wondering why the train hadn't departed – surely it was after 8.10 by now – the compartment door was flung open and the two men from the platform stood on the threshold, their gazes locked firmly on him.

They were dressed casually but regarded the scene with an air of purpose before moving officiously towards Anton. "Stand up!" One of them snapped. His hair was white blond, almost albino, and his complexion was pock-marked and doughy.

"Excuse me?" Anton feigned innocent surprise, although his heart jumped and began to race. Scaramouche must have sensed something amiss for he squirmed on Anton's lap and whined.

"Stand up," the other man repeated. He was shorter and younger than the first, with a ruddy complexion and ginger beard. The autumn colouring didn't look as nice on him as it did on Jessica. His manner was aggressive as he ordered, "State your name and purpose on this train."

Anton remained seated. The women around him had all fallen silent, mouths hanging open in surprise. "Tony Bird," Anton said, adding carefully, "what is all this about?"

"We'll ask the questions," the pasty man countered officiously.

The ruddy one added, "We're looking for someone fitting your description, a …" he hesitated, his eyes darting round at the intent faces watching him. "The man we're looking for is wanted for questioning. So, you either cooperate with us now or we hold up this train and physically haul you off it."

"Oi, who do you think you are!" Betty demanded, suddenly coming to life.

"Stay out of this ma'am," the first man warned.

"I will not!" she snapped. "This man is American. He's our ally – he's been fighting this war out there on the frontlines, which is more than we can say for the likes of you!" She jabbed a contemptuous finger at the white-haired man. "Why aren't *you* in uniform, doing your bit for our country?"

"I said, stay out of this!"

"And I said, I will not!"

"Do you know this man, ma'am?" the younger one asked suddenly. "If you had any idea who we suspect him to be, you wouldn't be so quick to defend him."

"I know him well enough," Betty said with a sly smile. "He has been my lover this past week – although I wouldn't be telling my boyfriend!"

Her two companions snickered while her questioner glanced with a flicker of uncertainty at his partner.

"It's true," Daisy leapt in, closing her paperback with a snap. "even though I met him first, but Betty here … Well, she stole 'im right from under me nose. Always does!" Daisy added throwing a rather genuine glare in Betty's direction.

"Is this true?" The older man demanded, eyes levelled on Anton's face.

Anton attempted to look shamefaced and nodded.

There was a pause and the two men seemed to weigh up the situation, then suddenly, "Hand over your dog tags." The younger man thrust his hand into Anton's face.

"Well, aren't you rude!" Betty admonished. "Anyway – he doesn't have them. In a fit of screaming passion," she clutched her bosom in dramatic parody of ecstasy, "one of my hands caught in the chain and tore it clean off. The tags went sliding across the floor and under the dressing table. I admit we completely forgot to retrieve them." She shrugged, not in the least repentant.

The younger man's ruddy face grew purple in fury. He opened his mouth just as the conductor poked his head through the door.

"If yer 'aven't found what yer lookin' fer, sirs, we needs to get underway. Th' engineer's on me back."

"This man is of interest to us," the blond one explained. "We –"

"This fellow?" The conductor said. "The one wi' the dog? Naw, this man's American. Meetin' 'is wife in Wakefield, 'e is."

The silence that followed was filled by Daisy's shocked gasp at the same time as Betty burst into a storm of tears.

Throwing herself against Anton's shoulder, she wept on his neck and pounded his chest in grief. "You're married! Oh ... I knew it ... I just *knew* it ... It was too perfect! ... You never said ... Oh this *always* happens to *meee* ...!" she ended on a pitiful wail.

Kate leapt to her friend's side, stroking her hair gently. "There, there, love ..." she glared over her shoulder at the three men.

The conductor gave a snort of contempt and turned away as the two men exchanged embarrassed looks. "Sorry, miss," the white-haired man murmured. "Er –"

"Just go, will ye!" Frankie spoke for the first time. "For 'aven't ye caused enough trouble wi'out delayin' the train too!"

***

The four women watched the conductor and the other two men leave the compartment. As the door slid closed on its tracks, they turned as one towards Anton. "Are you anyone we ought to worry about?" Betty asked. She was sitting upright, wiping the remnants of her inspired performance from her face with a handkerchief.

"No," Anton shook his head. "I have told you the truth."

"That *is* an odd accent," Kate observed, pensively. She'd been strangely quiet through the event but now she regarded Anton with suspicion. "I saw your face when the men were outside the window looking at you. You're not American and you're not joining your countrymen in the Pacific. Who are you?"

Anton exhaled in a gusty sigh. "I have not been honest. I am on my way to London. My wife is joining me at …" *careful*, "Wakefield."

"Say that again?" Kate said.

"Oh Kate, for heaven's sake, give over." Betty was checking her face in a compact mirror. "You did one semester of elocution and you think you're an expert on accents."

"I am from the mid-west," Anton thought quickly, assuming the women would be unfamiliar with such an accent. "Bridgeport, Nebraska." It had been a stopping point on his mail route.

"You see?" Betty insisted dabbing her cheeks with a make-up sponge.

Kate's retort was cut off by the train's whistle and, with a jerk, the carriage stuttered and began to move forward. "Thank God," Betty said, snapping her compact shut.

Danke Gott, Anton agreed silently. He adjusted Scaramouche on his lap and glanced up at Frankie sitting opposite. She hadn't said much but her eyes had been on him the entire time – searching and speculative.

Now she nodded. "Yes, thank God."

***

"What are you doing here, Robin?" Jessica demanded, deciding that attack was the best form of defence.

"I could ask the same of you," he said. He craned his neck to see around her into the shop. "Except that I know what you're doing here."

"This is my family's property. I don't need to explain myself to you."

"Where is he, Jessica?" Robin asked, menacingly.

"My father? He's back at Broughton Hall. He –"

"Don't play games with me," he ground out. "Where is the German?"

"*German?*"

Now he grasped her roughly by the upper arm and shook her to punctuate his words, "I said, *don't ... play ... games ... with me.*" Jessica's rucksack slipped down her arm, catching on Robin's hand but he disregarded it in his single-minded purpose.

"Robin! You're hurting ...!" Jessica grabbed at his hand, clawed at his fingers but they tightened and dug into her flesh. All the while, with mounting panic, she watched the bus over Robin's shoulder. It had pulled in at a stop further up the road. "Let go!" she cried, trying to pull away.

"Just answer the question."

"I don't know what you're talking about." She tried to shake him off. "Robin, please!"

"Tell me where he is and we'll go easy on you – I have connections, I can help you, we can get this sorted out."

"For God's sake, let me go!"

"Jessica! Tell me!"

"I have no idea who you're talking about – just ..." craning her neck, she saw the bus pull away from the curb and approach along the street. A woman and two men had alighted. They'd noticed the commotion and were looking curiously towards them. "Please, Robin … I need to catch that bus. I have an appointment. I –"

"Jessica!" He gave her arm another vicious shake and leaned into her face. "Enough of the lies!" Turning, he pulled on her arm, tugging her up the footpath behind him.

The bus was closer.

"You're coming with me," he insisted. "You refuse to answer … I'm taking you –"

She dug in her heels. The heavy rucksack was swinging awkwardly from her arm. The people up the street were now openly watching the unfolding drama. "Let me go! I'll scream!" She'd already raised her voice and the trio seemed to become more alert, the men glancing at one another uncertainly.

Rounding on her, Robin peered into her face, "You'll scream?" He seemed surprised.

"*Help*!" Jessica shrieked at the full pitch of her lungs. "*Help me! Help!*"

The two men paused only momentarily to assess the scene. Jessica jerked her arm, trying to break Robin's grip. "*Help me, please!*" she screamed again.

"You there!" one of the men called, and then they were marching towards them.

The bus was lumbering nearer.

"Stay out of this!" Robin shouted furiously, raising his free hand at the men.

"What're you doing?" one of the men called out. "Let the lady go!"

They drew steadily closer, evidently reluctant to get involved, but required, if only by chivalry, to do so. "Stay back!" Robin ordered but the men ignored him.

"*Help me*!" Jessica cried.

Robin was momentarily distracted by the men. Taking the advantage, Jessica wrenched her arm from his grip.

"*Run*!" the woman up the street shrieked.

The bus arrived at the corner. It was approaching the stop outside Eric's shop.

Jessica bolted towards it, waving frantically. Robin made a lunge for her and caught her swinging rucksack just as the two men caught up with him.

"Let her go!" One of the men grabbed Robin by the arm, hauling him round while the second made a fist and swung.

Jessica didn't wait to see what happened. "*Stop*!" she yelled at the bus. "Stop please! *Stop*!"

Quickly summing up the situation, the driver immediately pulled over. Jessica clambered into the door-well before the bus had come to a full halt. Grasping the pole in the entrance, she was flung backwards against the wall as the driver flattened the accelerator and the bus lurched forwards.

Collapsing on the floor to catch her breath, Jessica clung to the pole and looked back to see Robin and the two men standing on the street corner. Robin was gesturing furiously towards the departing bus, as he drew some kind of official identification from his inner pocket. The two strangers stared at it, wide-eyed and abashed.

"Eeyup, love." Jessica looked up, still gasping for air. The young female conductor stood on the step above, offering a hand. Jessica took it and allowed herself to be helped to her feet as the bus rocked and bounced down the road. "Wass tha' all 'bout?"

"Just a ..." Jessica panted, "A ... fellow who ... wouldn't take no for ... an answer."

"Oh, aye." The lass smiled sympathetically. "Don't we all gotta contend wi' tha' these days! Lads what's on leave from t' front – thinks we owes 'em summat."

Jessica made her way to a seat and all but fell into it. She was beginning to tremble and she felt cold all over. *I must be in shock*, she thought, hugging her rucksack. "Ticket?" she asked the conductor.

The girl smiled and shook her head. "Don' yer worry. Call't a public service, lass."

"Thank you. I … appreciate it."

In the aftermath of fright, Jessica now felt exhausted. Her left leg was jiggling uncontrollably, the rucksack on her lap bobbed up and down. Her throat felt parched and painful; she was about to cry.

And all she wanted was to go home.

***

"So, Tony, how long've you been married?" Kate was watching him from her seat opposite.

"Not long," Anton responded, vaguely.

Kate looked thoughtful. "I only ask as you're not wearing a ring."

"No, you didn't," Betty said. "You asked because you're trying to catch him out on something."

"Did not!"

Betty sighed. "Don't worry about her, love." She bumped Anton's shoulder playfully with her own. "She suspected her granny of being a Nazi sympathiser because she caught the old lady humming Beethoven's Fifth."

"Shut up, Betty. That's not true!" Kate flushed.

"Why don't ye take yerselves somewhere else if ye're plannin' a stramash." Frankie spoke up.

"You stay out of it, Scotland!" Kate snapped rudely.

"Sassenach!" Frankie spat.

"All right, ladies," Betty interrupted, looking past Kate to see out the window. "We're almost at Wakefield. Now we'll get to meet Tony's wife for ourselves." She threw him an encouraging smile.

The train began to slow. The scenery morphed from open

fields, to houses, to warehouses, and finally the platform stretched alongside them. Slowing, slower …

Anton breathed steadily, pulling the air deep into his lungs and controlling his exhale. As the train finally rolled to a halt, a group of servicemen and women was moving about on the platform. Anton tried to compose his face into a relaxed expression. *She will be here … She will come.*

***

The bus was approaching Wakefield station where a number of passengers were due to alight. Jessica's rucksack was on the seat between her and the window. She gathered it onto her knee and pulled out a scarf as she watched the station approach. The bus's brakes hissed and its gears ground as the driver manoeuvred the heavy vehicle onto the side of the road.

Looking beyond the station building, Jessica could see that the train was not yet there. She was either too late or too early, she suspected the latter – there'd been no delays on the road from Leeds.

The bus stopped and rocked on its wheels momentarily and Jessica was instantly on her feet, covering her distinctive hair with the scarf and eager to get onto the platform before the train arrived.

And suddenly she heard it. A wheezing, huffing sound in the distance and Jessica felt her stomach lurch with anticipation.

Many of her fellow bus-travellers were getting off and the line was moving slowly down the centre aisle between the seats.

To Jessica's stressed mind, they were shuffling, dragging their feet by inches, fussing and faffing with their belongings, chattering to one another, *As though they've got nowhere else to be,* she grumbled to herself.

Without warning, the line stopped altogether.

Jessica almost ran into the man in front of her. Stifling a groan, she craned her neck and she saw an elderly lady struggling down the stairs from the upper level.

I wouldn't've gone up there if I had mobility difficulties. Impatience made her uncharitable. The seconds ticked by. The lady then needed assistance lugging a cumbersome suitcase out of the luggage rack.

Jessica groaned with frustration.

The train had arrived. She could see it swaying gently as passengers alighted. Others queued to get on.

Urgency was rising up in her. Every five or so seconds, she ducked her head to see out of the window.

The train was still there; passengers were waiting to board.

Jessica's heart pounded. A cold sweat dampened the back of her blouse.

"Excuse me …" she tried to shoulder past the man in front of her. "I'm sorry – I must board that train."

He didn't budge. "Excuse me …" she tried again. The elderly lady was being helped onto the footpath.

The man turned to Jessica, levelling a sour look on her. "None o' us are goin' nowhere. Jus' 'old yer 'orsis."

"I –" she began but the old woman was out of the bus. The line edged forward and suddenly Jessica was on the side of the road, running for the station. She dodged a man and woman and navigated a family with a child mid-tantrum.

The last of the passengers had boarded. The rucksack bounced awkwardly on her back as she ran. "*Wait!*" she shouted. Several people turned curiously in her direction. Among them were two familiar faces and Jessica's heart stopped.

Turning so quickly she almost twisted an ankle, she moved furtively to stand beside the preoccupied family, trying to blend in. The mother was attempting to pacify the child while his brother and father watched on.

Jessica kept her back turned to the station praying that

the two men on the platform had not noticed her. Thank God, she'd spotted them first. They were two of the thugs that had accompanied Robin in his midnight raid on Broughton Hall.

Jessica fought to control her breathing as they drew closer.

They were behind her now. So close that Jessica fancied they could hear her heart pounding. "She could be anywhere," one of them was saying.

"Aye," his companion agreed. "Best we get back on board … in case she's meetin' 'im. Keep an eye out."

Jessica's hand stole up to ensure there were no stray hairs poking out from her scarf.

"I dunno," the first one said. "Robin reckons they'll be on this train but –"

"Well, I reckon Robin's on the wrong train. If she don't get on at the next stop I say we go 'ome. I got –" he broke off as the guard gave a quick blow of his whistle. "Come on."

The two men jogged onto the platform and climbed aboard, just as the guard blew again on his whistle. The train belched a cloud of steam. The great wheels turned in place, grinding steel on steel, gaining purchase, edging slowly forwards.

Jessica watched, her heart in her mouth and a dull headache starting behind her eyes, as the train disappeared down the tracks.

***

Anton frantically searched his memory. *I wasn't supposed to get off was I? No. She definitely said, don't leave your seat – I'll find you.*

Where was she, then? Something must have happened or … He hated the thought but it wouldn't go away, *she changed her mind?*

Anton's heart twisted painfully and he couldn't be sure he hadn't moaned out loud.

She has changed her mind. The notion clanged deafeningly

in his head and caused such an ache in his heart that he wanted to gasp.

Kate interrupted his thoughts. "So," she said, caustically, "time you come clean, Tony – or whatever your name is. Why were those men suspicious of you? Where's this imaginary wife? And what's with that phoney accent?"

"And what is this interrogation?" Anton snapped. He'd had enough of her insinuations and her smug looks. Worry didn't sit well with him and this woman was making it worse. *Don't let her get to you. Be careful of your accent.*

"Leave 'im alone, for Christ's sake," Frankie demanded. "A man's entitled to 'is own thoughts ain't 'e?"

Kate threw her a disdainful look. Returning her attention to Anton, she said, "Why don't you show *me* your dog tags … or do I have to call those men back?"

Anton sighed. "I am not wearing dog tags," he lied firmly, then settled back in his seat, stroking Scaramouche, as much to calm himself as anything else. His mind was racing ahead – he was on his way to London, alone. With no money, no belongings but for the clothes on his back, and a scruffy little dog that was pushing its nose into the crook of his elbow, as though sensing something terribly amiss.

And more than anything, more insistent than food or shelter … more painful than anything he'd been through over the last year, was the sudden realisation that she had let him go. Jessica was not coming.

The knowledge was like a hot blade stuck between his ribs. *Verdammte Scheiße!*

***

Wakefield … Sheffield … Derby … the words repeated themselves in her head.

Robin's men had said they'll go home if they didn't find her at the next stop. That would be Sheffield.

I could go to Derby ... and pray the captain has stayed on the train.

"Oh, God," she moaned aloud. *He'll think I've abandoned him.* She hated the thought but there was nothing for it. Looking behind, she saw the bus had already departed. It didn't matter anyway. Her bus had been bound for Barnsley; she needed one that went to Derby.

The bus stop was now empty – even the family with the squalling child had disappeared. There was a grocer's shop up the road but other than a handful of people gathered at its door, the street was empty.

Jessica stood on the spot, completely at a loss – she had no idea what to do next.

Unfamiliar with her surroundings, she didn't know how to get to Derby – she knew only that she had to get there.

I could wait for the next bus and ask the driver. She peered down the street again. No bus was in sight and she couldn't tell how frequently they ran. A woman pushing a pram was approaching. As she drew level, she glanced with mild interest in Jessica's direction.

"Can you tell me how often the buses run?" Jessica asked stepping forward.

"Not often enough," the woman quipped unhelpfully. She continued past and Jessica glared after her, aware that with every second that ticked by, the train was closer to Derby and Jessica would never get there on time.

Damn, she thought, glancing at her watch. *Damn ... damn ... damn!*

The panic twisted her stomach and her pounding heart was doing her headache no favours.

Stepping out onto the road, she squinted into the distance. No bus, only a couple of cars and a lorry. The morning sun was warm on her face; it promised a lovely spring day but Jessica felt like dropping to the ground and weeping.

What am I going to do?

The lorry lumbered past, spewing a cloud of acrid black smoke from its exhaust. Jessica coughed and leaned against a signpost.

She suddenly felt weak and exhausted. *Oh, God help me, what am I going to do?*

A car went by, another followed and Jessica suddenly became aware of one of them stopping on the side of the road.

Looking up, she realised it was a taxi, the driver leaning over, peering at her through the passenger window. "Yer all right, miss? Yer lookin' a bit ou'a sorts."

A taxi! Can I afford a taxi? Jessica, aware that she must have looked rather vague, stared at the man momentarily, while performing a quick calculation in her head.

"Miss …?" he prompted.

"Um …" Jessica pushed away from the post. "I …" *think quickly … it must be … sixty-five, seventy miles to Derby.* "I missed my train. I wonder …" she leaned down to see through the window, "how quickly could you get me to Derby Station?"

The driver stared at her incredulously. "Beg pardon?"

"I need to meet a train in Derby. I … How quickly could we get there?"

"Lady, it'd cost a fortune and it would cost me even more gettin' back without a fare."

"How much to make it worth your while?" Jessica calculated that it would take almost all the money she'd brought with her, but she had to meet that train. Now she came closer to the car and leaned on the window ledge.

The driver shook his head. "Not possible. Sorry."

She watched him put the car into gear. Before the thought had even crossed her mind, she'd wrenched open the rear passenger door and leapt onto the seat.

Outraged, the driver said, "Out! Now!" He pointed to the bus stop. "I'm not taking yer to Derby!"

"My husband is on that train. He's joining his unit – they're sending him to the western front!"

Unconvinced, the man glared at her. "Anyone with two legs an' two arms is going to the western front. Outta me car!"

Think! She commanded herself, and once again the words were spewing from her lips before she even knew they were there. "He doesn't know …!" she cried, in a panic she didn't have to fake. "They're shipping him out and he doesn't know I'm pregnant!"

The man pushed open his door and was in the process of climbing out when he stopped and stared at her. "You're pregnant?"

Jessica nodded and with absolutely no contrivance on her part, she burst into tears.

***

He'd introduced himself as Jake.

For a moment, he sat behind the wheel of his taxi staring at Jessica, his face a picture of surprise and uncertainty.

While Jessica's tears were genuine enough, Jake had assumed they were because her husband was going to war without knowing he was to become a father. Jessica's tears were in fact a result of relief because Jake's face had swiftly changed.

"We'll never get to Derby on time," he'd insisted, pulling away from the curb. "But I reckon we could get to Sheffield quicker. It's only twenny-five miles – we'll make that unner an hour!"

And so, Jake had driven as though his life depended on it. Jessica braced against the seat to avoid being thrown about as he took corners like he was channelling the ill-fated Dick Seaman.

All the while, he questioned her – When did she find out about the baby? Why hadn't she told her husband before he left? And so on. Jessica's inventiveness was beginning to run out. She managed to tell him was that she and her husband had quarrelled, and he'd left. In a moment of guilt, she'd run to the station to tell him but arrived just as the train pulled out.

"Which is when you found me at the bus stop," she finished. She was growing tired of her lie, wishing only to focus on not injuring herself as the taxi bounced at breakneck speed along the roads to Sheffield.

"Well," he said, glancing at her in the rear-view mirror, "you certainly looked dejected enough leanin' against that pole. Wouldna stopped, otherwise."

"I'm glad you did, Jake." Jessica felt the tears coming again and sniffed them away. "You'll never … ah!" she gasped as he negotiated a sharp bend. "You'll never know what it means … you doing this."

"Aye well," Jake said, swerving around a pothole, "my daughter 'ad 'er first only last month. Son-in-law's missing in action – never knew 'e were a father …" He shrugged. "S'pose I just didn't want to see that 'appenin' to someone else if I could help it."

He smiled sadly at her and turned back to the road. "Wife'll unnerstand if I'm late 'ome for dinner."

***

Jessica already had money in her hand as they pulled into the concourse in front of Sheffield Station's arched façade. Great blocks of stone, shattered, pulverised into dust, lay in mounds where teams of workers had pushed them out of the way, and Jessica remembered Sam saying that Sheffield had sustained considerable damage in the bombing raids.

"How much?" she asked, throwing a hand out to brace as

Jake applied the brakes in a screeching halt.

"Nothin' – get out. S'coming!" He pointed towards the north where a plume of black smoke, steam and smut heralded the train's approach. "Go! And good luck to yer, lass!"

Jessica didn't argue but she couldn't accept his charity – not after her lies. Dropping a couple of precious shillings onto the seat, she scrambled out, slammed the door and ran. The train was lurching and belching, slowly drawing up at the main platform.

She'd have preferred Derby to ensure Robin's thugs were well away, but with no choice, she'd just have to keep a look out.

The platform was accessed via a footbridge that was remarkably intact. As she ran, the rucksack bounced uncomfortably on her back but she ignored it. Flying along the footbridge, dodging and bumping startled Saturday morning commuters, she saw the passengers were beginning to board.

No ...! No ...! Not again! she begged the fates, all the while aware that Robin's two cronies could be anywhere, could be watching her at this very moment. *Blend in, don't attract attention!* It was a constant dialogue in her head as she ran down the bridge and onto the platform and –

Shit!

The two men stood side by side, next to the train, heads turning first one way, then the other, eyes narrowed, watchful.

Jessica stopped abruptly, checking her scarf, noting as she did, a sign on the wall indicating the parcel office at the south end of the platform. Squaring her shoulders, she adjusted her expression to that of a busy woman on an errand and began marching purposefully down the platform, directly towards the men.

As she came within their hearing range, she targeted a stranger and, gesturing towards the office, called in a bright voice, "Excuse me, is the parcel office this way?"

"Aye, love," the man responded and Jessica thanked him and

kept walking, eyes fixed on the office ahead, heart thumping, sweat beading her lip, directly past the two men waiting to arrest her.

But they'd heard her call out her enquiry. *They're only human, she told herself, and wouldn't expect a fugitive to be so visible. Or ask about parcel offices. Now ... wait till the very last minute. Make sure they don't get back on the train.*

And then she was outside the parcel office. The door was shut, a Closed sign on it, but from where they were, the men couldn't see that. Jessica stood, gesturing as though someone was in the office, answering her query.

The guard blew the whistle – one shrill pip. Jessica waited. She had to be certain the men would remain behind. She continued to stand, pretending to talk to someone, one eye on the two men some sixty-odd yards away.

The guard called out, "All aboard!"

And still Jessica waited. She was trembling ... She turned away from the closed office and took a step towards the train door. One of the men was watching her. Why? Perhaps he was merely curious. Perhaps he will come over to ask if she'd seen anyone suspicious.

The guard blew the whistle again – two loud pips.

One of the men said something to his companion. They both stared in her direction.

Hold your nerve. Look casual ... but she took an involuntary step towards the train.

The pair moved. Eyes fixed on her, their feet moving in unison, they started towards her, picking up pace as they did.

Shit! Damn and shit!

The engine driver leaned from his window, watching the tracks as the train's wheels spun in their place, pistons and drive shafts grinding, pumping, and Jessica waited ... waited. The men were intent on her.

With one eye on the men, the other on the train, she forced herself to hold her nerve until the very last moment.

One of the men called out to her. He began trotting down the platform. He lifted an arm and called again.

"Jessica?" he shouted. "Jessica Barrow! Wait! We just want to talk to you!"

Like hell!

The train was slowly moving past her, carriage by carriage. Carriage one … carriage two … carriage three … And Jessica stepped closer. The other man raised his arm in her direction. Now they were both running … calling, "*Stop! Stop the train*! Jessica … *Wait*!"

Jessica couldn't wait any longer. The last carriage was passing her. They anticipated what she was about to do and one of them bellowed, "*Don't …!*"

But Jessica did.

She ran at the train. Just as the last door drew even with her she threw herself forwards in a desperate lunge.

The rucksack thumped against her back, almost overbalancing her. Jessica grasped the hand rail beside the door, feet teetering on the lowest step, face pressed against the window and clinging for dear life.

The train was terrifyingly slow to pick up speed. Jessica began working at the door with her spare hand while the men shouted, sprinting now, down the platform, demanding the driver stop immediately.

Don't stop … she silently prayed. The engineer was way up the other end of the train and had fortunately disappeared within the engine room.

Gripping the handrail tightly in one hand, Jessica pushed on the door with the other. *Please open … please open*. Fumbling with the handle, she pushed again. Still it refused to budge. "*Lucifer's bloody balls …!*" she screamed. In a frenzy of panic,

Jessica began thumping the door but the window remained empty – no one came to help.

The men had almost caught up. They were running alongside now and one made a clawing grab for her. He missed but his forward motion caused him to trip over his feet and fall. His companion continued running – reaching for her.

But the train was finally gaining momentum, lurching and rocking, the gap gradually widening. Clutching desperately to the handrail, Jessica was tossed about like a rag doll when suddenly, in a jolting movement, the train rocked sideways and threw her backwards. The door suddenly swung open with a fluidity that took her by surprise. She had a split second to curse her stupidity – *of course it opens outwards* – and it was only her grip on the handrail that prevented her from being flung onto the tracks.

The door flew open to its outer limit, carrying Jessica with it. For a terrifying moment, her feet were suspended in mid-air and Jessica desperately grasped the interior handle. Then the door swung to again.

Carried by momentum, Jessica was thrown inside.

Crashing to the carriage floor, she lay in a crumpled heap as the door slammed shut behind her.

Shivering fitfully from fright and adrenalin, Jessica burst into tears.

Chapter 45

Anton did not look for Jessica as they pulled into Sheffield Station. He was trying to resign himself to the unwelcome knowledge that she'd abandoned him. Unprepared for the pain in his chest, he cuddled Scaramouche close and the little dog gave a sleepy grunt.

How could she have left you? he thought, burying his nose in the warm fur. *How could she have left us?* He knew it had been a lot to ask of her. She had a family ... children who depended on her. How could he have expected anything else?

But he had thought she loved him, or was, at least, fond of him. He'd overestimated her regard for him, just as he underestimated her maternal need to return to her children.

Yet the men had been looking for him, which meant they would have been looking for her too. Perhaps she'd been caught.

God, he hoped not. But then, if they hadn't caught her, she'd abandoned him. His throat constricted and he swallowed hard. Neither outcome gave him comfort.

At their arrival into Sheffield, Kate and Daisy had gone outside to stretch their legs and smoke a quick cigarette. Anton took the opportunity to turn to Betty.

"Why did you tell those men we were together?"

Betty smiled wanly and drew a deep breath. "I ... don't really know," she began hesitantly, then she sighed wearily. "Look, I don't know who you are but I'm pretty sure you're the one they're looking for." She shrugged. "I just don't know why."

She absently stroked Scarry's head and the guard blew his whistle. "I don't know much, but I've learned to trust my judgement. For some reason, whoever you are, *whatever* you are, I like you. I don't *feel* you pose a threat ... to me *or* my friends. All I know is that those men were government officials and they're looking for someone. I hope I'm not wrong about you."

Betty stared hard at him, but he said nothing. She paused to tuck her hair behind her ear, "I think you *could* be dangerous – not to me, though. I hope I won't regret protecting you."

Despite his inner turmoil Anton smiled.

Just then the guard blew his whistle a second time. Anton leaned forward, "Betty, I am not English, this is true," he glanced across at Frankie. She nodded grimly. "Even so, I am no danger to anyone. I am as I said, travelling to London." He looked pointedly at the sleeping dog on his lap. "I can only assume my wife missed the train. This is Scaramouche. He is her dog."

The carriage jerked and the train began to move. Betty grinned. "Nevertheless, I know that Kate is right – although I'd never tell her – that is a terrible American accent. I …" She hesitated, eyeing him suspiciously. "I hope I won't regret this," she repeated, looking at him as though she expected him to say something. When he didn't speak, she shrugged. "That accent … if I were to guess –"

She broke off as Frankie cleared her throat warningly. Kate and Daisy had returned. Daisy barrelled into the compartment full of scandalised excitement. Kate, more subdued, followed.

"Seems to be some kind of commotion outside," Daisy reported. "Those men," she looked significantly at Anton, "the ones questioning you … running along the platform, they were, shouting at someone and yelling, *Stop the train!*"

Kate was regarding him narrowly. She remained silent but by her expression, Anton knew he was in trouble.

He must get off the train.

***

Jessica took a few moments to pull herself together. If she was going to find the captain and pose as his wife, she must be controlled, convincing. Her scarf had blown off while she'd been wrangling with the door and now pieces of her hair stuck in sweaty rat's-tails to her temples.

At length, her trembling subsided and she pushed to her feet, legs spaced wide to balance against the rocking of the train. She mopped her tear-stained face on her sleeve and pulled her ticket from her pocket. It was crumpled but legible: carriage three, compartment two, seat eight.

Jessica didn't know what number carriage she was currently in, but she knew it was the last one and would need to work her way up the train. Adopting the spraddled gait of a sailor, she lumbered along the corridor – the doors to the compartments were on her right, the windows opposite looked out over the Yorkshire countryside.

At the end, a sign on the wall told her she was in carriage five. She opened the door to the coupling platform and stepped into carriage four. Through the door, along the carriage she went, rocking side to side, bumping from wall to window and back, passing compartments containing passengers – dozing, reading, eating. Ahead of her was another door. She bounced and jostled across the connecting platform and into the next carriage.

"Carriage three," she said aloud. "Compartment five, compartment four ...three ... two ..." She paused and peered through the glass.

Four women: three WRNS and a nurse, sat two on one side and two opposite with a man between them – a handsome, dark-blond man with a small scruffy dog asleep in his lap. Her heart melted with tenderness for him, and she expelled all the air in her lungs in a great sigh of deliverance. *Thank God!*

Weary with relief, she was lingering uncertainly on the threshold when the pretty blonde nurse looked up.

Jessica saw the woman's eyes widen as she leaned across to lightly touch the man's knee. Her mouth moved and all five in the compartment turned in Jessica's direction.

In an instant, the captain was on his feet, the compartment door slammed open on its casters and Jessica was caught in his arms so violently that they crashed together against the window across the narrow corridor. Scaramouche was wedged between them as the captain clutched at her with an intensity that shocked her.

It shocked Scaramouche too, for the little dog whimpered and wriggled. He was quickly rescued by the nurse who prised him away and returned to the compartment, closing the door discreetly after her.

***

"*Mein Gott!*" Anton breathed against Jessica's neck, "*Mein Gott.*"

"Shh," she warned. "Be careful."

"I love you. *Mein Gott*, I love you … I thought never to see you again …"

He felt her body quaking with emotion, felt her tears dampening his skin.

"I thought … I'd lost you too," she wept, "I … I was so scared …"

Moving her gently back, he lifted a trembling hand to brush the hair from her brow; he stared lovingly into her face. "I thought …" he was about to say something most unmanly. He gave a rueful smile and carried on regardless, "I thought you had abandoned me."

She sobbed in a breath to respond but he cut her off, "Me *und* Scaramouche. But you did not."

"I never would," she whispered, "because I love you too."

He tasted her tears as he kissed her, clinging to her. He wanted to shout with joy. He wanted to sob with relief. He crushed her to his heart, then took her face between his palms and rained kisses over her cheeks, her eyes and nose until she wept and laughed at the same time.

"I have been so afraid," she told him, whispering hurriedly. "Robin caught me at the shop. He tried to stop me getting on the bus. I had to fight him and then his men were at Wakefield and –"

"Shhh, *nicht sprechen* ... do not speak of it. I am so tired of those men. *Und* I am tired of speaking with a very poor American accent." He huffed a laugh, "I want only to kiss you."

And he inclined his head towards her once more and she raised her arms, coiling them round his neck. He allowed her to pull his face down and fused his mouth to hers.

***

After some moments, Jessica pulled away. She took his hand and Anton followed her to the end of the carriage, beyond reach of flapping ears.

"I caught a taxi to Sheffield," she summarised quickly. "The driver didn't want to take me, I told him I was pregnant."

At his expression, she laughed. "Come on, Captain, it was almost six months ago!" But his horrified reaction had caused her a moment's disquiet. *Of course, he wouldn't want an English child.* The thought was irrelevant. "Anyway, those men chased me down the platform. They know I'm on the train."

"Then they will know why. Did they hurt you?"

She shook her head and he asked, "Did *Tyler* hurt you?"

"No," she smiled and lightly touched his cheek. His skin felt warm against her trembling fingers. "I feel like it's been days since I've seen you." She dragged in a breath. "We can't stay on the train."

"I know. One of the women, Kate, she thinks she knows something. The men came to question me."

"They came into your compartment?"

The captain stood with his back to a wall. He was holding her so that she leaned against the length of his body, swaying in a gentle, almost sensual movement together. Jessica rested her forehead on his chest and drew in a long breath. *If only time would stop and allow us this moment.* But it would not. She raised her head to look at him as he continued.

"They had a … description of me … they ask things …" He kissed her again. "You have made me forget how to speak English."

Jessica laughed lightly. "Mrs Markham gave them your description. You're very distinctive, you know."

He gestured dismissively.

"Seriously. You have a face …" she felt the flush rise up her throat. "You have a face women would not easily forget."

"Ah." He smiled and squeezed her.

Jessica's heart stirred with a mixture of pleasure and pain. *I will certainly not forget that face.* "Now we need to get to Devon. Tell me about that woman, Kate."

"Kate knows I have not been truthful. She did not speak when the men came asking questions, but Betty told them she and I were lovers and had been together all week."

Jessica frowned thoughtfully. "Why did she do that?"

"I do not know. I do not care. But I am glad she did *und* I thanked her for it."

"And the others? What about the blonde who took Scaramouche?"

"That is Frankie. She is all right."

"All right," Jessica repeated, thinking. She turned her head to rest her cheek on his shirt. "You must introduce me to them. If they believe you are married to an Englishwoman, regardless of who they think you are, it will be better. They might suspect your accent, but they'll see I'm truly English. It should put them at ease."

"And now," he said, and she felt his voice rumble through his chest as he spoke. "We must get off the train at the next station."

She breathed in the masculine scent of him. "Mmhm. Derby is a junction. Perhaps we could change lines and lose them."

"*Nun, ja.* We can work it out later. Firstly, we must collect Scaramouche *und* be ready."

He led her back to their compartment and opened the door. Jessica felt his hand on her waist as he ushered her into the cabin where the four women sat eyeing them curiously.

Immediately, Scaramouche leapt off Frankie's lap and flew at Jessica. She picked up the bundle that squirmed and whimpered with pleasure, while laughing and dodging his lolling tongue. "Yes, I'm pleased to see you too, little fellow."

Frankie chuckled. "Right friendly, 'e is!"

"Oh yes, *urgh* ... enough Scarry!" Jessica made a face as she received a lick from chin to temple. "Here ..." She lifted Scaramouche so that his front paws hung over her shoulder and his bottom sat in her arms.

"Ladies," the captain said. "This is my wife, Jessie."

The greetings were warm enough, although as the captain introduced each of the women, Jessica noticed how Kate's eyes were speculative while Betty seemed relieved. Frankie's face was open and friendly with just a hint of envy.

Daisy was reading a novel. She looked up and her eyes crinkled as she smiled, "Nice to meet you, Jessie. 'Ere, there's a spare seat beside me."

"Rubbish," Betty said, getting up. "She must sit next to her husband. Sit here Jess – you mind me calling you Jess? Course not. I'll sit next to Daisy, you sit with your handsome hubby."

Jessica took Betty's seat and the captain sat beside her. Settling Scaramouche on his lap, he curled an arm round Jessica's shoulders and pulled her snugly into his side.

Across his chest, she watched the landscape of fields and farmhouses drift past the window, and felt the captain's lips linger beside her eye and his breath warm her hair.

***

Anton looked down at the woman tucked in beside him. It felt good to hold her like this; it felt natural. They were as genuinely affectionate to one another as a pair of newly-weds. Even Kate seemed to have relaxed and the ruminative frown had been smoothed from her brow.

"Looks like we're slowing down," Betty commented, interrupting his thoughts. The scenery outside their window had become more residential, farmland having given way to warehouses, which had become rows of terraces, one attached to the next.

Anton's arm tightened about Jessica's shoulders in a gentle squeeze. "I better take Scaramouche outside for a walk," he said.

"Good idea," Jessica agreed, sitting up. "He drank a lot of water this morning. I'll come with you."

They rose together and Jessica swung her rucksack onto one shoulder while Anton tied the leash to the dog's collar.

He could feel Kate's eyes on him, penetrating. Impossible to ignore, he glanced at her and found her staring at him. She got up and wordlessly left the compartment ahead of them.

Jessica threw him a quizzical look, but he knew the other women were watching and quickly smiled. "Come Scarry," he said, adding in his best American accent, "Time to take a piss."

***

Derby Station was an interchange between the Midland and the Cross Country routes. On that February day in 1942, it was a busy, bustling centre of transport. Easy then, for a young couple carrying a small dog to melt into the Saturday morning crowd that jostled and shoved shoulder-to-shoulder along the platform.

The captain removed his jacket and they covered Jessica's distinctive hair with it. Being a chilly morning, her unusual headdress attracted no curious stares as they moved against the human tide through the Arrivals door and out into the street.

Jessica glanced over her shoulder towards the red-brick façade of the old Victorian building. With the press of people coming and going, it was difficult for her to see if they were being followed. Equally difficult then, she reasoned, for someone *trying* to follow.

"Quickly," the captain said, placing Scaramouche on the ground. Holding the leash in one hand, he took her elbow in the other and the pair strode briskly along Railway Terrace, Scarry trotting cheerfully on his stumpy legs alongside.

"Café," Jessica said. She pointed towards a shop with lace curtaining and a swinging sign depicting a steaming teacup. "We can sit in there," she explained, "have a cup of tea and think about our next move."

***

Bernadette was rinsing cups as the couple came in. Her eyes lingered on the handsome gentleman as he directed his lady friend to a table near the window. They ordered a pot of tea and the woman added, "A bowl of water for our dog, if you don't mind, please?"

Business had been slow that morning. Bernadette was willing to welcome any distraction – and that laddie was just the tonic. "Visitin' are ye?" she asked, as she brought their tea.

"Yes," the woman responded pleasantly, but Bernadette only had eyes for the young man. He briefly glanced her way but didn't speak.

Blimey but 'e's an 'andsome devil, she thought. *An' that smile! Pity it were only fer the red-haired woman.* Bernie had never been the kind of woman a man like that would admire – but what she wouldn't do for one sweet smile – for her alone!

She sighed ruefully and returned to rinsing the dishes.

***

Across the room, Jessica was teasing him. "She's staring at you."

Anton ignored her comment. He leaned forward and whispered, "I think we should go back to the station … there is a train from here to Penzance. It goes through Exeter, which from memory, is in Devon – near Waterville Place."

Jessica narrowed her eyes at him. "I wouldn't've known where Exeter was. How do you know so much about England's geography?"

He stared back, mildly surprised and wondering if she were teasing him again. Apparently she wasn't. "I had reason to become familiar with the English coastline and major cities."

Realisation dawned on her face. "Oh," she murmured, and turned towards the window. "I suppose you would've. Look!" she indicated through the lace curtaining. "Isn't that one of those women from the train?"

Anton followed her gaze and stifled a groan. "That is Kate."

"The one who was suspicious of you?"

"Hmm."

At that moment, the waitress brought their tea on a tray. She set out two cups and saucers, and placed a small bowl of water on the floor for Scaramouche. Anton waited until she'd retreated behind the counter before whispering, "See those two men with her?"

"Oh no," Jessica breathed and Anton saw the colour drain from her face. "Robin's men." Her hand trembled as she poured the tea. She pushed a steaming cup towards him. "Drink up."

Anton nodded and turned back to watch. "She is telling them about us," he said. And then his heart skipped a beat. Kate was speaking, pointing towards the café and the two men turned to look. If not for the lace curtaining, they'd have stared right into Anton's eyes!

Jessica was holding her cup in two hands, blowing over it.

"We're trapped here," she said, looking hunted.

"I think Kate followed us." Anton took a quick sip from his cup – the tea was scalding.

The men seemed to be disagreeing. The red-haired one was gesticulating wildly, his ruddy complexion growing purple. "He's pointing this way," Jessica said, in a hissing whisper. "They're going to come in."

"We must leave," Anton said decisively, rising from his chair. Jessica looked up in alarm. "But, how –?"

"Wait here."

***

As the handsome man approached, Bernadette looked up from the bread she was slicing. She laid the knife on the cutting board and felt the uncomfortable flush creep up her neck as he smiled at her.

"Good morning, Ma'am."

Bernadette gave a wistful sigh. She smiled back.

A short time later, Bernadette closed the back door softly behind them. She didn't, for a minute, believe the handsome stranger's tale of being followed by the crazy lady out on the street.

His accent was odd – sort of American, sort of not. But she agreed to let him and his wife out into the lane and promised to deny ever seeing them if the lady and her two men friends came enquiring.

That were quick! Bernadette thought as the front door opened.

***

The café's back door opened onto a narrow lane. It was littered with boxes and bins and was shaded by a bedraggled hazel tree. A mangy, grey cat bristled and spat at them as they crept past.

The captain held Scaramouche's leash and hooked Jessica's rucksack over his shoulder. He took her hand and led her briskly up the lane. "If we go directly to the station," he told her, "we might get there without them knowing."

Jessica doubted they could be so lucky, but saw no alternative. They quickly made their way past the backs of shops, a stable yard and a broken-down old cart.

It was only a short distance to the station. As they approached, they slowed to an inconspicuous walk, heading towards the main board.

"There's a train to Penzance leaving in twenty minutes," she said. Hope made her heart beat faster. "We'll need to buy tickets – we'll have just enough money."

"Let me do it," the captain offered quickly. "I will ask for a refund of the London ones. Give me your ticket." He held out his hand.

"They won't do it!"

He smiled, "Not if we do not ask."

Jessica waited with Scaramouche in her arms, as the captain joined the line. She hoped he'd be served by the young girl behind the counter and not the grumpy looking older man.

Their luck held out.

Leaning casually over the counter, the captain seemed to be whispering intimately to the girl. She raised her eyes and met his gaze with a bold expression.

Jessica made a derisive noise in her throat. The war had made tramps of so many young women, it was almost criminal.

The captain continued talking, and as Jessica watched, she saw doubt begin to shadow the girl's face. Her eyes flicked towards the man serving at the next counter, before she seemed to make a decision.

Now she worked quickly, taking the tickets the captain held. She referred to a card on her counter, made an alteration to the tickets, then returned them.

Jessica thought the young woman seemed nervous and through the procedure, she shot furtive glances towards the man – probably her boss.

Meanwhile, Jessica kept one eye on the entrance doors. There was no sign of Robin's goons so she began to hope – just a little. Surely something will go right for them.

The captain was suddenly standing in front of her. Without a word, he took her hand and led the way towards the platform.

***

Jessica relaxed into her seat. Hard to believe she'd left Broughton Hall only the day before. There were no compartments in this more modern train. They were seated together, two seats side-by-side with enough room for her rucksack on the floor. The captain sat by the aisle that ran down the middle of the carriage.

This train was not headed to London so there were fewer people on board. Indeed, their carriage was almost empty; only a handful of passengers – older gentlemen, women with small children, talking quietly, flicking through magazines.

The seats across the aisle from where they sat, were occupied by an elderly couple, the gentleman greeted Jessica with a finger to the brim of his hat as he ushered his wife into the window seat.

Sitting beside the captain, Scaramouche wedged between them, Jessica rested her shoulder on the window and watched the fields and villages sail past, the landscape gradually changing as they moved further south.

The rolling dales of Yorkshire had long been left behind. Now, they swept past the rugged slopes of Derbyshire and the western pastures of Gloucestershire; lumbering ever southwards.

After a time, Jessica adjusted her position on the seat. Turning, she curled on her side in a small ball and laid her head in the captain's lap. She was instantly asleep, and Scaramouche tucked behind her knees, slept as well.

If the conductor came down the aisle, the captain must have presented their tickets with no incident and Jessica slept on, unaware.

**

Anton watched her as she rocked gently with the movement of the train. Her skin was silken, dusted lightly with freckles, her hand rested on his knee. Her nails could have been very pretty had they not been so work-worn, her fingers were curled like a sleeping baby's.

His heart ached for her – and for himself. He couldn't think of the rest of his life without her. Yet he couldn't imagine an alternative: a home where they could live, raise a family and grow old, surrounded by Thomas and Mary, and children they would make together.

The world would never allow such an appalling circumstance as a German Luftwaffe Captain and an English war widow cohabitating … God forbid they should marry! And what of their children? What little abominations society would label them!

The love between Anton and Jessica would be considered disgusting, unconscionable. They would be regarded with horrified expressions and treated as criminals.

Jessica murmured something and stirred, and he rested a gentling hand on her head. "Shh, my love, sleep," he whispered. She sighed and he allowed his hand to lightly stroke her coppery hair.

There had been a boy in his school with hair that colour. He'd been teased mercilessly by the other children, most of whom had hair in various shades of blond or light brown.

Anton remembered when the Nazis came to his school. Armed with their colour charts, they examined each student to identify those children whose hair colour fell outside the boundaries of what was considered Aryan.

Fortunately, Anton's school was a small rural establishment with only thirty-four children. One boy stood out as different – but not in a bad way for his hair was not dark. The colour was golden and russet and cinnamon depending on how the sun struck it. The Nazis went away that day, empty-handed.

The boy with the autumn hair had confounded them.

Anton shuddered, still haunted by what might have happened had the Nazis even suspected. For the boy, Josef, was his friend. His friend, *die Jude*. Had they known, the Nazis would have called him, *die unter Mensch*. And then they would have taken him away.

Anton hated Nazis. Only a few years after they visited the school, Josef's family had moved to New York. Many others had neither the foresight nor the means, but at least Josef's family had found safety and for that, Anton was grateful.

The fact that Jessica's father called him a Nazi still rankled, but the man knew no better. To Eric – to anyone outside of Germany – if you were German, it stood to reason that you were also a Nazi. It was precisely why he and Jessica were forced to make this journey; the success of which would be judged by his escape to France and their separation.

The train gave a slight lurch before slowing and Jessica's gold-flecked hazel eyes fluttered open. He watched as she blinked drowsily before focusing on his face, and his heart filled with such tenderness that he wanted to weep.

She pushed to a sitting position and snuggled beneath his arm, but he turned her face to his with a finger beneath her chin and kissed her.

He kissed her with such sadness and desperate longing that she gasped against his mouth. But she didn't pull away. Instead, she curled her arms about his neck and he felt his desire for her rising despite the awkwardness of their posture.

"*Ahem!*" the gentleman across the aisle grunted.

Slowly, reluctantly, Anton gently drew away. Jessica smiled at him. Her face was slightly flushed from sleep, her mouth reddened from his kisses.

God help me, he thought to himself, *how will I ever walk away from her?*

***

The journey to Penzance was expected to take about eight hours. Since they were not going all the way, but were alighting at Exeter, they anticipated leaving the train late that afternoon.

Relaxed in the knowledge that they'd managed to escape Robin's men, the captain and Jessica dozed in their seats, leaning into one another. From time to time, Scaramouche whimpered with boredom and a couple of hours into their journey, the captain took him for a walk along the aisle to stretch his legs.

Jessica watched the captain through heavy-lidded eyes, remembering how thin, how ill he'd been when she first took him into her house. With nourishment and the work he'd done around Broughton Hall, he'd filled out.

Though shorter than Jon, he wore Jon's clothes well, the shirt fitted across the shoulders, even if the trousers hung a little too loosely on his hips. His muscles moved with an easy fluidity as he strolled down the carriage; Jessica smirked realising she wasn't the only woman watching.

She exhaled with a grunt of bitter irony that she should find love with such a man; a man whom her children adored and who loved them in return, a kind man, intelligent and witty, and yet so dangerous.

And dangerous he was, even if he were not physically dangerous, the notion of him and everything implied by his being German was dangerous. If only the villagers of Wharferidge, Wolstone and their surrounds could see the man she saw.

She sighed.

"You are awake?" Consumed by her thoughts, she hadn't noticed his return.

Glancing up, she smiled wanly. His eyes were more grey than blue today and she wondered at their changeability. *He's sad too,* she guessed.

She extended a hand, took a fist full of his shirt and pulled him down, forcing him to crouch beside their seat.

"I love you, Anton," she said, using his first name to emphasise her point. "Don't ever forget that – no matter what happens in the future, I will *always* love you."

He shifted on his heels, flushed slightly and placed Scaramouche on the seat beside her. "*Und* I love you."

"Look," she said, pushing upright to a sitting position and levelling her eyes on his. "One day, if not Natalia, you will find a nice girl and you will marry – no, don't argue! You *must* marry and have a life, make a home … children." She was speaking quickly, an urgent whisper above the clackety-clacking of the train. Her eyes were beginning to sting. She blinked hard. "Just know that … oh, I don't know what I'm trying to say but … *please* remember me and everything we've shared this past year."

His arms came around her. "Do you think I could ever forget you? You are the only woman I will ever love." He buried his face in her neck and she felt a shudder run through him. "Frau Jessie, my Jessie …" he murmured into her hair, inhaling deeply.

"*Ahem!*" the gentleman across the aisle grunted again. "If you two don't keep your hands to yourselves I'll toss a bucket o' water over you!"

"Be still, you grumpy old curmudgeon!" Jessica retorted, feeling the captain twitch with mirth. The man grunted irritably while his wife gasped in exaggerated shock. Nevertheless, the captain pulled away to search her face.

"If I cannot marry you, I will not marry at all."

"You know that's foolish. Don't make promises that are impossible to keep."

"Jessica –"

She placed a finger against his lips. "Enough now. The train is slowing. I think we're coming into Bristol. We might have time to take Scarry outside for a toilet break."

***

It turned out they paused in Bristol for fifteen minutes. Jessica was almost cheerful in her relief at no longer being followed, although Anton maintained a wary lookout. They strolled along the street, hand in hand, beneath the beautiful towered façade of the station with its grand old clock. Scarry investigated likely posts and trees to cock a leg against, while Anton casually surveyed their surroundings – watching for anyone, anything that might suggest they were being tailed.

His military training had taught him that appearances couldn't always be trusted, and to take nothing for granted.

By the time they returned to the train, all had been calm and he'd seen nothing to concern him. They resumed their seats, for the last leg of their train journey.

***

The train pulled into Exeter St David's Station as evening was closing in. Mulberry-coloured clouds hung low in the sky and Jessica looked doubtfully at them. "We'd better find somewhere to spend the night." She pulled her coat from the rucksack and slipped into it. "Looks like rain. We can make our way to Waterville in the morning."

Anton nodded distractedly as she talked. He was studying a group of men a hundred yards up the wide street. It was Saturday night and they were servicemen – sailors by their uniforms – standing about, shoving one another and brandishing what looked like whiskey bottles. As a trio of young women alighted a bus, they hooted and called crude suggestions.

Anton scratched the stubble on his chin, thoughtfully. Young men, he knew, engorged with confidence and eager for diversion, were to be avoided. He turned and looked the other way. A sign caught his eye.

Pointing, he said, "Is that a …" he frowned, searching for the term that was not part of his daily vocabulary. "Is that *ein Gästehaus*?"

"A guest-house?"

"Similar word, then, guest-house."

Jessica squinted through the gathering darkness, as a chill wind blew across the nearby River Exe. He saw her shiver and hug herself. "I think it might be. We need to go … wind's cold. I think rain's coming."

Anton hiked Jessica's rucksack over a shoulder, gathered Scaramouche under one arm and took Jessica's hand with his other. They hurried along the street towards the sign swinging in the distance.

A brisk minute's walk revealed that it was indeed a guest-house. It also revealed the *No Vacancy* sign in the front window.

Pausing on the footpath, they considered their next move. "I could go in and ask if there's another nearby," Jessica seemed to be thinking aloud. "Come in with me?" she asked. "Don't speak, but smile a lot. You're irresistible when you smile."

"Ah … but so are you." He touched a finger lightly to her lips. "You do not smile enough." A flicker of sadness shadowed her face momentarily and he said, "Come. It is getting colder."

The entry hall was warm. It smelled invitingly of home cooking and anthracite heating. A middle-aged woman was standing at a table in the hallway. She was on the telephone, writing something on a notepad. She didn't look up as Anton ushered Jessica ahead of him, but raised a single finger in their direction as she finished her conversation.

Anton put Scaramouche on the floor but kept him close, although the little dog strained curiously towards a hatstand in the corner.

"Right y'are," the woman was saying down the phone. "You'll be the first to know."

She listened, "Mmhm … yes … Very well. Goodbye."

Hanging up, she turned to the couple standing close to one another. Her professionally assembled smile faded in an instant and Anton saw her gaze dart involuntarily towards the telephone.

Something was wrong, he knew it instinctively. Jessica hadn't seemed to notice. She stepped forwards with a friendly smile and enquired whether the woman knew where she and her husband might spend the night.

The woman frowned and seemed to deliberate. After some consideration, she introduced herself as Mrs Ellis and explained that a room was, in fact, available in her house. "A young lady … a farm girl, she was. Vacated earlier. I 'aven't 'ad time to do up the room."

"Oh that's perfect," Jessica said brightly, "And so lucky, isn't it dear?" She beamed at him, relief written clearly on her guileless face."

Anton nodded agreement but couldn't shake the feeling of disquiet hanging over him. Was it his imagination, or was Mrs Ellis avoiding eye contact with him? Nevertheless, he smiled at Jessie and gave her hand a brief squeeze where it rested on his arm.

"Right y'are," Mrs Ellis said. "Come, sit in the parlour for a bit, eh? Rest up while I prepare the room." Without waiting for their response, she ushered them into a small parlour with a comfortable couch and glowing fire.

"So where you heading? Having a bit of a break?" Mrs Ellis's chatter was casual. *Too casual*, he thought. Was she probing, or was it his own suspicious mind?

He wanted to hang back, but Jessica had broken away and was already taking a seat where Mrs Ellis indicated. "We're on our way to Waterville," she freely told the woman. "You wouldn't know the best way to get there, would you?"

Mrs Ellis thought for a moment while she poked at the fire and added a scoop of anthracite.

Behind her back, Anton gave Jessica's arm a nudge. She glared at him and mouthed, *What's wrong with you?*

Before he could respond, Mrs Ellis turned round and he quickly pasted a smile on his face. "There's a bus what runs from here to Astor. You want the southbound route, from Paul Street. From Astor, you get another bus – it's only an hour, but it don't run all that frequently."

"Thank you." Jessica shot a triumphant grin at Anton.

"Now," the woman went on, "you just relax here for fifteen minutes or so. I'll go make up that room."

"Thank you so much," Jessica said. "We thought we'd be wandering about all night."

"It's no problem, love, none at all." Mrs Ellis paused with her hand on the door, seeming to hesitate for a moment. Suddenly, she looked at Anton properly for the first time. Her mouth formed a grim line and the German knew, in that moment, that his instincts were correct. He forced a smile and sat beside Jessica, appearing to relax.

Mrs Ellis shut the door firmly on her way out.

"What the hell's wrong with you?" Jessica demanded *sotto voce* but he ignored her. He was immediately on his feet, ear pressed to the door.

"What are you –?"

"Shh!" Anton waved at her, continuing to listen. Then he heard it: The one-sided conversation of someone on a telephone and he swore colourfully under his breath.

"She knows about us," he said. "We must leave. Now!"

"But –"

"Come. Listen." He beckoned her over. Scaramouche trotted at her feet and stood wagging his stumpy tail and glancing from one to the other.

Jessica pressed her ear to the door beside him. He saw her eyes widen as Mrs Ellis's voice could be clearly heard.

"When will he be back, then? I mean, he only just called. Literally minutes ago."

A pause.

"No, I don't want to talk to Mr Johnson, I want to talk to Mr Tyler. It were he what told me –" she broke off with a frustrated sound. "To call him, if I saw –"

"Told you – in my parlour."

"No, just walked in … off the street. Look, I ain't got all night."

"Red hair, little dog … I'm certain."

Jessica gasped. She looked across at Anton, her mouth gaping.

"I'll try," Mrs Ellis continued.

"Wouldn't know. He hasn't spoken."

"No."

"All right then."

"Well, tell him to hurry."

"Thank you."

***

Anton heard the gentle replacement of the telephone receiver and his eyes locked with Jessica's.

"Oh, God," she breathed. "How does she know about us? How did Robin know we were here?"

"I think it would not be difficult," Anton reasoned. "Probably the ticket girl at the station told him we were coming to Exeter. Then all he had to do was telephone the guest-houses near the station."

"But –"

"Does not matter now. We need to leave." Anton looked around and spotted the iron fire poker. An idea was forming in his mind. Grasping the poker, he spoke quickly, "Carry the dog in your arms *und* do as I say."

With Jessica's rucksack over his shoulder, the poker in his hand, he went to the door, listened for a moment, and turned to her. "Now!"

Anton flung open the door and stepped into the hall. Mrs Ellis was sitting on the little stool next to the telephone. She gave a startled yelp as he appeared even though he held the poker behind his back.

Quickly gathering herself, the older woman seemed to make an admirable effort towards nonchalance. "Oh, hello. Can I get you something? Tea perhaps? I was just going upstairs to do your room."

"No, thank you," Jessica said. Anton was surprised at how calm she sounded. She stepped in front of him. "We've decided not to stay after all, but thank you for your kindness."

Anton watched the woman's eyes flit around as though searching for some way of detaining them. "Please, let me … how about a, a plate of –"

Jessica stepped forwards. "Look, we'll just – *ah*!"

She broke off in surprise as Anton impatiently grasped her firmly by the arm. The glare he shot at her was genuine as he dragged her against his side.

"That is enough!" He snarled, emphasising his accent. He knew the woman would give Tyler a complete report. This could be a way of exonerating Jessica's involvement with him while affording them a quick getaway.

The blood drained from Mrs Ellis's face and she let out a terrified squeak. Backing up against the wall, hands held defensively before her, she gasped, "Please … I …please don't hurt me!"

Anton felt sick at the thought of what he was about to do but having made up his mind, was committed to it. "You stay there!" he ordered, brandishing the poker like a club, and dragging Jessica closer. Scaramouche, still cuddled in her arms, stared at the scene from wide, bewildered eyes.

Anton gave Jessica's arm a rough shake. "You will com *mit mir*."

Jessica, thankfully, understood his intention immediately. "Please … let me stay here!" she begged him. "You don't need me anymore … *please*!"

Edging towards the door, Anton held Jessica as a hostage, with one arm about her waist, poker trained in the older woman's direction. "Move! *Schnell*!" he commanded, all but thrusting Jessica through the door and onto the porch.

Anton trusted that the mere sound of an aggressive German accent would spike fear into Mrs Ellis's heart. She'd have read the newspapers. She'd know the horrors being carried out by the Nazis. Let her fearful imagination do the rest.

"Can't you let that woman go?" Mrs Ellis tremulously called after them.

Why was she trying to be brave? Anton cursed under his breath. "Move!" he ordered Jessica.

"I won't stop you!" Mrs Ellis tried again. "Just leave the woman –"

Anton turned on the threshold. "*Nein, ist* out of zhe question. She coms *mit mir und* you vill stay zhere! Do not move!" He brutally slashed the air with the poker.

Mrs Ellis seemed to shrink, her face turning white while Anton took a menacing step towards her. Her eyes were wide and filled with terror as she slid down the wall before him.

"Do not move!" Anton bellowed again. He still held Jessica's arm. Now he yanked her viciously forwards and raised the poker in her direction.

The very gesture of threatening the woman he loved felt so foreign that it almost caused him to waver. He took hold of himself and growled in his thickest accent, "I tell you, I vill kill you both if you move *ein* finger!"

"I won't … I won't …!" Mrs Ellis cried in dread.

Now Anton turned to Jessica. "You! Move! *Und* no games!" He shoved her savagely out into the darkened street. Jessica stumbled down the front steps, landing heavily on her knees. Her gasp of pain turned his stomach. Scaramouche tumbled from her arms with a startled whimper.

***

Jessica was not play acting now. Her knees hurt and she gathered the little dog to her and remained crouching on the side of the road. For a terrifying moment, she wondered if something had snapped in the German's mind and he was no longer pretending.

But when he turned she saw the remorse flicker across his handsome features as he realised he'd genuinely hurt her.

"On your feet woman!" he barked, all the while apologising with his eyes. He shot a glance at Mrs Ellis who could be seen through the open door. She was cowering in a far corner of the entry hall. The captain snarled a string of indecipherable German at Jessica, pulled her to her feet and hurried off into the dark.

The absence of street lighting worked in their favour, rapidly absorbing them into shadows.

The captain discarded the poker under a shrub and they trotted down the street as quickly as they could, given the state of Jessica's knees.

She could feel them growing stiff with bruising and they hurt like the blazes. But she couldn't stop to worry about that now as they darted down a lane, zig-zagged along alleys, behind shops, warehouses and eventually came to a gasping halt in the shelter of a churchyard wall.

As Jessica collapsed against the brickwork and allowed Scaramouche to slide to the ground, the captain was immediately crouching before her, rolling up the legs of her slacks, a stream of German contrition issuing from his lips.

"I can't … under … stand you." Jessica panted. She unbuttoned her coat allowing the cool night air to touch her overheated skin.

"*Mein Gott,*" he murmured, peering close to examine her knees in the dark. "I am so sorry – there is blood. I have hurt you."

She touched his hair, "It's all … right. Honestly … Captain … get up." Her breathing was steadying, she grasped his coat at the collar and tugged, trying to drag him to his feet.

He resisted, and squinted up at her. "I am sorry … I was too rough."

"It's not that bad. Come on," she looked around anxiously and tugged again. "We need to find somewhere to hide for the night."

The captain got to his feet and suggested they head towards the river, "There should be buildings. Ones like …" he shrugged, his mind struggling with the term. His English usually failed him when he was tired or upset about something.

"Warehouses? Sheds?" Jessica suggested. Besides fatigue and the soreness of her knees, she was becoming very hungry.

She wasn't about to complain though – the captain and their dog would be equally tired and hungry.

"Can you walk?" He leaned towards her and took her hand. "I am so sorry. You know I would never intentionally hurt you."

"I know that." She smiled as he lifted her hand to his mouth and brushed her knuckles back and forth across his lips. "You're right," she agreed. "Let's go to the river. Maybe we can find somewhere to hide down there."

She pushed away from the wall and they started out.

The night was cold and thankfully, the clouds that had earlier threatened rain, seemed to have blown over. A gentle wind occasionally blew threads of music from some distant dance hall, but the night was otherwise silent. They found the river easily enough, but there were no warehouses or buildings to offer shelter. The best they could find was a riverside bandstand.

It was obvious, even through the darkness, that the place had seen better times. Its paint was peeling and plaster mouldings on the gables and balustrades were broken or missing. Jessica sighed regretfully; this place would have been lovely in its day. A lively gathering place for locals and visitors – yet another casualty of war.

But tonight, it would serve them well. They mounted the steps and moved about on the creaking floorboards and the captain looked at her with a question on his face.

She nodded. "It's as good a place as any."

They settled in for the night. Huddled together for warmth beneath their coats, Jessica served a meal of tinned beef and vegetables that they ate directly from the cans with the Digestive biscuits.

Scaramouche sat between them. After wolfing his own share, he wandered to the edge of the river for a drink and a sniff around, then promptly came trotting back.

Jessica and the captain munched their way through half a packet of biscuits and a couple of tins of beef, before snuggling down for sleep.

Spooned by the captain behind her, she cuddled Scaramouche to her chest, and despite the cold, despite the discomfort of the timbers beneath them, the trio rapidly descended into sleep.

***

Lingering on the edge of consciousness, Anton reflected wryly that he'd always hoped for the opportunity to sleep with his arms round Jessica. This night was the second such where he'd done just that, but certainly not under the circumstances he'd envisioned.

The thought made him sad. He tightened his arms round her and she stirred, more asleep than awake, and sighed sleepily with the dog in her arms. "Sleep my darling … My love," he murmured softly in German, before pressing a firm kiss to the nape of her neck.

Then he too slept.

***

It rained during the night, but the couple slept on, undisturbed by its steady clatter on the tin roof over their heads.

When Jessica awoke in the morning, it was still dark and she was shivering. She felt stiff and sore, as though she hadn't moved all night. Slowly, she became aware of the captain lying behind her, his arm draped over her hip.

The coats they'd huddled beneath were damp with dew but had fortunately trapped enough warmth in their folds to protect them from the chilly night air.

Scaramouche was missing. The thought occurred to her as she realised the lack of warmth provided by his furry little body, was what had awoken her. She didn't know where he'd gone but assumed he'd wandered off to relieve himself. She worried he'd get lost in the dark and her immediate reaction was to call him. She moved and drew a quick breath, preparing to call out.

Immediately the captain's arm tightened like a band around her, pulling her back against him. "Do not move," he whispered into her hair. "There are men down there."

Suddenly she heard it: the deep notes of casual male conversation. There seemed to be three, perhaps four individual voices. "What are they doing?" she breathed.

"Fishing, I think."

"Damn!" The sun would soon begin to lighten the sky and they would be discovered. Questions would be asked; nobody let a stranger loiter in their town these days without asking questions. "Where is Scarry?"

"He was down there ... but now I do not know."

"Damn," she repeated. The dog was likely to give them away, but just then, Scaramouche scampered up the steps, happy as you like, and eager to begin another day of his big adventure.

Behind her, the captain moved silently into a sitting position. He softly clicked his fingers and Scaramouche went to him.

Snatching the dog into his arms, he said softly, "Come. If we gather our things, we can leave while it is still dark."

Before they had settled for sleep the night before, Jessica had packed the rucksack. She hadn't anticipated having to make a quick getaway, her only thought had been to keep all their things in one place. But her forethought worked to their advantage.

"I have it all here," she pulled the rucksack towards her.

"Give it to me," the captain volunteered. "You take the dog – he is lighter."

They swapped bundles, then crouching low, moved as silently as the aged wooden flooring would allow. Fortunately, the steps to the bandstand were on the street side, opposite to where the men stood on the river bank, home-made fishing poles in their hands.

Jessica could just make out their silhouettes limned against the dawn sky as she and the captain slipped silently away.

"We must find the bus stop," she told him as they walked along Waggoners Way. "Mrs Ellis said Paul Street."

"*Ja, und* that is exactly where they will look for us. I think that Mrs Ellis will have told Robin Tyler everything. He will be here somewhere."

Jessica stopped abruptly as a heavy weariness fell over her along with the urge to sink to the ground and stay there forever. "What are we going to do?" she moaned. Forcing herself to remain upright, she told herself firmly, *You haven't the luxury of falling to pieces.*

***

Anton saw Jessica's shoulders slump; she was doing all of this for him. By rights she should be home, safe with her children and her cows. But, just as quickly, she stoically pulled herself together and he knew why he loved her. "We must find another way," he said, thinking. "We are assuming Mrs Ellis gave us correct directions."

Jessica's eyes widened. "Do you think …? Surely she wouldn't have lied?"

"She would if she were trying to trap us."

Frowning, Jessica chewed her cheek and seemed to be thinking. "I doubt she lied about the directions," she said at length. "I don't think she thought that quickly; probably why she tried to delay us long enough for Robin to get there. Remember, she had no vacancies? She made up the story of the farm girl suddenly leaving."

Anton nodded and scratched absently at his sprouting beard. "I think you are right. We must still find our way to this town." He looked at her questioningly.

"Astor – we were to take a bus to Astor."

"Now," Anton gestured to indicate the sun rising over the horizon. Daylight was banishing the shadows and burning off the light mist hanging over the river. "I want to see your legs."

She blinked at him and said coquettishly, "Why Captain, is that some kind of German courtship ritual?"

He was still feeling guilty over hurting her and was in no mood for teasing. He grumbled something guttural and hunkered before her.

"I can do it," she slapped his hands away. "And stop being so damn apologetic! I don't blame you, you know." She rolled up the leg of her slacks to reveal ugly pink and purple bruising and dried blood on her knee. "The other one will be the same so you don't need to look." She quickly rolled her slacks back down.

Anton made a rueful face. "I was too rough *und* I am very sorry that I hurt you."

"I know, and you're forgiven. Now, where shall we go?"

He thought for a moment. "To the station. If we take a train back to the previous stop – Cowley, I think, we can take the bus from there. Tyler will expect us to catch the bus from Exeter. He may not think we are already on it when it arrives. Just in case, we must sit separately *und* keep Scaramouche out of sight."

She regarded him steadily for a moment, weighing up his idea. "I don't think there's anything else we can do," she said at last. "So –" she took his arm. "Let's go."

***

As it turned out, they arrived at the station only to find the trains running to a Sunday timetable. There would be a long wait if they were to take a train back to Cowley.

Jessica studied a map of Exeter on the station wall. "I'm surprised they have this here given we're at war," she said as the captain stood looking over her shoulder. "Most town maps were removed."

"We are here *und* there is Paul Street." He indicated a spot on the map. "Not far."

She grinned. "Let's be adventurous! Robin knows what I look like. His men know what both of us look like. Why don't we go to the bus stop? I'll stay hidden while you check the timetable. If it looks like Robin or anyone is there, get on the bus alone – I'll catch up down the road. If there is no sign of them, we'll get on the bus together."

A slow smile was creeping across his face.

"What?" she demanded.

"You." He touched her nose with the tip of a finger. "Making daring plans. So unlike the shy lady I met almost a year ago."

She narrowed her eyes at him. "Harbouring an enemy fugitive will do that! So, are we going?"

"We are going."

***

There was no sign of Robin or his men when they arrived at the Paul Street bus terminal. A notice on the wall explained that due to petrol rationing, buses were running to a reduced timetable, but as luck would have it, one was due within the next ten minutes.

A young woman and her elderly mother were the only other people waiting. When the bus pulled in, exactly on time, Jessica and the captain – she carrying Scaramouche, he carrying the rucksack – boarded and sat near the rear door.

The bus moved off with a hissing lurch. A pretty lass in a conductor's uniform approached the captain. "Astor, two adults, please," Jessica leapt in before the girl addressed him.

The girl offered the captain a conciliatory smile and slight raising of one eyebrow. She'd evidently decided that Jessica was overprotective of her boyfriend.

The captain returned her smile and Jessica nudged him. "Were you flirting with her?" She asked quietly as the conductor moved away. She attempted a teasing tone but didn't quite manage it.

"Are you jealous?" he countered, grinning wickedly.

She made a contemptuous face and he laughed, saying, "I think she will remember me more if I were unpleasant."

"You think? Perhaps your face is common where you come from, but here you're considered very handsome. She will remember you regardless."

"So your solution would be to smile or frown?"

"Keep your head down and do neither."

"You *are* jealous." He bumped her playfully with his shoulder.

Jessica glared at him then turned away to look out the window; it made him laugh again.

"You need not be," he added. "Look at me ..."

Her mouth twitched but she stubbornly continued staring out at the houses on the outskirts of town as the bus navigated its way through the narrow streets.

"Jessica," he whispered in her ear. "*Meine* Jessie ..." with a finger beneath her chin, he turned her to face him.

His mouth covered hers as his hand cupped her cheek.

Jessica felt a stirring deep in the pit of her stomach as his kiss deepened and her head began to swim.

Suddenly he broke the kiss but murmured low and sensual against her lips in his own language. His breathing was shallow, his eyes slightly glazed. He closed them and settled back in his seat.

Jessica felt dazed and aflame. Her nerves were jumping and alive. He did this to her. When he kissed her like that – like the way he had that day in the orchard – her body reacted with such desperate longing that she felt she could explode.

But she was a widow with two young children. Surely such passions as the German captain ignited in her were the domain of loose women? Certainly not in keeping with the respectable young mother she was supposed to be.

She stole a sideways glance. He was resting with his eyes closed, head on the back of his seat.

Where did he learn to kiss like that?

That Natalia girl of his, I suppose.

And suddenly Jessica's heart clenched with a pain so intense she almost cried out. He was going home. To the loving bosom of his family, and the arms of the girl he'd left behind.

Jessica had never known jealousy before, but now she *was* jealous. Not of the pretty bus conductor or the girl in the café. She was jealous of the girl who expected to spend her life with him – the girl who had a right to him.

***

Anton rested with his eyes closed. He felt fatigued after two nights with little sleep, but he was also charged with the kind of adrenalin adventure and danger always seemed to fire in him.

He felt Jessica stir beside him and took a quick breath. Every day was a struggle to keep his hands to himself. These last two nights as he'd lain with her, if not for the precariousness of their situation, the discomfort of where they were forced to sleep, he'd have disregarded his promise to her.

That night she'd spent in his bed had only inflamed his appetite for more. That he was in love was undeniable. That he was in lust was equally undeniable. He wanted her … He ached with it and last night as she pushed her tight round arse against him for warmth he … well, he was grateful that she went immediately to sleep and was unaware of the insistent demands of his tormented body.

He exhaled in a long sigh. There were more important things to worry about because he'd noticed a car at the station. It had pulled away from the curb at the same time as their bus, and he was now certain it was tailing them.

Occasionally, he stole a glance behind and it was still there – had been for several miles.

It slowed and stopped when they did; it sped up when they did. And now they were on the open road, having left Exeter behind, it kept a constant quarter mile between them, coming in and out of view as they crested and dipped with the undulations of the road.

Anton knew Jessica wasn't aware of it, and he wanted to keep it that way. To rest here with his eyes closed, seemingly untroubled, would afford her precious time to relax.

She was exhausted. The purple shadows beneath her eyes contrasted sharply with the pale apricot of her skin. Her beautiful hair was a straggly mess, desperately in need of washing and her clothes were grimy from sleeping in rough, dirty locations.

She sighed softly and cuddled into his shoulder; he shifted, raising his arm to allow her to snuggle beneath. Scaramouche squirmed about before curling up beneath Jessica's coat. He also slept.

But Anton maintained a wary vigil.

It was midday by the time the bus pulled into Astor. It wheezed to a halt outside an old pub called The Coachman's Rest.

Jessica stood gazing up at the lumpy, whitewashed walls of the old place. "Must be at least four hundred, years old," she estimated. Scaramouche, happy to be off the bus, danced excitedly about their feet. "Mrs Ellis said there'd be another bus but I don't know …"

Anton wasn't listening. For the last several miles, he hadn't seen the car following them. He hoped he'd been mistaken and that the car's steady pace had been an innocent coincidence. Somehow, he doubted it.

He put a gentle hand on her shoulder. "I think we should keep moving. Why do you not go inside," he indicated the pub with his chin, "*und* ask the best way to get to Waterville."

She nodded and passed Scaramouche's leash to him. "All right. You wait here."

***

Jessica stood resting her elbows on the bar. Her nerves were jangling, making her feel a little sick. A woman was serving another customer down the far end, and through a door into the kitchen, Jessica could see two young boys – one was chopping vegetables while another swept the floor.

"Waterville Place?" the man in front of her repeated. He was built like a mountain, tall and broad, solid but not fat. The effect was intimidating and he knew it. "Army took it over about six months back … using it for an 'ospital for returned servicemen."

His tone was friendly enough but his face was guarded.

Please God, don't let this all be for nothing!

Jessica sighed. "I … I'd still like to see it.".

"Listen Ma'am," the man went on, "yer come down here to see an old mansion? I unnerstand: tourists love that old place – right jewel she is too. But if yer 'aven't noticed, there's war on and what the army wants, the army takes. End o' story."

He turned away to serve a customer leaving Jessica standing awkwardly alone. She felt foolish but reluctant to walk away … not yet. Something was nagging at the back of her brain. Something she couldn't put her finger on.

The publican finished with the customer and looked round. Jessica saw the impatience flicker across his face. "What?" he demanded irritably. "I ain't got all day. Yer gonna order a drink or yer leaving? Make up yer mind but I got nothing else for yer."

Jessica exhaled. She was about to turn away, when she tried another tack, "I'm a nurse." She even surprised herself. "I've been stationed at Waterville Place. I'm trying to find my way there."

The man leaned forward to peer at her. She smelt cigarettes on his breath. "That right? Well, yer lying otherwise yer'da known the place were an 'ospital."

"I …" Jessica hesitated. She was growing desperate and something was still nagging, echoing in her mind – words she'd read somewhere.

"That all? I got things ter do."

He gestured as though to dismiss her but Jessica was still

thinking. *What was it?* She asked herself. *What did I read? Was it in Alexandra's journal perhaps? Yes*! She remembered, but did she dare? How could she not? She'd come this far!

She swallowed and leaned towards the man. "I must go to Waterville Place," she lowered her voice but spoke clearly, "I want to see the early crocuses."

The man's expression transformed. His mouth fell open and his eyes darted rapidly left and right. "Say that again."

Jessica swallowed. "I um … want to see … early crocuses?" She wasn't so confident this time. If he turned her away now she didn't know what she'd do.

The man stared hard at her and seemed to be considering his next words. Finally, he drew a long breath. "I don't think they are out yet."

Chapter 46

"Where d'yer hear that line?" the barman asked. "Jessica, yer said yer name was, right?"

Jessica nodded. She was sitting at a table, a steaming cup of tea between her palms. The man was sitting opposite with a glass of ale, while the woman, Magda, served the handful of local customers. "I just read it." She was nervous but a thrill of excitement was coursing through her too. *Have I stumbled on the right person to help us?*

"D'yer know what yer said?"

Jessica nodded.

"No one *just reads* that."

"It was in an old memoir," she added. She blew on her tea as though completely at ease, chatting with an old friend over a cuppa.

"That right?"

She nodded again.

"What *old memoir*?"

Jessica smiled nervously. "You won't know the person who wrote it ... it's *very* old."

He cocked an eyebrow. "Try me."

"Her name was Alexandra Broughton. She –"

"I know 'er. Alexandra were well known and very popular. Down at The Bowsprit there's a paintin' of 'er above the fireplace. Right pretty she were too."

"Yes, I believe so. And the earl, Lord Patrick, he was her stepbrother."

"Aye, well, he's practically a saint 'round here. Seventy years since he died, but they still talk 'bout what a decent chap he were even though he was one o' the hoy-poloy. So yer have Alexandra's memoir, do yer?"

"I do, and she mentioned the ... the crocuses."

"Not surprising. Lord Patrick ... Well, it's unclear whether he were personally involved in *the business,*" he emphasised *the business* with quotation-mark fingers. "But he were known to be sympathetic to local goings-on. Times were difficult back then. People needed t'earn a livin'. The earl kept some kind of warehouse ... 'ad a cellar what were considered a safe 'ouse if the authorities ever came sniffin' about. So," he eyed her carefully. "Yer know that line means nothin' these days, don't yer?"

Jessica felt her hopes deflate. The man pursed his lips, watching her steadily. "Tell me then, what *really* brings yer here?"

"When I found the memoir," Jessica thought quickly. "I was curious about Alexandra and –"

"Nope." He raised a large, square hand to cut her off. "Try again."

"But –"

"The truth this time."

Her mouth went dry and she stared at him, swallowing nervously. *Can I trust him?* she wondered. *Why would he help me? He would hate Germans as much as anyone but what choice do I have?* She felt his eyes studying her.

His frown made him look fierce. His hands, cradling his ale glass, were large, the fingers short, stubby, calloused – two fingers on his left hand were missing from the first knuckle. His face was like old leather, his eyes were quick, black and sharp – they looked as though they could see great distances and his white hair was long and ... the word windswept came to her.

Lucifer's balls, he's one of them!

She knew he saw the realisation dawn on her face. She heard his intake of air as he awaited her next move.

Having decided, she said softly, "I need help. I have ... I need to send something very precious, to France, and I don't know any other way."

"What makes yer think I can help?" The man sat back in his chair, face inscrutable. The stumps of his missing fingers tapped the side of his glass.

Be careful, Jessica, she told herself firmly. Her hands were clammy on the teacup as she took a sip; its warmth, its tannin flavours, helped steady her nerves. "I don't *think*," she said carefully, "but I *hoped* you might … know someone."

He waved dismissively and moved as though he was about to get up from the table. "I can pay!" she said urgently. "Not much … but I have *some* money."

"There's no one here what can help yer." He went to leave.

"I've travelled a long way … I'm desperate." The tears sprang involuntarily into her eyes and he paused, pinning her with an intense, black stare.

"Yer accent is northern."

"Yes."

"How d'yer come t'ave that book?"

"I own Broughton Hall – it was Alexandra's childhood home. I found it there."

"And yer thought yer'd come down here …" he shrugged, speculatively, "meddle in things yer don't unnerstand? Sticky-beak 'round? Have yerself a bit of adventure?"

"No!" Jessica cried. "Of course not. It was Alexandra's story that made me hope I could find some way to …" she didn't want to say the word *smuggle*, but it hung in the air between them. "Some way to send my goods to France."

He stood staring down at her. Jessica knew she looked exhausted, grubby and dishevelled. Surely he could see she was genuine?

"These are dangerous questions yer asking. People've been known to disappear after asking the kinds of questions ye're asking – sniffin' about like this."

"I'm not looking for trouble –"

"Ye're *inviting* it."

She sighed wearily. Her throat constricted with a painful lump. *Don't cry*, she told herself sternly.

"I'm desperate," she croaked. "I have no choice." Looking up, she bravely returned his gaze, hoping he could see the sincere appeal in her eyes.

"I reckon I'm a pretty decent judge o' character," he said, after a moment. His attitude seemed to relax slightly. "I can see yer frightened o' sumthin', but what ye're suggesting is no small thing."

"I know," Jessica lowered her eyes to her tea. He was going to send her away empty-handed. After all she and the captain had been through she didn't think she could bear that. The backs of her eyes started to sting. One slow tear spilled onto her cheek. "I'm desperate," she repeated, in a whisper. "I don't know what else to do."

He resumed his seat, eyes never leaving her face. "Yer young and naive, foolish. And because o' that, I reckon yer tellin' me the truth. Everything yer do in this world's a gamble, lass. The roll of a dice, toss of a coin – yer could step onto the road and be run down by a lorry. Yer could be sleeping innocently in yer bed and some bloody Gerry dumps a bomb on yer 'ouse."

He drew in his breath, his voice dropped very low and he leaned forward in his chair. "All right. I'll bite. Where *is* this item?"

Jessica looked up suddenly. Her heart was hammering and her stomach suddenly convulsed. *God, I'm going to be sick!* She took a steadying sip of tea and swallowed over the lump in her throat before answering.

"Outside."

***

Jessica led the captain into the bar. She'd given him a hurried run-down on the man, their discussion and the situation. "It's a real chance," she told him. "I think we've found the right man, or at least, someone who *knows* the right man."

The captain didn't seem convinced as he followed her, Scaramouche in his arms and Jessica's rucksack on his back. She led him to the darkened corner, where the hulking man waited in the shadows.

"This the item?" The man eyed Scaramouche doubtfully. "A dog?"

Jessica's arm snaked around the captain's waist. "Not the dog," she said in a shaky voice. "This is Tony."

The man snorted rudely. "Yer wanna send *him* to France? Why isn't he there already, fighting fer his King?"

The captain spoke for the first time, "Because I am German."

"*What the fuck*!" The man leapt to his feet. He was at least a head taller and almost twice the width of the captain. His face darkened and he sputtered in a hoarse whisper, "Yer bring this … this …"

The captain calmly held his ground but Jessica felt the blood drain from her face. She began to tremble. "*Please!*" she begged but the barman continued to tower threateningly over them.

"A *fuckin' Gerry*? Yer bring a *fuckin' Gerry* into my bar and …!" he ended with a furious choking sound as words failed him.

One or two fishermen leaning on the bar looked up from their pints, attracted by the sudden commotion.

Perhaps it was Jessica's soft weeping, perhaps the way the captain pulled her gently into his chest, that caused the rough Englishman to finally close his mouth.

Yet he continued to stand there, and Jessica watched through swimming eyes as the man glared at them. His lips were drawn into a tight line, his great barrel chest rose and fell with outrage.

Finally, the large man pulled a deep breath through flared nostrils and seemed to take control of himself. Evidently, deprived of the bar-room drama they'd hoped for, the patrons returned to their drinks.

"All right," the man snarled. Then calmer, "All right. I'm sufficiently intrigued." He flicked a hand towards the bench opposite. "Christ!" he drew another breath and shook his head with angry disbelief. "Ye're a fuckin' Kraut, are yer? Well, what the bloody hell are yer doing with a decent Englishwoman? *That's* the question."

"He's with a decent Englishwoman because he's a decent man!" Jessica snapped smartly. As the publican's eyes swung in her direction, she modified her tone. "Look, we want to be together but we can't. We're running from the authorities. They won't leave us alone. They're hunting us … he *must* get to France. From there he'll be able to get home."

"That's yer plan?"

Jessica nodded. Her breathing was coming quickly and she felt mildly dizzy. "They'll take my children away …" the grief in her voice was authentic, and fresh tears dribbled down her cheeks. "They'll send me to jail and put him in a P.O.W camp."

"They would – we're at war," the barman said dryly, continuing to watch the captain's face through narrowed eyes.

***

"Yer seen action?"

Anton nodded slowly. The man was too astute to be lied to.

"Doing what? What's yer name, rank, company …?"

Drawing a deep breath, Anton felt Jessica stiffen beside him, but threw her a fortifying smile.

"Hauptmann Anton Vogel. Luftwaffe."

"A fuckin' flier, eh?" The man ran a hand through his straggly hair. "*Whew*!" he whistled and leaned back in his chair, regarding Anton through narrowed eyes. "Luftwaffe. Yer know I could kill yer on the spot and get an hero's medal?"

"I know it." Anton held the man's gaze.

"Ye're not afraid?"

"Oh, *ja*, I am afraid. I am afraid for this woman *und* her children. I am afraid for my parents in Germany. I am afraid for every man in the trenches, in the air *und* on the sea regardless of the land they call home. *Ja*, our countries are at war, *und* our politicians. But beneath our uniforms, we are just men."

The man snorted. "Idealistic ain't yer?"

Anton gave a wry, one-shoulder shrug.

"Dog tags." The Englishman thrust out a large paw.

Without hesitation, Anton reached beneath his shirt and pulled the chain over his head. The tags made a tinny sound as he handed them across the table.

The publican turned the tags over thoughtfully. "Are yer both mad, or foolish?"

"Neither." Anton's smile was mysterious. He leaned across the table, and said, "You need me."

The barman man raised bristling salt-and-pepper eyebrows. "That right?"

"You are the man we have been looking for," Anton said simply. "You are the one that will take me to France. I know this because you need a German speaker to help you evade the port authorities."

For the first time, the Englishman smiled. He was missing an eye-tooth. "Not just a pretty face, eh?"

Anton dipped his head in acknowledgement. "I can make it easier for you in your activities."

"And what activities are those?" The barman's tone was challenging but his interest was undisguised. He sat back, folding meaty arms across his broad chest.

"The smuggling of Jews out of France."

Anton watched in silent satisfaction as the Englishman leaned forward in his chair, his eyes becoming hard. "Is this what yer think?"

"It is what I know. I also know I can make things easier for you."

"Let's say ye're right about me business. How could yer make things easier?"

Anton arched his eyebrows in mock astonishment. "A German officer, working *with* you, *und* you do not know how that would make things easier?"

***

The Englishman and the German exchanged a long, assessing stare and Jessica felt a cold sweat break on her nape. Suddenly, the barman threw his head back and roared with laughter.

She gaped at him, then turned to the captain in confusion. He merely smiled and gave her hand a light squeeze. It was a gentle, loving gesture – not lost on the other man, and perhaps it was the decider because he suddenly rose from his chair.

"Make yer way down to Waterville Place. There's a bus'll take yer almost to the gate. When yer get orf, yer'll need to find a man called Sid. By the time yer gets there, he'll be expectin' yer. Tell him Wheeler sent yer."

"Wheeler?" Jessica interrupted. "That your name?"

Wheeler's eyes bored hard into her face. "What's it to yer?"

She felt the captain's warning touch on her arm but ignored it. "Alexandra's memoir mentioned a man – someone she protected from the excise-men. I'm sure his name was Wheeler."

"Probl'y some ancestor. Family's bin here fer cent'ries."

"Waterville Place, it's an 'ospital – *army* hospital," he emphasised, and Jessica saw his eyes travel over the captain. "Yer'll keep yer mouth shut, head down and respect our returned soldiers."

The captain's expression was contemptuous. "Of course."

"Hmph!" Wheeler snorted. "Sid'll drive yer round to The

Bowsprit. When yers get there, 'e'll int'roduce yers to a feller named Alf. He'll give yers a room and a meal. I'll join yers there tomorrow."

Jessica jumped to her feet. "Oh thank you, thank –"

Wheeler cut her off. "We'll talk more then."

Glancing down at the German dog tags in his fist, he tossed them in the air and the captain caught them overhanded. "Ye're going to need these." He paused, eying the captain narrowly. "If yer do anythin' stupid or I find out yer've been lyin' to me, they'll be usin' these t'dentify yer filthy carcass."

Nodding in apparent contemplation of his own words, Wheeler's eyes lingered on the captain. "No," he said at last. "Y'ain't mad nor foolish. That'd be me."

Chapter 47

The bus took less than an hour to get to Waterville Place. The route was winding and increasingly rugged, pushing ever southwards. For the last ten minutes, it lumbered along the road following the coast.

Looking out the window, to their left, the English Channel heaved and tossed, a murky grey expanse of water with white peaks. Jessica shuddered to think of the lives lost in its treacherous depths and automatically reached for the captain's hand.

It was their target: that deep, cold strait – the purpose of their journey. She wished there was another way. But there wasn't and she'd worn herself out fretting over it. Yawning, she slumped further into her seat and adjusted Scaramouche on her lap.

"Captain?" she said drowsily, having suddenly remembered some niggling detail. "How did you guess Wheeler was smuggling Jews out of France? You took quite a risk, didn't you?"

He shook his head. "No risk. Did you not see that woman, Magda, who was working there? She wore a Star of David on a chain about her neck. The two boys in the kitchen – they had a certain look, features distinctly Jewish. It was a guess *und* my guess was correct."

She nodded, impressed, and closed her eyes.

A short time later, the bus dropped them outside a great pair of wrought iron gates and a stone gatehouse. They had arrived at Waterville Place and Jessica's heart gave a leap of excitement.

***

At her first glimpse of Waterville Place, Jessica drew in a deep, awestruck breath. "It's a palace," she whispered.

From where the bus dropped them, it was a twenty-minute walk up a long driveway that twisted and wound through a forest of gnarled, bare-branched trees. Even with their wintery nakedness, the trees hid the house until a surprising moment when it suddenly appeared before them.

The afternoon sun cast the stone in a rose-gold glow and revealed the enormous building in all its stately glory.

For Jessica, who'd once visited Castle Howard, Waterville Place was strikingly regal with its symmetrical, three-storey wings standing like book-ends between a double-storey long gallery. Above the roof rose a glittering dome, reflecting the dying sun in a thousand sparks of light.

For centuries, it had been the seat of the earls of Thorncliffe and the home of Alexandra's stepbrother; a property of considerable significance with which Jessica felt a strange affinity.

Scaramouche trotted ahead. As Jessica and the captain continued along the driveway behind him, Jessica thought how grand this approach must have been in its day, although it now bore the ruts and potholes of heavy army vehicles, like the one roaring towards them.

They stepped aside to allow it to pass and found, not the sweeping, elegant gardens Alexandra had chronicled, but a veritable city of canvas tents bustling with army personnel.

The drive led to a large, colonnaded portico, before which was a once elegant, marble fountain.

Jessica remembered Alexandra's description of its cheerful tinkling as the water bubbled and played, jewel-like in the sun. Now, it was dry, soundless and stained with streaks of grime. Touching the captain's arm, she whispered, "Remember, don't speak."

He rolled his eyes.

"Sorry." She glanced up at the house. "Fancy a nose around? A look?" she added, seeing his confused expression.

He nodded.

With Scaramouche in Jessica's arms, they passed through a pair of iron-bound doors, into a dark-panelled entrance hall.

Rooms on either side must have once been reception or guest rooms but were now offices. Through the open doors, Jessica glimpsed cabinets and files; in one room, a group of officers leaned over a document on a desk.

Jessica and the captain moved, unquestioned, through a door directly ahead of them and here they paused in astonishment.

This room was a circular foyer, lined with mirrors that, albeit tarnished and age-spotted, reflected the afternoon sunlight in a million brilliant shards of colour streaming through the kaleidoscopic dome way above their heads.

Jessica was aware of her mouth hanging open as she gaped at the incredible room. Beside her, the captain exhaled in a low whistle of appreciation.

"This is just how Alexandra said it was." Although she whispered, her voice bounced sibilantly off the bright surfaces.

"*Ahem*!" A man cleared his throat behind them and they whirled round. Jessica found herself standing before a tall, overweight man with a ruddy face and long, drooping moustaches. "Lookin' fer sumthin'?" he asked, in a wheezing voice. "This's a military 'ospital. If yers ain't 'ospital people yer got no business gettin' in the way."

"Oh, I'm sorry." Jessica said quickly. "We were directed here – we're looking for someone called Sid."

"Sid, eh?" The man looked her up and down before turning to the captain and repeating the process.

"I don't know his surname. We were just told –"

"Only one Sid 'ere. Yers'll find'm in stables – out back. Now," he firmly ushered Jessica and the captain through the front doors, then turned on his heel and left them standing beneath the portico.

***

Jessica held Scaramouche's leash while she and the captain

freely wandered Waterville's grounds. With the number of military men and women milling about, the captain attracted no particular attention, and as it turned out, it wasn't hard to find the stables, or Sid.

He was surprisingly young – no older than twenty – with a glinting rat-like cunning in his eyes. His gaze sifted over the captain with more than passing interest and Jessica was amused to feel her companion shuffling uncomfortably beside her.

"Mr Wheeler told us to come to you," she explained. "We need to –"

"Get to The Bowsprit. I know. Wheeler tel'phoned."

Jessica raised her eyebrows. "He telephoned?"

Sid grinned, revealing stained teeth. "Yer think we ain't got tel'phones in the south?" He allowed himself another look at the captain, eyes lingering on the handsome German's mouth, before seeming to shake himself. "Right then. Follow me."

Chapter 48

The Bowsprit was desperately in need of repair. Its window sills and door were warped and split, paint that may have once been dark green was peeling away and several windows on the upper floor were boarded over. The white-painted façade was dirty-grey and the decorative, ship's wheel hanging beneath the eaves was missing several spokes. If she hadn't known better, Jessica would have assumed the building was derelict.

Yet in Jessica's current state, it could have been Buckingham Palace for it represented a bath and a proper meal. Sleeping rough over the past nights was telling on her now that the adrenalin of anxiety and fear was fading.

A bed, she thought dreamily. *A bath, a meal and a bed.*

The interior of the pub was in no better shape than its exterior. The floor was grimy; Jessica's boots seemed to stick to the boards. She grimaced and tried not to think about the years of accumulated muck under her feet.

A stooped, elderly man appeared. He and Sid bent their heads together in a rapid, whispered conversation. While the pair was talking, Jessica went to the fireplace and stared up at the painting above it.

"Look," she breathed, as the captain came to stand beside her. "It's Alexandra, but – she's about forty, I'd say."

Framed in heavy gilt, the painting showed the same Alexandra Broughton Jessica was familiar with, only older; she'd grown and matured into a very dignified woman. "She was pretty," the captain whispered and Jessica nodded.

Dressed in a tawny satin gown perfectly complementing her tumbling brown curls, she was seated on a low chair, one slim hand resting lightly on the brow of a blonde dog, the other lying across her lap. Jessica's eyes were drawn to a large emerald ring – the only jewellery she seemed to be wearing.

Alexandra gazed serenely from the canvas, a small, secret smile on her lips. "Wish we could've stayed longer at Waterville Place, looked round a bit," she thought aloud. "I know it's a long bow but I feel a connection with that place through the things Alexandra wrote about it."

The captain nodded.

Just then the two men approached. "This is Alf," Sid told them. "He'll take care of yers now." Sid cast a final, longing look over the captain's lean form, touched his forelock and departed.

***

"Aw-right," Alf said, in a slow drawl, looking first Jessica, and then the captain, up and down. His piggy eyes took in every detail. "If Wheeler says ter give yers a room, thass what'll do." He jerked his chin towards a rickety-looking staircase. "Room five. Two doors down on yer leff."

The captain nodded his thanks, while Jessica hesitated. "I'm wondering," she spoke politely, "would it be possible to have a bath?"

Alf curled his lip. "Oh, *you were wondering if it would be possible to have a bath*," he rudely mimicked her speech.

Jessica flushed and looked away.

"The lady would like a bath," the captain's tone was curt, guttural, and Alf's eyes widened in surprise. Evidently Sid had neglected an important detail about Wheeler's guests. "You do not care to mock *my* accent?"

Backing away slightly, the little man shook his head. "We 'ave a bathroom, we do. Across th'all from yer room."

"I hope it's cleaner than the taproom," Jessica whispered as they mounted the stairs.

"It will be, if we must clean it ourselves."

Their room boasted a double, brass bed with a lumpy looking mattress, a scarred wooden table by the window with two chairs, and a small vanity table and mirror. The window looked out over a rugged cliff to where a pebbly beach was visible below. Hooks attached to the wall, presumably passed for a wardrobe and the captain removed Jessica's coat, then his own, and hung them.

Jessica immediately turned down the bed and satisfied herself that the sheets seemed clean; even if they were so thin as to be almost sheer.

The bathroom, predictably, was filthy. The linoleum floor was gritty and the enamel bath was chipped and bore rust stains from a persistently dripping tap. A greasy brown ring indicated the water level of recent use. *One hundred years ago, by the look of it,* Jessica mused.

Surprisingly, however, it was connected to a furnace.

"Hot water!" she cried, delighted. She'd had visions of carrying pails up from the kitchen.

The captain smiled, but turned at a sound behind them.

Alf stood on the threshold, a rag and tin of Bon Ami in his age-crippled hand. "Thought yers might want these."

"Kind of you," the captain muttered sardonically, taking them.

"Wheeler reckoned 'e'll be 'ere t'morra mornin'." The little man turned and shuffled away.

Stripping off his shirt, the captain set to work scrubbing out the bath.

Jessica watched him; the play of muscle beneath the pale skin. There was a scar on his shoulder she'd not known was there.

He was nicely proportioned: the broadness of his smooth back and the way his hips narrowed. Her imagination could supply the rest; in the darkness of his bed that long ago night, she'd felt him beneath her hands, her fingers had traced the topography of his lean hips and buttocks, and she'd dug her nails into the muscles of his shoulders as he'd moved above her … and within her.

She drew in a sharp breath.

Jon's trousers were too big; they hung loosely on his hips and as the captain straightened to examine his work, he passed the back of a hand over his forehead and she glimpsed the defined lower oblique muscles and flat stomach with the line of soft hair, trailing from his navel, disappearing into the top of the low-slung trousers.

Once again, it occurred to her that he was not merely fit, but had the physique of a sportsman.

There was only one bed in their room. They'd spent the last two nights together, sleeping close for warmth. Now there was no need to do so.

The knowledge saddened her as much as it relieved her; she'd denied him so long. Yet, she'd found comfort in being held these past nights. She would miss it.

The furnace roared into life as water erupted from the tap. The captain gave a grunt of satisfaction as the abrasive cleaner and grime rinsed away. "It is cleaning well," he observed. "You see?"

Turning, he caught her gazing at him.

The heat rushed into her cheeks. Normally so perceptive, he would know her thoughts. "Um …" she stammered, feeling awkward. "I'll go back to the room. You …" she waved towards the bath. "You go first."

***

Jessica sat by the window, elbows on the table, chin in her hands, gazing absently at a flock of seagulls standing on the beach below. Scaramouche snuffled curiously about, investigating corners and crevices.

She was aware that her eyelids were growing heavy and a soft warmth was enveloping her like a comfortable robe. Behind her, the door opened and she jerked awake.

The captain came in. His hair was wet and he was carrying his clothes. He had a faded pink-and-green-striped towel wrapped round his waist. "I found this," he indicated the towel, "in a cupboard in the hall. I have left some in the bathroom for you."

"Was there soap?" she asked hopefully.

He shook his head. "No razors either." He rubbed his hand over the three-day growth on his chin.

"At least there's hot water." Jessica got up, slightly drowsy, to take her turn.

He must have cleaned the bath again after he'd used it for it was spotless now. She opened the taps and impatiently stripped off her slacks, her jumper and blouse and stood in her underwear waiting for it to fill, revelling in the damp steam rising round her.

At length, she stepped out of her knickers, unhooked her bra, and slipped with relief into the hot water. Settling with a long, replete sigh, she closed her eyes.

***

"Frau Jessie?" the voice startled her awake and water lapped up the side of the bathtub.

"Captain!" She attempted to cover her nakedness with her arms, but the door was only slightly ajar, and he was talking through the gap; she could see his face averted.

"You have been a long time. Did you fall asleep?"

"I … yes. Lucifer's balls! Water's gone cold." She sat up and opened the hot tap. The furnace in the corner fired up.

"Frau Jessie, do you mind if I come in?"

She paused, surprised and uncertain. "Why …? Did you forget something?"

"No. Sit up *und* cover yourself. I will help you wash your hair."

Jessica did not move. She would love to have her hair washed. It hung in dirty, stringy hanks about her face. She'd expected it would be virtually impossible to wash her long hair in this tub, but if he were to help … The thought was irresistible. "Wait a moment."

She wriggled to a sitting position and drew her knees up. Satisfied that none of her private bits were showing, she invited him in.

Closing the door behind him, he smiled and showed her the bottle he held. "You see? I have a gift for you."

Her eyes widened. "That's not shampoo! Is that shampoo?"

"*Ja*. It is. We are, after all, in a smuggler's house." He unscrewed the cap and sniffed. "Äpfel. Did you know *der* Äpfel is part of the rose family?"

"No, and right now I don't care." She bowed her head as the clean scent of apples mingled with steam and filled the room. It felt like heaven as the captain worked the shampoo into her hair, gently massaging her scalp, including the crusty patch where her hair had been torn out. He rinsed with warm water from a jug. The soap ran free, smooth, like cream down her back.

Not since she was a child, had anyone other than Jessica herself washed her hair. But the captain painstakingly lathered and rinsed again, combing the tangles out with his fingers. The sensation of his hands on her scalp, the silken water cascading over her shoulders, her chest, dripping off the peaks of her breasts, was one of the most sensual experiences of her life.

Perhaps *the* most sensual experience; she'd never shared such intimacy with Jon.

***

As he wrung the wetness from the length of Jessica's hair and turbaned a towel round her head, Anton thought he might explode from want of her. Every day was torture; he'd never before been forced to live so closely with a woman and not find relief in her body. Washing her hair had proved to be an unexpectedly intimate thing – he'd been unprepared for its delicious torment.

Much as he needed sexual release, his need for her to trust him was greater. If they were to be together again, she must come to him of her own free will – it meant more than momentary gratification.

If she didn't, then so be it because he wanted her to remember him with love. He wanted her to tell her children about the love they had shared, not try to wipe from her mind the guilt of sex with a man for which the world would brand her a traitor.

He rose and placed a second towel on the edge of the bath. "I will leave you now."

***

Jessica couldn't bear the thought of putting on dirty clothes after having bathed. Back in their room, she asked the captain to avert his eyes while she removed her towel and slipped into her coat. Then gathering her knickers, bra and blouse, she took them to the bathroom and washed them in the bath.

Now they were hanging over the backs of chairs, drying quickly before the fire the captain had lit in their room. She would sleep in her clean underwear tonight.

While she'd been completing her bath, the captain had gone downstairs to request a meal. The only hot food Alf could muster was half a national loaf and some bland soup that had been thickened with barley and had over-boiled carrots floating in it.

It might as well have been a succulent roast with all the trimmings the way the two of them fell on it. The captain soaked a lump of bread in the soup and offered it to Scaramouche who seemed equally pleased.

Along with the food, Alf had brought a newspaper and a bucket of anthracite for the fire. After they'd finished eating, the captain sat in the window and opened the newspaper. One thing Jessica could say about his sojourn in England was that his grasp of the language was almost faultless, as was his comprehension and reading ability.

Since the fire had warmed the room, Jessica's clothes dried quickly. She put on her underwear and blouse, and climbed onto the mattress; the bedclothes lay folded back at her feet. She'd been so exhausted, both emotionally and physically, that she was immediately asleep while the captain settled to working his way through the newspaper.

**

Perhaps it was boredom – he'd finished the newspaper. Perhaps it was the gradual darkening of the sky as night came down. Perhaps it was having a full stomach for the first time in days, or all of these factors combined that caused fatigue to weight Anton's limbs and blur his vision.

Jessica was sleeping so soundly that she snored, ever so softly. He smiled to himself as he eased onto the bed beside her.

The room was warm from the gently glowing fire and it wasn't long before he too slept.

Outside the window, evening brought rain and a wind whipped the Channel into a cresting frenzy, howling and clawing at the decrepit old building. But The Bowsprit had stood on its cliff-top roost for so long there was little damage to be sustained that had not already been done. The inhabitants of room five slept peacefully for the first time in what felt, to them, like weeks.

**

Sometime during the night, Jessica awoke, shivering. The fire had burned down and the room was chilly. Dragging the bedclothes over the two of them, she quickly fell back into unconsciousness, her body unthinkingly seeking the captain's warmth. She pushed back against him, in the familiarly comforting spoon position, and he moved in his sleep, arm curling round her waist and holding her close.

Chapter 49

Jessica woke before dawn having slept almost twelve hours. The light beyond the window was pearly grey. The rain had ceased beating against the glass and had left milky rivulets in the salty grime.

The captain continued to sleep; he had one arm under her, the other over, cradling her. Like this, she felt warm, secure ... so very relaxed, as though the world and all its troubles no longer existed.

But she had to move; she'd lain in one position so long that her left arm had gone to sleep. So as not to wake him, Jessica turned by inches in his arms until she faced him. He was bare-chested, wearing only Jon's trousers, and as she drew a deep, comfortable breath, she caught the clean masculine scent of his skin and felt a tightening between her thighs.

Unable to help herself, she burrowed her nose into the hollow at the base of his throat and inhaled slowly. His arms tightened round her and he muttered something soft in German.

"Shhh," she whispered against his chest. She pressed her lips to his throat and closed her eyes, feeling the steady pulse there.

But he stirred. "Frau Jessie ...?" His voice was slow and thick with sleep, his accent more pronounced. "What are you doing?"

"I kissed you," she whispered. "Go back to sleep, it's not morning."

"You kissed me," he murmured, only semi-conscious. He sighed against her hair and ducked his head.

When his lips fused with hers the current of desire that shot through her was so intense that she gasped against his mouth.

***

Anton's eyes popped open, instantly awake.

"Frau Jessie ... *was ist?*" He pulled back uncertainly to stare

632

at her, but with the heavy-lidded ardour on her face, he was lost. He kissed her again.

Her mouth opened and she made a small whimpering sound. He broke away again but she followed him, pressing her lips to his with a savage hunger that surprised him.

"*Verdammte Scheiße!*" he growled. His body was immediately on fire, his breathing erratic. She pushed her hips forwards and he moaned. "Frau Jessie, do not do this if you are not certain because –" But she did it again, and it was more than he could take.

Anton's hand found the junction of her thighs covered in cotton. He felt her heat through the flimsy material.

She sighed against his mouth, trailing her hand over his chest, and down … round his navel, lower … and lower still, to the waistband of his trousers.

He moaned, his hips thrusting forward with a mind of their own. His desire for her pushed eagerly against the front of his trousers.

"Frau … Jessica," he gasped, his mouth moving hungrily on hers. "I –"

"Shut up!" she panted. She fumbled with the button on his trousers; her other hand cupped him through the heavy drill cotton.

He groaned, then pushed aside the crotch of her knickers to slip beneath the sheer fabric. Her skin was hot and she writhed against his hand.

***

Suddenly the button on his trousers popped free, the zipper opened with ease. Jessica grasped him, crying out as his fingers probed her most sensitive place.

But she held him, distantly aware that he was breathing hard, while the sensations growing within her were causing her head to reel.

Suddenly he withdrew his hand and she immediately felt the loss. "Don't st –" she began but he unceremoniously tore off her panties. In one fluid motion, she was beneath him gazing into blue eyes that were bright with desire.

"Are you certain?" he gasped, poised above her.

"I'm certain to kill you if you don't."

He grinned. "I feel I have waited my whole life to hear you say that."

***

It was like going home, Anton reflected. Like the first time with her, only more urgent. The days they'd spent on the road together, living and sleeping in close proximity, had teased them so taut with sexual tension, that no sooner had he entered her than they had both cried out in simultaneous release.

Their coupling had not been the sensuous act of love he'd wanted to make with her. Like a dam bursting, it had been a torrid release of pressure, a hurried assuaging of instinctive animal need. They were seeking comfort in one another's bodies, and like animals, it was a purely natural sating of a hunger that was quickly over.

He had certainly needed it, from a physical point of view – and she too. But spiritually? Emotionally? He couldn't say how she felt, but he was far from satisfied.

Now, he lay on his back while she slept, her head on his shoulder, his arm curled protectively round her.

How was he ever going to leave her?

He tried to think of a way he could stay – as if he hadn't wracked his brain for most of the past year! He played scenario after scenario through his mind only to arrive at the same unwelcome conclusion: it was not possible to remain in England. There was nowhere they could go; no alternative country would allow them to live in peace. Indeed, the only country on earth that would accept *him* would be his own, thanks to the rampaging, obsessive destruction of *der Führer*. But Jessica and the children couldn't live there.

His chest rose and fell in a distraught sigh.

Jessica muttered something and stirred in his arms and his body sprang alert – eager as a horny teenager.

"You awake, Captain?" she asked, rolling onto her back and blinking at him.

"Oh, *ja*," he said, noting wryly that some parts of him were more awake than others.

"What time is it?"

Her watch was on the floor beside the bed. He reached for it and, squinting at the little mother-of-pearl face, read, "Twenty minutes past eight in the morning."

"Mmm," she responded, yawning. She rolled on her side and snuggled further beneath the bedclothes, and he moved up behind and curled lovingly round her. *We fit together so well*, he thought sinking into sleep.

***

They were awakened a short time later by a loud pounding on the door. Anton sprang from the bed, naked but for the dog tags slapping on his bare chest. Quickly pulling his trousers up over his hips, he fastened them as he went to the door and called out, "Who is it?" in a very poor English accent.

"Wheeler. Open the door."

The captain glanced at Jessica who was sitting up, hair awry, buttoning her blouse. At her nod, he unlocked the door and it swung open to reveal the hulking man standing in the hall.

He came into the room, seemingly filling it. Scaramouche danced about his feet, yapping at the intrusion but Wheeler didn't spare the little dog so much as a glance.

His piercing eyes sifted over Anton's athletic build. "You got a lousy English accent," he observed, striding to the window.

"I keep telling him that," Jessica said. Anton had tossed over her slacks and she was fighting into them beneath the bedclothes.

Wheeler ignored her. "C'mere." He jerked his chin at the water below and pointed as the smaller man came up beside him. "See that out there?"

Anton nodded.

"Whaddayer reckon she looks like?"

Anton knew nothing about boats. He studied the vessel lying some hundred yards out in the secluded cove below the cliffs. It was not large. It had a steering house in the middle with a mast before it, an engine room behind and another mast at the rear. There was a large net rolled into a ball lying on the rear deck – that was a hint. "Fishing boat," he said at length.

Wheeler nodded with satisfaction.

"That's what she is and that's what ye're gonner tell yer Kraut mates when she docks in Le Havre tomorra mornin'".

Anton nodded slowly. "And when they come snoopin' around," Wheeler went on, "yer gonner tell 'em yer've been ordered to oversee 'er comin' in with fish for yer fuckin' Kraut mates in Paris. Unnerstand?"

Nodding again, Anton continued to watch the water beyond the window.

"Yer try anythin' dumb, yer make one false move, I'll blow that handsome face right orf yer fuckin' 'ead, yer got that?"

"*Ja, ja.*" He gave a dismissive wave of his hand.

***

Behind the men, Jessica had scrambled into her clothes and now came to stand beside the captain. She looked at the small vessel bobbing a short way out.

"I also need yer ter keep 'em distracted while me cargo

gets loaded. Don't care 'ow yer does it. Just don't try no funny business."

"Human cargo." The captain spoke flatly and Wheeler shot him a sideways glance.

"Aye, human cargo. Yer got problems with that I'll just blow yer 'ead orf now an' save yer worryin' 'bout it."

The captain turned, unblinkingly facing the larger man. Light glinted on his dog tags. "Let me tell you something, *Herr* Wheeler," he spoke calmly but his blue eyes shimmered boldly. "I am *not* a Nazi. My best friend is Jewish. I learned to speak English while living in New York with his family before the war. Because I am German, does not mean I am the brute you want me to be. It may disappoint you to know that very few German people *are* Nazis. Many of us have risked our lives protecting our Jewish friends *und* countrymen. You challenge me, you judge me or threaten me one more time, *und* I will kill you with my bare hands."

Jessica held her breath as the two men regarded each other steadily for several long moments. Finally, Wheeler gave a respectful nod and clapped a friendly hand on the smaller man's naked shoulder. "Steady on there." His tone seemed conciliatory. "I were just testin' yer, yer know? I gotta test yer out."

"*Ja*, I know," the captain responded evenly. "Now," he turned and pulled Jessica against his hip with an arm about her waist. "I will do everything you ask, but I want this woman safely returned to Yorkshire."

Wheeler nodded. "Aye, I thought as much. I can arrange that. One o' the women back in Astor, remember Magda? She needs to get outta the district. I'll give 'er a car. They can go back to Yorkshire together."

"*Das gut.*"

The captain shot Jessica a smile that she supposed was meant to make her feel better. It didn't. She was feeling too sick with worry and the grief of his impending departure.

"Right then," Wheeler said, turning away from the window. "There's no moon tonight – thass what we want. Be on the beach – down there," he pointed with his thumb towards the sand below, "at eleven. Alf will meet yer there and int'roduce yer to Cap'n Miller. Path to the beach's about a quarter mile up the road. If yer not on time, she'll sail wi'out yer. No second chance an' yer better 'ave a good reason 'cause yer know too much now." He jerked his chin at Jessica, "And so does she."

"I will be there."

Wheeler grunted, glanced sideways at Jessica, then strode from the room.

***

"So that's it," Jessica said, almost to herself. She was dressed in her coat having taken Scaramouche outside for a run. The captain was leaning, arms folded, against the window embrasure, watching the vessel riding gently on the waves below.

"It's our last day together," she said, unnecessarily, as she hung her coat on the hook. She came up behind him and wrapped her arms about his waist and rested her forehead on his back. "How are you feeling about tonight?"

He laughed through his nose, and she said, "What?"

"I think it is funny," he told her, eyes on the fishing boat, "that American men complain women only want to talk about feelings. So do German men, Jewish men, Indian men, Dutch men – the different men I have met over the years, all say the same." He turned in her arms and draped his own over her shoulders, linking his hands loosely behind her head. "And it appears that even Englishmen would agree."

"In that case," she said softly, "perhaps we should talk about what happened this morning."

"Ah." Stepping back, he dropped his arms and rested a hip on the wide, stone window-ledge.

"You don't have to look so defensive."

"Do I not?"

"No. I ... I wanted you – as much as you did me." She blushed furiously with the admission, but pressed on. "I only wish I'd not been so ..." she looked away, throwing about for the right word.

"Stubborn?" he suggested, folding his arms over his chest.

She snorted. "Well, there was that. But I have been selfish too, and afraid. When I needed you, you did not reject me. Yet, over the past months, you have needed me but I've been too caught up in my own concerns. It was always about me."

She picked at the skin round a nail. "I wasted so much time being afraid when we could've been comforting one another. I was afraid of falling in love with you and being hurt when you left. But I fell in love with you anyway and will be hurt when you leave just the same. I've saved myself nothing and denied us the companionship we both needed."

He grinned, and she said quickly, "Oh, don't say you told me so!"

"I would never say that." He opened his arms and gathered her against his chest. "But I might think it," he added wickedly, before sobering. "Yes, you have denied us the chance to have loving memories of each other. But it is not too late."

"Hmm?" She looked up at him.

"We still have the afternoon. I want to spend the entire time inside you, loving you slowly *und* making memories for the rest of our lives."

As he spoke, she felt the warmth begin down in her core and rapidly bloom up through her stomach and chest.

Dipping his head to look directly into her eyes, he said, "Will you have me, Frau Jessie? Will you allow me into your body, to pleasure you, *und* myself, *und* then to sleep, sated – for once – in each other's arms exhausted by our lovemaking?"

She drew a long, shaky breath. "Yes."

***

Anton undressed her slowly, his lips tracing the path of his hands, exploring in daylight those secret, womanly places he'd only previously imagined in the dark.

He led her to the bed where they lay for a long time, curled around one another like serpents. They touched and talked; they made no promises.

Jessica trailed her fingertips over the ridges and contours of his body, and he stroked and sipped at her sensitive places before claiming her mouth, and as their kisses grew deeper, more urgent, he fitted so perfectly within her.

He was tender and slow, the way he'd promised. But their hunger for one another grew until their bodies became dewy and their hearts pounded.

And then she broke, biting down on his shoulder to smother her cries, while he arched above her, straining and shattering into a million pieces.

They lay gasping, clinging together while their breathing slowed and the sweat dried on their skin. *This*, he thought rocking her gently on the edge of sleep, *is where we both belong.*

The evening was beginning to close in as they rose and ran, naked, hands clasped and giggling like children, across the hall into the bathroom. They bathed one another, and found new pleasure in each other's company and the private conversation only lovers can share.

Anton requested a meal and Alf brought a tray laden with sausage and mashed potato. "Last meal of the condemned man," he suggested and she glared at him.

"You are returning to your family."

"*Ja*, this is true, but I am also condemned to a life alone."

***

Jessica didn't argue – nor did she believe him. She had no doubt that he loved her. But she was also under no illusions that once returned to the circle of his family and a normal life, he would eventually find his way back to Natalia.

He must make a future for himself – just as she must.

So, they enjoyed a picnic on the bed, inviting Scaramouche up to share the food, before he was sent back to his place before the fire and they rolled into one another's arms one last time, before drifting into sleep, sated with food and love.

Chapter 50

It was a little past ten when the captain rose. He dressed in the glow of the fire while Jessica sat on the bed hugging her knees. She watched: his body shone bronze and gold in the flickering light, the contours and valleys, the flexing and contracting of muscles as he moved, were all thrown into structurally elegant relief.

She knew every line, every dip and curve by heart now. She had caressed the concave hollows on the sides of his buttocks, she had kissed the brown nubs of his nipples, and more. These were the memories – all that was left to her after their afternoon of lovemaking and she had imprinted them on her mind, to sustain her for the rest of her life.

When he was dressed, he stooped to scratch Scaramouche behind the ears, but his eyes were on her. "I do not think it wise you come to the beach."

"I've been trying to decide whether I should go," she admitted. "I dread saying goodbye, but I want to have every last minute with you that I –"

She broke off at a sound outside their door and they stared at each other. It was a muted scuffling sound followed by an expectant silence; the heavy silence that accompanied fear of discovery.

The captain straightened and held a finger to his lips. He was edging slowly towards the door when without warning, there came a violent pounding on it.

Jessica gave a startled cry and the captain threw himself against the wall as the door suddenly crashed open in a splintering of brittle, aged wood.

Instantly, Scaramouche set up a tirade of vicious barking.

In less than a heartbeat, two men had barrelled into the room and Jessica pulled the blankets up to her chin. *"What the hell –!"*

she cried in outrage, as the men advanced towards her.

It was then she recognised them from the station – one white-haired, the other red-haired.

Scaramouche continued to bark, and now he lunged at one of them.

The man kicked out savagely. With a yelp of pain and alarm, the little dog slid across the room to slam into the opposite wall below the window.

Jessica screamed and leapt from the bed, sheet wrapped round her.

"Stay where you are!" the red-haired man bellowed, aiming a finger at her. She froze, but in the commotion, the pair hadn't seen the German pressed against the wall behind them.

Now the captain launched himself at the nearest. In a surprise attack, he crashed the white-haired man to the ground, straddled him and dealt a brutal, jaw crunching upper-cut, followed by two rapid-fire hooks; left and right.

The man howled as blood exploded from his nose. His companion turned from Jessica and flew at the captain, but the smaller man was ready. He bounded upright and stood positioned with fists raised, left foot forward and met the intruder's attack, easily ducking the man's fist, sidestepping, and sending him sprawling on his backside.

Ridiculously, in that moment, Jessica thought, *He's a boxer! I knew he was an athlete!*

And, just as suddenly, the thought became irrelevant as Robin Tyler stepped over the threshold, Enfield pistol aimed directly at the German's heart.

"I wouldn't move a hair if I were you," Tyler said calmly. "Hands above your head."

Slowly, the captain obeyed.

Jessica stood beside the bed wrapped in a sheet. Tyler glared at her, his lip curled in disgust before he swung back to his men.

The red-haired one had hauled himself to his feet while his wounded companion remained on the floor.

"Get up, George!" Tyler commanded irritably.

In the corner, Scaramouche lay whimpering, and Jessica adjusted the sheet and tried again to go to him. "Stay where you are!" Tyler growled at her. "Don't you move, you treasonous whore!"

The captain grimaced while Jessica sat on the bed, clutching the sheet to her neck.

With the gun steadily trained on the German, Tyler reached behind his back for a pair of handcuffs. He threw them across the floor to the red-haired man. "David, handcuff him!" he barked.

"Robin," Jessica tried to modulate her tone. "Please don't do this. He's –"

Tyler swung in her direction. "Jessica Barrow, you're under arrest for ...*ooof!*"

Tyler hit the floor hard, momentarily winded. He'd taken his eyes off the German for only a second, but it was all the captain had needed to throw himself at the man and knock him to the ground.

The gun flew across the floor, skittering on the old linoleum – Tyler, his off-sider and the captain all leapt after it.

"David!" Tyler shouted as his man snatched the weapon off the floor. "Here!"

But David was too slow. It seemed he'd hardly registered the gun was in his hand when the German danced towards him, swinging, left, right ... left, left ... hook, and David hit the floor. The captain snatched the pistol and turned to face Robin Tyler, the barrel aimed right between the Englishman's eyes.

"Do not move."

Jessica had never seen the captain so cold. His face was expressionless, his eyes glittered like chips of ice. This ruthless man was a far cry from her sensual lover – and he was frightening.

"Jessica, get up!" he commanded. The pistol never wavered from Tyler's face, although the captain sidestepped, keeping all three men in sight. "Get dressed."

Jessica slipped from the bed, keeping the sheet wrapped around her. She grabbed the pile of clothes on the table and ran straight to the little dog lying on the floor. Blood was seeping from a cut on Scarry's shoulder and he shuddered in shock but his little tail quivered at her touch.

"You three," the captain said, dispassionately, "eyes this way, if you please."

Jessica's hands were trembling, but she dressed quickly, blouse and slacks – no time for underwear – ignoring the stickiness on her thighs. She kept one eye on the men, the other on Scaramouche who lay staring up at her. She stood over him, uncertain what to do, and just then something beyond the window caught her eye.

It was a brief flash of light. It looked like … a lantern? *Oh, God!*

"Captain, the ship!" she pointed towards the beach. "They're signalling. You must go!"

"No." He hadn't taken his eyes from the men. His hand, holding the gun, was rock steady.

"You must!" she insisted. Her heart pounded in her chest and her hands flapped uselessly about.

The three men were fixedly watching the German's face, no doubt waiting for the slightest flicker of distraction. But he seemed too well-trained. He stood, expression lifeless, hand unwavering, gun pointed at them.

Jessica turned away, watching the signal on the water. Somewhere a bell tolled. Behind her, she heard the captain herding the three men into a corner. The panic rose in her chest.

"Captain, you must –" she started.

"No!"

What the hell did he think he could achieve by missing that boat? "For Christ's sake!" she cried, growing desperate. "What's wrong with you? *Go! Go!* There's nothing for you here but more trouble like this!" She flung a hand towards the three men huddled together; one of them snuffled wetly through a shattered nose.

"Jessica, come here." The captain modified his tone and held out an arm. She went to him without hesitation and he pulled her against his hip, leaning towards her ear.

"Don't you touch her you fucking Kraut bastard!" one of the men bellowed.

Tyler nudged the man lightly, "Easy, David," he spoke calmly. "He might be a Kraut bastard but he knows what he's doing."

***

"Take the dog and get out of here." Anton murmured, eyes never leaving the men in the corner of the room. "Go to Exeter … wait for me. I –"

"No," she responded flatly. "You have to leave – now. Before it's too late."

"Listen –"

"*No!*" Jessica shouted into his face and he flinched. "No I bloody won't. You go!" she sobbed. "There's nothing for you here. Nothing but trouble! I don't want you here – *Go!*" She suddenly lashed out, thumping him hard on the chest. "Just go!"

Grief stabbed Anton's heart.

"Jessica …!"

***

Across the room, Robin Tyler watched in astonishment. *He bloody loves her!* He thought. *The Kraut genuinely loves her!*

"*Please* …" Jessica begged. She'd stopped belting her lover and was now clinging to him, tearfully. "If you love me, you have to go!" She cupped his face in her hands, kissing his jaw, his cheeks, while the German's piercing blue eyes never left Robin and his two men.

Just then, George swayed on his feet. He gave a low moan and slid down the wall in a crumpled heap.

Useless, Robin thought uncharitably. *They knew how important this mission was and they saddled me with a pair of untrained farmers.*

Jessica and the Kraut were whispering to one another. She seemed to be pleading, while he offered monosyllabic responses. Then Robin saw a change flicker over the German's face.

Unexpectedly, he grasped Jessica by the back of her head and kissed her hard on the mouth. His eyes were still on the three men, even as he broke away and murmured something that caused Jessica's knees to almost give out beneath her.

Robin watched as the bastard grasped Jessica's arm to steady her, then thrust the gun into her hand. He adjusted her grip, pointed to something on the weapon and kissed her one last time.

The German spared not a glance for the three Englishmen as he dashed from the room.

Chapter 51

The night was perfectly dark. A chill breeze blew in off the Channel as Anton sprinted the five hundred yards down the beach. Shingle crunched beneath his boots and was awkward to run on. Sweating with effort now, he knew he'd be freezing once in the boat and would miss the insulating warmth of his flight jacket – bundled in the bottom of a box in Jessica's attic.

At the water's edge he stopped. Leaning over with hands on knees to catch his breath, he listened hard and heard the slap of water on a wooden hull. In the silence of the night, the sound was quite loud – if you were listening for it.

He straightened and tried to see through the dark. Alf must be here somewhere.

***

"You've never handled a gun before, have you, Jessica?" Robin taunted. He leaned casually against the wall, arms folded over his chest. It must have been five minutes since the Kraut left but she hadn't moved. "You're no more capable of firing that thing than you are of walking on the moon."

"Don't move, Robin. You don't really want to find out what I'm capable of."

He smiled and pushed away from the wall. "What would you do if ..." he took a step towards her.

"Stay there!" The revolver wavered but she held her ground.

"You're not a killer, Jessica."

She aimed the gun at his knee. "I don't intend to kill you."

"No, you probably don't. You're buying time for your lover to get away." Robin's eyes narrowed as he picked his moment.

In a split second, he leaped towards her, grabbed the pistol from her hand and twisted her arm behind her back.

Jessica roared and fought like a tigress, snarling, kicking, but she was no match for him.

"Well, that was embarrassingly easy," Robin sneered, as David pulled her arms around to the front and handcuffed her.

***

Anton waited at the edge of the water where it foamed in the dark like boiling milk. At a sound behind him, he turned and squinted. Two man-shaped shadows were approaching – one was small and stooped.

"Took yer time," Alf grunted. "Cap'n, Miller, this be the Kraut. If yer done wi' me, I'm gone." He turned and immediately melted into the night.

"Yer speak English?" Miller asked in a sibilant whisper.

"Yes."

"Fluent?"

"Yes."

"Right," the man hawked and spat onto the sand at Anton's feet. "Ain't fond o' Krauts, but I'm told ter take yer to Le Havre so that's what'll do. Yer gonner clear things wi' yer Kraut mates. That right?"

"That is right."

As they were whispering, a rowing boat materialised from the darkness. Someone leapt out with a splash and dragged it closer to the beach. "Cap'n Miller – yer ready? This th' passenger?"

"Aye, this be 'im." Miller looked at Anton and gestured towards the boat. "Get in."

The little boat bobbed in about three feet of icy water. Anton thought he should have taken his boots off to keep them dry but it was too late now.

He'd just settled himself in the boat when there was an angry shout from the beach behind them.

***

Jessica stumbled on the shingle. Robin heard her gasp as sharp pieces of it stuck into her palms.

"Get up," he snarled heedlessly, dragging her by one elbow.

From where he stood, he could make out the vague outline of a rowing boat, heading towards a larger vessel. It rode some hundred yards out and was softly lit by two or three small lanterns, which cast rippling gold lights on the water.

Squinting, he thought he saw the shapes of three men in the rowing boat and he silently cursed David and George for refusing to come down to the beach. Untrained as they were, they were better than nothing.

"I've got her!" Robin yelled suddenly as Jessica struggled beside him. "Hey Kraut, I've got your slut!"

There was silence from the water, as though the men in the boat had frozen in place.

"Hand yourself over ... she'll go free. I'll tell them she led me to you. She can go back to her children. Live happily ever after."

The silence from the rowing boat continued.

"Give yourself up and nobody'll get hurt. I promise you – I've orders to bring you alive." It was the truth but Robin had no intention of obeying orders – too late for that. After seeing the regard between the German and Jessica, it had become personal for Robin.

They'd made a fool of him, no doubt laughing up their sleeves at his expense, all the while carrying on their tawdry affair.

No, Robin wanted this Nazi bastard dead – he'd be satisfied with nothing less.

Suddenly there was a splash – someone was in the water, and Jessica screamed. "*No*! Captain no! Get back in the boat!"

"Shut up!" Robin hissed at her. He held her with an arm round her waist, the iron-cold muzzle of the Enfield hard against her temple.

"Captain, for God's sake!" Jessica cried. She was writhing about, fighting him, but Robin knew he was stronger

"Jessie …" the German's voice carried over the water and Robin smiled with satisfaction. *This was too easy*!

***

Robin released his hold on her and Jessica felt the gun leave her temple. But relief was replaced by horror as Robin's arm came up, aiming towards the man in the water.

"*No!*" She slammed against his side but the gun remained steady. "He's lying!" she bellowed. "He's going to shoot!"

"Yer comin' or not?" A disembodied voice called from the larger vessel.

Robin braced his stance and held his aim.

"*Yes!*" Jessica cried, frantically thumping Robin's arm. On the brink of hysteria, she shrieked towards the boat hidden in the darkness, "He's going with you!"

Snarling and gnashing like a wild animal, she threw herself into Robin's side again and again trying desperately to disrupt his aim.

Suddenly, in a flash of light, the night shattered as a shot rang out.

"Jessie!" the captain cried, and for the first time, Jessica heard fear in his voice. "Do not hurt her, I am coming."

"*Noo!*" Jessica wailed and instinctively bent her knees, dropping to the sand. Then scrambling to her feet, she lurched across the shingle towards the water. Obviously realising she had nowhere to go Robin merely watched.

"Go Captain," she bellowed as she ran. "If you love me … Go! *He's going to kill you!*" she ended on a piercing shriek.

"Come on, man!" The shout came from the distance. "Last chance if yer comin'!"

A second gunshot cracked across the water.

"No! Robin ... Please!" Jessica begged.

She heard the splash and the dull thud as the bullet hit something solid. When the outline of the man in the water dropped out of sight, Jessica bent double and howled like a wounded animal.

Through the traumatised buzzing in her brain, Jessica gradually became aware of the men in the boat calling to one another in confusion. Then she heard the oars cutting the water and lifted her head. *They're leaving without him*!

"Don't go!" Jessica shrieked. Sobbing hysterically, she staggered along the water's edge. *"Don't go!"*

Robin casually strolled after her. He fired again … and again. Jessica's ears rang with each explosion. She felt the bullets zing past her head.

One hit the water, another struck the wooden hull of the rowing boat. Almost demented with fear, Jessica's eyes darted crazily over the inky water – where was he? *Where was he*?

Blindly, Jessica stumbled over the ripples in the sand and tripped on a lump of driftwood. Falling heavily to the sharp shingle, she knelt, heedless of the stinging pain in her bruised knees, weeping uncontrollably.

***

Robin watched impassively as Jessica fell. He stood over her as she hunched, rocking back and forth like a madwoman, clenched fists cuffed before her.

The rowing boat had vanished into the dark with two men aboard, but Robin strained his eyes, scanning the black water where he knew the third man should be.

There was a heavy, wooden sound as the rowing boat bumped against the larger vessel. Tyler waited, watching as a lantern on board illuminated the first man clambering aboard the fishing boat. The second man followed.

Still, there was no sign of the German, but Robin knew instinctively the bastard was there.

He was right.

The German was small but surprisingly strong. Robin felt a pang of grudging admiration as he saw the swimmer reach the larger boat. He watched as the man hauled himself up the vessel's side.

Closing one eye, Tyler took careful aim and pulled the trigger.

"Shit!" he cursed as the bullet thunked into the boat's hull.

He continued to watch as a set of arms extended to assist the German aboard.

The Enfield had one shot remaining.

One shot; one chance to take the bastard down.

The Kraut's silhouette moved boldly against the side of the boat.

One shot, Robin chanted in his head. *One ... clear ... shot.*

He exhaled slowly. Raising his arm, he sighted down the gun's barrel. Steadied his pulse ... Measured the rate of his heartbeat ... Wait ... *waaaiit ...*

Now!

The Enfield jumped in his hand with a terrifying explosion.

At the same instant, Jessica grasped the lump of driftwood and swung it with every ounce of strength she had left.

Epilogue

September 1948 – Broughton Hall, near Wolstone, Yorkshire

Magda bent to retrieve the empty basket at her feet. As she straightened, a movement caught her eye. She flicked a hank of unruly black hair away from her face and narrowed her gaze against the sun's glare.

Sandy was sprinting along the gravel drive, arms pumping, knees driving like pistons. He mounted the porch steps two-at-a-time and disappeared into the house.

Magda made a tutting sound. "Child's got too much energy," she said aloud, though there was affection in her voice. She slung the basket over her forearm and turned towards the orchard.

***

In the kitchen, a willowy young woman had just removed a tray of scones from the oven and was laying them on a cooling rack. When Sandy blew into the room like a mini tornado, she jumped in surprise, hand flying to her bosom.

"Blimey, Sandy!" she gasped irritably. "Must you do everything at a million miles?"

"Sorry, Mary." He was not in the least contrite. "There's a man at the gate!"

"What man?" Mary set the cooling rack before the open window. "Did you tell Mr Clay?"

"Mr Clay's down the eastern paddock."

She tucked a strawberry-blonde curl behind her ear, removed her apron and draped it over the back of a chair. "All right. I'll go see what he wants."

"I think he's French," Sandy called after her. "He said, *bonjour.*"

***

The stranger leaned against the gatepost scratching absently at his thick beard. Having travelled for the better part of a week, he was tired and filthy, and uncomfortably aware of his odour and shabby appearance.

Yet the boy hadn't seemed to notice – perhaps the occasion of an unexpected visitor was too exciting to mind such details. He'd said, "Wait here," and disappeared at speed up the drive.

The man waited only a few minutes before someone emerged from the house and his heart began to pound. It was a young woman, slender and graceful. She strode confidently down the drive, regarding him steadily as she approached.

The man shifted his weight and removed his battered old hat, watching her as she drew closer. Her gait faltered and her mouth opened slightly. She stopped abruptly some five yards away, staring hard, her brow furrowed.

The man smiled. *"Bonjour, mademoiselle."*

The young woman didn't respond. She continued to stare at him but now her brow had cleared and her lips trembled slightly with each intake of air. Finally, she swallowed and said in a strangled voice, "Can I help you?"

Giving a one-shouldered shrug, he said, *"Oui.* That is, I hope so."

The woman made a small choking sound and swallowed again. "Well, you'd better come with me, then."

***

Jessica pushed to her feet and dusted the soil from her hands and knees. Her father's headstone was small by comparison with the others, but the grave was neater. She tended it regularly pulling out weeds and pruning the rose bush.

She enjoyed coming to this place, where she could talk to her father in a way she never could while he was alive. Strangely, she felt he understood her now, in a way he previously hadn't.

Her stomach grumbled – a sure sign that it was almost lunchtime. She turned towards the kisting gate, calling over her shoulder, "Scarry!"

The scruffy little dog came bounding from round the corner of the old chapel, where the vicar's fat old tomcat could be found lazing on a bench in the sun.

It was an unlikely friendship that existed between the pair and Jessica smiled to think of it. She knew all about unlikely friendships.

Scaramouche trotted beside her as she strolled along the well-worn path to Broughton Hall. And in the cool of the verdant woods, she lost herself – as she often did – in reminiscence.

They had been friends, for too brief a time, she and the German. They had been lovers too. But after that night on the beach in Devon, she'd never heard from him again.

She'd seen the men drag his limp body aboard the fishing vessel. She'd heard the thump of a dead weight hitting the deck.

That Robin had shot him she had no doubt. Whether he'd survived … well, she'd no way of knowing.

Once the war ended, she'd waited for word from him … *hoped* for word from him … eventually coming to realise that there would be *no* word from him.

She'd been so certain he'd find some way to contact her – if he could. Perhaps through his American friend, or … Jessica bent to pick up a stick; she threw it up the path for Scaramouche.

Of course, he'd been wounded, but maybe he'd been killed. She couldn't think about that. There was always the possibility that he'd survived and married that girl of his. Probably had a string of blue-eyed children toddling round by now.

The thought made the breath catch in her chest as she walked.

He had a right to his life although she hoped he thought fondly of her, now and then.

Scaramouche ran up with a slobbery stick in his mouth. It

was not the stick she'd tossed for him, but he didn't seem to notice. The little dog had attached himself to her after their ordeal six years ago. Along with Magda, the pair had returned to Broughton Hall, battered, bruised and exhausted, but they'd returned. That man, Wheeler, had seen to it.

He'd seen to other things too.

Jessica emerged from the forest onto Broughton land and rounded the barn to find Magda hanging washing on the line.

Even now, so many years later, Jessica's heart still clenched with pain as she recalled that dreadful night in Devon. She'd been in no fit state to drive all the way back to Yorkshire. If not for Magda …

As the military increased its demand for milk and Jessica's business grew, Magda's decision to remain at Broughton Hall had been a Godsend.

Magda glanced over and Jessica thought her friend had an odd look on her face. Nevertheless, Jessica continued along the path to the garden door.

***

The kitchen smelled delicious. Closing the garden door, Jessica sniffed appreciatively. "Mmm, scones, Mary. I'm starving …"

Mary stood by the range. Ignoring her mother's comment, she rushed forward with her arms outstretched. "Mum," she said, her eyes wide and haunted. "Oh, Mummy, you'd better sit down."

Jessica's heart lurched in her chest. "What –?"

"Here …" Mary pulled out a chair but Jessica resisted.

"What's going –"

There was a movement in the doorway and Jessica looked up. A man in black trousers and cream shirt stood towelling his hair.

He was lean and muscular, not very tall. His eyes were blue but weary, in a face that bore the traces of adversity and experience.

The pale skin on his chin evidenced a recently removed beard.

"*Dear God ...*" Jessica breathed before her vision grew fuzzy at the edges. She managed a step towards him but her legs buckled. She was unconscious before she hit the floor.

***

Jessica blinked. The face leaning over her slowly came into focus.

"Captain? It's you?"

"Yes. It is me," he whispered, adding, "though I am a captain no longer."

He smiled and it was the same beautiful smile sprung straight from her memory, though there was a hint of sadness in it too. And something else was different: his accent. Still guttural but not as much. More rolling ... French, perhaps?

He was watching her while she considered. Now he moved back a step as she wriggled to a sitting position and realised she was on her bed. "You carried me here?"

Nodding, he looked mildly uncomfortable, like he wasn't sure of his welcome.

Jessica, still coming to terms with his return, was uncertain what to say. There were so many gaps, so many questions. Involuntarily her eyes darted to his ring finger.

Following her gaze, he held up the hand. "I am not married."

"But you made it. You got away."

He nodded.

"And your family? They must've been overjoyed."

His expression hardened. "My family," he said pensively and drew a deep breath. "I have not seen them."

"But –"

"They know I am alive but it was not safe for them – or me – if I went home."

"But the war's over."

The captain shook his head and sat on the edge of her bed. "Jessie," he began and Jessica's heart turned over – she'd never thought to hear that lovely voice say her name again. "After I arrived in France," he spoke slowly, selecting his words with care, "I worked with Wheeler's men, as promised, but … it was too important. There were so many needing assistance – not just Jews, but German defectors, scientists, doctors, spies. We exported valuable documents, works of art, medicines … As a German speaker, I was invaluable. I remained in France to continue the work."

Jessica stared at him in mute astonishment.

"Then, one day," he went on, "I was in a bar in Paris, drinking with a German officer. The Gestapo arrived. I was arrested and taken to prison. I had been sharing German information with the United States, through Josef – my friend?"

Jessica nodded, stunned.

"The Nazis had suspected me for a while and had set up a false meeting. Along with another man, I was imprisoned and sentenced to be executed."

"Evidently you *weren't* executed."

He chuckled softly. "No. Two weeks after my imprisonment, Paris was liberated by the French and United States armies. I was released."

The captain allowed Jessica a moment to digest everything. Finally, she opened her mouth to respond but was interrupted.

Thomas stood at her open door, Mary behind him. Still wearing his cricket whites, the bowler's tell-tale red stains down the front of his trousers, Thomas murmured, "Mr Bird, you came back."

The captain slowly rose. "Yes, Tommy. I have –"

Thomas threw himself into the man's arms. "I knew you would," he gasped, emotionally. "I knew it!"

Mary's eyes were moist as she watched her twin embrace the

man whom, as children, they'd both loved.

Jessica swung her legs over the edge of the bed and sat, grief and despair churning in her stomach.

How she longed to go to him – hold him and be close to him like Thomas. But there was something she had to tell him first. He had a right to know, and she was uncertain of his reaction. So, for now, she waited.

***

That evening, Jessica, Thomas and Mary, Sandy, Magda, Sam and Marg, gathered about the dining table in celebration of the captain's return. Magda had prepared a delicious meal of roast beef and summer vegetables, and Sam had contributed a bottle of wine.

"Pity Granny's not here," Thomas piped up. "Mum you'll have to telephone her tomorrow."

"Where are your parents?" the captain asked suddenly.

"Grandad's dead," Thomas announced insensitively.

"Tommy!" Mary admonished, while Jessica glared at her son.

"My father passed away last year, Captain. Lasted longer than we expected. Mum's in Scotland with my cousin Sadie."

The captain nodded. "I am sorry about your father."

Jessica smiled then and returned her focus to her plate.

Around her, the mood was festive. Sam and Marg had been overjoyed at seeing their *adopted son* again and as the meal progressed, Marg, seated beside the captain, couldn't stop herself touching and hugging him – as though constantly reassuring herself that he wasn't an apparition.

Conversely, Sam simply watched contentedly, smiling as if to say, *I knew this day would come.*

Throughout the dinner, there was laughter, joyous tears and the clinking of glasses, yet Jessica felt removed from the celebration.

Seated opposite the captain, she felt ill from a combination of happiness and apprehension. Elated as she was by his return, there were too many questions in her heart and too much to confess.

She avoided his gaze, though if her eyes did inadvertently meet his, she wanted to weep for the appeal on his face.

He clearly didn't understand her reticence and she knew she was being unfair. *Tell him*, she ordered herself. *He deserves your honesty, tell him tonight and then he can decide for himself.*

***

Later, after the remains of the meal were cleared away, Mary and Magda volunteered to tidy the kitchen and Sam and Marg returned to their cottage.

Jessica was seated in the garden beneath a lush, verdant bough of the ancient oak tree on her front lawn. Scaramouche lay at her feet and she had a cup of tea in her hand.

She knew the moment of truth had arrived as the captain came down the porch steps and strode casually towards her.

How she remembered that walk of his. Lithe, she thought, though she'd never put a word to it before.

"May I join you?" he asked.

Jessica merely smiled and he took a vacant chair beside her. Scaramouche got up and waddled over, wagging his stumpy tail.

"Hello, boy," the captain said, ruffling the little dog's coarse coat. "It is very good to see you looking so fit and well. Do you remember our adventures all those years ago?"

"He's rather old now, Captain. He's physically well but I doubt he remembers breakfast."

The captain laughed. "We are all older, Monsieur Scaramouche, but are we wiser?" Suddenly he looked up at her. "Jessie," he said with the acuity she remembered, "you have something troubling you?"

Jessica carefully placed her teacup on the grass at her feet and exhaled with a long sigh. "Yes."

He waited while she considered her next words. "Captain, how long do you intend to be here?"

A small furrow appeared between his brows. "Well, I... I have not... I could return to Germany – it is safer now. But I can move about England relatively freely also. I can *appear* French – my French accent is rather good, *n'est pas*?" he said, his German accent eliding easily into French.

"Compared with your American one?" she asked, playfully.

He grinned and her heart gave an old familiar leap.

"I just wondered," she said. "You see, there's something you must know …"

The captain nodded encouragingly.

"It's about Sandy." Jessica saw the muscles in his jaw tighten. Mustering her courage, she said quickly, "He's my son."

She gazed anxiously at him, trying desperately to read his expression, but his face was like stone.

After a pause, he said, "I guessed at dinner, though he is fond of Magda."

"Yes, and she of him. Some believe she *is* his mother."

"Your son," he repeated, as though testing the words.

Jessica swallowed the hard lump in her throat.

The captain leaned back in his chair, legs extended before him, gazing into the lush green canopy above their heads.

The summer evening was mild, the sky tinted rose and lilac, a soft honey-scented breeze lifted her hair. Yet Jessica noticed none of these things, as she waited for him to speak. *Why wasn't he saying anything? What was he thinking?*

Unable to bear his silence any longer, she whispered, "Please say something."

The captain continued to stare into the branches, then he slowly closed his eyes. "You are married?"

His voice could barely be heard over the rustling of the oak leaves. Jessica leaned forward in her chair. "What? No! No, I'm not married," she stammered, surprised.

Equally surprised, he turned his head and met her gaze. "Then who is his father?"

Jessica opened her mouth to speak but he abruptly sat up in his chair. "Please," he interrupted. "Whoever's son he is, I will not judge you." He peered intently at her. "It was war, Jessica. People did what they had to do to survive." He shrugged one shoulder. "He seems a bright boy, a nice boy —"

"Captain — *Anton.*" It was her turn to interrupt.

She reached across the space between them and took his hand. "Sandy is *your* son."

***

The following day, Sam took Anton to visit the dairy, and Anton was pleased to see the herd considerably expanded; the milk and butter business had grown since the war ended.

As a result, Broughton Hall had prospered and was certainly in better repair than he remembered — it had electricity too!

Once the emotion of his reunion with Marg and Sam had worn off, Anton felt as though the six years of his absence had been a mere six days — but for the fact that they were all older: Sam a little balder, Marg a little plumper — and he fell immediately into his old work routine.

His relationship with Thomas was warm and loving, though he could sense that Mary was holding herself in check — as though waiting for something — and he thought he knew what she waited for.

There was still more Jessica wasn't telling him, and astute as Mary was, she evidently sensed her mother's caution and was equally wary.

Though Jessica's revelation about his son had shocked and

unsettled him, Anton was gradually getting used to the idea that he was a father. He wanted to reach out to Sandy, get to know him, but until Jessica was completely honest with him, he resolved to tread carefully.

He couldn't force her to talk to him, but when a few nights later her found her seated under that big oak tree again, he pulled up a chair and sat, content to share a companionable evening.

"I never saw Robin Tyler after that night in Devon," Jessica said without warning. She sipped a glass of iced tea. "And his father moved out of the old farmhouse in Jackson's Heath. I haven't seen him again either." Her voice was weary, as though she was tired of thinking about it.

"I suppose Wheeler took care of things with Robin," she said, matter-of-factly. "Wheeler took care of everything back then."

Anton nodded. "I worked for Wheeler for six years but we never spoke about that night."

"He never spoke about *anything*, he was so discreet – and thorough – he took care of *everything*." Jessica shrugged. "I had expected there'd be repercussions. I thought, after Robin and the beach and all, that I'd be questioned or even raided again," she shrugged. "Nothing. For a long time, I nearly fainted at every knock at the door …" she gestured as though mystified and repeated, "Nothing. You spent time with Sandy today?" she abruptly changed the subject.

Anton saw her face tighten, though she was trying to sound casual. He smiled reassuringly. "I am a father! It is an idea that is taking some time to get accustomed to."

Jessica smiled, cautiously. "I'll bet."

"What does Sandy know of his father?"

"Well," she took a deep breath. "Only that he was a pilot. He was brave and handsome and he went to war. We never saw him again."

Anton nodded pensively. "What will you tell him about me?"

She dropped her eyes to her hands, loosely clasped in her lap, and Anton frowned, speculating. "Jessica, what is troubling you?"

She looked up sharply and sucked in her breath. "I don't want you to think ... that is, I ..." She flapped her hands helplessly.

"Tell me."

"So many fatherless babies were born during that time. They were put up for adoption or ..." she stared into his eyes, drilling home her point. "*I* chose to keep Sandy. *I* made the decision, Captain, knowing I'd be raising him alone." She shifted uncomfortably in her chair, "I don't know how long you're staying, but I don't expect anything from you. Do you understand what I mean?"

Anton felt a twisting in his gut. He exhaled in a long sigh. "You are telling me I am not –"

"Sandy is not your responsibility."

Anton leaned back in his chair, thinking. *She does not want me in their lives.* The realisation caused his chest to hurt. *But what did I expect, coming here unannounced?*

The silence between them stretched for a long time. Finally, attempting to lighten the mood, he asked, "Do you think he likes me?"

"Oh, yes!" Her laugh sounded a little forced. "He thinks you're very dashing."

Anton nodded, quietly proud, but no less hurt.

***

That discussion with Jessie had been three days ago and since then, Anton hadn't been able to draw her into a personal conversation. He'd been at Broughton Hall well over a week and had slipped naturally into his old role of assisting Sam in the dairy and doing odd jobs about the property.

He'd easily reclaimed his place in Marg's heart and delighted in his growing rapport with Thomas and Mary, deriving an unexpected pleasure from their almost adult company.

Moreover, he was getting to know his son, even if the true nature of their connection had not been explained to the child.

Anton realised, unhappily, that he would soon need to leave Broughton Hall, though neither he nor Jessica had broached the subject. Conversations with her remained awkward and uncomfortable: they kept to impersonal reminiscences, skirting emotions and more intimate memories of one another. It couldn't go on like this.

They talked about that night on the beach in Devon and Anton confirmed that one of Tyler's bullets had found its mark. "Not badly," he told her. "Through the shoulder as I climbed onto the fishing boat. Odd," he said, remembering, "I knew at the time that Tyler had a clear shot. I could not believe his aim was so poor."

Jessica smiled and described the savage blow she'd dealt just as Tyler pulled the trigger.

"Broke his arm with a lump of driftwood," she ended with satisfaction.

"Ah," Anton said, grinning. "I wondered."

Slowly, cautiously, they began filling the gaps in one another's lives – although Anton's story was considerably diluted. There were moments, experiences he didn't want to think about, let alone share.

And there'd been other women too, although none that could ever replace his Frau Jessie, not in his heart.

Whenever he was with her, the urge to touch her was almost unbearable. Yet she'd given no indication she might welcome such intimacy – understandable after all these years, but …

Anton sighed. He'd never stopped loving her and had he found his way back to Germany, he'd have kept his promise: *if I cannot marry you, I will not marry at all.*

But he knew the issue of his departure must be addressed – it was now safe to return to Germany. He and Jessica couldn't keep circling one another like polite acquaintances.

***

But circle one another, they did, and even as they rekindled their old friendship, the uncertainty remained.

Jessica couldn't understand why the captain was still at Broughton Hall. It seemed to her that he was getting to know his son, and while she was content for the two to develop a relationship, until she knew the captain's intentions, she was not prepared to have *that* talk with Sandy.

Two weeks after the captain's arrival at Broughton Hall Jessica was sweeping up a small pile of dead leaves on the front porch when she heard Sandy's lilting, enthusiastic voice. Looking up from her work, she saw her son and his father coming up the drive together.

It warmed her heart to see them like that, though she grieved for the years missing to them both. One day, she hoped, she would be able to tell Sandy the truth about their visitor. But for now … she watched the boy and man approach.

The captain was walking in that graceful, relaxed way of his, while Sandy was doing his usual walk-run beside him, both were chattering like magpies over some commonly held opinion.

Nearing the porch, they paused and gazed up at her and for the first time she saw the resemblance between them: the curious tilt to the head, the curve to the lips with just a hint of mischief lurking at the corners. She saw light and laughter in their glistening eyes and felt a stab of sadness. She knew Anton was planning to leave; knew she couldn't stop him but wished, not for the first time, that things could be different.

And how good he looked, standing there in the afternoon sun, one hand resting on Sandy's slim shoulder. The entire scene was enough to cause the dull ache in her chest to become real pain.

"Mummy, Mr Bird said he'll teach me to play football! We just need to get a ball. I said we could get one from Wolstone."

"Football, eh?" Jessica said archly. "I didn't think you were interested."

Sandy slipped from under the captain's hand and trotted up the stairs. "Oh yes! I've always wanted to play football but Thomas's only interested in cricket. Can we go to Wolstone, *please*?"

The sun was shining on Sandy's hair. It gleamed with strands of cinnamon and copper inherited from her, but in this light she could also see the honey and gold from his father.

Her breath caught in her throat and she looked past her son to where the captain stood at the foot of the steps. He too, was watching Sandy, a pensive look on his face.

We need to talk, she thought. *Properly, honestly.*

"We'll see Sandy," she smiled down at him. "But right now I need to talk with Mr Bird. Go help Thomas break a hay bale for the cows, please, then go wash your hands for tea."

"Okay, Mummy." Sandy turned, took the stairs two at a time and bolted at top speed towards the paddocks.

"Okay?" the captain asked, smiling. He came up the steps to join her.

"It caught on and won't go away." She gave a mock grimace and swept the little pile of leaves off the edge of the porch onto the garden below. "Not the worst thing the Yanks left here, though."

She propped the broom against the stone wall of the house. "Captain, can we talk please?"

He nodded. "But not here."

"No. Not here. Meet me in my office in ten minutes."

***

669

"Why are you here?" Jessica asked tightly, trying to control her emotions. Having deliberately chosen the cool business-like ambiance of her office for this discussion, she was sitting behind her desk, the captain sat on a chair opposite.

After doing her book work yesterday, Jessica had closed her ledger and placed her folded spectacles on top. She saw his gaze rest unseeingly on them, his mind seemed elsewhere.

***

Anton hadn't expected Jessica to be so direct. Taken aback by the challenge in her tone, he hesitated.

"Well? The war ended three years ago!" she persisted. "It's been six years without a word and then you just show up out of the blue. Why? Why now? Why didn't you come sooner?"

He sighed. "Because I could not." He knew it sounded lame but taken off guard, he needed to arrange his thoughts."

"*Six years*, Captain," she emphasised. "You could've been dead for all we knew."

He nodded. "I worked with the United States, flying supplies, soldiers and civilians, into and out of France. They are rebuilding, there is much work still to be done..."

Jessica looked sceptical. She sat back in her chair, eyeing him narrowly. "You've already explained all of that."

***

"This discussion is not going as I expected," the captain admitted. He looked up from her ledger.

"What *did* you expect?" Jessica tried to moderate her tone. "What did you think happened to us?"

He shrugged one shoulder. "I do not know. I suppose I thought you would put everything behind you. That you would return to the way you were before we met ... forget everything that had happened."

Jessica gave a humourless snort. "I was pregnant. How could I possibly forget?"

"I did not know that. When finally the war was over I could not return to Germany. I was wanted as a spy, a defector, a traitor to my country. Life..." he seemed to search for the right words. "Life was unchanged for me."

"Well, life wasn't unchanged for me," Jessica snapped bitterly. "When my pregnancy began to show I was confined to this house. I couldn't go to Wolstone – those people! There was no way I'd be able to explain. After Sandy was born, I took him and Magda to Wolstone. I introduced her as my cousin and let them all think Sandy was her baby. It was *so* hard, and for a long time Sandy thought he had two mothers." She smiled ruefully, "I think he still does sometimes."

They fell silent for a minute. Voices from elsewhere in the house filtered through to them: a stern comment from Mary followed by childish laughter, a banging door, water splashing in the bathroom.

"We needed to hear from you," she reasoned. "We needed to at least know you were alive. But you haven't answered my question, Captain. Why are you here now?"

***

Anton exhaled in a long sigh. Why *was* he here now? How to collate all the thoughts tangled around each other? How to tell her that he still hoped, still loved, still wanted the life they'd once imagined together? How to explain that the time was right for him, when for her, that time seemed to have long gone?

"Were you planning to stay?" Jessica asked hoarsely, breaking into his thoughts.

He didn't respond immediately. He watched her restlessly rolling a pencil between her fingers.

If only he knew what she wanted.

***

Jessica waited, her eyes focussed on the pencil in her hands. She'd risked everything asking him that question. Her mouth had grown dry and her heart pounded painfully. She'd spoken abruptly and not how she'd intended.

He didn't respond immediately and a dull ache began behind her eyes.

Finally, he leaned across the desk and with a gentle finger beneath her chin, he raised her eyes to meet his.

"Do you want me to stay?"

"Yes!" she didn't hesitate and like a dam bursting, the words came tumbling out. "I want to grow old with you! I want Thomas and Mary to have you back in their lives. I want Sandy to know his father. It's *everything* I could want, but I don't want you to feel you *have* to – that's what I've been trying to explain. You must want us too which is why I need to know – "

"Shhh," he breathed, smoothing the sudden tears from her cheeks. "Of course I want you."

"That's how you're feeling now. But it's been so long... I thought you must be dead or... married. You showed up so unexpectedly and found you had a child –"

"Jessica –"

"What brought you here *now*?" she demanded again.

He sat back in his chair, studying her face. "I came back now because things have changed. Many of the Luftwaffe commanders, the SS, all those that would execute me as a traitor are in prison. I am now free to go home. But... " he sucked in a deep breath and waved his arm in an expansive gesture, "I wanted to make *this* my home... if *you* wanted *me*."

Her heart leapt with joy at his words, even as a small part of her still hesitated. She had to be sure. She pulled a hanky from her pocket and blew her nose.

Tucking it away she said, "Captain, it was my decision to

raise Sandy. You've had no say in it – no choice whatsoever."

"I had a choice." He leaned forward and caught her hand, weaving their fingers. "I chose to make love to you. We created Sandy together."

Jessica's breath hitched with emotion. "But what if you change your mind? What if you suddenly decide you don't want to be a father after all. You'll grow to resent Sandy. You'll hate me. That's what I'm afraid of!"

"*Mein Schatz*," he murmured, smiling. "Still so afraid of the future. Six years I have dreamed of you, imagined our children, our life together, never expecting that it could come true." He drew in a long, shuddering breath. "You, Sandy, Mary and Thomas, and whoever is to come next … that is all I could *ever* want. Remember my last words to you? That night in the Bowsprit? I put the gun in your hand and whispered those words just before I left you, remember?"

Jessica nodded, inhaled deeply and repeated, "I will love you till I die."

Releasing her hand, he rose from his chair and came around the desk. Cautiously, he leaned forward and softly touched his lips to hers. Immediately a spark flared between them and she gasped.

He felt it too and drew back slightly, searching her face. At her expression, he grinned and said, "Let us go downstairs now. They will be wondering where we are."

***

Thomas hated doing dishes. After tea, Mum asked him and Mary to clean up, and ordinarily he would've protested, but Mum had given him this strange pleading look as though to say, *I really need you to do this,* and then she and Mr Bird had taken young Sandy into the parlour and shut the door.

"What d'you think's going on?" he asked his sister as she

passed him a dripping plate.

Mary raised her eyebrows at him. "What do you think, eejit!"

"Well, I suppose they're telling Sandy that Mr Bird's his father."

"Pure genius, you are!" Mary taunted but she smiled fondly and wrung out the dishcloth. "Seriously though, I imagine this means Mr Bird is planning to stay."

Thomas was surprised. "Of course he's planning to stay! He *always* planned to stay." He finished drying the plate and reached for another.

"Mum wasn't sure." Mary placed a cup on the draining board and plunged her hands back into the soapy water. "If she didn't know, how would you?"

Thomas sighed with exaggerated patience, enjoying getting one over his sister. "Of *course* Mr Bird always planned to stay. Why else would he come here?" He put the plate down and began drying the cup.

"He came because his work in France was over."

Thomas looked archly at his sister. "But why would he? He didn't know about Sandy – we haven't heard from him in years, he had no reason to come. Wouldn't it've be easier for him to just go home? We would never've known the difference. But he came *here*." Thomas jabbed a finger at the floor to emphasise his point. "Why would he come *all this way* just to tell us he wasn't staying?"

As Mary handed him another cup, Thomas saw the realisation dawn on her face. He grinned smugly. "Who's the eejit now, eh?"

At that moment the door opened and Mum came in. She looked flushed but relieved. Thomas exchanged a look with his sister as his mother took a seat at the kitchen table and ran her hands through her hair, causing the bits at her temples to stick out.

"Everything all right, Mum?" Mary ventured.

"Is Sandy okay?" Thomas interrupted.

Mum nodded. "Sandy's all right. He just got a shock, that's all. He's gone outside for a bit."

"Where's Mr – " Thomas began as the door opened and the man in question came in.

Although he looked tired, Mr Bird seemed happy. But Thomas noticed Mary turn away. She pulled the plug out of the sink and remained staring into the water as it swirled in a vortex down the drain.

Still worried, Thomas thought. *Well, someone needs to get things sorted.* "Mr Bird," he asked boldly. "You're going to be staying with us, aren't you?"

Thomas shot a glance at his sister and saw her back stiffen. He heard his mother's quick intake of air.

Mr Bird didn't seem to notice. He responded immediately, "If you and Mary will have me, I would very much like to stay and be part of your family.

***

Jessica felt vaguely dizzy as her heart gave a joyous leap. She heard Mary exhale as though she'd been holding her breath and Jessica watched as her daughter turned to the captain.

"You didn't expect to be a father. What if you change your mind?" Mary asked evenly.

"I have had six years to think about this. I know my mind. I cannot replace your father, but I hoped you would have me... I hoped to be a father to you. To find that I am in truth a father... it is more than I ever hoped for. So yes, if you will have me, I want to stay."

***

Later that night, Jessica was reading in bed. Even after a year of electric lighting, it was still a novelty. Sleep was proving elusive and it was more than summer's warmth that kept her awake.

In the hall, a floorboard creaked and she glanced up expectantly. At the light knock on her door, she placed her book on the side-table and pulled the sheet up and tucked it beneath her arms. "Yes?"

The door slowly swung open and the captain stood on the threshold in only underwear and a T-shirt. Now in his early thirties, while lean and strong, he looked older than his years. *Still handsome, though*, Jessica thought, *but he looks like he's been through a lot.*

"Frau Jessie, may I ask you something?"

Her heart began to pound and her stomach clenched. She nodded, and as he turned to close the door, her eyes lingered admiringly on his strong legs and buttocks.

Whatever he's been doing, it's kept him fit. "What do you want to know?" she asked, patting the edge of her bed.

He sat, smiling, and warm colour crept into his cheeks. Six years suddenly fell away revealing the self-effacing young officer he used to be. "Frau Jessie, did you really love me … back then?"

It was her turn to blush. She drew up her knees, hugging them. "Yes," she admitted after a pause. "I loved you very much."

"And now?"

Forcing herself to meet his clear blue gaze, she saw hope and vulnerability there. "I never stopped loving you," Jessica said firmly. "I prayed for your safety, hoped one day I might hear from you. And every time I looked at Sandy, I thanked God because he was a living, breathing gift from you. The most precious gift – you gave me a child!"

Her eyes began to sting and she blinked rapidly. "You also gave me this."

Reaching into her bedside drawer, she took out a small velvet pouch. The captain shifted on the bed to watch as she pulled open the drawstrings and tipped out a miniature calf, captured in gangly newborn detail.

"Lil Dagover," he murmured fondly.

Over the years, its beetroot-juice stain had faded to a rusty brown but he recognised the carving he'd made her.

"I want you to know," he said soberly, "that I have loved you since I first awoke to find you leaning over me. You were frightened and worried and," he conceded with a wry grin, "you did not like me very much. But I loved you," he murmured. He reached out and caught a tendril of auburn hair, letting it coil around his finger. "And I wanted you."

Jessica drew in her breath. The old, familiar tingling she always felt at his proximity started in the pit of her stomach.

"Over the years," he went on, "I dared not dream you could have loved me, and could love me still. So yes," he whispered, fingers gently busy, "I would like to stay."

"Oh, good!" Jessica cried. "Now will you please stop talking and make love to me?"

She watched his surprised expression transform into delight. "*Jawohl!*"

It took only a second for the captain to remove his clothes and slip beneath the sheet.

Immediately folding her in his arms, he fused his mouth to hers.

They clung together in a passion fuelled by all the fears, uncertainties, loneliness and grief of the last years. Now, secure in the promise of a shared future, they moved as one, touching, sighing and caressing, giving and receiving that sustenance for which they'd been starved.

As their need grew more desperate, more fevered, Jessica clutched at his buttocks urgently pulling him closer.

He resisted and she cried, "Captain! I've waited six years for this!"

"Oh *ja*, but first I must know," his voice was rough with desire but he was holding himself in check. "Why did you call our son Sandy?"

"What?" Jessica demanded. "Not now!" She clawed at him, pushing her hips against his, but he merely grinned at her.

"Sandy," he insisted. "Is that not a girl's name?"

"Yes! No!" Jessica growled, writhing beneath him.

He kissed her again, teasingly, then pulled away.

Jessica moaned, her mind reeling. "*Please* …!"

"Why Sandy?" he persisted.

"Short for Alexander," she gasped. "His name's Alexander. We shorten it to Sandy... because... Broughton Hall has already known an Alex – *ahh!*" Jessica cried out as he plunged into her.

***

Later that night, the lovers slept in a tangle of damp limbs and sheets. Neither was aware of the abstract scent of the unearthly, the impossible, hanging in the air. Nor did they see the shadowy elderly woman, hunched over a desk, writing beneath the incandescent glow of an invisible candle.

Had they heard the scratching of her pen, they'd have guessed it was a mouse; her heavy sigh could have been the wind.

But their sleep continued, undisturbed as the old woman wedged a tin box beneath her arm and pushed up from the desk.

Drifting like scent on a breeze, she moved to the bedside where she gazed down on the naked couple.

"Hmm?" the man murmured. He shifted to cradle his lover, pulling her gently back against his chest, one arm curled protectively over her stomach. "*Schlaf, mein Schatz.*"

The old woman nodded with satisfaction…

… and was gone.

A message from Karen Turner

When thinking about all the people who indirectly contribute to a book like Stormbird, it's difficult to know where to start. Perhaps then, I should start at the beginning and thank my grandparents Olive and Eric, whose names I borrowed for this story. In addition are Grandma's recollections of war-time Yorkshire, of loves found and lives lived for the moment.

Stories also from my mother, Christine, whose memories of bombing raids and childhood games played among the rubble of peoples' homes, were irreconcilable with my fortunate Australian youth.

Though the veil separates us, your voices will live forever in my heart; your words on my page.

Thus inspired, Stormbird unfolded, against the backdrop of my fictional home, Broughton Hall, on the outskirts of real life Otley, West Yorkshire.

Getting down to business, my most heartfelt thanks, of course, goes to the one person, without whom, I would never have dared to dream. To Stuart, the best, most supportive husband in the world, thank you – more than I can say.

To my editor, Jane Woodhead, though a great geographical distance now separates us, we did it again. And we'll do it again. Thank you – again!

Special mention to Maggie Christensen my critique partner for your valuable advice. And to all those, too numerous to list, who along the way have held my hand, buoying me when I doubted and rejoicing with me as I succeeded. Thank you beyond measure.

A big fat thank you goes to Angela Conetta for the best one-liner I've ever heard - potty mouth!

Finally, I couldn't end this without saying a heartfelt thank you to you – my readers. I hope you enjoyed Stormbird.

If you did, I'd be very grateful if you could post a quick review on Goodreads or Amazon so that others can discover and enjoy Stormbird for themselves.

Feel free to visit my website, www.karenturner.com.au and drop me a line – I'd love to hear from you!

Other books by Karen Turner

ALL THAT & EVERYTHING

Ever wondered what life looks like from a cat's perspective?
What about the funny side of daily train commuting?
Are things really what they seem in the mirror?

From Regency London to the Australian bush, *All That & Everything*
is an enchanting collection of award winning short stories.

Karen combines a selection of her late father's sketches with
these carefully chosen stories to offer something for everyone.

Other books by Karen Turner

TORN

1808

When 14 year old Alexandra meets Patrick, her handsome and notorious step-brother, she is confused and resentful as he shakes the foundations of everything she has ever known. Driving a wedge between Alex and her brother Simon, he tears apart the fabric of her quiet world. Yet she is intrigued by the enigmatic Patrick and finds herself increasingly drawn to him.

These are the years between childhood and womanhood, during which Alex begins to realise that her growing affection for Patrick owes nothing to sibling fondness.

But these are turbulent times for England and Patrick and Simon, answering the call of adventure, join the fight against Napoleon with devastating consequences.

In a family ravaged by war and deceit, Alex finds herself betrayed in the worst possible way.

This is the story of one woman's passionate struggle for love and hope against all the constraints of her time.

Other books by Karen Turner

INVIOLATE

1813

Inviolate continues the story of Alex Broughton, the passionate and determined young woman readers first met in *Torn*.

This remarkable sequel continues from where *Torn* left you wanting more.

From *Inviolate*:

And in my quiet moments – those moments just before sleeping, or when I lay down my sewing to stretch my neck – the memories of Patrick came, unbidden, and always with the power to evoke intense emotions. In time I hoped they would fade to snatches of conversation or secret kisses, to be hidden away in a dusty, rarely explored corner of my mind. But when they appeared without warning, like glittering gem-stones, they were so exquisite that I forgot the hurts and betrayals and saw only the beauty so briefly enjoyed. And despite being deceived in the worst possible way, I remained haunted by a fleeting and impossible love affair.

Other books by Karen Turner

COUNTERPOINT

1808

When Alexandra first meets Patrick, her handsome and enigmatic stepbrother, he tears apart the fabric of her quiet world ...

So begins the epic love story that had fans of *Torn* gripping their seats. But there's another side to the story, a darker side: Patrick's side.

Welcome to a world of lust, decadence and violence.

Counterpoint is a retelling of *Torn*, told in Patrick's own words, and by those closest to him.

Just as *Torn* ushers readers into the very proper parlours of Regency England, where young ladies live within the bounds of the social restraints of their time, *Counterpoint* thrusts readers onto a rollicking ride through a clandestine world of wealth, privilege and dark passions.

In glittering ballrooms, sordid London backstreets and bloodied battlefields, Patrick Washburn comes of age in a time of licentiousness, when profligate young men, seasoned by war, live life for the moment, with no restraint and no regrets.

www.ingramcontent.com/pod-product-compliance
Lightning Source LLC
Chambersburg PA
CBHW060807120726
47909CB00006B/1813